September Day & Shadow Thriller Box Set
Books 1-3

A September Day and Shadow Thriller

LOST AND FOUND

Book One

AMY SHOJAI

Copyright

This is a work of fiction. Names, characters, places, and incidents either are the product of the author's imagination or are used fictitiously, and any resemblance to actual persons living or dead, business establishments, events, or locales is entirely coincidental.

Second Print Edition, February 2017
Furry Muse Publishing
Print ISBN 978-1-944423-17-9
eBook ISBN 978-1-944423-18-6

First Published by Cool Gus Publishing
First Printing, September 2012
COPYRIGHT © Amy Shojai, 2012

FURRY MUSE
PUBLISHING
P.O. Box 1904
Sherman TX 75091
(903)814-4319
amy@shojai.com

Chapter 1

Linda Birch raced out the back door into the snow. "Help, somebody help me!" She slipped and fell, struggled to her feet and left pink handprints when she levered herself upright.

The butcher knife had left a three-inch gash in her calf. Her stomach burned and she held her left hand hard against the stab wound in her side.

The screen door banged open. Benny stumbled down the slick steps.

She sobbed, held bloody palms toward her son. "Stop! Please!" Linda ignored the cold on her bare legs. Her bright pink Snuggie dragged through the snow.

Benny didn't mean it. His expression remained as serene and blank as the snow that blanketed the lawn. He drew his right thumb along the blade and stared at the red line that appeared. He repeated the gesture with his left thumb and crimson splattered onto the snow like the petals of a wind-shattered rose.

"No, stop, honey. Don't hurt yourself." Linda stumbled toward her sixteen-year-old son, her fuzzy slippers clotted with ice and clumsy on her feet. She stopped when Benny regarded her for the briefest moment.

Linda saw that glint of recognition, a connection, before his focus evaporated. Her eyes welled. She'd had the real Benny for such a short time before the money disappeared. But she had no choice, she couldn't pay more. Insurance denied experimental trials. Savings had lasted less than a year. They were monsters to hold a child's health for ransom.

Benny sliced his other hand. Linda ignored her own injuries. "Let me have the knife, Benny." She kept her words quiet, authoritative, despite the pain that made her tremble.

Her beautiful baby boy's five-foot-ten-inch height dwarfed her dumpy body. Snow whirled overhead and made her dizzy when she looked up. She grabbed Benny's arm to keep from falling.

"No!" He screamed. The knife lashed out and just missed Linda's cheek. She fell to her knees.

He slashed the air above her head, playing target practice with individual flakes as Linda huddled before him. She prayed the tantrum would pass so she could get him back inside before they both caught pneumonia. She coughed. Spat blood onto the snow. How could that be?

Linda pulled her hand from the warm wetness on the front of her Snuggie. It had been barely a scratch, she was sure. Benny had had his share of tantrums. He'd scared her with the knife, so she ran. That made him even more scared, she reasoned, and prompted him to follow her. He'd done so well recently, and even had a job at the local Piggly Wiggly bagging groceries.

She waited until he stopped waving the knife to hold out her hand. She didn't think her legs would support her, and Linda reminded herself to start that diet soon. Maybe the New Year's resolution would stick this time. "Help Momma up, Benny."

"Momma?" Benny stared at her and at the splatters around them. He stuck one hand in his pocket before he stepped directly into the blood spill. His shoes polka-dotted the ground. He tilted his head to see better and deliberately created stamp-art with his feet. Benny held eye contact for ten seconds this time before breaking to stare at his shoes. He paddled in the blood again.

Linda held out her hand again. Spoke words devoid of emotion, matter-of-fact. "Sweetie, let's not make more of a mess. Give your Momma a little boost up, honey."

His left hand moved inside his pocket. She could hear the click of shiny pennies under his busy fingers. Repetitive motions—spinning, rocking, twirling; what the experts called stimming—offered a focus that helped relieve stress. But Benny hadn't twirled, spun or rocked for over six weeks. He made direct eye contact, even let her touch him briefly—and touched her in return without prompting. He spoke. He made sense. They communicated. The butterfly had broken free, a true miracle.

Benny knelt down in the snow next to Linda. "Sorry, Momma. Sorry," he said. And then he stabbed her until she stopped moving.

Chapter 2

September Day sloshed another half cup of coffee into the giant *#1-Bitch* mug, and glared out the frosty breakfast nook windows. North Texas didn't get snow. That's why she'd moved back home—well, one of several reasons. She shivered, relishing the warmth of the beverage, and toasted the storm with a curse. "Damn false advertising." Her cat Macy meowed agreement.

The blizzard drove icy wind through cracks in the antique windows and made the just-in-case candles on the dark countertop sputter. She pulled the fuzzy bathrobe closer around her neck. Normally the kitchen's stained glass spilled peacock-bright color into the kitchen. Not today, though. The reinforced security grills on the windows and dark clouds outside transformed the room's slate floor, bright countertops and brushed-steel appliances into a grim cell.

Overhead lights flickered on, off and back on again. They'd done that for the past hour. Crap. More stuff for the contractors to fix. One candle guttered in the draft, and September mentally added window caulk to her list. She prayed the electricity wouldn't go out, since the backup generator in the garage would take finagling to find, let alone to start.

She added a dollop of flavored cream to her cup, and replaced the lid that kept Macy's paws at bay. The longhair sable and white cat sat like a furry centerpiece on the rose-patterned glass table. He mewed in frustration when September set her covered mug next to the muffin saucer he'd already licked clean. A white paw patted the cup's lid.

September plopped into one of four wrought iron chairs, and pulled the mug out of the cat's reach. "Nope, I know where you put your feet."

Macy paced. His tail dry-painted September's cheek and wove in and out of her long wavy mane. Green slanted eyes, coffee-dark hair, hidden claws and enigmatic smile—she'd been told more than once that she and the cat matched in both personality and looks. Mom wanted her to dye the white skunk streak at her left temple, but September couldn't be bothered, not anymore. In Mom's high-falutin' social circles of perfectly coifed dowagers it served as a thumb-your-nose warning to keep strangers at bay.

She gave the cat's elevator-butt pose a final pat, and opened the DayMinder. Macy made a disgusted *mffft* sound, gathered himself and vaulted to the top the fridge. "Sure, go ahead and sulk. You're wired enough without caffeine."

Outside, gusts flailed the November blooms of the Belinda's Rose against the window beside the new steel door. At least the cold couldn't sneak through that barrier. In fact, the temperature change had shifted the door frame so much that it took an enormous effort to latch. That was fine with her. If it was hard to latch, the door offered even more security.

The weather not only derailed her schedule, the cold hurt like a bastard. September wrapped both hands around the mug. Her fingernails had already turned blue-white, and she couldn't feel her toes despite insulated ski socks and slippers. Not even flannel PJs, long underwear and a thick robe proved adequate against the weather.

She checked the thermostat for the third time—68 degrees—to save money, for crying out loud. "Screw it." Some old habits she could afford to break. She cranked the dial to 78, blessing the contractors for the gas-fueled furnace and hot water tanks.

Her DayMinder was choked with appointments, notes, and prompts. She'd entered most of them on her new phone, currently charging on the counter, but preferred the old-fangled paper version. "Busy is good. Except on snowy days."

Hell, she didn't want to risk the roads in this weather either. But she could damage control other deadlines she'd have to miss. She'd already left a message with the lawyers postponing the deposition on the dog bite case since she couldn't evaluate the dogs at the shelter until the weather settled. But fast talk and a good phone connection might allow her to keep other appointments. September dialed, sticking her free hand beneath her armpit to warm her fingers.

"WZPP, you've reached ZAP105 FM Radio, giving you the best easy-listening 24/7, how may I direct your call?"

"Hey, Anita, it's September. Could you—"

"Feels more like December."

September rolled her eyes. "Ha ha, funny lady, never heard that before. C'mon, it's cold and I'm in a pissy mood. Could you cut the jokes for once?"

"I've been here all night, still wondering how to get home, so my bad mood trumps yours, kiddo." Anita paused to blow her nose. "You want to talk to Humphrey, I guess. I'll connect."

Before she could say another word, September was plunged into the station's easy-listening hell. The thirty seconds lasted a lifetime before Humphrey's Jolly-Green-Giant voice broke in.

"ZAP, this is Humphrey Fish."

"It's me, September. I can't make it to the station. We'll have to do a phoner for the Pet Peeves program today." Before he could protest, she added a sweetener. "I'll do it for free. And there'll be a bunch of calls today with everything shut down, so the sponsors won't care." Macy chirruped, and dove off his favorite perch to wind around her ankles.

"Did you bring this sucky weather with you?" Humphrey didn't soften his sarcasm. September imagined him bouncing up and down, a human beach ball with legs. "I thought Hoosiers drove in snow nine months out of the year, and now you're afraid of a little flurry?"

"There's a reason I moved." *Let him think the move was only about the weather*, she thought, swallowing a slug of the strong coffee. "Have you snuck outside your little glass box lately? It's the freakin' ice age out there."

Humphrey snorted. "Never took you for a weenie, September."

If only he knew. "I know how to drive. It's the local amateurs that scare the crappiocca out of me. Texans hit the gas to get out of it quicker." Macy mewed his agreement and patted her leg.

Humphrey's exasperation made him sound like a weasel on steroids. "C'mon, in-studio was part of the deal. And you've only been here once. Have something against leaving home, do you?" He paused. "Can we hurry this up? There's a live promo in thirty seconds."

September bit back a retort. She could leave the house anytime she wanted. It wasn't as if she lived in fear, not at all. She'd moved home to be closer to family. But when the Chicago habit of looking over her shoulder had been broken in South Bend, look what had happened.

She mentally shook herself. Once her hands and feet adjusted, she'd better tolerate the cold, and could run over to the radio station as promised. Besides, the Reynaud's episodes never lasted for long. And she wanted the radio platform. Her breath quickened at the thought of leaving the house. She hated driving on snow, that was why—but she told herself anything worthwhile came with hurdles.

"Okay. I'll get there. Just let me get caffeinated first. Oh, and put the state police on speed dial, ready to have them thaw me out of a drift come next May." She heard him snort back a chuckle and her shoulders relaxed. She wouldn't have to leave the house.

"Okay, okay already, you win. But call in five minutes before. No, make that ten minutes before air. Use a landline. Cell phones are shit on air. We'll run with an expanded Pet Peeves, and double-up on the calls. I'll promo between now and then to get email questions to start us off. Frog-on-a-stick, gotta run."

The sudden dead air ended the conversation. The ten-minute weekly pet advice show got the word out better than paid ads, although the tiny stipend Humphrey called a paycheck barely covered the cost of caffeine. Her pet behavior consulting business included advice by phone, although in-person training was ideal, and the radio show and her regular column in the local paper drove more than enough clients to her subscription-only pet advice website.

Besides, she didn't need much, and never would again. Chris had seen to that. She took a shuddering breath. Just a random thought bushwhacked her emotions. Christopher Day was supposed to have been part of her dreams, THEIR dreams.

September chugged half of the too-sweet coffee. She cradled the oversize mug, treasured for more than the warmth. Chris had bought it for her at a dog show. They'd often exchanged crap gifts for no reason, just to make each other smile. It was his last gift.

She set the mug down with a clunk. Macy grumbled and pressed his forehead against her socks. She stooped to smooth his fur, and her tight throat relaxed. "Thanks, buddy, but I'm fine. Later we'll play laser tag, okay?"

The cat reacted to the "play" word, and leaped onto the wrap-around counter that edged three-quarters of the kitchen proper. He trotted to the corner cupboard next to the fridge, and pawed open the door. Macy scrabbled inside, his plume tail drawing figures in the air, and backed out dragging the stuffed mouse toy by one ear. He pushed the toy to the edge of the counter, dropping Mickey at her feet, and meowed with expectation.

She waved one finger at the cat. He sat up and begged. "If you want it, then speak, Macy." When he meowed on cue, she tossed the toy across the room. "Kill it, kill it!" Macy raced after it, grappled the toy, fell on his side and bunny-kicked Mickey into submission.

September gulped another slug of coffee and checked her watch. Time enough for a hot shower before the radio show. Before she'd shuffled halfway across the kitchen, the phone chirruped. September hurried to grab the phone where it charged on the countertop before Macy decided to attack it like his toy.

September glanced at the display, sighed, and answered. "Hello, Mom."

"Holy catfish, we've already got six inches and it's still dumping everywhere! What's the weather like there?"

"I live seven miles away from you. What do you think?" The overhead lights remained a bright, steady glow. "I've got a generator in the garage if it gets worse, but so far the heat and lights are good." She watched Macy grab his Mickey and stash it back into his favorite cupboard.

"But you still have drywall to do. Doesn't the weather have to be good for drywall work?" She hesitated before rushing on. "I know you wanted the housewarming on Thanksgiving, dear. Maybe next year instead."

"Not a housewarming. We've been over this. I'm having the whole family here for Thanksgiving." Macy left the cupboard and returned to paw September's leg, one claw snagging the fabric. She bent to unhook the nail. "There's two weeks to get it done, Mom."

"We could gather at your brother's, or even one of the girls'."

"Mom, stop." She bit her lip, and struggled to keep her temper in check.

"I'll make some calls, honey. Don't you worry a bit."

"I said *no*." September took a breath. "Look, Mom, let me do this. I need to do this. It'll be fine." She'd only been back in Heartland for a few months, but it didn't take long to remember why she'd left home and stayed away for ten years. "I've got everything planned. The kitchen's finished, plumbing and electrical passed inspection, and the security system works great. Remember, I told you and Dad the password when I gave you the extra keys?" She kept talking when her mother would have interrupted. "Dining room furniture will be here next week." She noticed the candles dripping wax on the new granite countertop, and blew them out. "Macy's pet gates work just as well for kids."

"Don't be stubborn and spoil the holiday for everyone."

The doorbell bonged, followed by immediate pounding that made September's pulse thrum. "Mom, someone's at the door. Don't worry, Thanksgiving will be great. For once, just trust me."

She punched off the phone to stop further argument. Pounding knocks took turns with the doorbell chimes. Nobody in their right mind would be out in this mess. She carefully stepped through and latched the pet gate before hurrying to the front entry.

Three deadbolts secured the stained glass front door. September peered through wavy glass and her heart leaped with sudden nerves. This couldn't be good.

Two uniformed cops stood on the front step, their shoulders powdered with white. September tightened the belt of her robe and smoothed unruly hair as though that would calm her racing pulse. She pressed the button beside the door to activate the speaker. "Can I help you?"

The bigger man answered. "Ma'am. I'm Officer Leonard Pike, and this is my partner, Officer Jeff Combs." Pike was almost a foot taller than her own five-feet-six-inches. His bulky long coat didn't camouflage his extra sixty pounds. A single black unibrow rose above horn-rimmed glasses, and his earflap hat sat too high to fully protect his bald head.

"Do you have identification?" Chris had taught her well. Unexpected visits never brought good news. Police don't do social calls.

Both men pressed identification against the glass. "Can we come in?"

She unlocked all three deadbolts and cracked the door as far as the chain allowed, but didn't invite them in. September shivered in the brutal wind. If she invited them in, she could close and lock the door again. But she didn't want strangers in her house. "What can I do for you?" She hoped they'd take the hint and leave quickly.

"We're on our way back from an accident." Officer Combs looked half his partner's age. Despite the youthful expression and athletic carriage, worry lines and the cleft chin relieved an otherwise too pretty face. "There's smoke pouring out the side of your house. Over there." He waved.

"Smoke? Oh crap! Come in already. But lock the door behind you." She rushed back into the kitchen. "Has to be the clothes dryer." September fumbled with the pet door into the kitchen, racing to the adjoining laundry room, one of the first rooms the contractors had finished. When she opened the door, white smoke filled the upper half of the room. "Why the hell didn't my alarm go off?" The contractor would hear about this.

Officer Combs caught her arm to stop her rush into the room. "Do you have an extinguisher? Where's your breaker box?" He turned to the older officer. "Call it in, why don't you, Lenny?" He pulled off his hat, and his light brown hair crackled and stood off his head with static electricity.

September jerked away from his touch. "We'll have it out before they get here in the snow." She hurried into the tiny room where the clothes dryer nestled against the wall and couldn't be easily unplugged. "Aw, hell." She punched buttons on the dryer until it stopped, pulled open the door of the front loader, and watched with disbelief as acrid smoke flowed out. "The machine's not even three weeks old."

Bending low, Combs viewed September's unmentionables. "No fire. Caught it in time." He straightened with a grin. "I've been curious to see the inside of the Ulrich place since I was a kid. Didn't want it to burn before I got the chance."

September kicked the dryer and winced, remembering too late she was wearing slippers. "Need to call the company. At least it's under warranty." Just what she needed, a game of telephone gotcha with the store. Nothing was easy.

"Ma'am? Do you need us to call for assistance?" Pike leaned his oversize frame against the doorway, pulling off his gloves to fish a tissue from his pocket and honked his nose into it. "That's some smell. Might want to open the window or crack the door." He nodded toward the solid door in the nearby breakfast nook. "Smoke will set off your kitchen alarm if you don't air it out." Pike looked around the room, tossing the used tissue in the trash before adjusting his cap.

"That door stays locked." It was too hard to mess with once it finally latched.

"Why?" Pike raised his eyebrow. "Any putz could pop that lock in sixty seconds."

She flinched, and eyeballed the door. "That's not what the contractor said."

He shrugged with a "whatever" gesture. "Locks are a specialty of mine."

September pulled a step stool out of a cupboard to reach and open the small window. At least there was no intruder danger by leaving it open. Nobody could wiggle through but a Munchkin with wings. She shivered, stepped off and folded the stool.

Combs stared at September. "Are you okay, Ms.—"

"Oh. I'm September Day."

Pike cocked his head. "September, like the month, and—er, Day like the—uh, day of the week?" He jabbed Combs with an elbow. "Is she kidding?"

"Yes, the name's just like the month." September sighed. Her parents, Rose and Lysle January, cleverly named their kids for their birthday months. Her sisters born in the spring got off easy and by the time baby brother came along in March, Mom and Dad settled for the more conventional Mark. Meanwhile, she'd been stuck with September January, no middle name needed. After 28 years she'd heard every joke possible. Chris teased her that she'd married him just to change her name. She'd joked back they should name their first child Happy. At the time, it didn't seem important, since she had no interest in starting a family. . .

Combs frowned. "Are you sure you're all right? You can call me Jeff." He smiled again.

She shook off the memory and forced a smile. After all, the man had saved her house. "Jeff. Thank you. I'm fine, just pissed." She shooed them out of the laundry room into the kitchen and followed with the step stool. "If you'll excuse me, I've got cleanup to do."

He had kind eyes. Brown. Like Dakota's. She caught Pike's amused expression before he coughed into another tissue and looked away. Wasn't that just dandy.

"You're one of the January girls, right?" Combs wouldn't leave it alone. "My sister Naomi went to school with one of your sisters."

She considered him more carefully. Officer Jeff Combs might be a couple inches shorter than Pike, but his lanky frame and loose gait offered a boyish contrast to his overweight partner. Still tan from the past summer's sun, he had crow's feet that advertised humor, stress, or both. Combs was at least five years older than she, maybe more. "Probably May or June?" She'd skipped a couple of grades in high school, so she was younger than most in her class.

"June, that's right." He nodded. "You were behind us, but then you took off before graduation on that music tour thing." He pulled on his hat. "What brings you back to Heartland?"

She urged them to the front door. "Thanks again. Sorry, but I don't feel real sociable at the moment." She had come home to start fresh and get away from the ghosts that stalked her—real and imagined. She had no interest in rehashed history.

Pike pulled on heavy gloves, adjusting his hat and turtling his neck down into his collar as he duck-walked to stay vertical on the slick path back to the patrol car.

Combs paused. "Listen, Ms. Day—September. Is it okay to call you September? I wondered, you being new back in town and all—"

"Officer, uhm, Jeff. I don't mean to be rude, but I've got a phone call to make. Thanks again. You saved my bacon." She started to close the door.

"Sure, I understand. Busy day. Maybe another time?" He handed her his card, and a twinkle lightened the shadow in his expression. "At least it's a good day to wear hot clothes." He turned and hurried to the car.

Despite herself, September chuckled. So Officer Combs was a wise-ass; she liked that in a person.

She shut the door, shooting the deadbolts and rattling the knob to be sure it caught. Time enough later to throw out scorched laundry. She needed to call Humphrey Fish five minutes ago, and she'd better be scintillating as hell or he'd make her pay.

September raced back to the kitchen, climbed the step stool, pried the smoke detector off the ceiling and shoved it in a drawer. She didn't need sirens interrupting the phone call. September cut Anita off before she could say a word. "Patch me through to the studio line. I'm already late."

"Your ass is so dead." Anita put her on hold for ten seconds, which forced her to listen to Humphrey's on-air introduction. She seethed at his tone.

"Why looky there, furry friends and neighbors, September just blew in. She's finally ready to offer us the best kitty and puppy advice available. Nice of you to join us, your highness. Didja overindulge in the catnip last night?"

"Greetings and salutations your own self, Mr. Fish." Uh oh, this would be rough. "Catnip's not a bad idea. It's a kitty hallucinogen and will take your cat's mind off the nasty weather." She hurried on before he could interrupt with another crack. "I hope all the pet parents listening out there have brought their animals indoors for the duration."

"Hey, they've got fur coats, so what's the big deal?" He laughed. "Not like some of us hair-challenged humans, right?"

She jerked the phone away from her head. He'd turned up the volume to punish her without the audience any the wiser. Two could play that game. "Scaly fish are cold blooded creatures after all."

"Oooh, so you're gonna be catty, are you? Pull in your claws and give us some Pet Peeves de-tails."

"You step on my tail, I'll hiss back, Mr. Fish." A breath calmed and settled her into the rhythm of the show. "Even furry cats and dogs risk frostbite or hypothermia in weather like this. See, the fur helps hold body heat next to the skin to keep them toasty. Wind can strip that warmth away, and the wet keeps the fur from insulating them. Their ears, toes, tails, even the scrotum can freeze."

"Blue balls. I love it when you talk dirty. Let's take some calls. Hello, you're on the air with Pet Peeves and September Day, what's your question?"

September braced herself. God only knew what callers she'd get after that intro.

"Uh, hi, I got a wiener dog. I left him outside overnight. Now he's a pup-sicle." Maniacal laughter bubbled until Fish disconnected the call.

"That's a good one. This is Humphrey Fish with September Day's Pet Peeves. September, what do you have to say to our wiener dog fella? C'mon, I know he's obnoxious but toss him a bone."

She winced, but didn't hesitate. "All jokes aside, the smaller the pet, the greater the danger. Also, y'all may end up with some hit-or-miss potty behavior as a result of the storm, because little dogs just don't want to squat in a snowbank and get their nether regions cold."

"We've got a theme going." Fish guffawed, but it was forced.

She heard a beep-click on the line, and recognized the call-waiting signal. She checked caller ID, and rolled her eyes.

Fish broke in. "Thanks for your question. We've got to take a station break, but September will be right back with all the answers to your litter box woes. Keep those phone calls coming." The music swelled and the taped commercial played. "Got you a new attitude today, do you?"

"I've had a hellacious morning." September heard the beep-click again—same caller—and once more ignored it. "This won't happen again."

"You don't understand. The callers love the new edginess. The phone lines lit up. They love your catty comments."

September stared at the phone. "You're kidding."

"Swear to god, September. The bitchy comebacks are great. I can dish it out if you're up for it." He paused. "It's great radio. Trust me. Just keep it clean. Sorta."

"Uh, sure. Whatever you think works." She still wasn't convinced. "Let me get this straight. You're going to be snide, and I'm supposed to put you down?"

"Exactly," he said. "Now pin on your sparkly bitch pin, and turn on the wise-ass to answer that litter box question. We're going live in five."

A long pause filled the airspace before the Dr. Doolittle "Talk to the Animals" theme came on and faded out followed by Fish's introduction. "We're back with Pet Peeves. I'm Humphrey Fish trading barbs with September Day. Me-ouch."

"Don't get your tail in a twist." Better start off mild. She still didn't trust him and didn't want to get canned.

"I resemble that remark." Fish opened the door and waited for her comeback.

"I know you do. And I got to tell you, it's unattractive." The beep-click interrupted once more. September continued to ignore it.

"Oh please, September, talk dirty to me again." Fish chortled.

She smiled. This was fun.

"Enough already with the potty talk. We need to go to the next caller."

"Sure thing. For more information listeners can click on PetPeeves.com." There. She got in the plug since Fish wasn't inclined.

"Caller, you're on the air with Humphrey Fish and Pet Peeves. What's your question?"

Quick breaths filled the long pause. "Is September there? Please, I need to talk to her."

"I'm here. What's your name? And do you have a pet question?" Dang, September hoped another break came before long. She needed her own litter box after so much coffee.

"September? Oh my God, September you've got to help me. Please, oh no oh no—"

"Calm down, I can barely understand you. Stop crying and speak up. I'll try to help if I can." Forget about the bitchy delivery, this one sounded serious.

"I tried and I tried to call you but your line was busy. The babysitter fell asleep, I could just kill her." The voice broke. "I've looked and looked, but he's nowhere around the house. You've got to track him."

The call waiting. "April, is that you?" She'd blown off her sister three times. September's mouth turned to dust.

"Steven's gone," April cried. "My baby's out in the storm, him and the dog both are gone!"

Chapter 3

Shadow raced off the path and buried his face deep in the drifted snow. The mouthful stung, numbing his tongue, and finally melted. He barked with surprised delight, grinned from both ends of his body and repeated the game, grabbing and tossing doggy snowballs as fast as he could munch.

He paused, black tail still churning the air, and stared at Steven. Maybe his boy would invite him closer?

But Steven never looked back, just plodded down the tree-lined trail. His boy ignored Shadow. Like always.

Snow blurred the route, but Steven followed the twists and turns with the confidence of one who has traveled the same track hundreds of times. Almost as if he could smell-sense the right foot placement with the keen skill of Shadow's own nose.

A new game? Just the two of them to visit the happy-place with no big humans? And no itchy vest that pushed black fur the wrong way. Shadow danced his delight. He bent double to bite the snow that settled on his back like his gnawed tattered sock.

Before they had left the house, after the old woman had fallen asleep, Steven had reached for the vest. But it hung on a hook out of his boy's reach. So his boy hung something else around Shadow's neck. It bounced now against Shadow's furry chest with each paw step forward. The cord wasn't as long as the leash. Not nearly long enough for the other end to be attached to Steven's wrist the way they practiced. And without the connection, Shadow was free to explore each side of the path, range ahead or lag behind.

Such smells. Such sounds. The cold focused every sensation until the world turned shiny bright, clean and sharp. Each white flake landed with a quiet "thpp" that made his long ears twitch, and tingled his skin at each grazed hair. Warm furry smells, rich and pungent…creatures burrowed deep out of sight tickled and teased that deep smell-place under his eyes. More, he wanted more.

Shadow raced in a tight circle, leaped high in the air to snap a withered leaf from a tree, and then dug frantically for no reason with mutters of joy. He panted, offering a happy tongue-lolling grin.

He stopped, cocked his big head to one side, and willed his boy to look at him. The white stuff clogged the air, blurring Steven's distant figure. Wind shifted and scent—and his boy—disappeared. Another gust blew snow so hard Shadow couldn't see, but it also brought back the familiar comfort of Steven's signature smell.

Shadow barked, bounded ahead three leaps, and barked again. He saw Steven flinch and cover his ears with his bare hands, but continue to stomp forward. Shadow barked again, and bent low in a butt-high bow in the most blatant invitation to play he could muster.

They could chase each other. Eat the cold white stuff. Roll around on the ground until exhausted. Shadow wiggled, barely able to contain his excitement.

But his boy never turned to see. Steven stuffed his hands back into his pockets, and trudged on.

The pup's tail slowed. He understood. The silent message shouted louder than the mouth-noise humans used. So he stood up and shook himself hard in a doggy shrug of disappointment. It wasn't Steven's fault. It was a good-dog's job to teach his boy how to have fun.

Most humans didn't dog-talk very well. So Shadow learned to watch their faces for clues to what all the mouth-noise meant. But his boy rarely varied his expressions, rarely vocalized, and spoke a different sort of body language than the adults. That was okay, though. Shadow was multilingual.

He figured out what some of the adult's words meant, like "food" and "outside." But more often, the big humans confused Shadow when they said one thing with their body and another with words. He never knew which to believe.

Steven wasn't nearly so confusing.

But his boy still carried the fear-stink from earlier. Not as bad as the boy's mother, but nasty all the same. Outside the house the cold wind washed away his fear-smell. Shadow whimpered at the thought, his ears flattened, and he hurried after Steven. A good-dog protected his boy, even if—ESPECIALLY if—scary people threatened.

Fear-stink made Shadow's fur stand up and feel prickly. Prickly and ready to bite. But he wasn't supposed to bite, ever. So he hated the fear-stink.

Shadow wanted to play. At the thought, his hackles smoothed. The cold, sharp day was made for play. For jumping and running, barking and peeing and digging out nose-tickling smells.

And fetching. He liked that word. The big humans never said the fetch-word enough.

Maybe they'd play when they reached the open field, the place with the metal climb objects. The happy place. His tail wagged at the thought. They visited the happy place almost every day, sometimes with the old woman and sometimes with the boy's mother. Shadow played, and Steven made the swings move or stacked rocks. Like his boy, Shadow appreciated routine.

With renewed anticipation Shadow raced after his boy. Maybe Steven had brought the ball—that was another word he'd learned all on his own. Shadow loved his ball; it made the best fetch game ever. Almost as much fun as to grab and shake Bear-toy to kill it. Pretend kill it, anyway.

Shadow reached his boy's side and trotted as close as possible without contact. Good-dogs stayed close to their people, and Shadow wanted to be a good-dog almost more than life itself.

Steven reached down and caught up the short cord suspended from Shadow's neck, mimicking the leash walk connection they'd practiced so many times. The pup showed his teeth like the big humans did when they were happy. He'd practiced and learned to copy their smile. He was sad that they didn't have tails to show joy and sadness, to warn and welcome. Shadow wondered why they never play-bowed. So Shadow learned to show happy teeth to help humans understand dog-talk better. They liked it, too.

He liked how his breath puffed white into the air. Panted breath surrounded his head in a cereal-scented white cloud. His boy's breath did the same thing.

From the time he'd arrived at the house, Shadow had understood his world revolved around his boy. That's how his boy's mother wanted it. Shadow knew she was Steven's mother because they smelled so much alike and because she treated his boy with the same ferocious care his own protective dam had shown.

But his boy's mother was sad a lot of the time. Even when she smiled, the sorrow crept through. It confused him. Sometimes Shadow managed to make her laugh, like when he'd tripped over Bear-toy or chased his tail. Her laugh made a wonderful swell inside his chest. When she called him "good-dog-Shadow" the day Steven pushed cereal treats off the table for him to snap out of the air, that was best of all. He thought his chest would burst with happiness.

Another lady visited him every day—the treat-lady. She taught him words and special games with rules he tried to understand. Sometimes it took a long time for Shadow to figure out what she wanted. Once he did, she made him feel so smart and happy. She called him "good-dog" more than anybody.

Shadow pictured her face and wagged again. Thought of the treat-smell that clung to her clothes made him drool.

The treat-lady showed him how to understand the mouth-noises people called words. Every time he guessed right, she made a "click" sound with her mouth and fed him a treat. It didn't take Shadow long to figure out if he was a good-dog, he could make that click-treat happen. People had pockets filled up with yummy stuff for good-dogs, and hands made for scratching a dog's hard-to-reach places.

Steven didn't like the click noise, though. Shadow could tell, because his boy covered his ears. Shadow wished he could cover his ears sometimes, too. The big people didn't mind the loud-hurt noises. The scary-noises today made him squat-and-pee until it stopped. Maybe only dogs and youngsters like his boy could hear those noises.

Anyway, Shadow only got to play the click-treat game when his boy stayed in the other room. Every few days the treat-lady spent a bunch of time with him, even longer than the daily visits.

He wondered why she didn't stay all the time. He'd like that. A lot.

The treat-lady taught him what to do when she said *sit* or *down* or *wait* or *come*. *Come* was the hardest. Shadow always found something that smelled or sounded so wonderful that teased him to ignore the word, so he'd only gotten *come* right a couple of times. The treat-lady had been so excited and happy and called him "good-dog" many times. More times than he had paws—that was a lot—so he knew he'd done it right. She gave him tummy rubs and played fetch until his tongue hung to the floor and his tail was too tired to wag. But he wagged anyway. He couldn't help wagging when she was near.

Maybe if he got everything right all the time, the treat-lady wouldn't ever leave him. Wouldn't that be fine?

Lately they'd practiced with his vest. He liked to race around the big room and drag the attached leash. He made it crash into the wire crate or splash into his water bowl, pretending that it chased him. But the treat-lady frowned and shook her head when he did that. She didn't give him any treats or smile or anything. She ignored him.

Shadow hated to be ignored. It made his tummy hurt. That's how he knew what not to do. He was smart that way.

The first time she picked up the end of the leash, he pulled hard and wagged his tail and woofed, sure they'd have a tug game like with Teddy, his bear-toy. Yet she didn't want him to pull, either. How confusing.

But when he stood quiet and did nothing at all as Steven clipped the leash to his vest, the treat-lady laughed and rubbed his tummy, gave him a quiet "click" and a treat, and he knew he'd done something right. Imagine that—a good-dog for doing nothing at all? For walking without pulling and standing quiet until the treat-lady said "okay" which signaled Shadow to do whatever he wanted.

He liked the "okay" word almost as much as "good-dog."

Shadow hurried along the snowy pathway, keeping pace with Steven. He didn't pull against the makeshift tether and surge ahead or drag behind. He knew how to play this game. He'd learned the rules.

Overhanging trees and bushes bore the brunt of the wind, but Shadow's nose and ear tips stung with the cold. He shook his head and licked his nose to warm it, and pulled the makeshift leash out of Steven's hand. Shadow stopped and plopped his tail into the snow and waited, just as the treat-lady had taught. His boy paused, and felt along the line of Shadow's throat and down his chest until he was able to retrieve the line. The boy's touch thrilled the pup and made his tummy leap with happiness.

Shadow didn't know why his boy never gave him tummy rubs, and didn't like to play. But he figured out it was a good-dog's job to teach his boy how to give tummy rubs and to play chase and fetch and all the other stuff that made life an adventure for human-pups and dog-pups alike.

Treat-lady hadn't said so. Shadow figured that out all by himself. He was smart that way.

The pup wagged faster when they came out from under the trees into the open playground. He nudged his boy's side with his muzzle. Was the ball in one of his pockets? He detected something hard, not a ball, with the acrid odor of the scary "POP-POP-POP" from the morning. Shadow wrinkled his nose.

Steven shuffled to the gate, fiddled with the latch, and entered. He dropped Shadow's neck cord so the heavy end nestled into black fur. Nothing new here—his boy always let go once they arrived so Shadow could play and "take-a-break." He'd learned that meant he should squat. Only after that was he allowed to play.

But either Steven's mother or the old woman had always accompanied them before. The pup's large pointed ears drooped and he whined. Being alone with his boy made him nervous.

The old woman helped take care of his boy. She smelled of dusty powder and bacon, and made him sneeze and drool at the same time. Her loud voice hurt Steven's ears sometimes, but the pup knew she meant no harm. He liked her well enough, but would like her better if she shared the bacon.

Steven made a beeline for the playground equipment and didn't shut the gate. Shadow's unease deepened. His boy always opened it and the old woman always shut it. The gaped door looked wrong. But Shadow stepped through and slowly followed his boy anyway. Change to his routine, or to his boy's routine was bad, scary. Deep vertical lines furrowed his brow. Shadow searched the empty playground for the old woman. Maybe she woke up from the sofa and would meet them here?

Steven trudged to the snow-filled canvas slings hung from chains that clanked in the breeze. He brushed one clear and twisted the long chains around and around. Once wound tight, he let go, watching without expression. The swing twirled, unwinding in the wind. He stared until it stopped, and again twisted the chains.

Shadow cocked his head for a moment and was comforted by the familiar game his boy played. Being alone with his boy was a new game, he decided. He needed to learn the rules. He shook himself and immediately felt better.

The pup trotted through the field to the farthest point inside the fence, and squatted without anyone to tell him to take-a-break. He told himself, "good-dog" but it wasn't the same.

After an hour of doggy play and swing twirling, Shadow rejoined his boy's side, like always. It was time. They always stayed just this long.

Steven held his neck cord like they always did. And they left through the street-side gate like they always did and walked two blocks to where his boy's mother or the old woman always waited to drive them home. Shadow's tail wagged at thought of the toasty warm car ride to come. The cold bit his nose, and he flinched and squinted into the wind. Steven stumbled, braced an arm against Shadow's back to catch himself—and left his hand there. Shadow adjusted his pace to his boy's.

Within minutes, the wind and snow had swept away all evidence they'd ever entered the playground at all.

Chapter 4

September's red Volvo slid into April's driveway and skidded to a stop behind the yellow PT Cruiser parked in front of the blond brick ranch. Before she could climb out, April threw herself down the front steps and body slammed into the Volvo.

"He's gone, I don't know what to do, I looked around the house, the back gate's open, and–"

"Calm down, slow down, I can't understand you." September hugged her hard to shut off the typical drama-queen babbling. April was three years older, but you'd never know it by her behavior. "Let's get back into the house so we can talk." September nervously scanned the landscape. She'd feel less vulnerable inside with the door locked.

Dark stains on both of April's knees accented her soggy yellow sweats, and her frizzed hair and smeary makeup made it clear she'd been out in the weather without a coat. April, the "pretty one" of the sisters, had inherited Mom's wavy blond hair, blue eyes and perky figure that made September feel like an awkward giraffe in comparison. September and her brother both took after their dad's side of the family.

September urged her sister through the open door, locked it once safe inside, and immediately breathed easier. "When did you notice Steven was gone? Have you called the police?"

April twisted the ruby ring on her finger. "I left Steven with Wilma and drove to work just like always." Her expression scorched the dainty red-haired woman who stood nearby.

"My son drove me here." Wilma offered a half smile, before dabbing tears with a hanky.

"Really." September turned to April, and couldn't help the sarcasm. "You went to work in this weather? Did you expect folks to show up for jazzercise in the blizzard?"

"It's not jazzercise." April bulldozed on. "I had loyal clients scheduled; they'd show up on bobsleds to get there. I just left a sign on the door and a message on the machine that we closed due to weather, and I came home right away to find Wilma asleep and Steven gone." Her voice hiccupped to silence.

Wilma hunched at the whip-hard words. Tears streaked down powdered cheeks.

"Wilma, what happened?" September stepped further into the living room. April's house always looked ready for a photo shoot, but today a slurry of grime tracked over the bare hardwood gritted beneath her shoes. September wondered what had happened to the Persian carpet knockoff that usually covered the floor. September tried to draw the woman out. "I know it was an accident. But what happened before you fell asleep? Anything different, some clue why he'd leave or where he'd go?"

"*Nothing* happened. Same routine as always." April fell into a matching chair, and then immediately bounced back to her feet. "Why are we jabbering when we could be searching? You're the dog track expert, that's why I called you. Find him. Please." She whimpered the last word.

September tugged off her gloves and flexed her fingers to jump-start circulation. Wind rattled the picture window and peppered ice against its surface, and she shivered at the image of the tiny boy lost in the storm. At least the dog was with him. "We'll run circles without some starting point." If April hadn't found Steven hunkered down near the house, there were infinite places to look. In this weather, a twenty minute detour in the wrong direction could be the difference between life and death.

"I'd change things if I could." Wilma clutched the cover like a fuzzy shield. "Anyway, when I heard the door open and close I figured Steven let the pup in. I had no idea the child would go out in this icy weather."

"He'll freeze, he's going to freeze." April hugged herself. "I should have been here, should have protected him."

"His coat's gone." Wilma sounded hopeful. "It has a hood. He had on a sweater underneath and jeans with thick socks."

"But only thin tennis shoes. They'll soak through in no time." April's fierce accusation made the older woman flinch. "You know Steven hates having his hands covered; he won't wear gloves." She stopped at the front window. "Why are we talking about this? We have to find him!" She whirled to face September. "You have to find him."

"You gave the police his description for the Amber Alert. There can't be that many blond, green eyed seven year olds in yellow coats out alone in this weather, especially not with a big, black dog." September pulled back the heavy sleeve of her coat to check her watch, grateful for the down-filled parka more appropriate to Indiana weather. "So he left sometime after eleven." Steven's jacket was little more than a windbreaker, but he'd stand out bumblebee bright against the snow. The little boy preferred anything yellow. "He's been missing at least two hours, maybe longer. We can hope he's holed up somewhere out of the wind." Stuffing gloves into her giant pockets, she turned to April. "Where did you look? No need to waste time repeating the same search."

"We turned the house upside down. He wasn't in his bedroom or under the bed or in the closet where he likes to hide. Used to hide." A fleeting look of pride lit her face. "He stopped hiding. Hasn't for a couple of weeks now. He stopped stimming, too. Until, uhm, until this morning, and he started rocking again."

"So what happened today?" The question was rhetorical. Nearly anything could turn a seven-year-old autistic child into a runaway, or more likely, a wander-away.

April crossed her arms. "When I couldn't find him, I looked in the back yard. The gate was open. I went a little crazy then and ran around the outside of the house and yelled for him. The snow was only about three inches then but starting to drift, and I couldn't see any tracks. I made a big mess around the back of the house, in and around the fence." She paused. "I was afraid I'd mess up any way to trail him, you know, the way you do with dogs. So I stopped. That's when I called you. Tried to, anyway. You wouldn't pick up." She didn't hide the fear-fueled accusation.

"I thought Mom had put you up to bugging me about Thanksgiving." Outside the picture window, the manicured lawn, pebbled walkways, clipped hedges and decorative stone-lined flowerbed had disappeared beneath drifts. No blemish of kid tracks marred the white. Pole lights at the end of the drive stood like glittery chess pieces.

"I called you because Steven already knows you. He's scared of strangers. He hates change."

September flexed achy hands. Raynaud's was a damn nuisance and would only get worse, the numbness in hands and feet making her clumsy as hell. She couldn't imagine how little Steven and the pup must feel. "Did the police say how long before they'd send someone?"

April shook her head. "You know all about that tracking stuff. We're wasting time. Find my son!"

"I can't track without a dog." September struggled to keep her temper. "Dakota died with Chris."

"Find my son." Her chin jutted. "I helped you. You owe me. *Do* something."

September bit back a retort. She did owe her. And April must be going crazy with worry. "I know someone who has tracking dogs. Guess we could see if they're available."

Wilma mopped her eyes with the afghan. "I do make allowances, I really do. I know he's your son and all, but he's not all that lovable." Wilma's double chins quivered. "If I don't get out his puzzles at ten-thirty, feed him exactly at eleven o'clock, or—"

"Wilma, we're wasting time. He's a child. Lost. In a blizzard. We can debate shoulda-coulda-woulda later." September could see that April was near the boiling point.

But Wilma didn't stop. "He's a fanatic about routine. Always wears his coat, hooks the leash on the dog before they go out."

"That's right, Shadow's with him. Haven't you trained that dog?" April aimed the next words like darts. "You trained Dakota, why couldn't you do the same with Shadow? What good is he anyway if he can't keep Steven safe?"

To April, the dog was a magic wand without value unless she saw instant results.

"I'm his mother. And you owe me."

September ducked her head, again acknowledging the debt. "Shadow's a nine-month-old German shepherd. He's like a bright teenager distracted by shiny objects. You want to trust Steven's safety to that?"

Her sister spoke with quiet command. "*I'm his mother.* I know what's best. Either help me find my son, or get the hell out of here."

"Great. I'll call about the dog." She pulled out her phone. "September to the rescue. Again."

April crossed her arms. "You don't want to compare messes."

That hurt. "And you won't let me forget." Leave it to a big sister to always know what buttons to push. "Wait, is it Doug? Do you think he took Steven?" April and her ex-husband Doug Childress had an explosive history over their autistic son's treatment. "Have you called him?"

"No. And don't you call him, either. I don't know if he's involved." For the first time, April's momma-bear attitude faltered. "If he has Steven, then at least he's safe. If he isn't involved, Doug will use it against me. I can't deal with him on top of everything else."

Wilma levered herself off the sofa. "Will you listen to me? Praise God, I know where he'd go." She beamed like she'd won the lottery.

April sucked in a breath. "Why didn't you say so before now? Where?"

"Ten-thirty puzzles, eleven o'clock lunch, and . . ." She paused dramatically as if the words redeemed her soul. "Twelve o'clock the park. We go every day. That's the only time we leave the gate open, when we go for our playtime in the park."

April hurried to the closet and slammed open the door. She yanked a coat out so quickly that metal hangers jangled to the floor.

September grabbed April's arm to stop her. "You're wet and exhausted. It's way past time Steven comes home from the park, right?"

April shrugged on the coat. "I always pick him up. He expected the Cruiser."

"But what if he's on his way home?" September pulled on her gloves. "Or somebody finds him, and gives him a ride, and you're not here?"

Wilma shuffled an eager step toward them. "He knows the address if somebody asks. I'm happy to wait while y'all go look. My son won't pick me up until two-thirty."

April's frown cut unhappy valleys in her brow. "I'll wait here. But you hurry. Call me as soon as you find him. You *will* find him for me, September?" Her shoulders drooped until the heavy coat slid off onto the floor.

"I promise I'll find him." September swallowed hard. The last thing she wanted was to dive into the hateful cold, all alone. Unprotected. But April was right. She'd never be able to repay her sister.

"I can't lose him." April dashed tears away. "I waited so long to have my own baby. You know better than anyone. Find my son, and we'll call the debt even."

Chapter 5

Snow knifed Shadow's ears until he shook his head to kill the tickle. He had lost his balance, fallen, and now struggled to stand in the chest-high drifts. His head turned from side to side until sniffs located his boy. Steven hadn't made much headway. In two bounds Shadow rejoined Steven.

Steven raised his feet high to clear the snow. His shoes squeaked with each step. Their progress slowed to a puppy pace, and Shadow curbed the urge to leap ahead. After all, dogs with four paws traveled much faster than people with only two.

Shadow wanted to be inside the warm car. He liked the daily car rides at the end of park playtime. But Shadow's time sense jittered his hurry-up urge. It was late. Would the car wait? The old woman wasn't here, either. What other rules got changed?

Maybe the old woman would be in the car. Or his boy's mother. She'd make the car wait. The thought felt right. It was a good-dog's job to trust adult people. They knew things dogs couldn't know, even if they did miss out on all the good smells. Shadow relaxed.

Sometimes Steven's mother rolled down the window so just the tip of his nose could sift through wind-borne sniffs. Cars moved much faster than dogs. But they never left their smelly pathway, and the smells always came from distant places far from the car territory. He'd like to follow those smells to their start, and drink deep of the scent until he knew everything about them.

He and Steven traveled the same path as always. Houses—not their own but strangers' homes—stood along both sides of the road. No sound came from the houses. No smoke steamed out rooftops. No bundled figures passed by with smiles or offers to pet a good-dog's head. Today he and his boy were alone in a world of white.

On other days, cars raced back and forth next to them with strong smells and scary noises. Treat-lady made it clear that good-dogs don't trespass into car territory. Shadow didn't want to argue. He didn't think Steven could best a car, either, so Shadow always stood between his boy and the road. Cars were creatures of habit and never left their territory.

But today the empty road looked lonely. Snow erased its borders, but Shadow could smell the difference. Only a bit further, over there by the pole where other dogs left pee-smell, that's where they always met the car.

No car waited. No amount of nose-pokes hurried his boy along, so maybe the car came and left. Or maybe it got lost with all the white in the air. Cars didn't have noses to find their way. He hoped cars could see to find their way through the white stuff. If they couldn't see, would cars swerve onto the footpath where dogs and boys walked? He whined but the wind whipped the sound away. His boy couldn't leap away as fast as a dog. Shadow viewed the car territory with new suspicion. Still deserted. No danger for now.

Steven fell again. This time he disappeared. The white stuff got deeper and deeper, soft as cat fur but cold when it swarmed through the wind. Shadow woofed and watched for Steven's angry explosion of thrashed arms to swim himself upright. But this time Steven didn't scream and flail. He just lay there. Silent.

Shadow didn't like it when Steven screamed. It hurt his ears. But it hurt his heart worse. Steven screamed when adults didn't understand, and Shadow wanted to scream lots of times for the same reason. But his boy's silence made Shadow's tummy feel strange, and prickled his skin with worry.

He plowed to Steven's side. Snow fell so thick and drifted so deep Shadow had to sniff hard to locate his boy's nest. He sneezed. Nothing smelled right unless he stuck his face deep under to reach the ground. And that made his eyes smart.

The snow wasn't fun anymore.

Shadow struggled upright, pushed ahead another two feet until he could stare down at his boy. Steven's lips trembled. Shadow hesitated. But he couldn't help himself, and slurped his boy's cheek.

Icy. Salty. He licked again, but stood ready to dodge Steven's slap, or brace against being pushed away.

But his boy just sat there. Cereal breath puffed from Steven's slack mouth, and his nose ran. Steven's lips shuddered again, and his teeth clicked. Shadow cocked his head. Did Steven have treats? No, he didn't chew, he just breathed heavy. But his tongue didn't hang out the way good-dogs pant. His slight body trembled.

Steven must be awfully cold.

He wondered why Steven insisted on two-footed walks when all fours did the job so much better in the deep white stuff. How sad that Steven had no fur to keep him warm. His own black coat helped, but the cold bit into his toes, ears and nose.

His boy could grab fur and pull himself upright out of the white stuff. They'd practiced that trick before. He learned quickly, like a good-dog should. He told himself, "good-boy" because Steven wouldn't. His tail wagged at the thought.

He waited some more, but Steven didn't move. He just stared up at Shadow. His eyes half closed.

Maybe he'd decided to walk on all fours. At the thought, Shadow grinned, his ears flattened and his tail wagged. Wouldn't that be fine? He backed up to give Steven room.

Steven finally lifted an arm but his bare hand slid against Shadow's fur. The stiff fingers couldn't move very well. Shadow reached around and risked another lick but instead of gripping his coat, Steven dropped his hand. And he folded himself the way Teddy, his bear-toy turned floppy after a good shake. Steven drew up his legs, and hid his face against them, with his arms wrapped close. His body shuddered.

Shadow's worried whine went unanswered. He stretched forward to nose poke Steven, and danced sideways to dodge the slapping hand that didn't come. So he whined again. He barked. Still ignored, Shadow stuck his nose under Steven's arm and levered.

"No, no, no, no, go away, go away, no touch." Steven wailed, flinched and unwound long enough to flap hands at Shadow. Icy fingers struck his nose, and he yelped and backed away. He watched Steven curl up and cocoon himself inside the snowy hole.

Shadow shook himself, and the nose sting faded. This was wrong. He barked again and again, deep determined woofs mixed with uncertain yelps that dissolved into a bewildered howl.

Steven shrugged into a tighter ball. He covered his ears with his hands. Wind gusts dusted white over the top of his boy. But Steven didn't move.

Shadow considered his options. Houses stared back, eyeless windows without a blink of motion. He looked the other way. The car territory remained empty. He raised his muzzle, tasted the air for anything warm. Cocked his head, but the wind teased and swirled both smells and sounds into a directionless jumble. He whimpered.

With a final sigh, Shadow turned back to his boy, and huffed warm breath against Steven's neck. He didn't nose poke this time. When Steven shifted, Shadow placed one careful paw at a time into the snow nest, and snugged his body as close to his boy as possible.

Steven didn't have fur but Shadow had lots of fur. The cold bit into tender boy-parts and dog-parts when they were by themselves. But together they'd be warm.

Until the car came. A car always came. All Shadow had to do was wait. Cars were warm. And warm was good.

His boy's body relaxed. Shadow curled closer so his tail covered both his own head and his boy's white-blue fingers. He felt a tiny thrill when his boy didn't shrink away. They breathed together.

Chapter 6

Claire O'Dell disconnected the phone and set it on the table. She wanted to scream and throw the receiver but resisted the temptation. Any sudden noise might set Tracy off again, and it had taken longer than usual for her to settle down. Nerves over the trip. Or just Tracy being Tracy.

Their big purple bag sat at the front door, ready for Mike to lug to the car. She'd stuffed a week's worth of purple and green clothes inside to keep Tracy calm and happy for the five days they'd be gone.

Home in time for Thanksgiving dinner. A real celebration this year. A rebirth for their family.

That was the plan, anyway. "Now what?"

The door squealed open and banged into the luggage. "Ready to go?" Mike stamped his shoes free of slush and stepped into the mudroom. She wished he'd wear a hat. His buzz cut offered no protection for the flushed ears that matched the freckles he hated. On Tracy, the snub nose and freckles were pixie cute, despite her nobody-home stare. The little girl also had inherited Claire's pouty lips, black hair and blue eyes, but missed out on their mischievous sparkle. She wondered if Tracy would take after Mike's lean build or her own stocky stature. It didn't matter unless they could unlock the little girl hidden within.

Mike grabbed the suitcase and bounced on his heels with impatience. "Is she ready? Calm today?" He pulled the bag to the door, grinning. "I can't believe today's finally here."

Claire wondered how to tell him so he wouldn't explode. Both of them teetered on an emotional cliff. "We need to talk."

His grin dimmed several watts. "What?" Mike peered around the neat kitchen, noticing the new stain.

"Orange juice." She answered the unspoken question, and had already cleaned up the broken glass, but the spot on the wall hadn't dried. Her own fault. Tracy had yelled for a big girl glass instead of the Sippy cup. After all, she'd just turned seven, and Claire so wanted Tracy to have what other kids her age took for granted.

The dappled wall paper hid the worst of five years of damage. Most parents only dealt with crayon scribbles. Claire had planned to paint the walls after the trip, and wipe away the bad stains for a fresh start. Stains, though, were the least of their worries. She took a breath and told him. "The flight got cancelled."

"Cancelled. Why?" Mike glanced through the storm door at the cloudless blue sky. "Overbooked? Did you get another flight?"

"Snowstorm grounded all the flights. No, not here." She sighed. "Just our luck Chicago has great weather for November, and cowboy-land gets snow." Her hand caught his. "I've been on the phone the past two hours for a way to get there. Nothing's available."

"That can't be." Mike pulled his hand away and dropped the luggage. "It's all set. I got a half day off from work to run you to the airport. We've pre-paid for Tracy. Took forever just to get on the waiting list." His fair skin flushed to match his wind-burned ears. "Maybe they'll postpone—"

"Already tried that. I called Elaine. The other parents are in the same boat. Elaine tried, too, but they won't cancel, said too many are already on their way. We get no refund, Mike, and we go back on the waiting list if we don't show." Claire tightened her jaw and resolve. She wouldn't cry, not as long as they had one option left. She just had to convince Mike.

He flexed his fist, frustrated there was nothing to hit. You couldn't beat up the weather. "Took out a second mortgage. I'm already working double shifts." Mike's soft words punched the air. "We can't stop now. Tracy has a chance, maybe her only chance. There's got to be a way." He closed the door on the beautiful Chicago winter day.

The clear skies mocked them. "Elaine says three other families from here, five from Detroit, and two from Kansas City got grounded. Well, the ones from Detroit just landed at O'Hare. Probably others we don't know about. But that's eleven kids with their parents and none of us can afford to miss this chance."

"What do you suggest? Strap on boots and hike to Texas?" He pulled out his phone. "What's the number of the Legacy Center? Maybe I can explain—"

"Mike. Stop."

"But she's just a little girl. We did everything they asked." He coughed, trying to cover the emotion. She knew he hated to look weak. But this was a challenge he couldn't win with skinned knuckles. "You could drive. We can ask my dad to go. It's not that far. You take the car, and I can catch rides to work with one of the guys."

Claire grabbed the phone from him. "Our old car barely gets you to and from work. I already asked about car rentals. Solidly booked. Trains take too long." She grasped his hands again, smoothed the blunt nails stained with grease and rough from cold weather. "Elaine found a bus."

"A bus? What do you mean?"

She smiled, kissing his chapped fingers. "The Detroit group meets Elaine at O'Hare to board the bus. It's a church bus big enough for everyone. From there they go to Kansas City and on to the Legacy Center in Texas." He had to say yes. "We're supposed to check in tomorrow for orientation and first treatments. We can make it if we drive straight through. But we've got to leave now."

"A church bus." Mike's mouth fell open. "They're driving a friggin' bus from Chicago to Dallas? Through a snow storm? With how many autistic kids for hours and hours?" His shoulders hunched. "You know how crazy that sounds?"

"A dozen kids, a few more parents." Claire's words tumbled over themselves. "There are three more buses with kids coming from Las Vegas, Minneapolis and Atlanta. Some others will drive their own cars. You read the program, Mike. It's limited to two hundred children, and probably half that number got zapped by the storm." She toed the suitcase, packed not just with clothes but with their hopes and dreams. "We've got twenty-four hours, maybe a little more time, to get there. With luck the snow will melt before we arrive and we'll make even better time." She squeezed his hand until he met her eyes. "Tracy can be on that bus. Me and Tracy." Claire offered a faltering smile. "It's our best chance, Mike. For Tracy. You know it is."

"I can't get off work, babe. I can't lose my job." He pulled his hands away. "Three guys are ready to take my place. I had to beg to get the half day off today."

"You can still drive us to O'Hare just like we planned. Elaine fixed everything." She embraced him, and couldn't stem the eager hope. "Please. We won't be alone. We'll help each other." She laughed. "We've all got the same experience."

He hung his head. "I wish I could go, too. I need to be there for you and Tracy."

"You are, Mike. You're a great dad, and a great husband. Just get us to the bus." She hugged him again.

"God, I feel so helpless." He grabbed the suitcase.

Claire kissed his cheek. "Helpless? Not anymore."

Chapter 7

September stamped snow from her boots at the back door. She'd found no trace of either Steven or Shadow. The drifts against the Gentry Park fence measured three feet in some places, more than enough to hide a tiny child and dog. She'd searched them all. Either they'd never been there or they had already left the park.

If they were still nearby, Dakota would've sniffed them out. She rubbed away the thought with an icy glove to her forehead. It was a waste of time to wish ghosts back to life.

Her phone rang before she could reach the door. She tugged off her gloves to fumble it out of her pocket, glanced at the caller ID and almost didn't answer. "Yes, Mom. What now?"

"Did your sister call you?"

"I'm at April's now." September hugged herself and ducked her chin into the heavy scarf wound around her throat. The snow hadn't let up.

"Oh, good. She said you could use her good silver since you insist on doing the whole Thanksgiving thing yourself. But your brother wants to bring his corn chowder. Don't you dare hurt his feelings and say no. He's very proud of that recipe."

"Mom, I'm kind of busy." Mom must not know Steven was missing, thank heaven, or there'd be hell to pay. With luck, they'd find him quickly and she wouldn't have to know. "Corn chowder sounds good. I'll call him later, okay?" She disconnected and pocketed the phone.

September entered the kitchen by the back door. April never locked the door when she was home, no matter how many times September insisted. A woman's voice spoke in the front living room, so the police were here, a pretty good response time considering the weather. "I'm back," she called, pulling off her hat and gloves. She blew on her hands and hurried through the dog gate that separated Shadow's domain from the rest of the house, and nearly skidded to her knees when she stepped on a fork.

Drawer contents lay scattered across the floor; cabinet doors hung ajar, and even the refrigerator door swung open. The place looked like the victim of one of Steven's tantrums. "April? Did they find Steven?"

Mrs. Santa Claus appeared at the dog gate wearing a hideous holiday sweater covered with embroidered turkeys. "Oh my." She looked around the room, and then met September's eyes. "We made quite a mess in our hurry." Dimples bloomed in both cheeks when she tsk-tsked and smiled. "Steven's still missing, so come help strategize how to find him."

"Who are you?" The woman smelled like fresh baked cookies. "Are you with the police?" September unzipped her parka, stuffing her hat and gloves into a pocket.

"I'm Lizbeth Baumgarten, but you can call me Lizzie." She held out a plump hand to shake. "I don't think you girls know just what's at stake." She hurried into the next room.

September quickly followed, wanting answers. April sat at one end of the overstuffed sofa with Wilma beside her. Something was off. "What's going on?" Her chapped lips tasted salty, and she wished she had a tissue.

"You find him?" April eagerly sat forward. "Any sign?" September mouthed *no* and April deflated and indicated the stranger. "I called Lizzie to help."

 Lizzie turned to April with a frown. "Just how many folks did you tell?"

"Is that a problem? The more people who know Steven's missing, the better." September pushed the hair out of her eyes. "You sure don't act like a cop."

"She's Steven's…um, therapist," April said. "You've got to listen to her."

"His *therapist?*" September looked the woman up and down. "This is the high dollar treatment you needed me to fund?"

"And just who are you, dear?" There was steel beneath the woman's jolly exterior.

"I'm April's sister. Steven's aunt." September examined the disheveled room, shocked to see drawers from end tables midway open and spilling contents over the floor. "The kitchen's a wreck, too. What are you looking for? What's more important than a little boy lost in a blizzard?"

Lizzie's brow furrowed as she hurried to answer. "Of course Steven is important. We must do everything we can to find him. And we will." She squeezed April's shoulders in encouragement. "We're a team, I won't let you down."

April squeezed Lizzie back. "Thank you. And I'm sorry."

The therapist patted her shoulder, took off and polished her glasses on the hem of her sweater, and squinted at September. "April misplaced something that belongs to me. And that affects not just one child, but hundreds of little ones." She replaced her glasses.

September ignored the therapist. She glanced at Wilma, but the older woman seemed clueless. "April, what did the police say? Are they on the way?"

"The weather must have delayed them." She wouldn't look at September.

Wilma stirred. "I don't understand. The police wouldn't ignore such a thing—"

"Of course they wouldn't." Lizzie hurried to the front window and gestured at the icy vista. "Perhaps you should call them again, make sure the police understand the urgency." She patted her pockets. "I left my phone in the car."

"Do you know what the wind chill is?" September joined Lizzie by the front window, and touched frosted glass with her palm. "I nearly froze running to Gentry Park and back, and Steven's coat isn't as warm as mine." She retrieved her phone out of a pocket, thankful she'd thought to charge it.

Lizzie took a step, and slipped on the bare, wet floor. She grabbed at September to regain her balance, and smacking September's cheek in the process.

Rocking backwards, September dropped the phone, catching her weight against the window before she slid on her butt to the bare hardwood.

April cried out with alarm. "September, are you okay?"

The hardwood felt cold through her pants, and she wondered again what happened to the rug. She rubbed her face, more surprised than hurt. "Should have ducked." She flexed her jaw.

Lizzie flexed her hand. "That smarts. Sorry about that." She stooped to retrieve September's phone. She pushed wire rim glasses up her pug nose. "April told you about Steven's treatment?"

"She doesn't know any details." April shifted her weight from foot to foot. "Can't we go find Steven now? You promised to help."

Lizzie gestured with the rescued phone. "Don't get up, just relax and sit a spell." She considered the phone and then stuffed it into her pocket so the embroidered turkey bulged. "I think we got off on the wrong foot." She offered a hand to help September up. "Friends? We're all here to help Steven."

September levered herself upright, ignoring the offered hand. "You're his doctor?" She had never hesitated to fund Steven's treatment when April asked. She owed her sister that, and owed Steven, too. But something smelled fishier than Macy's Kitty Kaviar treats.

"Not his doctor, no. That's Dr. Henry Pottinger, or at least that was his doctor." She looked pointedly at April, who turned away. "But I'm on

Steven's team. His safety and well-being mean everything to me. Everything. We've got a twenty-four-hour window to make sure he's okay." Lizzie's eyebrows rose and fell like a pair of white caterpillars. "Right, April?"

April hesitated, and then nodded. Her lipstick was a stricken slash.

"Didn't we come through with every promise? Are you dissatisfied in some way?" Lizzie made a decidedly unladylike sound. "There's just no pleasing some folks. Now, you listen to me. Steven's made such great strides. We turned away others to make room for Steven in the program. I can't let anyone's cold feet take that child's future away."

Lizzie spoke in riddles. "What are you talking about?" Sudden suspicion heated September's face. "Is Steven really lost?" She whirled to face her sister. "You should be calling the cops every ten minutes. Is this some sick joke?"

"Oh, he's lost all right." But Lizzie looked relieved at September's confusion. "Good girl, April, looks like you kept your word after all." She abruptly crossed the room and stood over Wilma who sat with her eyes closed on the sofa. "You can just stop that right now. I said stop it."

Wilma jumped, opening her eyes and unclasping her hands. "I'm just praying for Steven to come home safe." Her chin quivered.

"Stop it. Now," Lizzie said. "We don't need that mumbo-jumbo muddying the waters. Prayers never helped me or my family. Science and taking charge of destiny, that's what makes things right."

Twisting the afghan throw in her lap, Wilma looked away, blinking hard. September could see the pulse flutter in her throat. She'd given up on prayers after Chris was killed, too, but there was no call for bashing the babysitter's faith.

Lizzie smiled and softened her words, turning to April. "This morning when you called, I sent you help to solve that, whatsit, little difficulty with Dr. Pottinger. Didn't I?"

April nodded.

"It's crunch time. Pottinger's right about the twenty-four-hour window. Steven needs his treatment on time, and if you miss that deadline, nobody can help. Just return what's lost." Lizzie's dimples had lost their charm. "Perhaps you made an error in judgment, but no harm, no foul, you can fix that. I'm reasonable, you know I am. After all, we all want what's best. For the children."

September fought the urge to clobber those dimples. "Is Steven with Dr. Pottinger? April, look at me, not at her." When her sister refused, September turned back to Lizzie. "Is this a shakedown? Where is Steven?" Her stomach fluttered with fear. What had April gotten into?

April spoke in a rush. "Dr. Pottinger showed up this morning, told me Steven needed his next treatments within twenty-four hours or—"

Lizzie shushed her, and finished for April. "—or else Steven will get sick. He might die."

September reeled. "He could die?! What sort of treatment is this?"

"It's a miracle treatment." April clasped her hands, unconsciously mimicking Wilma's prayerful posture. "Dr. Pottinger brought proof on a flash drive. He insisted I watch the video but I never got the chance, because Steven got . . . upset . . . so I got interrupted." She looked with anguish at Lizzie. "I don't know what happened to the flash drive. Something happened to it while Wilma napped." Her stony expression battered the babysitter.

Wilma mouthed something silently. She'd resumed praying.

September's frustration grew. "What's wrong with you people? So a flash drive is missing, just ask for another copy." She moved back to the window and glanced at her watch. The snow hadn't slowed in the least.

"Oh, we have backup." Lizzie dismissed September's suggestion. "I even found where the information got emailed to another party, somebody called bodaciousbody."

Bodaciousbody, September knew, was her sister's email address that she used for work. For some reason April emailed the drive's contents to herself. April shook her head, a silent plea for September to remain quiet.

Lizzie measured the two sisters' reactions and sighed. "April understands. We can't have just anyone stumble on this information. So that loose end needs to be dealt with."

Enough already. "Give me my phone." September held out her hand, but aimed her words at April. "Call the police, or don't. But Steven needs somebody to be the parent and go after him."

April flinched. "How dare you."

"Screw it." September pulled on her hat and gloves. She hurried to the front door and twisted the deadbolt. She could have canvassed half the neighbors by now. If Steven wasn't found, at least one of them could call the cops.

Lizzie followed, and gently put a hand on the handle to stop her. "Here's an idea. April and I will go find Steven. And you can find me that flash drive. You're right; you'll need your phone." She reached into the wrong pocket, though, and pulled out a gun. Her expression brooked no argument.

September froze. She slowly pulled her hand away from the door.

Lizzie's body blocked any view of the gun from the other women. The older woman nodded once, and waited until September moved away from the door before secreting the gun. She kept one hand in that pocket.

April had always been the pretty one, a smart girl who acted the ditzy bombshell with her baby-girl voice. But ever since Steven arrived, and April kicked butthead Doug out of her life, her big sis morphed into a do-or-die responsible parent. Now she'd gotten into something that involved a gun.

Wilma's chins Jello-ed a rumba. "It's all my fault because today I fell asleep, and he's out there lost in the snow, and it's my fault but I didn't mean it. I just leave everything in the Lord's hands. Would you pray with me?"

"I told you to leave God out of this." Lizzie waved September back into the room. "Sit with April. She needs some sisterly support."

September slowly walked across the room and perched on the arm of the sofa next to April.

Wilma turned to April. "You know how Steven likes to hide shiny objects. Was that computer thingy shiny? Remember that time you lost your watch? Didn't find it for two days, until you changed his sheets, and there it was under the mattress."

April got up and crossed to Lizzie, her voice urgent. "We've got to find Steven. He'll freeze. September said she'd get a tracking dog to find him."

"What a good sister she is. I'm sure she'll do anything you ask. Won't you, September?"

September nodded, her mouth dry. April hadn't a clue.

"We'll find him." Lizzie patted April's cheek, the epitome of caring grandma. "Children are my life." She held out her hand to April. "So let's go find him."

"Oh, yes! Thank you. With all of us looking we'll find him more quickly." April hugged Lizzie.

September held her breath, relieved when the gun remained out of sight.

"It's clear the flash drive isn't here, we looked everywhere. Maybe it's still with Dr. Pottinger."

"But I don't know where he is." April's expression crumpled again.

"I know you don't, dear. Let me worry about that. Put on your coat. We'll take my Hummer. It's got four-wheel drive. The little guy can't have gone far."

April gathered her coat, and hurried to open the door. Snow smacked the warmth out of the room with one fat breath.

"Go wait in the car, April, I'm right behind you." Lizzie shrugged a checkerboard woolen poncho over her head. She waited until April shut the door.

September stood up from the couch as Lizzie retrieved September's phone from the turkey pocket. She turned it on and fiddled with the display. "While we look for Steven, you retrieve the flash drive your reckless sister lost." Her tone had morphed from grandmotherly to sardonic.

"Who are you? What's really going on?" September noticed Wilma had once again started praying, even though she'd not seen the gun.

"If you care about that little boy, you'll find that flash drive and return it to me. I control access to his medicine. And in twenty-four hours if he doesn't get his medicine, Steven falls off the ugly truck."

"Then we need to find Steven, and stop bellowing about some mysterious flash drive. Screw twenty-four hours. You've got twenty-four seconds to give me answers—"

Lizzie stomped to the door, and then turned. "When you find the flash drive, call April. She went to work this morning, so you can look there for starters." She tossed the phone at September. "And don't call the cops."

Wilma flinched. She screwed her eyes shut, and redoubled the prayers.

September lunged to catch the phone before it cracked apart on the hardwood floor.

"Consider that flash drive your ever-most-special gift to all the little girls and boys. Right in time for the holidays."

Pulling herself upright off the couch, Wilma hurried to the corner phone. She still clutched the afghan in one hand and picked up the receiver in the other.

Lizzie watched her. "What are you doing? I said no cops."

Wilma dropped the woolen cover. "I'm not calling the police. I'm calling a higher power. I'm sorry you're not a believer. But like you said, we want the same thing, having him safe. I have to get Stevie on the prayer chain since I got him lost." Her face was serene as she dialed the phone.

Lizzie flushed. Her right eyelid twitched.

"If she won't call the cops, I will." September thumbed the phone to dial 911.

"That's not a request. Put down the phone, both of you." Lizzie pulled out the gun.

Chapter 8

Shadow's ears twitched. A car? He liked car rides. Cars were warm.

He burst from the nest, white as a Polar bear until he shook off the ice. Steven snugged into a tighter ball when Shadow's warmth pulled away, but he made no sound.

Fluffy snow had changed to tiny ice balls that sizzled like bacon when they hit nearby roofs. Shadow blinked. Round yellow eyes glowed. The shiny eye-lights lit up the snow in twin pathways flung far ahead of the growly car. The eye-lights were placed higher than the ones on Steven's car. This car was a giant.

Shadow liked his boy's car. It smelled like French fries. Maybe all cars, even tall ones with big yellow eyes, smelled that way. Or even had French fries for good-dogs and their boys.

At the thought, Shadow's tail moved faster. Steven needed a warm car place. So did Shadow's toes. He licked his paws and they tingled in response. He'd like a French fry, too.

Steven didn't respond to Shadow's nose poke, so he woofed under his breath, prepared to dodge a flung fist. But his boy clung tighter to himself, hugged legs with his hands while his knees pillowed his cheek.

The engine grew louder. Yellow eyes stabbed close.

Shadow barked. Nothing happened, Steven didn't even twitch.

The giant car grumbled, and made lots more noise than the small one Steven's mother drove. Shadow watched for a moment. It didn't pause, just rolled along the car path and pushed snow ahead of its nose-less face. Would it stop? Maybe not. How would his boy climb inside if it didn't stop?

Could a dog make it stop, or just people?

He pawed Steven. His boy needed to move. Steven could stand by the car path. That's how cars knew to stop and let them inside. That worked for his boy's car, anyway. Maybe it would work for the giant car, too.

He grasped Steven's sleeve and tugged. Up, get up, stop the big car and go for a ride. Cars carried dogs and their boys home. And home was warm, with bowls full of dinnertime. Home was Teddy, his bear toy. Home was treat-lady visits. Home was safe. Shadow wanted to go home.

Steven must get up, up, up!

"No-no-no-no, leave Steven alone." His boy barely lifted his head, the words so soft only good-dogs with big ears could hear.

Shadow turned away and bounded toward the growly car. He stopped near the pole that jutted out of the drift. It carried a faint smell of dog pee where others before him had marked. So the pole must be important, maybe the big car paid attention to dog signposts, too. Shadow barked as loud as he could, and danced back and forth from the curb to the sign. He kicked up flurries, and bowed low and stuck his butt high to wave his tail in the air. That way the big car could see his black shape and know he meant no harm. Would it understand and stop to play with him?

But it didn't even slow down. Shadow stared at his boy's huddled form and wondered if the big yellow eyes could see Steven. He figured not. They didn't move from the car path. It would soon pass them by and Shadow would be alone with his boy again. They'd have to wait for another car to come. Wait in the cold.

Shadow dove into the path of the car. He wasn't supposed to. Treat-lady taught him only bad dogs moved into the car path. But he didn't care. He didn't know what else to do.

Shadow stood his ground. Barks mixed with excited yelps. The giant yellow eyes bore down on him until he could see nothing else.

Chapter 9

September froze, terrified. Once the front door latched behind Lizzie, she scrambled to her feet, stumbled to the door and threw the deadbolt. The back door was still unlocked. Didn't matter, though, too late for do-overs.

Bits of bone, blood and brain created a Pollock pattern on the wall behind Wilma's shattered head. September gagged. Chris had died from a head shot, too.

If she had just played along, Wilma would still be alive.

Her tears wouldn't stop. She hazarded a peek through the frosted glass. April waved cheerily from the black Hummer's passenger window. The sound of the gunshot must have been muffled by the house, distance and being cocooned inside the car.

Lizzie climbed into the driver's seat, scowled at September and cocked a finger-mime gun at April—implication clear. She'd kill April unless September followed directions. The car left with a flash of taillights. Snow packed over the rear by accident or design obscured the license plate.

The cell phone clutched in September's hand rang, and she nearly dropped it. Mom. Again. She cancelled the call, and stared at the phone for a long hungry moment yearning for the police.

Wilma's body slumped next to the ruined sofa. September looked away. She buried the phone deep in her pocket. If she called the cops, April would die.

She looked at her watch, considering the impossible 24-hour deadline. Not nearly enough time to find a needle in a snowstorm—two needles, counting Steven.

Wilma's dead, open eyes stared, and a bloody tear rolled down one cheek as if in sympathy.

No choice, she had to do something.

Start at the beginning. That was Dr. Pottinger. The flash drive belonged to him; he'd been here to show April. Lizzie searched the house and didn't find it, maybe because April took it with her to work. September dropped her head in her hands. Think. She had to think.

April trusted Lizzie. She hadn't seen the gun or Wilma's murder, and hadn't a clue her life was in danger. The deadline had something to do with Steven's medication. But that made no sense either.

Ice peppered the window. She felt a draft. The back door, she had to make sure it was locked. She couldn't think clearly, not if someone could sneak up on her, they'd never caught her stalker. Wait, no—that was in Chicago before she'd moved to South Bend. Now she'd moved to Texas to get away from him and the memory of Chris's murder.

Lizzie could come back. April paid no attention to locks. Without Dakota or Chris around for protection, September had to be extra careful. But Wilma was already dead. Locking doors now wouldn't protect April. Locks wouldn't save Steven from the blizzard.

September flinched, and checked the time again. Wilma had said her son would pick her up at 2:30. She wouldn't have to call for help, but she didn't want to be here and face him finding his mother. Once the cops came they'd ask questions for hours. And Steven would freeze. She had no choice. And she had to make the minutes count because once she left, she couldn't get back into the house.

She skirted the bloodstains and hurried down the hall to Steven's room. The yellow tulip quilt made by September's mom jumbled at the foot of the twin bed. Buttercup sheets stripped from the mattress tangled in a mess on the floor. Dresser drawers had been dumped across the carpet. The shelf over his bed hadn't been touched. Steven's collection of small polished stones sat with military precision in a double row.

A mobile with gold foil dragonflies floated above the bed. Three bright yellow toy trucks rested on their sides to make the wheels easier to spin. His cache of treasures, contained in a yellow plastic soap dish on the bedside table, included a shiny gold wristwatch with a broken plastic strap, several copper-bright pennies, and three yellow M&Ms. No flash drive.

She'd have to check with Doug Childress. Maybe Steven was safe and sound with his father. If not, she'd get help to find Steven in the snow. Screw Lizzie's threats.

No dust bunnies nested under the bed. April inherited their mother's clean gene, while September got their dad's haphazard style. She reached under the bed and pulled out a small, dark stuffed bear, a surprise since Steven didn't like soft toys. The ears had been chewed off. Huh. *So Shadow spends time in the bedroom with Steven—good deal,* she thought. She'd worried Steven kept the dog at arm's length. A bond better predicted the pup would protect the boy.

The bear's lopsided head showed evidence of sucking. After all, the pup wasn't much more than a baby himself. Shadow's breeder said all the littermates used toys as pacifiers.

September tucked the teddy beneath one arm, and rushed to the bathroom's dirty laundry hamper to pull out a pair of Steven's socks and stuff them into her pocket. She hurried back to the kitchen, located a fresh plastic bag in the mess on the floor, and filled it with the soft dog treats. Next to Shadow's "Service Dog In Training" vest and leash hung April's keys. September grabbed them all.

Her foot hit a hard object that spun off her boot and hit the wall. The pill bottle came to rest beneath the table. Steven's medication. He needed his evening dose, and according to Lizzie, he needed it within that 24-hour deadline. "Please, I'm due some better luck." The whispered plea was the closest she ever came to a prayer anymore. If Steven was still out in the cold, it might be too late for him anyway, but she had to try. Steven had to be her priority. "Forgive me, April." Her sister would agree. "Once he's safe, it's your turn. I promise."

She hurried to the front door. If the bad luck fairies spread it around, Wilma's son would be delayed by the weather long enough for her to get a head start. She dashed out the front door and left it unlocked. Security no longer mattered. She plowed through the snow to reach her car.

It started on the first try. "God bless Volvo." September shoved it into drive, resisting the urge to speed away. The roads doubled as ice rinks. She lifted her foot off the gas and coasted toward the four-way stop at the corner, and let the car's momentum carry her into the turn. She caught her breath at the view in the car's mirror when a police cruiser slowed to a stop outside April's house.

Adrenalin jerked September's hands on the wheel. Her foot stomped the accelerator before she managed to regain some semblance of control. Years of Indiana winter travel prompted the instinctive twist of the wheel into the skid, and she managed to keep the Volvo on the pavement. She white-knuckled the wheel and the car slid to a stop.

"Chris, what do I do?" God, she missed him. Mom would say go back, talk to the police. She wanted to. She had seconds to decide. But it would take time to explain the bizarre story, and Steven had little time to spare. She caught a flash of her reflection and grimaced. The police would never believe her. *She* wouldn't even believe her.

Decision made, September babied the gas and the tires spun, the rear end crabbed sideways a foot and finally caught. She cranked the heater as high as it would go and flexed her hands to warm them. At a steady 25 miles per hour, she rolled through deserted streets without a problem. Sane folks stayed home and off the roads today. That spoke to her own state of mind.

Once she reached a main thoroughfare into town, her speed crept up to 45. September watched for potential pursuit. She needed to check April's office before the police beat her to the punch. After that she would see Doug Childress.

No stone unturned, Chris used to say. She just didn't want anyone she loved to get buried when she started to dig. Not again, not ever again. Not like what happened with Chris. He'd wanted to protect her, and instead she had gotten him killed.

Chapter 10

The big car slid from side to side like a tug toy. Shadow barked and danced forward and away, excited by the motion as much as the notion of a game. It traveled on all fours but didn't act surefooted like a dog. He wondered if it would fall over in the snow the way Steven did.

The car beeped like his bear-toy when he bit it. Then it slid sideways but stayed on the car path.

Shadow held his ground. He would make it stop. He was good at this game. He played dare-you-tag with dogs at the park and they always turned away first. Besides, the car had to stop so Steven could get inside the warm place.

It slid faster. And it beep-beeped and flashed eyes at him, though he didn't see them blink. Maybe it didn't understand? How else to tell it to stop? The twin yellow eye beams caught him full in their glare.

He didn't like the stare. Shadow's hackles rose. His alarm barks turned to snarled warnings to keep away.

It didn't slow. It would hit him—and then who would help his boy? At the last moment he leaped away and yelped when the car clipped his tail.

It didn't stop. It chased Shadow off the car-path.

He tucked his bruised tail and hop-scotched through the snow to stand guard over Steven. He bared his teeth, howled and barked. Spittle flew from his jaws.

The beep-beep hurt a good-dog's ears, like a hurting scream that wouldn't stop. The giant car shoved snow before its flat face, bumped up against the hidden curb, and shivered to a stop.

The door wheezed open and a short bundled figure clambered down the steps. Shadow lowered his head and growled at the stranger.

The woman stepped closer, and called to someone on the bus. "That dog nearly killed himself to get me to stop. In my book, that earns him a ride."

Chapter 11

April glanced sideways at Lizzie. The older woman gripped the steering wheel with fuzzy mittens as she squinted past the thwack-thwack of the windshield wipers.

"Buckle your seatbelt, April. Safety first."

She obediently secured the restraint. The irony wasn't lost on her. Steven wasn't safe. Not by a long shot.

"Tell me where to turn. We'll start at the park and go door to door." Lizzie's sympathetic smile crinkled the corners of her eyes behind her granny glasses. "We'll find Steven, don't you worry. And we'll get him over to the Legacy Center with time to spare, just like Dr. Pottinger explained. He'll be fine."

"Turn here." She prayed Lizzie was right. The car swerved around the corner, the tires spinning before they caught traction. April grabbed the door to steady herself, admitting that more than the car was out of control.

The day had gone south so quickly. Dr. Pottinger's horrible revelation. The blood. Steven lost. At least he'd eaten before he left the house. After she had poured orange juice into the dog's bowl—the silly dog loved the stuff—Steven sipped his own juice. He rocked, shared dry cereal with the dog, and she called Lizzie to clean up the mess.

Oh God, what a mess.

She watched Lizzie, comforted by her confidence and care. Not like her own mother, for whom appearance ranked highest of all. September had not been able to handle the pressure, and fled to Chicago to escape Mom's unrealistic expectations. But April had stayed and not only met them, but exceeded them. The divorce from Doug had been a setback, but she'd make it up to Mom—and it would be worth the heartache—once Steven was cured.

"Thanks for sending help. I didn't know who else to call this morning." April rubbed her bare hands against her coat. They still felt sticky from the blood, although she'd scrubbed for what seemed like hours.

Lizzie shifted the car into a lower gear. "Tragic, just a tragic loss, but there's no going back." She smiled. "The children come first, right? Can't let such an unfortunate accident derail our plans."

Yes, it was an accident. "I can't lose Steven now. He's come so far. Did I tell you, this morning he called me 'Mommy?'" Her heart swelled at that first-ever experience.

Lizzie beamed. "Honey, that's marvelous." Her mittened hand squeezed April's with encouragement. "See, didn't I tell you? Steven will be the child he was born to be. Just trust me, stay on track." She polished fog from the window that the defroster hadn't yet cleared.

April shivered, remembering the morning's heated revelations. "That wasn't true, was it? What Dr. Pottinger said? Steven will be okay if his medicine is a little late. He was exaggerating for effect." Steven had already been off his meds for nearly a day, but Lizzie didn't need to know that. It could have been the argument, not the missed medicine that triggered his stimming.

But Lizzie's tone was stern. "Dear, there's no fudge factor in the twenty-four hours."

"Nobody told me it mattered that much." April couldn't hide her resentment. She should have been told. Now they just had to find Steven. He couldn't have gone far. She rubbed clear a spot on her own window, and watched for the splash of yellow of his coat.

Lizzie shifted the car as they climbed a gentle but slick incline. "Dr. Pottinger cared deeply about you and Steven. He didn't want any back-sliding. That can get ugly, as you discovered." She sighed. "But Pottinger got ahead of himself. The Rebirth Gathering is the right time and place for explanations and persuasions and a careful glimpse into consequences. We've revised the program, so such things won't happen again. But he took matters into his own hands sharing the flash drive. And you can see what it got him."

April stared out the window. It wasn't fair. September didn't need the money. She didn't have a child that needed special care. She ran away from her mistakes. September had only come home to Heartland to hide from her past.

Not like April, who dealt with problems head-on; dealt with September's troubles, too, and transformed what could have been a tragedy into joy. By God, she'd do the same with Steven's treatment. But this time it was September's turn to be the grown up. Funding Steven's treatment was only a start.

Lizzie adjusted the heater. "Any further thoughts on the whereabouts of the flash drive?"

"Maybe it's in Dr. Pottinger's car?"

"Gerald looked. He's very thorough, you know." Lizzie turned on her headlights and set the low beams to help see through the thick snow. "Didn't you say Steven was with his babysitter when he got lost? Where were you?"

"My office." April rubbed her face when she caught a glimpse of her reflection. She needed a total do-over. "I had to change clothes. I couldn't leave those dirty ones in my house, and I keep fresh clothes at work." Burn them, yes, that's what she'd do. Once they found Steven she'd clean up the loose ends. "I told September I had to change the answering machine, and leave a note for clients."

"Well now, that's good to know. I'm sure September will check your office, just in case the flash drive found its way there. Besides, there's still the issue of that email, am I right?"

"Sorry." She emailed everything to herself at work, where she kept all important records. "I can delete it once the Internet server comes back up. Or September can, from my laptop at work. I can call her—"

"The information on that flash drive is proprietary. Only other parents understand. Critics will say what happened today was Steven's fault." She focused on the road "We know different, don't we?"

She'd only been out of the room for thirty seconds. "It's my fault. I'm his mother. But it was an accident." He was a little boy. Steven had no notion of consequences.

Lizzie smiled. "Outsiders could shut down the program. September is still an outsider. Do you really think she'd understand?" She took off her glasses and polished them with a mitten. "It's vital we recover that information."

"Don't worry. September doesn't have to understand." She smiled grimly. "She owes me."

"That's a relief, because the price for Steven's Rebirth Gathering just went up."

"What?" April's stomach flip-flopped. "I said that I'll get my sister to pay—"

"Money doesn't matter. The whole program goes away if that flash drive falls into unsympathetic hands. So Steven's treatment only happens if September returns the flash drive—without looking at what's on it." Lizzie adjusted the glasses back onto her button nose. "It's not just about your son. All those other children need the treatment, too."

Her mouth suddenly dry, April understood that if Steven's cure went away she'd lose her little boy all over again. It was all in September's hands, a woman who had spent her fortune on a fairytale fortress against a boogeyman left behind in Chicago.

"For now, just worry about Steven." Lizzie's tone became soothing. "You've done a good job with him, April. A mother's love is a beautiful thing."

April squared her shoulders. She *was* a good mother. The best. She'd fought Doug's notions, and when he'd balked, she had enlisted Mom and even persuaded September to help Steven become all he was meant to be.

Yes, she'd let September worry about the flash drive. She'd take care of Steven, the way she'd always taken care of him. "There." April pointed up ahead. "That's Gentry Park. We can start with the houses on the same side of the street." Maybe Steven's safe and warm in somebody's house. Her knuckles whitened on the car door handle, eager to begin the search.

"Great, you run up to the door and check. I've got to make a call." Lizzie pulled the car next to the curb in front of the first house, and April unbuckled her seatbelt.

Two blocks away, the yellow HART-line bus backed off the curb, and drove away.

Chapter 12

Officer Jeff Combs stood outside April Childress's house, isolated from the whirlwind of quiet activity. Three patrol cars, an ambulance, and two plainclothes vehicles crowded the drive. The victim had already been pronounced dead, and the evidence team was inside. He'd already seen enough to know nothing he could do would help.

When the stretcher emerged he looked away, wanting to blank out the sight of the shrouded victim. Frozen tears broke loose, dusting sparkles onto his dark coat.

Officer Leonard Pike followed the body down the steps but veered away from the ambulance and headed to him. "I'm off shift, heading out. Sorry about your mom, Combs. We'll get the bastard who did this. The putz has no chance." He clapped the younger man on the back.

Combs gritted his teeth to curb curses. He felt gut punched, and wanted to hit back. He'd seen drug killings, overdoses, child battery, spousal abuse, accidental homicides and planned ones including suicides. The worst of the worst. But nothing compared.

This was his mother.

Mom, who never turned away a stray dog or kid. A woman dedicated to the church prayer chain. Who prayed for absolution for saying "drat" out loud. So proud he'd made detective, yet never spoke of his shame when it was taken away. When Cassie filed for divorce over a disturbed adolescent's fantasies, his mom had never wavered. She convinced her brother Stan to go to bat for him, or he'd not have his badge today.

"You know what's right," she'd always told him, "God won't make you wait too long. Trust yourself, honey."

Mom. Her beautiful red hair matted and stained, her blood splattered against a stranger's living room wall.

Rage shook him like a seizure. Pike reached to steady him, and Combs reflexively swung before he could stop himself. His partner dodged, grabbed and pinned his arms. "Get off. Son-of-a-bitch, let me go." Pike moved well for being so overweight.

"Hey kid, take it easy. Hang on." Pike tightened his hug for a long moment until Combs's struggles stopped. "Okay?" He released his grip and stepped away with a quick gesture toward the still-open front door. "They want to talk to you."

He'd never realized seeing red was literal. Combs took a half-step toward where his mother's body waited in the ambulance.

"Leave her be. For now." It was the first time in six months Pike had showed compassion. He wasn't known to take it easy on himself or anyone else. Pike had troubles in his own life, including a doted on disabled grandson, but he mostly kept such things to himself.

Combs knuckled his eyes. "Sorry, man. And thanks." He'd been an albatross dumped in the old timer's lap. Pike didn't have the clout to object, and didn't want to rock the boat his last year before retirement.

Combs managed to rock everybody's boat without trying. Last year, he and his old partner had built a case against a Cheese factory by getting close to one of the young kids who'd been sucked into the drug life. "Cheese" was slang for a mix of black tar heroin and cold medicine that looked like grated parmesan, and had accounted for countless teen deaths in Dallas since it was first identified in 2005. The thirteen-year-old informant ended up dead, and shortly thereafter, Combs's own career was DOA. He'd become a political hot potato, and Pike made no bones about his opinion of "babysitting duty" as he called it. Now he acted almost human.

"Doty needs you inside. Go talk to the detectives."

Combs straightened, scoured his face with gloved hands, and marched into the house.

The medical examiner hurried out. "Terrible thing, Combs, terrible thing. It was quick, though. The boys will fill you in on my prelim, and we'll find out anything else ASAP. This tops my priority list, Combs. The very top."

Combs nodded, grateful the man hurried away so he didn't need to think of a reply. He wasn't sure how his voice would sound or how long it would hold up. He looked away from the bloodstained sofa that commanded the living room.

"In here, Detec…I mean Officer Combs." Detective Kimberlane Doty, a forty-something blond Amazon with close-cropped hair whispered to her partner, Detective Winston Gonzales, a bantam rooster of a man half her age. They waited in the nearby kitchen.

Great. *The bitch who destroyed my career and her whiz kid protégé get assigned to Mom's murder.* His anger ratcheted up another notch, and he cautioned himself not to let them push his buttons.

Gonzales checked his notepad. "Victim is sixty-three-year-old white female." He looked up. "I understand you found her. Pike called it in at two fifty-seven." He paused, and acknowledged Combs with a chin jerk. "Wilma Combs was your mother. Sorry, man."

Doty broke in. "Why didn't you call it in yourself? And why'd you wait so long to tell Pike?" She ignored her partner's surprise.

Gonzales recovered, his tone apologetic. "We have to ask." Doty's lips tightened but she didn't comment.

Combs gave a slight nod to Gonzales. He appreciated the gesture even if the man had replaced him in the detective lineup. "When nobody answered the door, I looked in the window but couldn't see anything. Too much frost. Tried the door and it wasn't locked, so I came in."

Doty peeled another stick of gum and added it to the wad she chewed. The whole department knew she'd quit smoking a month before. The smell of clove gum combined with blood stench was too much to bear, but she didn't seem to notice or care. "Did you have reason to believe there was a problem?"

"Hell no. She's my mother, babysits here five days a week, and I give her a ride when the weather's bad." He couldn't stand still. He paced from the sink to the small kitchen table and back again. His shoes crunched. He looked down. Dog food and Cheerios. "Today I was late. Twenty-freaking-minutes-late." His foot bopped a one-shoe jig until he consciously planted both feet. Calm down. Be a cop. For Mom. He looked away, unwilling to share his grief, and tried to speak without expression. "The wounds…" He swallowed hard and continued with effort. "Injuries were fresh. No pulse. But she was still warm." Better. He sounded like a professional even if he wanted to scream. Twenty minutes would have made all the difference. Damn the weather, damn the traffic, and damn Pike and his turtle-slow driving!

"What time did you arrive, Officer?" Gonzales maintained a neutral expression and matched Combs's professional tone.

By the book. Doty must have reformed. Combs cracked his knuckles at the sardonic thought, and cautioned himself not to pick further at the scab not yet healed. Screw the past. Only his mom mattered today. He recited the facts, drily, with no inflection. "I looked at my watch when we pulled up. It was two-fifty. I banged on the door for maybe two minutes. No answer. Tried the door and it was open. There was blood everywhere and the place was ransacked. I thought the perp might still be in the house. So I yelled at Pike to secure the outside while I did the inside." He puffed his cheeks and blew out breath, but the tension remained wound tight. "Mom was already gone, so there was no hurry to get her help. Once we cleared the area Pike called it in at two fifty-seven."

"You sure you didn't want to get a head start on the evidence hunt, Officer?" Her tone was mild.

But Combs bristled. "Give me a break, I was a good detective. You know that better than anyone." He'd smack that feral mouth if she said one more word. Why not? His career was over anyway.

"Cool your jets, Combs. Just saying I wouldn't blame you." She shrugged. "Rules are rules, but all bets off if something like that happened to my grandma. She raised me. Nobody messes with my family." Clearly her feelings included relatives of cops.

Combs took a long, shuddery breath. He hadn't expected that. But he'd take it. Just the facts, he told himself. Feed the team. "Pike didn't even come inside. He steered clear of trace. I didn't touch anything—except to check Mom for vitals."

Doty cocked her head and gnawed the end of the pencil, her brown eyes narrowed in thought. "You sure this doesn't have something to do with last year? Coming back to bite you on the butt through your mom?"

Combs winced. "That dog won't hunt, Laney." He wouldn't give her the satisfaction, but he'd had the same thought.

They'd caught two of the three brothers who operated the lab. One was in prison, the other dead. The third had a long memory, if Spider could be believed. Despite the tiny girl's venomous tattoos of her nickname, she'd been terrified of the brothers. "If Ghoul Patrol had something to do with this, they'd want me to know."

Ghoul Patrol. The code name fit the Goth kids. Spider had had a serious case of hero-worship toward him, and Doty had pushed Combs to encourage her. "Young girls always want to feel special," she told him, "so you give her what she wants, and she'll feed us what we need." But Spider didn't tell all her secrets, after all. She reserved her most intimate fantasies—about him— for her diary. *Water under the bridge,* he thought.

Gonzales tapped his pencil on the pad. "Pike found lots of footprints out there, boot prints and tennis shoes, small, maybe a size six." He waited a beat. "A child or a woman. We found similar prints in the front room in the blood."

Combs nodded. "April Childress lives here with her son Steven. Probably their prints. The kid's a little guy, maybe five or six years old I think. Maybe that's why they're both MIA."

"Yeah, the yellow PT Cruiser out front is registered to April Childress." Gonzales made a note. "Funny she left the car if she ran with her kid. Did she call a cab, or get a ride, or what? There's at least three other tire treads out there, besides your patrol car. But I can't see a soccer mom doing the deed, unless it was an accident."

"Naw, the ME said it was up close and personal. Takes a special kind of badass to shoot someone in the face." Doty jerked her chin at Combs. "Assuming your mom was an innocent bystander, my money's on a third party. Single mom, a kid—where's the dad? Custody issue and the victim is collateral damage?"

Gonzales flipped a page on his pad. "Trace found another single muddy print on the hardwood of a man's dress shoe, size ten or eleven. Nothing outside." He looked at Doty. "Maybe it iced up by the time he left."

"Good, that makes more sense." Combs noticed his leg once more jounced to its own rhythm, and he walked a few steps to stop the urge. "Besides, the whole house got trashed. Somebody tossed it and got mad when they couldn't find whatever they were looking for." *Good, good,* he thought, turn thoughts away from that final picture of Mom.

At least Dad wasn't alive to see this. But he'd have to call Uncle Stanley. And his sister, Naomi. Aw shit—between the two of them he'd be pressed hard for constant updates. He couldn't sit on the sidelines, had to be part of it, had to find Mom's killer. He couldn't let his family down again. This was bigger than a ruined reputation. Whatever it took, even suck up to Doty, it'd be worth it to get first crack at the bastard who did this.

He braced himself to eat shit and like it. "Doty, we worked together for what, five years? I won't pretend not to want in on this. Make room on the team." Before she could shoot him down he added, "It's my mother, for Christ's sake."

"Good reason to keep your distance. You know the brass won't authorize that. Hell, they'll put you on administrative leave as soon as they find out." She stared at him, and a slight smile twitched her normal icy expression, and for a moment he thought she might relent. "Even if I wanted to, that's not my call. And after last year you used up any benefit of the doubt."

"You're just covering your ass. Again."

"Bite me." She popped her gum. "Look, Combs, go ahead and hate my guts if it helps. It's my case whether either one of us likes it or not. I want the bastard who did this as much as you. Okay, not as much, but dammit, this is personal for me, too." She looked away, nostrils flared.

She was right. Using Doty as a verbal punching bag wouldn't help find Mom's killer. But he'd be damned if he'd let Doty freeze him out. Whether officially or not, he'd find the killer. He'd nail his balls to the wall.

The phone on the kitchen wall rang. The three looked at each other. Before either detective could react, Combs scooped up the receiver. "Who's speaking please?"

"Hey, there. Just checking in, I was worried about the little guy." The deep male voice boomed so loud, Doty and Gonzales easily heard. "Is September there? This is Humphrey Fish over at the radio station."

Chapter 13

September dropped the keys twice before her numb fingers managed to fit the correct one into the lock. She opened the door and a doorbell beeee-boooped. A hand-lettered CLOSED FOR SNOW taped to the glass corroborated April's morning visit. Shouldn't be too difficult to find her laptop and business files, and learn more about Pottinger. Five minutes, tops, and she'd head over to Doug Childress's place. He lived a few blocks away. She left the keys in the door.

Body Works contained more than a dozen exercise machines in the front mirror-paneled room, with cushioned jog-in-place boards situated in between. It was designed so that members moved from machine to machine, first working upper arms for thirty seconds, shifted to a jog-board for the next thirty seconds, and on to a thigh-master machine, and so on to complete the circuit. It provided a low-impact aerobic workout favored by middle aged and older women, and April had developed a dedicated clientele in the three years since she'd opened. It made sense that she would change the message machine to prevent any wasted trips.

The mirror was not her friend. Unlike April, September rarely wore makeup, but she admitted she looked like eight miles of bad road. She had a case of terminal hat-hair that could use a good brushing.

She found two smaller rooms at the end of the short hallway. One contained a pair of saunas, two showers, and a makeup area and sink, complete with courtesy towels and toiletries. She ached for the sensation of warmth. A sauna would be heaven, but the sink would have to do.

September pulled off her hat and gloves, ran warm water in the sink, added a dollop of coconut-scented wash and submerged her hands in the steamy liquid. Invisible spiders tingled over the blue-tinged flesh. Sensation returned and her fingertips became rosy. She cupped her hands and bent over the sink to splash her face. More soap increased the gentle lather and the pooled water turned pink as the soap stung and felt good at the same time.

Blood stained the white towel when she patted her hands dry. Nose bleed. Great. She held the towel to her nose until it stopped. God, she'd love to spend more time to get warm. She looked with longing at the sauna, gritted her teeth, tossed the towel in the laundry bin and moved on.

A file cabinet, phone and printer crowded the next room, with a laptop on the small desk. Two hand dumbbells served as bookends. An emergency fire exit with an alarm centered the back wall.

She turned on the laptop, tapping her foot as it pinged and sang to itself. She rifled April's file cabinet but found nothing other than client folders filled with contracts, workout plans and contact information. "Damn." She searched the desk calendar for any clue to appointments outside of the store—for a name or a "P" that might indicate the mysterious Dr. Pottinger. The desk was clear, and no flash drive hid within the single drawer. Crap.

April's biweekly hair or nail appointments crowded between infrequent lunch dates with girlfriends or family, mostly with their mom. To be fair, April's social life slowed with Steven's arrival. But compared to September's self-imposed lockdown, April's dance card overflowed.

Most notes had to do with Steven. School stuff, meetings after class three times weekly with a "therapist" she guessed must be Lizzie, and the weekend horseback riding lessons—equine-assisted-therapy. September recalled April's rant about the Texas school systems pressed into mainstreaming special needs kids, and how inadequately trained teachers were stretched too thin to be effective. Funding Steven's therapy helped September feel better about—well, things.

That's how the whole Shadow issue arose. God knew *she* wasn't ready for another dog. Love 'em and they leave you. Dakota was Chris's idea, and she and the big dog had quickly bonded.

It had taken much longer to trust Chris. He had worked for two years to break through her resistance to marriage, but they had six years together before her stalker tracked them down. The boogeyman was still out there, waiting for her. So when April called, she ran home like a cat diving under the bed, hiding from one threat only to run smack into another.

She wondered how April had connected with Lizzie and Pottinger. Maybe there was a computer file or an email.

April subscribed to dozens of e-lists about weight training, weight loss, aerobics, business markets, autism, camera techniques, knitting, and on and on. When not working out or dealing with Steven, her sister sent and received dozens of messages daily. An email filter dumped emails into separate folders.

September first tried a search for "Pottinger," and when that didn't work, she input both "Lizzie" and "Lizbeth Baumgarten," and still came up empty. She scanned the most recent subject lines in the filtered list headed "Steven" and found nothing.

She checked the clock on the wall. Time to get out of Dodge.

"Beeee-booop."

September froze. She'd left the keys in the door. She *always* locked doors. Why hadn't she locked the damn door? Please let it be one of April's diehard gym clients ignoring the "closed" sign.

No cheery 'hello' sounded. After a lifetime of silence, September inched forward, heart galloping in rhythm with quickened breath. The police couldn't be here, not so soon.

She closed the laptop and tucked it beneath one arm. As she tiptoed to the doorway, September hugged the wall before peeking around the corner.

There. In the mirror. A man so tall he had to duck to miss the ceiling fan. He wore a bat-black cowboy duster that turned pale skin and silver hair ghostly. Hunching forward, he peered around in a cobra's dance, poised to strike. He drew a pistol. Pulled back the slide to chamber a bullet. Screwed on an attachment to the overlong barrel.

Shit-shit-shit.

September pulled back from her vantage point. She didn't recognize Ghost-Man, and he sure as hell didn't belong in a woman's gym. That wasn't a cop gun. It looked like a .45 semi-automatic. She'd lived with a cop long enough to know, and the silencer was definitely not police issue.

Lizzie must have sent this reject from a spaghetti western. All the killer cared about was the flash drive when Steven had to be September's priority. If Ghost Man killed her now, Steven was good as dead, and so was April.

September frantically scanned the small space. The emergency exit wouldn't work. The alarm painted a target on her back, and the snow hobbled any ability to outrace him. Besides, she had parked right in front of the entrance and left the door unlocked for a quick getaway. Dumb. She should have realized Lizzie wouldn't trust her, and would send one of her goons to finish the job.

She stole another glimpse and jerked back—he was halfway to her hiding place. Her breath quickened. Another three steps and he'd enter the sauna. She could run past the doorway and out the front.

He'll hear. Shoot you in the back.

Damn call-waiting, she should never have answered April's call. Poor Steven, some days it didn't pay to get out of bed, and now it was up to her. If she could get out of here alive. September froze, only her eyes searching for something, anything, a way to distract or slow the Ghost Man so she had a chance to run.

There—the dumbbell bookends.

She dared another peek when he disappeared into the sauna room. *No time, no time . . .* September grabbed a dumbbell, and scurried down the short hall. She plastered her back against the wall beside the sauna doorway. Her breath jittered. She waited, the hand with the dumbbell cocked and ready.

The first door slammed open. "Come out." The next door crashed, echoed its twin. "I know you're here." This room was next. His pistol poked through the door, sniffed for her.

September swung and the dumbbell smacked the heel of his gloved hand. The handgun spiraled away. Shattered the nearest mirror. She dodged and squinted. Mirrored slivers showered a bee sting swarm against her cheek. September stumbled in the slick glass. She fell to one knee. As she struggled to get up, she palmed away tears and blood.

The gun. There, by her foot.

The Ghost Man. He dove for the gun.

September screamed. He grabbed the pistol. She kicked his hand and the gun spun away. His hand wrenched her ankle instead. He twisted and rolled, pulling her with him.

"No!" She belly flopped, and was punched breathless. But by-god she still clutched the dumbbell.

Scrambling, he scooped up the gun.

She flailed, sobbing in fear. Crabbed backwards over crunchy glass and sliced open her palms.

He strangled the throat of her coat. She twisted, flipped onto her back and he was there. He straddled her waist. She stared at the greenish barrel held level with her face. September looked up.

He had a beautiful smile. "Give me the flash drive." His knees pressed against her sides.

She struggled to suck in air.

"Where is it?" He smiled his perfect smile again, and pressed harder.

He patted the outside of her parka, searching the lumpy contents of her pockets. Bloody droplets and mirror shrapnel glittered his hair pink. He leaned close, relaxing the pressure enough for her to suck in a frantic breath. She could smell spicy aftershave. His eyes glowed like white marbles.

"You'd like to breathe again? So we're going into the next room where you'll empty those kangaroo-size pockets—"

September whip-lashed the dumbbell. It hit his temple like a ball bat thwacking a ripe pumpkin.

He dropped. Onto her.

She still couldn't breathe. Black sparkles danced behind her closed eyelids. The hard cold pistol pressed against her throat, snugged between their bodies as intimate as lovers.

She pushed him off and the gun slid to the floor. The dumbbell dripped red.

She filled her lungs at last, and noticed the bloody goose egg that marred his head. September released the dumbbell and it rolled away, crinkling through broken glass. She waited until his chest inflated, and breathed relief mixed with guilty disappointment that he still lived. She picked up the gun, hating the greasy weight. The weapon looked the same as Lizzie's weapon, only with the bonus silencer. He'd meant to kill her. She had to move, get out of here. He could wake at any moment.

She scrambled to her feet, and gasped when pain clawed her side. He'd done something to her side. She set the gun on the desk, grasped the chair with her right hand, and braced her left elbow on her thigh to pull herself erect.

The Ghost Man lay in full view of the glass entry. Best to get him out of sight, maybe confine him somehow, because once he came-to he'd be pissed and come after her with or without the gun. At that thought, she tried to pocket the gun but had to unscrew the silencer to make it fit. Then she grabbed the hem of his long coat and tugged his dead weight the short distance to the nearest sauna. She rolled him beneath the wooden bench, and dashed from the sauna. She slammed the door, jiggled it to be sure it latched, and jammed a flimsy laundry container beneath the handle. It wouldn't hold long, but it was better than nothing.

The movement jostled towels in the laundry basket, revealing a flash of yellow stained with red. Steven always wore yellow. She pulled the terrycloth aside. Beneath the white towels, she found one of April's signature size 4 workout outfits. It was covered with blood.

Chapter 14

Shadow whined and shifted on the floor between his boy's feet. He didn't like the stranger-danger smells in the big car, or the jerky motion when it moved. And his tummy told him dinnertime had come and gone.

He nudged Steven with his nose and whined again. But his boy didn't move. Steven stared out the window at the scenery, silent as when they'd entered.

The old man across the aisle stared. It made Shadow so nervous he yawned, licked his nose and turned away. Even then the man didn't have the good-dog manners to do the same. He reeked of scary-smoke scent, and he whistled when he breathed.

Not like Steven, who breathed quietly and smelled like soap and dog treats and boy-smell.

"Where you headed?" The old man sounded kind even if he did smell like smoke. "I like your dog. Used to have a German shepherd a long time ago. What's his name? My name's Teddy."

Shadow's head jerked up and he stared at the man. But despite the words, he didn't see anything that resembled his teddy bear toy. He yawned again, and averted his eyes in deference to the human, like a polite puppy should.

"Can't you tell me your dog's name? Or your name? I told you mine." The old man plucked some paper from his pocket, folded it, and wiped his nose. "Good dog you got there."

Shadow stopped listening. The stranger hadn't said "treat" or "food" or "play ball" or any other important words that signaled fun stuff. Steven ignored the man, too, and just stared out the window like he always did.

The grown-up's gap-toothed grin showed stained teeth and his breath smelled like onions when he spoke. "Good for you, son. Your momma taught you not to talk to strangers, right? That's good, real good." Teddy scratched the gray stubble peppering his jaw, and it made a gritty noise like a potato chip bag made. Shadow loved salty chips. His tummy growled.

"You're awful young to be on your own out in a snowstorm, even with a great guard dog. Right, pooch? Or are you a service dog? Where's your vest? You're just a pup yourself." His crooning tone reminded Shadow of treat-lady.

Unable to help himself, Shadow offered a tentative wag, signaling an uneasy truce, especially if Teddy offered chips or treats. It wouldn't be polite to refuse treats. Shadow licked his lips.

The big car stopped with a jerk. Shadow scrambled to keep his balance.

The old man sighed and stood up. Shadow's ears twitched at the pop noise in Teddy's knees when he shuffled down the aisle toward the front of the big car. The old man stopped by the tall door to chat with the driver.

Shadow's mouth relaxed into a gentle pant once Teddy moved away. Four other passengers sat near the front of the bus. He and Steven huddled in the last seat. His boy didn't like to be close to other people even if he knew them.

Shadow had never met any of these strangers. They stared, too, but from a distance, so his fur wasn't all prickly.

He watched the people exit one by one down the steps and out the car's funny doorway. Shadow liked that just fine. Car rides should be for dogs and their boys to relax with people they knew. Not for strangers to stare.

Shadow cocked his head when the odd-smelling man didn't get off with the others. Maybe his clicky knees made it hard for him to climb down steps? Their regular car, driven by Steven's mother, only had two seats. Shadow always sat in the back seat behind Steven's mom, and his boy rode next to him. Sometimes treat-lady sat next to Steven's mom in the front, too. All of them just hopped in or out, they didn't have to climb. Shadow watched the old man and the woman driver. Maybe if his own family had as many people in it as hers did, they'd drive a funny big car with steps, too.

"Freda, do you know the boy with the dog?" Teddy's glance brushed them, and Shadow thumped his tail again.

She shrugged. Shadow watched with interest when she pulled a fuzzy hat out of one pocket and tugged it over her short hair. He wondered what else might be in the pockets. Maybe a ball? Or treats?

She turned in her seat, and Shadow heard the cushions squeak. She looked at him.

He stared back for a moment. Fur rose on his back but smoothed down again when she looked away. The door whooshed open, and the old man's knees popped when he got off.

Always before at stops, people got off and new ones got on. Shadow's mouth closed with expectation. He knew they got off at Steven's house. That's how car rides always ended. Shadow's bowl should be filled with food by now. He wished they'd get there soon. His toes ached from the cold.

But this time the lady closed the front door before any new people appeared. Shadow stood up when she waddled down the aisle, turning sideways to fit. She stopped in front of them. "Kid, you've been riding the bus for—" She looked at her wrist. "Close to two hours now. Did you miss your stop or what?"

Shadow wagged and dropped his ears. She smelled good, like French fries and flowers. No smoky smell, and her voice wasn't rough. She didn't sound mad, but you could never be too careful with strangers, so he wriggled his butt. She smiled at him and cut her eyes away. He relaxed at once.

Maybe she'd pet him and call him "good-dog." Right now he'd like that. A good-dog was brave no matter what, so he stood between his boy and the stranger and pretended to be brave just like with the smoky man. When she leaned toward his boy, he woof-whined concern and wagged faster and higher.

She sighed, backed away and sat in a more distant seat. Shadow relaxed, but watched carefully. "I'm not supposed to let dogs on the bus. But I couldn't leave you both out in the cold." She smiled again. "Besides, I like dogs better than most people."

Shadow thumped his tail—she'd said "dog" so she must be speaking about him. Steven stared out the window.

"My shift's over. I wouldn't even be out in this mess, except I started the route before it got bad. I figured you knew where you was going, but maybe not, huh? Teddy's worried."

His head whipped toward her. But she didn't have his bear toy, either.

She waited. Steven didn't answer. "Just tell me where you live, son. Or a phone number so I can call your folks." She'd pulled a palm-sized object out of her pocket and waited expectantly.

Shadow stretched forward and sniffed her pant leg. She had at least two dogs of her own. He wondered if she ever called them good-dogs and rubbed their tummies. Or maybe fed them French fries?

"Steven Childress, thirty-three Bois D'Arc, Heartland Texas 903-555-6824." His boy sing-songed the words so quickly, the woman gasped with surprise.

"Well now, Steven, is it?" She smiled, and stood up. "Thanks for telling me, son. I'll call the number, okay?"

Shadow cocked his head when her body stiffened. Caution colored her words. Big-humans often changed the way they treated his boy after being with him. He wondered why.

***

"Am I speaking to Mrs. Childress?"

"You've dialed April Childress's cell phone. Who's this, please?"

"Freda Tybalt. I'm a bus driver for HART-Line services, and well, I've got your son and dog with me. Steven's been riding for the last couple hours."

"Thank God. We've looked everywhere for that little dickens. He's autistic, you know, wandered away in the storm. Where are you?"

"Here's the deal, Mrs. Childress. I'm at the Star Mall, my shift is over, and the next driver takes the bus on from here. But I'm late because of the ice. Dispatch says they're shutting down the runs for the rest of the day."

"I'll come to you. Be there in two shakes. Could you wait in your car if the bus has to leave? I'll pay you for your trouble, Ms. Tybalt—er, Freda."

"Naw, don't need no reward. I should have realized he was joy-riding earlier. But I had my hands full with the roads today, if you get my drift. Pun intended." She chuckled.

"Don't want to put you out, but I'd sure be obliged."

"It's no trouble to wait. I get something for dinner or snack before I head home. But my VW won't accommodate the dog, boy and big ol' me." She paused. "Probably some of the stores are closed but they'd keep the mall open. My friend Teddy is inside."

"You tell me. I'll meet you wherever."

"Okay, meet us at the mall. We'll wait at the north entrance, in the food court. I'll even treat the boy and his dog to French fries. How's that?"

"Perfect. Thanks again, Freda. I'll be there quick as I can. Sending my, uh, the boy's father. We'll insist on rewarding you appropriately."

Lizzie sat back in the car and hung up April's cell phone. She dimpled with relief. Outside the car, April plodded through the snow to knock on the front door of the next house. They'd already covered two blocks up from Gentry Park.

But April didn't need to know just yet that Steven had been found. The continued search kept April occupied until they could retrieve Steven and get him the treatment he deserved. She'd threatened to withhold the medication, sure—that's the way the game was played. But Steven was an innocent, and she couldn't punish him for the stupidity of his mother. Or his aunt. No matter what, the children's well-being came first. That was her mission, her life's calling. Nothing would stop that mission of mercy.

But Gerald was at April's Body Works to get her laptop. She needed to send someone trustworthy to collect Steven.

Who to send? Someone who wouldn't question. Someone who needed money—no, better than money. A parent who couldn't otherwise afford a miracle for a child. The answer came immediately, she knew just who to call. Lizzie smiled, and dialed the phone number.

Chapter 15

September downshifted, tires spinning as she sped away from Body Works. She wanted to curl up and hibernate for oh, about thirty years, and never think about snow or killers or guns—or little boys lost in the snow— ever again. But her hand's sense memory relived the dull "thwack" made by the dumbbell against Ghost Man's head. She clenched the steering wheel to still the tremors that rendered her already numb fingers even less effective.

"Think, get your brain in gear, and think." Blood seeped from the peppered shards of glass down one cheek. Luckily they'd missed her eyes. She drew close to the mirror to pluck a bright splinter from her brow and a hot wet thread tickled down. She palmed it away.

"Find Steven." Saying it aloud helped focus her blurry thoughts. "Then search the laptop for something, anything that can help." The computer sat in the passenger's seat next to Shadow's stuffed bear toy. She'd wadded April's bloody clothes and dropped them on the floor of the car. The clothes had to be the reason April hadn't called the police. September couldn't risk Ghost Man or anyone else finding the incriminating clothes until Steven was safe. What if the blood was Steven's? A sinking feeling made her clutch the steering wheel to keep her balance. No, she couldn't, she *wouldn't* think that way.

September pulled out her cell phone, scrolled through the programmed numbers until she found Pam, and dialed. "Please be there, please please please."

"Hullo, what's shakin', September?" The woman laughed. "Lordy, I love this new caller ID thing. How's the wonder-pup?" September could hear barking in the background.

"Afraid you were in Houston."

"Naw, the tracking trial isn't until the end of the month." The background barks increased. "Heike, Uschi, hush girls. I can't hear myself think." The barks calmed and finally stopped. "Sorry about that. I had to bring 'em inside. I've got Bruno in the garage with the two young ones, Uschi's in the kitchen with her babies, and Heike's due to whelp in another week. She's ready to pop, may go at any time."

Then it would have to be the old-timer, Bruno. The two bitches tracked better, but Pam wouldn't take them out when they had pups. And the young dogs, littermates of Shadow, barely had their noses wet in tracking. She took a breath. "I've got a huge favor to ask, Pam."

"Sure, what's up? Eugene's stuck at that veterinary conference. He finished his lectures yesterday but they grounded all flights so I'm twiddling my thumbs." She laughed again, a contagious bellow that was surprising from the slight woman. "He's going to miss our thirtieth anniversary dinner tonight, so I'm treating myself to lobster without him. I imagine he's hanging out with the other internists debating how to resolve the latest controversy over hot rum toddies."

September began to see a car here and there on the streets. "I've got a tracking challenge for you."

"Oooh, sounds fun! But in this weather?" Pam made a raspberry with her lips. "The girls won't like that. You know I can't risk Heike. And Freda's pups are two weeks old; I don't want her away from them."

"What about Bruno?" *Please, please, please,* September thought, she had to help. "I wouldn't ask but it's a matter of—well, life-and-death sounds dramatic, doesn't it?" She tried to laugh but it sounded as pathetic as she felt. She was no actress, but the less Pam knew, the safer she'd be, especially with crazies like Ghost Man lurking. "Shadow got out. I tracked him as far as Gentry Park before the snow erased sign." That, at least, was the truth.

"What? Did that dingbat sister of yours—"

"No, it's not April's fault." September cut off Pam's angry words. There wasn't time to explain.

"Bruno's retired. Besides, he's certified in human tracking. I've never trained a dog to track another dog, have you?"

"He's got a ninety-four percent find rank. It's the best shot we've got. I collected Shadow's stuffed toy and a couple of Steven's dirty socks." She slowed as a car passed. "A dog can generalize to the target scent. Bruno's savvy enough to make that leap."

Pam sighed. "I keep waiting for the punch line. You're not telling me everything."

September remained quiet.

"You've not spouted a single pun or wise-ass comment. What's really going on?" She gasped with understanding. "It's Steven, isn't it? That's what this is about if you have his socks. Am I right?"

"Pam, will you please bring out Bruno, give it a try? Please."

"I get it, say no more. You want to try before going Amber Alert. Maybe you don't want CPS involved, or you think April's ex snatched him or something. I don't need to know, long as you've got something for Bruno's old nose to snort."

September nearly cried with relief. "Thank you. I owe you big time."

"Yes, you do." Pam's good humor was colored by concern, but she still tried to lighten the mood. "Spring for a bottle of Merlot and we'll call it even. I'll expect you to give me all the dirty details when we guzzle that bottle together later tonight. Deal?"

"Deal." September coasted into the intersection. Traffic lights flashed a yellow caution so she didn't risk the brake. She could see Doug's townhouse halfway up the next block.

"I'll meet you at Gentry Park. It'll take me at least twenty or thirty minutes to get Bruno ready and slip and slide over to the park. Hopefully we can make it before the light goes. The dark won't matter to Bruno, but I sort of like to see where I'm going."

"Pam, you're a life saver." Please God, let that be true.

A half hour gave her time to check with Steven's father. April's ex sometimes acted like a jerk, but he loved Steven. And if he didn't have the little boy with him, he deserved to know about Steven's disappearance.

She drove past Doug's building. Parking spots were full except for one. The cops would want to talk to Childress if they hadn't already, and she didn't want her car to be seen when they showed up. She rounded the block, and parked in the rear next to the dumpster, right below the fire escape in the only available space. By the look of the mounded snow, the other cars hadn't moved in hours. Only the one next to hers had a semi-clean windshield. She recognized Doug's white corvette in one of the coveted covered parking spots. Good, he must be home.

Hell, maybe Pottinger was with him. He and April argued about Steven's treatment, and that's why she'd ended up helping out with the funding. That'd be luck unchained, to find the boy and the mysterious Pottinger at the same time. Folks said she was born under a lucky star—yeah, right—but this was different than a damn scratch-off game. Or the insurance policy she'd never wanted, or known about, until Chris was killed.

She checked the mirror again. Her swollen face looked lopsided. Blood crusted her forehead. September tugged her hat down, and poked coffee-colored hair beneath out of sight. Careful not to ding the car next to hers, she opened the door to scoop a handful of clean snow and scrubbed away the blood. She gritted her teeth but the numbness relieved the ache. She checked the side mirror and noted the improvement. Her flushed face just looked like a casualty of the weather.

September slogged to the rear entrance of the apartment building, jerked open the common entry, and found the elevator. Doug lived on the top floor five flights up. Thank God the building still allowed unannounced visitors. The mailboxes at the front weren't marked, so she had a fifty-fifty shot to guess which of the two top apartments he'd chosen.

A wide hallway split the floor in half. The large window at each end of the hall overlooked the dumpster and her car at the back, and office buildings and street at the front side. Doug would stroke out over the dumpster view, so she chose the front apartment, rang the bell and waited.

"Hold on, I'm on the phone."

September's jaw tightened. If he eyeballed her through the peephole he might turn her away.

"Doug, it's me, September." She buzzed the bell again. "I have to talk to you. Only take a minute."

The door swung wide, Doug Childress blocking the doorway, cell phone in one hand. Bright blue eyes nailed her from beneath groomed sandy brows. He was a perfect Ken doll to April's Barbie. "What do you want?"

She peered past him, hoping to see good news, but the living room was empty. No sign of Steven anywhere, even though she knew he got visitation each week.

"I heard you moved back. Sorry for your loss. But hey, at least you're set for life with the money, eh? Silver lining and all that."

Her nostrils flared. Yep, he was still an asshole. "Let me in."

He grudgingly moved aside, and waited for her to enter. "Not much warmer in here. The cold caught everyone by surprise, and it takes time to heat these rooms."

The living area boasted ten-foot ceilings, decorative columns and floor-to-ceiling windows facing the street. One corner held a desk and laptop, and another a big screen television opposite a hunter green leather sofa and chair group. The marble entry spilled into the kitchen side of the room, divided from the living area by a walnut counter. Hardwood floors covered by sumptuous oriental carpets—real ones, not fake like April's missing one— gave the room the air of a showroom.

September wasn't at all surprised. The man had always been as polished as his home, from cashmere sweater to alligator shoes. A decorator's dream, straight out of a magazine spread and just as real, with no room for sticky hands or imperfect kids. The glamor had dazzled April until Baby Steven's diagnosis spoiled Doug's ideal family portrait. April had been trying to retouch the picture ever since, until she finally gave up and cropped him out of the frame.

"What do you want?" He stood at the open door, inference clear.

"Have you heard from April?" September noted the small hallway. Steven might be there.

"Wipe your feet, would you?" Doug closed the front door with an exaggerated sigh. "No, I haven't heard from April. What's she done now?" He motioned with the cell phone toward his desk. "Hurry up. I've got work to do."

"When was the last time you saw Steven?"

"Last weekend for my regular visitation. Why?" He switched off the news channel on the widescreen. "What's this about?"

Maybe Steven was hidden away in a back bedroom. She strode toward the hallway.

Doug blocked her. "Why are you here? What's with the questions about Steven?" His puzzlement changed to aggravation and she stopped, realizing the boy wasn't there.

She noticed the laptop on the nearby desk, and took a closer look. No flash drive was in use, but there were several fliers that had to do with autism. She picked up one. "Meeting Dr. Pottinger? Any promotional flash drive to review?"

He stiffened. "Who? What the hell are you talking about?"

He knew the name. His body language told a different story even if he denied it. But what could she gain by challenging him, since Pottinger wasn't here? Short of knocking him down and searching the premises there was no way to find the flash drive even if it was here.

"Isn't Steven with April?" At her expression, Doug uncrossed his arms and stepped close. "Isn't he?"

It had been a wasted trip, ten minutes lost that she could have been searching for Steven at the park. Childress knew nothing about Steven's disappearance. September crossed to the windows to hide her worry and figure out what to say without further endangering April.

Childress crossed to September in three quick strides, agitation clear. "Answer me. Where is my son?"

The quiet street five floors below suddenly bustled with activity. Two cars, one a black and white, double-parked out front. A uniformed officer got out of the patrol car, and a short man and tall woman in plainclothes emerged from the other.

September whirled and dashed toward the door.

Childress stared out the window. "Why are the police here? It's about Steven, isn't it? What's happened to my boy?"

She rushed back, grabbed his arms, and shook him. "Steven's fine. I promise." She looked away, praying he didn't hear the lie in her voice. "But April's in danger. You have to help me." The police would be here any minute.

"Help you do what?" He shook her off. "Where is my son?"

"Stall the police, just long enough that I can get away and reach April." She squeezed his arm. "Helping April is helping Steven, do you understand? Will you help me?"

She didn't wait for his assent. He'd either help or he wouldn't. She dodged out the door and turned toward the elevator and noticed the indicator light showed its slow climb from the first floor. The police were already on their way up. She looked left and right for a way out. There, at the end of the short hall the EXIT sign flashed over the doorway. She bolted. Snatched open the stairwell door. Took two seconds to look back.

Doug watched, his cell phone clutched tight, his face white.

She held the door and tried one last time. "You've always been a button-down jerk. For once in your life, don't worry about how it affects you. Do something for somebody else. Not for me. But if you ever loved April, if you love your son now, trust me."

"What have you done?" He didn't bother to hide his dislike.

"Stall the police." She paused. "Please, Doug. Help me help Steven and my sister." She didn't hide her desperation.

He hesitated, and then made up his mind. "Get out of here. Before I change my mind."

She nodded and dodged through the doorway, loping down the steps three at a time. She banged out the stairwell door into the common area, and skidded to a stop. With studied restraint she strolled out the rear exit when she wanted to race for the car. The snow had slowed but the wind picked up, driving icy needles into her exposed skin. September looked up, fully expecting to see Childress or one of Heartland's finest watching through the fire escape window.

The snow had crusted the passenger door of her Volvo and sealed it shut. September tugged hard before it sprang open, banging into the adjacent car and jarring snow off the passenger window. Less than a minute had passed since her mad dash down the stairwell. She climbed into the car, hands shaking as she started the engine, backed out, and drove away as fast as the slick roads would allow.

Her phone rang. She took the call without checking the screen. "What?"

"Mark's jazzed about the corn chowder." Mom, again. "But he doesn't have a big enough bowl to serve from. Do you still have that ceramic tureen? Remember, that monstrous thing he made in college throwing clay around, or whatever it's called, before he got into the glass artsy stuff?" She waited. "September, are you there?" Her voice sharpened. "What's the matter? Where are you?"

"Just leaving Doug's place." Too much information. She immediately wished she could take back the words.

Mom tongue-clucked. "You didn't invite him to Thanksgiving, did you? April won't be happy."

"Forget Thanksgiving for a minute, will you?" She wanted to cry. Mom didn't have a clue. And she couldn't tell her.

"Oh honey, I knew it would be too much for you. I'll bring the oysters, Mark has his corn chowder and April can do the turkey. We'll do carry-in, it'll be fun." The told-you-so remained unspoken but obvious. Mom thrived on being right.

"Stop it. I don't have time for this. I'll explain later." September disconnected, and knew she'd pay for it later. But now it didn't matter.

Doug didn't have Steven. He wouldn't speak about Dr. Pottinger. But for sure he'd talk to the police, now that she'd stirred up his suspicions. "Crap, crap, crap." She pounded the steering wheel. He wouldn't be able to stall the cops for long once he realized Steven was gone. She should have listened to April and never gone to him.

April didn't want the police involved because something bad had happened this morning. Her clothes didn't get bloody by themselves. Tears spilled down September's cheeks in two scalding paths. It was the only warmth she'd felt all day.

September wished she knew how to fix this mess. Maybe she should have asked Mom. Rose January always had the right answers, and she'd tell you so herself. She just had to suck it up.

Just meet Pam at Gentry Park, and hope Bruno could lead them to Steven before he froze.

Chapter 16

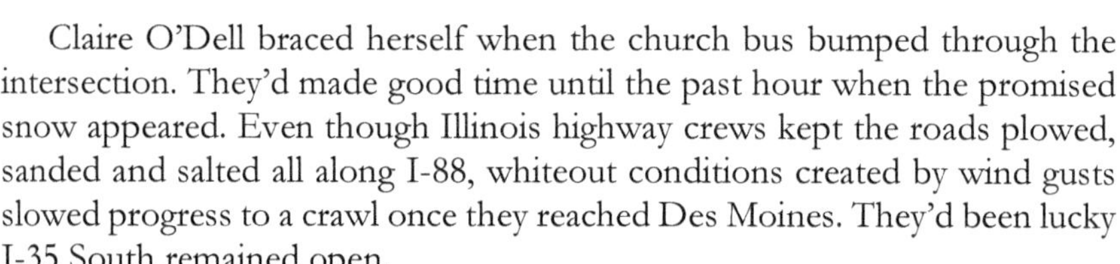

Claire O'Dell braced herself when the church bus bumped through the intersection. They'd made good time until the past hour when the promised snow appeared. Even though Illinois highway crews kept the roads plowed, sanded and salted all along I-88, whiteout conditions created by wind gusts slowed progress to a crawl once they reached Des Moines. They'd been lucky I-35 South remained open.

For this leg of the journey Elaine drove the bus while her husband kept tabs on their son Lenny. The old vehicle wheezed and rattled when it idled, and the driver's side window refused to seal. Elaine's tattered coat snugged close to fend off the bitter draft and her faded muffler, matching fuzzy hat and gloves turned her into a pudgy, gray Michelin Man.

Claire sat two seats behind the driver's seat across the aisle from Elaine's husband Dwayne and their son Lenny. She wondered how they could afford the fee on a clergyman's salary. Elaine couldn't work outside the home, not when Lenny was Elaine's full-time job.

Caring for Tracy also kept Claire homebound, and she didn't begrudge giving up her career. It's what parents do for their kids, after all. After this trip, once the treatment took effect, all of that would change. It wasn't only a new life for Tracy. It would be a new life of exciting opportunities for them all. Maybe she could go back to teaching, at least part-time . . .

Tracy sat next to the window, both palms flat against the fogged glass. Every few minutes she puffed out her breath to melt the frost and then drew concentric circles on the smooth surface until it froze once more. Puff-puff-puff, draw. Puff-puff-puff, draw. Her eyes flickered now and then but otherwise ignored anything or anyone around her. A bump rocked the vehicle and Tracy swayed and her head thumped the glass. She blinked. Then, puff-puff-puff, draw . . .

Claire breathed again; relieved Tracy hadn't crumbled into a screaming mess. She'd been surprisingly calm thus far on the trip. But Claire's own nerves remained raw, and not just from the anticipation of the unknown that lay ahead.

The roads had become treacherous. At each pit stop—and there were many bathroom rests needed with the nine children on board—Claire held her breath, hoping the hamster-wheel tire spin would keep the bus on the road. They couldn't afford delays, car damage or Triple-A.

As if on cue, a childish voice at the back of the bus sing-songed a demand. "Potty-potty-potty. Potty-potty-potty."

Tracy stirred beside Claire.

The chant was taken up by two more voices, followed by an adult's calm attempt to diffuse the growing clamor.

"Do you need the toilet?" Claire didn't touch Tracy, but offered the question as a means for her daughter to focus on something other than the disturbance at the back of the vehicle. Tracy's puff-puff, finger-swirl tempo increased, her agitation clear. "Tracy, you draw so well. Draw me another circle, honey." Claire kept her tone deliberate, just-the-facts to encourage her daughter to focus.

"Potty-potty-potty! Potty-potty-potty!" The volume grew. Across the aisle, Lenny added his adolescent voice to the chant, while Pastor Dwayne spoke with quiet intensity into his son's ear.

"We'll pull over at the next exit. Two or three minutes tops, hang on, kids." Elaine's conciliatory words did little to calm the growing unrest. Claire knew the comment was more for the parents than the children, and she heard murmured encouragement from the adults.

Tracy's breathing quickened. She began to rock.

"Oh, no . . ." Claire quickly pulled out the lumpy dinosaur toy from the carryall she'd stuffed beneath the seat. "Grooby needs you. Do you want me to sing a song to Grooby?"

Tracy rocked.

Claire rummaged further inside the carryall for the purple crocheted throw. Maybe if she could get Tracy swaddled quickly, she could head off the episode.

The bus swerved to the right, bearing down the off-ramp so quickly that Claire caught herself and had to brace against the seat ahead. Tracy's forehead made contact with the window again. She began to rock faster, each forward motion thumping her head against the glass while her keening protest grew in volume. The frosted surface shivered with each impact. Claire fought to regain her balance. It was too late to stop the tantrum. The purple throw could contain Tracy, though, and protect her daughter's head if she could get it around her.

"Potty-potty-potty!"

"Eeeiiiiii . . ." Tracy's nails-on-chalkboard cry traveled two octaves, punctuated by the head-thumping percussion Claire feared would crack the window, her daughter's skin, or both. As the bus shuddered to a stop outside the service station, Claire dropped a double layer of the purple fabric over Tracy's shoulders and arms, holding extra as padding against the window. Immediately Tracy's screams redoubled, but the rocking transformed to side-to-side head flails, eliminating the battering. Claire pulled the fabric into a makeshift hood, and the dark color muffled both sight and sound as the other chanting children were escorted off the bus.

Pastor Dwayne urged Lenny down the steps and paused to speak to his wife before he got off. "Can I get you anything, honey?" He leaned to give a brief kiss to Elaine.

"Coffee with cream, no sugar." Elaine turned in her seat. "Want anything, Claire? Something for Tracy?"

Claire nodded and spoke loudly over the keening. "Apple juice, thanks. And black coffee for me." She smiled weakly; still careful to dodge Tracy's thrashing head.

Once gone, Tracy's cries slowly lost their edge, and finally trailed off into silence. Her stimming continued while Claire braced the movement and prevented further self-battering.

A cell phone tweedled, and Claire flinched before she realized it belonged to Elaine.

Elaine looked at the display and her eyes widened with surprise. "It's the Legacy Center." She thumbed the device, and answered with caution.

Claire held her breath as she rocked with Tracy in the purple comforter, her emotions mixed. She hated the tantrums. But the brief spells after blow ups offered the only time she could touch Tracy with impunity. Rocking Tracy felt like a normal mother-child relationship, even though Claire suspected she gained more comfort from the situation than did Tracy.

"They haven't canceled the Rebirth Gathering, have they?" She'd be devastated if that happened after going to such lengths to arrive on time.

Elaine shook her head, and a smile covered her face. "Thank you so much. Yes, I'll have Dwayne call his dad immediately. It's a miracle!" She hung up the phone.

"What?" Claire felt Tracy slump against her, and fought the urge to hug the child. "A miracle? What happened? Is it postponed? Delayed? Do we have more time to get there?"

"They're deferring payment for Lenny's Rebirth Gathering. It's an answer to our prayers." Elaine wiped happy tears from her face. She glanced out the window and waved at Dwayne as he duck-walked on the icy pavement to escort their son back to the bus. The other children and parents straggled behind.

Claire squelched sudden jealousy. "I didn't know they did that. How lucky for you."

Dwayne climbed back onto the bus and traded places with his wife in the driver's seat. Elaine handed him the phone. "The Legacy Center called. They've got a security job in exchange for Lenny's treatment. Know anyone who could handle that?" She beamed.

"Really?" He crossed himself. "Thanks be to God. I'll call Dad."

Chapter 17

Officer Jeff Combs stood in the back of the elevator, Detectives Doty and Gonzales poised to rush ahead. They hadn't wanted to include Combs in this go-see with Doug Childress.

Doty changed her mind once he shared the phone call information from radio host Humphrey Fish. She had known if she shut him out completely, he'd do his own investigation, and admitted she'd do the same thing in his place. But Doty couldn't risk muddy waters, so he had to walk a fine line. Until they got word from upstairs, he'd keep sniffing around. And if the brass tried to sideline him, he'd take a leave of absence or quit to stay in the game.

"We do all the talking." She popped her gum. "Don't take advantage. You're not yet officially on a leave of absence, and not a part of the investigation. This is a one-time favor out of respect for your loss. Don't make me sorry I cut you some slack."

Combs nodded. "You're generous to a fault."

Gonzales smiled and quickly covered it with a cough.

The elevator opened before Doty could retort. She checked both directions, and marched to the man standing in the open apartment door. "I'm looking for Doug Childress. That you?"

Childress pocketed his cell phone. "What can I do for you?"

"I'm Detective Kimberlane Doty. This is my partner, Detective Winston Gonzales." She didn't bother to introduce Combs, but the slight didn't matter to him. He was here, that was enough.

Doty showed her badge when Gonzales approached and presented his own credentials. "We're investigating a homicide. Let's go inside, we have some questions for you." She didn't wait for permission, simply elbowed past Childress to the center of his living room, and Gonzales followed.

Childress didn't object. But he grabbed the door as if to counter the verbal punch. The word "homicide" had that effect on most people.

Doty counted on that reaction. She hadn't changed her brash approach; she still bulldozed her way through the job. Combs preferred a more subtle approach, and wondered how Gonzales liked the partnership. Combs waited for Childress to go ahead, following him silently into the room and shutting the door.

Doty took the lead. "We're looking for your wife, April Childress."

"Ex-wife." Childress approached the desk, tapped the keyboard of the open laptop, and closed the cover.

Doty bared her teeth in what passed for a smile. "Ex-wife, right. Do you happen to know where we can find her?"

Childress folded his arms. "April should be home. Or at work. What's she got to do with a homicide?"

"Have a seat, Mr. Childress." Doty waited until the man perched on the edge of an overstuffed leather chair. She sat opposite him on a matched settee.

Childress leaned back and crossed his legs in a calculated effort to appear calm. But his foot bounced until he grabbed his ankle to stop it.

Gonzales ran a finger across the spotless glass top table in front of Childress as though checking for dust. "Nice furniture. You have maid service? My wife would kill for something like this."

Combs smiled his approval. Childress was a detail man. The furniture gleamed, the pricy rugs shone jewel-bright. Even the desk's clutter looked organized. Childress was careful, and that would color his answers.

Doty aimed a "give me a break" look at Gonzales that would have wounded a lesser man, and then shined a high-wattage smile at Childress. "Where can we find your *ex*-wife?" She emphasized the "ex." "Do you have her cell number?"

Typical Doty. She rabbited through work with little regard for careful reflection. She concentrated on the big picture and missed details that mattered. For instance, why had Childress shut down his computer? Perhaps he had something to hide.

"She changed her cell number, it's unlisted now. She didn't want me to have it." Childress wrinkled his nose as though to a bad smell. "What's all this about? I have real work to do, as I'm sure you do as well, so if we can speed this up . . ."

Her smile slipped. "Steven's babysitter got shot in April's house. We want to talk to April. So we're asking."

"Oh my god, the babysitter?" Childress bounded to his feet. "What about my son? Is Steven all right?"

"We have no reason to believe Steven's in any danger. Do you think he'd be with your wife?" Doty's expression conveyed skepticism despite the earnest tone.

"What happened?" His hands clenched as he went toe-to-toe with Doty, but she didn't flinch.

Gonzales urged him back to the chair. "Sit down, Mr. Childress, you're understandably upset. But we're doing everything we can to find your son and ex-wife. We need your help."

Childress fell into the seat, stiff and unyielding. "I don't know where April is. How could she let something like this happen? She's changed." He paused. "Do you have kids? It changes things."

"Yep, I've got an eight-year-old boy and twin girls, who are four," said Gonzales.

Combs stepped forward. "You're right. Kids change everything." Find common ground with the man to build empathy and they'd make headway more quickly.

"I lost my wife the day Steven was born." His mournful tone seemed out of character with the earlier bluster. "You think I'm a monster, but that's the truth."

"Why is that?" Gonzales leaned forward, sympathetic. Damn, he was good.

"I love my son. I really do. I wanted that little boy more than life itself. But April and I argued all the time about the way he is damaged, and how to deal with his . . . issues. I still take care of him, I'm still his father." He took a shuddering breath. "You've got to find him."

"The way he is? You mean autistic?" Combs fell silent when Doty raised her eyebrows, reminding him of their deal. But he couldn't help thinking of his own kids, and his throat tightened. Melinda at twelve was a chubby miniature of her redheaded mother with a temper to match. Sensitive William, so much like his murdered grandmother, acted like he was nine going on forty. If either of his kids had been "damaged" like Steven, he couldn't imagine loving them any less.

Doty made a note, and looked over at Gonzales. "Pike's grandson is autistic. That's tough to deal with."

Childress picked a spot of lint off his trousers, adjusted his tie and squared his shoulders, the actions clearly designed to regain control. "Nothing like that in my family. It's her family's crazy DNA or something that scrambled Steven's brains." He stopped. "That's not what I mean…that sounds harsh. I don't know what I'm saying. April's a good mother. She'd do anything for Steven. Hell, so would I." He hunched forward in the chair. "Is that how the babysitter got killed? Did she step over the line with my son? April turns into a barracuda about Steven. As long as he's with his mother, he'll be fine." The last sentence served to convince him as much as them.

Dotty gave a slight head shake in Combs's direction. He gritted his teeth instead of smacking Childress, and waited for her answer for the team. "We aren't sure what happened. April's car is still at the house."

"The PT Cruiser? I got that for Steven. He loves yellow." He rubbed his temples. "She didn't take her car?"

Doty pressed for answers. "Mr. Childress, is there somebody April would call, somewhere she'd go for help? She may not have even been home at the time."

Childress started, and leaned forward. "You mean Steven might not be with her?" He blanched, suddenly matching the tapioca color of his sweater.

Gonzales held out his hands palms up in a "who knows?" gesture.

"I need a drink." Childress jumped to his feet again, and hurried to the kitchen, opened a cabinet, grabbed a bottle of scotch, and poured. He emptied the glass in two swallows. Without pause, he poured again and this time cradled the glass like a toddler with a binky. "Want some? It's early, but what the hell."

Doty's sour expression declined for all of them.

"You think someone kidnapped Steven? Was there a ransom note or something? Is that what this is about?" He drank again, and topped off the glass. "I mean, I do okay and I've got some investments. Maybe a hundred thousand liquid, but the rest is tied up. What are you doing to find my son?" Childress returned to the living area and settled on the arm of the chair.

"What about April? Does she have the finances?"

Childress laughed a high pitched nervous sound. "Hardly. I pay child support, and she got the house in the settlement. She has her own business, an exercise place. Can you believe it?" He rolled his eyes. "Just what I want my wife doing, dressing up in spandex and prancing in front of a bunch of fat old women. She opened the place after we split." He sipped again and some of the drink sloshed onto his knee, though he didn't seem to notice or care. "I'd never have allowed it."

So he's a control freak, wants a perfect wife and kid, and gets pissy when real life throws curves. "What's the name and address of the business?" To hell with hanging back, they needed to get moving on this. Doty said nothing, giving tacit approval.

"Body Works. Don't know the address, but it's somewhere near here. I never visited even though I'm told it's a nice location, I'll give her that. I've got the phone saved, that one's listed." He pulled out his cell phone, played with the buttons, and gave them the number.

Gonzales's mustache twitched as he jotted down the information. "We need to contact the phone company, get the records of calls to and from her number. If April's on the run, she may contact family or friends."

"September. That's what she meant." Childress whirled to confront the detectives. "April's sister September, they're tight."

"You think they might be together?" Doty made another note. "Where do I find September? What's her last name?"

Combs answered for Childress. "September Day. I saw her this morning. She's renovated the old Ulrich place, that historic brick monstrosity at the top of the hill on Rabbit Run Road. The renovations had to set her back a bundle."

Gonzales frowned. "You know her?"

He shook his head. "We'd just handled a fender bender this morning, and Pike noticed smoke at her house. Turned out to be nothing. But September got rid of us fast, said she had a busy day."

"You got to be kidding me." Doty gnawed her pencil, sighed and made the note. "September and April. Last name January?"

"You don't understand. She was just here looking for April." Childress rolled the cold glass against his forehead. "She promised me Steven was okay."

"Wait. She was here?" Doty's face turned red.

Ice clinked in the glass when he nodded. "She saw you out the front window and begged me to stay quiet, that it would help April. Crazy stuff."

Combs stalked toward the man. "She asked you to stall the police? And you agreed to obstruct a police investigation?"

Childress flinched. "I didn't know there was any investigation. She promised me Steven was okay, but said April was in trouble. She looked like she'd been in fight."

Doty hurried to the door. "Officer Combs, stay here with Detective Gonzales. Finish up with anything we've not covered." Her jaw tightened. "Which way did September…Day, is it? Which way did she go?"

Childress scooted to sit on the edge of the chair when Combs backed away. "You were coming up the elevator so she took the stairwell down. Leads to the back exit." He stood, wobbling before he caught his balance with a hand on the chair. "She must be parked back there if you didn't see her out front."

Glaring at him, Doty rushed out the door.

"You'll find Steven, right?" Childress finally noticed the stain on his trousers. "I need to change." He started toward the hallway and paused to check the time again.

Gonzales followed and reached up to pat Childress on the back. "Have a seat. We're not finished."

"What? I told you everything. You should be out finding Steven." Childress returned to the armchair and this time sank into it like a deflated balloon. "What am I going to do?"

"You're going to relax, take a breath, and tell us everything September said." Gonzales didn't say a word when Combs joined him.

Childress pulled at his tie as he gathered his thoughts. "She was looking for somebody, some weird name. And wanted to know if I had Steven." He focused on Combs. "Do you think that was just to throw me off, to confuse things?"

"Steven wasn't with her?" Combs watched as Gonzales took notes.

"Of course not." His tone was clipped, angry at the notion. "Like I already told you. She wanted a head start, didn't want to get caught up with your questions. Said it would help April and maybe Steven, too."

Doty burst into the room. "There's another body. I called for backup."

Childress sucked in a breath. "Steven?"

"There's a car by the dumpster, a body inside." She advanced on Childress, and he shrank backwards into the chair until it nearly swallowed him. "What the hell is your family involved in? That makes two in one day."

"Where's my son?" Childress's jaw worked as his fingers clawed the soft arms of the chair.

Doty took pity. "Victim's an adult male."

A relieved sob hiccupped in his throat.

"I didn't want to disturb things until we got the CSIs here. Boot prints in the snow all around, small ones, like at April's house." Doty whistled through the gap in her front teeth. "Gonzales, go downstairs and secure the scene until the coroner gets here." She turned to Combs, clearly pissed. "Okay, you're part of the team at least until the brass says otherwise. Plenty for everyone to do."

He nodded, and turned to Childress. "What car does September drive?"

"How should I know? Call the DMV."

Doty narrowed her eyes but kept her temper for once. "We need your help, Mr. Childress. To find Steven. Work with us. Can you tell us what September was wearing? What kind of shoes, for instance?"

Childress sniffed, cocked his head to one side and smoothed the soft fabric of his sweater. "That's something I still love about April. She always dresses like a model. September is a frump. I notice fashion."

"So?" Combs gave props to Doty for her patience. His own was at an end.

"September wore sweat pants, a stocking cap, and some shapeless overstuffed coat. Oh, and dingy little snow boots, no heels, just flat rubber treads." He pointed to the entry. "She tracked in snow, so I noticed."

Doty smiled. "That's a match. Betcha the prints around the body are September's."

Chapter 18

Shadow sprinted down the long corridor, scrabbled for purchase on the floor and skidded into the tiled wall. He gathered himself, dove for the glove, grabbed and shook it just like his bear-toy. It tickled his nose. He sneezed and dropped it so he could paw the fabric. It smelled like bacon and peppermint gum.

He'd decided he liked Freda when she suggested fetch. Shadow grinned around the fuzzy glove. He trotted back to where she waited at the glass doors, and pushed the glove into her hands so she could throw it again.

"Nice dog." A man on his way out stopped to button his coat, but kept his distance from Shadow.

Shadow paused, and cocked his head at the man's tone. The man was scared of him. Shadow had met a few adults who didn't like dogs or acted nervous. He didn't know why. So he dropped the glove and wagged his tail low to the ground to show he meant no harm.

Freda shrugged. "He's with the little boy over in the food court." She viewed the deserted place. "The mall's closing down early."

"Yes, everyone's leaving. I think the food court is the only place still open." He smiled, but backed away and hurried from the building.

He ducked his head against the gust that snaked inside when the man left. He was glad to be out of the cold. At the thought, Shadow sat down and licked one of his sore paws.

"You're just a good doggy, aren't you?" She crooned until Shadow lowered his ears and wiggled his butt. "Wanna fetch?" Freda called. "Bring me the glove."

Grabbing it, he pushed it into her hand and gently released it when she asked.

"Ew, you've got it all wet. You're as bad as my dogs." She stuffed the soggy glove into her pocket despite his dance to convince her otherwise.

Following Freda, Shadow leaped away when a chainlike wall rattled from the ceiling to close a nearby doorway. "It's okay, boy." She waited for him to draw close and sniff the metal.

Shadow returned to Freda's side. He'd visited buildings like this before with treat-lady, sometimes with Steven but often just the two of them. Those times he'd worn a special vest. Today he didn't even have his collar or a leash, and treat-lady wasn't here. Freda was okay, but she wasn't treat-lady.

He weaved between small tables and chairs set in the middle of the large open space to reach Steven. Smells of cooked food made his tummy rumble but he was polite and didn't beg. Shadow settled on the floor beside Steven, and laid his head against his boy's wet shoe. Familiar was good. He'd had too much newness for even a good-dog to manage.

Steven pulled his foot away. Shadow sighed. He wished his boy might— just this once—touch his head. A small touch, not even a full pet. He scooted closer and leaned against Steven's chair, comforted when his boy didn't move it away.

"Your lady friend didn't show, Teddy?" Freda pulled out a chair and sat next to the older man.

"The ice was too risky." Teddy coughed and slurped something from a cup. "You wore him out. Playing fetch?"

At the "fetch" word, Shadow raised his head and wagged. The old man laughed. "Can't get enough, can you, boy?"

"Any headway with Steven?" Freda unzipped her coat and pulled off her hat.

"Not a word." He swiveled, looked around the area. "They're shutting down the food court. I had to argue to get the French fries."

Shadow barked. In case they didn't understand—sometimes people missed the obvious—he stood up, whined and wagged. And licked his lips.

"French fries?" He barked again. "Hey, he knows what French fries mean." Teddy patted Shadow's head.

"Don't tease him. I tell my dogs French fries are bad for them." She grinned. "They don't believe me either."

"Noisy noisy, no, no, no." Steven spoke, and covered his ears when Shadow barked again. Freda's jaw dropped. "Steven's hungry. Steven's thirsty." He rocked, holding both hands over his ears.

"Drink your milk, Steven." Teddy pushed the cup closer. "I'll get you some French fries once they're ready."

Shadow barked again, and Steven's hand slashed the air and hit him. He flinched. He wasn't supposed to bark. His boy didn't like loud noises. Shadow's ears fell in apology but Steven didn't see.

Freda held out her hand to Shadow. "Shush, boy. Come over here."

After a quick glance at his boy, Shadow obeyed. "Sit." He did and placed his chin on her knee, and closed his eyes when she stroked his brow. "Steven, that wasn't nice. Never hit animals." Her words were angry but not at him.

Steven stopped rocking to grab the cup with both hands. He drank it dry. "Steven's hungry." He found the metal tag on his coat and zipped it up and down.

"He can't help it," Teddy said.

"I know. The boy's mother said he's autistic." She scratched Shadow's head. "I bet the dog's trained to help him." She massaged his ears and Shadow groaned. "But you don't know what the hell you're doing out here, do you?"

He whined and his tummy growled again.

Freda laughed. She patted him once more and stood up. "The French fries are ready. And I think this good dog deserves a couple for himself, don't you?"

Shadow wagged and woofed agreement. But he woofed softly, the way a good-dog should.

Chapter 19

September navigated the sharp turn toward Gentry Park, watching for Pam's Jeep. Her cell phone rang in her pocket, and she swerved to a stop. If it was April, she could always ask about the bloody clothes. Yeah, right, like that will happen. More likely it was Lizzie with more threats, but while she was wishing, why not hope they'd found Steven.

She dug for the phone without shedding her gloves. September fumbled Steven's empty prescription bottles before she found the phone. Caller ID said Humphrey Fish.

"Give me a freakin' break." She didn't need his crap, so she answered the call before it could go to voicemail and immediately disconnected. September tossed the phone next to the pills and laptop in the seat, pulling back onto the street.

The phone rang. Fish again. "Sheesh, can't you take a hint?" This time she let it go to voicemail. She'd delete it later.

The phone rang a third time. She needed a clear line for important calls. She punched the Phone, waited for the connection and yelled, "It's not a good time. Quit calling." September hung up before he could say a word.

The phone rang again immediately.

"Am I speaking Norwegian? What does *a bad time* mean to you?"

"Don't hang up."

"You're tying up the phone.

"Did you find Steven?"

She paused. "No." She didn't have time to explain, didn't want him involved. There was no time to waste, especially with a headlines-grabber like Fish. "I need to keep this line clear."

"I called your sister's house, and a cop answered, somebody named Officer Combs. So cut the bull. If you're in trouble, let me help. I've only got another minute or so, I put on a long-play record and told the engineer I needed a potty break."

She watched the rear view mirror for police cars, but the roads remained deserted. "What do you want, Fish? How can you help from the radio station?"

"The cops want you, September. They didn't know about you before. My bad."

"What do you mean, they didn't know about me?" So Doug Childress would come late to that party, if Fish had already outed her. Combs. . . why was that name familiar? "What did you tell them?"

"Just that you got a call during the radio show from your sister about the lost kid." He couldn't mask the delight in his next words. "The phones rang off the hook after that. I could use more on-air drama like that." He hesitated. "That's not to say I'm not genuinely worried about the little fella."

What a bozo. "Nice chatting but I'm seriously busy." She started to cut the connection.

"September, don't hang up. You need me. Let me help."

She held the phone up to her ear. "You just want the scoop, Fish. And that's low even for you."

"You got me all wrong. Sure, it wouldn't hurt my feelings to bump my image. Heartland isn't exactly a primetime market. Radio's dead anyway. It's a starter-job, or you land here at the end of a career. I need a facelift, a ticket out."

"And Steven's story would be your ticket."

"Shit, don't be that way. I care about kids, too. And small, furry Disney-esque creatures."

She didn't have time for this crap.

"Who went to bat for you for your little animal show? Sure wasn't the big muckity-mucks. We needed some warm and fuzzy and you were just the ticket."

"You? No way." She pulled back onto the road.

"Way. Listen, you need help, don't deny it. I'm sitting here toasty while you play slip-n-slide with the cops."

Her tires skidded as if to confirm his taunt. Fish had a point. And he wasn't the police. Sure, the man always had an angle, but if their different goals had a mutual benefit, what could it hurt?

"Okay, Humphrey. I'll give you the story if you give me a hand. But you have to promise not to take this public. Or go to the police."

"You're killing me." He sounded like a child threatening a tantrum. "What if they come to me? You already opened that door bailing in the middle of the show. Listeners already heard that."

"What's done is done. But not another word unless I give you the okay. You could get someone killed."

"Killed? Really? Don't tease." He sounded delighted, and then the teasing lilt disappeared. "Wait, you're not joking? Jesus-frog, September, what the hell is going on?"

September inhaled sharply. "What did the police say?"

"Nothing much. I've listened to the scanner, though. They found a woman dead at your sister's house." He hesitated, his concern real. "Tell me it's not your sister."

"No, not April." She squeezed the steering wheel and pressed harder on the gas. "The babysitter. Wilma." She glanced at the car clock, and guestimated she was still five minutes away from the park. Time stopped for nobody. "No more questions. You'll get all the details later, I promise."

"Sure. I've heard that one before." He sniffed. "Where are you, anyway?"

"Why? So you can broadcast my location?" She glanced at the seat at April's laptop and Steven's pills. "If you want to help, do a search for me on your computer." She caught up one of the pill bottles.

"Is that all?" She heard his footsteps echo, shoe lifts clip-clopping like Old Bessie. "Okay, I'm set. Google's raring to go, what d'ya got?"

"Type in Henry F. Pottinger, Ph.D." She spelled the last name.

Fish said nothing for several moments, making her antsy. "Well? Did you find anything?"

"Too much. He's affiliated with something called NeuroRealm. It's the research arm of a pharmaceutical company. They focus on neurological stuff, brain disorders, chemical brain imbalances affecting behavior, that sort of thing."

"Research? Drugs?" That made sense if he was Steven's doctor. "What do they treat? Does it say?"

"Let's see. Whole section on cancer. Something on Parkinson's, another on Alzheimer's. Then there's schizophrenia, ADD, OCD, they got all the popular initials. There's links to journal articles, you could get lost in all this frog-icity. Lots of money behind this group."

"What about autism?" September's pulse quickened. That had to be it. April hadn't been able to contain her excitement about Steven's recent improvements.

"Uh…don't see it here."

Damn, it had to be there. With an effort September refrained from urging him to look harder. The park was just ahead, and time for fishing had run out. "Is there any contact information, a phone number or name? Search the news or media page."

"Here you go. The public relations person, Martha Freemantle, has an email." He read the address quickly. "Got that? The NeuroRealm general number is 817-555-3421."

"Wait. Let me get something to write on." She coasted to a stop in front of the park and grabbed a pencil from the dash. When she couldn't find anything to write on, she grabbed the pill bottle again, and found a number was already printed on the bottle. "817-555-3421. Is that it?"

Gotcha. Lizzie spoke in riddles. So she'd bypass Mrs. Claus and go to the top.

"So—what's the deal? What does NeuroRealm have to do with you being in trouble?"

NeuroRealm had some by-damn explaining to do, and once they found out about gun-totin' grandma and her ghostly-goon, they'd pull Lizzie's fangs. She'd see to it. "Thanks for your help, Humphrey. I'll be in touch."

"Hey, I did my part. You can't leave me hanging."

"Have to run. I do appreciate it." September cut him off mid-whine. She knew her luck had truly changed for the better when she saw Pam's Jeep on the other side of the park. She took a deep breath. Time to find Steven.

Chapter 20

Combs leaned through the glass window to push his identification closer to the receptionist. "I spoke with Mr. Fish earlier. He expects me. I appreciate your cooperation. Anita, is it?" The nameplate spelled her name in tiny rhinestones that matched the accents on her glasses.

Anita sneezed and dabbed her nose with a soiled tissue. "Sweet talk all you want." Her voice was a Lauren Bacall baritone. "I already told you Humphrey's on-air." She punched a button on the phone, careful not to mess up the fresh magenta nail polish that perfumed the air. "I got a cold, got a headache, probably got strep throat, and got the crankies over a double shift. I got the don't-care-and-cain't-hep-it, so don't push me."

"The bluebird of happiness shit all over my day, too, lady." God, he didn't need attitude.

She batted red-rimmed eyes behind blue cat-eye glasses. "Quite the charmer, aren't ya?" She shuffled paper and ignored him.

He wished for a breath mint, or a cigarette. Hell, a shot of rum wouldn't be bad either. It might shave the fuzz off his tongue. He spoke in a conspiratorial tone. "Anita, I'll take responsibility. You won't get into trouble. But I need to talk to Fish. *Now.*" He underlined the word. Controlling access into the studio, Anita had to push the button to open the glass door. "Please." He'd kiss receptionist butt if it helped. Couldn't be worse than puckering up to Doty.

She covered her mouth, coughed, and grimaced. "Me and Humphrey and the engineer are the only ones still here. Others got out before all this weather. Should have hitched a ride with them."

"You're stranded?"

"For the night, looks like." She shrugged. "I can be sick here as easy as at home. The kitchenette has instant soup. I'll survive without my flannel jammies." Anita resumed busy work.

Combs paced the tiny reception area. He dreaded Uncle Stanley's call. His sister Naomi had already used him as a verbal punching bag when he told her. After her sobs quieted, his sister agreed to inform the rest of the family. He couldn't be distracted, had to step up the search to find Mom's killer or he'd shoot somebody. Maybe even a receptionist.

"I'm grateful for the company." Anita sniffled. "Humphrey's a one-man show 'til somebody else shows up. That's a lot of fish stories." She lifted an eyebrow, expecting him to chuckle. At his stony glare, she adjusted her glasses. "He'll need a potty break before long, 'cuz he's been drinking coffee for hours." She laughed. "But he'd rather hear himself than take a break—heck, wouldn't surprise me if he just whizzed in a cup."

Whizzed in a cup, sheesh. And she called him less than charming? No matter how satisfying, it would do no good to piss off the gate keeper. "I need a few minutes. Just tell him I'm here. If he needs a break, it won't get in the way of his program."

Anita held up one finger and turned away to sneeze into a wad of tissue, honking and wiping her Rudolph-bright appendage. She winced, reaching for the half roll of toilet paper stashed in the inbox on her desk when the first wad of tissue didn't suffice. "This storm, it's a dream come true for Humphrey. He's wanted to break into the prime radio time for years. Humphrey's making points keeping the station on air."

A headache gathered behind Combs's ears. Anita's voice irritated like new shoes on a blister.

"He's taking lots of call-ins." Arm wave. "Everyone's stuck at home, nothing to do but listen to the radio and jabber on the phone." Finger fling. "This could make things happen for Humphrey." She sighed and her hands settled in her ample lap, two fluttery birds grounded. "The man just doesn't take care of himself, though. That falls to me. Not that he ever notices," she said softly.

Aha. So Anita had designs on the radio king. And Fish didn't know she was alive. "He just doesn't appreciate what you do for him. That's a shame." Combs hoped she'd come around quicker if he showed a bit of empathy.

"Oh, I don't mind. He's got a lot to offer, such an undiscovered talent. And besides, I need the overtime."

"He's taking call-ins? I don't hear the phone ringing."

As if on cue, Anita's phone jangled. "It's a different number. He's got half a dozen phone lines in there." Her phone rang again, followed by a second line. Her shoulders clenched. "I can't get away from morons calling for school and church and who-cares closings. Humphrey's been making those announcements every fifteen minutes." She wiped her nose. "Why don't they freaking listen, huh?"

Everyone in radio must be nuts.

She punched a button, speaking into her headset, and transformed into a syrup-voiced sex kitten. "WZPP, you've reached ZAP105 FM Radio, giving you the best easy-listening 24/7, how may I direct your call?"

He reached through the window, and disconnected the phone.

"Hey!" She batted his hand.

"I'm not asking. This is a murder investigation. I'll run your ass down to the station, too, Anita, because I don't have time to wait until Fish's piss-cup runneth over."

"Murder? Lord, why didn't you say so, I thought it was another unpaid traffic ticket." She pulled off her glasses, and continued in her crow-rasp voice. "He doesn't pay me enough to run interference for murder. I'll page him, but he still probably won't reply till there's a pre-recorded station break."

"When's that?" Combs checked the time.

"Quarter hours usually, but today all bets are off. Knowing him, he got all the breaks in at one time to give himself more running-at-the-mouth room."

That could be another fifteen minutes. Maybe he should have gone with Gonzales to the Januarys' house to interview September's parents. Doty didn't want him there, though, and figured his follow up with the radio guy wouldn't get back to the brass. Hell, if this Fish character had just answered his questions when he called April's house, he wouldn't be here.

"So who got murdered?" Anita winced, and reached for a lozenge. Cellophane wrappers littered the floor next to the wastebasket that overflowed with used tissues.

"You don't know the victim." Victim. Not a victim, it was his mom. He coughed and turned away.

"Careful, honey." Anita tore off several squares from a roll of toilet paper and offered them through the window. "This weather, you could catch what I got." When he waved the tissue away, she folded it and honked. "Damn, it would just be easier to unscrew my nose for the duration." She tossed the used clump toward the wastebasket as the phone rang again.

This time he reached through the window and yanked the headset off her head. "I'm sorry you feel like shit. I'm sorry he treats you like dirt. But if you don't get Fish out here in the next thirty seconds, I promise you'll feel even worse." He didn't smile, didn't yell, and didn't need to.

Anita started to say something and hesitated. "Screw it," she murmured, pressing the buzzer to release the door lock.

Chapter 21

Gentry Park hadn't changed other than a bit more snow since September's earlier visit. She twisted in her seat to reach Shadow's stuffed bear in the back seat and winced. *It's only bruised ribs. It could have been worse.*

To keep her hands free she stuffed the bear inside her parka and zipped up the coat. She found Steven's dirty socks, still inside a baggy, deep in one massive pocket. The smelly bear and scented socks were the best bet to find Steven.

She braced herself for the temperature change. *Lordy, she hated the cold.* She unlocked the door, hyper-vigilant to any suspicious movement. Her blood drummed in her ears when she stepped outside into the open, unprotected, but at least the street, the park—hell, the whole world—was deserted. The street lights reflected in the snow shined like moonlight, so bright she'd see any interlopers in plenty of time to retreat to the car.

Snow fell thick as fog. No trace remained of her earlier search of the park. September entered the fenced area and waved at Pam.

The rail-thin woman emerged from her Jeep. She wore high black Wellingtons, leather gloves, a tan, down-filled jacket, watch cap, and hood drawn over the top of her head. A fuzzy scarf, blue as a bruise, peeked out from the collar. Warm, sensible, a fieldwork outfit Pam wore like a second skin.

September motioned to the gated entrance on the wooded side of the field closest to April's house. That's where they should begin. Pam saluted her understanding, and unloaded the sable shepherd from the back of her vehicle.

The old dog jigged for a moment at the sight of the harness, and stood patiently until hooked up. Old dog senses faded with years, just like people senses, but nobody knew how much scent discrimination diminished with age. Even a fraction of Bruno's youthful abilities could bring Steven home. Tracking dogs didn't need the light.

They had to find Steven, just had to. Once he was safe, September could concentrate on freeing April from Lizzie's control.

She trudged around the perimeter of the fence to meet Pam. September didn't want to confuse Bruno with more of her own tracks. She'd already muddied the trail.

"I owe you big time." September smiled at Pam, offering Bruno a gloved hand to sniff. The dog waved his amber tail.

Pam scowled when she saw September's face. "You run into a brick wall? C'mon, honey. Has something to do with all the cop cars around your sister's house, I bet. Surely they didn't call out the troops to find a lost kid. So spill."

September wavered. It would be such a relief to share the burden with somebody else, especially a disaster-savvy individual like Pam. Lizzie hadn't said anything about telling other people, only the police. And she'd already enlisted Fish. But Pam might call the police, and get sideways of Lizzie. September shook her head. Couldn't risk it, not when she'd already got Wilma shot by misjudging Lizzie.

"I heard your radio show today, September. Was that really your sister or was it Fish's idea of a publicity stunt. Or is it something else?"

September flinched. Breathing hurt, her face stung, and she couldn't feel her hands or feet despite the extra-thick socks and insulated gloves. But her heart hurt worst of all. "Yes, it's more involved than I let on."

"I knew it." Pam punched one gloved hand into the palm of the other, clearly upset. Bruno woofed, gazing with concern back and forth between the pair. "It's Steven, right?" She cocked her head and sucked in her breath. "Something more? Is April in trouble?"

"Here's the deal, Pam." September remained leery of saying too much. "Steven's missing, and we think Shadow is with him. Other stuff happened after they disappeared, and the police are sorting that out." She weighed her words. "We don't need to distract the police from their job, especially when you and Bruno have a better chance of finding Steven. Finding him, that's the most important thing."

"No wonder you're frazzled." Pam pulled her into a warm hug. "April must be going crazy. You're a good sister."

September froze for a moment, and then fiercely returned the embrace. She fought tears, the unexpected sympathy making her want to unburden herself completely. It would be such a relief to share her fear, ask for advice, and get some encouragement that she'd made the right choices. She pulled away, and opened her mouth—

"You'll tell me the whole story at some point?" The older woman absently stroked Bruno's gray muzzle.

The moment passed. She had to keep it light. "Sure, Pam. I promise. I'll give you a blow-by-blow over steaks the size of toilet seats. And a good bottle of merlot." Pam would be safer, and even April would be protected by keeping Pam in the dark. September checked her watch. It had been less than five minutes since she'd arrived, but every second that ticked by brought her nearer the 24-hour deadline.

"Make it prime rib." Pam turned to the dog. "*Sitz. Bleib.*" The dog planted his furry rear and waited. His tail scythed a half-moon in the snow that was already halfway to his chest.

September pulled out the baggy with Steven's socks. "I've got Shadow's toy bear, too."

She wrinkled her nose. "Bruno finds people, not animals. Keep it simple or we'll confuse him. He hasn't done this in a while." She seized the baggy from September, opened it, and presented it to the dog.

Bruno stuck his snout inside. He snuffled repeatedly, inhaling the telltale scent signature that spelled "Steven" in his canine brain. Pam looked up. "You stay here, and give me a twenty-foot lead before you follow."

September nodded. "I think Steven entered there." She pointed. "He played on the swings like always and went out the other side exit." She swung her arm toward her car parked in the middle of the street. She hadn't wanted to risk getting stuck by parking where the drifts grew deepest. And she wanted the car to have easy access to a quick getaway. Just in case.

Pam concentrated on her dog. Bruno sniffed and finally pulled away from the baggy and huffed, signaling his readiness. "Bruno, *such.*"

The "find" command triggered the dog into a low slouching posture. He shoveled snow from time to time to get a better scent. Bruno trotted through the open gate for five or six feet, nose skimming the snow, and paced first to the left and back toward the right. He cast a semicircle ahead of Pam to match the scent to the socks.

September held her breath, and let it out when Bruno made a beeline toward the swing set near the middle of the park. Steam puffed from his mouth. Pam's blue scarf covered the lower half of her face as she allowed the big dog to pull her in his wake by the long line attached to his harness.

Bruno spent several minutes around the playground equipment, paying particular attention to an area beneath one swing. September heard Pam repeat the "*such*-find" command, and the German shepherd cast back and forth on the far side of the jungle gym. Once he moved in a purposeful stride toward the far gate, September followed.

Bruno's nose assured them Steven had left the park. He drove through the open gate, trotting without hesitation, and September hoped he would lead them to a nearby house, where they'd find Steven sipping hot chocolate with kind neighbors.

But less than five minutes later, the dog stopped at a street corner. Hesitating, he returned to an indentation in the snow a short distance away, pacing a tight circle and then a larger one. Bruno whined. He shuffled into the intersection, poked and sniffed deep into the snow, and finally returned to the sign to lie down.

Pam waited until September caught up. "End of the line, September." She pulled a ball looped with rope out of her pocket, praised the dog, and tossed him the toy. He caught it with ease, and teased for a game of fetch, his reward for a job well done.

"You're sure?" September couldn't hide her disappointment.

Pam played tug with the eager shepherd. "Bruno's nose doesn't lie, does it, boy?" Her expression of pleasure at the old dog's success faded when she recognized September's desperation. "Sorry. Maybe somebody picked him up?" Bruno mock-growled, tail wagging happily as he pulled against the rope toy.

"Maybe a ride, sure. But who? Steven wouldn't climb into just any car. April has to jump through hoops to get him places. That's why she bought that atrocious banana-yellow Cruiser." September noticed the sign, cocked her head a moment, and stood on tiptoe to brush the white away, revealing hidden letters. She winced when her bruised muscles protested, but the effort paid off.

HART-Line Bus Stop.

"He got on the bus?" Pam wiped snow off the bridge of Bruno's muzzle.

"They're yellow. Or sort of a mustard color anyway, that could be close enough for Steven." That was better than Steven stuck in a snow drift.

"Makes sense." Pam tugged the dog toy, and then let Bruno keep it. "*Fuss,*" she said, and he trotted in a heel position by her side back to the park. "Steven must have hunkered down in the snow for a while. Maybe he waited for the bus there."

September followed Pam. "I came within sight of that spot, I should have kept going a little further." Instead, she'd returned to April's house to be bushwhacked by crazy Lizzie. "I didn't know those dumpy HART-Line buses came this far into the suburbs. Steven loves routine. A yellow bus is the next best thing to his mom's yellow car."

"So call the dispatcher, and have them contact the drivers. They'd remember a little boy."

"Maybe not if he was alone. But Shadow with him makes him memorable." Excited, September unzipped her coat and pulled out the toy bear. "Before we go back, you've got to check and see if they're still together."

Pam considered the toy dubiously. "I told you, Bruno's not trained for—"

"Let him try. At this point any info could be helpful."

With a sigh, Pam stopped. "Okay, okay, but it could also confuse things." She turned to Bruno. "*Platz. Aus.*" The dog belly flopped into the white, dropped the ball into her open palm, and Pam stuffed the toy back into her pocket. September handed her the bear.

Bruno sniffed the toy and tried to take it. Pam pulled it out of reach, moved away, and came back. She said, "*Such,*" and offered it to him once more. He reached out tentatively, sniffed, and leaped to his feet, grabbing the bear to shake it. Bruno danced away with the toy.

Pam turned up her palms in a helpless gesture. "He thinks we're playing. I'm sorry, September, he's not any help."

"Crap. Thanks anyway." September yawned.

Pam offered the ball-tug toy once more. "*Bring.*" After one final spine-shattering shake that certainly killed the stuffed bear, Bruno dropped the soggy toy at Pam's feet and eagerly reclaimed his rope-ball.

"Call the bus company." Pam returned the bear and jogged back toward the park as September struggled to keep up. "If the driver doesn't remember Steven or a dog, find out the locations of different stops on this route. We can take Bruno around to each one."

"Great idea." September thought her ribs might poke through her flesh with every bone-jarring jog, but she grit her teeth and kept pace with Pam. "I don't know if Steven would get off at a strange stop. But that's a good next step to check." She dug her phone out of her pocket and frowned. "It's nearly dead."

"My cell's in the Jeep. You can use that. Charger's there, too." Pam handed September her keys. "Phone's in the center caddy between the front seats and the charger's hooked into the front console. You can take that with you if you like. I've another at home."

September struggled for a response. "I don't know what to say."

"Go. I've seen you checking your watch, and I know time's wasting." The woman smiled gently. "I haven't known you long, but I recognize you. You're the one who pulls strangers out of fires." She paused. "It's what you do, it's who you are. It's *who we are.*" She held her palm up to stop any protest. "You'd do it for me, and don't dare deny it. Like recognizes like."

September palmed tears away before they froze. "Thank you," she whispered.

"Go on. I'll be along in a minute. I owe Bruno at least a ten-minute playtime for his good work."

The dog trembled with anticipation but stood steady as Pam removed his halter and unhooked the long-line leash. His tail lashed at the mention of "playtime." When she lobbed the toy high in the air, Bruno launched himself like a furry rocket. Pam's expression glowed when the fetch-game turned back the clock for the old dog.

September wished she could turn back the clock, too, to a more innocent time. Before stalkers, before lost dreams and lost loves, and little boys lost. She hurried to Pam's Jeep, climbed inside, and made sure the doors were locked. With the engine rumbling, she switched the blower to high, eager for warmth and breathed with relief for the first time after hours of stress. She was safe. She finally had a plan. Steven would be found.

She didn't notice the black Hummer that approached from the far side of Gentry Park and stopped in the middle of the road directly beside her Volvo.

Chapter 22

Combs shoved through the radio studio's glass door so hard it rebounded off the wall, and he felt vague disappointment when it didn't break. He jogged down the hall and stopped below the red "on air" light above another door. The organ-rich tones of Humphrey Fish recited a litany of area work and event closings, as the live broadcast was piped through office speakers.

The studio walls—glass—formed a soundproof enclosure where a pale, skinny kid with headphones sat before a computer bank of dials and switches. When Combs opened the door, the kid rose halfway out of his seat, and made frantic shushing motions. Combs ignored him. "Where's Fish?"

The recitation abruptly stopped. "Well, well, well, look what the storm blew in." Humphrey sat on the far side of the room on a padded rolling bar stool. A football-size fuzzy mic hung above his head. "We'll be right back with a surprise guest, right after a word from our sponsors." He made a hand motion to the engineer.

The engineer twiddled dials, sat back and chugged Red Bull. "You got ninety seconds," he told Humphrey. He pulled off his headphones and stuck out his jaw at Combs. It didn't improve his weak chin.

"You're Fish?"

"In the flesh. Who're you?" Humphrey hopped off the chair.

A poor man's Leprechaun, Fish stood just over five feet, and was nearly as wide as he was tall. "Officer Jeffery Combs." He shook the man's hand, and tried to mask his surprise.

"Yeah, I know, I know, you're shocked. I'm even more handsome than you expected, right? I got a face for radio, what can I say?" He scratched his bright red poof of chin whiskers.

"We spoke before."

Humphrey smoothed the freckles on his billiard-smooth head, and pushed the microphone away. "What the hell are you doing, breaking into a broadcast? Didn't your momma teach you any manners?" But his hazel eyes twinkled. "Makes for good radio, though."

Combs clenched and unclenched his fists. "My mom is dead and I'm here to find out who killed her." He'd like to grab the man by his silly chin whiskers, or some equally short hairs, and see how he liked that joke.

"Frog on a stick." Fish produced a green paisley kerchief from his pocket and mopped his brow. "Sorry, Officer, thought this was about traffic tickets." His innocent expression failed to hide the calculation. "It's about September? I already told you everything I know."

"You've told me diddly."

Fish hoisted himself back onto the booster chair. "Maybe I do know more than I think." He eyeballed the clock. "We've got some wiggle room before we go back on air, right, Craig?" Fish waggled his fingers at the boy-engineer's puzzlement until the kid's scowl cleared and he nodded sudden understanding. Fish swiveled in the chair to face Combs. "The power of radio could get us some leads from the citizenry out in listener land. Am I right?"

Combs shook his head. "I ask you the questions, Fish. This isn't quid pro quo or some reality media circus. Real people are involved. A woman is dead, a child is missing." He wouldn't be able to stop the DJ from flapping his jaws once he left the radio station, but while he was here, he'd stay in control.

"Fine, you ask the questions." Fish folded his hands over his tummy and smiled benignly. "What's your name again? Have a seat."

"Officer Jeffrey Combs, Heartland Police Department." He settled into the indicated chair, and bumped his head into another overhead microphone. He pushed it away. "What time was September—"

Fish grinned and interrupted. "We're back, friends and neighbors, and I've got a treat to warm the cockles of your heart." He paused, and pushed his own mic away momentarily. "Play along, it'll be painless. And you might learn something."

Combs's ears felt hot. He looked around and caught the knowing grin of the boy-engineer.

Back in carnival barker mode, Fish cleared his throat and continued. "On this bitter cold November day, we're gonna play "Clue" in a real-live murder investigation with our in-studio guest, Officer Jeffrey Combs, of the Heartland Police Department." His mocking tone set Combs's teeth on edge.

Combs stood abruptly.

"Sit down, sit down, Officer Combs." Fish shook his finger at Combs like a garden gnome chastising a Doberman. "I'm afraid I've taken the good policeman by surprise, since he planned to ask me some questions first. Or maybe he's been stricken with stage fright." He was in his element. "You can sit there like a lump, answer my questions or ask your own, officer. Since you're already here, why not make the best of it?"

Combs glared, but took his seat. He crossed his arms, lips tight.

Fish reacted like a car intent on beating a red light. "When I called earlier to check up on WZPP's very own Pet Peeves guru, you answered the phone. It appears, gentle listeners, that September Day got her tail caught in mayhem." He pushed the mic to one side. "Say something already." he whispered, "They can't see your gloomy face."

Combs glared but said nothing. He'd not agreed to be part of this orchestrated fiasco. Let Fish find his own way out of the maze.

"Speak into the microphone, Officer, so our listeners can hear." Fish beamed when phone lines lit up. "There's been a death, right? And it happened at September's house? Wait no, she'd gone to her sister April's house to hunt for the missing kid. Am I on track so far?"

Combs shifted in the chair, glanced at the door and debated leaving Fish to swing in the wind. But the show would go on whether he remained silent, left, or sang a solo and if he could get control of the conversation, perhaps he'd salvage something. "We are speaking with family, friends and neighbors to locate the whereabouts of Ms. Childress and her son."

"Steven, his name's Steven," prompted Fish. "What about September?"

"Certainly we'd like to speak with Ms. Day about her sister and nephew."

"So d'ya think April is the killer or what?"

Combs recoiled from the mic. "You damn prick."

"Okay, hold your britches there, champ. I was out of line. Sorry," Fish said, clearly anything but remorseful. "As a journalist I have to ask. You don't have to answer."

More phone lines winked. Combs stood to leave.

The little man rode his chair like a jockey. "Everyone out there in radioland, I must confess that I ambushed Officer Combs into a live interview with the promise of some answers. So fire away, Mr. Policeman, ask me anything." He waggled his fingers at the boy-engineer. "And in a bit we'll take some calls."

Combs breathed deeply, gathering his thoughts, and eyed the mic as if it was a snake. "Turn it off." He might already be dead but he'd be damned if he'd let Fish shovel more dirt on his grave. "Shut off the show, go to commercial and I'll talk. Or I'll walk."

Fish sighed. "Fair enough. Listeners, we'll be right back after these messages."

Combs waited until Fish nodded at the engineer. He stared over his shoulder at the "on air" light over the door, and once it went dark, he breathed more easily. Combs swiveled his chair to face Fish. "You said that September, uh, Ms. Day rushed out of the station after her sister called."

"Oh, she wasn't here. She called in from a land-line." He wiggled his eyebrows, enjoying the gossip. "Takes a lot to get her out of the house even without a blizzard. She called in late and left early, but we heated up the airwaves while she was here."

"What exactly did April Childress say?" Combs couldn't imagine either sister as the shooter. But they could have both called from April's house to alibi each other since neither was at the station during the show.

"She said—wait, I've got a better idea." He waved at the engineer. "We've got the show recorded. Craig, cue that up for us, will ya?" The engineer held up two fingers. "Okay, in two minutes we'll have a re-run of that gripping call."

Sweat tickled the back of Combs's neck, and he loosened his jacket. Fish kept the station shirtsleeve warm. "Can you tell where September called from? Her house, or somewhere else, a cell phone maybe?"

"Don't know. Don't care. Long as she phoned in on time, we ran with it. Not a cell phone, though. Reception sucks with those things." He swigged brown, vile liquid from a puce-colored coffee mug that must have been purchased from a yard sale and washed last during the great flood. "By the way, April mentioned a dog, too."

"Dog? What about it?" They'd found kibble all over the kitchen floor, but no sign of the pet. "Must have taken the dog with them."

"Taken? You think April and September are on the run with Steven? And the pooch? And you're dogging their trail, eh?" The round man forced a laugh.

What a piece of work. Combs finally sat in the chair beneath the guest microphone, trying to keep a civil tone. "What car does Ms. Day drive?"

"Volvo." Fish didn't hesitate. "It's a running joke between us but—um— not appropriate on-air." The engineer snickered. "Hey Craig, how you doing on that recording?"

The engineer gave a thumb's up and flipped a switch. Combs listened with interest. Fish's voice began the recording.

Caller, you're on the air with Humphrey Fish and Pet Peeves. What's your question?

Long pause. *Is September there? Please, I need to talk to September.*

Must be April, Combs thought, and leaned forward.

I'm here. What's your name? And do you have a pet question?

September? Oh my God, September you've got to help me. Please, oh no oh no—

Calm down, I can barely understand you. Stop crying and speak clearly. I'll try to help if I can. September sounded cool as a cucumber. She was either a great actress or she wasn't part of the setup.

I tried and tried to call you, but your line was busy. April spoke so fast she was hard to understand. *The babysitter fell asleep, I could just kill her, and Steven went out like he does and I've looked and looked, but he's nowhere around the house. You've got to track him.*

April, is that you? September sounded guilty, and Combs wondered why.

Steven's gone. My baby's out in the storm, him and the dog both are gone!

I'm on my way, I'll . . . September paused. *Fish? Are we still live? Shut the damn radio off, for God's sake, shut it down.* She softened. *April, sweetie, I'm on my way. We'll find Steven. I'll see about tracking, if we need to. But you need to call the police.* Another pause. *Fish, will you freakin' shut it down?* A click and a dial tone ended the segment.

Combs didn't say anything for a long moment. It didn't seem staged. April sounded frantic, and September no less concerned. So if the boy and dog—

"What kind of dog?"

"German Shepherd." Fish spoke with a bad German accent, and then reverted to Midwest twang. "Puppy was a gift from September to the kid, and I think she was training it to help the kid out." He mopped his brow with the kerchief again. "Steven's disabled or something. I never got the details. Hell, I've only known September for a few months, so it's not like I can quote chapter and verse on her life. She's sorta private for a radio personality."

The show aired before the shooting, but April never called the police about Steven. Neither had September. Partnered with April's threats, it was enough to raise the hairs on the back of Combs's neck.

Fish pulled his mic close. "This is ZAPP 105 Radio, with Humphrey Fish tap-dancing as fast as he can on this icy, blustery day. For those just tuned in, we're making history. My special surprise guest, Officer Jeffrey Combs of the Heartland PD, has been giving us an insider's view of a murder investigation. You hear it first, you hear it best, you hear it LIVE on WZPP Easy Listening." He slurped coffee, and sludge painted a nasty shine on his upper lip. He grinned and nodded at Combs.

With a muffled curse, Combs glanced over his shoulder to see the "on air" sign brightly lit once again. Sonofabitch! How long had they been broadcasting?

"To recap for you listeners-come-lately, our own Pet Peeves maven, September Day, bailed on the broadcast when her sister April Childress sent out a howl for help over the airwaves. That's the recording you just heard. We'll replay that again in the next half hour."

Shit. Must have gone live when the engineer cued up the recording. No going back now, dammit. "I need a copy of that." It wasn't a request.

"Sure, Officer, whatever you want." Fish's sarcasm was clear. "That's Officer Jeff being detective-like and official. The poor man's intimately involved because, you see, his mom—what's her name, Officer?"

Combs smoldered as he stood. He'd got what he came for. Time to get the hell out of Dodge.

Undaunted, Fish blustered on. "This defender of the public safety discovered his mother had been killed—in fact, murdered—at April's house." He faked a sympathetic tone. "And I am assisting the good officer any way that I can to help bring the perpetrator to justice."

Grabbing the microphone, Combs interrupted. "We would very much like to speak with September Day and April Childress. Anyone with information on the whereabouts of these individuals should call—"

Fish's bass voice rode roughshod over Combs. "Call the studio line here at the station, that's 800-555-ZAPP. Speaking of that, our phone lines have lit up. Sorry to keep y'all waiting, let's take some calls." Without waiting for Combs's approval, Fish pushed a button. "You're on the air with Humphrey Fish. Do you have a question or comment for Officer Combs?"

"Sounds to me like that April woman did it. Mark my words, when you find her, you'll see she done something to your mother. Maybe even to her kid."

"Thanks for calling." Fish stabbed another button, cutting off the call. "Folks, this is a trying time for Officer Combs. He's lost his mother, the murderer is out there, and two women and a child are missing, possibly accompanied by a German Shepherd, or the child may be alone with the dog. This ain't a good day to be out for man or beast so if you've got tips for us call 800-555-ZAPP."

He'd had enough. Combs strode to the door, and put his hand on the knob as Fish pushed another button. "Caller, you're on the air with Humphrey Fish—covering the biggest Fish-story of them all. What do you have for me?"

"Mr. Fish? Uh, this is Lucy, and I listen to that Pet Peeves show all the time. You really make me laugh." She hesitated. "Am I on the radio?"

"Lucy? Lucy, dear, I'm delighted you're such a fan. What do you want to tell Officer Jeff?"

Combs pulled open the door and took three steps down the hall back to the front waiting area. If he hurried, he could rendezvous with Gonzales. He could hear the broadcast continue over the hallway speakers as he neared Anita's desk.

"Oh. Well, I live over by Gentry Park, and I see a young boy out there every day, him and a big black doggy. They was here today, too."

Combs stopped. He half turned, attention focused on the overhead speaker. He willed Lucy to say more, anything that would make the radio station visit more than a waste of hot air.

"You think you saw Steven and his dog today? What time?" Fish gestured with one urgent hand toward Combs, beckoning him through the glass wall to return to the studio.

"I had to let my own Cleo inside, she was barking so loud. Cleo's a French Poodle, and she just hates this icy weather. Anyways, I seen the little boy with his yellow coat leave the park with his doggy. That was a little after one o'clock."

That's about the right timeline, Combs thought. He bounded back down the hall to the studio and banged open the door, ignoring the engineer's winced reaction to the noise. Combs grabbed the fuzzy mic as if throttling a snake, and drew it close to speak. "Lucy, was the child with an adult? Or did you see a car anywhere around?"

"He was all by his lonesome. That's not all, though. The real reason I called was there's somebody over in the park right now, with another dog."

Combs inhaled sharply. "Another dog? But people go to the dog park all the time."

The caller snort-laughed. "Not in this weather, they don't, and not at night in the middle of a blizzard. And besides, this is different. It's one of them tracker-type dogs."

Despite his excitement, Fish sounded calm. "A tracking dog. Maybe it's September trying to find Steven?"

"That's what I thought, after hearing y'all." Lucy's voice grew more agitated. "I looked out the back window again, and September—or whoever it is—fell down in the snow. I called 911 but they're taking forever to get here. I've been watching since you had me on hold. She ain't got up, and the dog's started to holler. You have to send somebody, make the 911 people speed up. The noise is making my Cleo awful nervous."

Chapter 23

Once September cranked the engine in Pam's Jeep, the blower quickly grew toasty. She loved the sports car look of her Volvo, but appreciated the utility of the Jeep. September pulled off her gloves with her teeth, and held her hands in the warm blast from the dashboard vents. The familiar prickly-painful sensation announced the return of circulation.

She located the charger, unplugged Pam's phone and connected her own. Bruno's happy bark made her smile despite herself. The fenced-in park was a perfect doggy playground. This side of the park's trees offered shade on hot days, and a windbreak against today's snow, while the other side where she'd left her Volvo had no protection.

But dogs don't care about such things. Bruno leaped and danced through drifts to retrieve his toy, ranging back and forth from the Volvo side of the park to where September sheltered in Pam's Jeep. Pretty good for an old doggy. His genes stood the Shadow-pup and Steven in good stead. She could see Pam bending to scoop and toss soft snowballs at the dog.

Using Pam's phone, September called information. "I need the number for the HART-Line Public Transportation, in Heartland, Texas." She punched in the number dictated by the recording. "Please let somebody be there." Chances were the office had closed early like everything else.

"HART-Line, how may I help you?"

"I'm at the Gentry Park stop, and need to know the route the bus travels from here. And if any drivers reported picking up a young boy and a dog."

"Dogs aren't allowed on HART-Line."

"I thought maybe with the snow—"

"It's not allowed." She was as cold as the weather.

September wanted to scream, but tempered her tone. "A little boy and his dog are lost in this mess and I think—hope anyway—they boarded the bus." She concentrated to keep her voice steady. "Could you at least check for me?"

"Lost in this blizzard? Seriously?" The dispatcher's attitude took an about face. "We've not had any reports from drivers. Hold on, let me check something."

September heard the keyboard clatter, and hoped her luck held after all.

On the far side of the field, Pam and Bruno raced around like kids on holiday. Dakota used to do that. He'd scoop up snow with his long muzzle until a little mountain of white capped his nose. She called him "shovel face." Last winter she and Chris made a snow-dog that Dakota promptly baptized yellow. Chris and the dog were so proud.

The dispatcher brought September back to the present. "All buses are accounted for, most en route to our terminal. We're shutting down early. My driver for that route didn't answer, but Freda's final stop is Star Mall, and the return route driver called in sick. So the bus will stay at the mall overnight."

"Star Mall?" Sheesh, that was clear on the other side of the city. "What stops should I check along the way?"

"Only made two stops for anybody to get on. Several got off. Do you want all the stops?"

"Yes, all of them. Thanks a bunch." Steven wouldn't get off unless he recognized his mom's car or house, but a Good Samaritan might have taken him off. Her heart hiccupped at the notion, knowing that too often, bad guys outnumbered good guys.

September jotted down the five stops on a notepad Pam kept on the dashboard. She reached for the Jeep's door latch and only then noticed the Hummer across the field parked near her Volvo. A tall man in a long dark duster clambered out, strode to her Volvo and tried the door. Ghost Man?

She scrunched down out of sight and risked a peek out the window. Pam and Bruno continued to play, oblivious to the threat.

Maybe she was mistaken. Other men wore long coats, and had white hair. It was too far to see features. Ghost Man and Lizzie didn't drive the only Hummer in town.

He eliminated any question when he hit and shattered the front passenger window of the Volvo.

September screamed, wishing she'd thwacked him harder. The Volvo's car alarm whooped but gave him no pause. He reached through the window and pulled out April's laptop.

Bruno barked at the commotion and started toward the vandalized car. Pam yelled. "Get away from there! What're you doing?" She trotted after the dog. "Drop that and get away from there!"

September scrambled to open the door, and finally managed to scroll open a window an inch or two. If it was Ghost Man, Pam had no chance. She yelled a warning.

He shot the front and rear tires on the near side of September's Volvo.

Pam cried out. Called over her shoulder to September. "Phone the police." She confronted the man, a fearless gamecock defending territory. "Bruno, *fass*."

September preferred the rabbit-hole safety of the semi-hidden Jeep to facing danger. But Pam's bravery shamed her. She bungled open the door, and promptly fell out into the snow, and her stomach clenched as another shot popped.

A thunk-twang hit the Jeep. So much for being hidden. No silencer this time—the distance didn't allow for that—Ghost Man had braced his gun arm on the top of the open SUV door to help his aim. The snow added inches to his height, giving him a giant's proportions.

"Pam, get away!" September scrambled and managed to climb back into the Jeep's open door.

"Bruno, *hier. Hier.*" Pam screamed the recall a second time, fear for her dog overriding any notion of her own safety.

September slammed the door. She flinched when another bullet struck the side of Pam's Jeep, and she quickly started the engine. Bruno's teeth were no match for bullets. He couldn't protect Pam. September jammed the car into gear. Wheels spun, dug deep and found traction. Up over the curb, across the sidewalk. She aimed for the open gate. "Didn't like the dumbbell? Let's see how you like two tons of car upside your head." The Jeep banged through a fence post, fishtailed, and steadied.

Bruno finally obeyed and raced back toward Pam.

Ghost-Man pointed his gun. At Pam. He shouted to her, something that September couldn't hear over the engine's roar. The gun popped, popped again.

Pam fell.

"No!" September slammed the brakes. The Jeep carved doughnut tracks in the field and then shuddered to a stop.

Bruno howled. He threw himself at Pam.

September stumbled from the car. Too late, she was too late. She wanted to run to Pam but instead stood frozen. Stared at Ghost Man. She'd rejoin Chris after all, and it was what she deserved.

Pam's moans broke her daze. September dove for cover as if the snow offered protection. She crawled toward her friend.

The pale man lowered his gun. "Find the flash drive. You won't get another warning." He climbed into the SUV and drove away.

September swam through the mounds of white until she could push Bruno aside and huddle next to Pam. "Honey, talk to me." Her bare fingers were nerveless sticks that smoothed Pam's scarf aside. Bruno continued to cry.

A woman from the closest house stuck her head out the door. "Is she okay? Is the dog hurt? He's making an awful racket. My Cleo's fit to bust over it."

"Call an ambulance!" Pam's skin paled to match the snow. Breaths shallow, slow. Bubbling. "Bruno, move." September again pushed the big shepherd. He slunk to Pam's other side. Bruno licked and nibbled the fabric of Pam's sleeve, nudged her arm.

"I done called for help. Even called that radio show with the policeman already. Should I call 'em again?"

"For God's sake, call nine-one-one!" September turned back to Pam. "Can you hear me? Where do you hurt?" She couldn't see the wound. Pam's bundled coat cocooned her, hiding the injury.

Tears spilled from Pam's brown-sugar eyes. "How's my dog? He shot us. How's Bruno?" At the sound of his name, the dog howled and tried to climb into her lap.

"Bruno *platz*. Down. Good dog." September tasted blood. She'd bitten her cheek. "He's fine, Pam. He's right here. What about you?" September held tight to Pam's hand.

"Hard to breathe." Pam coughed. "You're in deep do-do." It wasn't a question.

The guilt hurt worse than any physical injury. "I never meant for you or anyone to get hurt."

Pam's eyelids fluttered as if to clear fading vision. She breathed and gasped with the effort. Distant sirens wailed. "You go. Find Steven."

Another siren joined the first. EMTs must have been in the neighborhood. September tried to gauge how soon they'd arrive.

The neighbor lady stood nearby, jaw agape. "Bring a blanket," September shouted, turning back to Pam. "Help's on the way."

"Tell my husband—"

"Tell him yourself. This is just another SAR adventure. You'll have a great story to share over that merlot." She said the words out loud to convince herself as much as Pam.

The sirens grew louder. She could stay with Pam, should stay with her, but that meant giving up on Steven. And April.

The neighbor trudged through two-foot drifts to toss a green and red afghan to September. "I don't want to get close to that dog." She sniffed, nodded at the whimpering Bruno. "He looks like a biter." She stood several feet away, watching.

Bruno's focus never wavered from Pam as September tucked the blanket around her friend, propping her head out of the snow.

"September?"

"I'm here, right here." She squeezed Pam's hand.

"Get the hell out of here." Froth stained Pam's teeth red. "Police won't let you leave. Steven needs you." Her eyelids fluttered. "My dogs, the puppies. Eugene. He isn't home. Who'll take care of my dogs?" A single tear escaped down her cheek. Bruno licked it off.

"I'm so sorry." That bastard. She'd track down Ghost Man; he wouldn't get away with this. "Concentrate on yourself, Pam. Stay with me, Eugene needs you. The dogs are counting on you." That wasn't what Pam wanted to hear, so September gave her what she wanted. It was the only thing she had to offer. "I'll take care of the dogs, no worries. I promise."

Pam relaxed. Her lips moved, but nothing came out.

"What is it? Hang on, help's almost here." September bent close, ribs protesting, her ear next to Pam's mouth. "I can't hear you, say again?"

"Hurry, go after Steven." Pam gasped with the effort to be heard. "That man. He said they found Steven."

Chapter 24

Shadow sat patiently beside his boy's chair and drooled. He watched Steven pick up a French fry, dip it in dark sauce and munch. The treat-lady gave Shadow French fries when he was a good-dog and stayed quiet during rides. "French fries" was one of his favorite words. Shadow whined. He knew the next one was for him.

The bacon-smelling Freda and old man chatted. Shadow listened for familiar words, but he remained focused on his boy when he dipped another fry. He stood, wagged and stretched to gently take the greasy tidbit. Shadow chewed once, swallowed, and sat again. He licked his lips.

The smooth, shiny floor soothed Shadow's sore footpads. Clanky cook-noises from the nearby fast food counter echoed in the empty space. The sounds made Shadow nervous, and the smells painted the air with temptation, but Shadow stayed next to his boy, the way a good-dog should. Once the French fries appeared, it became a happy place, and Shadow became a fan of both strangers.

The old man sipped his drink, a burned-smell concoction Shadow recognized. Steven's mother drank the same hot liquid every morning. Teddy coughed and wiped his mouth with a tissue before sipping again. The old man sounded growly when he talked, but without the threat. It was just the way he sounded, like a big dog that meant no harm.

Freda sipped her own drink. It smelled sweet and when some sloshed on the floor, Shadow tasted it. He pawed her, hoping she'd spill some more.

"Steven, don't you want a sandwich? A kid needs more than fries for dinner." Shadow pawed her again, and she smiled and rubbed his ears and he leaned hard against her hand.

Steven shook his head. "Steven likes French fries. Steven likes ketchup. Steven feeds good-dog French fries and sauce." He dipped another fry, sucked off the sauce, and chewed the morsel. Shadow pulled away from Freda and cocked his head in anticipation.

The old man gestured at the basket of fries, now nearly empty. "Want some more ketchup?"

His boy ignored the question. He dipped fries. Offered one to Shadow. Shadow considered the gesture as nice as a tummy rub.

Teddy looked around. "Everyone's gone already, except us chickens."

"My relief driver never showed. The office said they're done for the night. Maybe for the rest of the week. That's a cut in hours right before the holidays I don't need."

Shadow's ears flattened at her tone. Big humans who worried meant problems for dogs. What would happen when the French fries were gone? What would he do…what would his boy do, if the two adults left? Shadow looked around. The clank from the kitchen had stopped. The open room with shiny-slick floors and food smells was big, empty, and nothing like home.

Adventure and new things were fun. Good-dogs liked to sniff new places. But Shadow wanted to go home. He yawned again and yearned for his soft bed in the kitchen, a kitchen that didn't clank. His bed smelled like him, a good-dog smell. Not like wet floor and old grease. Shadow watched Freda's wide, kind face and turned to the stubble-cheeked Teddy. He whined.

"Do you want a refill?" Teddy hooked his thumb to indicate the man at the food counter. "The manager knows me, and gives me freebies on refills."

Freda smiled. "I'm done. Besides, once Steven's on his way, we hit the road. Happy to give you a ride home, it's on the way."

Shadow checked his boy before he rose and padded after the old man to the counter. It smelled of chicken, fries and a touch . . . yes, it was bacon grease. Maybe if he asked his new friend in just the right way, he'd get some.

He sat down. He cocked his head and gently pawed Teddy's pant leg. Greasy, salty French fries tasted good, but nothing compared to bacon. He whined and pawed again.

"I don't think you like coffee, fella." Teddy showed his stained teeth in a grin. "Thanks, Carl."

"You're welcome, Mr. Williams. Everyone in the mall has already left. I'm out of here, too."

Teddy laughed. "Drive home safe." Carl rolled down a noisy cover, and exited out a back hallway.

Shadow sighed. That metal curtain cut off any hope of bacon. He heard a distant door open and close when the French fry cook left the building.

Teddy limped back to Freda and Steven, and set his cup on the table. "Have to take a potty break, be back in a flash."

At the table, Shadow sniffed carefully. Most of his boy's French fries were gone. Maybe the smoky-smelling Teddy knew about another food place? At the happy thought, Shadow shook himself hard. Freda would stay with Steven, so surely a good-dog could explore? Just a little? Shadow turned and trotted after his new friend. His claws ticked on the slick floor.

He followed Teddy to a nearby room without a door. The place smelled like pee. Not clean dog pee with all kinds of exciting messages, but human pee from many different people. Shadow sneezed, and sat down to wait for the old man to come out. He couldn't smell anything that resembled food. His ears drooped and he sighed.

A cold draft ruffled his fur. He looked back to where his boy waited. A big man approached.

Freda stood up and they grabbed hands the way humans sometimes did.

The stranger pulled a tissue from his overcoat and honked. He wore a short overcoat that fluttered open like crows' wings, and a hat with flaps like floppy dog ears.

Shadow's hackles rose, he didn't know why. Behind him in the cold, hard room, water hit water and he smelled fresh old-man-pee. Shadow whined but didn't move.

Something was bad wrong. The stranger's posture threatened despite his mild tone. Shadow didn't know what to do. The prickly sensation made him want to stand between Steven and the stranger. Instead, he shivered. Shadow fought the urge to roll on his back.

He wished the Teddy would hurry. He could be brave with a trusted friend by his side. People knew things, and could tell dogs what to do.

The stranger smelled of anger and something scarier. A sharp, pungent scent that rang alarms. Alarms that told Shadow to *do something*. Shadow's tail tucked tight, and he showed attack-ready fangs. He crept closer, his body low to the ground. He padded with care to keep his claws quiet.

They didn't notice him. People missed lots of important things. That frustrated Shadow sometimes. But this time being overlooked was a good thing. Mounting courage lifted his tail into a stiff bristle that matched the fierce concern of his silent snarl.

The big man pointed something at Steven, looked at it and then held it against his head and talked into it like it was a person.

Shadow crept closer and stopped directly behind Freda. They still hadn't noticed. He heard a faint but familiar voice come from the ear-object the man held still against his head. Shadow growled, and Freda started at his voice. She finally looked at him, worried brow wrinkles asking questions. He huddled behind her and dared himself to be brave. Be a good-dog. But he couldn't move.

The stranger reached out a hand toward Steven.

He growled again, and pressed against Freda's leg. He felt her tremble. She was scared, too. Shadow needed to be brave. He took another step forward.

Freda licked her lips, and Shadow smelled her sudden fear, and the slight tremor in her voice increased his agitation. "Mr. Childress, what about Steven's dog?"

Shadow flicked his ears toward her but didn't move his attention from the stranger.

"Dog?" The man frowned, finally noticing Shadow. He reached for Steven's arm.

"Steven, run!" Freda yelled, and backpedaled so fast she knocked over a chair.

Steven screamed. And Shadow leaped to his boy's rescue.

The man grabbed Steven and pulled him before him like a shield.

His claws clattered for purchase. Shadow's bark-demands escalated when Steven screamed louder, and he skidded into a nearby table, and yelped. He scrambled to his feet, and stalked within two dog-lengths. He snarled a demand for the man to let Steven go. Would he take Steven away?

Freda kept screaming. "Leave him alone!"

Shadow knew what "leave it" meant, but the strange man wouldn't let Steven go. He placed himself protectively between Freda and the threatening stranger. He lunged and feinted away from his boy's kicks, not wanting to injure Steven.

The man blocked Steven's pinwheeling arms and held his boy hard against his body. "It's just a tantrum." He had to shout over Steven's cries, but his worried eyes slid to Shadow.

Screams hurt Shadow's ears. The man's fear-smell spilled in waves but his steady stare threatened. For the first time, Shadow wanted to bite. Bite hard. He straightened his posture, arched his neck, and flagged his tail with just the tip jerking. He stared back. Ready.

Freda fumbled in her pocket. She held something to her ear.

So much fear-stink made it hard for good-dogs to think.

"Hang up the phone." The big man held the squirmy boy by the collar the way Shadow picked up his stuffed bear toy. He backed away with Steven in his arms.

Shadow danced closer. Aimed a bite. He dodged the man's kick, and feinted again. His ears pinned back. His tail wagged, stiff and frantic. He'd never attacked anything except his toy bear, but the bad man didn't know. He could bluff. Sometimes a loud growl was enough.

"Call off the dog." He pulled something out of his pocket and pointed it at Shadow. "I don't want to shoot anyone, not even a dog." The boy-thief's glasses glinted as he looked around the big room.

Steven's screams spiraled higher and higher. He turned red, and his eyes screwed shut. Shadow gathered his haunches. Good-dogs protect their boys.

Shadow danced closer and away again. Good-dogs don't use their teeth on people. He knew that. But what if the people were bad? He wanted to bite hard, hold on, and shake him. Grab and hurt, so his boy would stop yelling. Shadow leaped, and his jaws snapped.

The stranger yelled, flinching back. Steven wriggled and screamed, making the man's pointing hand jerk.

Freda howled and tackled the man. Something popped.

A gag-making stink burst into the air. Freda crumpled. Her head thudded on the shiny floor, and the ear-object cracked open and skidded across the slick floor.

Why'd she fall down? Shadow nose-poked her but she didn't stir.

The man pointed at Shadow, still struggling to contain his boy by the collar. "Look what you made me do."

He paw-danced around Freda's form and dodged in. Shadow's teeth snapped empty air before he bounded away. The gun continued to pop.

Steven slumped, finally silent. He hung in the stranger's grip, eyes closed like when he slept. But he wasn't asleep. He'd just gone to his quiet place. He did that sometimes, and hid for hours.

Teddy hid, too, out of sight in the entrance to the pee-smelly room. Shadow heard Teddy panting as though winded from a game of fetch. He whimpered, too. Shadow whined, wanting to join Teddy and hide his face against the man. But not while his boy was in the stranger's grip.

The whole world smelled like fear. And blood. It bubbled out of Freda. That made Shadow even more determined to bite. Despite the terror. Because of fear. He glared at the man who dared take his boy. He'd make the bad man go away. It was his job to protect Steven.

The stranger stared back. He threw Steven over his shoulder, turned and lurched away.

Shadow's paws bicycled for purchase. He lunged. His teeth clacked, snapped, and sought contact. He leaped, silent in pursuit. His fangs tore through cloth, sliced flesh. Salty skin, broken flesh, blood-taste and smell. He leaped high, grabbed again. Hung on.

The man screamed, he shrieked louder than Steven. He kicked, and a shiny shoe connected with furry ribs. Shadow yelped and rolled away. In the same motion, the man hit the mall door and pushed through.

The door slammed against Shadow's muzzle. He yelped and leaped against the glass. Flecks of saliva salted the glass when he grabbed the metal crossbar. How to get through? Go after them. He could see him, the bad man. The boy-thief. Close. Untouchable. *Taking his boy.*

A good-dog would know what to do. But Shadow hadn't a clue. He'd failed.

Bad dog. Shadow howled.

Chapter 25

September pulled into the Star Mall parking lot, and slowed Pam's Jeep to a crawl. One lonely VW squatted near the bus stop next to an empty HART-Line vehicle. Score.

Guilt flogged her for leaving Pam behind, even if EMTs were on the way. She'd left a message at the shelter about Bruno and the rest of Pam's dogs. She'd done all she could, at least while she was on the run.

Steven was priority number one. The flash drive was a lost cause. After Steven was safe, she'd concentrate on April. "Let him be here," she said, as if speaking the hope aloud would make it happen. It wasn't a prayer. Hell no. God never answered. Even Wilma would agree with her now.

Snow had changed to ice that chittered against the windshield. Wiper blades on the warm glass painted the mess into a frozen sheet except for the twin spots the defroster melted.

Light spilled from the mall's glass entry, but the stores inside looked dark. The place must have shut down early for the storm, but September didn't check her watch, didn't want to know the time. Each minute ticked closer to failure. And failure meant death.

September braced herself for the slap of cold and levered open the car door. By the time she'd shuffle-skated to the entrance, sleet sugared her hair.

Her phone rang. She looked. Mom again. She didn't answer. It was close to nine o'clock. Only 17 hours until the deadline.

The smeary doors gave her pause. How odd. Janitorial services kept entrances pristine, sensitive to shoppers' first impressions. Smudges covered the glass from floor to chest height on the two center doors, and muddy paw prints slurried the tile entrance. Her shoulders unclenched with sudden relief. They were here.

She pulled open the glass door and hurried into the mall. "Steven?" September's voice echoed. Metal accordion gates shuttered store fronts on both sides of the entrance, leaving only the massive hallways passable. If the individual stores had closed, that narrowed the search. She listened but heard nothing but the ambient buzz of florescent lights. The mall was empty. Maybe she missed them. Maybe they were safe with kindly strangers. "Where are you?" Steven might not answer, but if they were here, the dog would respond. "Shadow. Baby-dog, where are you?"

A yelp sounded, and September's heart leaped. "Shadow, good-dog. Shadow, *come*. Steven, it's Aunt September, don't be scared." She raced toward the yelps. Where the dog was, Steven couldn't be far.

The pup skidded around the corner, yodeling with emotion. His big paws slid out from under him. He regained his feet and launched himself, aiming slurps at her face as he wailed and *arooed* happy sounds mixed with something else. Her stomach fluttered with dread.

"Baby-dog, settle down." The jumping-jack behavior said he wanted her on his level, so she knelt to hug his shaking form. "Hush, it's okay." She eagerly scanned for Steven as she dodged the pup's frantic licks, stroking his throat until he rolled onto his back. He'd wet himself. What the hell? Her throat tightened. Something was off. "Where's Steven? Shadow, calm down. Settle. Where's Steven?" She steadied herself and spoke with command. "Find Steven."

"Steven's gone! You've got to help. Call for help, my phone's dead–"

September scrambled to her feet. Shadow rolled upright but continued to wriggle and cry.

"Who are you? Where's Steven?" She backed away.

The old man shuffled closer in a frantic jig that favored a bum leg. His faded blue eyes swam with tears. His overcoat swallowed a frail body bent with arthritis, defeat, or both. He held stained bare hands before him. And shuddered.

"Call the cops. Freda's cell phone is smashed. I don't have one." He stared at his dirty hands, wiped them against the front of his dark coat, and folded them together as though in prayer. "That's a good dog, he tried to protect Steven." His lower lip trembled. "That poor little boy." He looked at her, anguished. "Nobody's here! I've banged on every damn gate for somebody to call for help. But they closed early, nobody's here. Thank God you came."

"Is that blood?" She glanced at Shadow for his reaction, but his hackles remained smooth. "Where is Steven? He's not hurt, is he?"

The man stumbled toward her, his voice desperate. "My friend, Freda. I think she's dead." He braced himself against the wall to keep himself upright. "Call an ambulance." He whirled and nearly fell as he scrambled back toward the food court.

"Wait. Somebody's dead?" The room spun, steadied, and she dashed after him. "Where's Steven? And who the hell are you?"

"Are you deaf? Call the ever-lovin' police!" His stiff old-man gait moved more quickly than she could have imagined. "If it matters, I'm Theodore Williams. They call me Teddy."

The dog's ears twitched. He whined as he kept pace with her, insisting on contact as they moved.

"Who's dead, Teddy?"

He stopped abruptly and pointed, and September surged past. Shadow pressed so hard against her leg, she tripped.

Teddy pulled off his glasses and swiped his tears with a sleeve. "We only wanted to help the boy and he shot her!" He found a napkin on a nearby table and scrubbed his hands, then shredded the paper into confetti. "I tried to give her CPR. You've got to call nine-one-one. Help Freda." He gulped. "Stop that man who took Steven. God, the poor little kid was screaming, he was so scared." He balled his fists, white knuckled with anger and fear. "I couldn't stop him. He would have killed me, too."

They turned the corner into the food court that held a dozen or more café tables with flimsy chairs. Near a large central planter, spilled fries and ketchup mixed with brown liquid from a crushed cup. The HART-Line driver was sprawled next to an overturned chair like she'd attempted to sit and missed.

September rushed to the woman, brushing her lank hair aside. A neat hole just left of center marred Freda's smooth throat, blood pooling beneath Freda's head. She was still warm, but without a pulse or respiration. Nothing she could do.

 She slowly got back up. Her bruised ribs had stiffened. Teddy stood with his head bowed, hands clasped before him, mumbling in prayer. He wobbled, and she caught his arm, noticing Teddy smelled like wet wool and tobacco when his smoker's cough rattled his lungs. Afraid to ask, she forced the words out anyway. "Tell me, Teddy. Who took Steven?"

He crossed himself, and took a steadying breath. "I bought them French fries." He stuck his free hand in his pocket, still wary of bloodstains on the canary yellow sweater he wore under his coat.

Steven would have been drawn to that color, just as he'd been willing to board the yellow bus when April's car failed to show up. She frowned when Shadow padded close to the dead woman and sniffed her leg.

"Shadow, let's go." She waited until the pup made eye contact, and then led Teddy and the dog toward the exit. "It was kind of you and your friend to help. Steven and Shadow love French fries, it's their special treat." She was talking about snack food with a woman dead on the floor, and wanted to shake him, but there was no rushing Teddy. His frantic pleas for action had morphed into dazed confusion. He looked ready to collapse. Shock did that to people. "What happened?"

"Steven told us his name, address and phone number."

She nodded encouragement. April taught him to parrot the information in case he wandered away, something autistic children often did. German shepherds helped prevent wandering like a moveable fence, and were trained to corral their charges and alert them to unusual situations.

When she looked at him, Shadow cut his eyes away and whined. His tail beat a low-held fast wag. It wasn't the dog's fault. Training took time. Shadow was little more than a baby himself. She was responsible. For all of it.

"Freda called the number." Teddy's lips trembled so much he was hard to understand. "Steven's dad was coming to get him. I was in the men's room when he got here. I heard them yelling, Steven screaming, and I should have helped. I should have done something. He shot Freda. Why'd he do that? He would have shot me!" Teddy turned and vomited.

September supported the old man, her mind awhirl. April hated Doug, she'd never send him. And if Doug did show up, it made no sense he'd shoot somebody for rescuing Steven.

Then she understood. Steven repeated April's cell phone number. Since Lizzie had April, she must have answered her phone and sent Ghost Man, although it didn't seem possible he could have beat her here from the park. "What did he look like?"

"I only saw the back of him as he left. Tall, overweight, wore a hat with earflaps. Is it a custody battle? I know those things can get nasty."

She sucked in a breath, feeling sucker-punched. So it wasn't Ghost Man. Lizzie must have an army of henchmen and sent someone else.

Teddy pulled a linen handkerchief from one pocket, and dabbed his mouth. "I should have gone after him, I should have stopped him. Steven screamed. He didn't want to go."

He could have saved Steven. She wanted to smack him, but she deserved punishment even more. She'd frozen at the park, and hadn't saved Pam. She'd as good as led a killer to butcher Chris and Dakota. She was nobody's hero. How could she blame Teddy when he'd at least tried to help?

"He didn't even know I was there. He was busy watching Freda and dodging the dog. You call him Shadow?"

The pup's head swiveled toward Teddy at mention of his name, and back at September when she couldn't catch her breath. Shadow sniffed her gloved hand and shoved his brow beneath her palm for the comfort of a pet.

But she pulled her hand away. He'd failed Steven. But she'd trained him. He wasn't Dakota. Dakota would have saved Steven or died trying, just as Dakota sacrificed himself for Chris. And left her alone.

Bile flooded her mouth. September bent, hands on knees, and retched. Her empty stomach twisted repeatedly in a painful, unproductive knot.

Now Teddy supported her. "I'm not a fighter, I'm a teacher." She wanted to tell him to shut up, but couldn't get past the dry heaves. "Taught computer science, writing programs, what do I know about guns?" His bushy eyebrows rose and fell above the rim of his glasses. "Where's your phone?"

"It's dead." She had to give him a plausible reason for not calling. Had to get away from him. Now that Lizzie had Steven, she'd won and had all the cards.

"But you have a car. I couldn't find Freda's car keys. I didn't want to move her." He sobbed, and forced himself to continue. "You can get us to a phone; my house isn't far from here. The police will know what to do, right?" He wanted answers, wanted forgiveness, and she had nothing to give. "I'm so sorry about your son."

September didn't bother to correct him. It didn't matter. Nothing mattered.

"I want to make it up to you and your little boy. Make it up to Freda." Teddy straightened to his full height, assumed a professorial dignity with the small posture change.

She'd bungled everything. Blew off April's call, missed Steven at the park, taunted Lizzie into shooting Wilma, let April be taken, and involved Pam. This poor woman's murder and Steven's kidnapping, it was all her fault, too. Everything she touched turned to crap. She didn't have the flash drive, hadn't a chance in hell to find it, and without that as ransom, April and Steven would die.

September's knees turned to rubber, and she sat down hard on the floor. Her ribs throbbed. She had no tears left. Yes, call the police. That's what Mom would want. It's what by-the-book Chris would do, too. She couldn't stop Lizzie, couldn't save anyone. Hell, she couldn't even protect herself without triple-locked doors and window bars.

Shadow pushed his front half into her lap, and she stiffened and pushed him away. "I taught you better than that." But he wouldn't be denied. Shadow buried his muzzle in her armpit and cried.

She couldn't help herself and gave in, her arms clutching and then cradling him. September held him tighter and tighter. She buried her face in the soft black fur of Shadow's ruff. And it felt good, oh God it felt so good, it had been so long . . .

"That's a great dog. I think he bit the guy."

"Good-dog," September whispered fiercely, "You marked the sonofabitch." Her words spit venom but her hands remained gentle as they stroked his fur, and then hesitated when she felt something strung around his neck.

September parted the dog's coat. She followed the fine chain down both sides of his throat to where a pendant hung hidden in the fur of his chest. "Shadow, move. Move, baby-dog. Wait." He didn't want to, but finally pulled himself away from her body. She pulled the lanyard over his head to examine the 16-GB flash drive suspended on the chain.

"Good-dog, Shadow. You're such a good boy, good-dog." She quickly slipped the lanyard over her head, and dropped the flash drive beneath the front of her coat.

Shadow wriggled with delight, ears flat to his head. He banged his tail against the floor. He'd stopped shivering.

Teddy offered his hand and helped her struggle to her feet. "What's that?"

She pressed one hand over the flash drive where it nestled between her breasts. "A miracle, Teddy. It's life itself."

Chapter 26

Combs lifted the brass knocker on September's front door and fought déjà vu. He glanced at his watch. It had been less than nine hours since he and Pike had noticed the smoke. He banged four times and rang the bell and backed down the steps with one hand on his gun.

"She's not here." Gonzales joined him.

"You check the garage?" Combs kept his hand on his gun.

"Empty. I did a walk around." He paused. "Last word we got, she's driving Pam's Jeep, but so far no sighting."

Combs craned to see the brick carriage house September used as a garage. The old wood gates remained true to the historical design but must be a bitch to open and shut in bad weather. She'd been in a hurry when she left, and hadn't bothered to close them. One door moved in the wind to carve an icy wedge in the drift. A covered walkway didn't fit the architecture but connected a brick path from the outbuilding to a side door. He guessed it opened into her kitchen.

The two men climbed the steps together. Gonzales stomped his feet on the brick entry to knock off clots of ice. "There's a lot of snow blown into the garage. She's been gone for hours."

"Not enough for a warrant. We'll have to tread lightly."

Gonzales pulled a keychain from his pocket with several keys. "Her folks gave me the keys and alarm code. They want her found." He grinned. "I explained there's probable cause she's either kidnapped or on the run from killers."

Combs smiled back. That would have to do.

The security was over the top. It took several minutes for Gonzales to find the right key to open each of the three locks in the fancy brass key plate. "Her folks were surprised September even left the house. She's convinced some stalker from Chicago followed her to Indiana and killed her husband. No proof, though, they never arrested anyone."

Combs struggled to concentrate. Uncle Stanley and Aunt Ethel expected him half an hour ago. He was the oldest. He should host the gathering. But they'd want answers he didn't have, details he couldn't bring himself to revisit, that no victim's family ever needed to know. Mom's murder had Stan panting to join the investigation, to hell with retirement. Uncle Stan was even more outside official boundaries than Combs.

At least with Gonzales, he'd make headway on the investigation. So far he'd not gotten any grief about the Fish radio incident, either, since it led to the park victim. September Day was the best lead they had.

Gonzales opened the final lock and pushed open the door. He stepped one foot inside, gun drawn. "Haloooo." He listened for a beat, and holstered his weapon when the security system beeped a warning. "Feels empty. Play heads up, but I don't think anyone's here." He located the alarm keypad beside the door and punched in the code September's parents had provided.

The old two-story house, complete with a turret on one side, originally contained a warren of tiny rooms connected by narrow halls. From the outside, the gingerbread structure was the witch's castle Combs and his friends whispered about when they were kids. But September's contractors had gutted the house, leaving the massive vertical beams in place. The work-in-progress created an open airy floor plan of casual elegance. It must have taken a boatload of money. Combs followed the detective inside, and wiped his boots on the sisal "Cats Rule, Dogs Drool" welcome mat. "What else did the parents say?"

"Not a lot. Couldn't say where the sisters might go. The mother talked to September this morning, and said she had seemed distracted and evasive. Also said there's been recent friction between the sisters over the Thanksgiving meal. Both want to host it." He shrugged as if it was no consequence. "Sounds familiar. My wife and her sister go round and round about that every year. But otherwise, they get along okay. September's even helped with Steven's treatment."

"The dog, right?"

"Yeah, the dog. But also some pricy new treatment Childress refused to fund." Gonzales looked around the house. "Nice place."

"Money to burn, like Childress said."

Gonzales shrugged. "He only had part of it right. The lottery paid out fifty grand or so after taxes. The big money came from life insurance on September's husband, at least that's what the parents say." He smoothed his mustache. "Doty thinks the sisters cooked up the lost boy story."

"Why?" Combs shook his head. "Does she think Steven got hurt or killed so they need a reason to disappear him?" Evil thought, but it did make sense.

"Maybe. Still no clue why either of them would shoot your mother." Gonzales refused to look at Combs. "Some people go off their nut when they lose a spouse. September could have lots of guilt over that, and maybe the sisters fought, and April ended up dead so September ran with the little boy."

Too complicated. Simple cause and effect was more likely. "We're turning a couple of hoof prints into a zebra stampede. We're too close to see the big picture."

"So what do you call the bloody workout clothes in September's car? With that Body Works logo, they belong to April and she's missing. Why else would your girlfriend stash them?"

"Don't call her my girlfriend." His wet shoes squeaked. He knew about the evidence of a fight at April's business, and acknowledged family feuds could lead to murder, but it just didn't feel right. "Blood on the workout clothes looked more like it came from the outside, not that the person wearing them was injured. Next."

Gonzales consulted his notes. "September's husband worked special victims in Chicago before they moved to Indiana. He was off duty when he got killed."

"Makes no sense for September to run with the kid. On the radio play-back, April said Steven disappeared from the house. She called September for help. They both get Academy Awards if that was an act."

"Don't discount the possibility of a set up. Bet it's a custody thing to get Steven away from his dad. More ex-husbands kill their wives than sisters, and Childress was hiding something." He checked his watch. "Wonder if Doty's still at the hospital. If the dog lady from the park pulls through, maybe she has a clue where they went."

Combs shifted his weight. If anyone should feel resentful of moms getting custody over dads, it was him. He had to make an appointment to see his kids. "September's Volvo was at the park. She wouldn't shoot up her own car. Somebody wanted her stranded. The witness didn't see a child. Didn't see much." He opened his coat.

"So why'd September run if she has nothing to hide? Hell, she insisted the neighbor call nine-one-one, but didn't stick around to make sure her friend got help."

That part bothered Combs. A lot.

"She grabbed the Jeep and beat it out of there before the EMTs could arrive." Gonzales stepped further into the room. "She could have set up that rendezvous at the park just to get another car, trashing her own to make herself into a victim."

"That's a stretch." Too many unanswered questions. "What makes a woman, the widow of a cop for God's sake, go nuts? Kidnap a kid and kill anyone who gets in her way?" Combs hated the guesswork, and was eager for answers and hoped the latest vic would pull through and have some clues to share. "What's the word on the dog lady's status?"

"Last I heard, still in surgery. And it's not looking good. Doty will call with any news." Gonzales peered up the impressive front staircase, and his nose wrinkled like a silk shirt on a hot day. "Damn, smells like smoke. I'll take the back, you take the front—"

"—and I'll get to Scotland afore ye." Combs looked around.

Gonzales suppressed a smile as he took the stairs two at a time.

Combs looked around the ground floor. Sheet-covered furniture leaned against walls. The room smelled of fresh paint and new carpet. Cherry crown molding contrasted with the cream walls and the carved stone mantel above a massive fireplace. He flicked up a dust sheet that covered a burgundy leather sofa and a matching overstuffed chair. Nothing here.

Combs passed through an arched doorway into a smaller room next to the kitchen meant to be the dining area. Instead, September used it for an office and music room. The rest of the house remained a work-in-progress, but this space was lived in. The cobalt carpet and matching blue ceiling contrasted with yellow walls. A small studio piano on the rear wall perched next to a large stringed instrument—cello? Bass?—that stood upright in a carved stand in the corner. Books and sheets of music overflowed the bench and a basket on the floor.

The opposite wall held a large bay window. September's desk and chair, cherry wood again, took advantage of the view. The work space held a computer, phone, and a Tiffany-style rose lamp. Combs remembered how countless rose bushes used to turn the old house into a perfume factory each spring, and wondered if they'd survived years of neglect. The adjacent file cabinet also held a printer, and a wedding picture of a beaming man about Combs's age with his arm around September. Her expression looked guarded, not that of a radiant bride.

"Talk to me, September." Combs pulled off his gloves and sifted through papers on the desk. "Tell me why."

Three gunshot victims in less than twelve hours, and September was the common denominator. Maybe she hadn't killed his mom, but she'd been directly involved, he was sure of it, but no judge would issue a warrant based on a gut feeling. He and Gonzales were here because September, April and Steven were missing, and potential victims of foul play. That was the official version, anyway, and Doty signed off on it. She was as frustrated as the rest of them.

Combs flipped through September's DayMinder, and checked the haphazard Post-It notes stuck to every surface of the desk top. He heard Gonzales clomping overhead. The hardwood floors, high ceilings and empty rooms made for great acoustics. You couldn't sneak around in this house, unless barefoot.

People carry DayMinders with them. September must have rushed out the door to have left it behind. Today's appointments, highlighted in a variety of colors, included the Pet Peeves radio show, and something called a temperament test. Each of the appointments had a checkmark, and the middle appointment included a phone number.

He dialed and got the city shelter with a prompt to leave a message. He didn't. Combs flipped the pages. An appointment marked "deposition" also had a checkmark, so presumably it had been resolved. "Deposition" meant trial. That could be about child custody. Combs dialed. Gonzales's footsteps thumped overhead.

"McIntyre, Devries, Ellis and Freeman, office hours are nine to five, please leave a message and someone will return your call," said a bored-sounding woman.

Combs recognized the firm, one of the largest in Heartland. "This is Officer Jeffrey Combs. I'm investigating a homicide and need to speak with whoever had a deposition scheduled in two days with September Day." He left his number and hung up. It had been a long shot anyone would answer at this hour.

Gonzales clattered down the distant stairs and hurried into the room, cell phone pressed to his ear. "I got Doty on the line. There's news." He listened, and hung up. "The victim from the park just died. Never made a statement."

"Shit." Combs stretched and cracked his knuckles but it didn't relieve the tension. "September made several calls today, probably to cancel appointments because of the snow. Her DayMinder has the number next to a note about a deposition. "

"Her folks said she's been an expert witness on dog bite cases." Gonzales gestured with the phone. "Maybe some good news, though. Ran a search on gun registrations, and Childress owns guns. He's a collector."

"Gee, isn't it funny he didn't mention that. What's Childress say?"

"He lawyered up."

Oh goody, now there's a surprise. "That's convenient. Something to hide, after all. What about the park victim?" Gonzales had a rep in the department as a ballistics expert. He'd gone through FBI training and had an uncanny knack and passion for all things guns.

"Snow made it hard to recover any shell casings, but I'll get to eyeball them as soon as I get back. That's prelim until the hard science guys confirm, but the best we got under the circumstances. But we got an ID on the vic at Childress's place. Dr. Henry Pottinger, divorced, no local family. Works out of Plano."

"Plano? That's an hour away. Visiting a patient?"

"Don't think he's that kind of doctor. Doty's following up on that." Gonzales tapped his foot with nervous energy. "Like everything else, the weather's shut down most businesses. It may be tomorrow or later before Doty can find out about Pottinger. Hell, he got shot, wrapped in a knockoff

Oriental rug, and left for us to find at April's ex-husband's house. Is she that dumb?" He tsk-tsked with his tongue. "Even amateurs do a better job of it."

"Yeah, I can't see either of the sisters manhandling the body into the car." His eyes itched, maybe from the smoke still in the house. Combs noted the screensaver on the desktop computer—a gorgeous, brown German shepherd—and tapped the mouse. The password prompt came up. Shit.

Gonzales pocketed his cell phone. "Another tidbit. Animal Control showed up at the park after we left to take possession of the victim's dog."

"So?" That was standard.

"We didn't call. September did." He scanned the room, glanced at the musical instruments, the cluttered desk, and the baby gate entry into the kitchen. "Animal Control already knew the victim's name, her address, that her veterinarian husband's out of town and other animals in the home need attention. September clued 'em in." He shrugged at Combs's scowl. "She doesn't act like any killer I've ever seen."

"So maybe she feels remorse?" He didn't want to hear it. "She can be sorry all she wants in prison." Combs played with the keyboard, typed in a few common passwords. No luck. "Find anything upstairs?"

"Upstairs is mostly bare, in various stages of reconstruction. There's a finished bathroom and bedroom." He hooked a thumb toward the kitchen. "Been in there yet?"

He nodded. "This morning with Pike. Laundry room connects to the kitchen. There's another staircase to the second story, and an outside door to the covered walkway that connects the garage." Combs gestured to the computer. "Want to take a crack at it? Maybe you'll find something that points where the sisters might go." Computers were not his strong suit.

"Sure." Gonzales pulled out the chair and sat down. "Give me the DayMinder. People keep lists of passwords where anyone can find 'em."

"Sure, and maybe there's secret message in the coffee canister." Combs headed for the kitchen.

He'd seen the baby gate in the doorway, and walked through it that morning, but it hadn't registered. It looked similar to one at April's house, except this one stood taller—nearly four feet—and included a small inset latched gate in the bottom. It wasn't for infants, it was for pets.

Combs scanned the room before he open the metal barrier. No dog sounds, but that didn't mean a surprise wasn't waiting. He liked animals, but he had a healthy respect for dogs, especially big ones. So far, the only sign of a dog was the screensaver.

Black ceramic stovetop. Empty bowl on the counter beside the double sink. Brushed steel dishwasher, oven, microwave and refrigerator. A magnetic wipe-off board on the fridge. Swirly gray and black marble countertops matched the mantel in the living room. Dark blue-green slate floor. Floor to ceiling stained glass windows with a view of snow-covered roses. Wall phone, the long cord looped up and caught on a hook. Stained-glass tabletop and four chairs, a coffee mug and saucer on the table. Sterilite storage box on the floor.

No dog.

Combs opened the gate and moved to the table. He picked up the oversize covered mug and it sloshed. Nearly full. He checked the cupboards, opened and shut drawers and cabinets. Moved to the refrigerator, noted the magnetic notepad filled with a grocery list.

Something tapped him on the head.

"Shit." Combs ducked and leaped away. He leveled his gun in one smooth motion.

"What? Something wrong?" Gonzales was at the open gate in two long strides, hand on his own weapon.

Combs choked back a laugh and holstered his gun. Pointed at the top of the fridge.

A chocolate brown cat lounged on the perch, one paw still trailing down the front of the refrigerator. Green eyes shined. Yawning, the cat paused to lick his white front.

"Cat grabbed my hair. Scared the shit out of me." Combs realized the storage box in the corner, about a third full of sandy material, was the biggest damn litter box he'd ever seen.

Gonzales smirked. "My sister has cats. Go in her house and the smell grabs you by the throat." He sniffed elaborately. "All I smell is smoke. No wonder the big bad putty tat scared you." He returned to the computer.

"I thought September trained dogs. Weird she's got a cat, but no dog." The cat stood on tiptoes, stretched, and jumped down to the countertop. Nosing the bowl beside the sink for one last kibble, the cat sat down and regarded Combs. And meowed.

"Nice cat. That's a good girl. Boy. Whatever," he said. "Close the gate, Gonzales. If this guy sleeps on the refrigerator, he must be some jumper." His mom had a cat, big old Simba. She'd rescued the cat from the local shelter eight years ago and said Simba gave her someone to cuddle since her kids were grown and the grandkids on the go. Combs caught his breath. He'd have to do something about Simba, now that Mom was gone.

The cat mewed again, and cheek-rubbed the empty bowl. It scooted close to the edge and teetered.

"Any luck with the computer?" Combs caught the bowl before the cat's gravity experiments sent it to the floor. He opened and closed several cupboards and checked the refrigerator, finding the cat's food.

"We'll have to get the experts in here." Gonzales frowned. "What you doing?"

Combs shrugged. "Feeding the cat. With September on the run, it might be days before he gets fed." He jostled a cup of dry stars into the bowl, shoved the bag back inside the fridge, and stroked the cat. The creature purred and began to eat. "Whatever's going on with September, she didn't plan it." He hated to admit she wasn't to blame. He massaged the cat's shoulders, and his own loosened.

"So what changed your mind?" Gonzales stepped inside and latched the gate.

"Coffee cup's still full. She rushed out without finishing. No notes on the fridge, and she's a list maker, they're all over the desk. And the biggie—if she's an animal nut, why didn't she leave food for the cat? Or at least make arrangements for it?" To him, that was most telling of all. "She called Animal Control for the park victim's dog, but didn't leave a few days' food down for kitty?" He scratched the cat's chin. "No way. She's on the run, but it's nothing she planned."

Combs's phone rang. Uncle Stan again, he thought, and pulled it out of his pocket. He'd remind him about Simba. The old cat's arthritis needed watching and Mom had babied her—hell, they'd taken care of each other. Mom would have a fit if her cat was forgotten. When he didn't recognize the number, he almost didn't answer. "Combs here."

"Jeff Combs? Officer Jeff Combs?"

"Yes. Who's this?"

"We met this morning at my house when you saw smoke. You left me your card."

He waved at Gonzales. "September? Where are you?"

Gonzales gnawed his mustache. "You have to be shitting me."

Combs struggled to stay collected. "September, a lot of people are worried about you."

"Did you find Pam? At Gentry Park. Is she okay?" Somebody else, a man, spoke in the background, but Combs couldn't make out the words. "I…uh, you need to check out Star Mall. I've got to go."

"No. Wait!" So many things to ask, he needed to keep her on the line. "Pam, is that your friend with the dog at the park?"

"Is she okay? Please tell me she's going to be okay."

"What's at Star Mall?" Moving to the refrigerator, Combs jotted notes for Gonzales to read, and the man nodded and dialed his own phone.

"Tell me about Pam."

"Her dog's with Animal Control. You called them, right?" The cat mewed, and jumped back onto the fridge and began to wash. "What's your cat's name? Big brown and white fellow. He's a hungry cuss."

"You're in my house? Is Macy okay?" She sounded angry. And scared.

"Tell her Pam's dead," Gonzales prompted. "Tell her more people will die if she doesn't come in." He paused, spoke into his own phone. "Combs has September on his cell phone, and we've got the number." He read it from Combs's scribbled note on the fridge.

"September, listen to me." Combs paced. He had to get her to come in. "The police know you're in trouble. We found a body at April's house. Were you there when it happened?" If she knew the victim was his mother, she'd hang up. "We're looking for you, looking for your sister and her son. Whoever shot that woman might be after you. Are you safe? Are April and Steven with you?"

"Oh, no. . ." She whispered the words, defeated.

"We know you were at Childress's place, too. There's another body there." At Gonzales' pointed expression, he added, "Your friend Pam's dead, that's three—"

"Pam? Oh God, what have I done?"

"Stay with me, September. I can help you. Just come in, we'll sort things out."

"You're wrong. Nobody can help me. And it's not three. Go to Star Mall." Heavy breaths. "I'll make them pay." She hung up.

Chapter 27

September's eyes burned, her feet throbbed, and she smelled—no, scratch that. She stank. Amazing how pungent a person could get, even in icy weather.

Teddy's worn sofa soothed her sore muscles but did little to ease her guilt. So many dead or at risk, all because of Pottinger's damned flash drive. Now she'd involved Teddy, another innocent bystander.

She should have left him at the mall, but that would have been like kicking a puppy. It would have been better to drop him off at his house and leave, before he got hurt, too. But once here, he'd insisted on calling the police. She'd managed to beat him to the landline before the storm took out the phone, but he'd overheard about Pam and Gentry Park. She'd put him off for now. That was good, because otherwise he'd have insisted they kill themselves driving to the nearest police station, hospital or fire department.

In the nearby kitchen, Teddy dished cold cuts from a baggy onto a battered pie pan while Shadow watched and drooled. The pup must think he'd gone to heaven. She used slivers of cold cuts for training rewards. Shadow's butt hit the floor, the puppy-polite request she'd taught him. Once the pan touched down, he scooted it halfway across the kitchen to lick it clean.

Lovely to be a clueless dog delighted by simple things like treats from a kind stranger, not haunted with visions of brains splashed against walls, or the fear she'd doomed April and Steven to a similar fate just by coming here.

She'd gotten people killed. Cops inside her house meant Mom and Dad gave them keys. But she'd be damned if she'd drag more family into the mess.

September held the flash drive in one hand, and felt the outline of the phone in her pocket. She could end it now. Ring up Lizzie. She could reach her through April's phone, arrange to trade the flash drive for April and Steven and get them back safe. If she could do that, maybe it would assuage some of the guilt over Pam, Freda, and Wilma. She had beaten the 24-hour deadline when she found the flash drive, but that didn't count until the ransom exchange. Steven was still lost. So was April.

"You want coffee? I've got decaf or the real stuff. My doctor doesn't like me having caffeine, but I keep some gourmet around for guests." Teddy chuckled, a nervous unhappy sound. "Or, there's some diet Coke, or Dr. Pepper."

"I need to be fully caffeinated, so coffee would be great. Thanks." She'd never finished the mug from this morning. No wonder she'd zombied her way through the last several hours.

Teddy set a chipped ceramic bowl of water on the floor. Shadow's toenails ticked on the linoleum. He slurped.

"Hungry? I could scramble some eggs." Teddy pulled a cast iron fry pan off a wall hook. "When was the last time you ate?"

September realized she'd not eaten all day. "Been just a tad busy." Maybe the lightheadedness wasn't just from dodging bullets. "I'll grab a burrito later." She didn't want Teddy to waste any more time. Coffee would have to do. The sooner she got away from him, the safer he'd be.

"You need to eat." He stood in the doorway, pan in one hand and three eggs cradled in the other.

"Not hungry. Just the coffee will do me fine. High octane, the stronger the better." Decaf was a waste of beverage.

Shadow trotted to her, his ears flat. He shoved his wet muzzle into her arms to dry himself. He'd had a rough day, too. He offered a sly grin as he climbed onto the sofa beside her. "Shadow, off." She corrected him out of reflex. April didn't allow dogs on her furniture.

He flattened himself against the cushions, squirmed and wagged, doing his best to look pitiful.

"Let him be. More dogs have been on that sofa than people. Fur's part of the fabric by now." Teddy pulled a chair close. "Don't you ever let him on your furniture? On your bed? That's one of the joys of a dog, I always thought." He smiled. "Me and my wife had an old shepherd named Max. He'd start out all polite at the foot of the bed and by morning he was my pillow, shoving me half off the mattress." He showed stained teeth. "German shepherds are the best."

Like Dakota. He'd been more than a dog. Losing him and Chris at the same time nearly killed her. September considered Shadow, and her lips tightened. No dog would ever replace Dakota. The pup was sweet but he was no Dakota. "Shadow isn't my dog. I'm training him for Steven." She glanced at her watch, surprised it was closing in on eleven. "How soon will coffee be ready?"

"It's brewing. Steven doesn't live with you? Is this a custody fight?"

Her hands sought Shadow's black fur and rubbed his ears. "Not a custody battle. It's hard to explain." She stared at the dog so she didn't have to look at the old man. "It's dangerous. I don't want you involved."

"I'm already involved." He huffed. "I get that it's dangerous. Freda got killed. I would've got shot, too, if he'd seen me. I'd like to know why."

No you don't, she wanted to say. You really don't want to know.

"You owe me an explanation." Teddy took off his glasses and polished them on his sweater, and replaced them. "That friend you told the cops about, Pam, she got hurt, too. I heard. I might be old, but my ears still work." He pointed an accusing finger. "And now those goons have your son. Is it ransom? Where's your husband in all of this?"

She winced. Lord, what would Chris do? She missed him so much. . . Abruptly she stood up. "Can I use your bathroom?" She could make the call to Lizzie in the privacy of the toilet. Get out of here before Henchman #12 showed up. Lizzie could have dozens of bad guys on call. She had to get away before the phone lines were fixed and Teddy got fed up and called the cops on his own. That would get Steven and April killed. And him, too.

Shadow whined at the tension. He yawned and turned away.

Teddy didn't answer for a long moment. "Down the hall, to the right. I'll get you towels. And I've got some sweats that might fit you, once you get out of those wet things."

She struggled to walk but her balance was off. She grudgingly accepted Teddy's hand. Shadow hopped off the sofa and leaned against her as if afraid to lose contact.

"Coffee will turn on the brain cells. Everything feels like mush." She tried to smile and failed. "Don't trouble yourself over the clothes, I'm okay."

"You'll change clothes." He shrugged to soften the harsh tone. "Clean clothes will make you feel human again." He'd changed out of his stained yellow sweater and jacket as soon as they'd arrived. Teddy led the way and motioned at the open bathroom door.

Metallic owl wallpaper aimed dozens of creepy bird eyes at September. She shuddered, and Teddy smiled. "The owls came with the house. You get used to them." He pointed. "There's a new toothbrush, even some deodorant in the cabinet. I'll scramble eggs and pour coffee." He raised a hand to cut off more protests. "Later we'll discuss." He glowered at her. "No excuses." He hurried to a nearby bedroom, and metal coat hangers jangled when he rummaged for the promised clothes.

Shadow pressed into the tiny room with her, and September didn't have the heart to kick him out. She closed the door and waited until he'd settled, and then she sat on the floor beside him to pull out her cell phone. She leaned back against the wall and silently rehearsed what to say. It was time she called Lizzie.

Chapter 28

Claire gazed out the bus window at the Kansas countryside. Flat, a white desert as far as the eye could see, only stubbled fingers of vegetation poked through. Even the drift fences offered little contrast to the barren landscape.

The serene view calmed Claire and mirrored her expectations. Though dormant now, spring would reveal fields lush with crops, just as her hopes for Tracy would bear fruit.

They'd acquired another seven children and their parents in Kansas City, and had planned to spend the night on the south side of town. Tracy slept on the seat beside her, exhausted from the earlier tantrum. The trip ratcheted up stress in parents, but for children, the cross country trek was torture. The kids didn't know or care that the discomfort was for their own good. Thank goodness most had nodded off, or sat in a sedated stupor. Parents just sought to get them through this last awfulness before a hoped-for better future became a reality.

Elaine lurched down the aisle and stopped to chat here and there with any parent who was still awake. Her mouse brown hair matched her watery eyes. She'd yet to shed the frayed overcoat from her turn at the wheel. The driver's window wouldn't shut completely, and it sucked out the warmth the heaters struggled to maintain. But parents grateful for the ride bundled their children in extra layers and kept complaints to themselves.

When she tried to smile at Claire, deep lines cut canyons from each side of Elaine's nose making her look ten years older than her 38 years. They'd been friends even before Tracy was diagnosed with Autism Spectrum Disorder at twenty months old.

"Doing okay?" Elaine grabbed the back of the seat ahead of Claire to steady herself when the bus swooped through another intersection.

Claire flinched and returned a tight smile. "Tracy finally conked out." She whispered so she wouldn't rouse the little girl. "She got so wound up I'm amazed she can sleep at all." Claire loved to watch her daughter sleep. Tracy looked normal when she was asleep, a beautiful child no different than any other five-year-old. Only when she was awake did Tracy's differentness become obvious.

"Lenny's wired, too. I gave him his Rubik's cube. That should keep him focused for another hour. I hope." Elaine sighed and sank into a seat. "This is our last chance. He's fifteen, will turn sixteen next month."

"Oh, that's right. The program says children must be under sixteen." Claire hadn't thought much about the requirement since Tracy was so much younger.

"If Tracy missed this go-round, she'd have another chance at the next Gathering." Elaine swiveled to inventory the vehicle. "Most of the children are seven or eight. Only Lenny and Ricky Smith are older." She stifled a yawn. None of the adults had done more than doze.

Tracy was the youngest, and one of only four girls. "We can't afford to wait." Claire spoke with grim resolve. "We had to scrape together the deposit. But it's worth it. Did you see that before and after video on the website?"

Elaine nodded and sighed. "A miracle. That's what sold us on the treatment." She finger combed her messy hair but it didn't help. "Everything just fell into place: the timing, the location. My father-in-law lives nearby and wanted to help out, but he's near retirement and not made of money. He was thrilled when Dwayne called about the Legacy Center's offer to waive fees. Another miracle." Her face grew soft and she became almost pretty. "Of course, Lenny's his grandson, and his namesake. Dwayne insisted."

"How's Dwayne? He must be exhausted, too." Claire turned to see the lanky pastor. "I didn't know he could drive a bus."

"Better than me. He grew up on a ranch, and says this old bus reminds him of the tractor he drove as a kid." Elaine swayed when the bus picked up speed around a gentle curve. She grabbed the seat back again to steady herself. "Dwayne says driving a bus compares to preaching a sermon. You dodge potholes and ice along the way and pray you don't slide off the road getting home."

Claire laughed and stifled the sound with her hand. But Tracy didn't move. Most of the kids slept, exhausted both physically and emotionally. She noticed several adults were also nodding off at the back of the bus. At least three of the parents had more than one affected child.

"We're behind schedule. Two other parents offered to swap out driver duty." Elaine stretched and her back popped.

Her muscles always got tight from driving, too. "We're not stopping?"

"I cancelled the hotel. We've got to drive straight through." Elaine yawned again. "With good weather it's another eight hours. But in this snow we'll be lucky to get there in twice that time."

Claire adjusted the coat over Tracy's drowsy figure. "We can sleep after we get to the Legacy Center. I won't feel like resting 'til then anyway." Hell, she hadn't had a good night's sleep in four or five years. Why start now?

Elaine looked like she might cry. "It's got to work. I mean the treatment, it's got to work." She pulled a Chap Stick out of her pocket. "Our congregation raised funds for gas to get us there, did you know that?" She pressed her lips together to spread the balm. "Nice to have people care that much. They'll hold a prayer vigil for us Sunday, too. All of us, not just Lenny."

Claire's eyes glimmered with tears. "That means a lot. I can help with the gas." She reached for her purse.

Elaine stopped her hands. "They wanted to help. They love Lenny. He's a gentle soul like his dad, and sort of the church project." She propped her chin in her hand. "Other parents feel guilty, are relieved it's not them. I don't blame them. I wish it was someone else and not Lenny." She shrugged at the whispered admission. "Not very Christian of me, is it?"

"Lucky he's gentle." Lenny was built like a linebacker and could easily clear a room. Claire touched her own crooked nose, the result of one of Tracy's fits and her own inability to duck in time.

Autism Spectrum Disorders affected children in different ways, but those on the bus had the most severe problems. Claire, Elaine and the other parents had tried everything to help their kids, from behavioral therapy and nutrition changes to a variety of off-label drugs.

Most people knew nothing about off-label treatments. Food and Drug Administration clearance required years of hoop-jumping plus boatloads of money that prevented many promising drugs from ever reaching the market. Other times, unexpected benefits were exploited by savvy drug companies, such as when sildenafil citrate, initially marketed for hypertension, knocked it out of the park as Viagra.

Drugs just couldn't be advertised for a particular benefit unless they had government clearance. But they could be prescribed off-label by in-the-know doctors. Since there were no FDA-approved autism drugs, all treatments for the condition were off-label.

Claire pinned all her hope on this latest buzz-worthy treatment—an FDA-approved drug for Alzheimer's that had shown unexpected benefits in autistic children. She'd do anything to help Tracy, sign a waiver release and mortgage her soul for the opportunity. So would the other parents. No snowstorm dared stand in their way.

Chapter 29

September closed the lid on the toilet, gingerly sat down, and turned on the water in the sink to keep Teddy from hearing. No more delays. She locked the door and dialed April's cell. It rang once.

"Yes?" The Ghost Man. Her hand shook at the memory of his weird eyes so close to hers. September reminded herself he couldn't reach her, squeezing the flash drive in her other hand like a talisman to bolster her courage. She held the cards this time.

"I have what you want." Her voice wavered, despite her attempt at bravado. "Let me speak to April." Better. She needed to sound in control.

She heard him tell somebody, "It's the sister," and then Lizzie came on the line.

"April's in the other room." Lizzie was all business. "Describe the merchandise. Exactly what do you have?" The grandmotherly façade was gone.

September stared at the one-by-three-inch object in her palm. "A flash drive. Shiny, black, strung on a silver chain lanyard."

"Everyone has those. You get them at the grocery store. Tell me the truth, September. You wouldn't try to fob off a fake?"

The idea jarred her. Lizzie was right. Steven could've collared Shadow with the lanyard days ago. She couldn't prove it was the right flash drive unless she looked at the contents.

"Besides, I've grown quite attached to April, and now Steven has joined the party, so it's all in the family. Your sister's busy with her laptop in the room down the hall, removing all traces of Pottinger's information she accidentally-on-purpose emailed to herself. You remember the laptop, don't you? The one you nearly killed Gerald over?" The words were a slap.

September flinched. She'd never wanted to kill anyone, but if she'd hit Gerald-the-Ghost harder Pam might still be alive.

"April understands the stakes. Do you understand consequences, September?" She acted the part of fond schoolmarm teaching a hard but necessary lesson. "Steven isn't the only sick child, and you've endangered the lives, the hopes and dreams of hundreds of other children. If I have to sacrifice one little boy to save a hundred, what should I do, September? What would you do?"

Focus on April and Steven. That's what mattered here. "You want Pottinger's information, right? I swear to you, I have the flash drive. I can give it to you." She had to convince Lizzie. She looked closer, and found a logo pressed into the case. "There's a logo on the side of the flash drive case, a bird on fire." *A Phoenix?* "Just let them go, please don't hurt them." September ached with the effort to persuade Lizzie without alerting Teddy. Water from the tap gushed and gurgled in its race down the drain, rushing as fast as the hands on her watch.

September whispered more urgently into the phone. "I found Pottinger's information. That's what you wanted, and I did it. Steven looped the chain around Shadow's neck. I'll give it to you, but I have to know my sister and Steven are both okay." Her pulse thrummed. "I won't give it to you 'til I know, so let me talk to my sister."

"You're in no position to make demands. So Steven hid it on the dog. The treatment unlocks hidden talents. It worked for my Gerald, after all." She sounded delighted. "We could have resolved this amicably, but I can't forgive you for nearly killing my boy."

September licked her suddenly dry lips. "He's your son?"

"Gerald is brilliant. You should thank him for Steven's cure." Lizzie's pride blossomed with the opportunity to sing her son's praises. "Gerald couldn't speak, either. He had violent rages. He was locked inside his own head for years. Then a happy accident created the miracle we are now able to share with the world. I didn't even recognize it; Gerald figured it out for himself."

"Happy accident? What are you talking about?" Shadow woofed and pressed against her thigh. She welcomed the contact and her nerves steadied in response. September wondered if the pup recognized Lizzie's voice over the phone. Probably.

"That's right, September. Gerald took some of my dad's prescription medicine by accident." Her breath quickened. "He started talking. After twenty-five years of silence, he started talking. Are you listening to me? You need to understand what's at stake, September. Are you paying attention?"

"Yes. I hear you. He started talking, it was a miracle." She couldn't stop shivering. She wanted to speak to April but was afraid to interrupt Lizzie's grandstanding.

"That's right. Gerald told me what he'd done. Taken Daddy's medicine. We told the doctors and they refused to believe us, and they wouldn't give us more when we ran out." Her voice turned grim. "Can you imagine that? They spit on the miracle! And it nearly cost Gerald his life. I won't tell you what we had to go through to keep him well . . . never mind that. But we knew right away we had to share this joy. Gerald finished school in three years. Only three years and he's a doctor, a Ph.D. Can you imagine?"

September closed her eyes and nodded.

"I didn't hear you."

"Yes, I can imagine. Gerald's brilliant, like you said."

"That's right. My boy's a genius. He met Dr. Pottinger in school, and together they've brought Gerald's legacy to other poor children who can benefit from this miracle." Her voice hardened. "That flash drive has information that you don't need, that only parents of these special children would understand. April understands. You haven't looked at it, have you? Don't lie to me, I'll know. You must give it back. Don't make me spell out the consequences." She paused. "You didn't answer me, September. Do you understand consequences?"

"Yes. Yes, I understand." September stiffened her back. "But if you want the information, let me talk to April." She didn't bother to modulate her tone.

"For the love of . . . Oh all right, I'll go get her. Just wait a minute, but you must make it quick."

September waited several impatient moments.

"September?" The voice, though soft and hoarse, was April. "They found Steven. He's safe here with me. We're fine. Everything's fine." She paused, as though choosing her words with care. "Lizzie says you found Dr. Pottinger's flash drive information."

"April, are you okay?" September choked back tears. She was alive, Steven was alive. "Yes, I found it. Where are you? I'm ready to make the exchange."

"Of course I'm fine. We're both fine. We're at Lizzie's getting ready to drive to the Legacy Center." April said. "See? Everything worked out." She paused. "September, you must return that flash drive. You don't need it anyway, and I already know what's important. That information doesn't belong to us, it's proprietary. I signed papers. Once you give it back, Steven will keep getting his medicine, and he won't have those nasty side effects, and he'll be cured." She paused. "What exchange?"

"The ransom. They want me to trade Pottinger's information for your safety."

"Ransom? Don't be ridiculous. Just give back the flash drive, and you can go back to your life and we can go back to ours. Like I said, all debts wiped clean—"

Lizzie came back on the phone. "Satisfied? They're fine."

In the background September heard April's questions become angry and siren into a shriek that was silenced mid-scream.

"What's happening?" Shadow barked back at September's anguished words.

A breathless Lizzie came back on the line. "Everything's fine. Your sister's fine. Steven's fine. I promise. Trust me." She hesitated. "I'll call you back."

September stared at the dead phone. Do killers keep promises?

Teddy rattled the locked handle and pounded on the door. "Why are you yelling? Open up, right now." He banged again. "I'll pick the lock, break the door. Open it. You're scaring an old man." He juggled the door, and it finally opened. He stared. "What happened?"

"I don't know." She was numb.

He shut off the water that threatened to overflow the sink, and looked at the phone in her limp hand. "Who were you talking to? I thought your phone was dead."

She didn't answer. The phone dropped, and the flash drive followed, the chain snaking to the floor. She didn't care.

Shadow pushed himself into her lap, and September wished the doggy weight was Dakota. Her arms hugged his big, warm body. Cold, she was so damn cold. "I think I just killed my sister."

Chapter 30

Lizzie struggled to contain her anger and consciously smoothed her expression. She had cultivated the mild mannered persona for just such occasions. She dismissed April's body prostrate on the floor, and focused on keeping Gerald calm. Control, she had to keep control. Thank heavens Steven was locked in the bedroom. A child shouldn't see his mother get killed. "Give me the gun." Her tone brooked no argument.

"We don't need her now we've got Steven." But Gerald offered the pistol without protest. "She was a loose end."

"She didn't matter. She's a mom; she'd do anything to protect her child. Besides, we could hold Pottinger over her head 'til the cows come home. She was no threat." She sighed, and straightened her hair. "Spilt milk now, and no cleaning it up." She set the pistol on a nearby table. "You already lost one gun. At least they can't trace it back to you." She'd taken Daddy's old surplus .45 pistols away from him when his Alzheimer's got too bad. Funny how his disease had saved Gerald and hundreds of children.

She knelt beside April. "She's not breathing." Her mind raced. Yesterday, everything was under control, with lots of lost souls to save. Too bad Pottinger became smitten with Little Miss Perfect and her son, Steven, or he'd still be alive and they wouldn't be in this mess.

Gerald stood tall. No concern clouded his pale, handsome face. He looked like his father, and sounded like him, too. "We have two hundred clients scheduled to arrive at Legacy Center in less than twelve hours. That's the largest Rebirth Gathering yet. We can't risk that payday, Mother, not when we're poised to go global. April knew the consequences. And you didn't tell me not to shoot her." Gerald moved to a chair and sat.

"We've talked about this. You can't take everything so literally." She covered her exasperation. A consequence of his disability, she reminded herself, and his genius. "You didn't have to shoot that woman at the park."

"You weren't there. She sicced that dog on me. I couldn't shoot the dog. He reminded me of Neptune."

"Neptune's a Pomeranian. Dammit, don't distract me."

He tsked. "Bad word, lazy English."

She ignored him. "Murder is lazy."

"You shot someone."

"She tried to play the God card; you know how I feel about that." God hadn't saved Gerald, scientific medicine made him well, just as it would cure the children. "I won't have the true miracle devalued by some mumbo-jumbo-spouting bible-thumper. And besides, if she was right then God would have stopped the bullet, don't you think?" She waited for his nod of agreement. "We save lives, Gerald, we don't shoot people. Or dogs," she added grudgingly. "Your research saves other children. That's all that matters. Nothing else can get in the way."

Gerald rubbed his temple where a goose-egg purpled the skin. "My head hurts. I might have a concussion." He straightened and looked at his fingers as if he expected to see blood. "She deserved to die. Dr. Pottinger died because of her."

Lizzie frowned. Pottinger had been Gerald's PhD advisor, and they'd worked together—with her, of course—to make Legacy Center a reality. The treatment helped so many kids. But there was no way it would pass FDA screening, not with the occasional aberrant side effects. They couldn't afford to go public and have folks scared away, and prevent children from gaining the benefits. If a few children had adverse reactions because parents couldn't follow the rules, that shouldn't doom the thousands who could be cured.

Now that the FDA had released new off-label guidelines to the industry, it was even more vital that Legacy Center enlist parents to vote with their funds at Rebirth Gathering. Gerald had a point. April was a potential liability, but her sister was even more dangerous.

They couldn't allow Pottinger's flash drive to end the dream. "If April's dead, September won't cooperate." She couldn't stop the worry. The children depended on her.

"She doesn't have to know. We've still got Steven."

She nodded. They could hold the child over September's head to get Pottinger's flash drive. Until it was found, she'd never feel that Legacy Center was safe. Damn the woman and damn Pottinger. The information could derail twenty years of work, and sentence all those children to a lifetime of disability and pain.

Gerald was right. April broke the contract and she knew the consequences. They were better off without her. Once they got the flash drive back, she could refocus her attention on the program where it belonged.

But the spilt milk wasn't Steven's fault. He shouldn't be penalized. Steven deserved his miracle.

"What do we do with her?" Gerald nudged April with his foot.

Lizzie smiled. "Doug Childress killed her. After all, it was his gun that shot Pottinger." Yes, that could work. That wove all the threads together. "They fought over Steven's treatment and April's fitness as a mother when she let him get lost in the storm." She turned on the persuasion. "You took care of Pottinger's body so well—"

"Once he was garbage I dumped him like you said. But now my head hurts. Get someone else." He looked toward the bedroom where Steven was confined. "That fellow who collected Steven for us, get him to do it. He's connected. He can pull strings so she's never found, making sure the police connect the pistol to Childress." He smirked, and Lizzie admired the expression. It had taken Gerald years to learn to smile like that and fake normal emotions. "Who doesn't notice when guns go missing?" said Gerald. "Such stupidity deserves an appropriate reward."

Lizzie considered the option. The man had lots to gain by delivering Steven to them unharmed, but he might get a conscience with April dead. "No, you'll have to do it. You shot her. Clean up your own mess and put April on ice, out of sight. You understand?"

He nodded. "On ice."

She smiled again. What a good son.

Chapter 31

Several police cars, an ambulance, and a fire truck swarmed near the entrance to the Star Mall. Combs had needed a breather but now rejoined Gonzales in the food court. The little man didn't seem fazed by the lateness of the hour, and stood with his cell phone glued to one ear. They'd called Doty from the road and beat her to the scene. The victim was already dead, so they'd secured the area and waited. So far, she'd ignored him either by accident or design. That worked just fine.

"Damn. We're hamsters running wheelies today." Doty stared at the mix of blood, ketchup and fries swirled with mud, and whistled through the gap in her front teeth. "What's the latest on body count—I can't keep up?" She aimed the sarcasm at Gonzales, as if he should have anticipated and prevented the bloodbath.

"You know more than I do." Gonzales ignored her tone as he disconnected the call. "Same shooter for all of them?"

"God, I hope not. But too early to know details. Ballistic tests take forever, but you can see the caliber from the shell casings, so it's at least two different guns. Maybe three." Doty gave a nod, acknowledging Combs. "We found shell casings under a table at April's, .45 caliber consistent with a semi-automatic. Our prelim says the FBI's GRC database suggests it's from a Remington Rand."

Gonzales scratched his head. "That's a World War Two surplus pistol. Lots of them floating around."

Doty grunted. "Either the same one or similar shot the vic at the park. Shell casings look like a match. Want you to take a look, though, and do your gun voodoo, Gonzales. The lab takes forever." She watched impassively as the EMTs zippered the dead woman into a bag.

"This one's different. Looks more like a .380." Gonzales sounded surprised.

Combs couldn't stop himself. "That's two guns. Makes no sense it would be the same shooter."

"Actually, it's three guns. Number three is a bullet we dug out of the ceiling at April's. Don't think it had anything to do with your mom, but it does cloud the situation." Doty spoke directly to Combs for the first time. "Type of old bullet hasn't been made in years, a .32 caliber S&W short. Hell, the bullet's so old, it's oxidized."

"Yes they do. Still make the bullets, that is." Gonzales explained when Combs raised his eyebrows. "Guns are my passion. I grew up in my dad's gun shop, spent more time at gun shows over the years than my wife cares to remember. I can tell you anything about make, model, and ballistics." Gonzales smoothed his tie. "Comes in handy when ballistics is delayed."

Doty popped her gum. "He's been right, ten for ten. So far," she added as if the compliment pained her. "Lots of bets in the department riding on him getting something wrong. Including mine."

"Childress collects antique guns." The man hadn't been forthcoming about that little tidbit, and that bothered Combs. A lot.

"But thousands of those pocket guns were made from 1880 to the 1930s." Gonzales smoothed his mustache. "Still, there's a distinctive shaved slice on the bullet, characteristic of wear on the bolt action. Makes it freakin' easy to match to the gun. If we ever find it."

Doty took a breath and offered a bit of what-the-hell speculation. "My guess is the same antique gun killed the guy we found in the car over at Childress's place. One of the bullets was a through-and-through, and fell out of the carpet when they unwrapped the carpet around his body. Gonzales says it's a match to the ceiling bullet at April's house."

Gonzales continued the argument. "Too much of a coincidence for unrelated shooters to use the same kind of antique gun and hard-to-find bullet. I don't believe in coincidence. And if Pottinger was killed at April's, it ties all four together. But what was he doing there?"

Doty unwrapped another stick of gum and stuffed it in her mouth, talking past the wad. "Maybe your mom walked in on something she shouldn't have, and Pottinger shot her, so April shot him with that funny gun."

"Nothing came up when we checked gun registry in April's name." Gonzales clapped Combs on the shoulder. "Unless she's carrying unlicensed. Not unheard of in Texas, but surprising since she's got the kid."

"Childress left it behind when he got divorced?" Combs guessed.

Gonzales made a note on his ever present pad. "My wife was into guns when we first got married. All that went away when we had the first kid. My guns stay locked up now in a padlocked room, and as soon as I hit the door my service weapon goes nighty-night out of kid reach. And Mercedes hasn't been at the shooting range in six years."

Combs agreed. His wife—ex-wife, he silently corrected—felt the same about guns around kids. Hell, so did anyone with half a brain. His phone vibrated. Uncle Stanley again. He let voicemail take the call. He couldn't deal with family right now. Not until he knew more and had answers.

"Lots of old guns aren't in the system. If April had to defend herself, and there's at least one more shooter out there, that'd be reason enough to run." Doty consulted her own notepad.

"Best explanation we've got so far. September protects her sister, and they both run from whoever shot Pottinger. They must have split up." Combs rubbed his eyes. "September went to Gentry Park with her dog tracking friend to look for Steven. Meanwhile the shooter must have followed September, and maybe the dog lady got in the way?"

"Your mom. Pottinger. Dog lady. And now a bus driver at Star Mall. Four murders in less than ten hours." Doty began pacing, her frustration clear, as she watched EMTs trudge to the ambulance with the latest victim. "Who is she anyway? Do we know if there's a connection, or is this just our day for bodies?"

"HART-Line bus driver." Gonzales read from his notes. "The bus is parked outside, and that little VW belonged to the victim. Dispatcher said they shut down HART-Line service because of weather right after her shift ended."

"September called and pointed us here. There's a definite connection." Combs waited for Doty to connect the dots.

She whistled tunelessly through the gap in her teeth and then motioned Combs closer. "Your mom was killed at April's house. Childress says his ex-wife and September are close, and she came there to find April. We found Pottinger at Childress's place right after September was there. And her supposed friend, the dog lady, met her at Gentry Park and got shot. Then she calls you and directs us here, where we find yet another body. Maybe it's not some mysterious stranger chasing after the sisters. Maybe we already know who's shooting up the city." Doty's eyes narrowed. "You took the call. What's your gut on this?"

Combs considered the question with suspicion. Doty kept score. Whatever he said would be remembered to use against him later. He shrugged.

"Talk to me, Officer Combs. Sure, I told you to stay out of this, but you're up to your holsters in it, clearly against policy, and I'm not taking the blame for you messing with my show." Combs heard her teeth grinding. "In case you haven't noticed, I've run out of hands. And clove gum. That chaps my hide." She glared. "This weather has traffic snarled; we've got multiple crime scenes, Dallas PD cain't git here from there." Her broadened accent mocked his rural upbringing compared to her own big-city credentials. "We've more than enough work to go around, and I'll try to look the other way as long as you play fair with me. So spit it out."

"Part of the team?" He ignored Gonzales's smothered smile. Combs wanted in, but the info-sharing had to flow in both directions.

"No way, this stays unofficial. You're still poison, Combs. I won't burn my own butt so's you can play. It's still my sandbox." She paused, held up a hand when he would've argued. "Since September pulled you into the investigation, it's my duty to debrief you." Her expression remained deadpan, reminding Combs of how well she'd always covered her ass while cutting corners. He both admired and despised the talent. "Play ball, Combs. And maybe we'll talk to you." The hint of a promise in her tone was real. "Has September gone serial killer on us?"

He snorted. "Hardly. She's calling us, reaching out for help. Sure, September's involved, no question, but only indirectly. Probably covering for her sister." He looked around the chaos. "If she was in control, I think she'd come in. I get the feeling she's being coerced about something. Maybe threatened?"

"April's motivated to protect her son. That has to involve Childress." Gonzales spoke with conviction. "You think Childress holds something over April's head?"

"Wouldn't put it past him," Combs said. "April and Steven are in some kind of trouble, maybe on the run from Childress. I don't like the guy. I think September tried to dig them out of a hole, and fell in over her head. That's my gut." He stifled a yawn, and wished he had a drink. Hell, he needed a drink. But coffee would have to suffice.

Doty's nose scrunched up like a rabbit after carrots. "We got problems at April's. Need more than the antique bullets to prove Pottinger died there."

Gonzales pulled out his phone. "I'll call the coroner again; get them to check for GSR. If Pottinger's a shooter there'll be trace on his hands or clothes. He wasn't wearing gloves. Means he must have been inside the house where it was warm before any gunplay." He shook his head. "We need the connection between April and this Dr. Pottinger. Who is this guy? That should answer lots of questions."

Doty's glare raked the big room. "How'd September know to come to Star Mall? It's not Black Friday for two weeks." She considered the food court floor, and glowered. "Can't tell the blood from the ketchup."

Combs looked closer at the mess. There were distinct tracks of three or more individuals in the debris. And a dog. A good size dog by the paw prints. "Fish from the radio played the recording of April's call. She was hysterical about her missing son, and she mentioned a dog." He pointed at a paw print.

Gonzales sniffed. "September knew about the bus driver, so she was here. That's why she called you." He yawned, clearly feeling the same fatigue they were all fighting. "But I don't buy that she shot the bus driver. What reason would she have?"

"Isn't it obvious?" Doty painted a possible version. "September managed to track down her nephew and the dog to the mall, and shot the bus driver when she got in the way."

"No. Steven's not with her. You can't fake that kind of panic. September's still running solo." Or maybe not. Combs recalled that soft male voice in the background when she'd called. "I count two…no, three cups. There's one under the table." He pointed. "So that's the bus driver, the boy and September. Or somebody else."

Gonzales crouched to examine the shoe and boot prints at each of the chairs. "Remember those prints outside Pottinger's car, the ones we figured for September's? None of these match. Whoever was here sat long enough for the mud to dry. See, there's a kid's tennis shoe, and this is the bus driver's print. That third set, it's a man's size. Dry, too, so he was with them." He stood, and followed the prints back toward the entry until they disappeared.

Combs pointed at another. "Could be September's. But it's over top of the kid's print." He rubbed his jaw. "So she came after they'd been here a while. Or even after they'd left."

Gonzales tiptoed around the telltale prints. "Here's another man's shoe print, that's got to be a size fourteen at least. That's a big guy. Dress shoes, slick soles. In ice?" His phone buzzed and he listened and quickly ended the call. "That was Pike."

Doty looked up sharply. "Fast work. What's he got?"

"I thought Pike went home." Combs yawned again.

She shrugged. "Everyone's on duty until further notice. Pike lives near a witness—that kid manager of the coffee shop at the mall—so he handled the call." She frowned at Gonzales. "What's the kid say?"

"He served a boy, an old man, and the woman bus driver before he closed shop and left. The dog was with them."

"Any names?" Doty's nostrils flared when Gonzales shrugged.

"Pike says the manager didn't recognize them. But they mentioned the kid's father was on his way to collect him."

"Really." Doty popped her gum. "Mr. Childress just put his foot in it, literally. That asshole has more questions to answer."

Chapter 32

Water thundered in the small room until Shadow's ears hurt. Wet clouds billowed, and the hot air was hard to breathe. It tickled his nose. He blinked to clear away the steam.

Shadow paw-stirred the pile of clothes September had shed before stepping under the indoor-rain behind the curtain. He alternated deep sniffs with muzzle-clearing snorts, and read the clothes like a cryptic Post-It: fear-stink, and normal sweat, pee, perfumed lotion.

He sneezed, withdrew his muzzle, and whined. Why did she just stand there and let water gush all over her? He'd never do that. Rain made his fur itch.

Humans didn't have fur. They covered themselves with cloth, and shed it onto the floor before they washed. Maybe that's why she didn't mind so much. He wondered how it would feel to be tummy-naked all over.

His nostrils flared. Shadow stuck his muzzle past the curtain to squint against the water. He licked and discovered hot rain had no flavor. When she moved close, he nosed the back of September's bare thigh.

"Oh!"

Shadow jerked his head out of the shower, shaking off the wet that clung to his head.

"You okay?" Teddy stuck his head partway in the door.

The water stopped. "Shadow cold-nosed me." She peeked from the wet place, and hair dripped down her form. "Take him out of here, will you, Teddy? While I get dressed."

"Sure." Teddy opened the door wider, one hand beckoned. "C'mon, boy. Leave September alone."

Shadow whined. September was upset. And a good-dog's job was to make his humans happy. He'd like to make her happy.

Teddy spoke again. "You come with me." He paused, and his tone coaxed. "I have a cookie with your name on it."

Shadow's ears twitched at the "cookie" word, but he didn't move. He stared at September until she looked at him. She smiled with her mouth, but it wasn't a true happy face—he could tell the difference. He sighed.

"Go with Teddy. Be a good dog."

Shadow wagged in acceptance. He'd do what she asked. But he didn't have to like it.

"His stuffed bear is in the back seat of the car. He's more toy-oriented than treats, especially after a meal." She grabbed a heavy cloth from the wall and retreated once more behind the curtain. "His toy will keep him occupied."

Shadow reluctantly followed Teddy. The stolen sniff from September's leg was enough, anyway. At the thought, his tail wagged and his wrinkled brow smoothed. Indoor-rain washed away the fear-stink. Nobody wanted to wear fear-stink. That invited trouble. September stood under the rain to wash off scary smells, so she could smell happy again.

Happy smells made him feel better, too. That's why he rolled in happy smells like dead birds or cow stuff. Shadow wished Teddy had a dead bird around the house somewhere.

People didn't smell stuff the way dogs did, though. Steven's mom didn't like dead-bird-smell. Shadow was sad humans couldn't appreciate such things. Why, smells colored everything. It must be dreary to be scent-blind in such a scent-rich world. Instead, people liked odd bottle-smells they rubbed on hands, faces, and even underarms to cover up self-scent. He didn't know why. No dog would do that. A dog disappeared without self-scent.

Shadow liked people self-scent, liked to poke his nose at underarms and crotches to get to know them. People didn't like that, either. How odd. He wondered how people recognized each other, scent-blind to each other's most noteworthy spots. He shook himself hard, in a doggy shrug.

"Shadow, come. We'll get your teddy bear." The old man hurried down the hall.

He knew what "come" meant of course, but it was the prospect of his bear that hurried his paws. Happy words like "teddy bear" and "good-dog" were nearly as good as rolling on a dead bird.

He skidded to a stop once they reached the front room. Shadow sniffed and stared but didn't see his toy anywhere. His ears drooped. Sometimes people promises didn't happen. People sure were hard to understand. To figure them out made his head hurt.

"Wait here, pup. I'll be right back." The old man pulled on a heavy coat, still wet from outside.

Shadow danced around Teddy's legs, and pushed nearer. People used that "wait" word when dogs got left behind. He didn't want to be alone.

"Shadow. Sit. Stay."

Teddy's strong hand gripped the fur on his neck to hold him back as he opened the door and slipped out, shutting it against Shadow's nose. Yelping, he pawed the door and backed away, hurrying to the nearby window where he pushed aside the curtain to see into the darkness. Wet smears frosted the surface as Shadow listened to Teddy's feet crunch outside, followed by the slam of a car door. Shadow whined with anticipation, and woofed as the crunchy footstep sounds returned. When the door opened, he dashed outside in a rush to take-a-break.

Teddy gasped but smiled and waited until Shadow finished his squat and sniffed the spot. "Good dog, Shadow. See, I wasn't gone for long" Teddy urged Shadow inside and carefully latched the door. "Look what I've got. Is this your bear? Whew, it stinks."

Shadow cocked his head, and stared at the soft black object in Teddy's hand. His tail thumped until he couldn't maintain the polite pose any longer. He leaped, grabbed Bear by its head. He shook Bear hard and harder still, and shook it once more until his neck was loose and the tension drained from his body.

"You like that, do you, boy? Like your bear?" The man made happy laugh-noises.

Shadow killed the toy again and pranced about the room. He launched into a joyful doggy canter around the room, leaped from floor-to-sofa-to-floor with Bear clutched in his jaws. Laughter was good. Butt high and head low, Shadow sneeze-laughed. He held his teddy with both paws—claiming ownership—and gawked at the old man, daring a game of keep-away. Oh, it was good to play. A fun game always made everything better.

But the man turned his back, shrugged off his coat and tossed it over a chair. "Have fun, Shadow. Play with your bear, and I'll fire up the search engines." He hurried back down the hallway and passed the little room where September had showered. Steam was still escaping from beneath the door.

Shadow stared after. Then he grabbed the toy and padded after the man, stopping in the open door at the end of the hall. Shadow shook Bear a final time and dropped the toy in the doorway. Would Teddy take the dare, and grab for it? Play keep-away?

Teddy ignored the invitation. He limped to a desk and pulled out the chair.

A small bed occupied half the space in the room. He wondered if good-dogs could sleep there. Shadow hurried to nudge the man's arm. He nudged again, and leaned against him, moaning when Teddy's hand rubbed the hard to reach place at the base of his ear.

"Go on, that's enough." Teddy patted him and then pushed him away. "Let me do some work. Go talk to your bear. Bear is lonely."

Shadow grabbed Bear by the head, and sprang onto the comforter. A poof of dust rose, nearly invisible but implication clear. Nobody slept here. Too bad for such a soft spot not to have an owner. Maybe he could claim it. Shadow waited for the man to tell him to get off.

Teddy smiled. He shuffled stacks of paper on the desk. "Enjoy the bed for now, pup. When September comes in, she'll have the final say."

Shadow panted happily, turned three times, and sank with a groan against a pillow. He pretzeled himself to chew an itch, and tasted salt where September had wiped tears against his fur. He sniffed the spot, worried. It wasn't a good-salty taste; it had an acrid tang of fear. He grabbed Bear's head, and sucked until his own jangled nerves fell quiet.

The man fiddled with the boxy objects on top of the desk. Lights flickered; buzzes and whirring noises twitched Shadow's ears. Teddy's fingers made clack noises. Shadow's eyes drooped.

"Teddy?"

Shadow wagged his tail when September appeared in the doorway. His jaw tightened on Bear.

September was wearing different clothes, clean, baggy ones that flapped over her hands and bare feet. The fear-smell was still there, but not as strong. Her hair didn't drip but it smelled wet. Shadow wondered why she didn't shake off the water. Instead she rubbed her head with a cloth.

Did she want him off the soft bed? He pulled his ears flat to his head. Shadow rolled to show his tummy, Bear in his jaws. He wagged and the comforter bunched beneath his tail. He'd been a good-dog, couldn't he stay on the bed this once?

"S'okay, pup. No rules today." She sat on the edge of the bed beside him.

He dropped Bear, rolled upright, and pushed himself into her lap, licking her face and eyes. Her breath smelled stale, though, and he didn't argue when after a brief hug, she pushed him away. Shadow lay with his hip snugged against September's—needed the contact—and grabbed his toy once more. She stroked his brow. He shut his eyes. Bliss.

"Why does he do that? The bear's head is lopsided and it stinks."

The clack stopped when the man spoke, but Shadow didn't move. He had Bear, a soft bed, and September's touch. Nothing could be better. Except maybe bacon.

"I don't know. Why do kids suck their thumbs? Comfort, I suppose. Pam told me his dam did it, and all his littermates, too. He'd just about do backflips for his teddy. Gets real possessive."

"Backflips?" He chuckled.

"Figure of speech. Here, let me show you." She shifted on the bed, and Shadow pulled back when she tugged the toy. "Shadow, drop it. Wait."

He whined, but released the toy and sat up, watching with interest as she held his teddy. Now what?

She turned to the man. "His recall isn't solid, but he does a pretty good wait. Especially if he knows there's a cool reward for the job. Like Bear." September made eye contact with Shadow, crossed the room, and held up his toy. "Come."

He leaped off the bed and bounded to her. The closed-fist signal meant to plant his tail on the floor. He sat. When she pointed to the ground, he dropped into a down. His focus never left Bear.

"Good-dog." She tossed Bear, and Shadow deftly caught the toy, turned and hopped back onto the bed.

"Neat. Can I try?"

September nodded. "Drop it." She waited for Shadow to comply, and tossed Bear to the man.

No—she gave Bear to the stranger? Shadow cocked his head. Was it a game of keep-away after all? With a frustrated yelp, he hopped off the bed, loped to the old man, and leaped against Teddy's chest to grab his toy.

The old man rocked backwards into the desk. Bear fell from his hands—success!—and before it could hit the floor, Shadow scooped it up. He pranced to the other side of the room, tail wagging high and fast. He hoped Teddy would chase and try to grab Bear again. He loved that game.

"Shadow, settle. That's enough."

Shadow's tail fell at September's disapproval, signaling dejection.

"Teddy, are you okay? My fault, I didn't tell him to wait first." She moved to help him up.

Teddy seized her arm and staggered upright. "We're not thinking straight. Small wonder, with what we've both gone through."

He didn't know what all the words meant; only that Teddy sounded sad. Shadow slunk to the other side of the bed to keep a safe distance from grabby Bear-thief hands. He didn't like one-sided games. He settled with the head firmly in his jaws. His breath slowed. September's presence made it safe to rest.

She sat on the bed. "Thanks for the fresh clothes. The shower helped clear my head." She paused. "You could do me a huge favor, and keep Shadow for me. I'm on a deadline."

Hearing his name, he moved closer to September.

"I'm thinking more clearly, too, and did some research." Teddy turned back to the plastic box and clacked the keyboard. "You're famous."

September's hand tightened in his fur, rousing Shadow. She smelled scared again, and suddenly started sobbing and dropped her head into her hands. Shadow pawed September's hands, nudging them with his muzzle. He didn't like this. Loud words hurt, and weepy eyes made his tummy flip-flop.

Then Shadow froze. Noise from the box on the desk, one voice in particular, raised his hackles. He knew that voice. A low growl bubbled deep in his chest.

September jerked away. Teddy staggered backwards in fear.

Shadow glared, eyes hard, searching for the voice that was inside the box. He sniffed but detected no scent, despite that despised voice. Shadow's bubbled growls exploded into angry barks. His tail wagged with fury. He raged, wanted to punish, to make right what had gone wrong. But there was nothing to bite. No way to reach the hated voice of the boy-thief.

Chapter 33

Combs sat in his car in front of the brick ranch house. He'd put it off as long as he could. It was time to talk with Uncle Stanley and Aunt Ethel. He plugged his cell phone into the charger since he'd be in and out within ten minutes, just long enough to make an appearance and support the family. Doty and Gonzales didn't want him at the press conference anyway. He sighed heavily and left the car.

Before he could ring the bell the door opened. Light spilled into the morning gloom and haloed the tiny woman in the doorway. Combs gingerly embraced Aunt Ethel, careful her tears didn't breach the wall he'd erected around his own emotions. She offered a sad smile as she stepped back and motioned him into the hallway. He stifled a hiccupped breath despite his best intentions, so he turned away to latch the door and regain his composure.

"Aw, honey, I'm so sorry." Aunt Ethel again hugged him tight. Her close cropped dark head barely reached his shoulder. She wore a favorite green Baylor sweatshirt, jeans, and moccasins, and her high cheekbones and dark eyes needed no makeup. She smelled like sunshine, safety, family. Like Mom.

His first sob surprised him.

"Let it out, sweetie." Her arms tightened. "I've got you, you're safe. Let it out."

Oh God, it hurt. He couldn't catch his breath. Cops don't cry. But sons do. The dam broke, and he shook in her arms for endless moments.

He broke the embrace. Without a word, Ethel handed him a hand towel. He mopped his face and cleared his throat. "I can't stay." He handed back the towel, and straightened his shoulders. Didn't look at her. He had to be a cop again.

"I know. You're on the job. So go see your uncle. He's in the kitchen." Her hands fluttered a tattered tissue. "He's biting nails to be involved. You know Stan. They made him take retirement, or he'd still run things."

True. Uncle Stan always knew what should be done and he'd tell you in no uncertain terms. Other folks often fell short of what was expected. He'd failed in his uncle's eyes. Again.

"I appreciate you coming, I know you're busy. But tell Stan something, calm him down." She hesitated. "The rest of the family left hours ago. I sent them away. They just got each other more and more riled." She wadded the tissue and stuffed it in her jeans pocket. "All but Naomi. She's upstairs, asleep I hope. I gave her one of my magic pills."

Thank God Naomi was asleep. He hadn't the courage to meet his sister and uncle together. "Don't think I'm the best person to calm Uncle Stanley." His smile softened the understatement.

She raised her brows. "You mean all that business with your job? Never mind that. Stan's a hard man, a proud man. The stuff they said about you hurt him because he knew they were lies." She smiled but her lips trembled. "Your mom was so proud of you, and Stan worshipped her."

The scandal not only killed his career and marriage, it drove a wedge through his family, and by default tainted Stan's reputation in the police force. Combs didn't even know the informant's real name. He'd never seen "Spider" without the black-on-white makeup or spiked black hair, until that day in the morgue when he'd learned she was a lawyer's kid, a lawyer with juice. Hell, Combs didn't blame the parents, he'd have stroked out if he lost one of his kids. But after Spider's diary surfaced, Doty used it to point fault at Combs and away from her own culpability, and Uncle Stanley stayed silent when Combs lost his detective's badge.

"He could have done more to defend me." The old hurt was hard to ignore, but he shrugged an apology. Aunt Ethel always defended and believed in him, even after Cassie lost faith and left with their kids. And of course, Mom's support never wavered. "Old news doesn't matter. Today it's all about Mom."

"Yes, it's about Wilma."

"Somebody has to take her cat." He forced a smile. "She'd kick my butt if I didn't mention that."

"Never mind the cat, your sister has that covered. Simba is upstairs sleeping with Naomi. They'll be good for each other. No more foot dragging. You go to Stan before he has another coronary." She grabbed his arm, a grip surprisingly firm for such a birdlike woman. "It's okay to show you're hurt, too. You are more like Stan than either of you wants to admit." When he would have argued, she interrupted. "Honey, help your uncle by helping your mom. She's what held us together, and with her gone . . ." Her chin rose, and her blue eyes glinted with more than tears. "There's been enough hurt in this family, don't you think?"

"Who's there, Ethel? Any news?" Stan called out.

"Keep your voice down, you'll wake Naomi." She searched Combs's expression for something, and smiled as if she'd found it. "Jeff's home." She squeezed his arm and whispered. "Give him what he needs, what you both need." She pushed him down the dark hallway toward the bright kitchen. "It's what Wilma would want."

He braced himself and strode into the light. Uncle Stan towered above the sink, coffee pot in one hand and empty cup in the other. His barrel chest, covered by the trademark leather vest, belied the heart condition that forced him into early retirement. Iron gray hair held a permanent wave from years of wearing a cowboy hat. His trimmed and waxed mustache hid humorless lips. Uncle Stan was a taller, broader version of Yosemite Sam.

"About damn time. Sit. You'll be here a while." Uncle Stan always spoke in foregone conclusions, and had no patience with what he called weenie hedges. He poured thick, black liquid into his mug before a sip and grimace. "It bites. Want some? This is the fourth pot, I think. Not bad with enough sugar."

Combs sat at the pine table in silent assent. He accepted the cup, warming his hands with it, and braced himself.

"Tell me." Stan returned the pot to the coffee warmer. He remained by the sink, braced against the counter as his knuckles turned white on the handle of his mug.

Combs had practiced before he arrived. "Single shot to the forehead." He coughed to cover the quaver in his voice on the last word.

Stan's mustache twitched. "So it was quick." He breathed in and out, his jaw working. "What else?"

"We're looking for April Childress and her son. Been in touch with the sister, September Day, who's considered a person of interest." Combs stared at the mug in his hand. An oily film floated atop the liquid. He tasted the coffee. Vile. Just what he needed. He took another slug.

"You attended school with them." Again, not a question. Stan pulled out a chair, flipped it around, and straddled it. The posture strained the seams of his pressed and starched jeans. "Miz January already called to offer condolences. Their whole family is tore up something fierce, waiting for word."

Combs unzipped his heavy coat. Ethel kept the furnace cranked to shirtsleeve temperatures. After Dad died, he and Naomi spent lots of time at Uncle Stan's house with their friends, including some of the January kids. He wasn't surprised they'd been in touch.

Stan peered toward the kitchen doorway, checking for his wife before he spoke so she couldn't hear. "Who chatted up the ex-husband? Miz January ain't a fan, some disagreement about the grandson's medication or something." He cleared his throat. "Divorce can be a messy beast, so I'd take it with a grain of salt, but wanted to pass it on."

"Gonzales visited the parents. I was there for the initial talk with April's ex." Combs rose and carried his mug to the counter. Messy, indeed. He didn't get to see his kids like he should. It made a man do and say things, changed a man into less than his best.

"I remember Gonzales. Dapper little guy, straight shooter from what I hear. He's like a rat terrier but you don't want to mess with them either, especially not if you're a rat. Partnered with Doty after you . . ." He stopped. Reached for his hat, and smoothed his hair when it wasn't there. Stared into his coffee.

Combs stiffened but didn't rise to the bait. He found the sugar bowl—the fake sweetener stuff Aunt Ethel preferred—and stirred a spoonful into his coffee. He tasted the coffee, added more sweetener, and stirred.

"Hey, bring the pot over, will you?"

Combs returned to the table, his mug in one hand and the carafe in the other, and reheated Uncle Stanley's cup. "Naomi make this?" He smacked his lips. Sweetener didn't help.

"Yep. Nasty, ain't it?"

Combs sat down again. It'd been ten months since he'd had a decent conversation with his uncle. He'd missed this. Hell of a situation when Mom's murder brought them back to the table—literally.

"Argument between the divorced parents over the little boy makes for interesting dynamics, and motives."

"Tell me about it." Combs slugged down half his mug, and set it aside. Now it was too sweet. "Steven's autistic. He's got a dog that September trained that's supposed to help."

"Autistic. So they disagree about the dog as part of the treatment?"

Combs paused. "I don't know. Good question."

"At least he's with his mom." Gonzales looked surprised at Combs's expression. "No? The boy's on his own?"

"Gone lost in the snowstorm with his dog. We think he took off before Mom was killed." Combs recited the facts dispassionately. "That's why April called September. We don't know if they were present for the shoot, only that both are on the run, probably from the killer."

"Or on the run *with* the killer?"

He considered, and then shook his head. "Not September. Maybe April, though, and that would put the sisters in conflict instead of cahoots. We're flying blind until we figure out what they're running from—or with—and why." Combs rubbed his eyes. "Mom was just at the wrong place at the wrong time."

"I cain't see either sister putting the boy at risk." Stan reached to adjust his missing hat again, and scowled. "It's April's house, so she's the bull's eye, and everything else revolves around her."

Combs agreed. "Or her son. She's a mom, so anything that affects Steven motivates April."

Stan fingered his handlebar mustache the way Ethel played with her rosary. "Something she has, something she knows, that's what this is about. April won't give it up, so hc shoots Wilma to raise the stakes, and takes April hostage to arm-twist September to deliver the goods. The bastard."

Combs cracked his knuckles. That made an awful, chilling sense. He stared at his coffee as if the black reflection held answers. "Even if April partnered with the bad guys, the timing and body count doesn't compute with a single shooter."

"Body count? Wilma's not the only one?" Stan's hand slapped the table, and the cup sloshed. "Ethel? Turn the damned police scanner back on," he yelled. "I'm missing too much. Dang woman thinks she's protecting me."

"You should monitor the radio show, too. I'm sure that Fish character milked all the gory details to hell and gone." He carried the empty carafe back to the sink. "We found some doctor's body, and another shooting happened at Gentry Park, a friend of September's. And I just came from Star Mall after September directed us to a dead bus driver. Bloody paw prints and a kid's sneaker tracks all over the floor. But no dog, no kid, no witnesses. Except for the coffee shop guy that Pike interviewed, but he didn't really know anything. I think the killer kidnapped Steven."

"September called that in? Shit, I didn't buy her as the shooter."

"Nope, she came late to that party. We think Steven got on the bus with his dog, and got off at the mall. But he didn't drive himself away. Somebody took him. The bus driver objected and got herself shot."

"I'll buy that." Stan slurped his coffee.

Combs rinsed out the pot and left it in the sink. "That extra leverage—the kid—keeps September on task. She can't come in to the police, or her sister and Steven get hurt."

"So pressure's on September to produce—whatever it is." He wiped coffee from his mustache. "She didn't give you any hint?"

Combs's shrug sent a sharp twinge down his spine. Tension always settled in his back. "You'd think she'd know better. Her husband was a cop." He flexed and twisted but it didn't help. Only finding Mom's killer would relieve the unrelenting ache.

"A cop?" Stan frowned. "Not around here. What's her story, anyway?"

"You don't remember?" Combs leaned against the counter. "Lot of gossip at the time. She was a musical prodigy, ended up on a concert tour sponsored by her school. Must have jumped the tracks when she fell in love, ditched school to marry, and gave up her scholarship." Yep, love could derail even the best laid plans. "Childress was pissed that September had some little sister crises over a supposed stalker late in April's pregnancy. She flew to the rescue, and Steven was born in Chicago during the trip."

"He didn't get to see his kid being born? I'd be pissed, too."

"More than that. Steven was a premie, hospitalized for a month before he came home, and Childress says that caused the autism. Blames September." Combs shrugged. "Anyway, September married the cop, threw away her music career and ended up with dogs."

"Makes no sense. Music to cop hubby to dogs? That's screwy. How'd they meet? Was he security for a concert?"

"Nope. SVU in Chicago."

"Special victims? Huh." Stan's tone suggested you had to be nuts to prefer the big city. "What's she do here? Heartland's a sleepy 'burb compared to Chicago."

"You do avoid the gossip, don't you?" Combs smiled at his uncle. If it didn't happen in church or on the scanner, it didn't matter. "She and her husband moved from Chicago to South Bend."

"Fighting Irish?"

"Yeah, Notre Dame land. They won the lottery, and then he got himself killed. Scuttlebutt says the stalker followed September from Chicago and nailed her husband. But nobody got arrested for the crime. Anyway, between the winnings and his insurance, September's financially set for life so she moved back home and bought the old Ulrich place. She's got it tricked out with more security than Fort Knox. Locks, bars, you name it. Her folks think she's still antsy over the stalker, but they don't seem to take it seriously. I'm just surprised she doesn't have a guard dog."

She looked younger than twenty-eight, and he'd been charmed by her quick wit. She didn't remember turning him down for a date all those years ago, and he hadn't reminded her. "She's smart. She worked SAR with the police, but both her husband and the dog died in some hinky convenience store shooting."

"That explains the security overkill, I suppose." He paused. "Married to a cop. Worked tracking duty with cops. Why didn't she go to the cops?" Stan's ferocious look still had the power to castrate.

"If these bastards have her sister, and now Steven, she's not taking chances. She's a victim, too. They pull the strings and she dances."

"It's all these damn cop shows. Has the whole world believing they can solve crimes all by their lonesome." His brow wrinkled. "Wait a minute. Did you mention a doctor? One of the victims is a doctor? What sort of doc?"

"Yeah, we found Dr. Pottinger's body outside of Childress's place." He tugged at his collar. The fabric, wet from the snow, had begun to chafe. "Pottinger's a researcher. Probably studies cockroach races or how many nose hairs the average teenager grows. Not really any connection other than proximity to Childress. But we found an antique bullet in the ceiling at April's house that the in-house ballistics guru says may be a match to the bullet that killed Pottinger."

Stan slapped the table again. "That's it!" He dismounted the chair, crossed to Combs, and gave him a bear hug. "Pottinger's the connection. That's the name Miz January mentioned, the doc who helped with the kid." His mustache quivered like a hyperventilating squirrel. "Pottinger—sounds like that Peter Rabbit storybook writer I used to read to you kids. Beatrix Pottinger, that's how I remembered."

"That's Beatrix *Potter*. Shit." Combs reached for his cell phone and then remembered he'd left it to charge in the car. He checked his watch. "Doty's holding a press conference in about two minutes. I need to get over there."

"Take me." Stan drew himself up to his full 6'2" height. "Don't shut me out."

Zippering his coat, Combs headed for the door. "You know what the brass would say. And since when did you become a rule bender?" The cold words sounded more abrupt than he intended. Stan didn't deserve that.

"Please."

Combs stopped at the door, his hand on the knob, and turned back. He knew Stan's request took enormous effort. The man granted favors, not the reverse. And from his own experience, Combs knew a view from the outside, stripped of power, took an enormous toll. Might as well lie down in a coffin and wait for the first shovel of dirt.

"I can't. You wouldn't in my position." The words cut Combs to the core. They'd finally reconnected, found each other again, only to have this happen.

"Don't suppose you can make exceptions." Stan hitched up his jeans. "You always did follow the rules, more or less. You were always a good cop, and a great detective. I think I knew that all along." His mustache twitched. "Wouldn't Wilma just blow a raspberry if this got you back into the fold again?"

Yep, Mom would be tickled but that didn't change reality. "I can't take you with me, but I can by-damn keep you informed." Combs held out his hand. "I don't want either of us to ever get lost in the shuffle again."

Stan grabbed his hand, squeezed hard. Blinked back tears that Combs knew were reflected in his own eyes. Aunt Ethel was right, they were very much alike. No need for further words.

Combs opened the door and hurried back into the cold before he embarrassed them both.

Chapter 34

September stood and backed away from the agitated dog. They'd waited for hours for Lizzie to take the next step. Worrying about April had her nerves on fire, so much so that she'd nearly come out of her skin when Shadow tried to attack the computer. The dog's attention never wavered from the computer monitor. He'd stopped barking, but his growls shook the bed.

"Turn up the volume. Shadow, good boy. Hush."

"What the hell's wrong with him?" Teddy gingerly reached for the audio. "I didn't think dogs could see TV." He fooled with the keyboard again as the video clip finished, and the image returned to the live feed. A heavy cop moved away from the podium and joined two detectives. "That's the courthouse."

September leaned closer to the monitor. "The video they played showed Henry Pottinger, Steven's doctor. Shadow must have recognized him."

Doug Childress seized the podium. "I just want my son back." He leaned into the microphone, and a picture of Steven filled one half of the split screen. "He's seven years old, and has been missing since noon yesterday." His voice caught. "He may be with his mother, or aunt. But Steven needs to come home. To me. To his father."

Shadow continued to growl, but September's hand on his ruff calmed him. He licked his lips, yawned, and lay down, but his focus remained glued to the computer.

"You sure the dog recognized this guy? How do you know him?"

"I don't. But the doctor is the thread that ties everything together. Shadow couldn't have met anyone else in that video, so that must be what got him riled." Her mind flashed to the bundle of bloody workout clothes. Did the blood belong to Pottinger? That would explain why April wouldn't call the police when Steven got lost. "There's so damn many people involved, I don't know who to trust."

"Would the dog recognize people on the screen?"

"Doubtful. Flat faced breeds like bulldogs or cats more easily react to TV, especially the latest high definition ones. Something about their eye placement and retinal differences compared to longer-nosed dogs. Shadow must have heard Dr. Pottinger before." Maybe yesterday morning. That was the only thing that made sense.

On the computer screen, the spiky-haired detective moved Childress aside, and pulled the microphone close. "September Day remains a person of interest." A picture of September with a cello, and without the white skunk streak in her hair, filled the screen.

The detective came back on screen. "We're also looking for April Childress and her son Steven." April's glamorous picture appeared side by side with a somber photo of Steven. "We believe the little boy caught a ride on the HART-Line bus and got off at Star Mall. The child could be in the company of a large, black German shepherd, a service dog. The police welcome any additional information the public may have about the whereabouts of these individuals."

Somebody from the press shouted. "Detective Doty, what about the other shootings? One at Star Mall and another at Gentry Park. Are they connected? Is this drug related?"

Doty held up one hand for silence. "I have no further comment on other pending cases. The deceased have not yet been identified pending notification of next of kin."

"How are they related?" Several reporters called out the same question at once.

"We're not prepared to say at this time," said the detective. "We welcome information, and you can call the number on the screen."

Teddy reached for the desk phone. "My turn."

"What are you doing?" September lurched to grab for the receiver. "Please, you can't call the police." She might not be hero material, but she was Steven's only chance. "Give me half an hour head start—"

"I'm dialing." He punched numbers, and then paused. "Unless you want to clue me in. It's time."

He was right. She didn't know if April was alive or dead. She'd already failed her sister, and the only way she knew to redeem herself was to save Steven. Lizzie would call, and she'd obediently hand over the computer drive, and be left with empty prayers they'd keep their word and release Steven.

"Tell me." He hung up the phone. "I want to help."

Reaching for the dog, she sat on the bed. Shadow wagged his tail, licking her hand as she stroked his soft, black fur. September felt her stress slowly ebb to barely below the scream-threshold. "Okay, what do you want to know?" She checked her watch for the millionth time. Six hours until the deadline.

"From the beginning. Give me the digest version, because the way you check your watch, time's short."

"You don't know the half of it." She struggled to gather her thoughts. She took a big breath and spoke quickly. "Some bad people kidnapped my sister and her son."

"Dr. Pottinger?"

"No. Lizzie Baumgarten and about a million henchmen. There's a pale man who looks like a ghost. That's her son, Gerald." She reached into the top of her borrowed sweatshirt and pulled out the flash drive. "They want this. It belonged to Pottinger."

His glasses twitched. "That's why Freda was killed?" He reached for it. "Why didn't you just give it to them, for Christ's sake?"

She slipped it back under her shirt. "I just got it. Shadow was wearing it."

He scratched his head. "The dog had the flash drive? Wait, don't tell me." He wrinkled his brow. "Steven, right?"

September nodded. "April said Pottinger was at the house yesterday morning, so I think that's why Shadow reacted just now." She hugged herself, and spoke her fears aloud. "That detective said Pottinger was murdered, probably at April's house."

Teddy gulped. "Your sister killed him?"

"No. I don't know. Maybe." September forced herself to finish the story despite the bad taste it left behind. "April was frantic when Steven disappeared in the snowstorm. I think Steven got scared when Pottinger was killed, and ran away." She braced herself against a chair back, gripping the upholstery so hard her fingers turned white. "Lizzie shot the babysitter, and threatened to kill my sister unless I returned the flash drive." The room reeled and then steadied again, a side effect of unburdening herself. Or maybe she just needed more caffeine. "She gave me twenty-four hours. That's two o'clock. April doesn't know about the babysitter. She just wants to help her son."

"That's how you got beat up?"

"You should see the other guy." The joke fell flat. Sure, she smacked Gerald, but in retaliation Pam was killed. "They've been ahead of me every step of the way." Her hand covered the flash drive. "This is first break I've had, the only hope to save Steven and April."

Shadow whined and pawed her until she shushed him, and he leaned hard against her. She avoided Teddy's eyes. Lizzie may have already killed April. If Teddy called the police, Steven could die, too.

He picked up a glass paperweight and immediately appeared calmer as he massaged its smooth surface. "I can see why you don't want to call the authorities. But do you think these jerks will return Steven? You can identify them, right?"

"I've got no choice."

"You always have a choice." He turned back to the computer. "First things first. Let's see exactly who we're dealing with." Teddy gently kissed the paperweight and set it down. "Channeling my wife, she was always the brains in the family. That was a fiftieth anniversary gift from her." He smiled, touched the glass again, and then his fingers clacked on the keyboard. "The phone's dead anyway. So until I can call the cops, might as well do some research."

September breathed again. "What are you doing?"

"Find out about this Pottinger character."

"Hold that thought." She hurried from the office to the living room, rummaged in her coat for her notes from the conversation with Fish. Gerald's pistol came out first. The greenish parkerized finish looked dull even in bright light. She'd never liked guns but she respected them, and Chris had taught her how to use them. September stuck the pistol into a pocket of the borrowed sweatpants. She wanted it within reach. She returned to the office bedroom. "My friend at the radio station found Pottinger on the internet. He works for NeuroRealm."

"Why didn't you say so?" Teddy typed the company name into the search engine, and soon had the website on the screen. "Here we go—all sorts of research. Hmm."

"How does this help?" Her toe stuttered in rhythm with the silent tick-tock in her head. Lizzie could call any minute. She had to be ready.

"Interesting." Teddy clicked on the media button, found the list of press releases, and opened the most recent. "Looky there." He backed away to give her room to see.

She scanned the press release. "Rebirth Gathering. April mentioned that." She read further. "It's a retreat for parents with autistic kids, and hints at some breakthrough treatment that cures the condition, extensively quoting Dr. Pottinger." She devoured the information. "Holy shit, it also quotes Dr. Gerald Baumgarten" She read further. "Sounds too good to be true. And it is. There's the contact person—Lizbeth Baumgarten, RVT."

"RVT, what is that? Some kind of nurse?"

"Registered veterinary technician." September's gorge rose. They must be using veterinary drugs on kids. "Look at that fee. You've got to qualify for placement, Rebirth Gathering won't accept everyone."

"Oldest sales trick in the book." Teddy snorted. "Make it exclusive, so folks want to be part of the elite."

"Doug refused to pay for the treatment, so April came to me."

Teddy whistled. "You didn't blink at the price?"

September shrugged. "I've got the funds, I'm comfortable."

"But it costs twenty-five grand just to get in the door, and they limit it to the first two hundred who register. Enough reason to kill." He shuddered. "Wonder how much the cost goes up once the children qualify for the full treatment? The bastards."

September read further, and gasped. "The full treatment goes up to seventy-five thousand." When did April plan to hit her up for that amount? Chris left her okay financially, but not if Steven's treatment fees hemorrhaged her funds. "April said Steven improved tremendously on the new therapy. Snake oil? Maybe. But placebo can be a powerful persuader. Parents grasp at straws, and will try any crazy cure for their kids, even unproven stuff."

"I didn't know you could experiment on kids." Disgust filled his voice.

"FDA studies mostly use adults, true. To run the same trials with kids would increase the cost even more, so they extrapolate doses and go off-label with drugs approved for other things." She shrugged. "Happens all the time. I think parents just sign a consent form acknowledging they know the treatment hasn't been FDA-approved. Of course the insurance won't pay for experimental treatments, but desperate folks accept the risk." She re-read the press release. "My God, Rebirth Gathering starts this afternoon! That must be the reason for the deadline. Whatever's on the flash drive must be explosive."

"So let's see what's so important." He held out his hand.

September's fist closed protectively over the drive, and she walked away. April got herself into the situation, but Pam was already on her conscience. She didn't need to add more to her guilt. Once she ransomed Steven she'd retreat to her reinforced rabbit hole, bolt the doors, and never come out again.

"Do you think these yahoos will let you off the hook? Grow up." He shoved his glasses up the bridge of his nose. "It's not just about Steven anymore. People have died."

"Who made you the savior of the world?" She whirled to confront him, and chewed words through a clenched jaw. "Don't you dare play the guilt card with me. I didn't ask for this. I owed April. Steven belongs to her now, he never belonged to me. I never even wanted kids; don't even like them, how long can she hold that over my head?" She clamped her hands over her mouth. Shame heated her face.

Teddy made a face. "Yes, I can tell you're an evil person only out for yourself. You hate kids. Probably beat that dog." He waved at Shadow and the dog wagged his tail. "So do you want Lizzie to kill more kids with her treatment? Do you let Lizzie get away with murder?"

She looked away. He didn't know. Only God knew who she really was, and what she'd done, and there was a very good reason God didn't hear her prayers anymore. So be it. She slapped the flash drive into his palm. "It's your funeral. If you get killed, I'm not going to cry."

"I have no plans to die. But they murdered my friend. Freda only wanted to help."

"Don't you think I know that? I know it's my fault." The flush left her cheeks, and September grabbed the wall to steady herself. She needed an IV bolus of caffeine or she'd never be able to finish this race.

Teddy plugged the drive into his computer. "Information is power. That's the shovel we use to bury them. We not only look at what's on this thing, we make a copy as insurance."

Pottinger's information might offer leverage, but she wondered what other horrors it might reveal. September mentally shook herself. Save them first, and save worrying for later. Teddy was right. She needed every advantage possible to come out of the storm. "Go ahead and copy it, Teddy. But hurry." She touched her watch. "When they call for the exchange I've got to be ready."

Teddy tapped keys.

"They'll come after your computer if they find out."

"They won't find it on this machine." Teddy boasted, still hitting keys. "I have an online storage site, password protected. In fact, Pottinger password-protected the file." He bared tobacco-stained teeth in a wolfish expression. "They don't know who they're messing with. I am the original badass hacker. And I flat love a challenge."

She smiled despite herself. "How much time do you need?"

His fingers flew. "Half an hour, give or take, when it's an amateur job. Professional encryption takes longer." He typed some more. "This is amateur hour. Piece of cake. I can save the file."

September returned to the bed but didn't sit down. She stroked Shadow, needing the contact to calm down. "They have to keep them alive at least until I return the flash drive. I have to believe that." The circumstances of his birth weren't Steven's fault. She had to stop blaming him. And herself.

Shadow nudged her hand. What the hell. She always thought better, worked out problems best around dogs. She'd learned that during the dark time eight years ago, when even her beloved music had forsaken her. She'd been lost until Dakota found her and brought her back to life. Dogs have a way of connecting and healing the broken pieces of one's soul that people can't always reach, although it was Chris who brought Dakota into her world.

September picked up the glass paperweight. Fifty years married. Something she'd never know. Chris wanted kids. Desperately. He shouldn't have counted on her for that most basic dream. Chalk up another failure.

Stop it. Picked sores don't heal. And she no longer had the luxury of feeling sorry for herself. She couldn't hide this time. Locked doors wouldn't protect her from this horror.

Shadow waited on the bed and watched her every move. He was tuned in to her, even more than Dakota. She tamped down that disloyal thought.

Holding the paperweight in her right hand, she picked up his bear in the other. "Watch," she said. She held the glass paperweight high, out of the dog's reach. "This is glass." She held up the bear. "This is Bear." She lowered both hands within reach of the dog. "Show me glass."

Without hesitation, Shadow reached forward and poked the glass globe.

September "clicked" her tongue, and tossed Bear to him. He caught it and dropped the toy and watched for what she'd do next. His tail slowly waved. He loved games, loved learning. Shadow was a trainer's dream.

Pulling a tissue from the box on the bedside table, September repeated the drill. She held the requested item in the opposite hand this time. "This is paper. This is glass. Show me paper."

Shadow lunged forward, poked the balled tissue, and received the tongue-click. "Good boy. What a smart dog."

His wags grew more exuberant. He woofed and play-bowed.

September searched for another pair, and bumped into the bed when she turned. Her pocket thunked against the footboard. She paused. Couldn't hurt. She pulled out the pistol, and checked the safety was on, and held it aloft. "This is gun."

"What the hell are you doing?" Teddy paused from his keyboard dance. "Is that thing loaded? Put it away."

"The safety's on." She glared.

"Do you have a permit? Where'd you get that thing?"

"It's Texas, y'all. I've got a license, but this isn't mine. Gerald dropped it and I accepted his donation." Turning to Shadow, she began again. "This is gun. This is—"

"Good God, put it away, September! What are you doing, anyway?"

"Vocabulary." She set the pistol on the desk. "It's a mental stimulation game. Some words he already knows, like paper, but he's not yet generalized."

"Generalized?"

"'Generalized': a generic word to a family of similar objects. He's generalized "bear" to include any stuffed toy. With paper, there are so many kinds I wouldn't want to confuse him by making him pick." She considered other objects, grabbed two, and turned back to Shadow. "This is candle. This is book. Show me candle."

Shadow poked, she clicked, and Teddy stared.

Teddy turned back to the computer. "It's a trick. No dog learns something that fast." He typed even faster.

"Hard to believe, isn't it?" She replaced the book on the shelf, and the candle on his desk. "I watched a horse demo at a behavior conference once. This mare could even tell what group an object belonged to—if it was a food or a tool." She rubbed the dog's head, and enjoyed the silkiness of the clean fur under her hand. "Had to try with Shadow, since he already knows so many action commands. Once he learned "show me," teaching him object names was a breeze."

Shadow woofed again. He pedaled his front paws from side to side, anxious for the game to continue.

"Nice parlor trick. But what good is it?" Teddy turned back to screen. "Nearly got it."

She shrugged but he didn't see. "Good for lots of things, especially for a service dog. It's most important that he gets a kick out of learning. Naming objects and behaviors teaches language. Just like the commands "kiss" or "sit" have meaning once the action is named. You've got to have a common language to communicate with people, computers, and even animals."

"Like new software, or a different language, huh?" Teddy bobbed his head. "Okay, that makes sense, I guess." He poked the gun. "With the trouble we're in, you ought to teach him something helpful. When's a dog ever going to shoot a gun? Teach him something we can all use, like "sic-'em.""

His words punched a fist-size hole in the conversation. For a moment the dog play had pushed horror aside, but the upbeat mood evaporated quicker than fog on a sunny day. "He's already protective, Teddy. He's a German Shepherd."

"Can't you, I don't know, get him to go after the bad guys? Get him close enough, he could do some damage? He nailed that guy at the mall."

She smiled, but shook her head. "The man took Steven. Of course Shadow would go after him. But Shadow's a service dog, and he's been taught restraint. It takes more than a few drills to turn a dog into Schutzhund material." It had taken years to train with Dakota, herself more than him. They'd nearly read each other's minds, but it required time to develop that kind of rapport. "TV has you think it takes thirty minutes to bully a dog to behave any way they want. A lot of that's creative editing, and the rest is the dog with the pee scared out of him."

Teddy scowled. "Well, you know dogs. I know computers. Let's stick with what we know in the time we've got left."

Time. That defined her world. She could teach Shadow anything if she had time. He worked for praise, he was easy. Dakota wanted to be paid with his ball. Macy demanded treats. Even people worked best for pay. If she could figure out what payday would float Lizzie's boat and used it against her, she just might survive the deadline.

"Got it. By damn, I got the sonofabitch's password cracked." Teddy swiveled in his chair. "'Paddlefoot,' the name of Pottinger's dog when he was a kid. Go figure, he'd be a fan of Clutch Cargo."

"What? Never mind." It didn't matter how he'd cracked the code. "Let me see." She shoved Teddy away from the desktop to stare at the screen. Time to find out what was worth so many lives.

Chapter 35

April regained consciousness when an ambient droning sound stopped. It could have been hours, or minutes, but now she was back.

Glittery light refracted through translucent crystals piled inches deep over her face and body. Florescent lights flickered overhead through countless prisms. She was buried in ice cubes. She tried to move. Nothing. Maybe she was dead. But no. The ice anesthetized everything.

Her mind was mush. Dr. Pottinger's threats, his death, hiding his body, Steven lost—the nightmare kaleidoscope couldn't be real. Steven found, safe in her arms, letting her hold and hug him. . .

It was hard to breathe. *I'm dying. Who will take care of Steven when I'm dead? Who will give him his medicine, work with him, help him—love him?* She gritted her teeth. Not September. She didn't want him. And not Doug. He'd given up on Steven.

April tried to move again, and the ice shifted. Had the ice been shaved, or any smaller than cube size, she'd have suffocated. Nuggets melted slightly by her breath fused and created a small cave-like shell about her head. That had taken some time.

Ice had numbed everything. April moved her jaw, explored lips, cheeks and teeth with her tongue. She tasted salt, how odd, and then understood. It was blood. The gag-making flavor primed her memory of September's phone call telling her the flash drive was found, and of Gerald pointing the gun.

She'd been shot. Each breath rattled deep in her lungs. April coughed, choked, and warmth dribbled down her chin.

A sound. Somebody outside. Voices, at least two people. April couldn't make out the words. But a woman's high pitched complaint argued with a man's rumbled answer.

Move. Get up. Shake off the ice, climb out. But her body refused to obey the silent drill sergeant commands in her brain. She could manage only a few finger twitches. Her ring clacked against the side of the container, but ice hog-tied the rest of her body.

She moaned. The numbing properties of the cold didn't extend to the stabbing pain of internal organs. Despite temptation to drift away, April gathered herself to yell over the anticipated hurt.

"Help! Help me." The cry rasped her throat like a file on metal.

Footsteps. Shoes scuffing carpet. The sound of the argument drew near.

"Help. Me. Please." With each breath she inhaled glass. She had to tell someone. Get help. Not for her. For Steven. He needed his treatment. The cost was beyond money. September had the means. Doug never understood.

Lizzie was an angel. Saving children meant everything to her, so getting shot had to be an accident. What did the movies call it? She was collateral damage. Just like Pottinger was collateral damage, an unintended consequence. Lizzie cared about the kids, cared about Steven; she didn't really care about the money. What price could you put on a miracle? The children would be the biggest losers if Legacy Center shut down. People without special kids wouldn't understand. Legacy Center must survive—even if she didn't—to ensure Steven's cure.

The strangers came closer. "I don't care what your momma wants," the woman said. "She's never liked me anyhow. I'd rather stay here in the hotel, or just bundle up at home 'til the electric comes back on. Pete, I refuse to spend the night at her house. She'll make it like she's doing us this huge favor. I don't want to owe her nothing."

So she was in a hotel. That made no sense. Lizzie hadn't wanted her to go home to an empty house where Pottinger had died, but all the hotels were full. So April had accepted Lizzie's considerate invitation to stay with her until Steven was found. Lizzie's down-home kindness was nothing like Mom's insistence on perfection.

"Aw, Julie, we don't have to talk about that now." Pete's exasperated tone matched Julie's volume. "Momma tries to be helpful. She's got that big hide-a-bed and gas heat, leastwise unless the gas line freezes."

"She stares at me." The pouty tone could have been a teenager's complaint. "Gives me the willies. Always judging me, she is, like she thinks she's the queen of the world." They drew closer. "And don't you dare suggest we go to that woman's place for Thanksgiving this year. Never again. Nobody makes fun of my rhubarb pie."

Black spots told April another blackout was imminent. So much easier to let go. But when she closed her eyes, Steven's face filled her world. She tried again. Whispered a silent prayer they'd come one step closer. Her ring clanked again on the metal wall of the ice bin.

"I got the pay-per-view ready to go. Work's cancelled for the next couple of days. Might as well make a holiday of it. So just get the Dr. Pepper, will you? I'll get ice, and we'll raid the mini-bar and have us a party. At least the hotel's got heat."

"Oh, honey, I've got enough heat for the both of us." Shoes clopped onto the tile of the vending room. Smacking sounds, mumbling, and a giggle.

Something tore inside when April struggled to expand her lungs. Fresh blood filled her mouth, and she spat out the foul wet. She heard the rattle-thud of a soda machine relinquishing a can. Ice over her body shifted as Pete scooped.

April's fingers fluttered; her ruby ring a metal flail against the confinement. Her hand broke free and thrust above the ice.

"DAMN!" Pete fell backwards. Julie screamed.

Big rough hands scooped away ice. Pete grabbed the plastic ice bucket, filled and dumped it on the floor. April wanted to thank him, but it required every bit of will just to fill her lungs.

"Is she okay? Why's she in there? Liked to give me a coronary." The blousy woman with lavender lipstick leaned close. "Pete, is that blood? God almighty! I'm calling nine-one-one." Julie jabbed at a cell phone she'd pulled from tight jeans.

"She's bleeding, sweet Jesus, she's bleeding. Hurry up, Julie, make the friggin' call!" Pete turned back to April. "Don't talk, you can talk later. How the hell you get in the ice dispenser?" He lifted one of her numb arms and looped it over his neck. He grasped her shoulders and cradled beneath her knees to lift her free of the box. Ice clung to April's clothes, reluctant to let her go.

Her vision turned dark but her mind cleared. Everything made awful sense now. She knew what to do. To save Steven. Her son. "Listen to me." Pete's expression morphed from fear to pity and horror. "I need to tell you—" April coughed. Red spattered his face.

"Shit." He recoiled, and nearly dropped her, but then gently lowered April to the tile floor. He swiped his cheek with his sweatshirt sleeve. "Julie, move your butt, girl, tell them to hurry. And go get us some towels or a blanket or something before the lady freezes." He grasped April's hand, leaning close with a forced smile. "Hang on. Let's get you fixed up first. There'll be time to tell what happened later." He swiped at his cheek again, and grabbed the phone away from his wife.

April coughed again, and tasted blood. "A drink? Some water? Please, can I . . ." She was so thirsty. Warmth spread over the surface of her chest but coldness filled her insides.

"Honey, what happened" Julie knelt beside her.

"Tell them." April gasped. "Protect my son. Tell them who did this to me." Julie leaned close, and April strained to whisper until she couldn't make her voice work. But it was enough. April relaxed, and fell into blackness with a bloody smile on her lips. She'd kept her promise.

Chapter 36

September leaned close to the computer screen. She found the mouse and clicked to enlarge the text. "Damn, there's dozens of pages, all in ten-point, single spaced type. And it's in medicalese." She wrinkled her nose. "Do you understand this stuff?"

Teddy stood back, hands on hips. He removed his glasses and leaned closer. "It describes some test protocol." He pointed to the pertinent sentence.

She dipped her head. "The first page is an abstract. There's the medication—Damenia, and the dose. That fits. Same drug listed on Steven's empty pill bottles." She read farther down the page, but shrugged away from Teddy's old man breath.

"Damenia. That sounds familiar. I think Molly takes that." He shrugged at her raised eyebrows. "Molly is my wife."

She stopped. "I thought she was dead."

He adjusted his glasses. "Molly's got Alzheimer's. I take the bus every day to the mall, and on her good days she comes and we visit. Today wasn't a good day." His sarcasm cut deep.

A buzzer from the distant kitchen startled them both. Shadow woofed under his breath and hopped off the bed. "He thinks it's something for him." September smiled and then felt guilty. Had to be hundred years since she'd smiled. She shrugged an apology.

Teddy laughed. "Sometimes life's so shitty you got to laugh in the devil's face." He stood as the buzzer grew more intense. "The rolls will burn, I better get them. You want cream in your coffee or black?"

"Coffee, any way you have it is fine. Maybe that'll help clear the cobwebs."

"Be right back." He hurried from the room.

September puzzled out the text on the computer. The document listed no authors or co-authors. She paged down and discovered the document included Pottinger's own notes and conclusions. It appeared that Dr. Pottinger had simply cut-and-pasted from some larger document to include the initial abstract that detailed the study structure, subjects, expected outcome, and what had transpired.

The paper detailed research compiled from seven groups located in Dallas, Houston, Kansas City, Oklahoma City, Chicago, Indianapolis and Detroit, each composed of between nine to fifteen subjects. A mix of males and a handful of females aged five to fifteen, diagnosed with mild to severe autism made up each group. The children were not identified other than by group code, sex, and age.

In all, the measure of eye contact, verbal communication, and one-on-one interaction increased by at least three-fold within the first six weeks on the trial drug. Objectionable stereotypic behaviors—repetitious self-stimulating actions or "stimming," such as spinning, hand flapping, rocking—and tantrums decreased by twenty-five percent within the same period, and these symptoms were eliminated in fifty percent of cases by the end of the first phase study. A small percentage of children started to talk virtually overnight. No wonder April was excited by the new treatment.

Nothing on the flash drive seemed worth Lizzie's efforts to recover the information, though. Sure, the drug composition and test results were proprietary. But all the parents signed an informed consent to enroll their children. April would have been told of any possible adverse effects of the drug, and must have deemed the risks to be minimal compared to the potential for improvement. Hell, any parent would willingly risk a bit of diarrhea to have a normal relationship with their child.

The old guilt stabbed anew. Chris had been sure he could change her mind about kids. "But I'm a freak," she said. Chris saved her, and she couldn't bring herself to give him what he wanted. Then he was dead..

She shrugged off the pain. None of that mattered in this moment. She returned to the tedious copy. The conclusion with Pottinger's annotations began on page 29 and continued for five pages. September reached the last few paragraphs and stiffened. She re-read them.

September opened an email and attached the document. She addressed it to herself, her parents, and siblings and hit send. Whatever happened in the hours ahead, the whole family would know. They needed to understand, and protect themselves, especially when Steven came home.

If he came home. Because the consequences of missing the 24-hour deadline went beyond returning the flash drive. For Steven and the people around him, missing the deadline could be fatal.

Teddy hurried back into the room balancing a tray with two coffee mugs, a saucer of steaming biscuits, a tub of margarine and a beaker of honey. "Help yourself." He settled the tray on the desk. "So what did you find out?"

Shadow sniff-tested the air, and wagged a polite request for a taste.

September closed the file. Did she want him to know? "They've found a cure for autism. At least, that's what they say."

He looked so relieved she thought he'd dance a jig. "But that's marvelous!" Her expression tempered his joy. "Isn't it?"

"It's awesome for about seventy percent of the kids. But the others . . ." She stopped. Dear God, Steven had taken the drug for weeks. She forced herself to continue. "They can't stop the medication. Not ever. They price it low to get parents to sign kids into the program, and once they're hooked, they raise the maintenance fee at the Rebirth Gathering to stay on the drug. Without the drug the children revert to their original state."

"Like a diabetic needs lifelong insulin therapy. That means millions of dollars are at stake." He licked his lips. "People do awful things for money."

"It gets worse." She couldn't stop thinking about what this meant for Steven. "Withdrawal causes side effects. Bad ones. They develop severe— um, anger issues." She couldn't tell him. It was hard to believe something that cured autism also caused psychosis.

A little girl told to eat her vegetables stabbed her mother repeatedly with a salad fork. Another child set the family cat on fire. One boy Steven's age beat and drowned his four-year-old sister in the toilet. The document listed dozens of examples of explosive violence along with video evidence, but she couldn't bring herself to watch.

Pottinger brought the evidence to convince April, a drugstore blackmail to pay the extortion or risk Steven's sanity. And her sister must have gone ballistic and killed Pottinger when she didn't have the funds, and knew what would happen to Steven without the treatment. April was a victim, but she also must be a party to Lizzie's cover-up. God only knew how many other children were on the treatment, maybe hundreds of children with ticking time bombs inside their heads. Getting cut off from the drug would turn them into an army of psychotic youngsters. September shuddered.

Teddy plucked at the long sleeves of his sweater. "There are always side effects. Parents wouldn't mind risking a few problems for the chance of a cure."

"Even violence?" She didn't buy it. "Either the researchers didn't know about the problems, or the parents weren't told until it was too late."

"Don't autistic children sometimes have tantrums? That's not beyond the realm of normal." Teddy buttered a biscuit. "I know parents can be extra sensitive." He took a bite, glanced at Shadow's drooling face, and tossed him a piece. The dog snapped the treat out of the air and wagged for more.

"Parents didn't complain. The researchers documented it. Don't you see? That's why Pottinger visited April, to hold this over her head so she'd pay. It's all in his notes."

April would have held out for the promise of a cure. Steven was her world, and she'd do anything to protect his chance for normalcy. "Read it for yourself."

Teddy moved to the desk when she stood up. He adjusted his glasses.

"Worldwide distribution of the drug's already begun." September paced in the small room. "They've got plans for before and after interviews with miracle children slated for an international market push. Forget millions, that's billions of dollars and thousands of kids." She sat on the bed, patted the comforter for Shadow to jump up beside her. Smoothing his fur helped calm her nervous energy that had to go somewhere or explode. "I remember what you said about backups, so I emailed a copy of the document to myself."

Teddy picked up his mug of coffee, started to sip, and stopped as he read. "Oh, God." He set down the mug, sloshing some of the liquid onto the tray.

"I know it's horrible. Desperate people risk everything for a maybe cure. They don't know they could kill their kids or push them to hurt someone else. We can't let that happen." She glanced at the tray of food, but had lost her appetite, perhaps permanently. Still, she needed to eat or would crash, probably when she least expected. "I sent my email public to de-fang the snake. Doctors won't prescribe it, parents will sue, and the recalls would bury NeuroRealm." She picked up a biscuit, chewed fiercely and swallowed half before she washed it down with a mouthful of scalding coffee. She fed the rest of the biscuit to Shadow.

Teddy sat quietly and stared at the screen.

"They call it a cure. Meanwhile, the drug creates an army of children ready to go postal while their parents celebrate a miracle." She shuddered. "The liability is unbelievable."

He nodded, his face white. "Worth killing for."

Chapter 37

Humphrey Fish's voice blared from the speakers when Combs started the car. He'd left the radio on when he'd stopped to visit Uncle Stan. He reached to turn it off.

"Keep those tips coming, listeners. We're your up-to-the-minute, ear-on-the-air, reporting as the manhunt unfolds. Joining us is Carl Dorfman, with his eyewitness account of the shocking murder at Star Mall. He barely escaped with his life."

Combs's hand jerked away from the dial. "Sonofabitch." He over-corrected but managed to keep the car on the highway.

"Uh, yeah. I served them some drinks and f-fries." The kid's slight stutter rose from excitement. He had no reason to be afraid. "The cops asked me all about it. I could have been killed, you know."

Carl Dorfman must be the manager who served food to the victim, the kid Pike interviewed. "What the hell is he doing?" Combs turned up the sound.

"Must have been terrifying," said Fish. "How'd you get away?"

Combs seethed. Dorfman had been long gone before any shooting.

"That Freda lady got shot. She's a regular customer. And the old guy Mr. Williams shows up with his wife most afternoons. She's got that old-timers memory thing, you know?" Dorfman clearly enjoyed the celebrity. "I never seen that kid before that was feeding fries to his dog."

"Must have been the missing child, right?" Fish was joyful. "How did you get away from the killer?" He wheedled like a kid begging for candy.

"You never saw him." Combs slapped the wheel, disgusted. The Dorfman kid withheld information from Pike. The little shit knew Freda and the old man. They could have tracked this Williams fellow down by now. How had Pike missed that?

Combs found his phone, thumbed the number and cut off the connection when Doty's phone again went to voicemail. She must have turned it off for the press conference.

"Teddy and Freda was waiting on someone. The kid's dad, I heard them say. If I hadn't shut down early, I'd be dead, too."

Fish gasped. "Steven's father killed all those people? Listeners, are you getting all this?"

Old news, Combs knew. Gonzales already followed up with Childress. Steven's father hadn't been out of police sight, or his lawyer's presence, during the period in question.

Combs turned down the volume and increased the speed of the car. Doty needed to know that Pike missed the boat on his interview. He wondered why. He checked his watch. If he didn't slalom into a ditch before he got there, he should arrive about the time they finished the press conference.

His phone trilled. Doty maybe? "Combs." Combs lifted his foot off the gas and coasted.

"Jeffrey, I've waited for you to call. The children are beside themselves. Was Mom really shot?" Cassie's accusatory tone made it his fault. Again.

He couldn't remember the last time his ex-wife hadn't sounded pissed. This time she had every reason to be. "I'm on the job. Call Uncle Stan, and he'll fill you in."

"Is she dead? What the hell happened? Your own mother, Jeff, for God's sake." She breathed heavily. "I had to hear about it on the radio."

Shit. Didn't anybody have anything better to do than listen to Humphrey Fish flap his gums? That wasn't Cassie's style at all. "Sorry I didn't call. Yes, Mom's dead." He rubbed his face with one gloved hand, before quickly returning it to the steering wheel. The road straightened and his foot pressed the gas. Another three minutes and he'd be head-to-head with Doty.

"Jeff, we've had our differences, but couldn't you for once do the right thing for your kids? They've lost their grandma."

"And I lost my mother." He winced, wishing he could take back the words. Her quiet gasp told him he'd hurt her. Again. "I should have called, you're right." Too little too late, though. "I can swing by in an hour. Talk to the kids."

"They'd appreciate it. I didn't call for me, you know. Richard is here, and I'll get through this with his support." The subtext underlined that she'd moved on. "Whatever happened between us, you're still their father. They need you. Especially at a time like this. They love—loved their grandma. So did I."

Rick the prick. A damn CPA number cruncher, probably got off on the soap-opera style Humphrey Fish show. Cassie worked with him, and Combs couldn't help suspect the pair had plans long before his career-suicide tipped his marriage balance sheet into the negative column. "I'll be there soon as I can. Meanwhile, call Uncle Stan. Oh, and Cassie?" His voice turned hard. "Turn off the damn radio."

He pulled up to the courthouse. Media vehicles jammed all available parking spots. Combs slid into a disabled spot. Folks with mobility issues wouldn't risk this weather anyway. On the radio, Fish continued to take histrionic calls. Switching off the car brought blessed silence.

Combs hurried to the building and nearly wiped out on the steps. Nobody had shoveled or spread salt, and even the metal handrail shimmered with ice. One time, years ago before the kids, he and Cassie spent a memorable weekend in Salt Lake City at a ski lodge. Thirty minutes on skis convinced him snow was best experienced through a window, preferably accompanied by a roaring fire and an alcoholic beverage. This much snow all at once in North Texas was just wrong.

Pike came out of the building as Combs opened the courthouse door. "Watch out for Doty, she's in a mood." He started to brush past, ear flaps bouncing in the wind. He grabbed the rail and winced, stepping carefully.

He caught Pike's shoulder. "That Dorfman kid you interviewed from Star Mall blew smoke up your ass. He was on the radio just now, boasting he knew the vic and the old guy, Teddy somebody."

"Go figure." Pike shrugged off his hand. "I'll squeeze him for the address. Kids these days, too damn glib. They lie to your face and sound like choirboys. You're right; Steven might be with the old guy."

He noticed Pike's mincing gait. "What happened to you?"

The older man grabbed the handrail and took a careful duckstep downward. "Crap shoes on ice." Combs glanced down at the man's size twelve boats. "Doty's in such a rush, I didn't have time to change, and took a ride down some steps on my ass." He forced a rueful grin. "But can't let that stop this old warhorse. The kiddo is counting on me."

Combs stared after the limping man, frowning. Pike's kids were grown, but having a disabled grandson must make this case strike close to home. Maybe that distraction made him miss Dorfman's lies.

He stamped ice from his boots before entering the old building. Government offices closed due to the storm, but the press conference staged at one end of the great hallway drew a small crowd like flies to road kill. Doty was wrapping up.

"That's all for now." She stalked away from the podium with a phone to her ear.

"Doty." Combs called out, trying to stop her.

She held up a hand in a "one moment" gesture and turned away. He didn't see Gonzales, but Doug Childress stood to one side, his eyes downcast, cornered by a redheaded reporter.

"Have you received a ransom demand?" The reporter's buck-toothed smile pulled tight like a rat's. He shoved a digital recorder near Childress's mouth.

"Sly, why don't you crawl back under your rock?" Combs intentionally bumped into the man's beer belly. Sylvester Sanger had a reputation for creating bullshit to fill the holes in his less than meticulous research. He wrote for a tiny tabloid published in the next town.

"I've got a right to ask." Sanger pouted.

"Leave the man alone." Combs glowered. They'd gone to school together, and hadn't been friends then, either. "You just make shit up anyway." He'd been at the wrong end of Sanger's yellow journalism before.

Sanger sulked, turned away, and caught sight of Doty. He hurried in her direction, muttering into his hand-held recorder as he glanced behind him to be sure Combs wasn't on his tail.

"Thanks." Childress buttoned his top coat. He turned to leave, and pulled soft black leather gloves out of one pocket.

Combs stopped him. "A moment, please. What do you know about a Dr. Henry Pottinger?"

Childress dropped a glove. He stooped to retrieve it. "You can direct any questions to my attorney."

Combs scratched the stubble on his cheek. He needed a shave. "Mrs. January mentioned him. Said he's Steven's doctor?"

"Oh. Well, that could be true. April takes Steven to a slew of them." He pulled on one glove and flexed his hands. "April discussed that with her mother more than me, so I suppose she'd know." He tugged on the second glove and turned toward the door.

Combs blocked him again. "The body found behind your condo was Pottinger."

Childress sucked in a breath. "Steven's doctor is dead? My God, that's awful." He paused. "Can it have something to do with all this?" He waved one gloved hand to encompass the previous hours.

Combs waited. He wasn't disappointed.

Childress glanced toward the redheaded reporter held at bay by Doty. "Your detectives already questioned me. I have an alibi for when Steven was taken and that woman was killed."

Combs winced. Mom deserved better than "that woman."

"What reason under heaven would I have to kill Steven's doctor?"

"Yes, what reason?" Combs repeated. "I understand you and your ex-wife were not in agreement about Steven's treatment."

"I want the best for my son." His gloved hands clenched at his sides. "I will do anything to make sure he gets the best care." His visage glowed dusky red under the harsh fluorescents. "Right now, Officer Combs, I have more important issues at hand. If you were a father you'd understand that." He rushed toward the door, and this time Combs let him go.

Doty shut off her cell phone and strode toward Combs. "Good timing, Officer Combs." She leaned on the title, a perpetual dig she couldn't resist. She turned to the reporter. "Back off, Sly, or I'll run your butt in for obstruction."

The reporter saluted, but stood his ground. "Just doing my job."

She whipped around, glaring at Combs. "Walk with me."

He fell into step, pushed to keep up with her long strides. Something had happened. The information about Pottinger would keep at least until he knew the latest. All the reporters but Sly had dispersed, eager to file stories about something other than the blizzard.

At the door, Doty offered a death's head grimace. "We found April Childress."

Chapter 38

September's phone rang. She didn't recognize the number.

Teddy stared at her when it rang again. "Going to answer it?"

"Hello?" September held her breath.

"Deadline time."

Her throat constricted when she recognized Lizzie's voice. "You said twenty-four hours. There's still almost three hours left." She hadn't had time to set up her strategy, had wanted to run it by Teddy first. She waved at him, put her finger to her lips and switched the cell phone to speaker so he could hear.

"Change in plans." Lizzie's words crackled with authority. "You've got the merchandise early—hurray for you—so there's no reason to delay. You are not the only item on my to-do list, you know." She sounded surprisingly loud from the phone.

Shadow growled. His hackles rose.

"Wait. No, I can't. I need more time." September jumped up, leaving the phone on the bed. She had to call Fish and get him on task. He'd go for the plan. He wouldn't be able to resist.

"You've got until noon. Deliver by deadline or you can buy double funeral plots. Meet us at—"

"No." September's hands flew to her mouth as if to take back the words.

Shadow crept near the phone. Stretched his neck forward. Touched it with his nose, and growled louder.

September's heart stuttered before it returned to a steady rhythm. She stared at the phone. It sat on the bed six feet away. Maybe Lizzie hadn't heard what she'd said?

"No? Did you tell me 'no?'" Lizzie was incredulous. "You want them dead?"

She'd heard. "I mean . . ." September swallowed hard, and stared at Teddy with a silent plea for help. He held up his palms signaling he had nothing to offer.

What if her plan wasn't workable? She'd counted on brainstorming with Teddy for him to pick it apart first. September pantomimed a pencil and pad. Teddy juggled items on the desk and silently handed them to her. She scribbled quickly, and handed it back to him and turned back to the phone. No do-over. "I want to talk to April. Prove to me April's still alive. Or there's no flash drive."

"Is this déjà vu? We've already traveled this road, and you got April so upset she's indisposed."

Shadow snarled, and began to bark at the phone. He jumped at it, pawed and batted until September snatched it out of reach. "Are you still there?" She checked to be sure Shadow hadn't disconnected the phone.

"September, September, I thought we had an understanding. You're nearly at the finish line. It would be such a disappointment to have you renege at the eleventh hour, so to speak. If you insist on proof, Gerald could make April scream. Again. Or maybe you'd rather hear from Steven this time."

Her stomach flip-flopped. "Don't hurt him. He's just a little boy." September turned to the dog. "Shadow, shut up!" They were still alive, they had to be. But April couldn't protect Steven, and Steven hadn't asked for this, he was the real victim here. "I'll give you what you want." She looked over at Teddy, who frowned at her chicken scratch notes and scrawled a couple lines of his own.

"Of course you will. I never doubted that for a minute." Lizzie paused, and then spoke with deadly intent. "You understand that I. Do. Not. Bluff."

"I understand. I really do understand." She took the notepad from Teddy, read it, and nodded. He gave her a thumb's up and a grin. September crossed the fingers of both hands, and couldn't contain the quaver in her voice. "Lizzie, you're in control. Whatever you want, tell me and I'll do it." She inhaled sharply before she dove off the virtual cliff. She had one chance to make this work. Teddy said it was a go. Fish surely would help. But the plan would only work if Lizzie agreed to the location. "I name the place."

There was dead silence for a long moment before Lizzie laughed, a claws-on-chalkboard sound.

"Listen, you've got the power. You control everything else, haven't you proven that?" September bulldozed on. She had to convince the woman to agree, that it was in Lizzie's best interest. "It won't do either of us any good if I kill myself on icy roads on my way to reach you. You named the time.

You say how the exchange goes down. But I'm new in town, I could get lost, miss the deadline and then Steven loses. Neither one of us wants that, do we?" Dead silence. One more try. "I only want to name the place so I don't accidentally break your rules. Help me help Steven."

She prayed she hadn't just killed them, but she bet everything that Lizzie wanted the flash drive so much she'd concede the minor point in the game.

Lizzie blew out her breath. "Very well. But the cops show up, and everyone loses."

September smiled at Teddy. "Meet me at two-oh-five Rabbit Run Road. There's no other house within half a mile. Plenty of time for you to get away, watch for the police, whatever you want." She gave a thumb's up back to Teddy. "I don't care about the information; I just want my sister and Steven safe."

"I know you do, dear. Your sister told me why. She explained what happened in Chicago with you and Steven." She laughed. "Play by the rules, and maybe your debt to that little boy will finally be paid."

Chapter 39

Combs's car skated into the hotel lot. The EMT vehicle had already arrived, but only one squad car. The Heartland PD was stretched thin despite officers and detectives who were pulling double shifts. He recognized the ME's car snuggled into the narrow area beneath the covered entrance. The cars overflowing the lot made it looked like a damn convention. Doty and Gonzalez's unmarked car also crowded beneath the awning.

The nearest empty spot was next door at the Sonic, a football-field distance away. His feet protested at the thought. Like his partner, Pike, he'd not been home to pick up appropriate foot gear. "Screw it." Combs double-parked beside the ME's hail-dimpled Toyota and hurried inside.

Detective Gonzales met him before Combs could reach the desk. "Back in Doty's good graces?" Gonzales sipped from a Starbucks cup.

"Seems like. As much as anybody can be. For now we're working on the same side." Combs stomped his feet to increase circulation. He noticed the man's drink, and his stomach gurgled, a reminder he'd not eaten since late yesterday. His nerves already jangled with buckets of caffeine from Uncle Stan's. He didn't need more.

"Doty beat you by three minutes." Gonzales nodded.

Combs followed his gaze. At the front desk, the detective loomed over the clerk.

"Nobody knows much." Gonzales sipped his coffee. "The couple that found April is in the manager's office."

Combs waved a hand toward the parking lot. "I figured we'd have folks trampling all over. The hotel's packed."

"Yeah, it's the weather." Gonzales indicated his soaked topcoat. "Ice and snow knocked out transformers and power lines in three counties. Hotels booked within hours, and there's a run on generators. Most of the guests want to stay snuggled up in their rooms, thank God. Be a rash of babies next summer."

His stomach growled again, and Combs winced, unzipping his coat. They had the heat cranked to a tropical climate. "Maybe September's in a hotel. You got somebody to check?"

Gonzales frowned. "We gave up. Too many people sneak under the radar, more than you'd think with dogs. We don't have the manpower to follow all those leads." He pointed at the clerk. "Fella says there's a four-guest limit per room. But he's turned a blind eye a few times and doesn't want his boss to know. I'd bet more'n half are over the limit with six or even eight to a room, and can't afford to pay extra if they get caught."

"Yeah, this sure isn't a holiday destination accommodation." Combs braced himself when Doty finally noticed him and briskly approached.

"What have you got?" She directed the question to Gonzales but included Combs in a tight smile. Doty held her pad and pencil at the ready.

"EMTs are still with her. She's barely alive, unconscious and not talking. Touch and go if she'll make it." Gonzales waved toward the stairs and pointed at the elevators. "I've got uniforms on all entrances and exits. I had the front desk call all the guests and threaten them with arrest if they poked their heads out the door."

"Yeah, we'll want to interview some of them. No sense having rumors ruin any real leads." Doty jotted a note. "Let's be especially thorough with the guests near the vending machines." She closed the pad and slapped her thigh with it in rhythm. "CSIs found blood in the men's bathroom where someone washed up."

Combs stifled a yawn. Maybe another infusion of caffeine would help after all. He felt for the January family. He'd had to deliver the bad news too often, but when you knew the victim, it made things personal. "April's blood?"

Doty gnawed her pencil. "Probably, but could be the perp's." Glancing briefly at Combs, she turned away, reluctant to admit anything. "We need extra hands. But you're still not officially here. Don't make me sorry I cut you some slack, Combs, or it'll be my ass in a sling."

"Understood." Combs felt grateful he wasn't at home, shut out from information. Like Uncle Stan.

"It's damn frustrating." Doty showed her teeth in a snarl. "I flashed pictures, and the desk guy doesn't remember anyone who resembled September. He doesn't recognize Steven, either. Or a dog. But Steven must have been here based on what April told the couple who found her."

"She spoke to them? Identified her kidnappers?" Combs's stomach clenched. Damn, he needed to eat or he'd pass out. "What'd she say? Where'd they find her? Did they get a look at the perps?"

"On ice. Literally. Witnesses came for sodas and found her."

"Vending?" This case got screwier by the minute.

"She got buried in the ice case." Not a flicker of emotion revealed Doty's thoughts. "The killer used this freaky weather as inspiration. In public, no less, but the ice bit him in the butt on this one." She smiled. "The ice saved her life. She can't talk yet, but once she can—if she can—April will identify the bastards."

"That's a shitty in-your-face, all right. But why would they dump her here if they checked in? There's a camera in the lobby." He shook his head. "Makes more sense they'd dump her far from bad-guy-central. Maybe wanted to send September a message and have her found quick. Can't escalate much more." He pulled off his gloves and mopped his brow with them.

Doty had also opened her coat, and Combs knew they all felt the heat, in more ways than one. News sources had already dubbed them the "Blizzard Murders." His mother's name would be inextricably linked with the worst spree killer in North Texas history.

Combs turned to Gonzales and surreptitiously massaged his stomach to stem the complaints. "So? Crime scene first, or witnesses?"

Before the man could respond, the desk clerk waved them over with a telephone receiver. Doty took the call, listened and handed it back to the clerk. "EMTs moving her out and we can take a look at the scene." She started toward the elevator. "The witnesses who found her aren't going anywhere."

The elevator smelled of urine. Combs's head throbbed. Despite exhaustion, sleep held no allure. He'd gone sleepless for longer when his wife had left. This was different. He didn't want to sleep, not until Mom's killer was found.

They waited as a gurney flanked by medics rolled down the hall, emerging from an alcove already beribboned with yellow crime scene tape. The ME stopped and stared. "We have to stop meeting like this." He shrugged. "First time I ever got called for a live one."

"Not much room, is there?" Doty picked her way with care, and Gonzales and Combs followed suit. Foot traffic of guests, EMTs and responding officers mucked up any helpful evidence, but better to limit the potential for contamination.

"What's the scoop?" Doty didn't enter the alcove, just leaned over the crime scene tape. Combs, slightly taller than Doty's imposing height, could see just fine and almost wished he didn't have such a great view.

"She nearly bled out. Gunshot again." The ME grunted. "Not as much blood as you'd think, because there's no exit wound. She could have drowned on her own blood, and survival isn't a given. Bullet's still inside." He motioned a tech forward to share digital images of the victim in situ.

"What type of gun?" Doty glared at the pictures as if she had X-ray vision and could find the bullet if she tried hard enough.

"Entry looked consistent with .45, that's the gun of the day, seems like. But no shell casings so you'll have to wait for autopsy to recover the bullet."

"Same caliber as . . . ah, the first victim." As Mom, he'd almost said. Now Steven might lose his mother, too. He hoped the little boy hadn't seen it happen.

The photos showed April's body sprawled on the scabrous linoleum, muddy footprints mixed with crimson where spilled ice had melted and been tracked by a parade of shoes. Her glorious blond curls were matted and her makeup had run.

The ME asked, "She our missing person?"

Combs nodded. "One of them." September and Steven were both still out there. But if Steven was with his mother's killer, Combs doubted he'd last much longer.

"Hell of a way to go, but she got lucky. The weight and temperature of the ice packed around her body slowed the bleed."

"The Good Samaritans fished her out and watched her bleed?"

"That's the bottom line. Then they tracked blood and water to hell and gone, so the CSIs have to sift through that soup to find any trace the killers might have left. Found a bloody hand towel over there." He pointed down the hall. "Witnesses said they used it to try and stop bleeding and gave CPR." He shrugged. "Kept her going until the EMTs arrived. They were already here for somebody else. Like I said, it was her lucky day."

Gonzales pointed out the several prints on the cracked linoleum. "Lots of different feet, but only two are clear. A woman's sock prints and a man's tennis shoe, both consistent with the couple who found her."

"Wait, you said killers? Plural?" Combs homed in on that comment. "How many?" They'd found one size 12 men's dress shoe print at April's house that probably matched the shoes Pottinger wore. The shooter at the mall had been more careful, maybe more of a pro able to cover his tracks. They did have blood evidence near the exit, though, that couldn't have come from the bus driver. Combs figured the dog had nailed the sonofabitch. He'd be hurting pretty bad, if the dog latched on with any force. Once they located the dog, they could match dentals to the suspect when they caught the guy. And they would.

"Did Pike get back to you about that Dorfman kid from the Mall?" Combs got blank stares. "The kid was on the radio spouting off to Fish, said he knew the bus driver and an old man with Steven. The boy might be with the old man."

"Pike must not have followed up yet. He'll check in with anything new." Doty made a note.

Gonzales grunted. "Shoe prints here aren't even close to the ones found at the other crime scenes. You don't need CSIs to confirm that." His bloodshot eyes flicked away—he wasn't getting much sleep either. Combs knew the man had avoided mention of his mother.

"They'll have to get her stabilized before they can dig out the slug," said the ME. "Maybe we'll get another match." Doty caught Combs's look. "Wishful thinking. Reeks of amateur hour." She turned and stalked back to the elevator.

"It all stinks." Combs turned to follow her. "A professional hit team gets in and out quick, bing-bang-boom. They have a plan. It's done before anyone knows about the game. They cover their tracks, like at the mall." He waved at the vending area, his gesture encompassing the whole situation. "These guys don't have a plan. They're improvising."

Gonzales's grim smile agreed. "That's why we'll catch them. I just hope we get lucky before these assholes kill the little boy." He couldn't hide his anger. "Every time the phone rings, it's about another body." The smaller man took it personally.

Hell, they all took it personally. And something didn't fit. Lots of trace left at April's, at Gentry Park, and here at the hotel. But nothing at the mall. Two different teams?

"Combs, what about September? Any more calls from her?"

"I left a message we found April. Tried again on the way here and the mailbox was full." But he pulled out his phone to try the number again.

"Hey, Detective Doty." The ME waved them back. "The victim's phone is ringing, you want to take that?"

Combs dashed back and caught up the phone before Gonzales or Doty could react. He took the phone with gloved hands and peered with surprise at the caller ID. It was September.

Chapter 40

September waited as April's phone rang a third time. Teddy stared at her, unasked questions palpable. Lizzie had called on a different phone. There was a chance a call to April's cell would actually reach her sister.

"Hello, September?"

Confused, September nearly hung up when the man's voice answered. But it wasn't Gerald the Ghost. "Who is this? I want to speak to April. Is she all right?"

"It's Officer Combs. Jeff Combs. We've talked before. I've left you phone messages and I've been trying to reach you." He paused, and she could hear voices in the background but not the words. "Where are you? Are you all right? Do you have Steven?"

"Why do you have April's phone?" She ran a hand through her hair, pacing. Shadow tried to follow and nearly tripped her.

"April's been shot."

The words were a stomach punch. She suddenly found herself sitting on the floor, the big dog licking her face while Teddy patted her shoulder. September pushed the dog away. "Shot? Is she okay?"

"You need to come in. It's time." His calm voice sounded so reasonable. "April's been taken to the hospital. Steven wasn't with her. Is he with you?"

If they took her to the hospital, she was alive. "Is she going to be okay?" She shrugged off Teddy's comforting hand.

"Where's Steven?"

September closed her eyes. Lizzie had lied. Big surprise. "Shadow bit the big guy who took Steven, but he couldn't stop them." She struggled to regain her feet, fear for her sister quickly changing to angry demands. "Is my sister going to be all right?"

Combs didn't answer for a beat, and she knew it was serious. "You need to come in now, September. Let the police handle things."

"How? How will you handle things?" She turned away from Teddy's fearful expression. The time for fear was over. "You don't know where Steven is, either. How will my coming in help? Will it save my sister's life?"

"Come on, September, tell us what you know and let us take it from there. I can send someone to get you. We know you're trying to help April and Steven. But you're in over your head. What can you do? You're only one person."

She looked at Teddy, and placed a firm hand on Shadow's shoulders. "I'm not alone." She punched off the phone connection.

***

Fur bristling, Shadow raced after September. The fear-stink so recently washed away rose in waves, and September's wide eyes, quick breath and charging heart shouted louder than words. The excitement was contagious. He wagged with a short, high-held semaphore that punctuated his excitement.

Teddy followed, and watched as September reached for her wet shoes. Shadow sniffed her foot. Shoes meant going somewhere. He whined and licked September's hands as she tied the laces. He could hear her pulse sprinting fast and hard, even through the layers of borrowed clothes that smelled like a stranger.

Teddy paced. "Why didn't you tell the cop our plan?" Shadow cocked his head and watched.

She shook her head, bright spots coloring her cheeks. September pulled on the other shoe, stood, shrugged on her coat, and patted the pockets for the car keys. They jingled.

Keys meant a car ride. Too often humans neglected to include the dog. Shadow's fur smoothed, and he waved his tail and yelped, frustrated but determined. He danced his "take-me-with-you" request with whirls, twirls and whines. She needed him. And he needed to be with her. She acted frightened, and that made his tummy tighten, too. But she didn't have teeth, and he did—teeth that could protect them both. That's what good-dogs did, they protected their humans. He whirled again and yelped.

"Settle, Shadow." September held out her hand, and he stopped to push against it.

He'd always wanted to be a good-dog, not just for Steven. September said being a good-dog for Steven was the most important job in the world. But his boy wasn't here. Steven didn't even like Shadow, he could tell. And Shadow liked September, a lot more than he liked Steven. Good dogs do what they're told. But it felt wrong this time.

Shadow yawned, but it didn't help. He licked his nose, and slurped September's hand. He didn't know what to do.

Except watch her face. Smell her body. Listen for the special words that explained everything. The joyful "click" noises September made for good-dog behavior. Only September made the special click noises. Only her "good-dog" made his heart leap. Only September made his world right.

He would not leave her.

Teddy retrieved and pulled on his own coat.

Shadow's brow furrowed. Maybe they'd all go for a car ride together. He'd like that. Shadow pranced and twirled between September and the old man.

September grabbed Teddy's arm. "I won't get you killed, too." She guided him back to the sofa. She swallowed in a loud gulp even a human could hear. "Stay here with Shadow."

He didn't like that "stay" word. With a whine, Shadow stared from face to face and checked hands for hidden balls, anxious for the game to begin. He loved games. He didn't want to stay.

Teddy sat down so hard the sofa squeaked in protest. "They'll kill you."

September's jaw tightened. "They'll try. But I'm not running this time, not hiding anymore." She headed for the door.

Shadow woofed, and raced her to the entry. No game after all. Instead she wanted to leave. Not without him! He pushed between September and the wall. His tail hammered the door.

"Baby-dog." September's gentle words gave him hope. He pressed his head against her side, reveled in her touch. "You can't go, Shadow. Be a good-dog, and stay."

He yelped. The "stay" word hurt worse than a fist. He had to change her mind. Shadow leaped to reach September's face. He had to tell her, show her. His place was with her, how could she not understand?

She knelt on the wet tile, opened her arms. Shadow whimpered and washed the salt from her eyes. "I know, baby-dog, but you can't. You just can't."

He didn't understand the words, but her tone told him everything he needed to know. Shadow's hopes deflated.

Teddy struggled to stand. He held the gun.

September gasped. Her arms tightened around Shadow.

His hackles lifted at the renewed fear-stink that filled the room. Something had changed between the two people. He cocked his head, trying to puzzle it out.

Chapter 41

Combs stared at April's phone. September had disconnected before he could convince her to come in.

Doty shrugged. "At least the stupid woman's still alive."

Combs flinched, but covered it with a cough. Typical Doty, going for shock value. "She's gone to ground, but she's not stupid. She'll come up for air when she's ready."

Gonzalez and Doty stared at him, clearly doubting his grasp on reality, but he didn't care, and knew he was right. She had something planned. He just hoped she could stay alive long enough to make it work. "Let's find out what the witnesses have to say."

The herky-jerky ride back down the elevator made Combs's stomach leapfrog. He breathed with relief when the doors opened. The burn in his gut was an old friend, an ulcer born during the last months of his marriage. It faded once the divorce was final, but the gnawing flames announced its resurrection.

At the desk, the manager straightened when they approached. "They're still in my office. They wanted to leave, and I told them they couldn't until you said it was okay." His aggrieved tone implied great effort on his part.

"You did good." Combs tossed the fellow an atta-boy before following Gonzales and Doty to the employee entrance. He hesitated. Something smelled wonderful. His mouth watered and he swallowed hard.

The manager reached beneath the counter to the hidden oven. "Warm chocolate chip cookies. Specialty of the hotel. Guests get a couple when they check in, but I suppose we could spare some for Heartland's finest." He held out a small paper bag. Slow steam rose from the open end.

What the hell. Combs stuffed one in his mouth, chewed and swallowed before biting into a second and pocketing a third as he rushed after the two detectives.

"It's about time." The male witness wore a threadbare robe, and his sharp knees could cut fabric.

Doty waved the man to a chair. "We appreciate your patience, Mr. and Mrs.—" she checked her notes. "Pete and Julie Green. Can we get you some coffee? Cookies?" She smirked at Combs and pantomimed a napkin.

He flicked crumbs away.

"Don't have much of an appetite." Pete was oblivious. "Honey, you want something?" He leaned down and brushed a kiss against his wife's temple.

Julie ducked her head and refused to look at anyone, keeping her bare feet pulled under her overlarge Dallas Cowboy's sleep shirt. Her long, straight hair fell in pigtails past her collar. She chewed on one, her expression unfocussed.

Trauma witnesses suffered shock, too. She'd tracked through the gore and the CSIs collected her socks. Pete's CPR attempts left him stained with blood. Hence, the borrowed robe.

"We've been here forever. I want to get my wife back to the room to rest." He stood behind his doll-size wife and gripped her shoulders. "We can't go home until the storm quits. And now this happens." His eyes scoured the room like a trapped animal seeking a bolt hole. "The management won't give us a new room, either. Tried to be a good guy, and what d'ya get? This sucks."

"Mr. Green, Mrs. Green, Heartland PD appreciates your cooperation." Doty's conciliatory tone didn't hide the sarcasm. "A woman nearly died. That trumps your inconvenience. I ask the questions, you answer them. We'll get you out of here when we're through. Are we clear?"

Julie patted her husband's hand. She sniffed, and glared at Doty with distrust, but offered a quick smile to Combs. "She told us what happened."

"Good. That's real good, Mrs. Green." Gonzales scribbled on his note pad. "Did she describe her attacker?"

She shivered. "I've never liked them. Told Pete over and over they are dangerous. Was a dark one with pointed ears gave me this when I was only three." She pointed to her lower lip, and Combs saw a faint scar stitched on the flesh.

"Ma'am, I think you're confused—" Gonzales tried to interrupt, but she pushed on, growing more and more animated.

"Pete wanted us to get a baby and raise it up." Her gaze darted about the room. "But they turn into killers. You just can't trust them. I put my foot down. And I saw folks sneak the dirty things into the hotel. I did." Her husband started to speak, but she shrilled over top of him. "No more arguments Pete, we're never ever getting one. Look what happened to that poor lady. And to her kid, too. She had to climb into the ice to get away."

"I don't think that's what happened, honey." Pete's calm countered her strident tone.

Doty's brow creased with puzzlement, but she encouraged the woman to continue. "She mentioned a kid? What'd she say?"

"She did. She wouldn't have said it if she didn't mean it. You didn't hear." The tiny woman turned from haranguing Pete to confront Combs. "She grabbed my hand, pulled me down to whisper in my ear. I even got blood on my face when she . . ." She gulped, calmed herself with several deep breaths. "That poor lady was clear as glass, even if she was all tore up and hurt awful."

"So what happened?" Combs tried to soothe. "What did she say?"

"She said the dogs did it." Julie hugged herself.

"What?" Doty rocked back on her heels. Her exasperation startled both witnesses.

Combs couldn't hide his incredulity. Mrs. Green had, after all, experienced a shock. "What exactly—and I mean *exactly*—did she say? Not what you think she meant, but the actual words. It's important." He held out a hand in a placating gesture. "It's easy to misunderstand in moments of stress, but even if it makes no sense, we want to know the exact words she used. Okay?"

Julie stared up at him before squeezing her eyes shut, maybe to clarify the memory or to shut it out. "She said the dog did it. That it was the dog's fault." Her chin jutted at their collective expression of disbelief. "I swear that's what she said."

Chapter 42

Teddy's hand trembled unsteadily with the weight of the Remington .45 pistol.

September wanted to cry. Maybe it was time to give up. April was probably going to die; Combs had as good as said it. She couldn't win, not when even Teddy was one of Lizzie's henchmen. She leaned into Shadow's ruff. His breath warmed her cheek. His tension screamed beneath her hands, a coiled spring aching for release. With sudden clarity, she knew exactly what to do.

"You almost forgot this. I hate these things. Maybe you'll need it—"

"Shadow, show me…gun!"

Shadow sprang. He muzzle-popped the target. The pistol spun away.

Teddy cried out and grabbed his bruised hand. He staggered. Fell. The sofa softened his landing. "Why the hell did you do that?"

"Oh crap, sorry, Teddy. Are you okay? Sorry, I just reacted. Yes, Shadow, good-dog." Shadow leaped around, tail flailing with excitement.

September scrambled to retrieve the gun—the safety was still on—and stuck it back into her pocket. She dried her palms on the carpet. "I thought you'd gone to the dark side, Teddy. Are you okay?"

He rubbed his face, grumbling. "Guess that was good practice for the dog, huh? Glad he doesn't know 'sic 'em' after all."

Shadow wagged and wiggled. She crooned, "Good-dog, what a good boy, Shadow, good-dog."She pushed him away and waited for her pulse to slow. Now that the adrenalin rush had passed, all aches flooded back.

It took seconds to lever herself upright, and she steadied herself with one hand on Shadow's solid-as-a-rock back. She zipped up her parka. Her knees creaked. Growing old wasn't for weenies. Shadow stayed glued to her side, watching. September fumbled for words, repeating, "I'm sorry. Did he hurt you?" The gun in her pocket weighed a thousand pounds. It could have gone off. He could have shot her, or it could have shot him.

Teddy smiled, and the expression brought a sad beauty to his weathered skin. "Most excitement I've had in years. And I don't begrudge you or your sister's passion for helping Steven. I sort of know what April's going through. Molly doesn't know me half the time. But other days, she's bright as a penny, with the same sparkle when we first met back in grade school. If some drug could bring that back, keep me from losing her, well guess I'd do just about anything." He fumbled the buttons on his damp coat.

"What're you doing?" Her suspicious tone made Shadow's ears flick forward, and he yawned, nerves still strung tight. "Where are you going?"

"With you." Teddy pulled on his gloves. His stoic expression sanctioned no argument.

She turned to go. "I don't have time to argue."

"Then I suppose you'll have to hold a gun on me." Teddy headed to the door.

Shadow leaped at the handle with yelps of anticipation. His tail swatted the floor. He sat as taught, offering a polite "wait" to ask for the door to be opened.

September sighed. She hadn't planned to take him along. She might not have chosen Shadow, but he'd chosen her.

"Okay, Shadow, let's go." She'd leave him in the car once she got to the house so he'd be safe. Steven would need a service dog more than ever once this horror ended.

Lizzie and Gerald had forced her out of her rose garden fortress, threatened her family, and killed friends. Time to turn the tables, and flush out the rats with the flash drive as cheese. She'd run home to Texas to hide but it was time to cowboy up, before Lizzie called again. "You really want to help?"

"Of course. Steven's counting on us."

"Then c'mon." She opened the door, and dodged Shadow when he dashed ahead toward the car. "Do you have your phone?"

He patted his pocket in affirmation.

"Good. Make sure it's charged." September held open the rear door. "Shadow, kennel-up." She shut him inside one of Pam's dog crates. At least he'd be safe. She saw Teddy slide into the passenger side, and hurried to shoehorn herself behind the wheel. She started the car, and made one more call before pulling out of Teddy's driveway.

"Anita, it's September."

"Lady, you've got everyone worried sick. Phones here at the station have rung off the hook."

"Connect me with Humphrey." September turned the key in the ignition and it started on the first try. Maybe her luck had changed.

"Are you okay, honey?" Anita didn't wait for an answer. "Fish is still on-air, and you're still the star. I'll switch you—"

"No, let me talk to him off-air." She shoved the car into gear and did a doughnut out of the driveway.

"He won't like that. He's drooling over what this will do for his career."

"It's important, Anita. Life or death important. He'll want to take this call, I'm not woofin' you." September eased off the gas until the tires caught. "Just tell him . . . tell him I'm keeping my promise."

Chapter 43

Combs leaned his forehead against the glass in the hotel foyer door. The icy surface was a relief after the hothouse warmth of the manager's office. The several cookies he'd eaten to quiet his stomach instead turned to cement in his gut, and he hoped they wouldn't end up splattered on his shoes.

Doty and Gonzales finished with the Greens, and quizzed other guests, but nobody knew anything. They found a few illegal dogs, as Mrs. Green had said. A Chihuahua in one room, three Toy Poodles in another, a wirehaired mutt, two cats and a Greyhound in a third—all clearly killer dogs. What a colossal waste of time.

A tapping on the glass startled Combs. Gonzales hooked a finger, and Combs straightened and felt his back crack as he hurried back inside. "What?"

"A few more lap mutts, but that's all." Gonzales yawned. "Sorry."

Combs yawned back. Everyone was exhausted. "This weather, folks want to hunker down under the covers and blast some no-brainer TV show. It's only cops and killers out in this mess." Combs debated another cup of coffee to wash the old shoe taste from his mouth. His stomach gurgled. He dismissed the notion.

Doty strode toward them, buttoning her long coat. She growled into her phone around a fresh wad of gum, spearmint this time since she couldn't find clove. "You get this message, call me back ASAP. Screw weather excuses, I need answers now. Don't make me call you again." She disconnected, still scowling. "Thoughts?"

"Lots of 'em," Combs said. "All profane."

"Talk and walk." Gonzales moved off, and Doty and Combs followed. The little man couldn't stand still. Pacing helped Combs work out problems, too, but he was so tired he resented the request.

"Five casualties. What's the commonality?" Doty started the conversation. "Your mom, dog lady, bus driver, doc-in-the-box by the dumpster. Now April on ice." Recited facts stripped the victims of any humanity. Statistics, numbers, faceless puzzle pieces to manipulate and solve the riddle.

Combs used the same technique. It forced you to maintain distance. Emotion clouded judgment. But shit, he didn't want distance, not with Mom. He used that pain to razor through the fog.

"Commonality?" Gonzales held up his palms. "Steven. He's the connection to Combs's mom, the body at the mall, and April."

"Okay, but what about the dog lady at the park? And the doctor?" Doty asked, popping her gum.

"September called the dog trainer to track Steven, so it's still Steven. It all comes down to the boy, or something to do with the boy."

"Duh." Doty's sarcasm was born more of frustration than anger. "The perps kidnapped the kid. Let's come up with something we don't already know."

"But that wasn't why Mom was killed. April called the radio station because the boy went missing. That was before the first shooting, before April got snatched." Combs congratulated himself on taking a page from Doty's playbook and keeping his tone even.

"If September took Steven, she'd be out of town by now. The roads didn't close until a couple hours after he supposedly got lost." Gonzales increased his pace, reached the end of the hallway and turned. "No, I think September has something the killers want, and they kept April to make September comply."

That was the same general thought he'd discussed with Uncle Stan. "Meanwhile, Steven and his dog boarded HART-land bus to Star Mall with the bus driver, and she was killed when Steven was taken."

"Why was the kid taken? Killers already had April." Doty's yawn exposed an impressive cud.

"April wasn't cooperating? September didn't produce results fast enough?" Gonzales smoothed his mustache and loosened his tie. "Upping the ante."

"Then shoot April? They meant to kill her." Combs didn't buy it. "That's knowledge not in evidence. Unless this is personal and the bad guys have insider info, they'd figure September would risk everything to save her sister, and even more with a nephew at stake." He thought for a minute.

"September refused to work for them, and went looking for Steven instead. So they got to him first to arm-twist September."

"Makes sense." Gonzales headed back to the lobby.

Doty kept stride. "Sure, that scans. And once they had the kid, they didn't need April, especially if she foot dragged, too. Easier to haul and hide a kid than a grown woman. Wonder if they threatened to kill April?" She buttoned her coat. "Bet that's why she called her sister's phone, checking to see if April answered." Doty turned to Combs. "Still no answer on her cell?"

"She's either ignoring my calls, turned off the phone, or ran out of juice. At least she cleared her messages. Now it goes to voicemail every time." He made a note to call Pike and see what he'd found out about the Dorfman kid. It bothered him that his partner hadn't checked in.

Doty pulled on gloves and Gonzales did the same. "City's turned into a friggin' morgue. Nobody's in office, I can't get any answers. The PD might as well be shut down." She sucked her teeth. "Still need details about Pottinger. Can't see how he's connected to this mess other than he landed on Childress's back porch." She turned to Combs. "You missed most of the press conference. Turns out he's some sort of researcher, but nobody offered any details. Maybe he was a Frankenstein that needed killing." She gave an exaggerated shiver, mocking the words.

Combs stopped dead and stared hard at the two detectives. "But he is connected. I didn't get the chance to tell you. Pottinger was Steven's doctor. So it still points back to the kid."

Chapter 44

Shadow braced himself against the side of the wire crate at the back of the vehicle. He hadn't protested when September asked him to kennel-up, although he'd rather ride loose on the back seat. The cage reminded him of his bed-crate at home. Only this one smelled of a strange dog. Adult. Male. Potent.

He rarely understood why humans acted as they did. But he trusted September. She and Teddy spoke from the front of the car. Going for a ride. He liked the "ride" word. Shadow trusted that when the car stopped, they'd be in the right place. Maybe home? He'd like that.

Hanging his head out a window was more fun than sitting in another dog's crate, though. Maybe September would let him do that soon.

Shadow sighed, and sank to the floor. The motion of the vehicle and warm air made him sleepy. The excitement at Teddy's house wore him out, and traces of the other dogs, more than one, comforted Shadow.

He nosed wisps of tawny fur left behind. No scent of nerves or fear, but the freshest footpad smells shouted with arousal. What had excited the other dog? Maybe a ball? The other dog smells exuded confidence. Would that other dog growl at him and show his teeth if they met? Shadow whined. He wouldn't want another dog in his bed.

Another crate, empty, sat nearby. Shadow stretched his muzzle and tasted the air. Another dog, female, spent time in the space. His ears flattened, and he withdrew. She had a sharp special scent, one that prompted caution, but he didn't know why. Shadow would give her a wide berth should they meet.

He stood up to get a better view of September, and braced himself when the car skidded around a corner. He whined and yelped. Shadow wanted her connection, if only just a glance.

September answered with a toothy smile humans used. But it didn't fool him. The lines in her brow, the quick movement of her eyes and lip licking told a different story. Worry. Stress. Fear. He whined again.

September turned away. Her gloved hand fiddled with something at the front of the car and a man's deep voice began to talk.

Teddy didn't say anything, but Shadow could see him shiver. The back of the seat blocked Shadow's view, so he couldn't read Teddy's face. Teddy's teeth chattered, despite the blister-hot air blast that ruffled a good-dog's fur.

Shadow was sorry for humans who didn't have the advantage of warm fur. The cloth that covered the old man smelled wet and sour. No wonder he was shivering.

The big car slowed, turned and pulled to the side of the road. Shadow rose onto his toes to peer out the windows. He could see a two-story brick house across the field on the left despite the sheltering arms of snow covered trees. It looked different than the last time he'd visited September's house, but he'd recognized the route even before they'd stopped. He pawed at the crate to rattle the door, but September and Teddy paid no attention. The latch flopped back and forth. He nosed it, moving it slightly.

"Wait for my signal." September unlatched the door.

Shadow yawned and pawed at the door. Snow blew inside and leeched warmth from the car as she examined the gun, fiddled with it, and stuffed it back into her pocket. She handed Teddy a piece of paper. She turned to Shadow. "If something happens to me, get Shadow to my parents. He's such a good boy." Her voice broke.

Shadow wagged and slicked his ears when she said his name, and wagged harder at the "good boy." He whined and yelped with excitement when September stepped out of the car and shut the door. He waited for her to open the big door in the back of the car to let him out. He danced with excitement.

Shoes squeaked on the cold white stuff. Shadow cocked his head. Listened. But the steps drew away.

He howled, clawed and battered the kennel door. September had left him behind.

Chapter 45

September stumbled from the car and plodded through snow drifts. Her feet clomped like dead blocks of ice. If she fell, she might not be able to get up.

Shadow's hysterical yelps followed her. She worried his noise might give away her location, but wished she could bring him along. He gave her confidence the same way Dakota had kept nightmares at bay.

Screw post-traumatic stress. She'd been lost without Chris or Dakota, but had to do this without them; forget about fear, find Steven, and call the debt paid. She fortified her resolve and trudged on.

At the property edge, September scooted beneath loose strands of barbed wire supported by century-old bois d'arc fence posts. The open fields surrounded her house with a mix of short-cut winter rye and brambles, so she hugged the fence line for extra cover. Cedar elm, burr oak, hackberry and mountain ash carried mounds of white in skeletal arms. In the knee high grass, prickle vines hidden under the snow clutched her ankles and clawed her pants until her thighs and calves cramped before she'd slogged halfway home.

She slipped, grabbing a nearby tree branch for purchase, and spines of the honey locust speared through her glove. September barely noticed. Hurray for Reynaud's numbness after all. Too many injuries, along with the combination of cold and adrenaline, anesthetized everything, but her brain revved into crystal clear focus. She gripped the enormous thorn with her teeth, yanked, and spat into the snow. September flexed her hand. It still worked well enough. Time to move. Find Steven. Stop the drug. Save the children.

September plowed another dozen steps before she peeked from the cover of the trees. Light spilled from her office windows. In her rush from the house yesterday she'd left on lights, although she had remembered to triple lock the front door. The place looked empty. Not even the police visit had disturbed more than tracks on the drive.

The drive circled the house in a dog-leg turn to reach the garage, and she couldn't see inside. That created a blind spot where Lizzie's cohorts could wait. Danger hid in unexpected places, even places you thought were safe, as she knew from experience. Her breathing quickened, and she almost gave in to the temptation to hide in the bushes outside and call the police when Lizzie arrived.

Suck it up, sweetheart. The old fears wouldn't rule this day, not again. She'd lost herself for eight long years. She couldn't let the killers get away. The lives of countless children, not just Steven's, hinged on her decision.

She looked over her shoulder and satisfied herself that Pam's dark vehicle wouldn't be visible from the house. September sprinted in an awkward crab-shuffle to the side of the house and the kitchen side door, spending several nerve-wracking seconds unlocking deadbolts until she could hip-bump it open. The door was such a bitch to latch. For the first time in recent memory, she slammed the door closed but left it unlocked.

The floor was wet. Snow had drifted through the laundry room's transom before someone—the police?—shut the window. The acrid stink from the dryer still clung to the walls. The 78-degree thermostat setting turned the room into a steam chamber.

"Mrrring." Macy loped from across the room and wound around her ankles.

"Hey kitty, good to see you, too." September smiled despite herself when he dropped Mickey on her shoe. But she couldn't have him underfoot. She needed to stash him someplace safe.

September scooped up and tossed the toy onto the counter and gave the "jump-up" hand signal. The cat obliged. She pulled off her gloves, and spent ten precious seconds nuzzling the cat, thinking it might be their last time together. "We get through the next hour, I'll buy you a plate of shrimp," she whispered. "But right now you need to stay out of the way."

His carrier was somewhere in the garage—where possible bad guys lurked—and would take too long to retrieve. The bathroom wouldn't work. He could open the door. The rest of the unfinished house wouldn't contain him, not when he could leap eight feet or more from a standing start.

"Macy, come." He did, but dragged Mickey with him. She collected the toy. "Macy, jump." She tapped the top of the refrigerator.

Macy merrowed and vaulted to his favorite perch. He watched September fill his bowl, top it off with several smelly salmon treats out of the canister, and set it beside him. His purr rumbled. He patted her head and settled down to crunch kibble. She prayed he'd stay with the food.

September unzipped her jacket, and moved to the stained glass table. The Number One Bitch mug was still half-filled with cold coffee next to the saucer from yesterday's breakfast muffin. She emptied her pockets, and stuffed Macy's mouse toy inside out of sight. Otherwise, once Macy ate he'd demand a game of Mickey-fetch.

Her phone needed juice. September pushed aside the treat canister and coffee maker and plugged it into the outlet to charge. The flash drive was bait, but the phone would spring the trap and, if she was lucky, it would save her life. And Steven's. She switched the phone to speaker mode, dialed, and hid it from view before anyone answered.

"WZPP, you've reached ZAP105 FM Radio, giving you the best easy-listening 24/7, how may I direct your call?"

Macy mewed. His ears twitched.

"Anita, it's September. Put me through—"

"He's expecting you, hon." Fish's broadcast came on the line.

". . . So for the latest on the Blizzard Murders, keep it tuned to ZAP105 FM Radio. I'm Humphrey Fish servin' it up fresh." He paused before saying, "Caller, you're on the air."

"Fish, it's time. Can you hear me okay?" She moved away from the counter, testing the range.

The stairwell door squeaked open behind her. Footsteps clumped on the landing. "I hear you just fine."

Chapter 46

Combs stared at Doty. "Pottinger was Steven's doctor." Combs repeated it for emphasis.

Doty's words were curt. "Perfect timing, Officer. When did you plan to enlighten us?" She did sarcasm well.

"Uncle Stan heard from September's folks. I came directly to the press conference from Stan's, and before I could say anything, you got word about April." Combs knew he sounded defensive but Doty always had that effect. He made an effort to smooth his tone. "Since then we've been busy." He could do sarcasm, too.

"So all the deaths are connected." Gonzales stuck his hands deep in his pockets. "Kid has some seriously bad karma."

"It's not like Steven pulled the trigger. But yeah, there's something rotten. Childress denied knowing Pottinger, and claimed April picked all the doctors."

Gonzales smoothed his mustache as if that would help him think. "You believe him?"

"They fought over Steven's treatment." Saying it out loud made Combs more convinced the man was involved.

"Hey, I'd fight for my kids to the death." Gonzales looked at Doty. "So would you, if you had kids."

So would he. So far he and Cassie had kept it civil, but all bets would be off if she tried to take his kids. "Crime of passion, you knock off the ex-wife.

But all these other people? It's got to be something more. Something about reputation. Or money."

Doty's phone buzzed. "About time. Tell me you've got answers." She listened intently, and whistled through her teeth with exasperation. "So you don't know yet, but can tell me when? Thirty minutes? Ten? Bite me, we don't have the time. I need answers yesterday. And while you sit on your ass for some bureaucrat to answer his pager, add this to your to-do list. Do you hear me?" The angry pulse-beat in her temple thrummed faster. "Write it down. I want you to find any connection—anything—between Dr. Henry Pottinger and Doug Childress."

Combs muttered a curse. "That's it. That's what April tried to say." He pulled on his own gloves. "Gonzales, is anyone watching Childress? Do we know where he is?"

Doty spoke through gritted teeth, her patience at an end. "He's the father of a kidnap victim, so yeah; I've got a uniform with him. You know, in case there's a ransom call."

Ignoring her acerbity, Combs mentally connected the dots. "Check to make sure we've got eyes on him. I don't know how, or exactly why, but Childress is involved." Combs watched Gonzales make a call.

"How'd you come up with that?" Doty's tone softened into a devil's advocate role. "He's a victim here. Maybe an asshole for a father and husband, but that doesn't mean he's a killer."

Gonzales hung up the phone. "They lost him."

"What?" Doty's temple pulse quickened.

"They can't find Childress. They got separated after the press conference, figured they'd hook up back at his place. Pike's gone after him." Gonzales was disgusted.

"Damn it to hell. But why? He kidnapped his own kid? That's crazy." Doty headed for the door. "Gonzales, keep a watch on the guy's apartment, he still might show up. It's not like we know where else to go." She slammed through the door.

Combs dodged its rebound and followed. Gonzales hurried to catch up.

"I'm still not convinced. Childress wasn't anywhere near this place. Ex-husband goes after the wife to get custody of the kid. Why would he hurt the kid?" Her phone rang. "Talk to me." She listened, and then told the men, "They found two guns in Childress's car. One's a Remington Rand Model 1911A1, a .45 semi-automatic, shoots the same caliber that killed the dog park victim and your mom. What do you want to bet the other gun will match the wounds of the vic from Star Mall."

"Sloppy as hell, but that confirms it's him." Their breath fogged the air. Doty stopped and turned on Combs's next words. "April pointed him out with her dying breath. And I bet Steven's not his kid."

"Our witness never said…" Doty's brow furrowed. "What d'ya mean, not his kid?"

"My God, you're right." Gonzales slapped his forehead. "April didn't mean the dog. She wasn't talking about dogs at all."

Doty looked perplexed. Gonzales and Combs spoke at the same time, mimicking Doty's flat Midwestern accent. "April said it was *Doug's fault*."

Chapter 47

The stairwell door squeaked and thunked closed behind September. "Who are you talking to?"

She whirled and then hiccupped a relieved exhalation. "You scared the pee out of me." She wiped sudden wet from her brow with a shaky hand. Her nerves were fried. "Did Teddy already call? It's too soon." He'd spoil everything.

Officer Leonard Pike peered past her into the kitchen proper, and scanned right and left. "Been waiting for you. Where's Teddy?"

She stiffened. Nobody but Teddy knew she'd come home. Her breath quickened.

Pike examined the room. "I heard somebody else."

"You did." September spoke loudly in the small room. For once, please let Fish keep his big mouth shut. "The radio, it's a call-in show. Trying to steady my nerves, you know? But never mind, I'll turn it off." She chattered on the way to the countertop, and pretended to mess with the radio. "There, it's off, Officer Pike. No more noisy interruptions, we won't hear a peep out of the radio from this point on." That should be clear enough to Fish to go silent, just as they'd planned.

He limped further into the room. "I parked in the garage, but it's too cold to wait out there so I came inside." He smiled. "I told you the locks sucked."

"You can't be here, Officer. If they see the police, they said they'll kill Steven." She hesitated, her stomach an angry fist.

He rubbed his nose with a gloved hand. "Safer to let the police take it from here. You'll just get yourself killed, too." He limped toward her, his hand outstretched. "Give me the flash drive."

She backed toward the breakfast nook, avoiding his reach. Pike wasn't a detective. He was a beat cop, partnered with Combs. "Did Combs send you?" They could guess about a ransom. How did he know about the flash drive?

"Combs? He's clueless. He still thinks you killed his mom."

"What the hell are you talking about?" She sidled closer to the hidden phone, needing Fish's audience to hear anything that transpired.

"The babysitter. That was Comb's mom. But I can fix that, fix everything. You're in over your head." He took a step toward her. "When Dorfman, the kid from the mall, told me about Theodore Williams being a regular coffee customer, I figured you two hooked up, so I stayed mum and didn't tell nobody else. Nobody else needed to know if you'd just stayed put. I could have come to you, collected the merchandise, no muss, no fuss." He sighed. "That would have saved everyone lots of heartache."

She couldn't breathe. Wilma was Combs's mother, and his partner Pike worked with Lizzie. She'd been out-flanked again. She eyeballed the kitchen table where Gerald's gun sat next to the bitch mug in plain view.

"I'm all you got." He tilted his head sideways, his tone persuasive. "You've done enough, September. There's still time to get out clean. Give me the flash drive." He held out his hand again.

Shit. "But you're a cop."

He stopped any attempt at pretense. "Steven's safe. I delivered him to Lizzie myself." He sounded so sane, so normal. "I can save you, too. Just hand it over."

"You killed Freda at the Mall? Sonofabitch. How much did they pay? Murderer!" She screamed and picked up a ten-inch wooden pepper grinder, knowing Teddy would hear and call the cops as they'd planned. But it would take time for them to get here. September lobbed it at him. God, she was stupid, dumb to think Lizzie didn't have someone on the inside when so much money was at stake.

He easily dodged the grinder. "I didn't set out to hurt nobody. Didn't take no money. Didn't even shoot the damn dog when it bit me." He held out both palms to her—cards on the table. "I'm a good guy, never did nothing sideways before. But I got a grandson. He's like Steven, autistic, ya know? This is for him, for his future. Okay?" He advanced on her. "Amateurs get involved and it all turns to shit, and I won't risk my grandson. You've got thirty seconds to hand over the flash drive and get the hell out of here. I got no way to protect you once Lizzie's crew shows up."

September was incredulous. "You turned your grandson over to those killers? You trust them to keep him safe? Do you even know what's on the flash drive?" She hefted the matching salt cellar, and threw it at him. "Steven's my responsibility. I won't turn my back on him again. Do you think they'll even let you out of here alive?"

He stopped short. Pike hadn't considered that notion. "I can take care of myself."

She fumbled open a cupboard, grabbed a crockery teapot and brandished it. "You sent those psychos after me, after my sister—after Steven." She hurled it at him.

He batted it away. It crashed on the floor. "Dammit! I didn't send nobody after you! I just protected Steven and got him back where he belonged, with his mom. Nobody was supposed to die. It's about saving lives." His face turned red. "We couldn't afford the treatment. But your precious putz of a sister opened the door when she killed Pottinger."

The words slammed the air. "That's not true." She took a half step toward the table. He hadn't pulled out his own gun. Yet.

"Don't make this any harder than it already is, September. Don't make me hurt you. Give me the damn flash drive." He lunged.

She dashed to the table. Snatched up the gun. Fumbled the grip when her numb fingers wouldn't work.

Pike pounded after her. His wet shoes slid on the slate floor. But he reached her in four strides, gripping her hand and twisting her wrist.

September screamed. He wrenched her arm behind her back. The gun fell. Her cry rose to a shriek.

She ground her boot into his instep. He snarled, and loosened his grasp.

Once she started, September couldn't stop the screams that burned her throat raw until she gasped for breath. She twisted, shimmied, and left Pike with the empty sleeves of her coat, and stumbled away.

He parachuted the coat at her.

It smothered her head in a damp snare. Stumbling, she fell against a chair and blindly shoved it toward where he'd been.

"Oof." He grunted and fell.

She whipped the coat away from her face. It settled across the stained glass table.

His hand caught her ankle.

September yelled, kicked, kicked again, but was pulled on top of him. She rolled off. Pike came up with the pistol.

She scrabbled for something, anything, to pelt him. One hand found the plush toy in the coat's pocket. She cocked and threw. Wished Mickey was a brick when it hit Pike on one ear, and rebounded harmlessly onto the table.

He didn't pause. Struggling to rise, he lost his balance—one leg was injured, from the dog bite perhaps—he limped forward and pointed the gun at her.

September clambered to her feet. She threw the muffin saucer and dumped another chair in Pike's path. Sobbing, she hop-scotched to the door, thankful she'd left it unlocked. She had to get away, stay out of reach, and keep the flash drive until Lizzie arrived so she could trade it for Steven. She was his only hope.

To catch Pike wasn't enough. She needed Lizzie's broadcast to the world. Needed that for April, for Pam, for Teddy's friend Freda. And for Steven. And for herself, by damn. She'd lost too much to let those bastards get away with murder. Pike wouldn't risk shooting her as long as he believed she had the flash drive. September spun the last chair at him, and dashed to escape.

The door swung open. She skidded to a stop.

"Hello. How nice to see you again." Gerald smiled, and seized her throat.

Chapter 48

Combs banged the dashboard with frustration. Ice covered the front and back windows, and his defroster didn't work for shit. He drove hunched over blinking through the dinner-plate-size hole scraped with a credit card, and prayed nobody else was stupid enough to be on the roads.

Gonzales had headed to Childress's apartment, while Doty drove downtown to chew techie ass and update brass. He suspected his name would be conspicuously absent from her report. He finally could visit with his kids. Cassie would be pleased. He'd rather do nearly anything but tell them how their Grandma died.

He jumped when the phone rang, not recognizing the number, and answered cautiously. "Officer Combs." Combs pulled the phone away at the sound of ear-piercing barks. "Hello? I can't hear you. Is this a joke?"

"Hello, hello, hello, please help us please. Hello? Is anyone there?" He turned away from the receiver. "My God, shut up. I can't hear anything." He sobbed.

"Calm down, who is this?" The yelps and howls spelled the canine version of frantic. "Who are you? How'd you get this number?"

"I'm Teddy Williams. September told me to call. The nine-one-one people won't answer." Teddy wailed.

"Sonofa—Okay, quiet. Take a breath, Teddy. Where are you?"

"I don't remember the address. They're going to kill her, and I didn't get the damn address!" He blubbered. The dog howled. "Shadow, shut up!"

That was the dog's name, Steven's service dog. This must be the stranger from the mall. "Calm down, sir. Where are you right now?"

"In the car. A brown Jeep, she said it belonged to Pam." He stopped as whines sounded. "Guess you can hear, she left me with the dog." He paused. "Oh, God. Oh, God. Somebody else just passed on the road, they pulled into the drive. It's the killers, I know it is, oh, God, oh God . . ." The dog continued to yodel.

"Teddy, listen to me. Stay with me." Combs stopped his car in the middle of the road, and punched on the hazard lights. "Who just came? Can you see them? Describe the car—do they see you?"

The old man's voice was hard to hear over the crazed dog's yelps. "They drove right past me up to the house. I can't see their car anymore. But it didn't show up at the other end, so it must be at her house with Pike."

Combs sat up straighter. "Pike? Officer Pike, the policeman? You saw him?"

"No. I heard him. On the radio." Teddy cleared his throat. "September set up a phone line to a radio show. I can hear her over the car radio. That's why the dog's going nuts. She's screaming at somebody named Pike. He was waiting for her when she got home."

"Wait a minute. She's at her own house?"

"Yes." Teddy wailed again. "I'm sorry I don't know the address."

Combs stomped the accelerator. He left the hazard lights on.

Chapter 49

Shadow howled frantic harmony to September's cries. He didn't know how he could hear her in the car. She wasn't here. And she couldn't hear him, though he barked loud and long.

His fur stood at furious attention. He showed his teeth, snapped and snarled, eager to defend. She was his person. A good-dog protected his people. He had to find her. Shadow keened and paw-punched the cage.

"Stop it." In the front seat Teddy clapped his hands over his ears. "Shut up. Be a good-dog."

A good-dog obeyed people. Shadow paused and flattened his ears. He licked the wire of the crate and whimpered. September screamed, and Shadow threw himself against the wire again. The latch jiggled. So he did it again. And again.

"Quiet, no, no, no, no. Bad dog."

Shadow ignored Teddy's growls. He didn't care. He'd be a bad-dog on purpose. How could he ignore September's screams?

"Shadow, please stop. You'll hurt yourself." Teddy turned around in the seat and his brow wrinkled. His eyes rained wet.

Shadow paused. He whined. Maybe Teddy did understand. His tail wagged the hopeful question, and he tap-danced in place. He willed Teddy to understand.

"I called the police. They're on the way." The old man made no move to open the door. He just sat there, and ducked his head each time September screamed. "We just got to wait."

Yelping in frustration, Shadow bit the wire mesh of the door, growled, and snarled. Tugged—like with Bear-toy. His gums split on the sharp wire. Salt-copper tang raised his arousal. His tail churned the air and battered the cage, a drumbeat counterpoint to the tug-contest.

The old man's scent chemicals choked the stale air, and cried "uncle" louder than puppy pee. Teddy had given up.

Shadow grabbed the wire and shook it. Bloody drool spattered the floor of the crate.

Teddy covered his ears. He surged forward, fiddled with something, and September was silenced.

Shadow cocked his head. He licked his lips, shuddered at the copper taste, and stared at Teddy. Shadow woofed, yawned and whined, the most persuasive tone he could. He pawed the door. Two claws had torn loose, and added to the blood on the floor. He couldn't make it any clearer. He needed out.

The old man waggled his head.

That meant no. Shadow furrowed his brow, cocked his head. But he was right. He knew it. To protect Steven, he'd learned to think for himself, to make right choices, no matter what. It was a good-dog's job to know when to disobey. That time was *now*.

Shadow laced back his ears, lowered his head. He hurled himself against the front of the crate. Backed up and did it again. He'd force the door open. Get out. Go to September. Because he belonged with her. Because they belonged together. Because he *must*.

His body battered the cage like a furry mallet, and jiggled the clasp open increments at a time. The fastener worked like his kennel at home. He'd get out. He didn't need Teddy. Shadow wasted no further breath on howls.

"Please stop. I can't let you out. Be a good-dog, shush, just calm down."

Shadow knew the man was staring at him, but didn't pause. Each grunted impact moved the hasp closer to opening.

Teddy swiveled, flung open the door, and lurched out of the car.

Shadow redoubled his efforts. He pawed the hasp. It moved in his favor. Another claw caught, and he yanked it free with a yelp. But the latch almost opened. He uttered frustrated whines, and he switched paws to continue the onslaught.

Teddy rushed to the back of the car and opened the tailgate. "Damn dog." He reached to secure the fastener. "Hell, it's nearly open."

Shadow roared.

The old man flinched and yelled, "Back off!"

Teddy's sudden command stopped Shadow dead. He watched, suspicious but hopeful. The man stared at him.

"You convinced me, dog. It's your choice. And your grave." His voice caught. "So okay, you crazy sonofabitch, you want out?" He reached for the crate door.

Out, yes! Shadow didn't wait for Teddy. A final body-slam rocketed open the latch. The metal grate whipped into the man's glasses and sliced open his cheek. Teddy toppled backwards into the snow.

Shadow vaulted from the car, and cleared the sprawled figure with one joyous leap. He found September's scent, and hop-scotched and bulldozed through snow so deep it scraped his belly. But the bloody paw prints left in his wake spelled a message of fear, hope, and determination only good-dogs could read.

Chapter 50

September clawed the gloved hand at her throat. She stared into Gerald's pale visage—nobody home—and staggered backwards into the laundry room. Squeaky shoes on snow announced Lizzie before she was framed by the open door.

"Did you miss me?" Gerald squeezed harder.

"Careful, Gerald." Lizzie caught his arm. "She has the flash drive."

Dark sparkles floated before September's eyes. She struggled to draw breath, but no air moved in or out. She forced herself to go limp before she passed out. And when Gerald juggled to balance her sudden shift in weight, she stabbed her clenched knuckles into his windpipe.

He gagged, thrust her away and clutched the injury.

"Gerald. Honey-pie, are you okay?" Lizzie bustled into the room.

September wheezed. She fell hard against the clothes dryer, and her palm slammed against the "start" button. The stink of scorched fabric sparked a smile-worthy idea. She swallowed, and then swallowed again to soothe the ache. Her mouth was West Texas in August, drier than stubbled field corn. "Where's Steven?" She barely croaked the question.

"Locked in the car with his father." Lizzie turned as Pike limped into view. "Good job delivering Childress. Did he give you any trouble?"

Pike shook his head. "He just wanted to see his son, was grateful for my help." Pike glowered at September. "Not like some people." He adjusted his glasses. "Don't worry, Childress won't wake up for a while. That headlock restraint puts 'em lullaby every time."

Lizzie straightened, and she nodded at September. "Bring her back inside." She shivered elaborately. "And shut the door, Gerald, you're letting out the heat."

Gerald bared his teeth, but the smile didn't reach his faded eyes. "I will enjoy this." He swung the door shut but didn't notice that it caught in the jamb and didn't latch. "Show time, my dear." He gripped her arm.

Her stomach was knotted with butterflies. She was outnumbered, but her plan was still in play. Show time, indeed.

Gerald shoved her, and she crashed into the kitchen table, skinning her palms on the mosaic glass surface. He stood sentry behind her so she couldn't retreat. Lizzie blocked the stairway, and Pike stood before the gate to her office. She was trapped.

"Where is it?" Lizzie leaned toward her, the table between them. She noticed Steven's pill bottles, and pocketed them with a smile. "Time's up. Where is it?" Her whispers were more threatening than shouted demands.

September looked toward the hidden phone and away. Lizzie's soft words might not be picked up by the phone. She had to get them to incriminate themselves, put it all out there for Fish's audience to hear. Lizzie would clam up if she suspected anyone could hear beyond this intimate group. "Your cop lapdog, Leonard Pike, mugged me around so much, I can't hear so well. Say again?" She spoke with exaggerated volume.

Pike scowled. "She's up to something." He aimed the pistol. "Only the kids matter. So give Lizzie the damn flash drive."

September took a breath, ready to play the game. Keep them off balance. Keep them guessing. "Show me Steven. Or there's no deal." It wouldn't work if she gave in too quickly. Besides, she had to give the police time to arrive.

Lizzie dimpled a smile at Gerald. "Perhaps your special persuasive skills will do the trick."

"As you wish." Murderous intent shined in his expression.

"Wait." Her voice jumped an octave. "I'll tell you." This was it, no more delay. "I hid it. There, in the canister." She pointed and was gratified when Lizzie strutted to the counter, well within range of the hidden cell phone. "I never would have believed Steven's therapist would sell him out. You're a bitch, Lizbeth Baumgarten, and your son Gerald is a damn killer." She let the vitriol pour forth, unedited. "And you, Officer Pike, selling out for some pie-in-the-sky dream-cure. Don't you dare justify it helps kids." Fish damn-well better hear.

Gerald strode forward and grabbed her hair. He heaved her into the table, and she landed across the cat's tattered toy and barely caught the #1-Bitch coffee mug before it crashed to the floor. September grabbed and hugged Mickey like a magical shield. They'd kill her now. But she'd named them for all the radio-world to hear. She smiled; satisfied that Steven and the other kids would be safe.

Lizzie's double chins jiggled with rage. "Help her up, Gerald. I taught you better manners." She dumped flour over the counter, and finger-sifted for the hidden flash drive.

September grasped one of the toppled chairs and pulled herself upright. She didn't want Gerald to touch her.

Pike looked with contempt at the remodeled kitchen. "You have any idea what a cop salary is? Don't judge me."

Lizzie looked up. "You can't put a price on a miracle, the chance for normalcy. A real life." Pride added inches to her height. "Gerald was the first. And now he's a doctor, spreads the cure to other children." Joy lit her face. "Rebirth Gathering will give hope to two hundred children and their parents."

The woman believed her own sales pitch. "Psycho kids aren't my idea of a miracle." September deliberately picked at Lizzie's weak spot. "If he was the first, you should have stopped while you were behind."

Gerald shrugged. "No reason to second-guess a miracle over a few bad reactions."

Pike was worse than the others, selling out his own honor and his grandson's health for empty promises. "Did they tell you about the risk of your grandson going psycho?"

Pike turned away. He crossed his arms and leaned against the refrigerator.

Lizzie glowered. "You don't understand, being childless and all." She returned to the counter, combed through the last of the white powder. The drive wasn't there. "Which canister, September?" She dumped the next and hand-stirred the sugar. Nothing. Lizzie picked up the cat treat jar and shattered it on the tile. She mixed the morsels with her foot.

September thought she heard a bark. Wishful thinking.

Pike stepped forward, but his injured leg wobbled. "Can't you see, she don't got it? She lied the whole time, just to get the boy back. Hell, it's what I'd do." He braced himself against the refrigerator, and held the gun steady.

Macy roused from his perch atop the appliance. The cat yawned and stretched. Sniffed, and gave a silent hiss at the smoke gathering high in the ceiling space.

"But even if she don't have the flash drive, she'll tell. And that will spoil everything for my grandson, Lenny. For all the other kids."

September saw the cat's focus as Macy stared down at Pike. His ears turned sideways, furry airplane wings of disapproval. The cat's coffee-strudel tail twitched.

The spark of an idea flared. "I understand about your grandson, Lenny, is it? Here, I've got it, you can have it. It's here." Her shaky left hand pulled out the lanyard chain from beneath her collar. "Don't shoot. Here, take it."

She held her other hand palm outward toward Pike, but the signal was meant for the cat perched above him.

He smiled with sadness, his voice gruff with what needed to be done. "That won't stop a bullet."

September's palm signal steadied and didn't waver. The cat's attention left Pike and followed the hand with intensity. She closed her outstretched hand into a deliberate fist around the drive.

Macy sat.

September hid her elation. She thanked heaven for all the foolish tricks she'd practiced with the cat. Maybe God answered prayers after all.

Green cat eyes monitored the lanyard's pendulum swing, tail twitched in a syncopated rhythm. Macy waited, forward pointed ears and whiskers eager with interest. Macy wanted the game to begin.

Chapter 51

Combs skidded through the intersection, and shouted into his phone. "They're broadcasting now. From September's house."

"How'd Fish manage that?" Doty laughed, but there was begrudging admiration in the sound. "That opportunistic jackass would sell his mother for a story."

Combs agreed. "September set it up. The secretary at the radio station said it's all via speaker phone." He approached an overpass and held his breath the tires wouldn't skid. "September got them to confess with radio listeners as witnesses. Including Pike."

"Save Pike for me." She and Gonzales were ten minutes behind him.

He didn't answer. He should have told someone else his suspicions. Pike doted on his grandson, it was the one soft spot he showed the world. Pike was a career cop, though, and you don't destroy a career over a suspicion, not like his own had been.

"Okay, Gonzales dialed up the radio show. We'll monitor the creeps as we go. Aw, shit." A thump and yelp from Doty followed.

Combs waited. "You okay? Hey Doty?"

"Sonofabitch. We're okay. But a mailbox is DOA." She snorted. "Can't see anything, and it's slicker than snot out here."

Combs removed his foot from the gas and waited until the tires regained purchase. He could hear the radio broadcast over Doty's phone, and dialed his own down to avoid the echo. "Fish is keeping his mic muted so they don't hear him over September's phone." The self-imposed muzzle must kill him.

"Ought to run Fish in for obstruction. The little shit should have called us, not waited until Teddy-come-lately decided to clue us in." By the garbled sound of things, she was up to four or five sticks of gum. "Gonzales has the old guy on the line trying to keep him calm 'til we arrive. Teddy's dictating a visual for us, but there's not much to see." She paused. "He's bent out of shape over the dog running away. What do I care about a stupid hound when we've got murdering scumbags to corral?"

Combs pressed the gas. This straight stretch of road, devoid of traffic or sudden curves, begged for speed. So did the situation. "We need backup. Pike is a crack shot." His teeth ached, and he forced himself to relax his jaw. "No sirens, Doty. They don't expect us, and our best chance is surprise." Besides, he wanted first crack at whichever asshole murdered Mom.

"We're pedaling fast as we can." Doty's tone, accompanied by more gum-popping, revealed her own frustration. Combs could hear a man in the background before she spoke again. "Gonzales is asking about the kid. Any word? Here, Gonzales, you take the phone."

Combs's grip tightened on the steering wheel. He couldn't help but think of his own kids. "Steven's onsite. Supposed to be locked in a car in the garage, with Childress."

"Hey Combs." The detective sounded as frazzled as Combs. "The garage is on the backside of the house, right? That's where they got Steven?"

Combs nodded, before realizing the man couldn't see him. "You saw the same thing I did. Old carriage house, big double door that opens out. We can't go in that way. Childress is with his kid. He's a part of this. He'd alert the goons in the house."

"There's a workshop door on the far side. Doty agrees we should target that entry."

She took back the phone. "Combs, you're what, about five or ten minutes head of us? Find this Teddy character, and wait." She paused, and must have removed her gum because the next words came direct and clear. "Wait for us. Do not—I repeat, do not go alone. We'll stage from Teddy's car and coordinate backup from there."

"Uh, say again? You're breaking up." Combs disconnected before Doty could argue. He wouldn't wait. There'd already been too much wheel-spinning. They owed him first crack. For Mom. Besides, Doty made it clear he wasn't on their team. With his career already down the toilet, he had nothing to lose. More than that, September and Steven were out of time.

He turned up the radio in time to hear September's contemptuous tone. "If Gerald was the first, you should have stopped while you were behind."

Combs sucked in his breath. "Don't do it, girl. Don't bait them." She wanted them on the record and so did he. But September was dancing a fine line. Just because she'd set up the sting with Fish didn't mean help would arrive in time.

"Toss it." The man's command lacked inflection. Must be one of the shooters.

"Tell me first. What does it hurt? Soon as I give you the computer drive, you've won. And Steven loses." September's voice caught on the child's name. "Your investment stands to make millions. And I'm dead. So humor me. Just who the hell are you people?"

September had courage, he'd give her that. "Hold on, I'm almost there." Combs growled at the radio, willing her to survive.

Chapter 52

September's hand remained steady as Macy's attention fixed on her closed fist. The cat's pupils dilated with sudden arousal. Pike stood in front of the cat's refrigerator perch, in perfect position. Then he moved. Damn.

"He said toss it." Lizzie's attention locked onto the lanyard. She made an imperative give-it-to-me gesture.

September stood in the center of a triangle with Gerald, Lizzie and Pike positioned at each point. As soon as the flash drive left her possession, she'd be killed. But she hadn't any choice. Fish had better be recording everything. It'd suck if she got killed and didn't nail the bastards. No. It'd suck no matter what. She held her breath, and tossed the flash drive to Lizzie.

Lizzie snatched it from the air. "It's a shame September kidnapped Steven, and Childress butchered all those innocent people." She pocketed the flash drive. "Not our fault she wouldn't give up Steven without a fight, and just lucky that Officer Pike was able to save the little boy. Too bad the dad died in the battle."

September gasped. "Doug's dead?"

"No. Childress is fine, just unconscious in the car with Steven." Pike raised his eyebrows.

Lizzie stared at him. "Work with me here. You said you'd do anything for your grandson."

"Childress doesn't have a clue. He just went through hell to get his kid back." Pike's sympathy was clearly with the father.

"Give me the gun. I'll do it." Gerald sniffed. "You smell something?"

September stifled a smile.

"Burning. That's smoke." Gerald returned to his point of the triangle near the laundry doorway.

Pike coughed. "It's the damn dryer again. Shut it off."

Gerald glared at the smoke that thickened near the ceiling. "Leave it alone." He turned to Lizzie. "Let's burn the place. September dies in the fire trying to save Steven from his father. Pike gets the boy out just in time. That'll take care of any unanswered questions and destroy any evidence to the contrary. These old houses are such fire traps." He turned to Lizzie. "Don't you just love it when a plan comes together?"

A cold gust shivered September's skin. The unlatched door had blown open. All heads swiveled at the same moment.

Shadow stood in the doorway. His hackles bristled from fang to staccato tail.

Pike pivoted and shot.

The tip of Shadow's left ear exploded. He shrieked. He shook his head and crimson flowers bloomed against the wall. But he stood his ground.

"Shadow. Look at me." He blinked through the pain and met September's gaze. It was enough.

September hurled the Mickey toy at Pike's head.

He caught the toy with one hand.

Shadow followed the arc of the toy. Her voice a whip-crack, September shouted, "Shadow, get Bear."

The dog sprang. His 80-pound weight slammed Pike square in the chest.

The cop's gun spat. Shadow howled.

Pike's head hit the wall and the floor in a hollow ripe-melon double thud. The pistol spun away. The stuffed toy skidded.

Officer Pike didn't get up. Neither did Shadow.

September scrambled to reach her dog.

"Get her, stop her!" Lizzie's command was a verbal slap.

Gerald's hand wrenched her shoulder, his other hand aimed Pike's recovered gun. He twirled her like a dance partner. And September let him.

She whirled to increase the velocity of her spin. Her outside hand played crack-the-whip with the hefty #1-Bitch coffee mug. The crockery hammered Gerald's temple. He dropped like an egg from a tall chicken.

September's knees gave way. She caught herself against the table, and stepped around Gerald's body to reach Shadow.

Shadow lay atop the unconscious Pike. He stared up at her, woofed and wagged his tail. "Good-dog, Shadow." She felt dizzy with relief. Despite his bloody ear, the dog seemed without further injury. Shadow sniffed the man. Satisfied, he directed a solemn stare at Lizzie.

September marveled at the pup's composure. That mangled ear must hurt like a bastard. Her own body throbbed in places she didn't know could hurt.

"You killed my boy, you bitch, oh my poor Gerald." Lizzie reached toward her fallen son, but Shadow blocked her way. The woman shuffled side to side, looking for escape.

"It's over." September choked on thickening smoke. She noticed Pike's fallen gun and lunged for it in the same moment Lizzie dove for it.

The older woman won the race and came up with the handgun. September rolled, and backed away. "You won't stop the miracle." She turned, aiming the gun at September's forehead.

September realized Lizzie was in the perfect position. "Macy, kill it!"

The eighteen-pound Maine Coon sprang from the refrigerator onto Lizzie, and hugged her head.

Lizzie screamed, and dropped the pistol.

Pike gathered himself, levering himself to his feet. He staggered to regain balance.

Lizzie yanked double fists of cat hair.

Macy yowled and the play attack became real. Cat claws thumbtacked Lizzie's face. Rear feet dug bloody furrows through fabric into flesh. Teeth sank deep and met in the middle and the woman's screams ratcheted to window-shattering proportions.

September scrambled and retrieved the dropped gun. "You're on the air, being broadcast to the world. You're through. The police are on the way."

Panic filling his face, Pike loped from the kitchen and pounded to the front exit.

She had to let him go. He was no danger to Steven. September heard Pike struggling with the multiple locks and flinging the door open.

Lizzie wrenched Macy off and hurled the cat across the room.

The cat's brain shifted into panic mode, and Macy pin-balled around the kitchen for a way out. He careened into Shadow, hissed and slapped a paw, and the dog flinched backwards with a confused expression. With a mighty leap, Macy levitated onto the counter, clawed open a cupboard door and disappeared inside.

Screams whooped from Lizzie as blood guttered from her cheeks.

Shadow tucked his tail. He slunk as far from the crazed Lizzie as he could get. September didn't blame him. Her own ears hurt. The dog's sensitive ears must be aching.

September crouched on the floor on the opposite side of the kitchen. She trained Pike's gun on the woman, surprised her hands didn't shake, and waited for Lizzie to shut up. Waited for Fish to send the cavalry. Waited to believe she was still alive.

The screams trailed off to intermittent gasps. Lizzie flushed tomato bright, and she braced against the counter directly in front of the hidden cell phone.

"Fish, are you getting all this?" September cocked her head. More shouts, this time from the front of the house, and sounds of a brawl. She grinned when Pike stumbled back into view, hands behind his back, escorted by Combs.

A gunshot stopped Lizzie's sobs. The woman gripped her arm. Wet soaked through the fabric.

September stared at her gun, confused. Had she pulled the trigger and didn't know it? Her eyes met Combs's, but he looked equally puzzled. A cold wind blew snow into the room. They'd never shut the door. She pushed to her knees, swiveling to see.

Gerald was gone. A car revved in the sudden silence, and the engine's grumble faded into the distance.

None of that mattered when September saw the revolver. Shiny. Kid-size. Pointed at Lizzie.

"Loud. No loud. Loud hurts Steven's ears." He fired again.

Chapter 53

Shadow whined and pressed against the wall. The gunshots hurt a good-dog's ears. So did the woman's screams. The men at the kitchen doorway yelled, adding to the confusion, even though the boy-thief from the Mall had his wrists bound. So much noise it made his fur stand up and his teeth ache to bite.

But Steven was here. He focused on his boy. They could be together again. It was a good-dog's job to take care of his boy. He should be happy.

But Steven wasn't happy. Steven was—what? Steven wasn't Steven. How could that be?

He tuned out the woman's screams. Ignored the men's yells. Tried to center himself. Shadow watched. Sniffed. The air prickled his fur. Beneath the smoke-filled air, his boy smelled different. Moved different. Not like his boy at all. And he had the gun. Like before.

His torn ear throbbed, a hot and hurty reminder of what guns could do. His muzzle burned from the angry cat's claws. Broken toenails screamed with each step. He should go to his boy. But that boy wasn't Steven, wasn't his boy at all. Shadow whined and pressed harder against the wall.

Shadow looked to September for direction. She called him good-dog. That made up for the hurts. But he was confused, uncertain. Tired.

"Steven. Drop the gun, honey."

September wasn't scared. She sounded in charge. He liked that. Human pups like Steven would, too.

Shadow paced a hopeful step closer to September, her confidence adding to his own. He watched Steven. He jumped and yelped when his boy made the gun pop again.

The gun reached out somehow, the way guns do, and bit the bloody-faced woman in the tummy. Her mouth opened in a silent disappointed "oh" shape as if somebody had stolen her favorite toy. She fell against the counter and slowly slid to the floor. She screamed again. "Steven, please, Steven. No."

"No-no-no, no-no-no." Steven parroted the words. His boy still pointed the gun at the lady.

Shadow yelped. A question—what do I do? His hackles bristled. He barked a high-pitched warning at his boy. But he kept his ears and tail low, respectful. He didn't want that gun to bite him again.

"Shadow, shush." September was quiet but forceful. "Combs, get Pike the hell out of here. Everyone, be quiet."

Shadow stood, his tail waving fiercely, as the two men backed away from the doorway.

"He shot me. I can't believe he shot me."

"I should let him shoot you again, Lizzie." September stood, held out her hand, palm down toward the boy. "Steven, drop the gun. And we'll make everything quiet, okay?"

But Lizzie kept yelling. "Shot me! How could he shoot me? After all I did for him and his bitch mother, how could he shoot me?"

Shadow wanted to bark back, but September's finger-to-lips signal stopped him. Instead, his front paws tap-danced his frustrated indecision. He felt lost. Should he go to Steven? Run to September? Flee out the door? The bristled hackles caused an itch that could only be scratched with action. But good-dogs follow the rules.

"No-no-no-no." Steven's free hand covered one ear, the other still pointed the gun. He flushed, and a sudden, sun-bright rage burned the fog from his expression. "Stop the bitch-noise stop the dammit hurty noise Steven says stop-stop-stop-STOP!" He ranted, the words repeated over and over again.

Shadow stood tall, his tail high. He moved toward Steven, woofed under his breath, and backed up and repeated the action. He stared at September. Steven's tantrums weren't new. But this wasn't a tantrum. He waited for September's signal for what to do.

September gulped. Even the shot woman fell silent at Steven's rant. The boy sidled forward and pointed the gun at the woman's bloody forehead.

September's eyes cast about the room. Shadow woofed again—pleading 'look at me.' When she did, he wagged and willed her to understand. He was ready.

And then she was ready, too. He saw her chest expand with a subtle breath. His head cocked, intrigued, when she scooped up the toy at her feet. He was ready for whatever she asked.

"Shadow, this is Bear." September held up the toy.

He stared at her, focused, ready.

September held out her other hand. "And this is gun. Show me gun." She pointed at Steven's revolver with the final command, and held her breath.

Shadow's ears came forward. He launched himself. His nose-punch spun Steven's gun across the room. And then, because it just seemed the right thing to do, Shadow pinned his boy to the floor and dodged screams and flailed limbs until within seconds, Steven calmed down.

"Good-dog, Shadow." September hurried to the tangled pair and knelt beside them. "What a smart dog, good boy." She reached to touch Steven, hesitated, and stroked Shadow's brow instead. "Good boy, such a good boy."

Shadow thumped his tail, licked her hand. She tasted of tears and pain, blood and joy. Nothing else mattered, not his ball, not his bear, not even his boy. Nothing mattered, only this. Approval in her voice. Her touch. Her scent.

Sudden sunlight spilled through the bars of the stained glass windows and bathed the room in a warm peacock glow. The storm had ended.

Shadow's hurts didn't matter, not anymore. Home wasn't a place. Home was a person. And Shadow was home.

Chapter 54

Claire O'Dell awoke with a start. It took a moment to realize where they were, but the bus had long since stopped moving. She sat up, swinging her legs off the side of the bed, and checked Tracy on the other side of the mattress where she'd nested in the purple comforter.

Yawning, Claire consulted her watch, and started. She had to hurry. Orientation began in less than ten minutes.

They'd arrived at the Legacy Center a little after 10:30 that morning, only an hour and a half late for the official check in time. The complex looked more like a refurbished motel than a medical facility, but was clean and felt luxurious after so many hours bumping on the drafty bus. She'd lain down beside Tracy for only a moment to settle her, and drifted off.

Quickly she stood, donned the lanyard with her registration number and name tag, and jostled the bed to rouse her daughter. "It's time, sweetie. Let's go see the other kids, okay? Grooby is awake and ready to go. Shall I take Grooby and you'll come later?" Claire held out the green and purple stuffed toy just out of reach. Tracy rubbed her eyes and strained to grab the now-shapeless dinosaur. "Ready to go? Need the potty?" Claire smiled when Tracy rolled out of bed, snatching the toy to her chest and ignoring the potty offer as she followed Claire to the door. Claire grabbed the folder with her daughter's medical records and clutched it to her chest.

Several other parents and children filled the hall, all moving in the same direction. The adults offered tight-lipped nods of acknowledgement, identical hopeful expressions stamped on their faces even as often beautiful youngsters registered very little. Each kept a respectful distance from one another and spoke in whispers, if at all; cognizant their children were in a strange, and therefore stressful, environment.

The tide swelled as it spilled into the lobby area, and began to flow into an adjacent meeting space that held classroom-style seating. Claire urged Tracy to a nearby spot where the little girl began play with one of the pens, rolling it back and forth, back and forth. Two enormous screens hung at the front of the room, with a slide of the Rebirth Gathering logo centered on each display.

Claire saw Elaine enter with Dwayne and Lenny. She waved and stood to catch their attention, not wanting to cry out and break the taut atmosphere. Her heart thumped as they hurried to join her at the table. She and Elaine silently embraced, and Dwayne wiped his eyes and grinned. She guessed every parent in the room felt the same excited anticipation.

The lights flickered, and the soft murmurs fell silent as everyone took their seats when the room grew dark. Her stomach flip-flopped, and Claire saw Dwayne hug his wife with excitement. She wished Mike could be here, holding her hand and sharing this special time as a family. Tracy rolled the pen back and forth, finally picked it up and began drawing circles within circles within circles, cloning the window art from the bus. Claire wondered if Tracy's fascination with circles would stay with her, after the successful treatment.

An hour later, Claire felt dazed but happy. She watched the clinic personnel escort Tracy and Lenny along with four other children out of the meeting area to a nearby examination room. The treatment sounded so simple: twice daily medication for six weeks, dosed specifically to each child's age, weight and metabolism, monitored by home-care visits every two weeks to adjust the dosage based on individual improvement. Claire eagerly signed the authorization for the off-label protocol, and handed over Tracy's medical records to the nurse. Not a single parent balked at the opportunity.

Claire had counted 178 children in the room. She figured the storm had prevented some of the 200 from keeping their appointment. Her heart ached for the absent parents and their missed opportunity.

The children were processed in shifts by last name. Tracy and Lenny had to wait until they reached "O" and "P" to be examined and cleared for the treatment by staff physicians. Claire felt comforted that the doctors were so careful.

"So far, none of the children have been turned away." Elaine spoke aloud what the other parents also worried about. Claire wouldn't be able to breathe, either, until Tracy returned and had received her first dose.

The treated children were returned to their parents in the large meeting hall, and served a light meal. The orientation explained that the medication should be taken with food to prevent upset tummies.

"Mac and cheese. Tracy loves that, thank goodness. Does Lenny like it?"

"It looks like they've got two or three options." Elaine pointed to a distant table where the children were offered hot dogs or chicken nuggets. "Lenny likes chicken, so we're okay." She hesitated. "Did they mention the side effects? I mean, just so we could watch for them, just in case?" The presentation emphasized the importance of sticking to a strict regimen, and that side effects could occur if doses were missed or given too close together.

"No. I didn't hear any details about side effects." She wouldn't have cared if the consequence was growing a tail, though. Side effects would never touch Tracy. Once she got on the medicine, Claire was determined to follow the directions to the letter, and give her child the best chance for success.

"Randolph, Ronald, Rudd, Rudd, please proceed to the exam room. After them, please have Salk, Salk, Schultz, Simmons and Sultani take your turn. We will take the Ts in three groups of three each, and then the Ws. Thanks for your patience."

The PA system announced the children's names as Tracy, Lenny and the other two kids were escorted back into the room. Tracy clutched Grooby, and it was all Claire could do to keep from hugging her daughter. Instead, she urged her back to the nearby table, requested the mac and cheese, and watched with a happy smile as Tracy ate. She knew not to expect any change for two or three days—the reason for staying at Legacy Center for that period—but couldn't help thinking that Tracy already seemed calmer and more focused. Claire couldn't wait to call Mike. Once again, she wished he was here. Lenny eagerly munched chicken nuggets while Pastor Dwayne hugged Elaine as she sobbed happy tears.

The lights in the room flickered, and general conversation died when the screens at the front of the room lit up once again. Claire frowned. Why would the presentation begin before all the children received their first treatment and were back in the room?

"What's going on?" Elaine voiced her concern as murmurs from other parents grew louder. "That's not part of the presentation. That's some sort of broadcast with Skype."

A broadcast of not particularly good quality flickered on the twin screens, and a pale face pulled back from a laptop video-cam. One of the assistants herding children in and out of the examination room stuck his head out the door, glanced at the screen and his mouth dropped open. "That's Dr. Baumgarten. What's going on?" He rushed to the side of the room and checked the AV connections, tapped keys on a keyboard, and suddenly the figure on the screen could be heard.

" . . .unexpected events beyond our control, this session of the Rebirth Gathering has been suspended."

"What?" Claire felt heat rush to her cheeks. "What's he talking about?" Her words joined the cries of denial from other parents. "We've already paid for the treatment. They can't take it away from us, not now!"

"Shush, be quiet. Let's hear what he's saying." Dwayne's pastoral voice boomed over the assembly, immediately silencing the discord.

Claire noticed the attendants had gathered in a knot, heads close together, urgent hushed discussion too quiet for any of the parents to hear.

"Again, my name is Dr. Gerald Baumgarten, and I developed the treatment that will give your children their rebirth. But as I speak, forces are at work to stop this miracle. Those who don't understand seek to stop me, and will go to any lengths—even fabricating lies about me—to discredit this medical marvel." He paused, his face an icy mask. "I know that it works because I myself suffered from autism the same as your children. The treatment gave me a rebirth, and it will for your children, too." He held up a vial of bright pills. "I have instructed the attendants to dispense the medication immediately. You must be responsible for dosing your children appropriately. I cannot caution you strongly enough to follow your dosage instructions."

Elaine covered her mouth with her hand, her eyes wide. She looked as shocked as Claire felt. Tracy continued to stir circles into her mac and cheese, oblivious to the growing tension.

Dr. Baumgarten continued. "My apologies that the full three-day Gathering and training isn't possible, but we—you—must work quickly if you want your children to receive their legacy and their right to a healthy future." He paused, and the parents in the room once more began to murmur. "I will not let you down. Never fear, I will find you, help your children to recover from their affliction. Have faith, they will be healed. And don't let anyone's lies persuade you to betray your child's future. I am their only hope—and I won't let them down! Tell the authorities nothing about me. Protecting me protects your chil—" The connection was broken.

Immediately the room erupted. Parents called to their children, attendants rushed out with trays laden with medication vials. The PA system spat to life. "In an orderly fashion, please line up according to alpha-list and wait for your name to be called. Stay calm. Your children's medication will be dispensed per Dr. Baumgarten's orders. You must show your identification number, to ensure each child receives the proper dosage."

Despite the called-for order, tempers flared, and shouts and shoves grew more frequent. "Stay with Lenny." Elaine barked the order to Dwayne, and moved to the line forming at the mouth of the exam room.

"Please watch Tracy, too." Claire rushed after her friend. The ten minutes they waited seemed like hours, but finally they each claimed a precious vial of pills—enough for six weeks—for Tracy and Lenny. The two women hurried back to Dwayne. Claire felt like she'd run a marathon.

Dwayne's face was gray. "What? Is Lenny okay?" Elaine immediately turned to her son, but the boy sat quietly having finished the last chicken nugget.

"It's Dad." Dwayne swallowed, and gestured with his cell phone. "I just got a call from the hospital."

"Oh, no. Was he shot?" Elaine held Lenny's pills in her fist like a talisman that could wipe out all horror. "I've always worried he'd end up shot. Is he okay?" She turned to Claire. "Dwayne's dad is a cop."

"He wasn't shot." Dwayne rubbed his eyes, and pulled out a chair and collapsed. "He was bitten by a dog."

"A dog?" Claire almost smiled at the outlandishness of the situation. It sounded like the punch line to some weird joke, but Dwayne wasn't laughing.

"He's in the hospital and under arrest. For kidnapping."

"What?!" Elaine gasped.

A police car, siren blaring, pulled up outside the Legacy Center. Claire carefully tucked Tracy's precious vial of pills into her bra. Parents all around her secreted their own vials and fell silent, arms crossed and lips tight. None would risk betraying their children's miracle.

Chapter 55

April opened her eyes, and licked her desert dry lips. She looked around the darkened room, taking in the plain walls and metal railings on the bed. In the dim light an IV drip beside the bed and beeping monitor offered the only motion in the room.

She tried to turn, and gasped as fire laced through her side. She'd been shot. This was a hospital. It hadn't been a dream. The nightmare was real.

"Steven? Steven!"

A figure roused from a nearby chair.

"Where's my son?" She grabbed the railings and tried to pull herself erect. But the stabbing throb of her injury sapped strength from her arms. "Please. Tell me about Steven, where's my boy?"

"Steven's in the hospital, too." Childress levered himself from the chair and stepped closer to the bed. "The doctors are taking care of him. Relax, April, you need to rest." His face was drawn and gray as the putty-colored walls. "You were in surgery for hours. I thought I'd lost you." His voice shook and then steadied, and he carefully clasped her hand as though it might break.

She fell back against the pillow and took several shallow breaths. It hurt, God it hurt. Were they at the Legacy Center? Lizzie's state-of-the-art medical team was the best, but how had she gotten here? "Where is Steven? I want to see him."

"April, you were shot and the ambulance brought you here, to Heartland General. Steven's here, too. He's in . . . in another ward, they had to sedate him. He's under observation."

"But he's okay? Steven's fine?"

Childress hesitated and then nodded. His hand tightened on April's.

As she relaxed on the bed she squeezed his hand back. "Good. Then he's safe." Her eyes fluttered. She felt so tired.

"He's going to need help, April. He's been through a lot. God, I love him so much." Childress's voice broke.

She levered her eyes open, surprised. "But Steven's cured, Doug. I found a miracle for him. You wouldn't listen to me, but I found a way to make it happen." She sighed. "I don't want to fight with you anymore. What's done is done."

He stared at her, lips tight, then nodded. "You're right, April. What's done is done. You rest now. When you feel better we'll talk about next steps." He smiled. "We'll get through this together, for Steven. Whatever he needs, April, we're a family."

"My son . . ." Her eyes drifted closed.

"OUR son." He squeezed her hand again, and to April it felt like she'd finally come home.

Chapter 56

Two Weeks Later, Thanksgiving Day

September poured coffee, added a slug of flavored cream, and pulled out a chair at the stained glass table. The new clothes dryer hummed in the next room with a load of clean towels. The door stayed closed with the laundry room window open, though. Two weeks' worth of odor neutralizers eliminated most of the stench, but she'd rather keep it confined to one room. September didn't mind. She considered it a badge of honor. The roasting turkey had already masked any lingering smell in the rest of the house.

Memories took longer to erase.

The scrabble tap-tap against the stained glass window brought her halfway to her feet. Coffee sloshed, hot on her thigh, and she yelped. The tap-tap came again—the Belinda's Rose danced in the 68-degree breeze. It sported three bright pink blossoms as if to celebrate the unseasonable Thanksgiving weather in proper style.

"Crap. Get a grip." September grabbed a towel and dabbed the stain as Macy stared from the top of the refrigerator. He yawned, shifted his weight, and burbled annoyance. He always had to have the last word. "Sorry I disturbed your nap, your highness." She jumped again when the wall phone rang.

September ignored the phone. The machine on her desk would pick up.

The first week after the Blizzard Murders the phone hadn't stopped ringing with demands from reporters. The second week, parents of autistic children took turns praising her heroism and cursing her for dooming their kids. The parents and their 178 children found at the Legacy Center, though, stayed strangely silent.

The doorbell made her stomach drop. Nobody was due to arrive for another hour. She had set the new dining table with five places. Side dishes remained to finish, and she'd fix whipped cream later for the warm gingerbread dessert. September checked out the wine bottles on the counter, debating the benefits of an early beverage. Instead, she sighed and hurried to answer the door.

Macy leaped to the floor and dashed ahead. The pet gate had come down after the contractors finished in record time. Everyone in town wanted an excuse to rubber-neck the house, inside and out.

September peeked through the glass, relieved it wasn't reporters, but still on guard. She sighed, unlocked the deadbolts and cracked the door. "What are you doing here?"

Combs stood on the lowest step. He shifted his weight and fiddled with a brown paper grocery bag. He looked more relaxed out of uniform in the gray windbreaker and jeans. "Wanted to check in." The lines on his forehead looked deeper, but September guessed she'd gained some crow's feet, too. He looked around. "Doty pulled off the surveillance?"

"Yeah. I asked." September blocked Macy with one foot, frowning with exasperation. "Come in before the cat gets out." She scooped Macy into her arms and draped him like a tawny mane around her shoulders. "Guess you don't have good news." She waited until he stepped inside, and then shot the bolts and jiggle-tested the door.

"No sign of Dr. Gerald Baumgarten. Alert's still up, but he could be out of the country by now. He transferred Legacy Center funds to an offshore account within an hour of his disappearance."

Lizzie's son had melted away with the blizzard. "He won't come after me. No percentage in it." September sighed, stroking the cat and relishing the purr that relaxed her shoulders better than a masseuse.

One eyebrow went up, questioning. "If you believed that, you wouldn't be peeking through windows before answering your door."

"Just because you're paranoid doesn't mean they aren't out to get you." She smiled to show she was joking. "But I am getting better about that." Hiding from the maybes and what-ifs just meant you'd be trapped when they found you. Better to keep watch and have your boots ready for the storm clouds.

Macy's tail stroked her mouth, and she spat out hair before gently moving him to the floor. He raced away up the entry stairs, and she heard the thunder of him clawing a favorite scratch post outside her bedroom door. Now that the pet gates were gone, she needed to add more cat trees to keep him happy throughout the house.

"The offer of a gun still stands." The paper bag crinkled in his rough hands.

She shuddered, and wondered if a gun was inside the package. "No thanks. I've had enough of guns to last me nine lives. And enough funerals." She walked back to the kitchen to retrieve her coffee cup, and he hesitated before he followed. She didn't offer him any, didn't think he'd accept it. Maybe he'd go away.

She'd be polite because Combs had been supportive, but his presence made her uncomfortable and wary. "I'm sorry I missed your mom's funeral." She was, but the words sounded stiff. Hell, she'd not been welcome at Pam's memorial service. Eugene tried to be cordial, but couldn't help blaming her for his wife's death. After all, she blamed herself.

"You would have been welcome. Aunt Ethel asked about you." His smile took ten years off his face. He looked sincere.

She was grateful for the kind gesture, and wanted to believe him. It was more than her family had offered. She'd tried to visit April in the hospital and been turned away.

"None of this was your fault. You've got to stop blaming yourself." He set the paper bag on the table, and cracked his knuckles. "I thought you'd want to know. Lizzie came out of the coma."

Tears pricked. "Thank you." She had no love lost for the woman, and cared not a whit if she'd ever see her again. She'd scrubbed the spot on the slate floor until she'd erased the blood reminder, but a death in her home would have left a stain she couldn't have lived with. She sat down and motioned him to a chair. "What about Pike? He'll stand trial with Lizzie?"

"Eventually. I think they'll want to try them together." Combs pulled out a chair on the other side of the glass table. "The court wants bad guys fully recovered before they sentence them to death. You got to love the Texas judicial system." He snorted. "The lawyers will have a field day. Both sides want you to testify. NeuroRealm, of course, denies any connection."

She wasn't surprised. "It was extra-label use and April signed a waiver. So did the others. Suing NeuroRealm makes as much sense as you taking aspirin to cure cancer and yelling foul when it didn't work."

He glowered. "Give me a break. Pottinger worked for them, they had to know." He sucked in a big breath and blew it out to calm himself, and forced a tight smile. "Preaching to the choir, right? But they say the drug is FDA-approved for Alzheimer's patients."

"Yes, Teddy said the drug sounded familiar. His wife Molly took Damenia for a while."

"Well, NeuroRealm won't pull Damenia from the market just because Lizzie went bat-shit crazy and gave it to kids and made them nuts." He looked stricken. "Sorry. How is Steven?"

"Stabilized, I think. I hope. I'm really out of the loop on Steven." September propped her chin in one hand and stared into the cold coffee.

"His father has custody, of course, until April's situation is resolved. Steven's in a mental treatment facility."

"Poor kid. He's the big loser in all this."

"Yes, but the doctors say there's hope. They're weaning Steven off the drug little by little to try and avoid the side effects of cold turkey withdrawal." She rubbed her face. "Steven won't be prosecuted for shooting Lizzie. He's just a child, and he was under the influence of medication. Besides, they've got enough real bad guys to prosecute without the bad PR of targeting a child that's more a victim than anyone."

"I keep thinking about my own kids." Combs looked haunted for a moment and then shook it off. "Parents will do anything for their kids."

September agreed. "The drug does work wonders in some cases. With all the publicity, parents are clamoring for clinical trials. More research might eliminate the side effects." She prayed that would be the case. But it would be years before they'd figure all that out, and in the meantime some parents would continue to jump off the ledge without further tests. At least it would be more difficult with all the extra scrutiny. "It could be a long time before anyone knows what damage Steven has suffered, or if it's reversible."

"But you think kids might benefit down the road from this craziness?" He looked incredulous. "Sounds like wishful thinking. But Mom would like that. Crises bring families together."

"Maybe it does in your family." She snorted. "Doug Childress wants nothing to do with any of us, and especially me. April will have to stand trial for Pottinger's death. She insists Steven had nothing to do with it. I want to believe her. We'll probably never know, unless Steven someday is able to tell us." She really didn't want to know. She sipped coffee. "Actually, you're right in a way. This did bring April and her ex back together."

Combs looked surprised.

"Yep. Childress splits his time between Steven in the psych wing and April in ICU. Mom says they're talking again. Instead of fighting over him, they're determined to get Steven help and plan for his future."

"That's got to be a relief."

She glared at him. "What the hell is that supposed to mean?" But it *was* a relief that Steven was taken care of. And that he was no longer her responsibility. And that made her feel guilty as hell.

Combs spoke softly. "I know what happened in Chicago."

Deep breath. She didn't want his sympathy, didn't need this, let the past stay buried. "Lizzie's a liar." She looked away. April should never have told anyone. They'd had a pact.

"Lizzie didn't need to say anything. Nobody believes her rants anyway. But cops talk." He leaned forward over the table. "When you were on the run, questions were asked. Uncle Stan has connections all over the country, even the Chicago Special Victims Unit."

She inhaled sharply. "Jeff, that's private." She glanced at her watch. "I've still got mashed potatoes and creamed corn to fix." She pushed away from the table and stood. "What happened in Chicago wasn't your fault, either." Combs leaned back in the chair, not going anywhere until he'd had his say. "You were a kid when you got pregnant. April helped you out of a tight spot."

"Let it go, Jeff." She felt heat flood her cheeks.

"It should have been a happy ending."

"Well, it wasn't." She strode to the stained glass window, and put her hands against the cool surface to stop their trembling. The sun played hide and seek with clouds and created dark hideaways beneath scraggly overgrowth. The garden needed an overhaul. Maybe a flame thrower. "This is none of your business." She crossed her arms to cut short the conversation. "Maybe I do need that gun to keep out obnoxious visitors."

"September, look at me." When she did, he smiled and held up his hands in a *what can you do?* gesture. "Doesn't take a rocket scientist. I'm just saying others might notice and ask questions. April and Doug both have blue eyes. Steven's eyes are green. Like yours." He cocked his head sideways. "That's a hell of a secret to keep."

She stared at him. "Are you quoting your high school science to make a point? Check your genetics, Jeff. That eye color stuff doesn't prove anything."

"No. But April's medical history does. She had never been pregnant. But you already know that."

She crossed her arms. "Everyone has secrets. I hear tell you've got some doozies." She felt satisfaction when he flinched.

"Yes, I know what it feels like to be a target." He took another calming breath. "I know it's not my business. But I like you. You shouldn't blame yourself. Most rape victims that get pregnant—"

"I don't want to hear this."

"It wasn't your fault."

"Children of rape are reminders of the worst moments of your life—and that's not fair to the kid. Not fair to anyone. It wasn't Steven's fault, either," she cried. "Look, I know I'm a terrible person. Because I can't love him. And April could. Damn you!" She rounded on him and flung the words like stones. "You can't say anything. Doug can't know. When April is indicted for Pottinger's death, Doug Childress is all Steven will have left." She shuddered. "His biological father is still out there somewhere. I lost myself for a lot of years hiding away from that scumbag. But Steven doesn't need to know that. God knows what Doug would do if he knew."

"You saved your son. You're not a terrible person. But I won't tell anyone. It's not my secret to tell."

She relaxed just a little. "That's it? That's why you're here?"

He stared at his hands. "I'm here because you caught Mom's killer. I never said thank you, and today's the day for it." Combs cleared his throat. "I'm here because Doty pulled surveillance. I'm here because I like you and don't want you to hurt anymore—that includes beating yourself up." He hesitated and poked the paper bag on the table. "And I'm here because I got nowhere else to be."

Despite herself she was touched and a little sad. "What about your family?"

He shrugged. "Kids are with my wife. I'm still suspended until further notice, and honestly, not sure I want to go back. Anyway, I'll go over to Uncle Stan's tonight for dessert. I don't feel too much like celebrating this year. Nobody does." He cracked his knuckles again. "You understand. We don't have to explain anything to each other. Right?"

She nodded. "True, that."

He sniffed the air with appreciation and his stomach growled. "But you've got guests coming, so I'll get out of your hair." He stood.

She laughed ruefully. "Mom finally agreed to let me host Thanksgiving this year, but nobody feels like gathering. Too many unanswered questions, too much suspicion and blame. It'll take a long time to sort out all the crappiocca, if ever." She shrugged. "But I already had the turkey, and it was a shame to let it go to waste." Galloping thumps sounded overhead, and September pointed at the ceiling. "Besides, Macy loves turkey. He once stole a frozen bird out of the fridge and I had to serve a lame bird after he amputated a drumstick."

"No way." Combs chuckled.

"Way." She smiled back. "Don't get between Macy and dinner. Anyhow, it's too much for one person. I invited Humphrey and Anita from the radio station, and Teddy and maybe his wife if she's having a good day. There's plenty. I could set another place. " She hugged herself and said softly, "Sometimes you have to find your own family." Something banged into the kitchen door. "There's the rest of my family now."

Combs wrinkled his brow in puzzlement, and watched when she hurried to the door and grabbed the handle without reaching for the deadbolt. "You don't have it locked?"

September grinned. "Like I said, I'm getting better about that. But I've got extra security now." The door banged again, and she timed the next bump with the doorknob twist.

Shadow burst into the room.

The dog stopped short in the doorway and stared at Combs. The missing tip of his left ear lent him a rakish expression. His hackles began to rise until September stroked his brow and spoke with soft authority. "Shadow, settle. It's okay." He looked into her face with adoration. His tail waved.

"Steven's service dog, right?" Combs stood still when Shadow came close to politely sniff-inspect his pants. He backed away, wagging his approval.

September pushed the door closed and hip-bumped it to latch. She didn't bother with the lock since the back garden had been securely fenced. The '*beware of dog*' signs kept strangers at bay, especially when they saw Shadow's size. His recent experience made him more cautious, but he was far from a guard dog. But nobody had to know that.

"I guess Steven will need him now more than ever."

She shook her head. "Doug doesn't want him around. It's his decision. He's Steven's father." Her hard look brooked no argument, and she smiled. "I'll just have to put up with the goofy baby dog, won't I?" She rubbed Shadow's undamaged ear, and shrugged. "Sometimes your family chooses you."

As if on cue, Macy thundered down the kitchen stairs. He spun around the landing with his Mickey clutched firmly in his jaws. But when he saw Shadow, the cat dropped the toy, hissed, and sprang atop the table.

Shadow woofed, tail waving, and grabbed up the toy. He pranced around the room, daring the cat to play keep-away with the stolen Mickey.

"Shadow, enough. Macy is the boss of you." September's voice was stern. She traded the Mickey for a dog chew, and tucked the toy inside Macy's favorite cupboard hideaway. She couldn't help being tickled at Shadow's antics. And the pup knew it. Shadow grinned, and began to gnaw his rawhide treat.

"He's big." Combs eyed the dog with a dubious expression. "I dunno about the cat being the boss."

"Believe me; Macy puts him in his place." Curiosity finally got the better of her. She nodded at Combs's paper bag. "What is that?"

He looked sheepish. "In case I got invited to dinner. Can't blame a guy for hoping. It's a house warming gift. Don't worry, it's nothing pricy. Just a joke replacement for that rude coffee mug you liked so much."

"Really?" She looked at him with wary suspicion. Nothing could come close to replacing the #1-Bitch mug from Chris.

"I couldn't find a duplicate." He suddenly acted nervous. "The fancy wrapping was pretty dang pricy, too." He handed her the grocery sack.

She gingerly looked inside, and pulled out the thermos-size mug. September read the printed legend out loud. "Son-Of-A-Peach."

Jeff Combs was a wise-ass. She liked that in a person.

EPILOGUE

The camera loved her. Haunted green eyes, sweet uncertain frown, tumbles of dark silken hair...and a ripe, unwilling body. His tongue slicked across wet lips, gazing with hunger at September's visage on the television news. The memory of her taste, her smell, her touch haunted him. Oh, how he'd missed her.

The fear still lived on within her. He could tell. Good! His breath quickened.

She'd shown unexpected courage when she ran. And surprised him when she married that cop—the sonofabitch got what he deserved. She'd disappeared before he could collect her, and hidden herself away for months and months. But now, nothing stood in the way of his desire, of his revenge. He wasn't sure which mattered to him more.

His plans would quickly come together. He'd prepared for this ever since that night she betrayed him. He already had new name to go with his changed, buffed appearance. Nobody outside of Chicago ever heard of *Vince Grady*, the actor. He stroked his bald head, and flexed his abs. Even September would be hard pressed to recognize him now. Perfect.

This time, he'd make her *earn* his trust. His eyes narrowed and he licked his lips again. He'd been played, lied to, and publicly humiliated. But still, he forgave her. He'd choose a new name for her, and change her appearance in case anyone objected to her sudden disappearance. Nothing would stand between them, ever again.

He'd teach September, oh how he'd teach her a new symphony of sensations. And she'd welcome his music this time, for each command performance. She'd never leave him again. He could hardly wait.

ACKNOWLEDGEMENTS

After 24 award-winning nonfiction books I thought I had "acknowledgements" down pat. But fiction writing is a whole different animal. I'll do my best to be concise.

I must first thank Cool Gus Publishing, Bob Mayer and Jennifer Talty for the opportunity, and my parents Phil and Mary Monteith who always believed I had a novel in me. I've been part of the incredible Cuchara writers group for more than twenty years, and these savvy writers continue to inspire and support my crazy notions and helped birth this book. Special thanks to my editor and friend Jessie Stephens, and first readers Kristi Brashier, Carol Shenold and Frank Steele for your eagle eyes, spot-on comments and unflagging encouragement and support.

I am incredibly indebted to International Thriller Writers and the Debut Authors Program. The people who make up this organization are some of the most generous and supportive folks I have ever met, and my novel journey and LOST AND FOUND would never have become a reality without this organization.

A vast number of veterinarians, behaviorists, consultants, trainers and pet-centric writers and rescue organizations have helped me help pets over the years, in particular members of the IAABC, APDT, DWAA and CWA. The Kayce Cover SATS seminar presented some years ago at an IAABC conference inspired the dog training vocabulary game described in the book, which my own dog loves to play. Much of the story is based on science, including behavior and learning theory, the current use of "off label" drugs in children and the benefits of service dog partnerships. Since this is a work of fiction, however, be aware that liberties have been taken to further the plot.

I am delighted that Gillian Salling, a tracking dog expert and owner of Fernheim German Shepherds, graciously allowed her gorgeous and talented Uschi Von Fernheim, TD to serve as the LOST AND FOUND cover dog.

I am also grateful to my readers for embracing "Name That Dog" and "Name That Cat" contests to help me find the perfect choices for some of the furry characters in the book. More than 85 terrific names were suggested with close to 800 votes resulting.

Caren Gittleman suggested the winning dog name Dakota because it means "trusted friend" and is also the name of her lovely Sheltie (who helps her co-write Dakota's Den Blog). Raelyn Barclay offered several dog name suggestions including Bruno, which won the second hero dog spot. Patricia suggested the winning cat name Macy, garnering more than a hundred votes from readers, wow! Macy is the name of Patricia's seven-year-old yellow tabby, and named after a character in the *Bold and the Beautiful* television show. Karyl Cunningham has been one of my most faithful blog followers and her suggested name Simba is the second cat name winner. Simba is the name of Karyl's slightly chubby, arthritic senior citizen kitty, a perfect choice for this character. The four winners received advance copies of the book, their pets' namesakes serving heroic roles in the book, and my eternal gratitude.

Finally, I'm grateful to all the cats and dogs I've met over the years who have shared my heart and sometimes my pillow. These days, Magical-Dawg and Seren-Kitty are my furry inspiration for all-things-pets. And of course, deepest thanks to my husband Mahmoud, who continues to support my writing passion even when he doesn't completely understand it.

I love hearing from you. Please drop me a line at my Bling, Bitches & Blood blog https://www.AmyShojai.com or find more pet-centric books at https://www.Shojai.com where you can watch for the latest *Thrillers With Bite*!

SEPTEMBER'S STORY CONTINUES in HIDE AND SEEK...

A mysterious contagion will shatter countless lives unless a service dog and his trainer find a missing cat . . . in 24 hours.

"...a creepy must read mystery for animal lovers...Shojai knows her stuff."
–J.T. Ellison, New York Times Bestselling Author

A September Day and Shadow Thriller

HIDE AND SEEK

Book Two

AMY SHOJAI

Copyright

**FURRY MUSE
PUBLISHING**
P.O. Box 1904
Sherman TX 75091
(903)814-4319

amy@shojai.com

HIDE AND SEEK

Prologue

Tommy Dietz grabbed the car door handle with one bloody fist, and braced his other hand against the roof, worried the carcasses in the back would buck out of the truck's bed. Despite the precaution, his head thumped the muddy window. He glared at the driver who drove the truck like he rode a bronco, but BeeBo Benson's full moon face sported the same toothless grin he'd worn for the past two weeks. Even BeeBo's double chins smiled, including the rolls at the nape of his freckled neck.

The ferret thin guy in the middle snarled each time his Katy Railroad belt buckle chinked against the stick shift he straddled. Gray hair straggled from under his hat and brushed his shoulders. He had to slouch or he risked punching his head through the rust-eaten roof. Randy Felch's snaky eyes gave Dietz the shivers even more than the freezing temperatures spitting through windows that refused to seal.

Three across the cramped seat would be a lark for high school buddies out on the town, but the men were decades beyond graduation. Dietz was in charge so Felch could either ride the hump or share the open truck bed with two carcasses, and the new Production Assistant.

Dietz stifled a laugh. Not so high-and-mighty now, was he? The man must really want the job. Vince Grady had turned green when he was told to climb into the back of the truck. Just wait till he got a load of the dump. Dietz remembered his first visit three years ago when he'd been out scouting locations. He wondered how the spit-and-polish Grady would react.

He'd hired locals for the rest of the crew. They needed the work, and didn't blink at the SAG ultra-low pay scale, the shitty weather, or the stink. In this business, you took anything available when pickings were slim. Then the show got picked up and union fees grabbed him by the short hairs. Amateur talent screwing around and missing call times cost even more money, so he needed a Production Assistant—PA in the lingo—with more polish and bigger balls to keep the wheels greased. A go-to guy able to think on his feet, get the job done. No matter what.

If Grady wanted the PA job, he'd have to be willing to get his hands dirty, and stand up to BeeBo and his ilk. Riding in the open truck bed was illegal as hell, though here in North Texas even the cops turned a blind eye unless it was kids. This was an audition, and Grady knew it.

He had to give Grady props—he'd not blinked, but clenched his jaw and climbed right in when they collected him at his hotel. He'd been less enthusiastic after following the hunters most of the morning, tramping to hell and gone through rough country until his eyes threatened to freeze shut. Something drove the man, something more than a PA credit for piss-poor pay and worse conditions. Hell, something drove them all to work in this unforgiving business. Dietz didn't care about anyone else's demons as long as they let him feed his own.

Dietz craned to peer out the back to be sure the man hadn't been tossed out the tailgate. Grady gave Dietz a thumbs-up. *Probably wants to point a different finger,* Dietz thought. Grady wore the official *Hog Hell* blue work gloves and ski mask—dark blue background and DayGlo red star on the face—or he'd be picking his frostbit nose off the floor.

Prime time in the back woods. Dietz's quick smile faded. Nothing about this trip was prime, not even the butchered Bambi in the back. Deer season ran November through early January, and it was always open season on hogs, so they were legal for any follow up film footage. The two deer hadn't looked good even before BeeBo dropped them, but that's what viewers wanted. Crocodile wrestlers, duck dynasties, and gold rush grabbers with crusty appeal and redder necks.

Nobody wanted actors anymore. Casting directors looked for "real people." So he'd caught a clue, jumped off the thespian hamster wheel, moved to New York and reinvented himself as Tommy Dietz, Producer. He'd found his calling with a development company relatively quickly.

A movie star face didn't hurt. Everyone these days had a little nip-and-tuck; it was part of the biz. He'd been selling his version of reality for years anyway, and always came out on top. He hit it out of the park on his third project. *Hog Hell* kicked off the next step with a Texas-size leap. He'd show them all, those who'd laughed at his dreams, calling him a loser. And he'd make them sorry.

The shabby pickup lurched down and back up again, and its engine growled and complained. Dietz was surprised the seat hadn't fallen through the floor. The overgrown road the hunters called a pig path consisted of frozen ruts formed from previous tire treads. They damn well better not get stuck out here.

"Don't worry, she'll make it." BeeBo talked around the stub of his unlit cigar. "This ol' warhorse made the trip so often, she could drive herself. Ain't that right, Felch?" BeeBo reached to downshift and Felch winced as the other man's ham-size fist grabbed and jerked the stick between his knees.

Dietz sighed. Out the window, skeletal trees clawed the pregnant sky. Weird flocks of blackbirds moved in undulating clouds, exploding from one naked tree after another to clothe the next with feathered leaves. Spooky.

Thank God the icy weather stayed dry. Heartland, Texas had dug out of a record-breaking snowfall, and the locals hadn't quite recovered. It put a kink in *Hog Hell* filming and they'd barely met the deadlines. Delay turned his balance book bloody with red ink.

Back home in Chicago they'd been hit with the same blizzard and so had NYC. But big cities knew how to manage winter weather. Apparently North Texas rolled up the sidewalks with even the hint of flurries. He wondered if BeeBo and Felch knew what to do in the snow, and didn't want to find out. The thought of hunkering down overnight in the truck with these men turned his stomach.

Dietz adjusted his own ski mask. He'd folded it up off his face so the blue cap hugged his head while the red star painted a bull's-eye on his forehead. He wore the official coat, too; dark blue and a bright hunter-safe star on the front and back, with the *Hog Hell* logo. The Gore-Tex fabric crackled with newness, and his blistered feet whimpered inside wet, dirt-caked boots. No way would he wear his new $300 Cabela's, purchased for photo ops at the upcoming watch party. He had a gun, too. In Texas nobody cared if you carried. They expected it.

BeeBo's preferred weapon, an ancient short barreled shotgun loaded with deer slugs, contrasted sharply with Felch's double gun he'd had custom made last season. Felch shot 44 Magnums, and the cut down double barrel rifle boasted enough firepower to take out an elephant, or a charging feral boar hog. They sleeved the guns in canvas cases stowed in the back of the truck, but the hunters cared far less about their own attire.

BeeBo and Felch would wear official *Hog Hell* gear at the watch party in five weeks, but not before. Dietz didn't want them stinking up the outfits. Today they wore wash-faded coveralls, heavy work coats, earflap hats, clunky boots with thorn-tangled laces, and frayed gloves with fingertips cut out. A bit of peeling DayGlo tape formed an "X" on the back and front of each coat after Dietz insisted on the nod to safety, even though he knew the two hunters paid little mind to official start and end dates during hunting season.

That was the point of the original reality program *Cutting Corners* that focused on people forced to skirt the rules to make ends meet. The unlikely stars of a single episode, though, turned Felch and BeeBo into overnight sensations and birthed the new show after *Cutting Corners* tanked. The two hunters were experts at skirting rules. Dietz was no slouch, either.

In the truck bed, Grady swayed back and forth. He'd pushed up the ski mask enough to expose his mouth. White breath puffed out in a jerky tempo, and Dietz wondered if the man would pass out. If Grady took a header off the truck bed, the liability would kill the show. "Find a spot to stop, BeeBo. I think our new team member has had enough."

Felch grunted. "No place to stop till we get there. Unless you want us to get stuck." He grinned, but the expression never reached his eyes. "You don't want us lugging that shit back to your hotel. The stink ain't something you want close by."

BeeBo guffawed. "Got that right. With all the hunters unloading, it's what y'all might call a 'renewable resource.'" He twisted the wheel and the truck bucked, jittering the decades old pine-shaped deodorizer suspended from the rear view mirror. "The critters take care of the stink pretty quick, though." His hairless wide-eyed face was a ringer for the Gerber baby. "It's around that next bend. You might even catch a whiff of Jiff by now."

Dietz wrinkled his nose. The pungent aroma wasn't assuaged by the air freshener that had probably come with the vehicle. He shielded his head from another thump, and squinted ahead through the crusty windshield. Wiper blades had torn loose on the passenger's side and smeared the detritus rather than clearing the view. It didn't bother BeeBo.

The trio remained silent during the final bump-and-grind through the trees. They pulled halfway into the clearing, and Dietz waited impatiently until BeeBo cranked the steering wheel, turned, and backed beneath a massive tree with pendulous clusters decorating the branches. Grady ducked, or he would have been scraped off by low limbs.

Several similar trees bordered the clearing, and another smaller truck squatted at the far end of the area. An elderly man stood in the truck bed and flailed tree branches with a long pole, while the woman dodged and weaved beneath to gather the resulting shower in a bucket.

"What's that?" Grady wasted no time jumping off the truck bed. He gagged when the wind shifted.

"Nuts." Felch unfolded himself from the cramped middle seat. "Pecan trees. They're gleaning the nuts."

Dietz's stomach clenched. He pulled the ski mask over his lips and breathed through his mouth, imagining he could taste the odor that closed his throat. Neither Felch nor BeeBo seemed to notice the stench.

Grady wiped his watery eyes. The breeze paused and he gulped a less contaminated breath. "Pecans? To eat?"

The truck squeaked, rocked and grew two inches when BeeBo stepped out. "Back in town they'll pay $8 to $10 per pound, once shelled. I got my daddy's old commercial sheller—held together with baling twine and spit, but works okay. I only charge fifty-cents a pound to shell." He shrugged. "Every little bit helps. It's too early for most of the big-name commercial farms, but for the gleaners, if ya wait too long the squirrels get 'em off the trees, or the pigs root 'em off the ground. Pigs eat lots of the same stuff the deer and turkeys eat, acorns and suchlike. But they get ground-nesting bird eggs, too. Pigs'll root up and eat damn near anything." He jerked his chins at Felch. "Gimme a hand." He lumbered toward the back of the truck and waited by the taillights.

Felch vaulted in the bed of the vehicle, and adjusted his gloves. He pointed. "Smorgasbord, y'all. Hey Slick, you might want to get video of this. Bet your big-city cronies never seen the like." His yellow teeth gleamed. He bent low, and grunted as he pushed and tugged the black plastic bag to the tailgate, hopped down and joined BeeBo. Together they slung the truck's cargo into the pit.

Yipping and growls erupted from below. Dietz stayed back, he'd seen it before. This stuff he wouldn't put on the air. This'd be too much even for the hardcore viewers without the added value of aroma.

Grady covered his mouth and nose in the crook of his elbow. He edged closer to the deep trough, a natural ditch-like runoff that sat dry three-quarters of the year. Piles of gnawed and scattered bones mixed with carcasses in various stages of decomposition. A family of coyotes tried to claim BeeBo's tossed deer remains, but was bluffed away by a feral boar.

Grady ripped off his ski mask, puked, wiped his mouth, and grabbed his camera with a shaking hand. He spit on the frozen ground and jutted his chin at Dietz. "So?"

Dietz smiled. "You got the gig."

***

The damn ski mask dragged against his hair so much, the normally clear adhesive had turned chalky. Victor had removed the wig after dissolving the glue with a citrus-scented spray, a much more pleasant olfactory experience than the afternoon's visit to the dump. A shower rinsed away any lingering miasma, but he gladly put up with the stink, the rednecks, and the sneers. The payoff would be worth it.

Until then, he couldn't afford for anyone in Heartland to recognize him. His tool kit of fake teeth, makeup and assorted hairpieces kept him under the radar. For the price, nearly fifty bucks for a four-ounce bottle of adhesive, it damn well better hold the new wig in place for the promised six weeks. He rubbed his hands over his pale, bald head and grinned. Even without the wig, she'd be hard pressed to recognize him.

Muscles had replaced the beer gut, Lasik surgery fixed his eyes, a chin implant and caps brightened his smile. He'd done it all, one step at a time, over the eight years it took to track her down. He'd even changed his name and transformed himself into a man she couldn't refuse.

He'd done it for her. Everything for her.

He dialed his phone. "I want to order flowers. Forget-Me-Nots, in a white box with a yellow ribbon. Got that? And deliver them December eighteenth. It's our anniversary." He listened. "Use red ink. The message is *'payback.'* Got that? No signature, she'll know it's me." He picked up a news clipping that listed the address, and admired the picture. She was lovely as ever. "Two-oh-five Rabbit Run Road, Heartland, Texas. Deliver to September Day. The name is just like the month." He chuckled softly. "Yes, it will be a lovely holiday surprise." He could hardly wait.

Chapter 1

Five Weeks Later

"I'm dreaming of a brown Christmas, just like the ones I used to know . . ." September stopped singing when her voice cracked. There was a reason she played cello.

She settled the instrument between her knees and caressed the silk-smooth wood. The pungent scent of the Christmas tree, a cedar cut from the back of the property, made her smile. After the recent freak Thanksgiving blizzard, a holiday without snow would be a gift. Boring would be nice, too.

The phone in the nearby kitchen rang, and she let the machine answer. "You've reached Pets Peeves Behavior Consulting. We're closed for the holidays. If this is a medical issue, please call your veterinarian. For new behavior clients, please complete the questionnaire on the PetsPeeves.com website or leave a brief message after the tone."

She'd stopped leaving her name. People thought *September Day* was a joke, and lately, she agreed. Her maiden name made it worse. Growing up with the name *September January*—no middle name needed—created its own kind of kid hell. But at least her parents gave up the birth-month names by the time her brother Mark came along.

The caller began to speak, quiet and determined, with an underpinning of anger. "This is Clare O'Dell again. You're the only one that can help Tracy. Please call me back!" She left the number, and disconnected.

September wrinkled her nose. Too many pet owners expected miracles.

Was Tracy a cat? A dog? What was the problem, was it new or long-term, had a veterinarian been consulted… The questionnaire saved so much time if only people would use it. She hated to ignore the calls, but most of them never followed through with the required information anyway. She made a note to include a referral name for all those frantic pet parents, though.

The cool surface of the cello would warm as she played. The Reynaud's syndrome meant her fingers needed help staying warm even though the furnace kept frigid outside temperatures at bay. She wore light blue sweat pants, a matching top, and insulated socks but no shoes in deference to the new carpet she hoped to keep fresh. September tugged on funky hot pink knit gloves—they'd been cheap, so she'd bought half a dozen. Each fingertip poked through the cut-off portions and resembled pink paws with claws poking through. She leaned forward, and long hair matching the rich chestnut of the aged wood spilled over the instrument until she tied a ponytail over her right shoulder to keep from tangling the strings.

The familiar routine unclenched her shoulders. She breathed deeply, thumbing each string, cocking her head to judge the tone, and made small adjustments with the tuners before picking up the bow. As she drew the horsehair across the strings, the cello's rich voice warmed the room, baritone to tenor vibrations resonating in September's body until she became part of the music.

"Ah Melody, I've missed you." She breathed the words, eyes half closed, and welcomed the slight discomfort when her tender fingertips smarted after a finger-slide shift to thumb position. They'd soon regain the string-fed calluses necessary for optimal performance. Nobody else would notice or care, but Melody deserved her best.

"Ack-ack-ack-ack-ack…" Macy prowled into the room from the adjacent kitchen, ducked under the Christmas tree and stared through cedar greenery like a jungle creature, his chocolate ears twitching with kitty criticism.

"Yeah, sure, everyone's a critic." September paused, arms embracing the cello, and grinned at the Maine Coon. "I'm not a big fan of your singing, either, big guy. But I've only got a week to get ready for the performance, so lion-cough all you want."

She reached for the *Son-Of-A-Peach* oversize coffee mug on the piano bench beside her and sipped the hot beverage. The cat eyed one of the ornaments, nosing it before patting it with a white paw to make it dance. It was one of the unbreakables she'd placed on the lower branches, but September didn't want the cat practicing potentially dangerous behaviors. "Macy, come."

Macy's ears swiveled forward. He left the ornament and trotted to her, and sat when she signaled him with the closed fist as he'd been taught. She rubbed the base of his tail with the back of her bow, and he responded with an elevator-butt pose. Macy mewed and stroked the length of his chocolate-furred body against September's leg and then pawed her bow arm with sugar-dipped toes.

His claws snagged her sleeve, and she had to set down the mug before she could unhook him. "You need a claw trim." She leaned down, and they did kitty Eskimo kisses, rubbing noses as she stared into the cat's green eyes that looked so much like her own. Sometimes she thought Macy could read her thoughts, too. Didn't all pet lovers feel that way? "Here, why don't you go scratch your log? Macy, go scratch."

She picked up one of the many pen lights stashed around the house for the cat's entertainment, and flicked it on. He'd follow a light beam anywhere, and it wouldn't hurt his eyes like a laser might. It worked better at a longer distance than the retractable treat sticks she used for clicker training.

Macy followed the light beam with interest, raced across the room, and pounced on the length of cedar log that lay against the wall. "Kill it, Macy, kill it! Good boy." He shredded the papery bark, making a mess she'd need to vacuum later, but it was worth it. "I know you'll make me pay a treat for each claw clip. Why don't you go find Mickey?"

He stopped and his tail drew a semaphore of disappointment in the air. She shouldn't have said the "treat" word when none were within reach. But after a quick grooming lick to smooth fur and hurt feelings, Macy dropped to the floor and dashed back into the kitchen. September smiled when she heard his claws at the cupboard door where he stashed his favorite toy. Too late she remembered what the *skreeee* of the opening cupboard signaled.

Overhead, a loud THUMP shook the ceiling, the sound of a seventy-pound dog's vault from bed-to-floor. Shadow's scrabbling claws clattered the length of the upstairs hallway, and his paws thundered down the back stairs into the kitchen proper. He slid on the slate floor, thumping sideways into the island at the center of the room and then levitated in a rear-paw dance to reach the cat teasing from the counter.

"Shadow, settle! Leave the cat alone. "

The black German Shepherd remained focused on Macy's stuffed toy mouse. The cat hissed at the pup, grabbed Mickey by its one remaining ear—the other ear a victim of the dog's gnawing—and dragged it out of reach when Shadow braced massive front paws on the counter.

The pup barked, frustration and excitement coloring the sound.

"Guys, enough!" September stood but she couldn't risk leaving the cello unprotected with the dog so aroused.

Macy dropped his toy in the kitchen sink, the risk of a hated dunking less onerous than dog drool. But September knew that wouldn't stop the pup.

At ten months old and still growing, Shadow easily accessed the sink. He'd grabbed a thawing pork chop from the sink two days ago. Never mind previous training as an autism service dog, Shadow had entered doggy adolescence and embraced canine delinquency with all four paws. The teasing cat made things worse.

Shadow snagged the Mickey toy and raced away with Macy in hot pursuit.

The black dog loped toward September and barely skidded to a stop, nearly taking her out at the knees. She lifted the cello and turned away, sheltering the fragile instrument with her body as the dog shook and "killed" the toy.

Macy stalked forward and crouched in the kitchen doorway, back paws treading like a racecar revving its engine. He launched himself at the dog, a silent flash of coffee fur that dashed beneath the dog's tummy before rearing up on his hind legs to box Shadow's face—but with sheathed claws. Shadow growled around the Mickey toy and wagged, big tail nearly clearing the piano bench.

The dog dropped the toy and open-mouth grappled the cat as Macy hugged his neck. Macy, still silent, retaliated with bunny-kicks from pistoning rear paws, escaped and launched himself into the middle of the Christmas tree.

"That's enough!" September's roar stopped the dog in his tracks, but it was too late for the tree. After teetering to and fro, it crashed to the floor, Macy leapt clear and sprinted from the music/office area to the front of the house, perhaps fearing the tree would give chase. Shadow gathered himself to follow.

"Wait. Down." Her whip-crack voice brooked no nonsense.

Shadow dropped to the ground. He gazed longingly toward the doorway and fidgeted when Macy returned to view and washed himself with a studied nonchalance.

"Don't even think about it." Her disapproval dragged the dog's attention away from the teasing cat. He squinted sideways at September with ears pressed flat and tail thumping. He scooted two feet on his belly—without getting up from the "down"—and grabbed the Mickey. The expression mimicked a doggy apology, and may well have worked on a less savvy human.

"You blew it." She carefully set Melody down, turning the bridge of the cello toward the wall. "Yes, I know Macy teased you. And you fell for it, again. Outside. You can go outside and cool your jets."

She grabbed up the toy on the way to the kitchen, pointing ahead so Shadow would move to the back door. Bright light spilled through the stained glass windows, courtesy of her brother Mark. She shoved the cat's tattered plush toy back inside the cabinet and set her coffee mug on the stained glass tabletop.

Although Macy could easily stay out of dog reach via the granite counters and his favorite refrigerator perch, teasing the dog had become his game of choice. The cat knew getting the dog in trouble banished Shadow to a scary uncharted outdoor land Macy rarely wanted to visit.

Spending time outside wasn't punishment to Shadow. It was more a break for both of them. He helped September deal with the PTSD, but she knew service dogs became emotionally drained and suffered burnout if not provided with their own downtime to recharge. It was good for her to practice being alone, too. Shadow could burn some energy sniffing out varmints. She'd probably have to hose him off, his paws anyway, before he'd be fit to return inside.

Mark's partner, Aaron Stonebridge, had begun the garden redesign after she threatened to finish pruning with a blow torch. The dug up portion of the rose garden proved irresistible to Shadow's digging. The feral hogs had had field day, too, and had torn out one corner of the fence.

September sighed. Shadow and Macy were bored. Wasn't that rich? She solved other folks' pet behavior problems, but neglected her own.

On cue, the wall phone rang again. There'd been a rash of pet runaways recently, and she'd been called to track missing dogs, cats, and in one case, a guinea pig. Shadow had loved that one after he figured out it was legal to follow the weird smell. The behavior advice requests still came through, but she'd had an equal number of crank calls and even a few death threats so now she screened everything.

September recognized the number before picking up the receiver. "Hey Combs, today's the big day?"

She'd met Officer Jeffery Combs during a day-long nightmare after his mother's murder a week before Thanksgiving. Instead of blaming her, as was his right, he'd become a friend.

"Yep, soon as I drop off the kids. They're not happy, and I don't blame them. We'd planned on another few days together. But I can't blow off my first day back."

Combs was one of her few friends in Heartland. She ignored hints he'd like to be more than that. Her world these days had no room for further complications.

September grabbed her coffee mug, a gift from Combs, and took a swallow. "At least they reinstated you as a detective. That's what you wanted, right? Vindication."

He laughed. "More likely punishment. Still waiting to find out about my new partner." He hesitated. "We still on for tonight?"

Her forehead wrinkled. She'd put him off twice before, and couldn't reasonably get out of it this time. "Sure, you can tell me all about your new partner—we can celebrate or bitch and moan, your choice. Anita dropped off some of her famous lasagna, and I've got wine. Bring beer if you want that." She hung up the phone. She'd have to change clothes. Sweats were fine for dumping around the house, but she should make an effort to be presentable now and then. Not date-clothes—it wasn't a date. But jeans and a nice sweater would be an improvement.

It was time she got back to a normal routine. That's why she'd agreed to bring Melody out of retirement and play the cello for Mom's church Christmas cantata. She sipped her coffee, not sure what constituted "normal" for her anymore.

September struggled for nearly thirty seconds and finally managed to unlock the reinforced steel door to take Shadow out. She shrugged on her coat, but didn't bother with gloves since she still wore the cello mitts. After hooking the leash on his collar, she slipped stocking feet into garden shoes, closed the door behind them and automatically dodged one of the low-hanging wind chimes suspended outside the door. Shadow tugged toward the car, anticipating a ride.

"Nope, this way. To the roses." He corrected himself and hung a quick left to the garden entry, his tail a happy flag.

She hugged herself in the forty-degree wind. Felt like thirty or less. The dog leaped and bounced at the gate two or three times before he managed a wriggly sit, a doggy request for the gate to be opened. "Wait." She unhooked his leash, gratified when he didn't move. At least he remembered some training.

The rusty gate squealed and Shadow's nose twitched with anticipation. She gave him the release word before he lost his composure. September crossed her arms, smiling despite herself as he raced into the three-acre garden to explore. She noted the time and shivered. A twenty-minute romp would have to suffice in this weather.

She hurried back to the kitchen. Wind had pushed the door ajar a few inches—the door was a bitch to latch—and once back inside, she hip-bumped it closed. She didn't bother with the kitchen door's cranky lock since Shadow would need to come in shortly. She congratulated herself that the unlocked door didn't bother her. Well, not much anyway.

September left the muddy shoes in the laundry room, and shed her coat and dropped it over her office chair before she returned to her cello. "Ah Melody, sorry for the interruption." She took her place once more on the piano bench, embraced Melody and tried to recapture the feeling of reverie.

But before she could draw the bow across the strings, the doorbell chimed. Her shoulders hunched. Aaron wasn't due for another twenty minutes, and he wouldn't ring the bell. Carefully she set the cello aside, replaced the bow on the bench, and hurried to the front door to peer through the stained glass sidelight.

For a while after the recent trouble she'd had uninvited visitors, especially after she stopped answering the phone. Her family knew to call first. Strangers had seen pictures of Shadow in the paper and remained cautious of the imposing black shepherd. The ragged gunshot notch in one ear made him appear ferocious.

Nobody waited on the front stoop. The front circle drive remained deserted. Maybe a kid on a dare rang the bell to her notorious 'house of blood.' That's how the local papers reported the tragedy. With Christmas next week, kids on school holiday had another week of boredom to fill.

She caught the motion of a fluttering sticker glued to the stained glass and felt cranky the ground delivery guys couldn't be bothered to wait. They pitched the package, rang the bell, and ran like she was an ax murderer or something.

September unlocked the three deadbolts, and swung open the door. A cloud of jackdaws, black tails as long as their bodies, descended onto surrounding trees like an invasion of ants, bending limbs to breaking, their raucous cries polluting the air.

But she saw only the package sitting on the top step. The long, narrow white box boasted a yellow ribbon and bow.

Her heart hammered. She whimpered and couldn't catch her breath. When the world tilted, September grabbed for the doorframe but fell to her knees and scooted away from the poisonous package. The yellow ribbon could mean only one thing.

He'd found her.

Chapter 2

Dietz watched impatiently as BeeBo unzipped his new official *Hog Hell* hunter's coat, doffed his blue and red cap, and took a good sixty seconds to squeeze into the provided chair. His massive thighs spilled over both sides.

The tiny office barely accommodated a single person, desk and computer set up, let alone two more grown men. BeeBo's girth should count as at least two and maybe even three. Thankfully, Grady's athletic but slight build easily perched on one side of the desk with such grace one would think it had been designed for such a purpose. That left the third vacant chair available.

He'd gotten lucky when Grady answered his plea on a national email list that served as a kind of Craig's List for the industry. Grady handled all the scut work Dietz hated, and was a problem solver of the highest order, especially the niggling details necessary to make a reality show seem real but run smoothly. The locals couldn't handle or understand some of the tech issues that challenged original programming. Once they got this next season rolling, worries would be behind them all. Grady understood that.

"Where's Sunny? And Felch?" He wasn't too worried about Sunny Babcock. The token girl on the team was little more than eye candy, and never stepped out of line. It made for great TV when she shot the lever-action Winchester deer rifle, never mind that she rarely scored with the cut-down barrel. But the last empty chair in the room looked ominous. Felch's loose cannon behavior helped make the show a hit but kept Dietz on pins and needles wondering whether he'd continue to produce. "This isn't an optional meeting."

Grady sipped his double skinny cafe latte. He was never without coffee, and between that and the energy drinks, the man fairly bounced off the wall. Now he grinned, teeth dazzling in their perfection, and pulled out his ever-present phone and dialed. His teeth were his best feature. That and his wavy blond hair, a style that was too young for him. Somehow he pulled it off along with the yuppie cargo pants and sweater. He disconnected the phone. "Sunny texted, running late. Nothing from Felch. He's not answering." He rolled a silver pen in his hand, a nervous habit he might have inherited from giving up smoking.

"I thought you got him a phone."

"Yep. But Felch hates it, leaves it off most of the time." He shrugged in a *'what can you do'* expression. "Promised to be here. Should be here any time."

"Better be." Dietz groused, and rubbed a hand over his stubbled chin. They all played at this like a second rate drama club when it was his life, by God. He needed a shave, hadn't slept well in days, and wanted to get this meeting behind them. He had to impress upon them the importance of the next two days. How they behaved, and what they said, would make or break the show and they couldn't go freelancing and shoot off their mouths. That's what got them into this mess.

Felch needed the dressing down more than BeeBo. The huge man was a cross between Frankenstein's monster and Jonathan Winters but despite a scary appearance, he only wanted to please. Felch, an Ichabod Crane clone, needed someone to ride herd on his free spirit. Of all the reality stars, Felch needed the money the most but hated the limelight the worst, and routinely dodged anything that didn't involve wind-in-his-face he-man activity.

Dietz didn't have time to play nursemaid. Grady handled the talent, got them where they needed to be, so Dietz could manage the money matters. He checked his knockoff Rolex. In six months, the watch would be real. With diamonds.

"That reporter came to see me last week. He talked to Felch, too. He's all riled up about us." BeeBo stared at Dietz, a kicked puppy expression that begged for a comforting word. He shrugged out of the coat, letting the DayGlo fabric slide off and fall over the back of the chair.

Dietz sighed, an exaggerated sound that ruffled the wavy fringe of hair that spilled over his brow. Leave it to BeeBo to point out the elephant in the room. "Let me worry about that. I told you, Grady sets up all interviews. I've got media appearances lined up to promo the big pig roast launch party for the new season." He leaned forward over the tiny desk. "BeeBo, we need to coordinate our messaging. Let me put it this way: It's like fishing—you got to use the right bait."

BeeBo nodded, eyes glued on Dietz, but still acted puzzled.

Patiently, Dietz explained. "If you throw all your bait out in the lake at one time and the fish gobble it up, they won't be hungry when you drop in your empty line."

"Why would I dump my bait…oh wait, I get it." BeeBo smiled, the gap of two missing front teeth a perfect fit for his stubby unlit cigar.

Central Casting couldn't have picked better. "We want the news people hungry, ready to swallow every word we feed them. If you grant interviews to everyone, we won't have any fresh bait to feed the big fish. And some of them are sharks so we have to be extra careful." Words would be carefully practiced, no room for error. "I don't want you or Felch or any of the production crew or talent—" His scowl included Grady, who crinkled sparkling green eyes at him. "Nobody talks to anyone without my say so. Got it?"

BeeBo agreed. "If you say so, Mr. Dietz."

Grady fingered his phone again. "Got a text. Felch is on the way; Sunny found him. Go ahead, I'll fill them in later." Grady pocketed his phone, slid off the desk and appropriated the empty chair.

Dietz breathed again. One less thing to worry about. He could count on Grady to get it done, no nonsense, no excuses. That was a pro. "Good. Give them this." He handed over several copies of the preprinted calendar with media and shoot dates noted. "Distribute to the rest of the staff. Have them clear their calendars and be on call for the next two days, until we get the big-ass launch behind us."

Grady's claim to fame included a number of indie films during the height of the martial arts craze, and a few guest star roles in TV cop shows as the victim or bad guy du jour. But like Dietz, when Grady reached the purgatory age—too old for romantic leads, too young for character roles—work dried up despite the obvious cosmetic work he'd had done. Facelift on a budget was never a good thing, and Dietz wondered how bad his face had to be to warrant such a gamble. Grady had to switch to behind the scenes work anyway. Turned out, he was good at it.

"What if he's right?" BeeBo turned his cap around and around in his meaty fingers. He tried to shift his pose in the chair, and it rode his butt until he gave up.

"Who? Right about what?" Dietz handed BeeBo his own copy of the calendar and sample questions and prepared answers.

"My dawg acts like he said. That reporter has a cat that's sick. What if it is our fault?" BeeBo folded the paper until it fit easily into the breast pocket of his shirt. "Hunting hogs is different. They tear up property, hurt folk's livelihood. And we don't waste 'em, just butcher what we bag and pass it on to folks that needs the food. But I never hurt no dawg or cat in my life, not on purpose anyhow." His lower lip stuck out, cherry red and wet, trembling a bit.

"Aw man, don't let reporters rattle you." Grady leaned forward and rested his forearms on muscular thighs. "The press always want an angle to get Joe Blow excited." He turned to Dietz, kicking his argument into high gear.

"Besides, it could be good for us. Get the warm-and-fuzzy crowd shouting about their poor pets. No such thing as bad publicity, right?"

Grady's smile made male investors open their wallets, and women open their legs and thank him for the opportunity. Dietz wished he had that charisma. Money worked as well, though. Once *Hog Hell* became the cash cow he expected, no woman would refuse him.

Better put the brakes on Grady's publicity notion. That would make the rumors worse when they needed to be erased. "You're killing me. The only publicity I want pre-launch is *good* publicity. Got it?" Dietz's slapped the desk for emphasis, and BeeBo jumped at the whip-crack sound.

Grady's toothy smile pinched white at the corners. "You're the boss."

"Got that right." Turning to BeeBo, Dietz softened his tone to a placating purr. "Nobody's hurting pets. Hell, you've been feeding your dogs the same ol' same ol' for how many years?"

"Thirty." BeeBo whispered.

"How many? Speak up, put some of that *Hog Hell* holler into it, brother." He played the part of cheerleader and hard-ass coach in turn, whichever was needed.

"Thirty years I been feeding my dawgs the same food. And they done good!" BeeBo raised his voice, the baritone rich and thundering in the small office. He stood up, scraped the grabby chair off his butt and slapped the desk with his own beefy palm. "By damn, they done fine!"

"That's what I'm talking about." Dietz beamed, his brow smoothing. "You don't talk to anyone, especially the media—I mean reporters or TV or radio people—unless I'm there and say it's okay. Grady will help you practice answering questions so you won't get stumped."

"Want me to take a meeting with that reporter? Get him to bury the story?" Grady straightened in the chair. "I can discourage him from bothering the talent. Maybe give him some new stories to chase, until after the launch."

Dietz rubbed his face and waved BeeBo back into the chair. The big man's looming height and girth made the room even more claustrophobic. "We want publicity, so you'll have to finesse it. I don't want any negatives about the show to surface in the next five days. Media appearances today, tomorrow night the launch party, and over the weekend build positive buzz. I want positive impressions about 'local boys make good and help the economy.' You know, a feel good Christmas story."

"Hogs for the holidays." BeeBo's gap-toothed expression was a sharp contrast to Grady's high-dollar caps.

Grady barked a laugh. "Not bad." He stood. "I'll take care of it, Boss. Better follow up on Felch. And I'll get the talent together with the staff later today for some media training fine tuning."

"Lots riding on this." Dietz stood as the two men headed for the door. "Hang back a minute, Grady. BeeBo, he'll catch up, so go wait in your truck."

They watched him lumber out of the room. He moved quickly for a big man, he moved quickly, and probably could take down a hog without the help of one of his several dogs. He turned to Grady. "One down, two to go. Make sure Sunny gets to the TV studio on time for the satellite media tour. The rest of us need to be at the radio station a half hour early." He scowled. "You've got to get Felch squared away."

"It's covered, no worries."

"Sure, you say that, but he's not here, is he?"

"Not my fault. The reporter got to him before I could, and hustled him into his car. You said no scenes, no bad publicity, and there were too many people around."

Dietz groaned. He needed a drink, never mind the morning hour. "We can control BeeBo—just tell him what he wants to hear. Sunny's a mercenary bimbo, and a paycheck will keep her in line. Felch takes convincing."

"He's a dumb ass."

"Hardly! Sure, he's unsophisticated, but he's not stupid. Behind that ugly face is a thinker. And a conniver. Find out what he wants and give it to him."

Grady shrugged. "Whatever. I can handle him." He sipped his coffee. Rolled the pen.

"You haven't so far. I need a cutthroat attitude, someone willing to get his hands dirty to get the job done. Are you hearing me?" He tried to calm his breath and failed. "Felch had me fooled. Makes me wonder if he's even from around here. If he's not a native Texan, that could blow up and derail this whole deal."

Grady didn't need to know Felch came out of nowhere and contacted him with the idea for the *Cutting Corners* show. You can't copyright ideas, after all. And it was Dietz's connections and expertise that turned the "idea" into *Hog Hell*, Dietz who got the barbecue sponsorships, Dietz the spin-off *High On The Hog* cooking show. And this season's show launch would announce the Piggy Panache gourmet gifts franchise during the watch party at the local Hog Heaven BBQ Restaurant, right in time for the Christmas rush. "We need Felch to stay in the show one more season, and make an appearance at the launch. The other guys get the job done, but Felch and BeeBo have star power."

Grady blew a raspberry. "'Star power?' Hell, they don't know what camera to play. You want an on camera backwoods goof? Just say the word." Grady pooched out his gut, let one eye cross and jutted out his chin, assuming a shambling gait and lisp. "Dem hawgs be the devil, sho' 'nuff."

Dietz sucked in a breath, shocked to momentary silence. The mimicry was uncanny. If not for the expensive hair style and clothing the man could be a smaller version of Felch. He shook himself. "They're the golden goofs. They're why viewers tune in, and viewers keep sponsors happy, and sponsors keep producers funneling in the big bucks."

Grady straightened and turned sulky. "I could do it."

"Sorry, we went in another direction." The words were familiar to every rejected actor, including himself. Even the love of his life had gone in another direction. Literally. She'd be sorry, soon enough.

Dietz brushed off the memories. That was then, this was now, and as a director and producer he had a responsibility to the show and everyone involved, and couldn't let personal feelings get in the way. Not yet, anyway.

"Didn't hire you to be the talent; I hired you to manage the talent. If you can't handle the job, there's a dozen like you lined up to take your place."

"So what else is new?" Grady's jaw tightened.

"It's your paycheck, too, you know. Hell, I'll double your salary for the next week for the extra aggravation. Deal?"

The younger man twirled the pen, considering, and then grinned.

"All righty, you get your designer butt in gear. Go catch up to BeeBo, and do what you need to do to keep a rein on the talent before him and Felch tank everything."

Chapter 3

Shadow cocked his head at the sound of the distant doorbell, raised his tail and woofed with concern. Doorbells meant visitors. Visitors might be friends with treats. But a visitor could be a scary stranger. It was a good-dog's job to know the difference.

He listened, but nothing else tickled his nerves. He yawned and then shook himself in a canine shrug until his shoulders relaxed. Some visitors didn't matter. His tail began to wave as he returned to sniffing the frozen mud, happy to stay outdoors and explore.

At first he didn't want to leave the house. His tummy hurt if he couldn't see September, and she didn't like the outside. He'd only take-a-break to potty if she clipped on his leash and stayed by his side. That way he kept her safe from scary strangers. He barked with loud ferocious warnings at anything that moved or made noise or smelled different, anything that made September startle—just in case. She'd make the CLICK-sound with her mouth, and say, "Good-dog, Shadow," and stroke his cheeks.

September's CLICK-sound meant he'd done something right, and often meant treats, too. He'd already learned lots of things, like how to walk on the leash without pulling ahead or lagging behind. He knew how to "sit" and "down" and knew what "wait" meant, though he didn't like that word even when he got a treat. Shadow liked treats, but he liked making September happy even more.

Playing games made her laugh. Shadow's tail waved harder at the thought of Frisbee-fetch. If September said, "Where's your ball?" he'd race to bring it. Other times she asked him to find objects he'd learned in the *show-me* game, like *book* and *paper* and *gun*.

Lately September partnered the *show-me* game with *hide-and-seek*. She let him examine a scented sock and it was a good-dog's job to track down the same scent hidden somewhere in the house. He'd learned how to play the game by following trails of smelly treats dribbled along the floor. Sometimes the puzzle-smell was treats like cheese, or some stranger's socks, and one time a strange dog's toy. He wondered if he'd get to meet the dog. Wouldn't that be fine! Or maybe even a cat. Macy wouldn't let him but Shadow wanted a really good sniff of cat-butt.

The best part about *inside* was September's bed at the top of the narrow stairs. She always asked him to jump up and share the sleep spot with her; especially late at night after she cried out in her sleep and her eyes rained water and her fear-stink made him start awake. When that happened, he nose-poked her and then dodged her fists until she knew him again. He'd figured that out on his own. Shadow was smart that way.

His bruised paws healed, but torn nails took longer. He trod carefully, and flinched when one of the thorny branches whipped close to his nose. The wind puffed through bone-dry overgrowth, shaking the prickly branches against each other in a rattled staccato.

Lately, the world outside teased more than Macy's sly looks. Shadow spent hours staring through windows. He longed to run and play, snap leaves out of the air, and roll to scratch his back against smell-rich ground. Once he knew everything about *inside,* it became harder and harder to be a good-dog the way September expected.

September didn't like it when he sneaked treats from the cat's sandbox. She'd made it clear that good-dogs steer clear of all-things-cat. Shadow hated to disappoint September, so he practiced paw-stealth to sneak close and snack on the yummy bits. But treats and sleeping on the bed, and sucking on Bear-toy, even sneaking quick tastes of cat-stuff weren't enough entertainment for a good-dog.

The icy vegetation crunched beneath his paws. Tough clumps of tall grass brushed his belly and parted for him when he ducked and weaved between scraggly thickets that crowded each side of the narrow path. Wind stroked Shadow's fur, and he slicked back his ears and squinted into gusts that carried scent-glimpses of distant treasures. Naked shrubs shivered in the wind, and limbs bristling with thorns claw-combed his fur if he misjudged the opening.

The pathway wound down a gentle slope hidden by bristling overgrowth and surrounded by a battered metal fence. When Shadow push through the final bushy barrier, he huffed and tasted the air with anticipation. He bounded toward the farthest fence pole.

Shadow sniffed the base before balancing on three legs and letting fly with a poorly aimed stream of urine. Lately, he wasn't sure why, it felt right to lift one leg. He sniffed his work, appreciating the steam that rose into the frigid air, and then moved further along the edge of the cleared fence line, and paused to sniff and pee, sniff and pee until he had no more pee to spend.

The center of this bottom half of the garden served as a morgue to brittle bodies of dead rose bushes stacked higher than the fence. Brown grassy areas bled across the lot where something had ripped into the thick sod leaving roots bared to the frosty air. Shadow padded to inspect the irregular furrows. His hackles raised at the rank odor that spoke of odd creatures—too many to count—that trampled through muddy soil before the clotted surface froze. He pawed the icy dirt for a fresher sniff, and stifled a yelp. He dropped his head to lick his tender toes.

Car tires screeched at the front of the house, a loud BANG echoed, and September screamed.

Shadow whirled. He drove back through the pathway toward the sound. Thorny branches tore at a good-dog's fur like an angry cat, but Shadow bulldozed on. He had to reach September. He could tell the difference between play-scream and scared-scream, and September was scared. She needed him.

Shadow reached the gate. He slammed into it, but it didn't move. The latch rattled when he pawed the metal and tried to push his long muzzle through the bars. The cross pieces, too narrow for him to squeeze past, stopped him dead. He turned his face sideways to try again, yelping with frustration.

He listened. Nothing. September hadn't called out to let a good-dog know everything was fine. So Shadow leaped up, placing his paws on the top of the gate, rear legs searching for purchase to climb over, but his paws slipped down and made no headway. Dropping to the ground, he backed away from the gate as far as he could, but the tangled shrubbery blocked a solid running start.

He couldn't go through. He couldn't vault the gate. Shadow dropped his nose to the dirt, checking for a way under. Yelps turned to barks and finally howls as he pawed the frozen ground. He had to reach September.

Chapter 4

Theodore "Teddy" Williams sat in the car for a long time, listening to the cooling engine tick long after it had been shut off. One of the women inside the two-and-a-half story brick monstrosity flicked the curtain to peer out, and then quickly ducked out of sight. He took off his wire-rimmed glasses, and rubbed his weary eyes. Unruly eyebrows bristled beneath his fingers.

Molly always trimmed his eyebrows. She could no longer be trusted with scissors, let alone something sharp near his eyes. Giving away Molly's garden stuff seemed wrong. It signaled giving up, meant he'd finally accepted she wouldn't get better.

He hunched his shoulders, gripping the steering wheel with gloved hands until creaky arthritic joints popped. After a long, shuddery breath, Teddy opened the car door and pried himself out of the driver's seat, popping the trunk. He limped to the front steps, slowly climbed them and fixed a cordial smile on his face. It wouldn't fool anybody, but he needed to make the effort.

The door swung open, and he faced half a dozen women ranging in age from thirty to seventy. Cassie held the door wide and motioned him inside, and his smile slipped. Teddy cleared his throat. "Thanks, but I can't stay. Molly's expecting me."

No, she wasn't. Molly likely wouldn't know if he visited or not, but he couldn't stay away. He visited every afternoon. On good days when the nursing home scheduled an outing, they used to meet at the local mall for coffee and a walk. Today they'd called to tell him to meet at the mall, and he couldn't wait to get there. Good days didn't happen so much anymore.

"We talked and Molly wanted me to bring her stuff over for the club to use. It's in the trunk of the car. Help yourself."

She should be here. Molly loved her Master Gardener club meetings, and delighted in sharing tips and bringing in expert speakers. After these special meetings, his wife came home filled with as much excitement as a teeny-bopper sighting Frankie Valli or whoever the young kids liked these days, and gushed about pruning timeliness, mulch components, grafting and the latest in weed pre-emergent technology.

"Thanks for coming, Teddy. We all miss Molly so much." Cassie folded her arms. "She was a driving force in the club. How generous to share her materials." The other women murmured agreement, but their sympathetic expressions stiffened his spine. "Maybe with Molly's secret ingredients, the rest of the club will carry on her legacy of winning blooms." Cassie's warm tone contrasted with her flinty expression. Despite her groomed yard and manicured flowerbeds courtesy of a hired army of lawn care specialists, Molly beat the pants off Cassie time after time.

"Molly never shared her garden secrets with me. Probably had something to do with her singing to the plants." A couple of the ladies smiled at his comments. "Me, I can't carry a tune in a tin bucket, but Molly and Patricia challenged the birds with their singing." He glanced around the room. "Where's Patricia?"

Cassie shrugged.

An older birdlike woman—he thought her name was Ethel, he couldn't keep all of Molly's friends straight—came forward and gave him a hug. "Patricia hasn't been here for the past several meetings, either. She and Molly were very close. Well, we all were. We miss her."

He swallowed past the lump in his throat. "Thanks. You meant a lot to Molly, too. She loved these meetings."

Molly wanted to share the supplies and pass on the savings to her friends, because not everyone in the club lived in mansions like this one. Cassie married up after her divorce, but acted like she'd been born lady of the manor. Others in the club pinched pennies and shared resources to create showcase gardens for boasting rights more than any income. The quiet rivalry between the iris club and the rosarians culminated at the spring garden tour each year. With only a dozen slots available, the gardeners angled for every advantage, and in the fall and winter months prepped the soil for winning blooms.

"We just started the meeting. Would you care to stay? I've got coffee brewing, and one of the ladies brought cookies." Cassie's crossed arms tightened, and she made no move away from the door. The other women, with the exception of Ethel, wouldn't meet his eyes.

He was a reminder of their mortality. They'd already pruned Molly out of the little clique before the disease infiltrated the rest of the group. Teddy spun on his heels, pushing Cassie aside. "Sorry," he mumbled. But he wasn't. "Come get what you want. Maybe some of Molly's magic will rub off on you."

She'd always been magical to him, a creature out of a fairy tale that somehow agreed to marry him, a mere mortal more adept at talking to computers than people.

He rushed back out the door, and had to consciously slow himself to keep from pitching headfirst down the brick front steps. The gaggle of biddies inside jostled each other, four finding coats to then clamber out the door after him. He stood at the trunk waiting for the women—they did remind him of geese, muttering and honking under their breath to each other—to line up and each grab a sack before trundling it into their own cars to stow.

Molly talked him into buying the truckload of fertilizer three years ago from the local man making the rounds. Mostly, she'd wanted to help out the hard-luck fellow. With the economy tanking, folks turned to all kinds of homegrown moneymaking schemes. But with the Molly magic, the contents of a dozen or so burlap bags labeled with neon yellow tape made a huge difference in the blossom production.

Their house had been on the tour four times in the past seven years Molly had been a member. Her roses rivaled any they'd seen in Tyler, Texas, arguably the rose capital of America. She kept her garden small due to the limitations of their postage stamp backyard, and used vertical space to advantage. Cherokee Rose took over the north side of the yard, spanning more than twelve feet in height and width, while Fortune's Double Yellow and Seven Sisters rambled up each side of an arched trellis that framed the back patio. Miniature roses lined the paving stone pathways painting carnival colors everywhere. But when she became ill a year ago, the garden took a back seat.

Teddy smiled when one by one, four of the women filed past the car to return to the house. Cassie and Ethel stayed at the door. "There's still a few bags left. Some gardening tools, too." He wanted all of it gone. It reeked of normal, happy times that would be no more. The reminder hurt too much.

"I don't want to mess my clothes." Cassie hugged herself, not budging from the doorway. "Leave a bag there on the drive. I'll have one of the kids tote it to the garage when they get home."

He adjusted his glasses. It would serve her right for him to accidentally-on-purpose break open the bag and dump it all over her sidewalk. But when Ethel hurried down to join him at the car, he stifled the impulse and offered a weak smile.

"Don't mind Cassie. She's all tied up in knots trying to be someone she's not." Ethel spoke softly, for his ears only, and patted him on the shoulder. "Molly always knew exactly who she was, and what she needed. That was—and is—you. She adored you—still does, I'm sure."

He grabbed up Cassie's bag of fertilizer and carefully set it on the ground so he wouldn't have to look at Ethel. "There's two more bags." His voice cracked and he cleared his throat. "I could carry them to your car."

"Just leave the rest here for Cassie, if you don't mind. I'll pass on the fertilizer, but would love to have one of Molly's gardening tools. Not to use. But as a memory, you know?" She patted him again. "As an honor to her. What happened to Molly could happen to any of us. That's got them scared. But she'd be pleased what you're doing here. Never doubt that, okay? Let your heart lead you and it'll never fail."

He smiled, blinking hard, and covered her hand with his gloved one and squeezed. "Is that what you do? Let your heart lead?"

She nodded. "Been with my cowboy for going on forty-five years, through the fat and thin times. The heart never lies, not if you listen close enough." Ethel leaned closer. "Even when it seems mighty silent, you can hear the echo."

"Thank you." He indicated the open trunk, filled with a variety of gardening implements. "Help yourself." He muscled the last two bags out of the car and dropped them beside the others.

At first, he and Molly laughed about the memory lapses. After all, neither of them were spring chickens, and he had nearly a decade on her. When she left her eyeglasses in the microwave they chuckled about "see-food" for a week. Then she called the pastor by the wrong name, and the embarrassment stopped the laughter dead. Shortly thereafter, he found notes she'd made to herself to keep track of the must-do items of daily living. The list included "take a shower" and "turn off stove." That scared him.

He'd begged her to see a doctor. Molly refused. She'd always been pig headed—it took him nearly three years to convince her to marry him. But after she drove across town to a dentist appointment and had a meltdown when she couldn't find her way home, he scheduled the appointment despite her protestations.

They'd held hands in the waiting room, anchoring each other against the desperate tide that threatened to sweep them away. The diagnosis drowned their hopes, and they'd been treading water ever since, knowing the time would come when they could no longer stay afloat in the flood.

Ethel picked out an old pruning shear, the yellow handle grip stained with sweat and scarred from use. "I remember seeing Molly use this." She hugged it to the breast of her coat. "I'll treasure this, and take good care of it. Betcha it's full of Molly magic, more than that old dusty fertilizer."

He saw Cassie in the doorway, waving a hand at the stacked bags. "You got that right." He slammed the trunk of the car. "Everything had to be yellow, or have sparkles. I'm proud you'll have it. Molly will be glad." If she could remember, that is.

It developed so quickly. Even the doctors whispered puzzled conversations in the face of Molly's swift decline. Teddy kept her at home as long as he could, but his age prevented him from providing the care she needed and deserved. Finally he'd found her a nursing facility, and continued to see her every day.

Some days she was bright as a penny, the Molly he'd always known. Those days they packed every moment with fun and laughter, memories of good times. The medications supposed to slow down the disease progression gave them hope for the future, a future they measured in days and hours, no longer months or years.

After cracking computer code for decades and figuring out circuitry and neural networking puzzles, Molly's brain disease thumbed its nose at him. Alzheimer's played fast and loose with logic, a moving target that stymied the doctors and wrung emotions dry.

He climbed back into the driver's seat, and watched until the ladies disappeared back into the house. Ethel pushed aside the blinds and waved the yellow-handled pruner, and he waved back. Teddy started the car, but before he could push it into gear, his cell phone rang.

The number wasn't familiar. Teddy still consulted with a few companies, and figured it might be an unlisted number from a client. "This is Theodore Williams, how may I help you?"

"Mr. Williams? This is Alison? Over at SunnyDale Nursing Home?" She spoke in constant questions, a young person's habit that drove him nuts.

"Yes, Alison, I'll be at the mall in another twenty minutes. Is the group already in the food court? I've got my car today since it's good weather, and can park around back." He shoved the car into gear and pulled out of the drive.

"Well, there's a change of plans. That's why I called." She hesitated, and then hurried on. "How soon could you get here? I mean, to the facility?"

"What's wrong?" His heart quickened.

"Nothing is wrong. It'll be fine, I'm sure? I mean, don't worry at all, not at all. But, could you come here instead? Soon as you can?"

He disconnected the call without a word and gunned the engine.

Chapter 5

September's heart thumped and she held onto the door as blood drained from her face. She backed away, unable to breathe, slamming the door to fumble the locks closed with palsied fingers. She didn't have to open the beribboned package; she knew what it contained.

She won a place on a prestigious concert tour but Mom didn't want her to go. September should instead give music lessons to children of the town's elite, volunteer in the right organizations, meet the right sorts of people, marry a fellow with the right social standing and the ultimate goal for Rose January—produce grandbabies. After weeks of arguments and cajoling and promises, Mom agreed on one condition: that a family friend watch out for September while she was far from home. And thus, the nightmare began . . .

The squeal of tires and metallic crash startled a scream from September. She should phone…who? Who could she call? Not even Chris had known the whole story, but he loved her and married her anyway, tried to protect her, and got himself killed along with their dog Dakota. April knew, but her sister would never help, even if she could. Hard to help from a hospital bed and pending arraignment. Combs knew some and probably guessed even more. She couldn't bear to share her shame with him.

The package waited on the front steps, identical to the cheery deliveries she'd learned to dread. That's why she and Chris had left Chicago, yet he'd followed them to South Bend. She braced herself and moved closer to peer through the front door, quickened breath fogging the stained glass.

The circle drive boasted a screen of newly planted live oaks on each side of a recently installed metal gate that fronted Rabbit Run Road. A car engine revved, wheels spinning, but the accordioned hood wedged between two gnarly cedar elms on one side of the open gate. Like a coward, he must have dropped the package and run and crunched his car. Good!

She'd changed after the recent Thanksgiving debacle. She wasn't the trusting innocent any longer. Afraid of him? Hell, yes! But more than that, she hated him for wrecking her life, or trying to. If he came after her this time, he'd get the surprise of his life.

"Uncle" Vic looked like six miles of bad road, his cheeks pocked with acne scars, crooked teeth, and a lanky string bean physique with massive belly more Peewee Herman than the leading man he wanted to be. He was a stray mutt so ugly and needy, folks bent over backwards to be extra nice to him and make up for the short straw he'd drawn in life. He chaperoned outings, vetted parties, and steered September away from missteps. Mom and Dad considered Uncle Vic the ideal shepherd. They'd been wrong.

She heard Shadow barking, his yelps and cries testament to the shepherd's protective nature, and her spine stiffened. She wasn't alone. She wasn't sixteen. This was her house, dammit!

September picked up the office phone and without taking her eyes off the distant gate, dialed Jeff's number from memory. She didn't have to give him details. But the phone went to voicemail. She fumbled with what to say, and instead hung up without leaving a message.

Her gun was in the car. Just the thought of the gun ratcheted up her nerves, and made bile burn the back of her throat. She hated guns, but Victor made owning one a necessity. September retrieved her coat, shrugged it on, and unlocked the deadbolts again, her fingers still clumsy with fear.

She shuddered, but grabbed the baseball bat left within reach by the door. It felt like an old friend, and her pulse steadied. She stuffed sock-clad feet into tug-on rain boots left at the entry. Her grip on the bat whitened her knuckles, but she took a deep breath, and strode out the door.

To reach the gun, she'd lose sight of the front gate, and risk Victor doubling back and trapping her in the garage. September hefted the bat, liking its weight. Shadow's barks grew more insistent, bolstering her courage. But she had to do this herself. Victor had killed Dakota, a trained protection dog, just to hurt her. She wouldn't risk Shadow by bringing him along.

September grabbed up a pair of binoculars she kept near the door, and trained them on the distant car. Red spiky hair. Victor was bald. Huh. He'd sent a delivery boy to do his dirty work. She'd confront him, find out more about Victor. This had to end. No more risking those she loved. No more excuses. And no more hiding. She clomped toward the crumpled vehicle, jaw tight and breathing fire.

Her face grew hot the closer she got to the Gremlin. It sat nose down in the slight depression between the trees. The engine made a hissing sound as it revved, trying to back out of the ditch, and she dodged clotted dirt kicked up by spinning wheels.

The driver's door butted against a tree trunk, blocking his exit. He'd need to clamber out through the passenger's side. She positioned herself to meet him, and held the bat ready. September ducked to see inside. He faced away from her, red hair moussed into spikes, and wearing a yellow windbreaker. She rapped on the window with the bat, resisting the urge to hammer the glass, and he spun around, a panicked expression on his face.

She stepped back, deflated. "What are you doing here?" September checked all around, but saw no other car or anyone else nearby. They were alone.

Sylvester Sanger gave a sheepish buck-toothed grimace. "You wouldn't phone me back. So figured I'd make a house call." His face was burned, probably from the airbag deployment.

"I don't talk to sleazy tabloid reporters about my personal life." Her shoulders remained hunched. She searched both sides of the road for signs of her stalker. "Was anyone else out here?" September forced herself to loosen her grip on the bat. Her hands had begun to hurt, and she flexed them, suddenly conscious of the goofy pink gloves.

"Some delivery van nearly T-boned me racing out your drive as I pulled up. That's how I ended up in the trees. I should have put the seatbelt around the kitty carrier." He jerked his head to indicate the back seat, where a pet carrier canted on its side, the door sprung open.

"Really? You brought a cat bribe?" She scanned up and down the road, nerves thrumming. She should get back to the house. The front door was unlocked. She turned to go.

"Wait. No, wait a minute. At least hear me out, now I pried you outta that fortress of a house." His voice rose in a whine, and he struggled to wiggle across the seats to get out of the car. "You made the national news last month. Sure, I wanted a piece of the action. The whole country wants to know what makes September-the-hero tick, her secrets, the tragic story of lost love."

She stiffened. The brisk wind whipped hair into her mouth, and she pushed it out of her eyes. He'd pestered her for an exclusive, wanting to raise his own credibility, and she'd dodged him for weeks. She eyed the battered car and flourished the bat. "Don't tempt me, Sly. Your car's already totaled and I need to work off some steam."

Sly levered open the passenger door, tumbled out, stood, and dusted himself off. "Never mind that. Your secret life, whatever it is, got trumped. Me and Fish are working on something bigger. Ginormous! It'll put us on the map and make us heroes. And it's right up your furry alley." He lisped with excitement, again gesturing to the pet carrier.

He fear began to abate, replaced by anger. "I can't believe anyone bought your line of crappiocca." Humphrey Fish, a local radio host, helped save her bacon during the recent blizzard, but he couldn't care less about her personal life. He only cared about the next story and getting out of Heartland to reach the big time. He still called her a couple times a week to push a return to the Pet Peeves radio show spot, but she'd had enough media attention to last a lifetime. What pet story would be big enough to tempt Fish to work with a sleaze bucket like Sly?

"You wouldn't answer the phone, or return my calls. So I came to you, but I'm not empty-handed. I brought you a gift." He jerked a thumb toward the back seat, pleased at his ingenuity. "I figured you'd come running to see who left it. I didn't count on ramming the tree before—"

"Wait. That package was your idea?"

"Package? That's what you call it?" His brow furrowed, and then cleared as he shrugged. "Well, yeah. Totally my idea."

"Son-of-a-bitch!" She swung the bat, and relished the satisfying "thunk" when it dented the hood of his old car.

He flinched and dodged. "What are you doing?" His voice sirened two octaves when she walloped the car a second time, even though the bat's whoosh never came close. "Stop with the bat, lady. If you don't want it, say so! Sheesh, I thought you were an animal lover."

The words stopped her third swing in mid-air. Animal lover? She had no compunction about putting the fear of God into Sly, but no pet deserved being scared spitless even if the owner was a clueless piece of toilet fish.

She lowered the bat and craned her neck to see into the car. On the back seat, the carrier jittered slightly as something inside shifted weight but remained reluctant to leave the security of the open carrier. It wasn't just a prop to enlist her attention.

She'd gone from fear to anger and now disgust at Sly's attempt to manipulate her. Even so, her shoulders unclenched with relief. Better the clueless reporter than the alternative. She hated to let him off the hook, but threw the bat to the ground so hard it made her arm ache. "Did you think a fancy-wrapped gift and cute puppy—"

"Cat. He's a cat." He opened the rear door, and struggled to maneuver the plastic container out. "He's my kitty security force, keeps interlopers out of my private office. That's why I named him Pinkerton. That, and his bright pink nose."

September put up both hands in a warding off gesture and backed away. "I don't need another pet. You don't show up with a cat like a box of chocolates. What were you thinking?" She tried to calm her hurried breathing, still fuming. What were the odds Sly would use the same wrapping as Victor? "You're trespassing. Clear out of here, and don't come back." She whirled, clutching her coat close against the chill. Her pink fingerless gloves and dumpy rain boots lent a ludicrous air to her retreat.

"But Pinkerton is sick. Don't you want to see him?"

September stumbled, but forced herself to keep walking. She couldn't rescue the world. And she wouldn't expose Macy to a strange, sick feline. "Take him to a vet. And get the hell off my property before I file charges for stalking." It wouldn't be the first time.

Chapter 6

Nikki scrubbed her tearful face with mittened hands, and stepped into the three-wheeler's path with hands overhead to flag down her brother. Twice he and his friends had raced by as they ran the track. She risked getting run over, but it was better than being ignored in the icy wind.

Hank applied the brakes. His fair skin flushed from wind-burn and embarrassment, but Nikki didn't care. "I'll tell. It's not fair." She had to shout over the engine noise.

"Quit following us." He forced a nonchalant expression when Zeke and his no-neck older cousin zoomed past on their own spanking new four-wheeler, and then Hank turned to scowl at her. "Mom told you to stay home. I can't babysit while me and the guys run the course."

"It's my turn. You always let me ride. I'm as good as those guys, you said so." She hated the whiny way she sounded, but couldn't help it. Hank was only three years older, but he treated her like a baby when she was nearly ten. He'd been riding since forever, while she'd stood out in the cold until her nose turned snotty. "Mom said to share."

"No, Mom said you should go shopping with her." He revved the engine like he wanted to spin out and leave her in the dust. Except the ground was froze solid.

"I already got my Christmas shopping done. Mom told you to watch out for me, and instead you ditched me soon as she pulled out of the drive. Maybe I should take back your present." She stuck out her tongue. He wasn't going to let her ride. Not with his friends around to see.

Nikki's friends had left town with their families for the holiday, except for her bestie Gina, whose mom just had a new baby. Gina was all, "Oooh, the baby this and the baby that," until Nikki wanted to puke. It was bald and prune-faced, and smelled like pee. Nothing cute about it, as far as Nikki could see. Not like the kitties over at the barn. Nothing was cuter than kitties.

Mom wouldn't let them have pets, especially cats, because she got sneeze attacks. Nikki didn't care about being with the popular kids at the barn. She wanted to spend time with the cats. So as long as Hank let her tag along to visit the kitties, she'd keep his secret.

Usually Hank was pretty decent, for a boy. He didn't mind when she tagged along, and she took seriously being sworn to secrecy about the barn hangout. That's where the older kids, boys mostly, hung out and smoked dope and bragged about all kinds of things that would make parents' eyebrows curl. Mom would have a cow if she knew Hank hung out at the barn, and she'd totally stroke out if Nikki did, too.

"I gotta catch up with the guys." Hank adjusted his blue and white Dallas Cowboy's gimme cap, the one he got for his birthday four months ago. "Sorry. I'll make it up to you later. Promise." His eyes shifted away and he ducked his head. "It's Zeke's rules, ya know. His trail, his four-wheelers..."

"Zeke's a stupid-head." She bit her lip to stop the tremble.

Hank smiled. "True. But he lets us ride, and got us both into the barn. He says his cousin visiting from Austin gets dibs over my kid sister." He shrugged. It made perfect boy-sense, she guessed. "You gotta wait until he goes home. Then it'll be back to normal, okay?"

"Promise?" She wouldn't cry, she wouldn't.

"Swear on my Cowboy's cap. Dustin—that's the cousin—he's heading out day after Christmas." Hank touched his hand to the cap, and saluted the way Daddy taught him. Daddy had bought it for him before he left.

She smiled. He looked like Daddy, too; they both did, with white-blond hair and freckles. Looking at Hank made her miss Daddy even more.

Hank revved the engine again. "Now go back home before Mom finds out you're here. She'd ground both of us." He pulled away in an impressive cloud of dust. She guessed it wasn't that frozen after all.

Ever since Daddy got deployed—a fancy word for "gone away to serve America"—Mom got this pinched expression on her face. She didn't laugh so much anymore, and mostly said "no" to anything new. Mom said she had a lot on her mind, keeping everything going till Daddy got home. She didn't want any bad surprises, and said Hank and Nikki had to suck it up and pull together like good soldiers right along with Mom. They all had their fingers crossed (toes too, and eyes if it'd help) that Daddy could come home for a holiday visit. That would be the bestest Christmas present of all.

She and Hank tried not to be any trouble. But the barn was too good to resist. You only got invited by the cool kids, how could anyone turn that down? If Mom found out about the barn hangout, that would be a *very-bad-thing*. Even though Hank and his friends didn't smoke or anything, Mom said an omission was bad as a lie. Nikki wasn't exactly sure what that meant, but she didn't want to find out.

Nikki watched Hank go. She scrubbed her salty cheeks where the tears had dried and itched in the cold air, and waited until he turned the corner over the hill out of sight. Since he wouldn't let her hitch a ride, she'd hike to the barn by herself. It wasn't *that* far. Up the hill and down the path to the left. She knew better than to ask Hank to look after the kitties. He wouldn't stop the trail ride for such a thing, and even if he did, she didn't want the boys to know how much she liked the cats. Hank was okay, but some of the older boys acted mean sometimes.

With school out until the Monday after New Year's, most of the big kids had better things to do than sneak out to the barn. She should have the place to herself. Hank, Zeke and his cousin wouldn't stop riding until the sun started to set. She checked her pink sparkly cell phone, the one Mom said only to use for emergencies, and saw she had at least an hour before dark-fall. There was plenty of time to travel there and back home without anyone being the wiser.

Twenty minutes later Nikki arrived at the old barn. The walk took longer than she'd figured, and chilled her to the bone. Before going in, she did what the big kids did, and walked all the way around the structure to be sure nobody else was there. The weathered wood had long since lost its original color, and the gray planks blended with the bare bois d'arc trees. Its witch-claw limbs grabbed at the shaky walls, and drooped clear to the ground as though to gather up the horse-apples shed around its gnarly feet.

Nikki shivered, from the cold, not the spooky trees. After all, she was nearly ten years old, and stupid trees were nothing to be scared about. She didn't see anybody else around, but listened carefully at the door anyway for whispers or boy laughter before shoving aside the loose wall plank enough to bend low and squeeze through.

She straightened, and turned her head this way and that. Nikki hadn't noticed so many shadows before when she'd been here with Hank. "Just shadows, nothing scary." Her voice didn't even shake. See? Nothing to get stupid about.

A soft mew replied.

"Mama Kitty? It's me, Nikki. I brought you treats." It wasn't proper cat food, but she'd discovered the cats liked baloney and cheese during her first visit when she'd dropped part of a sandwich.

The fluffy gray cat eeled out from one of the empty stalls and padded toward her. "How are you? Where's your family?" When they'd first met last spring, she'd had half a dozen babies, but over the weeks and months, some had disappeared.

Nikki brushed off a wooden box and sat, crooning to Mama Kitty when the cat cheek-rubbed her ankles. "Kitty-kitty-kitty?" She called again, hoping the three remaining young ones would come out of hiding when she pulled out the plastic baggy of food. Unlike their mother, the kittens remained shy and she'd not managed to pet a single one, although they would sneak close enough to grab a treat or two she tossed in the dirt pathway down the center of the building. "Guess you need a new name, huh? I mean, if your babies are all grown up, I can't call you 'Mama Kitty' forever. So what's your name?"

The gray cat hopped into her lap and nosed the plastic bag, trilling and mewing with excitement. "Always hoping for treats, aren't you?" The cat's bony hips stood out prominently beneath the fur. Nikki shredded the cold cuts into strips, and hand-fed her two before the first kitten appeared. Two more kitten-shaped shadows hung back in the doorway to the stall.

Nikki tossed a cube of cheese near the first youngster, and he pounced on it, crouching over the treat to lick and finally pick it up and chew, head turned sideways to more efficiently munch. She offered another strip of baloney to the gray cat on her lap, and thrilled at the sound of cat purrs.

Like always when she visited the cats, she fantasized about taking them home. "I keep hoping you could come live with me. Would you like that? Hey, I'll call you 'Hope' for luck. Maybe that'll make it happen."

Hope purred and head bumped Nikki's hand, as if approving the new name. Nikki had researched on the internet and found out some cats didn't cause allergies. There was one called a Siberian that people said was a safe kind for sneezy people like Mom, and the gray cat had long hair like a Siberian.

She tossed another piece of cheese to the kitten, and made trill sounds with her tongue. The blond again pounced on the food. "You like that, don't you?" She smiled when the two other furry figures finally dashed out of the shadows toward the food.

The blond kitten screamed, and raced away. Only then did Nikki realize the other two creatures weren't kittens, but raccoons.

Hope dug her claws into Nikki's pant leg and arms, and puffed up to enormous proportions. Screaming, Nikki scrambled to stand up, dumping the terrified gray cat off her lap.

The raccoons hissed and fought over the cheese, gulped it down and then stared up at Nikki. They took wobbly steps toward her. They acted sick, bad sick. Maybe they had rabies.

Nikki backed away, one slow step at a time, fearful the sick raccoons might attack her. She should never have come alone. She was just a stupid nine-year-old kid, and made a baby mistake. Hank would know what to do. She wanted to find the loose board and make her escape, but was afraid to turn her back on the threatening animals.

She still clutched the baloney and cheese baggy, and flung the plastic toward the sick raccoons. The creatures fell on the treats, making awful noises, and the gray cat pressed against her leg, wailing. Without further thought Nikki scooped up the bony feline, turned, and dashed to the loose board and backed out of the barn butt first.

Panting, she straightened and whirled to run back home. She nearly ran into the man, and stopped dead, juggling the yowling, struggling cat.

"What y'all doing with my cat?" The giant scarecrow-man leaned forward, long scraggly hair flying, and shrugged off a heavy sack slung over one shoulder so it slammed to the ground. He scowled, revealing broken, stained teeth. In the other hand, he held a gun.

Chapter 7

September broke into a run back to the house when Shadow yelped. "Baby-dog, I'm coming, everything's okay." He sounded frustrated but without the warning snarls she'd learned to recognize and heed. He fed into her emotional state and mirrored it back, and she felt equally attuned to the pup. She no longer questioned it. They were family.

He paw-punched the garden gate and his woofs punctuated the metal jangle. At least his torn claws had healed, but she winced at the memory of the bloody damage. September trotted around to the garden.

Shadow flattened his ears when he saw her. He yawned and voiced a squeaky trill and wagged with clear relief.

She took a big breath herself, mentally shedding the stress from the argument with Sly. "I'm fine, baby-dog, did you worry about me? Sorry for all the noise." She unlatched the gate and knelt for a moment to thwart his impulse to jump up, squinting her eyes shut and laughing as he nosed and washed her face in a proper exuberant doggy greeting. "Okay, already, I love you too. Ready to go inside? Gotta call somebody about Sly's car." He stood tree trunk solid when September braced against his broad shoulders to lever herself upright.

Shadow raced her to the back door, sat, and waited for her. "Good-dog, Shadow." He wriggled and grinned, watching with expectation for her next words. "Shadow, open." She coupled the command with a wavelike hand signal, and the young shepherd lunged onto his rear legs and punched the door with his chest and paws.

The door rebounded from the dog's weight. September bit her lip to keep from smiling, instead tipping her head with one raised eyebrow until Shadow backed out of the open doorway and planted his tail. "Good-dog! Inside." She gave the final command in the chain, and watched him sprint across the kitchen's slate floor, nails a tap-shoe clatter on his way to slurp mouthfuls from the oversize water bowl.

She hip-bumped the door closed, kicked off her boots and walked past the stained glass table to retrieve her cell phone from the dark counter. September noted the missed call. Humphrey Fish. She made a face, and deleted without listening. If he'd partnered with Sly on some hair-brained scheme she had even less inclination to return the call.

Her website traffic exploded after the national news turned her into an overnight superhero, and the real pet problems got lost in the tidal wave of curiosity seekers. Good for Fish, his dream came true, but she didn't need the aggravation or the money. Well, maybe the money. At some point, the lottery winnings would run out, even with her careful investments and management. Meanwhile, the news coverage painted her with a huge bull's eye. Anyone could easily find her now. It was only a matter of time before she'd have to deal with Victor, for real.

Shadow whined and pressed close as if he could read her mind. He wiped his wet muzzle on her sweats and she absently stroked his head as she dialed the insurance company and explained the situation. Sly would pay for the damage.

The big dog stiffened, muscles rock hard against her thigh. A low growl bubbled in his throat.

"What?" She disconnected but hung on to the phone as she followed the trotting shepherd from the kitchen through the music/office to the front door. His hackles raised, he stared at the door, head tilting to one side. The growls erupted into alarm barks, and he danced around the door with his tail flagged high, begging for it to be opened.

She thumbed one of the deadbolts home before peeking through the adjacent window. A huge cobalt pickup pulled into the drive, and September's shoulders relaxed. Aaron was early.

He swung down from the driver's seat with the practiced grace of a cowboy's dismount. She knew Aaron still rode as often as he could despite her brother's worried disapproval. She pasted on a smile, opened the door, and used one sock-covered foot to boot Sly's gift box inside. She'd toss it later.

Aaron loped toward her, one hand waving behind him toward the highway. He yelled something unintelligible.

"What?" She shivered. Despite the clear sunny day, the wind cut like glass.

"Nearly hit it." Sun-bleached eyebrows shaded his gray eyes, and the corners of his mouth turned down, accentuating his dimples. Women still hit on Aaron, and it drove Mark crazy, but Aaron laughed it off.

"Oh, that car off the road? I called for help." She gestured with the cell phone. "He missed the curve."

He didn't act mollified. Aaron never lost his composure. He balanced Mark's emotional highs and lows the way her husband had steadied her. When she'd lost Chris she'd run home to Heartland to hide. She bit her lip, and stared at the box she'd kicked into the corner. She hadn't run far enough. Reminders, even fake ones, reached out to bite when least expected.

She and Mark shared dark hair and a tall slim build, and had also inherited Dad's tender heart. In the past few months, she'd managed to toughen up. Aaron knew she'd kick his butt if he hurt Mark, and it didn't bother him because, well, Aaron was that genuine and nice, despite her own initial suspicion of anything good. She hoped Aaron would never lose his fresh-faced optimism.

Now something beyond bad driving had him riled. "Come on inside, you'll freeze your nibblets."

He finally laughed. "Yeah, I hate when that happens." Aaron pulled the door shut behind him before he noticed Shadow's raised hackles. His scowl returned. "Are you okay? Where's Macy?"

Aaron was a cat guy and Macy knew it. "He's around somewhere. Had to separate them for a while, so he's probably sulking somewhere with his Mickey toy."

White eyebrows climbed higher, but Aaron had the good manners not to say anything. "You don't let Macy outside, do you?"

"Perish the thought." She gave a theatrical shiver. "He'd take on a coyote if he got the chance, but Macy's no match for them. Shadow's run off a few, and I worry they'd gang up on him, big as he is."

"I nearly hit an animal up by the gate. Maybe it was a big skunk, but it's the wrong time of day. I only caught a glimpse. Yeah, I know Macy isn't black but it was in the shadows and moved more like a cat." He craned to see up the sweeping front staircase, and then turned to scan the living area. "Are you sure Macy's inside?"

September glanced around, uneasy. Unlike many cats that dove under the bed with anything new, Macy loved visitors. And the big cat especially loved Aaron, almost to an embarrassing degree. "Macy? Kitty, where are you?"

When he didn't appear, Shadow kept by her side, the frown on his furry brow mirroring her own concern. She checked the cat's favorite perch atop the refrigerator. Empty. She opened the cabinet and pulled out Mickey, but the cat wasn't there. She crossed to the kitchen stairwell to call. "Macy, come! I have treats." She waited, head cocked to listen. Shadow woofed under his breath at the "treat" word and licked his lips.

Macy wouldn't snub both Aaron's visit and the promise of treats. Granted, even a trained cat wasn't above blowing off requests now and then. She peeked back over her shoulder, where Aaron leaned against the kitchen island with an odd, vacant expression on his face. "You're sure you saw him, that he got out?"

Aaron raised his eyebrows as if surprised to see her there. "Who got out?"

Shadow whined, and barked more sharply. He poked his nose at September's hand for the mentioned treat.

The dog's bark sharpened Aaron's focus and he straightened and blinked hard. "That's…Shadow, right?" He shook his head. "Not firing on all cylinders latcly, haven't been sleeping too well. Better keep the dog inside, he'll get in my way. I brought the fertilizer mix for the first section of the garden."

"You said a cat dodged across the road on your way in. I can't find Macy."

"Oh, yeah." He rubbed his eyes. "He's not in the house after all? I'm sure it was a cat."

"Maybe he snuck out when I let Shadow into the garden. Macy loves spending time in the garden, but at least it's fenced and more or less cat-proofed. He's only been out there on leash, though, with Shadow to keep tabs on his furry butt." At his name, the dog barked once more.

"Want me to go out the front? You do the garden. We'll cover more ground that way." Aaron held up his own phone. "I'll call you if I catch a glimpse."

She waited until Aaron left before pulling on heavy tracking boots from the laundry room, and grabbing Shadow's halter and leash from the wall hook. He cued on the tools and could barely contain himself from bouncing up and down, muttering doggy comments under his breath. The newly trained *hide-and-seek* game had become one of his favorites, almost as adored as Frisbee fetch or Bear-tug-o-war. "Calm down, baby-dog. Sit."

He sat. His tail polished the kitchen floor, ears slicked back against his head as she put on his halter and attached the leash. Shadow's muscles trembled with the effort to contain himself. The dog finally exploded in joyous bounds aimed at her face when the last clasp snicked into place. "Shadow, settle." He leaned against her, sighed heavily and slurped her hand. "I love you too, baby-dog." She whispered so that only he could hear, and then stood and squared her shoulders. "But you're not the only fur-kid in my life. Shadow, want to play *seek*?"

His head cocked to one side, ears came forward with interest and his happy panting paused. She'd begun teaching him the *hide-and-seek* game so he'd be able to track missing pets, a skill that would have saved her much heartache a month ago. He'd been successful a few times, but now Macy counted on her, on both of them.

Most cats that got out of the house stayed close to home but remained hidden, and wouldn't even answer a beloved owner's call. A tracking dog, one trained to trail pets, was the answer.

After she grabbed Mickey, she led Shadow to the kitchen door, manhandled it open, and stepped outside. If Macy got out, it would have been from this door. September took a deep breath, and waited a moment until the dog's full attention focused on her. She held the stuffed toy for him to sniff, just as they'd practiced, so that he'd know the scent to track. "Where's Macy? Macy's hiding. Shadow, *seek Macy*!"

Shadow's eyes lit up, he woofed understanding and his nose dropped to the ground.

Chapter 8

The young woman fidgeted with the collar of her pink-koala-print smock, and glanced over her shoulder toward the closed door of the administrator's office. She whispered. "Mr. Williams? Mrs. Bradshaw doesn't know I called you?"

Again with the question. "We've known each other for almost a year now, Alison. When will you start calling me Teddy?" He adjusted his wire-rimmed spectacles, set the iPad on the counter and unbuttoned his lightweight jacket. "It's okay you decided not to go to the mall. Probably easier to spend time with her here; she prefers the familiar these days. Maybe take Molly for a walk with Trixie, and then take a trip down memory lane." He forced a smile and gestured at the album.

"You know the policy? We got to be respectful. Always Mister or Miz?"

"Good golly, she hates being called Miz Molly." He waited for Alison to giggle at the old, tired banter. Molly would have hee-hawed with delight.

But Alison busied herself with a pencil and pad, averting her eyes. "Could you take a seat for a minute?"

He'd worried for nothing. Allison would have said something, or the administrator Mrs. Bradshaw would have met him if there were a problem. He shrugged, grabbed the photo-filled tablet from the counter and shuffled over to one of the uncomfortable orange Naugahyde chairs, and lowered himself slowly with a grunt. His old bones didn't take kindly to the up-and-downs of sitting these days, and it irked him that the usually perky Alison was so prickly. Besides, the assisted living facility depressed him. He'd never imagined life would come to this.

Theodore Williams, maverick computer nerd, loved the predictability of technology. He'd been an early adopter of all things cutting edge when pocket protectors weren't cool, enjoyed the challenge of cyber-anything, and delighted in the ability to upgrade, re-boot, and download the latest advances. Hard drive failed? Replace it with a newer model. Software infected? Re-write the virus code to ricochet and destroy the sorry-assed wannabe player. Never mind Teddy officially "retired" from his teaching job ten years earlier; he still got called for freelance jobs from time to time, often from white-glove entities that needed discretion. His reputation as Mr. Fixit hadn't dimmed, although his hair had turned to snow and his knees made popcorn sounds.

But he couldn't re-boot Molly. Alzheimer's had stolen her away.

They met a lifetime ago. The girl with the giddy-making smile and ballerina grace made him crazy-happy for more than forty years, she the sequin shine to his stark practicality. Teddy liked to think he'd balanced her impetuous impulses as much as Molly had taught him how to laugh, laugh at life, laugh at failure, laugh at success, but always laugh together. Their happy expression had two F's, the "laff" a code for a personal shared hilarity nobody else understood.

Alzheimer's stole the laffs.

It happened so fast. Within six months, Molly disappeared, locked in a void of vacant stares, crying jags and fist-flung waking nightmares he couldn't breach. Most days he spent researching the digital world for the latest options, until his eyeballs bled from strain and he wanted to take a baseball bat to the computer. He hoped the iPad pictures from their happiest moments might spark a smile.

The front door squeaked open, and Teddy looked up. "Lewis? What're you doing here?" He struggled to his feet, and held out his hand to the much younger man.

"Same as you, I suppose. Visiting." Lewis's big hand swallowed Teddy's when they shook. He tugged off his gimme cap to reveal a well-worn groove in his brow. "Patricia finally got the point . . ." His throat worked and he turned away.

"I didn't know. God, I'm sorry." The news was a blow, although he hardly knew the man. As the local high school football coach, they frequented different circles, and Lewis's much younger wife worked in social services. But Patricia and Molly called themselves "professional volunteers" and spent hours together in various club meetings. "Patricia can't be more than forty year's old." His voice quavered with the shock.

"She's thirty-seven." Lewis throttled the cap in callused hands, but the words were void of emotion, as though he'd already used up futile anger and must conserve any remaining energy for grief. "They tell me it's a particularly aggressive form of the condition." Dark bags under Lewis's eyes aged him a decade beyond his mid-forty age.

Alison returned to the front desk. "The administrator wants a word, Mr. Williams. Through that door." She pointed, and then turned a full-wattage smile on Lewis. "Miz Patty is ready and for waiting your visit? Follow me?"

Lewis stuffed the hat into his pocket and followed Alison down the left hallway. Molly's room was at the end of that same corridor. The patients—or "guests" as Alison characterized them—needing more advanced care stayed on that side of the facility.

Teddy reclaimed his iPad from the chair before he hurried to the administrator's office, the first door on the right-hand hallway. He'd visited the office only twice before: six months ago when he realized Molly needed more than he could give, and a week later when together they'd introduced her to the facility. Neither visit had been pleasant.

"Mr. Williams, come in, have a seat." Mrs. Bradshaw met him at the door. Stiff decorum that served as her professional mask—and emotional protection, he guessed—had fled. Her hands fluttered, birdlike, smoothing the front of a dark tailored blouse and matching slacks. No koala print for her.

"I'll stand, thanks. What's this about? I want to see Molly." He gestured with the iPad. "I brought her favorite photo album. Is she having a bad day?"

"Actually, she's had a very good day." Mrs. Bradshaw moved around the tidy desk and perched on the edge of the overstuffed rolling chair. She scooted it back and forth, back and forth until Teddy wanted to nail her feet to the floor.

"A good day. Terrific. So what's the problem? You want me to authorize adjustment to the medication?" She'd been taking Damenia until the blowup in the news over the off-label use of the drug caused the company to pull it from the market. Maybe the new drug had better results? His heart jumped and he cautioned himself against false hope.

She pursed her lips. "We're doing everything we can, and I'm sure she's fine. You know how she loves Trixie."

His heart thumped louder. "I'm not liking your tone, Mrs. Bradshaw. What does Trixie have to do with this?" The resident Golden Retriever had been the deciding factor between this facility and others, and Molly acted much calmer when in the dog's presence. He put his hands on the desk, and leaned toward her. "Where is my Molly?"

She shrank back. "Like I said, I'm sure everything will work out fine. But you see, at the moment, we don't know exactly where Molly is."

He straightened. The iPad dropped to the floor with a loud crack.

Mrs. Bradshaw stood, the rolling chair rebounding from her narrow butt. "Truly, Mr. Williams, it should be fine. I've already called in a Silver Alert, and the police should find her quickly. Besides, the day's pretty mild, and she talked about walking the dog. Before we could get an aide lined up, she and Trixie were gone."

Chapter 9

Shadow snuffled, drawing the cool air deep, tasting the flavor of the paving stones. His own signature odor and that of September remained fresh, where they'd recently trod this path from the back garden. Cat smell drifted from the door, and he cast first right and then left in a semicircle, seeking the odor that identified Macy like a name-tag.

In his before-life, when he lived with his-boy at that other house, he'd learned what to do only because September visited and taught him what a good-dog should know. She taught him what special words and hand signals meant, like "sit" and "heel" and "come" and called him "good-dog" more than anyone else. Shadow liked to learn, liked hearing the "click" noise September used to tell him he'd done something right. He worked and worked, so hard it made his head hurt, to show September he could be a good-dog so she wouldn't ever leave him behind again.

She'd left him behind in his before-life, and he didn't like that, not at all. He still worried sometimes that he'd be left behind. He'd finally found his family. It was a good-dog's job to stay with his family—even cats could be family—teach them how to laugh and play fun games that kept dogs and their people from feeling bad.

Nobody taught him that. Shadow figured it out all by himself. He was smart that way.

The *hide-and-seek* game made September laugh and call him 'good-dog' a lot. He wagged at the thought, and huffed another breath. It wasn't as exciting as Frisbee-chase, but finding Macy always prompted the cat to make interesting noises.

When he'd first come to live with them, Macy scared Shadow with paw-thumps as he raced by, until he figured out that was cat language for wanting to play. Macy-talk confused him, but he learned quickly. He figured dog-talk confused cats, too.

He liked to steal Macy's mouse toy, a guarantee Macy would play with him. That game he invented all by himself. Macy slept with the toy and the aroma of cat fur and spit smelled almost as good as the real thing. So far, Macy only allowed long distance sniffs. Shadow was certain if he played the game right, he'd get to sniff Macy up close and personal, push his nose deep into the cat-fur-body, and not have to make do with second hand sniffs. Wouldn't that be fine!

September missed out on lots of smells and sounds that made the world such an interesting place. Shadow figured that the *hide-and-seek* game was a way for her to understand. It made him happy he could teach her, like she taught him. Family helped each other like that.

Shadow found nothing on the sidewalk, so he began pulling steadily toward the front of the house, towing September behind. The tug of the long line at his shoulders provided a direct physical connection with September he relished. Tension vibrated the line, more than when they'd played *hide-and-seek* in the house. It puzzled him that he couldn't immediately target Macy-smell but maybe the game had changed? September did that; made simple tasks harder to test him. He liked surprising her with success. His tail swept back and forth at the happy thought.

At the front of the house, September asked him to sniff bushes along the windows on both sides of the entry steps, even though he found no Macy-smell. He did find interesting bunny stuff, and a place where two raccoons had slept for a time, but no evidence of the cat.

For the first time, Shadow worried he might fail the test. He trusted that September knew lots of things, more things than a good-dog could discover, so it must be his fault he couldn't find Macy-smell. He didn't want to let her down.

From there he ranged back and forth on the hard circle pathway where cars arrived and left. Shadow liked cars. He got to ride in the back of September's car and stick his nose out to taste rushing wind when she made it go fast. He'd rather stick his whole head out, but the narrow opening wouldn't allow more than the tip of his nose. The pavement spoke of bird droppings, people shoes and coyote urine. Shadow's hackles bristled a bit, wanting to track the interloper. But he resisted the urge to pee over the mark, and concentrated on the job.

The garden-man's truck sat to one side, and it smelled of chemicals and mice poop and green growing things. But no cat. He spent several moments huffing and testing spore surrounding the vehicle anyway. He paid particular attention to the doors, and even jumped into the back of the truck to see if Macy had found a hidey-hole inside. Macy did that a lot, finding and curling up to sleep in tiny places a good-dog wouldn't fit. He snuffled up potting soil and dust that coated stacked bags, and sneezed twice before he hopped back out onto the ground.

September pointed underneath, and he sniffed a second time but found no Macy-smell, only the trail of the garden-man's boots. He whined and stared at September's face. Had Macy stopped smelling like Macy? How could that happen, for a cat to become invisible to smart-dog noses? Maybe this was a game he couldn't win.

Deep lines in September's forehead spoke of worry. Tension in her hand fed down the line and made his shoulders clench. Shadow's tummy hurt at the thought he might fail the test. He had to find Macy. Then the cat would hiss and paw-pat his face, September would laugh and stroke his brow and call him 'good-dog.'

"Shadow, *seek* Macy." She held out the cat's toy again for him to sniff. He licked it, too, in case that made a difference, but Macy-smell must still be the same. September's voice sounded fearful. He understood this wasn't the usual game, and sniffed Mickey again to please her. Nose-to-ground hadn't worked, though, so instead he lifted his face into the breeze.

His mouth opened and he panted quietly, sorting the threads of scent that tangled the breeze. Some were neon bright and shouted for attention while others barely nudged the itchy smell-center deep inside his muzzle.

He turned his head around, huffing out and discarding those that held no bearing, and—there! He came to attention, nose poised with purpose, and inhaled deeply, holding and tasting and teasing out the one thread that came oh-so-close to what he sought.

Cat. He'd found cat smell. He turned to September, and she'd already read his intent, and her half smile mirrored his anticipation at winning the game. That was the puzzle! She wanted him to find this other cat, and Macy-smell was the clue.

He pulled hard, letting his nose lead him to the origin of the cat scent, tugging September in his wake until she had to trot to keep up.

"Good-boy, Shadow! That's it!"

Her happy tone spurred his paws faster until they were both running down the long car path to the front gate. He slowed momentarily when he reached the strange car half in the ditch and crushed against the gate. Two of the doors swung open, and he took a moment to compare the scent he'd found on the breeze to the one strongest in the back seat of the car.

"Shadow? What're you doing, boy? *Seek* Macy, your kitty. Macy. Please, let it be Macy you're tracking!"

He didn't let her worried tone slow him down. Scent firmly in his brain, Shadow obeyed the command to find the lost cat. Nose barely skimming the ground, he located the freshest paw-treads.

Sick, the cat smelled scared and sick, not like Macy at all. Maybe that's why September wanted it found. He pulled hard to follow the trail, towing her so fast behind she stumbled and he had to slow down so she could keep up. The cat had run from the car across the road into the bushes of the nearby field. Shadow dug in his paws, leaping ahead with excitement that the goal was so close.

Chapter 10

Despite the pink gloves, September's hands hurt with the effort to hang on to the tracking line as Shadow eagerly led them to the source of the scent. Her hope took a hit when he stopped to investigate Sly's car. She didn't see the man anywhere, or his cat. She debated aborting the hunt. But Macy could have made it this far, perhaps even investigated Sly's abandoned car on his way to explore the great outdoors. That could be Macy's scent near the car.

No, she couldn't stop now. She couldn't take the chance. It wasn't the dog's fault if she'd given mixed signals. Besides, it was Shadow's job to track, and it was her job to believe the dog. She needed to reward him if he found any cat.

The field across the road from her renovated Victorian house offered a maze of Johnson grass hummocks, and cedar trees sprouted everywhere, an unwanted green plague ranchers fought to eradicate. She nearly turned her ankle in a pig wallow, thankfully dry, where a sounder—feral pig herd—must have recently camped and uprooted turf seeking food. Between the hogs and the armadillos, the field offered ample opportunity for injury.

Shadow tugged her steadily toward the center of the field where a gigantic bois d'arc tree held court. Spiny branches scratched the sky. As kids, she and Mark had called them "witch trees." Like most cats, Macy wanted to claim the highest perch possible. It made sense Macy had headed for the tallest tree around.

Parts of the old tree split, exposing the gnarly orange wood inside.

Shadow slowed, sniffed and pawed the trunk and stared up into the tree branches. He jumped up, placing front paws against the rough bark, and whined before dropping off. He lay down and stared at her with a happy grin, his signal of a find.

"Good-dog, Shadow. Good boy." She offered the praise and stroked his throat and he wriggled with delight. She stared into the dark, bare branches overhead, trying to see Macy through the twisty jigsaw. "Macy? Macy-cat, come." She waited. Nothing happened. She'd expected at least a meow response. "Macy? I've got treats." A shadow on one of the branches shifted, revealing the silhouette of a large fluffy cat. "Thank God!" She dropped the tracking line, and searched for a way to climb into the boughs. Cats often acted like it was too undignified to come down once they managed to climb aloft.

"Shadow, wait." She found a scraggly branch so heavy it drooped nearly to the ground, and pulled herself up onto the broad wood. Careful with hand placement to avoid the spikes, September tight-roped toward the trunk of the tree until she was able to use smaller ladder-like limbs. "Macy, I'm here. Hang on, kitty." She realized Shadow had wandered some distance from the base of the tree, probably enamored of some critter scent now that he'd nailed the *hide-and-seek* game.

She climbed twenty feet into the tree on the opposite side of the cat's perch. September inched around the girth of the trunk, finally at eye level with the furry miscreant. The cat hissed—not Macy, but a strange longhaired tabby cat with a bright pink nose and crusty eyes—and leaped from the tree to the ground. Crap. This must be the cat Aaron had nearly hit, probably Sly's sick cat, Pinkerton.

September grappled to maintain her balance, and bear-hugged the trunk. Below, Shadow's head jerked to follow the cat's flight, and without a backward glance, he leaped after the cat in a joyous chase.

"Dammit, Shadow, no!" She struggled to dismount the tree, her descent less graceful than the climb up, and jumped the last five feet in her hurry to stop the dog. Not only was Macy gone, now Shadow had disappeared.

"Shadow, come." He knew the command, but wasn't particularly reliable. She should have tied the line, she knew better.

He yelped—a sound of frustration, not pain or fear—and September dodged through the cedars and burr oak stands, eager to catch up. Vining brambles festooned cedar elms like overdone Christmas garland, smothering and bending saplings double. She ducked beneath swags of the prickles, and tore through green drifts that clawed her pants and scored her ankles. Shadow's tracking line must have snagged. That was good and bad; good that she'd be able to catch him, but bad if she hadn't been around. A caught line could trap the pup and make him easy pickings for coyotes. "Shadow, where are you, boy?"

He barked an answer, then twice more, and barks morphed to yodels of distress.

"What the hell?" September redoubled her effort, leaving torn fabric and skin behind, and broke through into a grassy opening.

Shadow barked and cried, leaped forward and back. His tail thrashed with conflicted emotions, his hackles erect. She bent to gather the long line of the lead that trailed in the grass at her feet. Three strides closer and she saw her wooden baseball bat creasing the tall grass. Puzzled, she retrieved the bat, and then dropped it with revulsion at the sight of the dark stains and clotted matter covering the business end of the wood.

The big tabby and white cat hissed from its perch. Shadow had cornered the feline against a downed barbed wire fence, the deadfall offering shelter but no easy escape. "Shadow, come." The dog turned his head, and backed up to press his shoulder against her thigh. She could feel him trembling.

The strange cat hissed again, and shifted to face them. Its enormous paws worked rhythmically, treading in the universal feline kneading behavior against the soft yellow fabric upon which it rested, perhaps in an effort to self-calm.

"Pinkerton? Hush, kitty, I'm here to help." She cautiously drew near, her boots crunching on dry vegetation, not wanting to spook Sly's cat. Finding Macy would have to wait until she caught this stray cat. She couldn't let her dislike of the reporter keep her from saving a needy animal.

September nearly tripped on a hummock of Johnson grass, and caught her balance on Shadow's broad back. He whined, and licked where her fingertips poked out of the gloves. The breeze died for a moment, and a smell smacked her in the face, the stink so thick she gagged. She stopped, heart hammering. She'd know that smell anywhere. Blood.

The cat's bright pink nose tested the air, but its eyes never stopped scanning, scanning, head turning first left and then right with a vague unfocussed expression as though blind and unable to see. A low keening sound, more growl than purr, made her scalp itch and mouth go dry. She gagged when Pinkerton's furry toes squished, and red liquid pooled beneath its paws steaming in the cold air and soaking into the yellow cloth. September prayed the cat was crouched on a still-warm deer carcass. Cats were heat-seekers, and sometimes a hunter's aim failed to drop prey in its tracks, and it ran for miles before collapsing.

But deer don't wear yellow. Or have spiky red hair.

Pinkerton cheek-rubbed and head-butted the figure until a gloved hand fell sideways in the brittle thatch. He stared into the bloody mess where a buck-toothed smile had been, and yowled a feline lament for Sylvester "Sly" Sanger.

Chapter 11

Shadow followed closely beside September, nearly tripping her on their rush back home. She'd taken off her jacket and wrapped the sick cat inside, even though it wasn't Macy. The cat smelled scary-bad, not only sick, but coppery rich with the dead man's blood.

He'd smelled that awful odor before. It made him want to squat-and-pee like a puppy. Instead, he growled to boost his courage, and his confidence increased when September touched his neck and smoothed the bristling fur.

"Aaron? Aaron, call 911." September barged through the kitchen door, waiting for Shadow to enter before bumping the door closed with one hip.

But the garden-man wasn't in the house. Shadow knew the big man worked among the dead plants inside the fenced back yard. When he didn't answer, September hurried into the nearby laundry, set the cat on the floor and shut the door before she picked up and held the small talk-box to her ear. She played with his tracking line as she talked.

Shadow drank deeply of the house smells, snuffling the slate floor with deep inhalations quickly huffed out as so much background noise. Acrid detergent. Spilled coffee trace. Lingering bacon—he licked his lips—but that scent, faded with time, had no merit in the current *hide-and-seek* game. No, he needed Macy-smell. His person—she who made all things right—had asked him to *seek* Macy. He'd found the sick cat, but read September's disappointment. He wouldn't pass the test until he found Macy.

He unraveled skeins of scent painted across the floor and floating at nose-level throughout the house. Macy smell filled the house. Only the freshest mattered. Shadow found the brightest trace, nose glued to the invisible trail, and pressed forward. The tracking line unraveled behind him, but stopped short and pulled against his harness when September's grasp anchored him in place. He stared back at her from the kitchen doorway, and whined.

"Shadow? What are you—" She dropped the line to finish talking.

He barked once, twice, impatient for her to grab the line so he could show her. She had to follow, he'd found Macy just as she'd asked. He barked once more.

"Give me a minute." She said something else into the talk-box and then pocketed the object. "Shadow, we've kind of got an emergency here. If you found Macy in the house, everything is fine and we'll play another time." But she picked up the line and let him tug her after him, despite the scary tension he heard in her voice.

Claws clicked across the cold hard floor of the kitchen, paws padded past plush carpet with the funny inside-tree, and onward to the smooth wood near the front door. He both heard and felt September hold her breath—everything traveled down the leash-line—and then she breathed again when his nose lead them away from the exit.

There! The freshest scent yet, at the bottom of the entry stairs. He huffed loudly, and scrambled up the staircase, slowing a bit when September dragged on the line. Good-dogs with four feet moved much faster than their two-footed people.

Shadow paused at the landing, wagging with low, loose wags as September caught up, and then he turned the corner and surged on up the remaining steps. He pulled and pulled—it was okay to pull with this halter but not the collar leash—and led them past September's room. He could tell she wanted to go into the sleep place, but the Macy-smell wasn't as fresh there as the paw-treads in the hallway.

Close now, and closer still. He even heard quiet cat breath, quick and jerky like Macy had run a race, and followed his ears down to the last door at the end of the hall. He nosed it open, walked to the cold shiny potty seat next to the cabinet, and lay down. That's what September taught him to do when the game ended. He woofed softly in case she didn't understand.

"Macy! Kitty, what are you doing in the sink?" September dropped the leash, and hurried past Shadow to reach the cat.

The cat roused enough to offer a half-hearted mew. But he didn't get up, and leap away to invite another tag-and-chase game as Shadow expected. Macy panted, eyes half shut, like he was sick. Macy's head fell forward, chin thumping the sink basin when he passed out.

September made a choking sound in her throat, and carefully gathered Macy into her arms. Shadow followed after, dragging the long line as she bounded down the stairs with his cat friend.

Chapter 12

The first dozen notes to the theme song of *Hog Hell* identified the caller before Dietz heard Grady's voice. "So? Did you find Felch? What's his excuse this time?" Heavy breathing but no words sounded. "Grady? You there, brother? Did you butt-dial again?" He started to disconnect, when the man finally spoke.

"Yeah, I'm here. Boss, we're screwed. Oh God, we are so screwed!" Grady's tone squeaked and broke like a voice-changing adolescent, the stampede of words muddled in the rush. "It's Felch, the crazy son-of-a-bitch. Christ, don't know what to do, couldn't stop him."

"Slow down, I can't understand you. Get a grip." Dietz sat and pulled the chair closer to the desk. He'd been prepping for the radio spot, but that could wait. "What'd he do? How much will it cost me this time?" Lord, couldn't the man stay out of trouble longer than a few hours? Three days, they needed three days of calm.

Grady's anguished voice broke again. "Remember I told you how he got in the car with that reporter? Felch called, said there's been an accident. Wanted me to pick him up." Heavy breathing again.

Dietz groaned. "So pick him up, take care of any insurance or cop reports, and send me the bill. And then don't let Felch out of your sight. I don't have time for this; that's your job."

"You don't understand. Took a while to find the place. They slammed into the front gate at this old Victorian monstrosity. Felch tells me he beat up that reporter, maybe killed him."

Breathing stopped for a lifetime. Then Dietz licked his lips, and whispered. "What did you say?"

"Felch went off on that reporter. I'm trying to tell you! He says the guy had this story ready, drove here to talk to some woman about it, and planned to release it before the show launch. Felch had to shut him up, protect the show. We all have a lot to lose if that story gets out."

"But he made it up! There's nothing to the story, Felch has to know that." Dietz stood up so fast, the rolling chair hit and dented the back wall. Even a fabricated story would ruin everything, though. "Felch beat him up? He can't be dead." He sat on the desk and put his head in his hand. "This isn't happening, I don't believe it."

"Believe it, all right." Grady's voice grew steadier. "I got Felch calmed down, got him in the truck, and he says the reporter spilled everything to this animal expert. What do you want me to do?" He paused, and then added, "Want me to talk to her? Warn her off? Hell, the reporter probably has notes stashed somewhere, too." His voice had gone squeaky-high with excitement. "We call the cops on this, and the show's toast. You know that, right?"

"Let me think, let me think." Dietz ran his hand through his hair until static electricity crackled. "Wait. Animal behavior expert? September Day?" He straightened. She could spoil everything. "Does she know about Felch and the reporter?"

"No. Maybe. Hell, I don't know." Grady rushed on. "Nobody's going to stumble across the body. Took all my powers of persuasion to get Felch in the truck and get the hell out of Dodge."

"Where's Felch now?"

"Haven't a clue. I dropped him at his place, but for all I know, he's circling around ready to jump me." He breathed heavily. "I'm sitting here in my car, with the doors locked, wishing I had a gun instead of this phone. If we're lucky, Felch is halfway to Mexico by now." Grady paused, and Dietz could almost hear the wheels turning. "You want me to call the police? Why don't you call the paper, give them the scoop about Felch getting fired from the show. That would distance us from him. I mean, before the body shows up. And it *will* show up."

The timing couldn't be worse. "The press will want to know why he got fired. When the reporter's found this will come out anyway, or even sooner if that woman talks to anybody." Think, think! Dietz stood up from the desk, and paced. Damage control, he needed time to manage and massage the story, discredit the reporter, and delay any negatives until after tomorrow night's launch. Longer, if possible. "First, get hold of the reporter's pack of lies, and burn them." He ground his teeth, silently cursing the whole situation. "Where are you?"

"Rabbit Run Road, half a mile from the behaviorist's house. Sunny's getting her hair and face done for the TV gig so I got to take her place talking

BeeBo down about his sick dog. You know he's a baby about his mutts." His grim tone spoke volumes. "I know the job can get down and dirty, but I never signed on for this. We gotta call the cops."

"We will, of course we'll call the police. But if the man's dead, waiting a day or three—until Monday, after the launch party—that isn't going to hurt him any worse, right?" He waited a long moment, and then prompted again. "Right, Grady? Tell me you understand."

"If somebody finds out before we report it, we're screwed even worse. I'm not going to prison for your stupid show."

Dietz groaned. "I have more to lose than any of you. My name's on the show. I cast *Looney Tunes* Felch. We need some wiggle room. If the news doesn't come out until after the launch party, and until after the holiday premium orders roll in, it won't matter. We can handle BeeBo. We can manage Sunny. And we can re-cast Felch."

"So you want me to keep a lid on it until. . .when?"

"Hell, until forever! What do you think?" He wanted to punch the wall. Success within his grasp, finally after years of failure, and now this. "Fix it. Find Felch, put a sock in it, make sure he talks to no one." He thought for a moment, and then added, "Especially keep him away from that September Day woman. You know, it'd be terrific if she left town for a while."

"Sure. I understand." Grady hesitated, as if weighing his next words with care. "Say the word, and I can arrange for her to take that trip. I can make the reporter's body disappear. But I need some guarantee this won't come back on me. I'm taking all the risks."

Dietz sank back into the chair. "What are you saying?" But he knew.

"I want to bury this problem as much as you, but a little more incentive would go a long way toward making the risk worthwhile. Don't you think that's fair?"

Blackmail? "I already doubled your pay this week. But that was to keep Felch and BeeBo in line. Haven't handled that too well, have you?" Dietz's face flushed with heat, and he was glad Grady couldn't see him.

"Do you want to argue the point? What's it worth to have this problem go away?"

Dietz took in the stack of bills on the desk in front of him, and the notes for the upcoming media events. He didn't have time to argue. And Grady knew it. "All right. Triple your weekly salary."

"I want a cut, too."

"You want *what*?" Dietz leaned his head in his hand. Damn Felch! The man better stay in Mexico or he'd beat the shit out of him, too.

"Triple salary. Named as a full producer on the show. And a fifty percent—"

"You're bat-shit crazy!"

"—or I could call the cops and let them handle it."

Dietz blew out his breath. Grady waited. He didn't need to say anything else.

It occurred to Dietz that he had no way of knowing how much the other man might be making up. Maybe he'd better have a private conversation with Felch before he slapped the snot out of him. Meanwhile, he had no choice. Promise whatever it took, for now anyway.

"What'll it be? Boss? I mean, *partner*?" Grady's words gloated.

"I don't want a sniff of my name or the show connected. And I don't want to know how you do it." Dietz slapped his palm against the desk and stood up. "Just make it go away, Grady."

"Done."

Chapter 13

Jeff Combs pulled the car to a stop in front of the brick colonial, and checked in the rear view mirror. Twelve-year-old Melinda sat with her arms crossed, red curls a jumble as she turned away to stare through the passenger window. Her lower lip pooched out, and high color on pudgy cheeks offered silent testament to the angry set of her shoulders. She looked so much like his wife, Cassie—ex-wife, he corrected himself—with a temper to match.

His eyes met William's serious expression, and the nine-year-old shrugged and leaned to pat his sister on the arm. Melinda jerked away from her younger brother's comfort, and her lip trembled with the effort not to cry.

The divorce had blindsided them all, but hit Melinda particularly hard. While William was a glass-half-full kind of kid and forgave pretty much anything, Melinda held each disappointment tight to her heart, taking it personally when life proved unfair. In that, she took after him, (Lord help her) and these days nothing seemed fair.

The custody arrangement gave him the kids for the two weeks leading up to Christmas. That would have worked out great except his leave of absence was cut short when Detective Kimberlane Doty took a new job in Chicago. His former partner's defection left a hole the department wanted to fill fast. Ironic that Doty not only got him busted from Detective down to beat cop, but her departure gave him back his ranking sooner than he could have hoped. He couldn't say no, the opportunity wouldn't come again anytime soon.

He unbuckled his seatbelt and strained to turn around, and tapped Melinda on her knee. "I'm sorry. I'm disappointed, too. But I'll make it up to you."

"I'll believe it when I see it." She wouldn't meet his eyes.

Hell, the sulky tone even sounded like Cassie.

"It's okay, Dad. Like you said, we'll make it up with an outrageous New Year's celebration." William addressed the words to Jeff, but pointed them at his sister. Always the peacekeeper. Like his grandma, God rest her soul.

Jeff blinked hard at that thought. This would be the first Christmas without Mom, and the first year after the divorce. Melinda had a right to be a cranky-pants, and he'd like to join her. But sadly, he had to be the adult. He sighed and opened the car door. "C'mon, troupes, I gotta get to work. Your mom's expecting us." In fact, he'd seen the curtains twitch and appreciated Cassie giving him time for private goodbyes before beckoning from the door.

The kids unlatched their seatbelts, grappled backpacks from the floor (a pink kitty-theme for Melinda, and the latest super-hero-du-jour for William), and tumbled out of the car. Melinda slammed her door extra hard and stomped toward the house, but William ran to Jeff's open window for their traditional "man-hug" and knuckle-bump. "Go get some bad guys, Daddy."

"You got it, champ." Jeff called hopefully after Melinda's back. "Hugs?"

She paused, hand on the doorknob, and glanced back. The scowl slipped, and she dropped the backpack and took a half step down the steps, tremulous smile fighting to blossom. Then Cassie opened the door. And the moment passed.

Melinda grabbed the backpack and shoved past her mother through the door, quickly followed by William. Jeff held out his hands, palms up, and shrugged, but Cassie said nothing. The door swung closed, blocking off the view of the sumptuous hardwood entry and formal appointments her new husband could provide.

"Happy holidays to you, too." He rolled up the window, threw the car into gear and left tire treads on the brick drive that Cassie's husband, Rick-the-Prick would pay someone to scrub clean. He scowled. Petty? Sure, but he had to take his pleasures where he could.

Forty minutes later, Jeff shook hands with his new partner, Detective Winston Gonzales, and his shoulders relaxed. He could have been partnered with anyone, even one of the cronies who still blamed him for the department's black eye that had led to his demotion a year ago. Maybe his luck had changed.

Gonzales smiled past his carefully trimmed black mustache, handshake firm, tidy suit and tie matching the studied assessment as he met Jeff's eyes. He sported a big dog attitude despite his small stature, and Jeff recognized his ability to face down most opposition with a steady stare, like a Chihuahua besting a Doberman on its home turf.

"Deja vu. You look a whole lot better than the last time I saw you."

Gonzales led the way to desk space on the far wall. "You still on that diet of caffeine and cookies?"

"Don't knock it till you tried it. Sleep is highly over-rated. Trying to measure up to Doty's standards." Combs pulled out the rolling chair in front of the bare desk where the blond Amazon used to work. "How ironic is that? Both of us partnered with her until she takes credit for the bust, and moves on to greener pastures. So to speak."

Gonzales snorted, and shed his suit coat, hanging it carefully on the back of his chair. "From where I sit, you measure up just fine. Doty is what she is. Let her take the credit. Got you back in the saddle, didn't it?" He planted his narrow butt on his own chair and trundled back and forth, his version of a hamster burning energy on a wheel.

They'd briefly worked together last month to investigate Jeff's mother's murder. When Doty froze him out, Gonzales at least met him halfway despite the rumors around the department. The younger man treated Doty with the respect reserved for a more experienced partner, but everyone in the department knew she maneuvered for high profile cases to help her climb the career ladder.

Gonzales cared as much or more about justice for the victims as he did clearing a case. That reason alone was enough for Combs to like the younger man. He envied Gonzales's ability to capitalize on the good and ignore the bad of the job—a glass-half-full kind of guy.

There it was again, he needed to be more like his son William and new partner Gonzales. Maybe that would balance out his own innate pessimism and suspicious nature. But it took a lot to balance getting kicked in the balls by your peers, wife leaving you, and kids' disappointment.

"Here's the current cases." Gonzales shoved the stack of files on his own desk closer to the edge and watched Combs cage the first one from the top of the pile.

Before he could give more than a cursory read, a shadow fell over the desk. Combs stood quickly and held out his hand. "Thanks for the opportunity, Captain." He had to raise his face to meet the towering man's flint-gray eyes.

"We needed to fill the hole. I trust you won't step in a big ol' pile of stink this time?" Captain Felix Gregory crunched the offered hand, dropped it and addressed both detectives. He nodded at the pile of cases. "That can wait. We've got a body."

Chapter 14

September stroked Macy's tawny fur, cradling the big cat in her arms and rocking him gently. They sat huddled together in their favorite overstuffed chair in the living room. It faced the floor to ceiling window view of the circle drive. Normally the cat preferred to snooze on the back of the chair above September's head, giving him an added elevation for scolding the dog. He rarely agreed to lap sit, except on extra cold or cloudy days. The fact that he didn't protest her arms spoke volumes. Macy was sick.

She'd thrown away the bloodstained pink gloves and hurriedly changed into stone washed jeans and a green sweater that matched her eyes, and now wore boot-cut zipper boots. She'd wanted to race to the emergency vet with Macy and the dead man's cat. But with the police on the way to address the murder, the cats had to take second place no matter how much she wished otherwise.

Pinkerton remained sequestered in the distant laundry room, meowing now and then in protest at the incarceration. September had belatedly scrubbed her hands and changed out of her shirt, but worried she'd exposed Macy to whatever had made the tabby cat sick. Feline illnesses easily transferred from cat to cat, and any virus or bacteria contamination of her hands could also infect.

Shadow lounged beside the chair, his stuffed bear braced between front paws, and mouth around the toy's soft, misshapen head. He sucked the fuzzy pacifier with eyes half closed, body leaned against one of her legs. The contact that usually calmed September's nerves did nothing to ease her tension.

"Please, don't let my cat die." She whispered the words, more of a hope than a prayer, not convinced God listened to her after all the awful things she'd done. But Macy was innocent. God had taken Chris and Dakota, but had spared Shadow. Maybe she'd been punished enough.

A car pulled into the drive, and September recognized Jeff Combs when he got out. When Detective Gonzales followed Combs, a dizzying sense of deja vu rocked her, and she squeezed Macy in reaction. He mewed in protest, and kicked with his rear legs, showing a bit more energy than he had in the previous twenty minutes. September soothed him with a soft murmur before placing him inside the fabric pet carrier she'd set next to the chair.

Shadow beat her to the front door. He still wore his halter, although she'd removed the tracking line and stuffed it in her coat pocket. When the doorbell bonged, he woofed twice, checked in with September, and sat quickly, anticipating the closed-fisted signal that always followed a doorbell chime. "Good-dog. Away. Go to bed." She waved one hand, and pointed across the room and he reluctantly trotted over to settle on an overstuffed dog pillow near the fireplace.

She unlocked the deadbolts, unlatched the chain and pulled open the door. Managing a weak smile, September motioned the two men inside. As soon as Combs entered, Shadow wiggled his body with ears pressed flat, and woofed a greeting. But he didn't break, and kept his butt planted.

"Hey Shadow, good to see you, too." Combs kept his eyes on September, though, raised eyebrows requesting answers. Gonzales already had a notepad and pencil out of his pocket.

"Thanks for coming so quickly." She motioned to the pet carrier. "Macy's sick. So could we speed up the statement? I can answer any follow up once I get him to the vet." Her voice caught. "I don't mean to be unfeeling, but the man is beyond help."

"If needed we can do follow up at dinner tonight." Combs entered and crossed to the wagging Shadow to pat the dog's neck before turning back to September.

September caught Gonzales' surprised expression. Great, now the whole police department would think she and Combs were an item. But he only smoothed his dapper mustache, and didn't move from the doorway. "Where's the body?"

"Across the road." She pointed out the open door, past the gate. "There's a bois d'arc tree about a third of the way in the field, and his body is a few yards to the left of it. West of the tree, I mean, near an old fence."

As if through a prearranged signal, Gonzales tucked his notepad back into his pocket and hurried down the front steps toward the crime scene. September slowly closed the front door after him. She latched each lock before taking a deep breath and turning to face Combs.

He'd settled on the arm of the sofa, and motioned her to take a seat.

Combs pulled out a digital recorder, and took up the questions. "Start from the beginning."

"This morning I heard a crash." She pointed out the front window. "I ran out to see what happened—"

"By yourself?" Combs stared pointedly at Shadow. He knew she took self-protection seriously.

"Shadow was in the garden. And I'm getting better about that." Her words sounded defensive, even to her own ears.

Shadow thumped his tail against the floor at the sound of his name, and she dropped a hand to touch his back. Should she tell Combs about the bat? Maybe she shouldn't have thrown away the pink gloves. Then it was too late to mention, as he prompted her to go on.

"You spoke to the car's owner? You know this person?"

"Sylvester Sanger." The name left a sour taste.

"Sly?" Combs grinned. "He's a piece of work. What'd he want?"

"He's been calling and hounding me ever since…well, you know. Wouldn't leave me alone, wanted to write a big tabloid piece, and didn't respect my privacy." Her cheeks heated at the memory. "He was a worm, but nobody deserves to die like that."

Combs paused, pencil in the air. "Killed in the car crash? That his Gremlin by the gate? Nobody inside when we drove up."

September stood from the sofa, and Shadow followed her pacing with his eyes, whining in response to her agitation. "Sly was fine, a little bruised up but out of the car and talking and walking when I saw him. Had his cat in the car with him and said he wanted my help researching some lame story. I was so mad he'd messed up my new gate, I didn't listen. I blew him off." She turned away sheepishly. "When I got back to the house, Aaron said he saw Macy outside."

"Your brother's partner, right?" Combs craned to look toward the kitchen. "He still here?"

"He wanted to wait in the garden. I can get him." She started toward the kitchen but Combs called her back.

"That's okay, we'll get his statement later. He didn't talk to Sly or see him?"

"I don't think so." September rubbed her face, and settled back in the overstuffed chair. She let her hand press the mesh top of Macy's carrier, anxious to grab him up and go. "When I couldn't find Macy, I had Shadow search for a trail outside the house. We found Sly." She shuddered.

"Did you touch the body?"

She ducked her head. "Didn't have to. I could see he was gone." Now would be the time to mention the baseball bat, but at that moment, Pinkerton yowled from the laundry room. She gestured that direction with a grimace. "The cat made contact, though. It was crouched on top of his body like a furry guard." She shivered. "I couldn't leave it out there. I called the police, and then Shadow found Macy." She finished in a rush. "He's sick. So's the other cat. That's all." She waited. "Can I please take them to the vet?"

Combs shook his head. "You need to sit tight. Sorry about that, but you know the drill." He stood.

Yes, she knew the drill all too well.

"Do whatever you need to do while I talk with Aaron. Gonzales will secure the body. We need you to stay out of the way. Stay in the house until I give you an all clear." He started toward the kitchen.

At least she could get the animals ready for the trip to the clinic. September picked up Macy's carrier and hurried after Combs to the kitchen, setting the carrier on the stained glass table before turning to the laundry room where Pinkerton continued to wail. She waited until Combs disappeared out the door, and resisted the urge to lock it behind him. He was a cop, after all. Another cop was across the road.

The sick feline's tortured cry sounded again when September carefully entered the laundry room, prepared to block any escape attempt. But the tabby cat continued to yowl, tail held high—for the first time she could see it was a boy—and the kitty's head pointed into the far corner of the room. He pawed the wall, crying with a frustrated vacant stare as if convinced a doorway should open for him. Shadow stuck his nose into the doorway, but politely kept his distance from the strange cat.

"Kitty? Pinkerton? I'm over here." When the cat didn't acknowledge her presence, she stamped the floor and slammed the door in case the cat was deaf. The tabby boy flinched from the sound, but continued to dig at the wall.

September wondered what sort of illness the cat had caught. *Please don't let it be contagious to Macy.* The cat had no collar or tags but the white blaze on the cat's muzzle and chin spotlighted the bright pink nose Sly had described. The vet clinic would be able to scan for a microchip—sadly, not all cats had them—and hopefully confirm if he belonged to Sly or not.

She found a clean pillowcase, held it open, and slid the bag over the top of the cat. The dazed creature walked right into the opening. September gently lifted the big cat, which began to purr and finally settled in the cradling material.

After she washed her hands one more time, September picked up the bagged cat, and deposited it on one of the cast iron chairs next to the glass kitchen table. She sat in another one. Her leg bounced up and down. She stood and paced, Shadow following her and whining. She opened the door and stuck her head out—technically, she hadn't left the house—and saw Combs in the bare spots through the fence. He stood dwarfed by Aaron. She couldn't hear what they were saying, but the tone of the bigger man's voice sounded confused and strident.

September hated that she'd somehow managed to get family once again involved with her troubles. She'd make it up to him later.

She saw Combs pull out his phone. He listened a moment before whirling to look toward her. September quickly ducked back into the house, gently pulling the door closed, not sure why she felt guilty. She'd done nothing wrong. Thirty seconds later, Combs pushed open the door with one foot and stood in the opening, phone in one hand and recorder in the other, and said nothing for a long moment.

"What? Did Aaron know something?" She licked her lips. "Can I go now? Take the cats to the vet?"

He dropped the recorder in one pocket, and gestured with the phone. "Gonzales called. There's only one big-ass bois d'arc in the field. You said west of the tree, right?"

"Right."

"Are you sure he was dead? If you didn't check for a pulse, didn't touch the body, you can't be sure."

"He had no face!"

Combs dropped his phone into his pocket. He wouldn't look at her, and instead waved a hand at the pet carriers. "Go on, you're in such a hurry, get out of here. Any other questions, we can cover tonight."

"Wait, tell me what happened."

He finally met her eyes with his own. Cop eyes. Hard. Questioning. "Gonzales can't find anything. There's no body."

Chapter 15

Tommy Dietz paced in the waiting area of the WZPP (aka "ZAP105") radio station, and checked his watch for the third time. BeeBo had yet to arrive, but the interview would go on with or without the big man. He had to make nice with the locals, especially with the kickoff to the new season imminent.

The brunette—wait, did she have blue hair?—stood behind the glass partition. She leaned forward and spoke with a nasal twang. "We're ten minutes away from air. Where's your guys?" The smell of a peppermint-scented candle clogged the room. She finger-combed her metallic blue nails through the matching streaks in her wavy hair.

"On the way; don't worry. And I can fill in until they get here." The radio show could barely be heard in the waiting room but grew louder when he walked to the counter and leaned toward the receptionist. Dietz eyeballed the nameplate on the desk. "After all, Anita, I'm the host with the most, and the brains behind *Hog Hell.*"

"Yeah, that's great." She waved one hand in the hair to speed the drying time of the nail enamel. "But Fish wants the stars. He wants the on-camera characters the listeners recognize, not the producer or director or whatever. No offense, but nobody cares about you. They want to hear all that down-home redneck talk."

Dietz hid his irritation with a bright smile, the practiced expression calculated to melt female hearts. "You like the redneck attitude, do you?" He turned up the wattage, knew that his blue eyes proved irresistible to women of a certain age. His bad boy good looks and expression promising a dangerous good time had booked him countless TV commercials back in the day.

Anita cocked her head and stared at him for a long moment. "Nice try, honey, but I've been schmoozed by the best. Better save your A-game for Fish if your talent is a no-show." She returned her attention to painting the nails on her other hand, holding up the middle finger in a mocking gesture. "I'll give you another two minutes, and then y'all need to get your cute boy buns back to the studio."

His anger seethed and he turned away and took several calming breaths. That's what he got for working with amateurs.

He'd turned BeeBo, Felch, Sunny and the others into stars, but the fickle tastes of the public could reduce them to has-beens twice as fast. Never mind the network ordered another six shows—they could and would cancel in a heartbeat if sponsor money dried up, and the whiff of scandal puckered wallets faster than anything. He couldn't let that happen.

In a way, Felch did the show a favor by getting rid of that rumor-mongering reporter. As long as Grady kept everything under wraps, the show had nowhere to go but up. Sponsors would beg for a dozen more episodes, book two or more years out. When that happened, he'd sell the property outright and be set for life.

"Hey there, Mr. Dietz, you ready? I'll let Fish know you're going solo." She arched one thinly plucked brow and pointed toward the security door, releasing the door-lock buzzer with the jab of one blue nail. "Down the hall, glass studio booth, wait for him to wave you in. He's live right now." She smiled with sympathy. "He'll want to cut the interview short. Probably would've given the lovely Sunny a whole hour." Her expression soured a moment before she added, "But I'll buzz your guys in right away if they show."

Dietz ignored the heat that warmed his neck. He grabbed the door handle and hurried through before she changed her mind. BeeBo would pay for this.

The radio show that had been muted in the waiting area overwhelmed the hallway at full volume. The host's voice boomed in a basso profundo so low that Dietz could feel sympathetic vibration in the studio windows.

"I have a tasty treat for you today, boys and girls. We'll be talking to the stars of the hit reality show, locally filmed *Hog Hell*. So hang tight. I'm Humphrey Fish, and we'll have a scrumptious knee-slapping interview after this brief message from our sponsor."

Dietz paused, surprised by the host's appearance when a bowling ball-shaped man waved for him to enter the studio. Fish hopped off the tall stool, and held out his hand to shake.

"I'm Fish. You must be Tommy Dietz." His bald head barely reached Dietz's shoulder. Fish jutted his red goatee toward the door. "Where's

BeeBo? And what's-his-name, the other guy?" He made a point of craning his neck right and left, pretending Anita hadn't alerted him to the situation.

After shaking his hand, Dietz took the chair Fish indicated. "I told Anita they're on the way. Thanks for having us on the show. We wanted to give you the scoop and first crack to share the exciting news." He knew Fish craved the limelight as much as his TV colleagues. After last month's notoriety with the Blizzard Murders, the glorified DJ considered himself a journalistic star in his own right, and a bit of flattery couldn't hurt. Fish's show, now syndicated and aired both live and via the internet, reached a wider audience than the local TV affiliates, and his audience shared similar tastes with the viewers that had put *Hog Hell* on the map. "Nobody else could do the story justice."

"My listeners expect the best. Let's not disappoint them." Fish motioned to the engineer, and reclaimed his tall perch. He pulled the football shaped fuzzy mic closer to his mouth and signaled Dietz to do the same with his. "We're live again in fifteen. I'll intro, pitch to you for a quick comment, and we'll go from there."

Dietz tugged at his collar. No matter how many media appearances he'd done over the years, nerves never went away. He noticed Fish sipped something murky from a puce colored mug, and wished he'd thought to stop for a decaf chai. He'd been trying to cut down on the caffeine and finally found a local cafe that did justice to his favorite blend.

"We're back, gentle listeners, and as promised, help me welcome Tommy Dietz, the producer, show host and creative genius behind *Hog Hell*, a reality show that's made stars out of local hunters BeeBo Benson, Randy Felch, the lovely Sunny Babcock and a host of other characters. Welcome to the show, Mr. Dietz."

"Call me Tommy. Thanks for the opportunity." He licked his lips, took a breath, and settled into the prepared pitch. "*Hog Hell* has won a huge following thanks to fans like your listeners. The show began as an experiment in edu-tainment that celebrates the unique culture of the hog hunting community."

Fish widened his eyes. "I didn't know hogs had culture. But that show really brings home the bacon."

"Ha, right. Good one." Dietz faked a laugh, and pushed on. "Feral hogs damage property and cause enormous financial hardship to the tune of $52 million a year, and that's in Texas alone. Nationwide, conservative estimates of annual cost damages due to feral hogs reaches $1.5 billion—yep, that's with a B. Hog hunts help manage the problem, and combine a dog sport— everybody loves dogs—with a worthy charity that benefits the community. The pigs harvested during the show go to local food banks. That barbecue is not only tasty, it's a win-win for everyone."

"The pigs might disagree." Fish slurped his coffee. "Listeners, what do you think?" He nodded over at the engineer. "Caller, you're on the air. Do you have a question?"

A female voice spoke with soft determination. "This is Gracie. I listen to your show all the time, Humphrey, it's such a delight. But I watched that Hog H-e-double-toothpick show one time after my son turned it on. Disgraceful!"

Dietz started to reply, but Fish held up a hand to stop him. "What didn't you like?"

"Everything! The guns, the violence, the vicious dogs biting those poor little piggies. Those Pit Bulls are killers, you know. Now my son wants one."

"Thanks for your call." Fish pointed at Dietz to speak.

"We take great care to manage the hunt in a humane manner." This wasn't the interview he'd envisioned. "The pigs are not dispatched on-camera. Feral hogs in this situation are much more dangerous to the people and the dogs than the other way around." He'd bet a year's salary the caller wasn't local. Probably some bleeding heart wanted the piggies adopted out in some hog sanctuary.

"Caller, you're up. What do you have to say?"

"Thanks for taking my call, Mr. Fish. I've got real problems with these so-called sportsmen playing target practice with the pigs. That won't solve the problem."

"Is that right?" Fish again held up a hand, cutting short Dietz's comments. "You have a better solution? And what's your name, sir?"

"Fred Jones, I'm the County Ag Agent. Now, I agree the rooting behaviors cause no end of habitat destruction, but shooting a stray pig now and then won't control them. Only way to control 'em is to round up and trap the whole sounder."

"Sounder?" Fish cocked his head.

"Sounder, that's a herd of wild swine. One sow can have two or three litters a year, or about thirty piglets, and even with fifty percent attrition, that's fifteen more pigs for every sow. Feral pigs are so smart, if you only trap one at a time, you educate the other pigs to be more wary and avoid the traps. The best way to control them is to trap the entire sounder at once."

Dietz sniffed. Viewers wouldn't tune in to watch a corn-sprinkled pig lot and wait for the piggies to stroll into the trap. But he'd play along. "Mr. Jones, we've had this conversation before. We're on the same side. And I applaud the job you're doing with the traps, and we'll keep on going after our pigs one by one."

"Sounds reasonable enough. Next caller, what do you have to say?" Fish twirled his finger in the air, and the engineer cued up the next guest.

"This is BeeBo Benson, y'all. Don't you be talkin' down my dawgs."

Dietz started. "You're supposed to be here, doing this interview."

"Sorry, Tommy. My best dawg got sick, so Grady drove me over to the vet." His voice caught on the last few words. "I don't think he's going to make it. But I can't have Mr. Fish's listeners thinking bad about my dawgs. That's a shitty thing to say about a man's dawgs, especially when they're sick and all." He paused and blew his nose. "Mr. Fish, I am right sorry that I missed out meeting you. I got to go now, but maybe I can make it up to y'all sometime?"

Fish shrugged a "what can you do?" gesture. "BeeBo, thank you for calling in. I'm sure all the listeners out there will send some positive vibes out to your dog." He turned pointedly to Dietz. "What do you know about this rash of sick critters everywhere? Now even your star hounds are affected. Some of my listeners complain about diseased raccoons and coyotes out and about, maybe infecting their pets. Since you and BeeBo are out amid the varmints, so to speak, is it contagious to pets? Did BeeBo's dog catch a critter cootie? Rabies, maybe?" His tiny eyes shined with excitement.

Dietz counted silently to five. It was that damn reporter's fault, raising suspicion for no good reason. "You'd have to ask a veterinarian about BeeBo's dog. There have been reports of raccoon distemper in the south part of the county, but that doesn't affect our show in any way." Had the reporter talked to Fish, too? This was his chance to put a lid on potential bad publicity before it went viral.

Fish was on a streak. "Here in North Texas, guns, dogs and barbecue go together like prom night and shotgun weddings. I kid. Well, maybe not. There's been some talk that the actors, I mean stars of the show, are scripted."

"Wait a minute, I—"

"We're still waiting for your other stars to show up. At least one had the courtesy to call in. BeeBo Benson, the lovable three hundred-pounder with the eagle-eye aim, rock hard gut and soft spot for his hog dogs. Randy Felch, thin as a copperhead with a temper to match. And the lovely Sunny Babcock, hotter than a coal stove even when covered in muck. Are you telling me they're not from Central Casting?" He glared. "Now, if BeeBo's dog is sick, my sympathies. Listeners know I'm a big fan of pets—you could say that "putting on the dog" put me on the media map. So I hope your stars will deign to show up and prove my suspicious nature wrong."

Dietz returned the stony expression. "If they were professional actors, they'd be here. These are real people with real feelings and allowances must be made. That's the tradeoff for getting the unexpected, exciting show our fans love. Believe me, BeeBo, Felch and Sunny are as real as they get." He lightened his tone. Wouldn't pay to piss off Fish before he'd gotten the news announced. "Two years ago to celebrate the wrap of the first season, we held a pig roast and barbecue locally to thank everyone for their help."

"I remember that. It was over at the Hog Heaven BBQ Restaurant." A beat. "I wasn't invited."

Aha. That explained some of the man's attitude. "My bad. Let me make it up to you, Humphrey."

"Don't be a tease. What do you have in mind?" Fish raised his eyebrows.

Dietz smiled. "The first show of our new season airs Friday, tomorrow night—right in time for Christmas. We're shipping out a special Piggy Panache Premium Package, official holiday gifts to Super Fans with sausage, jerky, bacon and more samples. You can't buy these. Viewers must watch the first show to find out the Piggy Password to order."

"A piggy password?" Fish nearly fell off his stool, guffawing. "Let me guess. Pig-in-a-blanket? Pig-in-a-poke? Porky Pig. Pig Newton?"

"Not even close, Humphrey. Guess you'll have to watch the show." Dietz's shoulders relaxed a bit. The little man had bought into the promotion. "Tomorrow night we have a watch party barbecue celebration once again at the Hog Heaven restaurant with an invitation-only audience. I've got spots for 200 guests—199, actually, because Humphrey Fish will be the first guest in the door." He noted Fish's pleased expression and continued in a rush. "The guests will also be on-camera in a future episode of the show as extras— so get ready for your close-up!"

"Now Tommy, that sounds like my kind of party. Can't wait to pig out at the big event! But what about those other 199 tickets? Do I sense a whole hog give-away in the offing?" Fish put his hand to his ear, pantomiming a phone.

Dietz grinned. "You read my mind. What do you say we give spots away to your listeners?"

The phone lines lit up.

Chapter 16

September rocked back on her heels in surprise, and had to consciously close her mouth. It wasn't possible they couldn't find Sly's body. She should have led them to the place. Hell, she would have missed it if the cat hadn't led Shadow to the crime scene.

Before she could say a word, Combs pushed past her and hurried out of the kitchen to the front of the house. She heard the door swing open and shut, probably on his way to rejoin Gonzales. Her lips tightened. Fine. She'd reported the crime. The police didn't want or need her help to do their job. She had her own job to do taking care of the cats.

"Shadow, wanna go for a car ride?" September looped his leash over the back of her neck, gathered up Macy's carrier with one hand and Sly's cat-bag in the other, and nearly ran out the door to the car. The big pup bounced and twirled in response, following so close behind her she nearly tripped. "Stay with me, baby-dog."

Shadow jumped into the back seat without prompting. After belting Macy's carrier in the front seat and setting the pillowcase on the floor, September deactivated the passenger side airbag just in case. Even a minor fender bender deployed the airbag and would crush a small pet, but she couldn't have the cats in the back with Shadow.

Her car swung out of the renovated carriage house garage. She carefully threaded the needle past Aaron's big truck to the front gate, avoiding the sight of Sly's battered car, which was now a crime scene. Combs didn't look up from collecting evidence, and Gonzales joined him by the car as she drove past.

Once on the road, she fished out her cell phone from a pocket and dialed the veterinary hospital. "This is September Day, and I'm bringing two sick cats in for exams. Yes, I'd call it an emergency. I'm on my way, should be there in ten or fifteen minutes." She briefly outlined the two cats' symptoms before disconnecting.

She set the phone on the dash and pressed the accelerator, ignoring the speed limit to make the twenty-minute drive in record time. The tires slipped on wet pavement, and September leaned into the turn. She glanced in the mirror when Shadow lost his balance. He yelped when he bumped against the door.

"Sorry."

He put his ears down and thumped his tail. Shadow stuck his nose through the pet barrier and poked her arm, and she smoothed his muzzle.

While her left hand steadied the steering wheel, she braced Macy's cat carrier nested on the passenger seat with her right hand. The cat's green eyes peered out of the mesh webbing, and he head-bumped the material and mewed, trying to reach her fingers. Sly's cat in the pillowcase on the floor said nothing.

Macy's breathing problems seemed to have resolved and now he seemed normal. But she didn't want to take chances, and Pinkerton needed a look, too. Besides, it had been too long between checkups. Macy loved meeting new people and enjoyed vet visits where strangers complimented him and offered pets and treats.

She couldn't bring herself to visit the vet clinic back in South Bend. She knew it was wrong to blame them but couldn't help it when they couldn't save Dakota. At the thought of his name, her heart skipped a beat. She still missed him. Always would.

"Macy-cat, feeling better?" She steadied the carrier as they again rounded a curve. When he meowed, Shadow nosed her once more. Although the pair had only lived together a short time, they'd already become fast friends.

Macy had always been healthy, and at four, he was the picture of a strapping adult boy cat. Maybe he'd eaten something toxic. Her own mouth tasted bitter at the thought. She knew all the holiday plants to avoid—holly, Jerusalem cherry, mistletoe—and decorated with an eye toward pet safety. She didn't even have the fake plants in the house.

She'd been rocked by Combs's revelation. It made no sense for the body to disappear. She hadn't fumbled for a pulse, it hadn't seemed necessary with the state of his concaved face, but if Sly had managed to stagger off, Gonzales would have found him.

Combs didn't mention the baseball bat, either. That thought chilled her. There had been plenty of time between her finding Sly's body and Gonzales's arrival for someone to move it.

Someone who stumbled upon the crime scene would raise the alarm and call the police, would get help, not hide the victim. Instead, they didn't want Sly found maybe because they killed him. And that someone had the murder weapon that could incriminate her.

"Shadow, tell me I'm paranoid." He woofed happily, and she smiled despite herself. The pup always knew how to lift her spirits. "We're a team now, right? We'll protect each other."

She felt lucky to have survived Uncle Vic with nothing worse than PTSD, although *nothing worse* seemed like an oxymoron. She shivered.

He'd listened to her teenage angst. He'd cheered her musical successes, and kept would-be romantic wolves at bay, deeming none good enough for his "princess." After being overshadowed for years by her sister—April was the pretty one—September felt flattered and vindicated by Uncle Vic's attention and fierce protectiveness. Her folks thought the world of him. And so she trusted him completely. Until her eighteenth birthday dinner, when everything changed.

"He can't hurt you." She said the words aloud, the mantra one she'd recited for more than eight years. But the package, another crappy joke from Sly, brought everything back. He couldn't hurt her. But he had. Because of Victor, she'd never feel safe again; never open herself to such hurt. Never trust again, not fully.

She kept the horrific memories buried and had no intention to share what sort of damaged goods she truly was. Chris had known, and ended up dead. "Safest to stick with cats and dogs. Right gang? You don't care about the past." And pets never lied about love.

She pulled into the parking lot of All Creatures Veterinary Hospital. Shadow's breeder had been married to the clinic's owner, Doc Eugene, an internal medicine specialist. Heartland didn't have a pet emergency center, and instead several smaller clinics rotated after-hours emergency availability. They'd treated Shadow's gunshot wound last month, along with his paw injuries, and she'd been relieved not to see Doc Eugene. For sure, he didn't want to see her.

September put the car in park and cracked both rear windows two inches before turning off the engine. The warmth of the heater followed her briefly as she stepped into the cold. Her breath puffed in white clouds when she hurried around to the passenger side to heft the twenty-pound Maine Coon's carrier out of the car. The cat in the pillowcase weighed less than half that amount. She slammed the door, and briefly touched a gloved hand to Shadow's nose sticking out the window.

"Wait here, baby-dog, I'll be out soon." Shadow's worried whine fogged the window, but he quickly settled to await her return.

The door squeaked open on a tile-floor waiting room lined with padded benches on three walls. Large windows on the front side gave September a clear view of her Volvo and the black doggy nose stuck halfway out one rear window. Clenching the pet caddy in one hand and the bagged cat in the other, she lugged them to the front counter—deserted—and waited a moment before setting both gently onto the floor.

"Anybody here?" She leaned over the chest-high counter, craning to see into the back room where muffled voices droned.

A hidden door squealed opened. "September, that you? Be right there." The youthful voice belonged to Timothy Beamish, the office manager and vet tech September had called on the way to the office. "Meet me in the cat room, exam three." The door clunked shut.

Macy's meow turned into a drawn out yowl as his carrier swung in September's grasp and accidentally bumped into a wall. "Sorry, buddy." She balanced Macy in one hand with Pinkerton in the pillowcase in the other, and hurried down the hall to the last small room on the left and elbowed open the door.

Three people stood in the room around a stainless steel table upon which a brown and white Pit Bull reclined. An enormous man, at least 250 pounds, turned a tear-streaked face toward her. The white-coated veterinarian's nostrils flared in aggravation, and September sucked in her breath and backed out of the doorway. "Sorry."

A short stocky man wearing a smock covered in pink and blue puppies and kittens saw her and smiled, and September glimpsed his name-tag. Timothy didn't move from his cradling grasp of the recumbent dog. "Cat room is across the hall. We'll be with you shortly."

"I'm so sorry." Heat flooded her face. She pulled the door closed and hurried to an identical room that smelled faintly of alcohol and cat pee. She shut the door and leaned against it. So much for dodging an encounter with Doc Eugene.

She busied herself getting Macy out of the carrier and onto the metal table for the exam, but left the tuxedo cat in the bag on one of the chairs. She settled into the other chair. The voices in the room across the hall carried, and it made her uncomfortable intruding on the big man's grief but she couldn't block out the sound. Obviously something serious afflicted his dog.

"He got all his shots. I give 'em myself, except that rabies one that y'all have to give." His voice trembled. "He's my best hog dawg, a real natural on the hunt. But he's been off the past couple weeks, you know? Not himself."

"Mr. Benson, we'll have to run tests. What kind of changes have you noticed?" Doc Eugene was all business.

"Wandering, can't get settled. Acts deaf, or at least he don't pay attention too good. Used to beat me to the truck. Now he trots on over, but don't know what to do once he gets there." BeeBo's voice had steadied. "Can you fix him? He's only four-years-old, but acting like an old fogey with half a brain."

"Like the others." There was a pause before a defensive note crept into Timothy's voice. "Well, it is. The other doctors said so, too."

September paid closer attention. Macy jumped into her lap and began kneading rhythmically against her thigh, acting fine. Maybe she'd over-reacted, but she couldn't take a chance. Macy had been with her through the bad times. She'd been alone, adrift, and he provided a furry anchor. September smoothed his dark neck and shoulders and scratched his white chin and chest. She wondered if the other pets Timothy had mentioned also suffered fainting spells.

"How's his appetite? What do you feed him?" Doc Eugene continued his no nonsense tone, intent on collecting an accurate history.

"Raw, it's healthier." Defensiveness crept into Benson's voice as well. "I fed that way thirty years, before it was a fad. My dawgs do good on it. This ain't the food, Doc."

"That's fine, Mr. Benson, we want all the facts so we can figure this out. I'd like to admit him. We need to run some tests, take blood samples, run a urinalysis, and go from there."

A long silence followed before the big man managed a choked answer. "Do what ya gotta do, Doc." His voice hiccupped, steadied and went on. "I'll pay whatever's needed. Just fix my dawg."

September heard the door across the hall open and close and pictured the big man returning to the front lobby area. She felt for him.

The door in the opposite side of the room opened and Timothy stuck his head inside. "We'll be with you shortly, we're getting that dog squared away. We're a bit shorthanded today. Only me and Doc Eugene scheduled, but lots of weird emergencies." He bit his lip. "I didn't say that. Doc wouldn't want me talking like that."

"Weird stuff?" September struggled to keep Macy on her lap when the big cat wanted to race over and greet Timothy. "Weird how?"

A canine whine turned into a drawn out howl. "Tim, I need your help." The veterinarian's soothing baritone murmured and the dog's distress calmed. Timothy handed her a form on a clip-board with a pen. "Fill out the basics about the cats, and we'll be back in a flash." He ducked out the door without answering September's question.

After another fifteen minute wait, the door opened again, this time admitting Doc Eugene. His long, narrow face masked emotion, and he wouldn't meet September's eyes. She'd feared his reaction. She'd seen him last at his wife Pam's funeral, where she'd been turned away.

"This is Macy." The cat wriggled out of September's grasp and leaped onto the exam table to meet Doc Eugene with a trill of welcome. The big man's eyes softened when the Maine Coon met his offered hands with head butts and cheek rubs.

September stood, and took a deep breath before speaking. "I gave Timothy the history over the phone, and completed this form. But I brought another cat—in the pillowcase. He needs an exam, too. I think it's Pinkerton, a cat that belongs to Sylvester Sanger."

"Tim?" He waited until the technician came in, and handed the bagged cat over. "See if we have a chart for owner Sylvester Sanger. If not, make a Good Sam chart, and get the basics." The door closed and he turned back to Macy. "Tell me again." He still didn't meet her eyes, but stayed focused on the patient, deftly examining the cat from nose to tail.

"Macy's four. He had his last exam a little over a year ago in South Bend, Indiana, a wellness exam with updates on his vaccinations. He got a three-year rabies at that time so isn't due for at least another year."

"You said it was an emergency when you called." He finally looked at her. She could tell it took great effort for him to keep his voice neutral, but his manner could have frozen fire. He had reason to dislike her. Pam would still be alive if not for her.

"I thought it was an emergency." September kept her eyes on the cat, anywhere but at the vet. Macy purred and trilled, delighted by all the attention. "He acts fine now, but he passed out at home."

His hands tightened on Macy, and he pulled the stethoscope from its necklaced position to listen to the cat's heart. "Has he ever fainted before?"

"No. He's always been active; he eats well. Chases the dog, teases Shadow, they're still testing boundaries. But they played this morning racing around and around, and he had no problem. This is the first time I've noticed anything." She paused. "I overheard what Timothy said. Is there something going around? Sly—I mean, Sylvester—mentioned that his cat had been acting odd."

He held up one hand to silence her, and continued to listen to Macy's heart. A half smile transformed his face for a split second. "He won't stop purring. But there's a distinct murmur." He flipped the stethoscope back around his neck. "Did the previous exams detect any abnormal cardiac sounds?"

"Nobody mentioned it, no." September's stomach clenched. Maine Coon cats could be prone to heart defects.

"I want to get a cardiac ultrasound." Doc Eugene scribbled a note on the chart, all business once again. "I don't like guessing, would rather get all the facts before we speculate. There's also a DNA test for Maine Coons that can tell us if he has the gene mutation responsible for HCM—hypertrophic cardiomyopathy, a heart ailment. That okay with you?" He continued to scribble, taking her silence for agreement.

She buried her face in Macy's mahogany coat, and her hair spilled over him, the color a perfect match. She struggled to maintain composure. *Just breathe.* "You want me to leave him here? Can't I wait while you run the test?" The three of them, as a unit, felt right. Leaving Macy behind took away one leg of their virtual three-legged stool.

He shook his head. "He's so friendly he probably won't need to be sedated. But I've got a kennel full of cases ahead of him, also the other cat you brought in. We need to mail the sample for the DNA test, and won't get results for at least a week." He opened the door and beckoned Tim before coming back to September. "We'll call you when we're finished. If it's what I suspect, we can get Macy on some medication to help relieve the symptoms and slow progression of problems."

Leaving Macy felt like a mistake, but September had no good reason to argue. Even if Doc Eugene didn't like her, she couldn't question his professionalism and dedication to furry clients.

When Timothy came into the room, Doc Eugene took September's completed form and strode out as though he couldn't wait to get away. The tech smiled and scratched Macy's chin before gathering the cat into his arms. "I'll meet you at the front desk as soon as I get kitty-kins squared away. Oh, I found Sylvester Sanger in the database. His tabby Pinkerton is the same age as your boy." Macy's big head bobbed over Timothy's shoulder and he blinked and meowed before disappearing into the rear clinic area.

September's throat tightened. *He'll be fine.* She collected Macy's pet carrier and returned to the front desk, heart as hollow as the empty container. She forced a smile when Timothy bustled back into the reception area, brandishing the paperwork for Macy's tests.

"What a sweet cat. Lots of them get stressed and hard to handle. Pinkerton won't stop yowling." He wrinkled his nose. "Cats don't like all the strange smells and critters."

"Macy's always been a people cat. He'd run up to an ax murderer and ask for a pet." She dug in her handbag for her wallet. "Thought I'd lost him out the door this morning. Scared me to death."

"You should microchip him." Timothy read the chart. "Wait, he already is."

She smiled. "So's Shadow."

He crossed to a shelf behind the counter and returned with a brochure. "What about these? Got in some trial packages, they attach to the collar. Kind of big for most cats but Macy's huge. You can get one for Shadow, too."

"Tracking system for pets? Couldn't hurt."

"They're sort of pricy." He sounded apologetic. "I can get it set up for you, though, no charge."

"Thanks." September handed over a credit card, barely glancing at the total. The amount didn't matter. Only getting Macy the right help mattered. Besides, between Chris's life insurance and the lottery winnings, she'd not have to worry about such things ever again.

A car engine roared and September started. She checked out the front window as a large truck revved outside.

"That's Mr. Benson." Timothy shook his head and frowned. "He's one of the stars of that local reality show, where he hunts with his dogs. He's pretty torn up. Sad situation." Timothy sighed. "I think he's got someone driving him, thank doG, or else he'd probably skid right off the road, the state he's in."

September strained to see around the truck until she saw Shadow poke his nose out her car window. Her shoulders relaxed. At least he was healthy. "What's the deal with Mr. Benson's dog?" She pushed her hair back behind her ears. "I couldn't help overhearing. Is it something that Shadow could catch? Or Macy?" Maybe she should get out the bleach and disinfect everything when she got home.

Timothy shrugged. "Something's going around, we don't know exactly what. There's been increased reports of sick raccoons, too. Maybe other wildlife."

"Rabies? Should I get Shadow another booster?" He'd cornered a raccoon in the garden a couple of weeks ago but he'd not had any contact before she called him off.

"Not rabies. The wildlife guys think it's a mutated dog distemper because there's more neuro signs than anything else. Raccoons can get dog distemper, but it's not contagious to cats. The feline distemper is a different disease—the panleukopenia virus usually causes vomiting and diarrhea and can make raccoons sick, too, but it doesn't cause the neuro signs like the dog disease. This illness has neurological signs like dog distemper but affects cats, especially the feral colonies, so maybe it's a variant. So sad." Timothy leaned pointy elbows on the counter and lowered his voice, enjoying a fresh audience and freedom to share juicy gossip. "The hospital's full of cats and a few dogs with similar weird signs like Mr. Benson's dog. Doc Eugene won't confirm or deny, and he's sent off a bunch of labs and been talking with some of the other internists." He whispered. "Don't say anything; he hates me to speculate."

September thought of how Pinkerton had acted in the laundry room, lost in one corner and unable to find his way out. "They catch it from raccoons?"

"Haven't a clue." Timothy handed back the credit card. "It'll be late this afternoon before the doc can run the echo. But don't you worry; we'll take good care of Mr. Macy. Oh, and honey? Don't let the Doc get you down. He knows it wasn't your fault. He's still hurting."

September flinched, but forced an unsteady smile that quickly crumbled.

"Oh dear, I shouldn't have said anything. Honey, it's okay." Timothy hurried from around the counter, ignoring the fact they'd only just met, and enveloped September in a bear hug. "You don't have to hide your feelings, it's safe here." He stood back and grabbed up a box of tissues. "We should buy stock in Kleenex."

She choked a laugh, grabbing one and smashing it against her eyes. "It's the worry over Macy." That, and Sly's ill-timed yellow-ribboned delivery. And disappearance. She scrubbed her face with the wet tissue as if that would also erase the helplessness she couldn't quash. "He's such a good kitty. Got me through some pretty desperate times, you know?"

"Don't they all." Timothy patted her on the shoulder, grabbed up the cat carrier to set it on the counter. "Want me to keep this here for Macy?" She agreed, and he escorted her out the door to the car. He gave her another quick squeeze and hurried back to the clinic, hugging himself against the chill.

BeeBo sat on the passenger side of the huge truck next to September's car. His shoulders shook, and September turned away to give him the privacy she'd want. The truck's engine revved, shuddered into gear and peeled out of the parking lot.

Shadow stuck his snout out the cracked window and whined. Her heartbeat a trip-hammer, unable to catch her breath, she clutched at the car door. *Get inside, get arms around Shadow, hands against his warm fur.* She needed contact to counter the chill in her veins. She should have brought him inside with her. She knew better, but had been overcome with worry over Macy, the strange cat's symptoms, and Sly's disappearance.

The pulse in her temple pounded, pounded, vision narrowed to a pinprick tunnel, and invisible bands crushed her chest. Numb fingers and toes betrayed her intent, and September stumbled, fumbled, failed to get IN—*must get INSIDE!*—the car's safety. A scream built in her lungs that she couldn't release past the constriction of her throat—*can't breathe! can't see!*—blinded by tears, sweat drenching her body despite the freezing air. Suffocating, dying, falling forever, no escape from the abyss that claimed her body, her soul…

A lifetime later her heartbeat slowed and breathing eased, and she found herself in the car's back seat with no memory of how she got there. The dog's weight pressed into her. "Sixty, fifty-nine, fifty-eight…" She counted backwards, out loud, a trick she'd used before she'd had Shadow. In those days, Macy's solid weight in her lap anchored reality so she could find her way back from the darkness. Now it was Shadow who licked her face, and she smiled and pushed him off her lap. "Good-dog, what a good-dog. Thank you, Shadow, I'm okay now."

Opening the door, September slid out of the car. "Wait." Shadow cocked his head but didn't attempt to leave the car, and sat when she latched his door and climbed into the driver's seat. "I'm ready to go home, how about you?"

Shadow woofed. Before she could start the car, her phone rang. She noted the display before quickly answering. "Hi Teddy, what's up?"

"I need you to bring Shadow." He sounded as breathless as she'd been moments before. "I'm at Sunnydale Nursing Home. Molly's gone, her and the dog are both gone."

Chapter 17

Teddy limped as fast as he could from the overly warm building when September pulled into Sunnydale's parking lot. He waited impatiently for the car to stop. Despite the clear blue skies, the December weather made the inside of his nose freeze, and he buttoned the front of his wool coat with stiff fingers.

Shadow's black muzzle poked out a rear window. Teddy hurried to the car when it jerked to a halt, and scratched the dog's chin. "Who's a good boy? Gonna help me find Molly, aren't you, fella?" The dog licked his hands and thumped his tail.

Blinking back grateful tears, Teddy smiled when September clambered out of the car. "You got here quicker than I thought. Thank you."

"Don't thank me yet." September straightened and flexed her back. "We were at the vet, a few blocks over when I got your call. Macy's sick." She pulled a scrunchy out of one pocket, gathered her long hair and bound it up with a practiced motion, all while taking in the cramped parking lot and shiny modern facility. "How long has Molly been missing?"

"They won't say. Covering their asses." He didn't hide his disgust and worry. Her own expression was pinched. "Sorry about Macy." He knew her animals were the world to September, but right now all his concern was focused on finding Molly.

"They're running tests this afternoon. So, what do you know? Have the police been called?"

He held his palms up with a helpless gesture. "The administrator called in a Silver Alert, but the police haven't shown up yet. I called them again right after I talked to you. They said all the units were out on other calls." He couldn't help the indignation.

"Maybe a police team will be available shortly." She wondered how many men had been deployed to her house to search for Sly.

"What's more important than finding a sixty-two-year-old Alzheimer's victim? She's not dressed right, she'll freeze in this weather." He shivered elaborately as if to illustrate the danger. "A couple of the staff said they canvassed the immediate neighborhood, and I'd go, too, if it wasn't for this bum knee." Between the arthritis and a needed hip replacement he'd put off, Teddy had enough trouble getting on and off of the HARTLine bus. He didn't like to drive at night anymore, didn't trust his eyes. "The police don't have a tracking dog unit, either. Said they used to contract that out, but the person shut down the service."

She flinched. "That was Pam and her dogs."

"Oh. Right." He avoided her eyes. "I guess her husband doesn't work the dogs now that she's gone."

"Doc Eugene doesn't have time to run the dogs and the vet hospital." She stroked Shadow's face. "Remember, Shadow isn't trained to track people. I drilled him on tracking lost pets. Lately there's been a lot of those and he's getting very good at it. But since he's the only dog available, I'm willing to give it a shot if you are."

"Molly's with Trixie." He couldn't help the hopeful note. "That's the resident therapy dog. Molly loves dogs, and the feeling's mutual. She used to spend hours and hours in the garden with our old dog, Rocky, and Trixie could be his twin. Dark red Golden Retrievers, not the pale yellow that's so popular now. Trixie spends as much time in Molly's room as she can. I think it helps remind Molly of the good times, you know?"

Shadow whined and pushed his face further out the car window when he saw September retrieve the long tracking line from the front seat. "Baby-dog, settle. You want to play *hide-and-seek*? Three times in one day, how fun is that?" September jollied the dog, getting him keyed up for the challenge, but Teddy could sense her worry even if the hunched shoulders hadn't revealed her stress.

"I appreciate this." He stuck his hands in the pockets of his long coat. "Wish I could tag along but I'd slow you down."

She let the black shepherd out of the back seat. "Shadow, sit. Wait." The dog obediently plopped his tail onto the cold pavement. He had a hard time containing his excitement, but allowed her to clip the long line to the D-ring centered between his shoulders on his halter.

Shadow seemed bigger than the last time he'd seen the dog over Thanksgiving. That had been one of Molly's good days, and they'd enjoyed the family dinner atmosphere. He hadn't tried to explain to his wife why the giddy, celebratory dinner meant more than the usual turkey-day holiday. Teddy noticed Shadow's gunshot ear had finally healed, although the ragged end lacked fur. It gave the dog a more grim appearance. "He's not a puppy anymore."

September paused. "I see him every day, so it's hard for me to tell the difference. He still has some filling out to do. He won't be a year old until Valentine's Day." She smiled at Shadow. "This is a game to him, though, we want to keep it fun so he always wants to work. What exit did Molly use? Also, I need something to cue in to Trixie's scent. A dog brush, or a toy that smells like the therapy dog." She led the way to the front door of the nursing facility. "Otherwise he won't know what to track, and might generalize to who knows what. We've been tracking cats today, including Macy."

The black shepherd's ears flicked at the name, and he nudged her thigh with his nose. She dropped her hand to stroke his brow. "That's right, you played hide-and-seek with Macy, didn't you? But this is a new game."

Teddy hurried to catch September's arm before she opened the lobby door. "Let me find the administrator and give her a head's up first. She's a piece of work." He pulled hard on the door. "I don't want her screwing our chances to find Molly by citing some weird rule book." He limped inside, and September and the dog entered right behind him. "Wait here." He whispered. "They're strict about animals." He arched one eyebrow. "I know he's your service dog, too, but Molly doesn't have time for arguing the case."

September spoke softly to Shadow, and he sat and panted happily.

At the front desk, Alison smiled at Teddy, and then half stood when she noticed Shadow. "You can't bring that in here."

Shadow's black nose twitched, he sneezed, and his tail swept the spotless floor.

The smells Teddy now took for granted would be odd to most folks. Institutional smell; a mix of disinfectant, urine and maybe desperation, if emotion could have a smell. He gritted his teeth and crossed to the administrator's office without acknowledging Alison.

Teddy knocked briskly, cracked opened the door and stuck his head inside without waiting. "Mrs. Bradshaw, a tracking dog is here to find my wife." She started to say something, and he spoke over her words. "I'm not asking permission, this is an FYI as a courtesy. I'm taking them down to Molly's room."

"That's fine, Mr. Williams. Of course we'll help any way we can. Tell the police dog team they have the run of the place, whatever is needed." She didn't get up, and acted relieved that Molly's recovery was out of her hands.

Alison stood behind the counter, attention moving back and forth between Shadow and Teddy when he shut the administrator's door. "It looks ferocious…does it bite?"

"Only bad guys." September's humor attempt fell flat. She crossed closer to the counter, Shadow in tow, and the girl shrank back. September made a fist gesture, and Shadow sat, cocking his head up at Alison. "Can you tell us where Mrs. Williams—Molly—left the building? She's with a dog, right?"

Alison smiled at Shadow despite herself. "Probably through the side entrance, 'cuz I never saw them pass through here. Trixie is our therapy dog, she's certified through Delta Society." She dropped her voice to a whisper. "She belongs to Mrs. Bradshaw. I think she's as worried about Trixie as Mrs. Williams." She pursed her lips and made kissy noises, and Shadow cocked his head and thumped his tail. "Is he going to track Mrs. Williams?"

"Actually he's going to track Trixie. So we'll have to keep our paws crossed the dog stays with Molly."

"Oh, Trixie adores her! She spends a lot of time with your wife, Mr. Williams. That is, when she's not raiding residents' rooms. She's a sneaky thief, but it's not out of meanness. She only borrows stuff. I think she does it so they'll tell her how pretty she is when we make her give stuff back." Alison sipped from a large cup, and then giggled when Shadow licked his lips.

"We need something that smells like Trixie." Teddy wanted to get Shadow on the trail. Too much time had already passed. "Does she have a toy or maybe a dog bed where she spends time?"

Without answering, Alison ducked down behind the counter, scrounged for a moment, and came up with an oversize blue ball on a rope. "She sleeps with this, carries it with her, and even eats with it. I'm surprised it's not with Trixie now." She offered it to September.

She took it gingerly, holding it carefully by one end of the rope in her gloved hands. "Perfect." She turned to Teddy. "Take me to Molly's room. We'll get a sense of the start point, and go from there."

He felt better once they began moving. "She's in the room at the end of the hall." He led the way and stopped at the designated door. Inside, a small bed with a garden themed spread dominated the room. A small table contained a picture frame of one of the last family portraits they'd had made before. . . Well, when Molly was still Molly.

Teddy furnished the room with things that mattered to Molly, or used to matter, anyway. Pictures from her garden. One of her posed with a tail-wagging Rocky—God, how she'd loved that dog, and he'd loved her back. A crocheted pillow cover that had spent years on their shared four-poster and now kept her company in her lonely twin bed. A tattered robe—her favorite that she wouldn't give up. The small vanity in the corner contained an assortment of toiletries, scented hand lotions and perfumes, a hair brush. A small blown glass bowl of jellybeans held court. He had a glass paperweight in the same colors on his desk at home. They'd purchased them as a pair on a trip to Scotland years ago, and Teddy wondered if she sometimes held the bowl and thought of him as he thought of her when holding the glass globe. They'd had to remove the mirror when Molly's reflection, a stranger looking at her, caused her first panic attack.

Sighing, Teddy made room for September and Shadow to enter. "This is it." He waved a hand at the towel on the floor. "I think the dog spends time lying on that, too. Now what?"

September brought Shadow into the room. She showed him Trixie's ball-on-a-rope toy. "What's that, Shadow? Time for *hide-and-seek*?"

She watched him sniff the ball, but he didn't attempt to take it as he might have when he was younger. Shadow was all business, inhaling with purpose. She showed him the towel on the floor, and he moved over to it and explored with snuffles and snorts. She showed Teddy her crossed fingers and he answered with his own. This had to work!

She waited until the dog signaled readiness with an expectant expression. "Shadow, *seek*!"

He dropped his head, returning to the towel, and then moved quickly toward the door. September had gathered the long line, taking up the slack with one hand, and kept him on a short leash as he guided her through the doorway.

Teddy followed, stumbling in his effort to keep up. He saw Shadow cast first one way and then the other on the immediate outside of Molly's doorway, and held his breath. Suspecting that September might accidentally cue the dog in one direction over the other, he was surprised when Shadow hesitated and then drove forward—the wrong way.

"Wait, September, the door is—"

She glared at him, finger to her lips, as the dog towed her past the rear door that Alison had indicated. Instead, Shadow padded quickly, sure of his nose, toward a rear area with a crash bar on double doors. "Seek, good-dog Shadow, seek!" She repeated and encouraged him, and he wagged without lifting his head when she pushed through the barrier.

The kitchen. Shadow had led them into the kitchen. The staff were nowhere to be seen, since mealtime was still hours away. Teddy's anger grew. Trixie wasn't allowed in the kitchen. There was no way Molly and the therapy dog had passed this way. But before he could speak, the dog towed September faster straight through the wide corridor, paying not the slightest attention to anything but the invisible trail on the floor.

A second pair of double doors on the far wall stopped Shadow, but he leaped up, pawing the crash bars and whining with excitement until September banged them open. She rushed behind the dog, playing out the long line but keeping it taut, and jogged to keep from frustrating his eagerness. Teddy struggled to keep up.

The doors opened on a hidden courtyard off the kitchen. A tiny garden, currently barren due to the time of year, shivered behind one concrete wall. Sacks of bone meal fertilizer created a second wall, forming a small alcove that sheltered from the wind.

Shadow abruptly stopped at the entrance to this cave-like opening, made eye contact with September, and planted himself in a down. He woofed, his tail banging happily.

"Good-dog, Shadow! What a good boy!" She knelt beside the black shepherd, rubbing his throat and letting him lick her face.

"Good-dog, Trixie, good girl, what a pretty girl." Trixie raised her shaggy head and wagged back. She deftly caught the rope-ball toy when September tossed it to her, but didn't stray from the woman's side.

Teddy pushed past September, relief palpable. "Molly! Are you okay? I was so worried." Finally he could breathe.

Behind the Golden Retriever, Molly had a child's orange plastic bucket and toy shovel, something that might be used at the beach, and had broken open one of the bags of fertilizer. "We must get rid of it. Rid of it all. It's bad, makes you crazy." Her ghostly face glowed dusty white with the bone meal, tears tracing wet tracks down her cheeks. "Isn't that right, Rocky...I mean, Trixie?" The dog licked the powder from her face and sneezed.

Chapter 18

Back in the Sunnydale parking lot, September waited as Shadow sniffed the front tire for the ideal spot to take-a-break. He'd done a great job finding Teddy's wife. Rather, finding Trixie.

"Good boy, Shadow. Ready to go?" She stroked his neck as he paused beside her before leaping into the back seat. "Pull in your tail. Good boy." She slammed the door, and he immediately turned around to stick his muzzle out the three inches of open window. He didn't care but Shadow risked eye damage if he stuck his whole head out.

She knew Teddy worried about Molly. How awful to have someone you love no longer recognize you. What if it happened to Shadow? Very old dogs did develop cognitive disorder, but she wouldn't have to worry about that with Shadow for years and years.

She started the car, shoved it into drive, and slowly pulled out of the parking lot. By the time they'd left, Molly had started talking nonsense to Trixie while calling her Rocky. The dog didn't care, though, and Trixie refused to leave Molly's side. Heartbreaking. She wondered if Molly knew, or was beyond recognizing what was happening to her mind. September hoped it was the latter. Bad enough that Teddy knew.

Thank goodness Molly stayed with Trixie. Shadow loved tracking other animals, and it had been a big day for the pup.

She hadn't known what to tell Doc Eugene about the reporter's cat. She probably should let someone know about Pinkerton. September rolled to a stop sign, pulled out her phone, and dialed. The reporter's number was stored in her phone even though she'd never returned his call. She left a message for whoever might get it through his service, and disconnected. It'd be hours before they could return to the vet clinic to get Macy. "What should we do now, baby-dog?" She smiled at the happy doggy expression reflected in the mirror. Nobody was around to see her talk to him, but she wouldn't have cared if they were. Shadow listened with more attentiveness and intelligent expression than most people she knew.

She still felt responsible for Sly's cat, and was curious about his investigation, especially if it might affect Macy's wellbeing. She could talk to Timothy about the reporter's suspicions. He acted more open to speculation than Doc Eugene, but she'd have to wait until it was time to retrieve Macy.

"Wait. Sly said he talked to Fish. He's got to know more." She dialed the radio station by memory, prepared to dodge the DJ's pressure to return to the radio show.

"WZPP, you've reached ZAP105 FM Radio, home of THE Humphrey Fish, bringing you easy-listening 24/7 with your favorite Fish Stories. How may I direct your call?"

"Hey Anita, it's September. Oh, and Shadow's with me."

"You want to talk to Fish? He's on-air for another twenty minutes or so." The brassy voice was pure West Texas, and turned honeyed when she asked, "How's the big guy? When you going to bring Shadow to visit again?"

September took one hand off the steering wheel long enough to make a "speak" signal, and Shadow woofed and wagged. "There, he said 'howdy.'"

The other woman laughed. "Seriously, you know Fish hates returning calls. So how about you stop by? I want to show you my new hair-style. Oh, and bring the baby-dog. I need a puppy fix. Tell Shadow I've got treats."

The dog tipped his head to one side as if he'd heard the magic word. He probably had. September laughed at his selective hearing. "Okay, I'm already halfway there. Shadow's ready for some treats and love." She teased. "Didja get tired of being a redhead?"

"I need to mix it up."

"So what color this time? Blond? Silver?

"Brunette with blue streaks. Thinking about getting my nose pierced, too. Maybe some tats."

September grinned. Nothing Anita did got Fish's attention, but that didn't stop her trying. "I'm sure it's stunning." She hesitated. "We had to help Teddy with his wife at the nursing home."

Anita tsk-tsked. "How's she doing? I feel so bad for them. For him especially."

"Not good. I think our Thanksgiving was the last good day she's had." She hesitated, and pressed harder on the gas to beat the light. "Sylvester Sanger came to my house this morning."

"That weasel? He's been here confabbing with Fish off and on the past few weeks, too. What does he want?"

"You don't know?" September's tires crunched as she turned into the gravel lot, pulled up to the brick building, and parked. "He had his sick cat with him. Said he and Fish needed my help on some story, so I guess it's about pets." She felt guilty now for whaling on Sly's car with the baseball bat. "I thought he wanted an interview about, you know, Steven and the other kids. He'd left several messages I ignored, and frankly, it pissed me off to have him show up and run into my gate."

Anita hee-hawed. "He ran into your new gate?" Anita laughed again, and then with an effort, stifled the guffaws. "Not funny, I know but—Jeez, what a piece of work." She hurried to add, "I've got other calls. Phone when you get here and I'll buzz you in."

September pulled off her seatbelt. "We're here. Give me sixty seconds to get Shadow out of the car."

When she exited, Shadow whined and paw-danced on the seat and clawed at the door. "Settle, Shadow." The insides of the doors carried scars from his impatience, but at least she'd remembered to set the child-proof lock on the windows. He'd been known to hit the button and scroll open the window.

Opening the door, September caught up his leash before he hopped out, but when Shadow tugged the line on the way to the radio station entrance, she didn't argue. She chose her battles, and actually preferred having him take point. She suspected, though, that he was focused on the prospect of treats, but trusted he'd alert to anything untoward in the vicinity.

Besides, she was so much better. Today she'd been out almost all day, with only one knuckle-biter episode. Having the big pup nearby did more for her than the dozens of locks and security system she'd installed at the house. Still, her heart always galloped anytime she left the relative safety of a building or her car.

They entered the empty lobby and her pulse slowed to a more reasonable rhythm. Shadow wasn't a "certified" service dog, and she had no documentation. There wasn't any official certifying body for service dogs. Those that had graduated from a program sometimes carried documentation, but self-trainers like her wouldn't have any proof. Nor did the law require it. Oh, she had his halter with the "service dog in training" badge from his short-lived partnership with her nephew. September didn't feel right using that since Steven would never need Shadow's services again.

The law said you weren't required to reveal your specific disability, but business owners could ask if the dog was a service animal or used for a disability. To avoid the whole issue she told them she was a service dog trainer. They didn't need to know it was for her.

She released the leash. "*Check it out*, Shadow." His head came up. He scanned the small waiting room—chairs, table, out of date magazines, glass wall and counter below, closed inner door, speakers mounted on the walls— and then he sniffed the perimeter of the room. September smiled. Her confidence rose in the security of the empty room, but every opportunity to train helped ensure Shadow's behavior would become automatic.

September crossed the empty reception area to the glassed-in counter next to the locked inner door. Shadow returned to her side, and at her signal, performed a "paws up" at the counter. He nose-smeared the glass, tail wagging, and September figured he recognized Anita's scent and anticipated the treat to come. "She'll be here soon. Meanwhile, want to play *show-me?*"

The pup pushed off, backed away and sat, cocking his head with expectation. He enjoyed these training games as much as she did. September examined the sparse room. Not much to choose from, but she finally crossed to the small table and picked up the vase of fake flowers in one hand. Quickly she pulled out the artificial blooms, holding them in the other. "This is *glass.*" She held out the vase. "This is *flower.* Shadow, show-me *glass.*"

He bounced forward, nose-punching the vase so hard that it nearly fell from her hand.

"Good-dog! You're so smart." She paused, and said, "Show-me *flower.*" He obligingly poked the blooms.

"You like?" Anita had returned, and peered at them through the reception window. She stopped, indicated her billowing dark bluesy curls, and twirled.

"Stunning."

Anita took a seat at the desk. "Fish's show winds up in another ten minutes." At her voice, Shadow bounded to the window, tail swinging, and woofed softly. She laughed, and leaned forward toward the small opening in the glass. "How's my boy? I got treats for my buddy." She crooned, her copper-bright voice softening. "What were you doing now?"

"Playing the show-me game."

Anita's eyes widened. "Teddy told me about it. He said Shadow's a canine Einstein or something." She waited, expectation painting her face. "Is that how you taught him to take away Steven's gun?"

Chapter 19

Nikki sat in the back seat of the car, arms crossed and still shivering over the encounter with the weird guy at the barn. She hadn't told Hank. Not yet, anyway. Not till she could tell him in private.

Hank sat beside her, but leaned forward with his head between the two front seats to talk with Zeke, while Zeke's cousin Dustin drove. They'd gotten permission from Zeke's folks to run into town for BBQ from Zeke's favorite restaurant. Several of the popular kids would be there, and Zeke acted all puffed up to introduce his older cousin to the gang. Big whoop.

Once again, Nikki was a tag-along, and not by choice. Mom wasn't home yet from shopping, so she had no choice and neither did Hank. But she didn't want to say anything in front of the others. They wouldn't believe her. Even worse, they'd make fun of her, maybe even tell Mom. Then Hank would get in trouble, too, and be mad at her. That'd be even worse than not getting to see the kitties anymore. No, she'd better wait to tell Hank in private.

When the stranger showed up, she'd nearly peed her pants when she saw his gun. It had two barrels but was way shorter than Daddy's rifle. She rubbed the deep scratches on her arms, hidden by her jacket, where the gray cat had gouged her. She hated leaving Hope-Kitty behind, and worried the sick raccoons might attack her. But when she saw the gun, she'd not thought, just ran. And the loud "boom-boom" that followed after made her think the scary stranger might have shot at her!

Hank had to believe her. He couldn't go back to the barn, not with the crazy man there. She didn't want him to get shot. Or tore up by attacking rabid raccoons.

"It's up the block, turn right at the light, and it's on the left." Zeke twisted halfway around in his seat to talk to Hank. "Did you hear about the watch party? I think maybe we can score tickets. Xavier's going to check it out, he's working today."

Zeke's older brother Xavier worked holiday hours at Hog Heaven. He got them discounts on hot wings and fries, and free drink refills, but only on Tuesday nights. Today was Thursday so they'd have to pay full freight. That's what Daddy called it, paying full freight.

"What's a watch party?" Nikki rubbed her throbbing arms. Once they got to the restaurant, she could go to the ladies' room and wash off the scratches. The cat didn't mean to hurt her, but she didn't want the sores to get infected. The barn wasn't all that clean. She thought again about the sick raccoons.

"Watch party for the first episode of the new season for *Hog Hell*. Doncha know nothing?" Zeke rolled his eyes, and turned back to the front. "Dustin, turn there. No, don't park under the trees or we'll get nailed with bird poop all over and have to wash the car."

Nikki blinked hard. Zeke was a stupid head, why'd he have to be so mean?

"It's this reality show, Nikki, a hunting show where they shoot wild pigs." Hank explained with quiet kindness. "Mom won't let us watch, says it's too violent."

"Ka-pow! They shoot the sons-of-bitches, and then barbecue their ass." Zeke licked his lips and made smacking noises. "Hank, ol' buddy, you're missing a great show. I got some of 'em TiVo'd, so you can watch at my house if you want."

"Barbecued oinker, huh?" Dustin grinned.

Nikki thought he had a hot smile. That's what Gina said about the boys when she wasn't talking about the new baby.

"Those feral hogs destroy lots of property. They eat anything." Dustin preened in the car mirror and smoothed his hair, and then winked at Nikki when he caught her staring. "Might even want to chomp on a cutie like you, Nikki."

She blushed and turned away. Dustin was cute, with his curly brown hair down to his collar. And he was seventeen, nearly twice as old as she.

Zeke smacked his lips again. "They'll be serving special eats at the watch party. The stars will be here. That Sunny Babcock is smokin'." They got out of the parked car, and he pretended to aim and fire an invisible gun. "Maybe they'll bring their guns. Nailed your butt, Porky-Pig!"

"I'm hungry. Let's go." Hank yanked open the car door and scooted out, impatiently waiting for Nikki to join him. He whispered as they followed the other two toward the entrance. "Never mind Zeke. He's trying to be a big man around Dustin."

She caught at his sleeve. "Gotta talk to you." Maybe he'd hang back a minute and she could tell him about the guy at the barn. The car door slammed, and a cloud of blackbirds rose from a nearby tree, swarming like bees until, as one, they roosted domino close, turning power lines into a creepy clotted string.

"Sure. Inside, where it's warm." He caught the door before it slammed shut, and hurried into the place.

She didn't like the birds. About a million beady birdy eyes stared at her like in a scary movie she wasn't supposed to watch but did anyway.

Nikki wasn't fast enough getting through the door, and it caught her sore arm. She hissed with pain, and her eyes watered, but she wiped them before anyone could see and call her a crybaby. Once inside, she found the boys had already claimed one of the tin-covered picnic-style tables at the back of the space.

Zeke grabbed the head of the table as well as the bucket of peanuts. He popped the nuts into his mouth, tossing shells on the sawdust floor. Nikki made a face. He chewed with his mouth open. What a pig. She giggled and covered her face. Daddy would have liked that; he said puns all the time.

Hank took a place next to Zeke, while Dustin grabbed a menu. When Hank waved at her to come over, she shook her head and pointed to the ladies' room.

There were only two stalls, both occupied. That was okay. She no longer needed to pee. Nikki shrugged off her jacket and tied the sleeves around her narrow waist, and then gingerly shoved the sleeves of her favorite purple unicorn sweatshirt halfway up her arms. She winced at the deep angry gouges, still seeping red. At least the inside of her purple top wouldn't show the blood. Mom would want to know what happened, and that'd be the pits.

She ran the water in the sink, and shivered when it wouldn't get hot. Nikki soaked one of the brown paper towels—they always smelled funny, but beggars couldn't be choosers. That's what Mom always said. She applied greasy pink soap and gently washed each forearm. It stung, and she gritted her teeth. "Means I'm killing germs," she whispered. That's what Daddy always said.

After drying off with another wad of the brown paper, Nikki carefully pulled down the sleeves. Mom would demand an explanation so she better keep her arms covered up until the sores healed. At least the cold weather meant she could wear long sleeves without getting weird looks. They still stung, but at least the wounds were clean.

One of the ladies came out of the stall, and Nikki hurried out of the bathroom before the woman could say anything or ask about her arms. Grownups were always so nosy. When she grew up, she'd give her kids some privacy. And a cat, if they wanted. Maybe even two cats.

She rounded the corner, clumping in her muddy shoes, and stopped when she saw the table now crowded with kids. The populars. All older than Nikki except for the cop's kid Willie Combs. She knew Hank had a crush on Willie's sister Melinda, even though he'd never admit it. But why else would he get the stutters and turn red around her?

Nikki slowly approached, keeping her head down so they wouldn't notice her. Having all their eyes on her would be worse than the gazillion birds outside. Maybe she could blend in and hang back behind Hank? But Willie's face lit up when he saw her, and she groaned.

"Hey, Nikki, you going to go to the watch party, too?" He bounced around like a kitten chasing a moth.

Melinda saw Nikki, and her mouth made a funny fake pout. "You had to bring your kid sister, I had to bring Willie. At least now they can keep each other entertained, right?" She batted her eyes at Dustin.

To Nikki, the gesture looked so fake she could have puked.

"Why don't you two kids find yourself a kiddie table?" Melinda made shooing gestures with her hands.

"Sure thing. C'mon, Nikki. It'll be our private place." Willie skipped to the next booth. He didn't act bothered at all.

When Nikki turned to Hank for help, he shrugged, handed her a cup with soda, and turned away. The back of his neck turned red when Melinda accidentally-on-purpose bumped into his arm.

Give me a freaking break. Nikki huffed and dragged her feet but it was easier to give in and join Willie than argue and create a scene. Besides, they could still hear the conversation from their so-called kiddie table.

"Are you?" Willie had his own drink. He'd taken the plastic lid off, and tried to stab his straw through one of the hollow ice cubes. "Gonna come to the watch party? Lindy says there'll be autographs from the stars, and a red carpet entrance, with a limo and everything. We'll get to see the first show before anybody else. It's a sneaky preview, with surprises and stuff. Mom's bringing us. She got tickets and my step-dad has to work, so we get to go. So, you coming?"

"Sneak preview." She automatically corrected him. "To watch somebody shoot a pig?" She shuddered. "Pigs are cute. My grandma used to have a pet pig named Pinky, and he wasn't stinky or dirty or anything. I don't even like bacon anymore."

"They're not shooting the pigs in the restaurant. It's a TV show." He dropped his voice. "I think it's special effects, you know, with green screen. I watched this behind-the-scenes special how they made that movie *Life Of Pi.*"

"C'mon, how do you think they get ham sammiches and pork chops? From the pork chop tree?" Willie was so immature, she thought, brushing off the cat hair stuck to her unicorn sweatshirt.

"Here's your food." Melinda carried a basket of fries and messy buffalo wings over to Willie.

"Tell Nikki about the watch party, Lindy. It's gonna be killer, right?" He grabbed one of the tiny sauce-covered drumsticks, dipped it in ranch dressing, and chomped down.

Red sauce dribbled from the corners of his mouth. Like blood. A boy-vampire. Nikki shivered at the thought. Hank said vampires were made up stories but she wasn't convinced.

"I don't know if they can let just *anyone* come." Melinda arched her brows and cocked her head, taking in Nikki's stained jeans and the frayed sleeves of her jacket. "The show is so gruesome. The stars are so bad-ass."

"So, I'm not invited?" Dustin sauntered over, hands stuck in the pockets of his leather jacket, peering out from under the curly shelf of his hair. "I'm not *anyone*. Am I?" He smiled at Melinda, and when she turned away, briefly flustered, Dustin winked at Nikki.

Nikki covered her mouth to keep from laughing.

Melinda grabbed up one of her brother's fries, dipped it in sauce and bit off a taste. "I bet my mom could get you a ticket. You've got to come! It's going to be THE BEST!" Her voice rose, and the rest of the other table turned to listen.

Now the "kiddie table" had become the place to be. Nikki liked being part of the crowd. Her arms didn't sting so much, either. Being included worked better than aspirin. She sipped her drink, happy Hank had decided to drag her along after all. Dustin didn't treat her like a baby, he saw through Melinda, too. Nikki smiled to herself.

Melinda rattled on, delighted to be the focus of attention. "You know they harvest the hogs and give away the food to needy people. That's why my mom is such a fan; she works at the Hot Meals soup kitchen. Volunteers, I mean. She doesn't work anymore since we moved in with my step-dad." Her words faltered a moment.

Nikki started to say something when Willie punched her softly. She shut her mouth, surprised when he shook his head. So she didn't say anything.

Hank didn't notice. "Could your mom score me a ticket?" He gazed back and forth between Dustin and Melinda, his face stricken. "I've never seen the show, but Zeke said he'd let me watch his TiVo."

"My fave is that tall guy, Mr. Felch." Melinda ignored Hank, and he shrank a bit, even as she turned her face up to Dustin. "BeeBo is sort of gross, he's a ginormous Michelin Man." Her laugh tinkled. "Mr. Felch, though, he's a creeper." She shivered delicately, for the benefit of Dustin.

"Sounds spooky. Feral hogs are dangerous, too, so anyone goes after a tusker must have some brass balls." Dustin showed his teeth again.

Zeke barked a laugh. "Texas size!" He made a rude gesture at his crotch, and Hank slugged his arm. "Hey! What's the deal? Oh." Zeke shrugged when Hank jerked his head toward Nikki. "That's what she gets for tagging."

With one pinprick word, Nikki's bubble of belonging burst. She bit her lip. Why'd Hank have to punch him? She wasn't a baby; she'd heard Daddy use worse words when he didn't think she could hear. She had to do something, show she deserved to be here. "You got pictures? Of the show stars?" Nikki jutted out her chin at Melinda, acting like a big shot around Dustin and making Hank get all weird. "How scary can they be? Bet it's fake TV like you said, Willie."

"Yeah, show us some pictures." Dustin smiled at Nikki, and she liked him even more. "I never saw the show, either. But if the pictures are as good as you say, maybe I do want to come to this little watch party soiree."

He said the word with a foreign accent and everything. Nikki hugged herself with delight.

"Sure, I can show you pics." Melinda dug in her tiny purse and pulled out a phone case with her initials in glittery sparkles. She fiddled with the buttons to engage the browser, typed in a search, and quickly had the TV show website on the screen. "There. See? I told you. Creepy as all get out. Doncha love it?" She held out the phone to Dustin and he took a quick look and then, despite Melinda's irked expression, handed the phone to Nikki.

"That's BeeBo with one of his dogs. He's got lots of dogs. Hounds that track them and Pit Bulls that hold them. The nice kind, though, his Pit Bulls aren't mean at all. He's always talking about how he wants his dogs to represent the good side of the breed." Melinda pointed, before changing the picture to the next frame. "And that's Mr. Felch, with his favorite piece. Can you imagine? He says he named the gun 'Trudy' after his lost love because she always shot off her mouth." She giggled.

Nikki leaned close to the picture, and then jerked backward. Her lips trembled. "That's him. That's the scarecrow man. He…he shot his gun at me."

"What? Where?" Hank pushed Melinda aside to hurry to Nikki. "What are you talking about?"

"At the barn." She whispered. Now everyone would know. "While you were riding the four-wheelers. I had to visit Hope, that's what I named the momma kitty, and there were sick raccoons and this scary man came with a big sack and carrying a gun. Maybe there was a body in the bag!" She'd just thought of that. Could it be true? He didn't have blood on his face, but he was white like a vampire. "I know it was Mr. Felch. I swear, Hank, it was him."

"She's lying. Can't you see she's lying?" Melinda, no longer the center of attention, had been pushed to the outskirts of the circle. "Give me back my phone. Why would a big movie star bother with you? You're making it up to get attention." She pocketed the phone and crossed her arms.

"I'm not lying. He was there, and he scared me. He was at the barn."

Dustin grabbed her arms to make her sit down, and she flinched and cried out. He backed off like she had cooties. "What'd I do? I only touched her. Sorry!"

Hank gently pushed her onto the bench. "Are you hurt?"

"My arms." She shoved up her sleeves. Now Mom would never let her see the cats again.

Dustin's face drained of color while Hank's turned rosy. Melinda's mouth dropped open. Willie said, "Ouchie," and patted her on the shoulder.

"Get in the car." Dustin pulled out his wallet and tossed a couple of bills on the table.

"What? Why?" Melinda found her voice. She reached out a hand toward Nikki's gouged arms, and stopped before she touched them. Brow wrinkled, she asked, "Does it hurt? We need to wash that."

"Already washed." Tears coursed down her face, hot and sticky. "Hank, you can't tell Mom. She'll never let me see Hope again." Her voice hiccupped.

"Get in the car. Now!" Dustin grabbed Zeke's coat sleeve and tugged, and pushed at Hank's shoulder. "Melinda, get your brother. Nikki, come on." He put one gentle arm around her shoulders.

Heaven. It was almost worth getting scratched by Hope. Almost. "Where are we going?" Her voice sounded so small, like a baby, she thought. But Dustin didn't act like it mattered.

"To the barn." Dustin hugged her. "We're going to kick some pig-sticker ass."

Chapter 20

September frowned at Anita. The news stories made Shadow out to be super-dog.

"So he grabbed Steven's gun? Shadow knows how to disarm bad guys?" Anita covered her mouth with her hand. "Sorry, I don't mean to imply Steven is a bad guy. How could a little kid like that…"

"It's okay, I know what you mean." She tucked stray hair behind her ear. "It's complicated. Shadow knows what the word means. He sort of nose-poked the gun at the right time."

At the word *gun*, Shadow cocked his head and his ears flicked backwards. The word probably had unpleasant connotations if he associated it with his shot ear. "The *show-me* game helps teach Shadow vocabulary. By holding two different objects, one in each hand, and naming them, he learns what each is called." Shadow knew nearly a hundred name-words by now. She scanned the room, and then turned back to the patiently waiting dog. "Shadow, show-me *paper*."

His mouth clicked shut and he danced across the room to the small coffee table, and nosed the stack of magazines.

"Good-dog!" September turned away to speak over her shoulder to Anita. "He prefers to learn new words, but we need to practice the known words to keep him sharp."

"He needs new ones?" Anita shuffled around her desk. She held up a coffee mug, and raised her eyebrows.

"Cup, he knows that one. But okay. What else you got?" September reached through the opening when she pushed it through.

Anita moved a few items around the desk, and then opened the drawer. "How about this? Got it on a trip to England years ago."

"Nice." September took the shiny silver letter opener, shaped like a hand wielding a sword. She turned to Shadow, the coffee mug in one hand and letter opener in the other, and he backed away and sat down, anticipating what would follow. "Shadow, this is *cup*. This is . . ." She hesitated, fingering the cool metal. She held it carefully, not wanting Shadow to hurt himself. "This is *knife*. Show-me *knife*."

He leaped forward, and nosed the hand with the letter opener.

"Good-dog!" She handed the objects back through the window. "I want him to generalize objects. No matter the size or shape, they're always cups. Not mugs, or glasses, just cup." She shrugged. "Could get fancy and add colors, the ones dogs see anyway—blue cup, yellow ball, green Frisbee—but at this point I don't want to confuse him."

Shadow woofed. He stared hard, probably willing her to produce the Frisbee. "Sorry, baby-dog, that wasn't nice of me, I shouldn't tease the dog." She scratched the top of his head and he tipped it sideways and pressed into the satisfying scratch.

Anita took the items, her blue highlights waving. "So now he'll identify any letter opener as a knife?" She dropped it back into the drawer.

"You got it. He already knows *knife*. I don't want to confuse him using terms like dagger or machete or butter knife."

He wasn't suited for Schutzund work—the type of training typical of police and protection dogs—and September wasn't interested in training an attack dog. During his temperament tests at seven weeks old, Shadow's breeder chose him as the best suited of his litter to be a service dog. He needed to have a confident but biddable, loyal and focused personality to partner with an autistic child like Steven, and bite-work had never been in his future. Dogs trained to help those suffering from PTSD often were expected by their human partners to offer warnings of perceived or imagined threats. But protection training wasn't necessary. The bond between human and dog partners grew so strong that feeling protective of each other happened as a byproduct of their love.

Even protection trained canines like Dakota weren't super-dogs. She wanted Shadow to know enough to alert her and protect them both, but not so much that he'd rush in and get himself killed.

It had taken every bit of courage to open her heart to another dog after Dakota died with Chris. Caring so much, loving so deeply opened the heart to future hurt. So much safer for her to keep others at a distance. Safer for them, too.

The phone rang, and Anita adjusted her headset on her blue-striped locks before her accent disappeared and she morphed into her husky-voiced alter-ego. She beckoned September closer and pointed at the door, pressing a hidden button to unlatch it. "Go on in. Maybe if he sees you, Fish will get the hint." She punched the phone line. "WZPP, you've reached ZAP105 FM Radio, home of THE Humphrey Fish, bringing you easy-listening 24/7 with the best Fish Stories. How may I direct your call?"

September held the door for Shadow. She hadn't bothered to switch to the short six-foot leash, and had to stoop to reel in the long tracking line before it got caught. Anita winked as they walked by, and tossed a treat that Shadow snapped out of the air and gulped in one graceful motion. September laughed when Anita lobbed a second treat at the end of the hall. "You're spoiling my dog." But she dropped the line, said, "Okay!" and he bounded after the prize.

Anita hung up the phone. "Spoiling them, that's what dogs are for."

"That's my line." Laughing, September hurried after the pup to the glass-walled studio of the radio station.

The red "on air" light over the outside of the door was off. A dorky headphone-wearing young man straddled a tall bar stool while he fiddled with the controls on the U-shaped bank of controls that surrounded him. Fish stood behind the engineer's shoulder, making notes on a computer tablet. He saw her and visibly tried to stand taller and suck in his pear-shaped abdomen. It didn't help.

She opened the door but didn't want to go inside. Fish had a history of ambush-interviews, telling visitors mics were off when in reality they were hot and broadcasting. When Fish saw Shadow, his hopeful expression shuttered to a scowl. "We'll wait till you're done." September let the door swing closed.

Fish tucked the tablet under his arm and strutted to the door. "It's about time. Are you allergic to returning phone calls?" The petulance turned his bass voice into a cartoon.

"I told you, I'm done with radio."

He wilted, and then brushed by her, swerving to avoid contact with Shadow's inquisitive nose. "You mean you're done with me? Then we've got nothing to talk about."

"Humphrey, don't be that way. I appreciated you giving me the Pet Peeves spot. But I don't need it anymore."

He whirled. "Did you ever think maybe *I* needed it?" Two bright spots of color sat high on his cheeks, and he blinked hard. "Might as well bury me now. My life is over."

Was he crying? Humphrey Fish, king of his little fiefdom, overnight sensation, needed her? Before she could ask, he turned away and entered one of the small offices at the end of the hall. She followed, catching up Shadow's leash to prevent the pup from returning to Anita-the-treat-dispenser.

The short man walked around his desk, keeping his back to September when she followed and shut the door. He stared out the small window.

"Why in the world do you need me?" Shadow dropped his nose to the carpet and began vacuuming crumbs. She wrinkled her nose. The place smelled of stale French fries and something sour. Fish was a pig. "You're the radio king, flying high after saving the day. Like the ad says; *all the best Fish Stories*. Right?"

"Don't be catty." He turned around, eyes hard. "What'd I do to get kicked to the curb? We had something good, September, good chemistry. You owe me—"

"What? I *owe* you?" Shadow whined and pawed her leg, reacting to her tone. "This place is like a chemistry experiment gone bad. I don't owe you anything." She turned to go. "I *thought* we were friends."

"So did I. When you asked me to help, I was there. But you can't even return my call, and then show up here to rub my face in it."

That stopped her. She hadn't realized how he must feel. "I'm sorry but I can't come back. Holy crap, it was only a stupid five-minute weekly slot." The weirdoes already phoned her with relentless glee, determined to get a rise out of her. "We did have chemistry. You're right. I'm sorry. I should have called and explained."

What made for great local radio banter risked her sanity once it went viral. The national publicity killed her privacy, and opened the door to the past finding her again. She shivered.

"Radio's dead. My career, anyway." His choked words stopped her.

"And Pet Peeves would save your career?" She couldn't help the sarcasm. He had to be joking, playing the victim in the hope for a pity favor.

"Hell, radio's been on oxygen for the past couple of years. Now the owners issued the station a DNR. Unless there's a miracle healing." Fish waved his hands in the air like a televangelist, but quickly dropped the campy imitation. He set the tablet on the desk. "You became a star last month. The station got lots of attention."

"Attempted murder on live radio will do that for you."

Fish winced at her dry tone, but didn't take offense. The little man's usual buoyant personality kept him higher than helium, but he'd deflated into a sad balloon cartoon. "The station owner got some offers. He's going to sell."

She sat down so she wouldn't add insult to injury making him crane to meet her eyes. "But that's good, right?"

"You'd think so." After a moment he sat down, too. "The new owners want to take it to a younger audience. And they're cutting staff. They'd keep *you* as long as your star power lasts, and I figured maybe as a favor you could say we're a package deal." He wiggled his eyebrows and they squirmed like dark caterpillars. "Barring that, I need another killer story, something that knocks their stinkin' socks off. Otherwise I'm gone as of the first of the year."

Her mouth dropped open. "But that's only a couple of weeks. What'll you do?" He'd been the voice of ZAPP for twenty years.

"Make a deal with the devil. Actually, he's not the devil. Maybe one of the devil's minions." He pretended to shudder. "Can't believe I'm so desperate I'd even consider working with the likes of him." He leaned forward over the desk. "Sylvester Sanger brought me a killer story. His editors won't touch it."

"That's hard to believe." Must be a doozy if his sleazy tabloid got cold feet. "That's why I'm here. He came to see me this morning." She scowled. "Did you put him up to that?"

"Yeah. I told him to talk to you, sure. You're the go-to pet person. I figured once you heard his theory, you could tell me if it's a load of fertilizer, or there's something to it." He fell back in the chair after seeing her expression. "You thought it was bogus, huh? Well, that settles it. I'll start packing."

Shadow whined again, and September stroked his brow and immediately her pulse slowed. "I didn't give Sly the chance to say anything. Thought he was someone else, so I went all Babe Ruth on his car." She pantomimed swinging a bat, and when Fish winced, she became defensive. "He deserved it. Ran his car right into my new front gate." It sounded lame when she said it aloud, and she felt ashamed since the man was dead. "Anyway, he mentioned his sick cat had something to do with a story he researched with you. I left Pinkerton at the vet."

"Pinkerton. Good name for an investigator's cat. Not a great writer, but he sure can ferret out the dirt." The old fluorescent lighting flickered, and he pursed his lips. "Damn place is ready to crumble, and the new owners sit on their thumbs." He cleared his throat. "So, why'd he leave Pinkerton with you?"

She paused. Fish wouldn't help unless she met him halfway, and he was already more than a little pissed at her. Better go all in. "Pinkerton slipped out of Sly's car after the accident, and Shadow tracked him."

"Oh, that's right. You're doing that pet tracking deal now. Hope it pays better than radio." He slurped coffee, making a nasty sound. "Sylvester ask you to track Pinkerton? Did he pay you yet? Careful he doesn't stiff you. His job's as precarious as mine."

September took a breath. "He's missing."

"Missing?" He laughed. "That's one way to dodge paying."

"Look, I found his body, okay?"

Fish's mouth dropped open. She could see the wheels begin to turn.

"I didn't realize the car crash was that bad…"

"It wasn't. Someone murdered him." Before he could interrupt further, she rushed on. "Fish, he was dead. I think he was dead." She rubbed her face. "I know he was dead, had to be, with that head injury." She held up a hand to stay his questions. "I called the police, they came to investigate and couldn't find the body." He didn't need to know about the missing baseball bat. She couldn't very well tell Fish about it when Combs remained in the dark.

"Somebody killed him, let a witness see, and then hid the body? That makes no sense."

She shrugged. "Tell me about it. If Shadow hadn't tracked the cat, there'd just be an abandoned car at my gate. Nobody would look for him, at least not right away."

Fish's eyes sparkled with excitement. "He made lots of enemies over the smear journalism he wrote. Nothing to kill him over, though. Unless the new story struck a nerve. Someone wanted to shut him up before he published."

"Exactly." She leaned forward, ticking off items on her fingers. "His cat is sick. Sly's dead. His body disappeared at my house. You sent him to me for help with a sick pet story." She didn't list Macy exposed, sick and at the vet, but couldn't help feeling there must be a connection. "Whoever came after Sly probably thinks I'm involved, too. You made me a target by sending Sly."

He held his hands in a prayerful pose, teasing. "So you need to help me. Work with me. Come on, September, what do you say? We make a good team. You said so yourself."

She'd had enough of high profile publicity and yearned for peaceful anonymity. "No more radio." Before he argued, she added, "But like you said, I owe you. I'll help get you the scoop, if there is one. So tell me what you know. What were you and Sly working on?"

He jumped to his feet, the bounce back in his attitude, and fairly rubbing his hands together with glee. "It's not only pets, September. Not by a long shot."

Chapter 21

Dietz shoved the truck into gear. The tires squealed like a pig and it handled like a rhino in heat. No way to sneak around town in this bad boy, so he had to hope nobody would be home at the behaviorist's house. He hoped Grady had already gotten rid of the reporter's body.

The extended cab truck made Dietz feel like a king on a mountaintop staring down on ant-like traffic. The truck could handle equipment needed for shoots in the field, or serve as a rolling office with his laptop, files and other equipment in the back seat.

But it was a truck. A blood-red truck with a snarling blue feral hog plastered on the door, and flaming *'Hog Hell'* emblazoned the length of each side. The vehicle took up nearly two spaces so he had to park on the street at his apartment. It guzzled so much gas he suspected a hole in the tank. A date would need a ladder to get in.

He'd dreamed of riding in a limo to his triumphant launch where he'd sip champagne or throw back some high-dollar beverage at an exclusive venue. Instead, he'd vroom up to a glorified take-out joint wearing a *Hog Hell* getup complete with ski cap and shit-kicker boots.

He'd choked down disappointment when his acting career cratered. For a time, he'd tried his hand at mentoring other artists, and got kicked in the teeth for his efforts. Writing and directing indie productions kept him busy but frustrated. Like others in his shoes, when unable to pay for top-of-the-line, he'd settled for in-kind trades with other wannabe film pros, yet despite his comatose bank account, Dietz continued to fantasize about awards, invites to the best parties, appearances on Letterman, a home on the beach, and above all, to rub the naysayers' noses in his success. Payback would be sweet.

After years of failures, *Hog Hell* could take him all the way. He'd smile and be gracious at the pig jokes, and proudly wear the stink of "reality show" in exchange for a fat bank account. Money was freedom.

And then the reporter threatened to take it all away. If Felch hadn't killed him, Dietz would have been tempted to arrange a little hunting accident. Now the sweet taste of almost-success soured so much, the thought of the watch party gave him hives.

He couldn't allow September Day to interfere. He'd watched her from a distance, just in case. Always good to keep your friends close and your enemies locked up. Time to put the fear of God into September Day. Make sure she shut the hell up or better yet, left town for good. She'd run before, more than once. After the new season launched, he'd have offers to sell his interest in the show, and get away clean to start new projects.

He drove fifteen minutes before he found the small road sign, and turned right on Rabbit Run Road. The road snaked through brown countryside where only a few scattered houses with ramshackle outbuildings dotted the landscape. At the rise of a small hill, the road pulled a dog-leg turn and sloped downward. Dietz saw the tall gate at the bottom of the curving road. He'd been told that the reporter had run his car into a metal gate. That must be it.

He slowed the truck, hoping to avoid other traffic. His God-awful pig-mobile stuck out bright as a blister. Best to park on the road and walk in, so she didn't discover any connection to the show.

He found a spot a few hundred yards from the entry, pulled off on the shoulder, and stopped. Dietz swung down from the truck cab, gently latched the door, and jogged toward the waiting sedan. He winced. The car's dimpled hood and door panels must have lost a fight with a hailstorm. Golf ball size hail wasn't unusual here in Tornado Alley but these were fresh dings. Maybe Felch had warmed up on the car before going after the reporter.

Dietz adjusted his blue gloves before cranking open the passenger door to the car. The floor to the sedan, littered with candy wrappers and empty fast food containers, smelled rancid and he found no notes on the back seat, under the front seats or in the glove box. His luck, the guy kept everything digital, and that would complicate things.

September wouldn't recognize him, so he could claim to be Sanger's boss. He could do this; he was still a damn good actor. He'd be pissed Sanger wasted her time on a story with no merit. That way he could pump her for what she'd been told, and debunk it at the same time. Yes, that could work.

Dietz jogged down the bricked drive, and circled around to the front, seeing the results of lots of cash. So that's how she'd spent the lottery winnings.

A pair of trucks sat in front of the house, one old and well-worn with a tree logo on the driver's door advertising garden services. The other could have been held together with baling wire and spit, and he wondered how it passed inspection with the exhaust pipe trailing and a rear headlight gone. Before Dietz could make his way past the two trucks, someone approached from the side of the house. Tall and gaunt, shaggy gray hair. Shambling gait. Unwieldy sack balanced on each narrow shoulder. A stained paisley bandanna covering his nose and mouth turned him into a cartoon bandit.

Felch.

Dietz froze in the middle of the drive, and resisted the urge to duck behind something, anything. The tall man had his head down, though, and hadn't yet noticed. Instead he carefully placed his big feet to keep from losing control of either or both of the sacks. He reached the falling apart truck, slouched forward, and shed first one and then the other bag into the truck bed with a muffled thump. White dust poofed in a cloud and immediately settled. It turned the truck's rust to ocher.

Felch straightened, saw Dietz, and stiffened. He held his hands out. "Stay back."

"What're you doing, Felch? Everything okay?" Dietz didn't make a move. He kept his voice calm. Had he already spoken to September? If she knew he and Felch were together, the show was toast. And his future gone.

"Nothing's okay. It's all gone t shit." Felch kept the truck between them. "You clear out of here. I'm trying to clean up, that's all. What ya call it, damage control."

"Where's Grady? He called me, said he's taking care of things. Didn't Grady tell you to go home and chill?"

"Can't remember." Felch's forehead creased and his sunken eyes searched the sky for the missing memory. "It's getting worse, don't you see?" He pulled down the kerchief around his neck and it became his trademark Western accent for the TV show—but it fell flat. "Don't know why I bother with this. Too late, figured it out too late. And now it's too late for that poor sonofabitch back there, too." He flapped one hand toward the house.

"Who?" Dietz took a step toward the man.

"Didn't believe him. But I saw coyotes go loco. Raccoons, too. My cats and deer and hogs and BeeBo's dogs caught it. With critters it's humane to put 'em down, right? And I caught it bad." He rested his head in his hands, and then pounded his temples. "Can't think! Got to do something, got to fix this, got to remember before I disappear." His voice turned to gravel and tears spilled unnoticed as he forced the words past sandpaper lips. "I had me a lady friend once. Love of my life, till she disappeared. If I disappear, too, maybe we'll find each other again."

Dietz's mouth tasted like he'd chewed cotton. "Uh, right. Whatever you say." They were screwed, they were absolutely screwed and ruined and going to jail if he couldn't get this nut-job the hell out of sight. He took another step toward the man. Where the hell was Grady, anyway?

"No! Stay away!" Felch pounded his head again. "If I can remember how to get her back, I know she'll keep me from disappearing. Ain't that right, Grady?"

Dietz started when Grady appeared, dragging another sack along the drive. "Whatever you say, Felch. You're the boss, the star of this drama." He nodded pointedly at Dietz and held a finger to his lips. "This is the last one, need some help here." He whispered to Dietz, "We're fine. Nobody's here, and I got all the reporter's notes from his car before I grabbed the body. But we have to work fast." He raised his voice to add, "Move that out of the way first, will you?"

Dietz grabbed one end of the baseball bat and tossed it to the other side of the truck. He bent to catch one end of the sack, Felch supported the sagging middle, and the three of them lifted and slung it into the battered truck. In the bed of the truck Dietz saw stacks of gunnysacks with white powder spilling out, cardboard boxes of fabric-wrapped objects, a rolled up rug, and even some sort of guitar case. "Moving day?" He grinned.

"It's your plan. Scare her off. Take a few things special to her, items she'd never leave behind. Just having someone poke around her house should make her run." Grady's tight sweater showed off an impressive six-pack before he zipped up his coat.

Dietz brushed white powder off his hands and sneezed. "What you got in that thing? Must weigh a couple hundred pounds."

"Get in the truck, Felch." Grady waited until the fellow had clambered into the passenger side and managed to shut the door, and then turned to Dietz. "Got back here too late."

Dietz felt a chill. "Too late for what?"

Grady shook his head. "Felch had a breakdown. You saw it. All I could do was clean up once I got here. Or did you want me to call the cops?"

"No, you said you'd handle it." He paced away from Grady, and back again. He should never have come. Now he'd been at the scene, maybe left incriminating evidence. "What's in that bag?"

"You don't want to know. I'll take care of it. Nobody will be the wiser."

"Christ! I want out of this." Dietz jammed his hands into his pockets to keep from punching something. "I'm making calls soon as I get back to the office. And I'm taking the first offer and selling this god-forsaken show. Take a loss if need be. But getting out from under." He whirled and started back through the gate.

Felch's ramshackle truck started with a grumbling roar, circled around the gardener's truck and drew abreast Dietz as he stomped back up Rabbit Run Road toward his monstrosity of a truck. Grady cranked down the driver's side window. "You won't sell the show."

"The hell I won't." Dietz kept walking.

"You forget. I'm part owner now."

Dietz stopped, and the truck stopped with him. Felch faced the passenger side window, head turned away with his forehead pressed against the glass.

Grady smiled, a bright sickly expression without humor. "Mr. Felch and I will dispose of our *problems*." He jerked his head to indicate what now rested in the bed of the truck. "I will see you back at the office, where you will have drawn up a legal agreement making me full partner in everything to do with *Hog Hell*." He held up a hand to stem any protests. "That show is my way out of limbo. Yours, too. Trust me."

"Do I have a choice?"

"See you back at the office. *Partner*." Grady gunned the engine, and was gone.

Chapter 22

Shadow fidgeted in the back seat of the car. It had been an eventful day and he yawned loud and long.

In the front seat, September made the car go, turning the wheel this way and that, while peering at him in the mirror now and then. Each time their eyes met, he beat his tail on the soft throw that covered the car seat. He couldn't help it. Looking at her made his chest thump faster. Maybe his tail was connected to that thump-place in his chest?

She'd told him "good-dog" many times when he found the dog and lady. The Teddy-man did, too, and patted his head but only for a minute before he took the lady inside. Shadow wanted to play with the other dog—they called her Trixie—but he could tell Trixie wanted to stay with Teddy's lady. He understood. That other dog fretted about Teddy's lady the way Shadow worried about September.

He worried about September sometimes, too. Earlier when they'd been in the car together, she'd grabbed and squeezed him hard, but not to wrestle-fight the way dogs do. Instead she shook and trembled, raining tears and spilling acrid fear-stink that made him wrinkle his nose. He stayed still and quiet, licking her face to show he meant no harm until her breathing quieted and she pretended to be all right.

But it was pretend. A good-dog knew the difference.

"Tired? Ready to go home?" She met his eyes in the mirror again and smiled.

He thwacked his tail. The tension in her voice had faded and her shoulders relaxed. He turned and lifted his nose to the window where wind blew through the crack. Most of the fear-stink washed away in the cold air but some clung to his fur where she'd grabbed him. He shook his head, flapping his ears hard, and breathed deeply to clean the stink from his nostrils. Shadow liked sticking his nose out the window, liked to drink sips of the many smell-flavors they drove through as they sped along the car path.

Cars stayed on these paths and never veered off. Well, mostly. Sometimes cars got confused. He sniffed hard again as September slowed and turned the wheel to the driveway. She stopped and stared for a moment at the stranger's car squashed against the gate.

Turning from the window, he pushed his nose through the grill barrier, as much as would reach, to get a closer sniff of where Macy had rested on the front passenger seat. He was confused by much of the cat's behavior, but September cared about Macy, maybe as much as she cared about Shadow. Even if Macy paw-swatted a good-dog's nose for trying to get a sniff, Shadow didn't like having his cat gone. He wondered why September had left Macy at the clinic. Why didn't Shadow get to go inside? The people inside always gave him treats.

He wondered if Macy got treats, too. He'd like a treat now. Maybe he'd get a treat when they went back into the house. Shadow licked his lips.

"I can't get my gate fixed until the police tow Sly's car." She made the car go again, and they drove into the big building where the car slept when they didn't use it. Shadow woofed. He didn't know what she said, but it seemed polite to talk back when she spoke to him. She talked to him a lot, and he only understood some of it. People knew lots more than dogs. September was always right. Well, almost always.

He waited impatiently for her to climbed out and open his door. For a moment he thought she might leave him to wait in the car again, and he yelped and pawed the door. The window smoothly scrolled down, and he happily stuck his head and chest out of the opening.

"Crap! Shadow, wait." She hurried to open his door before he managed to climb out on his own. He'd done that before, and didn't understand why she objected.

"You're too darn smart. Forgot to engage the child-lock on the windows." Her voice scolded but she couldn't hide her smile so Shadow knew she wasn't mad. He hopped out, and offered a butt-high invitation to play. "Go on, big guy. I'll meet you at the door."

He bounded away, taking advantage of the opportunity to sniff the area. The garage smelled of small furry creatures tucked away in shadowed nests. Nothing new there. Shadow dashed through the double barn doors, and despite her permission to forge ahead, he waited for September. She got nervous if they were apart, and that made Shadow feel funny, too. So instead, he pretended to sniff the pavement until she made the big doors slide closed.

The usual sounds and smells filled his world. Fresh cut and burned cedar—the gardener had cleared the scrubby trees behind the house. A coyote. Sick raccoon. Shadow wrinkled his nose and wanted to investigate but wouldn't leave September.

Metal creaked and squealed from the swivel atop the car house, screaming like an angry Macy. And something else. He lifted his nose from the spore and paused, waited until the wind shifted. The several sets of toys hung all around the house echoed in bongs, chimes and cricket-chirp pitches, some glittery like shattered ice falling to the ground. In the *show-me* game, September named them 'wind chimes.'

"Shadow, let's go." September stood beside him, tapping her foot and swept a gloved hand toward the front door.

There! Floating on the wind, now strong and then gone, but definitely there. A familiar scent, from the back garden, Aaron the gardener again. But different. He growled, his notched ear twitching with sense memory, and his hackles rose. He pressed against September's legs, putting himself between her and the smell.

Blood. Lots and lots of blood.

Chapter 23

September took a step backwards. Shadow's rumbled growl shook his fur. He never growled, except when playing tug with Bear-toy. His tail carved a scimitar in the air above his back, jerking back and forth while his head lowered, pointing toward the back of the house.

"Is anyone there? Aaron?" His truck was still here. September kept one hand on Shadow's neck, and could feel his slight trembling.

A loud screech made her jump, and she ducked and then half laughed when she looked up and saw the rusty weather vane swinging in the wind. The dozen or so wind chimes that hung every six feet around the house played a clanging concert.

She'd hung the chimes for several reasons. The sound helped identify her home with a distinct sound for both Shadow and Macy, to help them find their way home, just in case either got out. The low hangers also doubled as early warnings of intruders if someone ran into them in the dark. And finally, she liked the sound.

Combs questioning what she'd seen irked her no end. It scared her, too. The police should have found some evidence of the attack—tracks, blood, something—even if the body was gone. At least they'd treated Sly's car like evidence and designated the field a crime scene, so they hadn't totally discounted her story. Someone had been very careful if they'd found nothing. She took a breath and had to consciously relax her jaw, and flexed her neck to shake off residual nerves.

Shadow must be feeding into her emotions. They tuned into each other in the same way she'd known Macy was in trouble, and sometimes September thought they could almost read each other's mind. She'd been so much better the past weeks, but today, nothing had gone right. Two steps forward, and three back. Crap, she hated PTSD. Sometimes she hated her life.

Stop. Suck it up, sweetheart. Nobody said life was supposed to be easy, and she had Shadow and Macy counting on her to hold things together.

"I'm okay, baby-dog." If she said it enough, she'd start to believe it, and that could make it so. "For I wish it to be so. Let's go in." She nudged him with her knee, and pushed past on her way to the house.

At the door, she gave the command. "Shadow, *check it out.*" It had become a habit, to send Shadow into the house ahead of her after they'd been gone. Usually he used the exercise to flush Macy from nap time. He'd never found anyone in the house. But no matter how much better she got, September couldn't bring herself to go in until Shadow "woofed" the all clear.

By the time she'd keyed open the last deadbolt, Shadow was tap dancing with impatience. September swung open the door and he didn't wait for her to repeat the command. He burst into the entry, nails scrabbling for purchase on the slick wood, and leaped without hesitation into the living room. Growls and barks exploded, echoing in the high ceilinged space.

September froze. This was a first. She didn't move, scanning the rooms from her vantage in the open door, poised to backpedal and race to her car. She dug in her coat pocket for her phone. Combs was on speed dial.

Shadow quieted only long enough to thoroughly nose the area immediately to her right, beside the entry. Then he whirled, raced back across the hardwood into the office-music room and again put on the brakes as he kept his nose to the floor. Nobody here, or he would have already flushed them out, but she yelled anyway.

"I'm calling the police!" She yelled, proud her voice didn't shake. "Better clear out before my dog nails you." Shadow wouldn't bite without a good cause, but the intruder wouldn't know that.

She heard no reply. Heard nothing but Shadow's snorts and low growls, and then the dog returned to her, huffing and whining. He pushed his head beneath her hand for a pet, his signal for 'all clear.' Although his hackles stayed raised, his loose tail wags and forward-pointing ears showed no immediate threat. She clutched the phone and took a careful step to follow him into the room and recoiled. Someone had been here.

Melody—her cello—was gone.

"Oh, no." She wanted to weep. Other items had disappeared. A sob hiccupped in her throat with the aching absence of the small Persian carpet, one she'd chosen during her exile in Chicago. She'd painted the jewel blue ceiling to match, and now the room appeared top-heavy without the balance of reds, blues and greens covering the floor.

Another empty spot shouted the absence of the stained glass desk lamp

Mark had made as a going away present when she first left home at sixteen. The wall above also looked bare—the Eichenberg wood engraving, "The Peaceable Kingdom" was gone, a gift from her father to celebrate Macy's adoption.

A stupid burglar. A robbery. Fear bled away, replaced with anger. He'd chosen only those things with special meaning for her, and left behind the desktop computer, CD player and other impersonal items. She wouldn't cry, she wouldn't. That gave the jerk power over her.

Shadow hurried to nose her, and shoved his head beneath her hand to force a pet. She smoothed his ears. "The perfect end to a crappiocca day. Anything else?" His hackles had smoothed, telling her the house held no strangers, only their scents.

He woofed, and bounded into the adjoining kitchen and she slowly followed, noting the kitchen door stood ajar. "Dammit." Combs knew better, so did Aaron. They'd blame themselves and probably offer to pay for everything, even though neither could afford it. Besides, nothing could replace such personal items any more than a new kitten would make up for Macy. *Don't even think that.* She jerked the door the rest of the way open, ducked to dodge one of the wind chimes, and hurried to follow Shadow when he raced to the garden gate. It also stood open.

Aaron had been back and forth from his truck to the garden all frickin' day. She strode through the garden gate with mounting anger, ready to chew him out and her brother be damned. Noticing the white powder on the walkway that needed to be swept up, she added that to her list of complaints. He knew how she felt about security.

September fought through the overgrown roses, following Shadow as closely as she could. He'd traded growls for whines, and kept his ears flat, clearly concerned. He could duck beneath the worst of it, while her legs and ankles caught thorns the jeans couldn't thwart. She stumbled to keep from tripping.

She floundered into a small clearing at the back of the garden, breathing heavily. "Aaron?" No answer. And no big man wielding tools. Hard to hide someone his size.

"C'mon, baby-dog. Let's go inside, and call the police. Again." She turned and fought for several steps back through the vegetation before noticing Shadow lurking in one corner of the cleared space. "Shadow, let's go." He ignored her, nose to the ground, and finally lifted his head and howled.

"What the…" She hurried to his side. "Shadow, what's going on?"

He pawed her leg, whimpering. His paw left a blood smear on her light colored jeans.

The wind died for a moment, and September smelled it, too. Coppery. Cloying. Oh God, she'd know that smell anywhere. With a trembling hand, she reached down to touch the still damp earth, warmer than the weather should allow, and stared at her crimsoned fingers.

She recoiled, falling backwards on her butt in the soiled earth. From her new perspective, furrows in the gore-soaked soil marked the path the big man must have been dragged. Shadow leaped around her, whimpering and barking until she managed to scramble upright. She raced back to the house, ignoring torn shins and thighs, scanning for shadowy figures and prepared to fight them off should they leap from the scraggly shrubs.

The house, she had to get back into the house, lock the doors. And call Combs, who cares what he thinks. She tried to speed dial her phone but dropped it into thorny undergrowth. Sobbing with frustration, she left it behind.

Shadow beat her into the house and whirled, tail wagging a frenetic tempo and barked with excitement as she slammed the kitchen door and struggled to shoot the lock. September whirled, ready to race to the front door and secure her stronghold. That first, before calling the police.

The sight of the beribboned package, now open on the center of the kitchen's stained glass table, stopped her dead. A card lay inside the box of carefully arranged clusters of tiny blue flowers. Forget-Me-Not blossoms.

September whimpered. Her knees turned to rubber. "Please God, no."

She didn't need to read the card, didn't care what it said, she knew Sly had lied. The package wasn't from the reporter. It was from her past. The simple message, on a cheesy anniversary card, spelled out the *why* in blood-red block letters:

Payback.

Chapter 24

Combs cursed under his breath. Late again. September expected him a half hour ago. He'd tried to call, but her phone kept going to voicemail. That bothered him. She never went anywhere without her cell phone. Last month, that had saved her life.

No matter how much he planned, Combs always ran out of time. Not on the job, that was different, and partly why his private life came last. He knew she'd been screening calls on the business line to avoid the sickos badgering her over her fifteen minutes of fame from last month. But she wouldn't answer her cell, either.

It had taken him a long time to get her to agree to this "not-a-date" as she insisted on calling it. The earlier visit with Gonzales might have been too much deja vu for her. She saw threats in the shadows. Not good, not good at all. He liked her too much, wanted more for her, than hiding from the world.

He didn't think she'd told anyone the whole story about her stalker, certainly not him, and not even her family. Last month during the Blizzard Murders he'd found out more about her past than she'd want him to know, and out of respect he'd not pressed her for details. But Combs understood why September kept relationships at a distance. Besides, the circumstances when they'd met were hardly conducive to dating. He hoped someday September would trust him enough to share her burden. That's what friends were for.

Combs was ready to move on from his divorce. The internal affairs investigation that derailed his career had been the final straw, but to be honest, his marriage with Cassie hadn't been healthy for a long time. He'd been so angry and defensive at the injustice of it all that he'd had no interest in dating again. How ironic that the horror that introduced him to September also ultimately caused the Department to reinstate him.

He switched on the turn signal for Rabbit Run Road, and waited for a huge flame-red truck to pass. He hoped September's failure to answer the phone meant she was pissed he'd questioned her story about Sly's body. Combs saluted the truck driver, and made his turn.

The gate stood sentry at the bottom of the twisty road. Sly's car still squatted like a crushed bug against the gate, ready to be towed as soon as the department got the chance. They'd found nothing in the car to suggest any reason for his disappearance, and canvassing local hospitals had produced nothing. The crime scene in the field had been processed, and a few blood samples collected, but it would take time to know if the evidence would help.

Once he got out of his car, Combs grabbed the carton of cold beer, skirted the gardener's truck and headed for the front door. His steps slowed when he realized no downstairs lights brightened the interior of the house. And the front door stood ajar.

He fell back two steps, dropped the beer and drew his gun. Combs dug the cell phone out of his pocket to call for backup. He hesitated, and instead dialed September's number again.

Combs heard the phone inside the house ring, ring, ring, ring, before the machine clicked on. He disconnected, and once more approached the front door, slowly climbed the steps and pushed the door open with his foot, screening himself as best he could by standing next to the door but away from the leaded glass sidelights.

"September? You there?" His cop voice switched on with sharp authority. "This is the police. Show yourself."

No answer.

He quickly entered low, stopped on the wooden entry and swept the room from side to side with his gun at the ready. Down two steps and to the right, the living room area with adjoining dining room stood empty. The table's place settings for two was a nose-thumb jab at the evening that apparently wouldn't happen.

To the left, September's music/office space was different, something was off—and then he saw it. The carpet was bare, a bright throw rug missing from the room.

"September? Where are you?" He took the steps to the left at a near run. Items were missing. He couldn't pinpoint the changes. But not a burglary. The expensive computer equipment hadn't been touched. Something else. Like she'd packed away items or rearranged the furniture.

"What the hell?" He holstered his gun and scratched his head. He noticed the bunch of blue flowers on the stained glass kitchen table, probably for a centerpiece for their dinner. Maybe she considered it was more of a date than she'd wanted to admit. The dinner table settings said she'd planned to be here, so her absence must be unexpected.

That's right, she'd been in a rush to take Macy to the vet. The pets won over dinner with him, paws down. "Some date." More disappointment than anger made him wince. It'd been years since he'd been stood up. "Guess I'd better get used to it." Thank God he'd not called Gonzales for backup after all. The man would never let him hear the end of it.

Combs headed back to the front door to collect his beer and stopped short at the sight of the gardener's truck. Aaron seemed scattered earlier during his questioning, but that happened when people talked to the police. Nothing like a cold one to get a guy to talk. He took two, and popped the top on one can as he walked, wishing he understood women better.

His face smacked into the seashell wind chimes hung at head level directly outside the door. "Bastard!" Combs made a point to dodge the others, and rubbed one eye that got nailed.

A fine white powder dribbled a path along the paved walkway from the front drive to the back garden entrance. Before Combs pushed open the metal garden gate, he stooped closer and touched some of the powder to his glove. It coated the fabric, almost like talcum. He stood, noting the trail led beyond the gate into the garden proper. A new trail had been torn through the weedy overgrowth. He could see why September wanted to get a handle on the mess. It was a far cry from the rose arboretum the place used to boast.

The old house was a landmark as a showplace until it fell into disrepair. They'd called it a haunted house when they were kids. He remembered lobbing stones to crash windows, ashamed to have broken into the place with other high schoolers to smoke and drink beer out of sight of their parents. September hadn't been part of that crowd, though.

For the past dozen years, the place stood vacant until September came back home, bought it and began renovations. Complete with triple locks that even the gardener should know to keep latched.

The hairs stood on the back of his neck. He couldn't see any movement. "Hey, is anyone there? Aaron Stonebridge, this is the police!" He pushed through the fresh path, holding the beer away from wicked thorns that grappled his pant legs to trip him up.

When he broke through into a cleared spot at the back of the fenced enclosure, he saw nothing and no one. The ground had been plowed and then raked. A towering stack of dried cuttings piled against the fence spilled to the other side where dead roses and other vegetation had been dug out by the roots. Dozens of blackbirds played hopscotch inside the prickly bundle, tree lice colonizing the dead and probably debating the merits of nest building within thorny protection.

"Hello?" He called once more, turning 360-degrees to capture any human motion. He idly wondered if any of the old roses were worth saving, or if all would be discarded and new ones planted. Somehow, the thought made him sad. The old house's garden was a reminder of his childhood.

As he trudged back through the weeds he pulled out his cell to try September one last time. When her phone rang, he heard an odd echoing ring-tone nearby. After three rings it stopped, going to voicemail, and Combs canceled the call and immediately re-dialed, this time standing still and cocking his head.

There! He dropped the beer and hurried back the way he'd come. Combs had to dial a third time and listen before he was able to pinpoint the source of the ring-tone. He knelt in the mud, reached through the undergrowth and pulled out September's ringing cell phone.

Chapter 25

September drove aimlessly. For the first time in memory she'd run out of the house without latching or locking the door. Hadn't even bothered to pack.

She'd been careless, let down her guard. He'd been in her house. He could have killed Shadow, done with her what he wanted. Security be damned, he could reach her anytime, anywhere. She was at his mercy.

What could she do? Nothing. Nothing at all. She couldn't even call for help. The loss of her cell phone plunged her back into the helpless void she'd left behind eight years ago. The flowers, the message, all brought into focus the hell she'd escaped and hoped never to see again.

Victor Grant. Or whatever the chameleon called himself today. He sucked you in, became what you wanted and only then shed his mask to play snake to your mouse. September shuddered. Her wrists and ankles throbbed with the memory of the restraints—that, and what came after.

Publicly, Victor lamented her "nervous breakdown" while gloating how grateful her parents were for his care and protection, his superb mentoring of her career. Weeks locked away schooled her in what he expected. She learned not to fight. She learned to please him. And she learned to despise herself, loathed herself even more than the monster. September believed him, knew it must be her destiny, that she owed him everything. She never doubted he'd hurt her family. That she had no choice.

Shadow's whimper brought September back to the present. She reached through the pet gate to stroke his face, but this time not even Shadow's touch helped.

Victor had found her. He wanted her to worry, wonder what he'd do, guess whom he'd hurt next. She choked on a sob. She couldn't ask the police for help without Combs finding out. He'd try to help and end up a target, like Chris. Everyone she touched, anyone who got close to her, was in the line of fire. Nobody in her family would expect danger from dear old "Uncle Vic." After all this time, nobody would believe her if she raised the alarm. By staying silent for eight years, she'd given Victor even more power.

She should never have come home. It would have been better to disappear without a trace. For a moment, her eyes pricked, and she pushed away the feelings. She'd been right to keep Combs at arm's length.

She had to get Macy. Her breath quickened. Victor knew she had a cat, probably knew about Shadow. Victor knew the best way to hurt her. The pets would be his first targets, just as he'd focused on Dakota.

If she could, she'd hide them away but Victor would find a way. The crippling thought of separation from Shadow or Macy made her throat ache. No! They were her family; they'd stay together, no matter what. She'd already lost too much because of Victor. She wouldn't give them up, too.

God, her head hurt! Glancing in the mirror for vehicles, she worried that Victor might be on her tail. Two copies of Fish's file, a copy of Sly's research, sat on the passenger seat. She'd made an extra copy to share with Combs and hadn't told Fish. He'd hate the police 'scooping' his story, but saving lives—including his—trumped any job.

Victor changed everything. He'd expect her to run.

To run meant Victor won.

Stay, and she risked everything.

September pounded a fist on the steering wheel. "Shadow, I'm not letting him win. Not this time."

She'd stay. Victor's sudden appearance the same morning Sly disappeared couldn't be a coincidence, there had to be a connection. Blowing the whistle on a potential epidemic could save lives. She owed it to the animals, to the pet owners, and the people who might also be affected. Besides, September had little she truly cherished, other than her pets, but she always kept her word. Somehow she'd help Fish investigate and find the proof to break his story. More than that, she owed it to Teddy and his wife Molly.

She slowed and stopped at the light, knee jittering with eagerness to move. The roadway remained clear. To reach the clinic and pick up Macy, she should turn right. If they called her to get him, she wouldn't know. "What should we do, baby-dog?" Shadow woofed, and his tail thumped the back seat. September adjusted the mirror to see him more clearly. He still wore the tracking harness from finding Molly.

"Teddy! Of course." The light changed, and September swung left and headed toward the man's house. He might not be home yet from the nursing home. She'd been saddened by Molly's condition, but because of it, Teddy was the perfect person to connect with Fish's investigation, and find the connection to Victor, too. Teddy could be a bulldog when he devoted his mind to a cause, and his computer-hacking skills should cut down any time needed to dig out juicy pieces that mattered.

The fifteen minutes it took for September to reach Teddy's comfortably shabby ranch house felt like hours. The crick in her neck from straining to watch all directions at once made her back ache, and she flexed and arched her spine until it popped. She pulled into his narrow drive. The closed garage door and light in the front living room indicated he was home.

September checked both ways, but none of the other houses in the neighborhood showed activity. Quickly she gathered one copy of Fish's file, and raced Shadow to Teddy's front door. She rang the bell, and danced from foot to foot, craning to see over her shoulder until the old man opened the door.

"September, what're you doing—" Teddy's mouth made an "O" of surprise when she pushed past him into the house. "Don't let me get in the way," he said, offering a sweeping bow to punctuate the sarcasm. "Hey, big fella. How's the super-pup?" He shut the door and offered his hand to the dog to sniff, followed with a chin scratch that Shadow clearly enjoyed.

"Sorry for coming without notice. I lost my phone, happened to be in the neighborhood..." She hesitated at his puzzled expression.

"My house is not in your neighborhood. And I saw you today, so I can't think this is a social call. By the way, thanks again for helping with Molly."

"How is she?" September followed him into the living room, fell into the squishy sofa cushions and scooted to make room for Shadow when he climbed up beside her. She crossed her legs, and when Teddy stared at her jigging boot she uncrossed them. She leaned forward with elbows on her knees. That also gave her a view of the front window. It was all she could do to keep from jumping up to close the curtains from prying eyes. A cloud of blackbirds fluttered onto the front lawn to graze for whatever buggy morsels they preferred.

"Molly is sometimes here and other times not. Today was a "not" day." He settled in the big La-Z-Boy that had clearly seen better days. "Very agitated. Kept saying somebody poisoned her. Frantic to keep *Rocky*—the dog we used to have—from being poisoned, too." He took off his wire-rimmed glasses and rubbed his eyes. "She confuses Trixie with our old dog. But at least we found Molly before she got too cold, got her cleaned up and settled. Trixie helped a lot; Molly loves that dog." He cleared his throat. "Sometimes I wonder if old Rocky didn't look down from doggy heaven and send us Trixie, they're so much alike."

"I thought you had a German Shepherd." September let him talk, giving herself time to figure out how to ask him for help.

"Yes, that's when we were first married. The dog of our youth. Lots of dogs between him and Rocky. We adopted Rocky for our thirty-fifth anniversary from a rescue group. He was already seven when we got him. At our age, we didn't want to deal with a puppy, and knew he'd probably be our last dog. Can't imagine why he lost his home, he was as close to perfect as a dog could be. Something special about those old guys. Rocky used to help Molly with the housework, picking up, collecting bits of trash or stray socks from the laundry. Should have seen him Christmas morning, all that stray wrapping paper liked to drive him nuts." The memories transformed his face to a peaceful glow. "Now Trixie does the same thing when she picks up stray socks or towels or stuffed toys at the nursing home, what Alison called thievery. I think Trixie wants things neat, especially herself. That dog loves getting spiffed up, coat groomed, nails done." He laughed. "Molly calls it Trixie's spa day. Never knew a dog to sit still for having her teeth brushed. She's calmer around Trixie, always more willing to talk to the dog than anyone else, even me." He brushed off the hurt, reconciled.

At the word "dog" Shadow raised his head and thumped his tail, and Teddy smiled. "You're a good-dog too." He polished his glasses on the hem of his yellow sweater and put them back on before he turned to September. "What's this about?" He blinked pointedly at the stack of papers she'd set on the coffee table.

She could stand it no longer and jumped up, crossed the room in three long strides and swished the curtains closed over the window before turning back to him. "This morning I had a visit from Sylvester Sanger." She indicated the folder of loose pages on the table. "He'd been working with Humphrey Fish," she returned to the sofa and sat down, "on an investigative report involving sick animals. Pets, wildlife. And maybe people, too."

"Okay." He shrugged. "And this matters to me, why?" He glanced at Shadow, and the pup yawned and panted gently. "Is Shadow sick? Or the cat?" His neck wattle turned rosy with concern.

"No." She shivered, and prayed she wasn't lying. "Well, Macy is at Doc Eugene's."

He eyeballed her. "Isn't he the husband of that tracking woman? Your friend killed last month? He's your vet?"

"Pam, yes. A lot of people got hurt. Pam was Shadow's breeder, so Doc Eugene was the vet of record. I hadn't found anyone else since moving here, so . . ." She shrugged. "Anyway, Macy's sick but it's not related to Sly's investigation. The doctor ran some tests and should know more soon."

"That's too bad." He stared at her, lips tight, and said nothing else for a long moment until she began to fidget. "You going to tell me about the investigation?" He finally stood up. "Or are we going to sit and stare at each other?"

"Yes. I mean no. Crap, Teddy, I'm tripping all over myself, but this could be important." She bit her lip to stop its trembling. "Guess I'm more worried about Macy than I thought." At least that part was true. She took a breath, grabbed the folder, and opened it. "I need your help on a project, something I promised to help Fish out with. There's nobody better at digging out the facts than you."

He blinked. "You're laying it on a little thick, my dear. Be straight with me. What've you got yourself into *this time*?" He underlined the last two words, but smiled, and took the file she handed him. He probably thought nothing could be as bad as the events that first brought them together. She hoped he was right.

"Okay, here's the Cliff's Notes version, but I'm sure there's more detail in the file." She cleared her throat. "Critters are sick. Wildlife first, and now pets. It's like they're aging super-fast, and going senile. But it's not only the old cats and dogs. I mean, that can be a normal part of aging." She hesitated, and then added, "Really old dogs and some cats develop cognitive dysfunction. Similar brain changes, with amyloid deposits, as in people diagnosed with Alzheimer's disease."

Teddy carefully closed the file in his lap, and placed both hands on the cover. "Why me? What does this have to do with me? I don't have pets. Not anymore." The quaver in his voice said he already knew, but wanted her to put it on the table.

"Fish says people are getting sick, too." She had trouble meeting his eyes, and hurried on. "He could be full of it. You know how Fish loves those hand-waving kinds of stories. People who don't have pets also are affected, so there must be something else in common."

He stroked the file but didn't open it. "What sort of symptoms?" He closed his eyes.

"Forgetfulness, losing things. Mood and personality changes. Problems completing familiar tasks. Confusion about what time it is, or where they are."

"Like Molly." He blinked down at the file in his lap. "She's younger than me, you know. The doctors say it's progressing a lot faster than normal. Whatever 'normal' is." He didn't hide his bitterness.

She leaned forward. "Fish says it affects younger folks, too. And Sylvester Sanger disappeared after investigating the story for Fish." She pointed to Fish's file in Teddy's lap. "He started getting calls to his radio show, and kept track. Fish said it's almost night-and-day with some of the people, some way younger than Molly. He thinks the medical community hasn't picked up on it yet because the cases are too scattered, and symptoms too similar to Alzheimer's. So when Sly called him having already done some legwork, he decided to investigate further and sent the reporter to me. Fish thinks it's something different, it happens so fast. "

Like Aaron. The thought shocked her. Aaron had struggled with his memory for several weeks now. Mark laughed it off at first, and later grew concerned. But he said Aaron was in denial, and refused to see a doctor. She'd noticed Aaron's vague behavior this morning. Now Aaron had disappeared, just like Sly. "There's a man named Victor Grant. He's involved somehow with Sly's disappearance. I'm sure of it. This can't wait. Can you help?"

Teddy stared for a long moment at the folder, but still made no attempt to open it. Finally he said, "I'll see what I can find out."

"Great, thanks! I've got to go get Macy, but I'll be right back." A pulse throbbed at his temple, and September worried she'd upset him too much. "Are you okay?"

"Just peachy." He breathed heavily. "You've implied that my wife's Alzheimer's could instead be caused by some weird brain-frying zoonosis spread by wild animals and pets. I'm over the moon with delight." He glared at her, words so soft she had to strain to hear him. "And on top of that, you dump this on me," he slapped the files in his lap, "and run off to get your cat? Because you can't be bothered? Because your life is more important than an old man who only has his dying wife to care about?" He rose, roaring the last words and brandishing the file like a club.

"That's not what I meant. I don't know—"

"That's right. You *don't* know. And you don't care to find out."

"Teddy, don't be that way. I'm not dumping this on you. I just have to get Macy first, and I'll be right back. We'll work together." God, this had been such a mistake, she should never have involved Teddy. He didn't understand.

Victor hid her scars beneath long lacy sleeves and flowing floor-length concert skirts, and she hungered for each public concert, respite from his oppressive presence. Victor escorted her onstage—having concocted a story of her neediness—but had to wait for her in the wings while she performed, only returning to collect her during the applause. She reveled in sharing an intimate musical conversation he couldn't orchestrate. But his threat to hurt anyone she told—her parents, the other musicians—kept her bound to him as securely as the ropes he used to punish imagined infractions. She concocted elaborate escape plans but never dared do more than dream . . .

She couldn't go back to that. He'd never let her escape again. "Macy's sick, I have to get him and make sure he's safe."

"Then you better go get him." Teddy strode to the closet, shrugged on his coat, and grabbed keys off the wall hook. "Lock up when you leave."

"What? Where are you going?" She jumped off the couch, surprised he'd not raced to his computer to work his magic.

"Where am I going? Where you should have gone. The police." He scooped up the file and stomped to the door. "I'm not playing amateur sleuth, not again. Last time it nearly got you killed, and this time Molly . . ." He stopped abruptly, cleared his throat and opened the door. "You're a terrible liar, September. You're not telling me something, and I'm not in the mood to fly blind, not when it's about Molly." The house shook when he slammed the door.

Chapter 26

Combs wiped clots of mud off September's phone, crumpled the paper towel, and dropped it into the garbage container hidden under her kitchen sink. In the short time he'd known her, she'd never been without her phone. Or her pets.

He hesitated only a moment before scrolling through recent calls. He could apologize later for intruding. September had always been a twitchy rabbit ready to bolt, the fallout of a stalker experience she refused to talk about. Someone so careful about locks and being responsible wouldn't disappear without any explanation. Maybe her phone would offer a clue as to where she'd gone.

The phone logged his own call early that morning, and the one she'd made to 911 that brought him and Gonzales running later that same day.

September had also phoned All Creatures Veterinary Hospital. "That's it," he breathed, and his shoulders relaxed. Quickly, he hit re-dial and waited for the vet hospital to answer.

"September? Did you forget something? Doc Eugene's getting ready to run Macy's tests right now. He should be ready shortly."

The clinic must have caller ID. He'd used September's phone. He hesitated, not sure what to say to the chirpy young man. "I'm a friend of September's. Is she on her way home?" Combs wondered what was wrong with Macy. Leaving him couldn't have been easy.

"I guess so. She didn't say. We expect her back anytime now. I left her a message on her home phone, too."

"Tell her…" He smiled. "Tell her dinner's almost ready." Combs disconnected. Getting the meal ready would make up for his snooping and help take her mind off Macy's health issues. He started to shut down the phone, but noted her most recent call to the radio station. "Huh. She's talking to Fish again?"

She'd been adamant about quitting the Pet Peeves show, just when her notoriety would make it take off. That burned Fish's butt, especially since September had dodged his calls for weeks. What made her decide to call him? He set aside the phone. Maybe she'd tell him later, but if he asked, she'd know he'd snooped.

He collected the beer cooler, carried it to her refrigerator—she called it 'Macy's Perch'—and loaded up the door with the beverage. Several covered bowls rested inside, each with plastic or foil covers, most small sizes that held a serving for one. He juggled a few, lifted lids, and moved some around. "Leftover, leftover, leftover, salad." He made a face at the last. It had tomatoes. He hated tomatoes. Combs hoped September wouldn't expect him to eat those red, nasty things.

A large covered dish on the bottom rack looked promising. Combs tipped up the foil. "Jackpot!" He carried the deep-dish lasagna, Anita's specialty, to the oven. After debating temperatures and considering the fancy settings for duration, temperatures, bake/broil/who-knows, he made a guess and set the dish inside to heat. Bake-and-eat frozen pizza was his forte.

The blue flowers would soon wilt. She'd taken the trouble to get the bouquet. The least he could do was put them in a vase. Combs rummaged in one of the overhead cupboards, but didn't see anything resembling a vase. She should have bought a vase when she got the flowers. He rinsed out the Son-of-a-Peach coffee mug that sat in the sink and congratulated himself on choosing a silly gift she'd actually use. He filled it with water, and stuck the handful of blossoms in the container before he carried it into the dining room and centered it on the table.

A phone tweedled. Combs searched his pocket, but it wasn't his cell. He hurried back into the kitchen, and caught up September's ringing phone before it went to voicemail. The caller I.D. said it was Mark. Must be her brother. He answered tentatively. He'd met the family only briefly during April's arraignment, and probably was not their favorite person. "Hello?"

"Hi. Um, who's this?" Mark had a pleasant unremarkable voice. "I think I mis-dialed."

"No, wait. This is September's phone. Are you her brother?"

"Yeah. Who're you?" Suspicion clouded his voice. "Let me speak to her."

"This is Jeff Combs. She's not here right now." He knew the stained glass windows in the room were also courtesy of the man on the phone.

"That cop." Long pause.

His jaw tightened. "Right. I'm that cop." *That cop* who had saved one of

Mark's sisters, September, and arrested the other. He waited. Combs crossed to the stained glass table, another Mark creation, to clean up the flower box debris.

Mark broke the silence. "Where is she? Is Aaron there?"

Combs paused. "I'm the only one here."

Then a pause. "Look, sorry for being such a prick. September says you're a good guy, and I trust her judgment. Aaron should have come home hours ago. It's his night to cook—vegetarian goulash. He's not answering his phone."

The prickling at the back of Combs' neck returned. "His truck's here. But he's not." It must have taken a lot for Mark to admit his worry. "Maybe he's with September?"

"Right, and she left her phone at the house? Why'd she do that? She and that phone are joined at the hand—or ear, I guess you could say. Besides, Aaron's acting odd." Mark sounded scared.

He put on his cop voice. "Odd how?"

"I'm coming over. You're at my sister's?" Sudden determination deepened the man's voice. "Maybe he's hurt. He won't listen to me, I tell him and tell him to take it easy." Combs could hear opening and closing doors as though the man retrieved his coat.

"Mark, I've already canvassed the grounds. Neither is here and her car is gone. September lost her phone in the garden, and I bet they're together." Combs gathered up the flower box garbage, crushed it together in one hand while cradling September's cell in the other, and opened the wastebasket cupboard with his booted foot. "No reason for you to run over here, I'm sure Aaron will turn up soon." He stuffed the trash into the basket, and bent to retrieve a card that had fallen out.

"You don't understand." Mark hesitated, and then explained in a rush. "Aaron forgets. He forgets a lot. Not only where he left his keys, or someone's name. He forgets what he's doing, right in the middle of stuff." He plowed on, once started unable to stop the outpouring. "Aaron won't see the doctor. Last week he turned on the burner and left the house, forgot about the oatmeal on the stove. He forgets to put on his pants and leaves the house in his boxers. Jesus, what am I going to do? Aaron's losing his mind. And he's using gas-powered chain saws and God knows what else. He could forget what he's doing and cut off his freakin' leg!"

Combs barely heard the other man. He stared at the crumpled hand-lettered anniversary card in his hand, block red letters screaming as they spelled out *payback*.

Her cello was gone. A bright lamp she loved, and the colorful carpet from the music room. An anniversary commemorated something special, to honor and celebrate a joyful wedding.

September's wedding anniversary had been in June, and the anniversary of her husband's death had passed weeks ago. The card was no celebration, the flowers were a taunt, a bullying threat born of anger and fed by obsession. *Payback.*

He knew what that meant. He didn't know the man's name, but Combs knew exactly who and what this was about. So did September. No need to lock the door when the invader had already breached the walls.

He licked his lips and cleared his throat. "Mark, your sister ever tell you anything about her stalker?"

"What are you talking about?" Incredulous. "You mean that business from when she lived in Chicago?"

"Don't know, Mark, but it's about time we found out." He crossed to the oven and switched it off, and returned the lasagna to the refrigerator. He gazed longingly at the beer, and then closed the door. September was on the run, she wouldn't be home any time soon, and he had no way to find her. But Mark might have a clue. "Can we get together? I'll buy you a steak."

"I'm a vegan, so's Aaron."

"So I'll get you bean burritos. Give me an address. We need to talk."

Chapter 27

Shadow whined and ran after Teddy, but the old man shut the door in his face with a loud bang. What happened? He checked over his shoulder at September, and furrowed his brow. They'd talked loud at each other. Before he left, Teddy's smell changed to an acrid fear-stink that made a good-dog's hackles raise. Shadow didn't like that.

September carried a cloud of fear that clung to her body and didn't wash away even when icy wind blew against her. In the closed-up car, the smell spoiled the fun of a car ride.

He whirled away from the door when a car started outside, and nosed past the fabric fluttering over the windows to see Teddy drive away. Shadow whined again, puffing warm breath against the cold window until his breath-fog froze white and blocked the view.

"Shadow, c'mere baby-dog. I need a kiss." September sounded sad and tired. He bounded to her and pushed his head and shoulders—as much as would fit—into her arms, tail whipping back and forth as she scratched the hard-to-reach itchy spots on his back. He licked her cheek, her mouth, and her eyes. Tasted the salty rain she shed. He nose-poked her, trying to make her laugh. But she hugged him tighter. He didn't struggle; he'd become used to her touch and knew it made her happy.

Finally, she pushed him away, and he sat down without her asking, and tipped his head from side to side, curious what would happen next. She stood up from the sofa, and walked down the long hall to a familiar room. Shadow eagerly padded after her, and hopped up on the bed. He sniffed the comforter, and could still smell his own signature odor, even after the long time since their last visit here. Shadow didn't know exactly how long, but many days and nights, more than he had paws. That was a lot. This time, she didn't ask him to get off the bed, and he sighed, put his head against the cover, and rubbed his face to get rid of the fear-stink her hands had left on his head.

"Maybe Timothy would bring Macy here. What do you think?" She picked up something from Teddy's desk, pushed buttons on the handle, and held it to her ear.

He whapped his tail against the cover when she smiled at him, and fine dust rose in the air. Shadow sneezed. Not a 'let's-play' sneeze, only a tickle sneeze. He heard when someone inside the ear-handle object spoke, and wondered again how people could get inside such tiny objects. A dog wouldn't fit inside.

"I'm September Day, calling about my cat Macy." She listened. "So the test is done? Macy's ready to go home?"

Shadow cocked his head and sat up. He was ready to go home. He yawned. It had been a long day.

She frowned into the mouth-piece. "Can I speak to Timothy? I'll wait." She sat on the bed beside Shadow and gently scratched his chest. He liked that.

"Timothy, it's September. I've had something come up and wondered if there's any way you could bring Macy to me . . ." Her hope-filled voice changed to disappointment. "Oh, I understand. I saw how short-staffed you were. Can Doc Eugene talk now? When I get there? Okay." She made a face. "How long will you be there?" She stood up abruptly. "I didn't realize you closed so soon. I've not had my cell phone with me." She listened again. "No! No, I can't leave Macy overnight. I need to get him now." She ran a hand through her hair, pacing to the desk and back again. "Please, wait for me. Don't close before I get there. I'm maybe twenty minutes away."

She clopped the receiver back on the desk, said, "Shadow, let's go!" and rushed from Teddy's office.

He bounded from the bed, squeezed around her in the hallway and galloped to the door, dancing with eagerness until she could get it open. Shadow raced to the car while September reached inside a metal box beside the window before she fiddled with the doorknob, and then dropped something back in the box with a clank.

"Good-dog. Let's go get Macy." She opened the car and nearly clipped his tail when she slammed the door.

The car moved fast. He liked that and stuck the tip of his nose out the small opening of the rear window. Shadow had to brace himself to keep from being thrown off the seat when September made the car swerve. When they slowed and pulled into the parking lot of the vet clinic, he nose-poked her.

She had to take him inside this time. He didn't want to stay alone in the car, not again. They were supposed to stay together.

She slammed open her door, stuffed a folder with papers into her pocket and grabbed Shadow's leash before coming to him. He pressed his ears flat and grinned when she opened his door, and waited impatiently for the long lead to be attached to his harness.

"You be a good-boy, okay? No schmoozing the staff for treats, and no rude nose pokes to the clinic cat, she hates that. Quick trip in and out, pick up Macy, and then we hit the road."

He wagged at the words he knew—*treats* made his tail wag the fastest. September stood back for him to hop out, and scratched under his chin as she closed the car door, and he leaned into the sensation. She hadn't asked him to "seek" anything, so he knew not to surge ahead even though he wore his tracking harness. Shadow walked beside her, not dragging September forward or lagging behind.

He couldn't resist inhaling the orgy of smells surrounding the clinic, though. They were especially plentiful in the bushes right beside the front door. Most of the pee smelled nice, a few spoke to him of nerves. Shadow understood that, a new place could scare dogs that weren't brave like him.

But a few of the smells screamed "different" in a way that itched his fur. Shadow raised his head, sampling the air. Were these different-smelling dogs nearby? The pee smell wasn't fresh, but they might wait to jump at him— jump at his person—on the other side of the door.

Shadow stiffened, watching September's hand reach for and push open the door. He leaped in front of her, barking loudly to warn off any different- scented dogs lurking in the room.

"Shadow! What's wrong with you?" She tightened her grip on his leash. "Sorry, everyone. He's usually a big push-over."

September's disapproving tone stopped his barks, but he remained cautious. She couldn't fool him, she was concerned, too. He scanned the small room from side to side, sniffing the air and staring at the other occupants.

Two women and a man sat on cushions against one wall. One held a cat in a canvas bag. He huffed the air. It smelled scared, but otherwise had the usual weird-cat-smell, nothing the way a good-dog should smell.

At the front desk stood another lady, this one with a bad-smelling curly- furred dog the size of Shadow's head snugged tight in her arms. It made an ear-hurty keening noise and gazed around the room without focus on any one thing. The little dog's hind end, swaddled in soft white fabric, smelled of poop and pee, and she shook and shivered even though the room was toasty- warm.

Shadow wondered what it was like to be held so far above the ground. Was she shivery-scared about being dropped? Maybe that's why she smelled bad? He stretched his neck as far as he could to get a clearer sniff-picture without risking contact.

"Timothy, I'm here for Macy." September touched Shadow's neck, and he followed to the far side of the room, away from the sick-smelly dog and nervous cat. He placed one paw on the cushioned bench, and then took it down when September shook her head. He licked his lips and instead stared out the large floor to ceiling window to watch their car in the lot outside.

"I'll tell Doc Eugene you're here. Go down to room one. Glad you made it before closing. Oh, some guy called looking for you. He said dinner was waiting. Hiya, Shadow." Timothy waved, and then turned to the woman with the dog. "I'll meet you with Butterscotch in room three."

"Crap, I forgot about dinner with Combs." Shadow followed September, and put his ears down and slung his tail back and forth at Timothy. Sometimes he got treats when he did that. This time, though, Timothy turned away and disappeared into a back room as the woman took her keening dog down the hall.

They didn't wait long. Doc Eugene bustled into the room, and stopped with surprise when he saw Shadow. "He's grown, hasn't he? You know, he was one of Pam's favorites."

September didn't say anything, but flinched, and Shadow wondered why. When the tall man in a white coat squatted down and held out his hand, Shadow went to him and happily accepted butt scratches. He turned around, and nailed the man's face with a slurp, and was rewarded with a laugh. Returning to September to lean against her leg, Shadow reacted to her tension and whined.

"But you want to know about Macy. It's what I always fear with Maine Coons. It's his heart." Doc Eugene stood up and placed something on the nearby wall before flicking a switch.

Her breath caught, and Shadow pressed harder against September's leg. He didn't understand the words as the conversation continued, but they kept mentioning Macy and he worried something bad had happened to his cat. That's how he thought of Macy. They were family, so Macy belonged to him like September belonged to him, and he to her. Family belonged to each other.

Finally, Doc Eugene left the room, while September led Shadow out the other door and back to the front desk. Where was Macy, where was his cat? He woofed with concern.

"Shadow, hush. Settle, while I pay the bill and get Macy's medicine. Then we'll go talk to Combs."

The room had emptied. September dropped his leash and turned toward the counter, so Shadow padded across the room and jumped onto the cushions in front of the window. He waited for her to tell him "off," and when she didn't, he smeared nose prints and watched the outside view.

A big truck loomed over their small car outside, like a big dog bullying a puppy. He could hear the engine snarl, the vibration rattled the window and tickled deep inside his ears. Shadow shook his head, and the metal tags on his collar jingled with dog music.

Behind him, the door squealed open, and Shadow whirled and hopped off the seat. Timothy had Macy in the canvas carrier, and the cat meowed and pressed a paw against the front webbing. Shadow panted happily.

"Macy! Kitty, you sure scared me. But you're going to be okay." September smiled, relief in her voice and posture, and held her palm flat against the other side of the webbing. She stuffed the pages from her pocket inside one of the carrier sleeves as Macy rubbed his face against her hand through the fabric.

Timothy held the carrier in nose-sniffing range. Macy didn't even hiss, just made the rumbly sound Shadow could feel as well as hear. "Want me to take him to the car? You've got your hands full."

"That'd be great. I'll unlock it." She fumbled out her keys, pointed them at the window and Shadow saw the car's eye-lights flash. "Shadow, wait with me, I still need to get Macy's meds."

Shadow wagged and huffed, sniffing Macy as best he could through the webbing, while the cat continued to face-rub. Other than the strange hospital smells, Macy smelled like himself, not scary-sick. He was happy his cat would come home with them, and they'd be together again. Family stayed together. Shadow wagged harder, and tried to follow Timothy out the waiting room door but was blocked.

While September stayed at the counter, Shadow returned to the window perch. He tipped his head from side to side, panting softly, following Timothy's progress to their car as Macy's carrier gently swung in one hand.

Someone got out of the bigger truck and walked to meet Timothy. The stranger's face had funny colors. Holes for eyes and nose and mouth. Not like a person at all.

Shadow's mouth closed. His ears came forward. He stood up. The man wore a hat pulled over his face. The two spoke for a minute, and then Timothy shook his head and tried to back away.

Shadow whined. His tail rose, jerky wags, and he whined again deep in his throat. They bubbled into growls and then angry barks when the stranger grabbed Macy's carrier—his cat!

"What? Shadow, settle, what's wrong?"

But he wouldn't stop. There, out the window! Timothy and the stranger played tug-o'-war with Macy's carrier! Shadow paw-pounded the window, barking and snarling so loud that spittle stained the glass.

"Oh my God, no!" September raced to open the door, but Shadow beat her through the opening.

"Stop! What're you doing? Help, someone help!" Timothy yelled and flailed ineffectually at the much bigger man, who shook him off like water from a bath.

Shadow galloped toward the pair. He barked warnings, but his leash tangled in nearby bushes and stopped his rush to protect his cat from the stranger. The man-with-no-face wrested Macy from Timothy and tossed the carrier into the back of the big truck.

Timothy pulled at the man's arm until the strange man snatched up a big digging stick from the truck's open door. He swung. Timothy fell.

Behind him, September screamed and froze in place. But Shadow never paused. He tore free of the leash tangle, and leaped at the man stealing his cat.

The shovel swung.

Chapter 28

Nikki sat in the back seat squeezed between Hank and Willie. Dustin drove like they were in a video game so the tires squealed on sharp turns. He'd promised to drop everyone off after they visited the old barn. Nikki wanted to sit next to Dustin, but Melinda claimed the middle front seat. Zeke sat on her other side.

Melinda was all "Oh, Dustin, you're so great Dustin, sit next to me Dustin" it made Nikki want to gag. She couldn't help giggling when Dustin paid attention to her instead of Melinda, happy he believed her story about the barn. The others probably would have ignored her.

This way, at least they all would share the secret. Nobody would tell on Nikki without getting themselves in trouble.

The barn was spookier at night. Chatter in the car died away when Dustin pulled to a stop and set the brake. Nobody made a move to get out, and Melinda finally giggled, a high-pitched nervous sound that made Nikki jump.

Dustin cleared his throat. "I got a flashlight in the trunk." Nikki was surprised to hear a slight quaver in the older boy's voice, but when he swung out of the car, his swagger remained intact. "Zeke, you and Hank come with me. The rest of you wait in the car."

"No way." Melinda followed the boys out of the car, her jaw shoved forward with determination. "What you gonna do, clobber him with the Eveready?"

Dustin shook his head, and popped the trunk, his voice hushed. "Take care of the little kids. Probably shouldn't have brought them, anyway."

The words were a stomach punch and Nikki blinked back tears. Willie sat quietly in the back seat, and seemed happy to do as he was told. She got halfway out the door before Hank could shut it. "I'm not a little kid!"

"Shh! Quiet, Nikki." Hank narrowed his eyes, and whispered. "This could be dangerous. For you too, Melinda." He threw out his chest and tried to lower his voice but it came off pathetic.

Melinda made a rude noise, and Nikki giggled. "Girl power. Right, Nikki?" The older girl put her hands on her hips. "We're not going to wait around for the pig-sticker to sneak up on the car. We're all in this together, or we all go home, right now."

Nikki held her breath. Maybe Melinda wasn't so bad after all.

Dustin rolled his eyes, but gave in. "Fine. But you're in charge so keep them together. Willie, come stay with your sister." He switched on the flashlight, and it flickered a moment and then burned steady after he thumped it softly against the side of a tire. "Stay close. Hell, we've made enough noise, I'll be amazed if we find anyone lurking around. Lurking in the barn." He said the word again, as if relishing the sound. "Lots of bushes to lurk in."

The group slowly circled the rickety old structure. They startled a hidden animal once, and even Dustin jumped and cried out. "It was nothing." He lowered his voice to a gruff growl, compensating for the loss of he-manliness. Nikki thought it was funny, but was glad he couldn't see her smirk. He'd called her a baby, but she didn't scream and pee her pants. She thought of the sick raccoons and her smile faltered.

The flashlight beam swept back and forth, keeping the path around the barn illuminated as much as possible. A big iron pot rested against the back wall of the structure, blackened wood scattered beneath. Nikki thought it must be a witch's cauldron like in Harry Potter spells, but hadn't been used in forever.

"Don't step in a hole and break an ankle. The armadillos turned the ground into a moonscape." Dustin stayed ahead of the small group, and every few yards stopped and turned back to light the way for those following. It didn't take long before they'd returned to the front of the building. He held the flashlight under his chin to make a scary face. "Nobody here but us chickens."

Nikki giggled. "Don't you want to go inside? Bet the scary man's hiding in there." Her nerves had calmed, but she didn't want the forbidden excitement to end.

"Inside?" Dustin turned to his cousin. "This the hangout you told me about? It's deserted."

Zeke nodded. "It's pretty cool. Cobwebs and creepy crawlies. And cats, like Nikki said."

Hank agreed. "The outside door's padlocked and nobody uses the place anymore, far as we can tell. But we always check before going in. Whoever owns the place would have to unlock the barn door, so we'd know to keep driving by."

"How you get in?" Dustin shined the light over the bleached gray of old boards. Any paint had long since worn off.

Nikki pointed. "There's a loose board." She led the way when Dustin shined the flashlight in that direction. "It sort of swings back and forth on an old nail, wide enough to get through. That's where I ran out today, and Mr. Felch stood right there."

"Nobody's here now." Hank reached the board, pushed it to one side, and eyed Dustin. "Might be a tight fit for you. It's wider at the bottom. You're wearing your good clothes, man. Your mom'll be pissed if you get all grunged up."

"Screw that." Dustin stared at Melinda. "Seriously? You hang out in this dump?"

She crossed her arms and tossed hair over her shoulder. "City boy all scared?" She poked an elbow gently in Nikki's ribs, and Nikki giggled.

His jaw tightened, and he thrust the flashlight at Hank. "You know the place. So go on through, then hold the light for me." He blinked at Melinda. "Unless one of you wants to go first?"

It was a dare. Nikki thought Melinda might go for it, but she laughed instead. "Be my guest," she said.

Hank took the light, pushed the board aside, and turned sideways to sidle through. The light inside the barn made gaps in boards show up in the darkness like a Jack-o-lantern toothy smile. Nikki shivered with delicious chills. She couldn't remember ever having so much fun. Even the stinging of arm scratches faded. The earlier scare was worth it, her admission to being an official member of the cool kids.

Dustin knelt on the damp ground, turned and crawled in sideways with a one-handed posture through the narrow opening. She waited her turn, watching as Zeke followed Hank. She hurried after her brother, and helped hold the board for Willie and then Melinda last.

"Nikki, it's show and tell time. What happened?" Dustin's words were teasing, but not mean. She could live with that.

"There's these cats live here, see? And I feed the mommy cat. I call her Hope. I think they live in that horse stall, because she always come out of there." Nikki pointed and walked toward the area. "I sat right here to feed the kitties. A kitten came out, too. But then these raccoons followed the kitten. Sick ones." She couldn't help shivering. "Maybe sick with rabies. They scared Hope and she clawed me good trying to run, and I got scared and runned. I mean, ran. Out the board. And I saw that man with the gun. Mr. Felch."

"Wait a minute." Dustin held up a hand. "The *cat* scratched your arms?"

She nodded.

"I thought you said this Felch guy hurt you." He glowered.

Nikki licked her lips. They hadn't asked her what had happened. "I only said he had a gun. Maybe even he shot the gun, you know, while I ran away. I heard a boom." Her voice sounded whiny, and she hated that. "He scared me!"

Dustin made a disgusted sound. "Got dragged all the way over here for nothing, for some cat scratches." He took a step closer to her and she reflexively stepped back. "You sure it was cat scratches?"

She bobbed her head again.

"Not raccoon? Not a creepy man?"

She wrinkled her nose. "I'm sorry, but you didn't give me a chance to explain—"

Melinda cut her off. "Never mind, Dustin. Give her a break. You should be glad it's nothing serious." She bent down toward Nikki and whispered, "Girl power," and Nikki didn't feel so bad after all.

"You're right. Sorry Nikki. Friends?" Dustin held out his hand.

Nikki stared at the big, seventeen-year-old boy's hand, and hesitantly put her small girl hand in it and shook. It felt very grown up. Maybe he didn't think she was such a baby after all.

"While we're here, do I get the tour?" Dustin shined the light around the inside of the barn. "Not much to see. Pretty clean, too. I expected it to be trashed."

Hank waved a hand to encompass the entire barn area. "Don't want anyone to know about us, so we always take out any trash we bring."

"How environmentally friendly of you." Dustin laughed. He walked down the center of the barn, shining his light inside each empty stall, three on the left and two on the right.

Nikki gasped. "The door's open." She pointed and ran to the far end of the barn. "Come on, bring the light!"

Next to the stall where Hope and her kittens lived sat a room she'd always imagined must house wonderful secrets, maybe treasures of sparkling jewels, or bags of gold coins. She remembered the bag that Mr. Felch had carried. Maybe this was his stash of treasure. He sort of looked like a pirate, only not as handsome as Johnny Depp.

The wooden plank door to the room had always been closed with a padlock, twin to the one on the outside of the barn but not so rusty. Some sort of grinder with gray-white powder inside sat next to the steps, and now the door swung open, and the lock was gone. If they found money inside, that could change things for her and Hank, and Mom. Especially Mom. It might make that worry spot between her eyes smooth out and go away.

"Hurry up!" She stepped from foot to foot, impatient for the light to come. Tentatively, she stepped up onto the wooden block that served as the single step into the room. Her nose wrinkled. It smelled dusty, powdery.

Dustin reached her and held the light high, illuminating the room. Nikki stepped on something brittle that cracked beneath her feet, and cried out and fell back into his arms, hiding her face.

Bones. The room overflowed with piles of blackened, charred bones.

Chapter 29

The small but tidy workroom held hand crafted items and brilliantly colored stained glass windows and lamps. Combs feared he'd break something, and shifted uneasily, crossing and then uncrossing his legs in the antique cane-back chair.

"Excuse the mess." Mark January sat opposite him. "I'm covered up with holiday orders, so every surface has projects in various degrees of being finished."

"That's okay." Combs shifted again, and then gave up and stood. "I'm worried about your sister."

Mark stood, too. "Mind if I work while we talk? I got a few more pieces to cut for this panel, and like I said, I'm up against a wall. Besides," he wiped his hands on the stained canvas apron, "keeping busy helps keep my mind off Aaron. You're sure I can't file a missing person's report?"

Combs shook his head. "He's an adult. You can file immediately, and missing kids or developmentally disabled adults will get attention right away." He shrugged. "Hate to say it, but depends on the workload how quick the police would get to him. Playing devil's advocate here, they'd argue maybe he took the day off, or his truck wouldn't start and he caught a ride with a friend, or had a tiff with a lover. No offense." He walked to the nearest table, solid, made from rough unfinished pine, and gently touched the jigsaw of cut glass pieces. "Christmas wreath?"

"Yeah, it's a wreath." Mark adjusted safety goggles over his eyes before he scored a large sheet of green glass with a "screeing" sound, lifted it, and broke it cleanly. "He could call me to pick him up. I've left messages, he's not answering his phone." Deft hands turned half the sheet a three-quarter turn, scored it again along a gold-painted line, and split it again.

"Well, I bet he's with September. She left in a hurry. She took a few things. A rose lampshade that was in her office."

"I made that." Mark paused, puzzled. "Why pack a lamp?"

"I didn't see her cello, either. That's what makes me think she ran." Or someone took her. Combs had a bad feeling. "What can you tell me about her stalker?"

Mark shrugged. "Not much." He manipulated a long, thin strip of swirly green glass he'd separated from one end of the larger sheet. "The stalker thing, that was her story, but Mom figured it was an excuse to explain when she messed up." A row of leaves drawn with a gold paint pen marched down the long strip of glass. With quick, sure strokes, Mark scored each in turn, cracked them free, creating a loose pile of rough leaf-shaped pieces. Combs came closer, and got waved back. "Watch your eyes. Shards fly in unexpected directions."

Combs reflexively blinked and took a step away. "She messed up, how? She left school early for some music scholarship. A tour, too, right?"

"Yep. A sixteen-year-old cello prodigy, that's our September. But too young to be on her own." Mark chose one of the small rectangles of green glass and began to shape it, scoring and breaking off bits at a time until the proper inner and outer curves defined each leaf. "My folks had this family friend." He made a face. "Older. Kind of a creep, if you ask me. He was supposed to watch out for September, but apparently he couldn't handle the job. She started spending more time partying than practicing, was a no-show for a couple of concerts, and they kicked her out of the tour."

"A party girl? Drugs?" Combs raised his eyebrows. That didn't sound like the responsible woman he knew today.

"Don't know. Maybe. Probably." Mark added another rough-cut green leaf to the growing pile. "Hell, I did my share of booze and pot growing up here in Heartland, and later in college. A teenager virtually on her own in Chicago? It's likely. Anyway, September finally got scared and called April to rescue her." He peered over the goggles. "You remember April?" The question had extra teeth.

Combs stared back evenly. "September returned the favor, didn't she?" April nearly got herself, her son, and September killed. April remained in the hospital, and probably faced jail time once she was well enough to face a judge.

"Why didn't this family friend help September? Who is he?" Mark had no clue what kind of real trouble September had faced, or how April helped her out, and it wasn't his place to enlighten the man.

Mark stopped, holding the glasscutter in one hand and another strip of glass in the other. "It's been eight years. I haven't a clue where Uncle Vic might be. The family sort of lost touch, and who could blame him? After September's meltdown, she hooked up with Christopher Day, they moved away and eventually got married. What does this have to do with anything?"

"Maybe nothing. Maybe everything. Might have something to do with Aaron. She left her front door unlatched. Not only unlocked, Mark, but unlatched. And I found this." Combs held out the red-lettered card. "On the table, beside a bunch of blue flowers."

"Flowers? Blue ones?" Mark set down the glass cutter, and took off his goggles to examine the note. "Anniversary? What anniversary is that? Today's December eighteenth."

Combs's phone rang. He dug in his pocket, and saw it was Gonzales. "Gotta take this." He walked away from Mark to the front of the room, speaking in a low voice. "Combs here." When Mark held up a hand and then pointed to an adjacent room, he watched the man go. "What's up?"

"You remember Theodore Williams, right? He's here with me and he's got quite a story. Ties in with Sly's visit to September this morning." He chuckled. "Hate to break in on a date with your girlfriend—"

"She's not my girlfriend." The inside joke fell flat. "She stood me up." He hoped that's all it was.

"So she's got better taste than we thought."

Combs cracked his knuckles. "What's Teddy into now?" He'd been instrumental in helping catch his mother's murderer, and become a good friend to September as well. Combs's breath quickened. "Does he know where September is?"

"You're ahead of me already. Yes, as a matter of fact, says he left September at his house."

His shoulders relaxed, and he leaned against one of the tables. She hadn't left town after all. Had he jumped to conclusions on the stalker angle?

"She gave Teddy notes from Humphrey Fish for some story Sly planned to write about animals making people lose their minds." He laughed again, the way kids whistled past a grave. "Crazy, right? Sounds like something Sly would make up. We found nothing in Sly's Gremlin, nothing at his work computer and his laptop is missing. We still haven't found the man. Looking more and more like somebody shut him up. Maybe Fish's notes will tell us why."

Crazy-ass memory loss. Like Aaron? When Mark returned, carrying a picture frame, Combs replied softly, not wanting the other man to hear. "Take Teddy home and I'll meet you there. We can talk to September, too." He pocketed the phone and turned to the other man. "What's that?"

"You said blue flowers." Mark held out the picture, a professional portrait of a somber teenage September with her cello held protectively with one hand, and a bouquet of blue flowers clenched in her other white-knuckled fist. A hatchet-faced balding overweight man with piercing green eyes, bad skin and worse teeth loomed behind September, his hand possessively on her shoulder.

"Who's he?"

"Victor Grant, the man my parents asked to watch out for September when she went on tour. I had to call Mom, and she recognized the date." He tapped the photo. "You said blue flowers, and it reminded me of this picture."

Combs must have looked puzzled.

"Blue flowers. Forget-Me-Nots. Uncle Vic gave her a bouquet of blue flowers after every performance." Mark tapped the picture again. "Eight years ago today September walked out of a concert in Chicago. She hasn't played since."

Chapter 30

September froze, the scream scalding but refusing to leave her throat. She couldn't breathe; terror transformed the action into stuttered slow motion.

Shadow. Ski masked man. Shovel.

Wielded like a club, the wickering sound ripped the air as it swept back and forth at the dancing dog. The stranger's broad shoulders rippled beneath his padded fleece jacket, and his tight jeans revealed muscular thighs as he aimed each swing at Shadow. She braced and flinched, each time anticipating the dull thud against Shadow's furry body and helpless to stop it.

But Shadow managed to dodge until it finally connected a glancing blow off his tail. He yelped, spun away, and launched himself at the man, teeth catching his sleeve. He hung on, snarling and shaking his head, suspended half off the ground with rear paws pin wheeling for purchase. For an endless moment, the attacker juggled the shovel.

The sleeve fabric gave way, and Shadow dropped to the ground, quickly regaining his balance but not fast enough.

Timothy lay crumpled on the ground. He moaned and tried to roll over. The shovel descended and connected with a sodden thump-crunch against his shoulder, prompting a shriek.

Shadow yelped, an echo to the vet tech's cry. He placed himself between the supine figure and the attacker, snarling a warning to back off.

The sound unfroze September's feet as well, and she raced forward. And then stopped, afraid to get too close. "Stop! The police are on the way!" She hoped they were, anyway.

She peered over her shoulder, and saw Doc Eugene through the window with a phone pressed to his ear. She turned back to the masked man. "Why are you doing this?" She heard Macy yowl from inside the truck's bed, and prayed the cat wasn't hurt when the carrier was flung.

Victor was heavy and limped; this man was lean and athletic. "Who are you?!"

He put a gloved finger to his lips and remained silent. Perfect teeth gleamed through the red and blue knit mask for only a moment before he tossed the shovel into the truck bed, climbed inside, slammed the door and peeled out of the lot.

September rushed to Timothy, barely registering the clomping footsteps approaching from the clinic. "Help is on the way. I'm so sorry." She shouldered the dog out of the way. "Shadow, stay back." She had to push the pup away again when he tried to climb into her lap and lick her face.

Doc Eugene grabbed her shoulder and pulled her aside. "I called 911." He knelt beside Timothy, examined him quickly, and then covered him up to his neck with several clean but tattered towels. "He's breathing. Barely. Don't see any bleeding. But I don't want him moved, he got hit in the head." The blunt force trauma left the young man's arms at weird angles when he'd tried to deflect the spade. "Why would anyone do such a thing?"

September sat on the cold pavement, arms around Shadow. "He took my cat." Tears spilled unchecked down her face, freezing in the wind.

Doc Eugene crossed his arms, trying to stay warm. "That makes no sense. Why would he take your cat?" He scowled. "He must know you."

Timothy stirred, blood pooled at his mouth and he blew red bubbles at the corner.

"Be still, Tim, help's on the way." Doc Eugene's voice was unsteady, but his hands held Timothy's head immobile, not allowing movement.

"I didn't recognize him." She wiped her eyes, dodging when Shadow tried to lick her face again. "He had a mask. And gloves. He didn't say anything."

"Yes he did." Timothy's voice, reedy and faint, startled them.

"Don't talk, hang in there." Doc Eugene sounded desperate. "Where the hell is the ambulance?"

One of Timothy's bare hands grabbed September's knee and she flinched before she bent close when he tried to speak again. He mouthed, "Macy?"

She blinked hard, but forced a smile and put her hand over his and gently squeezed. "Don't worry about Macy. You need to take care of yourself."

"I'm sorry." A bloody tear escaped one eye. The other had already begun to swell closed. "He asked if Macy was yours. Couldn't stop him. So sorry . . ."

"Asked about me?" It was Victor's doing. Her heart broke. The monster had targeted Macy, and Timothy had also fallen victim to his payback. She reassured him with lies she didn't believe, and choked on the words. "Macy will be fine. I promise."

"Stop making him talk." Doc Eugene checked Timothy's respiration that grew ever more strained. "September, think. Think! What did he look like? Did you get the license? What color was it? You'll need to give a statement to the police."

The police. That's right, they'd be here any second, and keep her repeating her statement over and over and the son-of-a-bitch would get away. If she followed now she could catch him. How dare he hurt Timothy, and take her cat! Macy's damaged heart could give out at any time.

Timothy's hand flexed under hers, and she leaned close to hear. "Payback," he whispered.

She felt her face blanch. "What?"

"Hurt Macy." Gasp. "Unless." A breath, and he choked. "Meet you." He stopped breathing. His hand fell from her knee, dropping a scribbled note with the same red block lettering as the anniversary card. September grabbed it, stuffing the note in her pocket.

She poised to begin CPR when Doc Eugene shoved her aside and took her place. "No, oh no no no." He took charge, feeling for a pulse before tipping back Timothy's head.

"Let me help." She moved closer.

"Haven't you done enough?" His voice cut her to the quick.

Doc Eugene began rescue breathing as the ambulance arrived. Within seconds, the parking lot swarmed with EMTs.

"You're right. Nothing I can do here will help." September grabbed the end of Shadow's leash. "Let's go for car ride." She whispered the magic phrase and the dog rushed to her car.

Nobody noticed when September slowly drove away from the clinic. She couldn't help Timothy. She'd probably gotten him killed. Besides, Doc Eugene knew as much about the attacker as she.

Payback. Sent by Victor. If she'd doubted before, the note confirmed the author, and she had to do what he demanded. He had Macy.

Chapter 31

Teddy pulled into his driveway and saw Detective Combs climb out of the unmarked car parked at the curb. He unfastened his seatbelt when Detective Gonzales pulled in behind him. What had September gotten him into? Again?

Her car was conspicuously absent, though. She'd dumped this mess in his lap, and run off on an errand to get her cat. He understood her reluctance to get involved in another police investigation. Last time she'd nearly died and still managed to save her nephew, but she hadn't survived unscathed. Hidden injuries hurt worse and took longer to heal, if they ever did.

He got out of the car, and waved at Detective Combs with the folder of notes from September. "Not a reunion I particularly welcome, gentlemen. No offense."

"None taken." Combs stepped to meet Gonzales, and the two waited until Teddy unlocked the door. At least September had seen fit to secure his home. That was the least she could do.

"September's gone." Gonzales stated the obvious. "Slippery little devil." He turned at Combs. "No offense."

"None taken." Combs frowned, forehead wrinkled with worry. "She's hard to keep up with, for sure."

They followed Teddy into the living room, and he waved them to the sofa while he got rid of his coat. "Yep, September's done it again. No offense." He couldn't resist the sarcastic tone.

Gonzales didn't smile this time. "I wanted Combs to hear this, too, since it's related to the call we made out to her house. We never found Sly's notes."

"These are duplicates of Mr. Sanger's notes from Humphrey Fish, out at the radio station. Another familiar name. Deja vu, indeed." He polished his glasses on the hem of his sweater, put them back on, and opened the folder. "She said Mr. Fish enlisted Mr. Sanger to investigate his listener's concerns about wild animals infecting pets. And possibly people."

Gonzales nodded at Combs, who took the lead. "Sick how? That's something the city pound or county extension agent should handle." He frowned at Gonzales. "As for people illness, that's the Health Department's purview."

"Fine." Teddy slapped the cover of the file closed, and offered it to the men. "Take it to them. My wife's not well, and I need to be on call for her, not gallivanting around playing Mr. Marple." He breathed heavily. "September only gave it to me because Molly's got Alzheimer's, and Mr. Fish thinks this is some new variant of the disease."

"Wait. Alzheimer's?" Gonzales held out his hand and took the file. "My wife's aunt has that. Terrible, heartbreaking condition." He spoke sharply to Teddy. "I didn't know animals got Alzheimer's."

Combs leaned forward. "That's not something you catch from your pet, or another person. This is bogus." He stood.

"Don't shoot the messenger." Teddy held up his hands, palms out. "Sorry, bad word choice. The fact is: September dumped that in my lap. I'm being the good citizen and turning it over to the authorities. You want to take it to the health department, I'm all for it."

Gonzales handed the file to Combs, and watched as he quickly scanned the contents, flipping pages. "He's got names. A lot of them. He's been careful to avoid anything litigious, but he's making a case for intentional poisoning."

Combs paced as he quickly read through the notes.

Teddy hesitated, feeling his heart rate increase. "Do you think someone would poison people intentionally?" Molly had been diagnosed only a year ago. Heat flamed his cheeks.

Gonzales stood. "Too soon to tell." He turned to Combs. "Take that to the health department. But first make a copy."

Combs agreed. "With the recent cut in funding and personnel, they can't move too fast, and with the holidays, it could sit for weeks."

"It was the pet owners complained first." Teddy walked them to the door, both relieved and a bit disappointed the puzzle had been handed off. "Bet animal control would have some insight."

"Yeah, or a veterinarian. Someone who treated the pets." Combs's phone buzzed and he searched a pocket for it while he continued to talk. "September told us Sly had a sick cat she took to the vet. Maybe the kitty has some clues." He added drily, "Just call me the pet detective." He shoved the file at Teddy to hold while he found the phone. "Combs." His eyes widened. "Shit. Okay, on our way." He scowled at Gonzales. "Deja vu strikes again. Or is that redundant?"

Teddy opened the door for them. "What? A big case?"

"Could be." He spoke angrily over Teddy's head to Gonzales. "Assault over at a local vet clinic. September fled the scene."

Chapter 32

September drove quickly, following the single word prompt on the scribbled note the attacker left behind. She gripped the steering wheel so hard her hands began to cramp. After she'd survived last month's horror, she dared to hope God had forgiven her. That she'd atoned for whatever she'd done to deserve Victor's attentions. She'd even attended church a few times, figured she owed Him that much for getting her through the worst. Mom convinced her to play the holiday concert, and actually got her to practice Melody again.

But bad stuff kept coming. She hung on with virtual fingernails to a cliff that threatened to collapse and dump her into a place from which she'd never claw free. Her teeth chattered and her sight shrunk to tunnel vision. "Ten, nine, eight, seven . . ." She tried the counting trick, and bit the inside of her cheek, anything to keep the roller coaster of emotions from jumping the tracks.

"I don't know how to pray," she whispered. "But this is me, trying. Please don't let anyone else get hurt because of me." In the mirror she saw Shadow tipping his head from side to side, and laughed bitterly. "Yeah, like praying's going to help. But can't hurt when we've got nothing else." He barked and she liked to pretend he agreed.

She knew what Victor wanted. He'd professed to love her, his definition of it anyway. He basked in the reflected glory of her audiences' appreciation, and when she left she'd betrayed that love. His humiliation kept him from pursuing her, kept her safe for a time because he expected her to tell, to file charges with the police.

But she couldn't tell, not the whole story anyway. Oh, she told everyone she'd been stalked, including Combs, but never identified him. She'd lied and claimed Victor tried to protect her—otherwise, she knew he'd hurt her family.

She told only enough to get by. To her parents, that she'd been stalked. To the police and her sister April, that she'd been raped. It was the only way to explain giving up her music. The only way to get police protection. And the only way to explain the baby.

Victor didn't know about the baby. His son. Given to April to raise as her own. Combs had figured that out on his own, and she hated the look in his eyes, judging her. Mom would disown her if she found out. She might be damned for not loving Steven, for giving him up, and staying away for eight years. But she'd not destroy April's family or damn that little boy by revealing the secret of his parentage.

She shuddered at what Victor's payback would be if he found out Steven was his son.

Once Victor learned she hadn't identified him, he waited, plotted, and when she'd relaxed her guard, he'd murdered Chris and Dakota. She couldn't prove it was Victor, he'd been too careful. Since she'd never pointed a finger at him before, identifying Victor at this late date would never float.

She knew what he wanted: To humiliate her as she had him. Payback for his hurt. Killing Chris and Dakota was the appetizer, she was the main course, and Victor orchestrated this menu like a virtuoso chef. Now they played a deadly game of hide and seek, this time for keeps.

But this time, she wasn't a frightened child. She had Shadow. And a gun. She'd serve Victor a dessert that would blow him away.

She hated guns. Chris got her one before they married, and made her practice. Here in Texas, she had a carry permit, but in Indiana, she'd felt safer leaving the gun at home and relying on Dakota's Schutzund training. She'd learned the hard way a dog was no match for a bullet.

Last month she'd stashed her gun in the car's glove box, just in case. At the time, her house's security as well as Shadow's presence made the gun less vital. For the first time, September knew she'd use it without hesitation.

September picked up the note in the car seat beside her—*Gazebo*—the one word conjuring memories of happier times. Her first public cello performance took place at the outdoor pavilion, affectionately known as The Gazebo, in the city park next to Heartland Middle School. After that, she'd played at The Gazebo many times. She'd even played for the Middle School graduation. The Gazebo represented the time before the bad; when her future was hopeful and only good lay ahead. Now it, too, was tainted with Victor's special brand of poison.

She turned at the corner. Heartland Middle School sat on the outskirts of town. With school closed for the holidays, and the weather so cold, visitors weren't likely so it made cruel sense to choose the spot.

The man had slung the cat carrier into the back of the pickup like so much trash. With Macy's diagnosis, he might already be dead.

No! She wouldn't think like that. Doc Eugene said the tests showed cardiac changes, but not as severe as they could be. It was the same heart condition that caused young athletes to drop dead on the basketball court. Macy had received his first dose of the medicine before they left. His required exercise restriction would be the biggest challenge—over-exercise could kill him. So could stress.

How much stress did Macy feel right now? Damn Victor!

"You hurt my cat and it's on," she whispered. He could terrorize her, threaten the people she loved, and she'd warn them and sic the cops on him. People could take steps to protect themselves. Well, most people could. Her throat tightened with guilt at her failure to warn and protect Timothy. Like a trusting pet without a clue, Timothy walked right up to the killer. Taking Macy crossed the line.

September sucked in a breath. "You're stupid. Stupid! What were you thinking?" Victor had her so rattled she couldn't think straight. But nobody had to know about Steven. April's secret would stay hidden.

She'd been a terrified kid, beaten down and ashamed to tell her parents. She'd believed Victor's assertions she'd asked for the attention, but she'd been a child. Mom didn't speak to her for years, angry she'd blown off her music career and blamed it on what she called "that stalker fiction." Even April believed the pregnancy to be a result of some bad-boy romance. She didn't need to know Steven was a child of rape.

September's reputation meant nothing, not in the face of murder. She *could* turn in Victor. Press charges. April was an expert at believing what she needed to believe and she'd protect her son with her life.

She didn't care if they never proved Victor murdered Chris and Dakota, or hired Timothy's attack. Pressing charges would shine a spotlight on him, and the public embarrassment alone pulled his fangs. To Victor, that would be worse than anything else. He'd be caught, or disappear for good.

She'd make him pay for all the pain he'd caused. And she'd get her life back.

No need to tell him that, though, not at first. "It's not a sin to lie to the devil, is it, Shadow?" He thumped his tail and she smiled for the first time in hours. That's what she'd do. Two could play at blackmail, because that's how he surely meant to use Macy, as leverage to get her to submit to him.

The school parking lot was deserted. Safety lights illuminated both the school property and the nearby park. As she slowly pulled through the park's high arching entry, she saw a ramshackle truck parked along the back exit beneath a pool of light, like a cat seeking a sunning opportunity.

September took a big, shuddery breath, steeling herself for the confrontation to come. She'd demand he give Macy back, and she'd keep his dirty secret. If he refused, she'd threaten to tell the police about him. *Everything* about him.

And once she had Macy back—and Melody, she wanted her cello, too, dammit!—she'd tell the cops all about his sorry ass.

Finding her own wash of light, September pulled to a stop near The Gazebo. Only the truck across the park showed evidence anyone was here, but there were plenty of dark shadows produced by the buzzing overhead fixtures. The single word on the note mocked her. It had no time for a meeting, no signature, nothing. It would be like Victor to lead her to this deserted place—and never show up.

September opened the glove box, pulled out the gun, made sure it was loaded, and put it in her pocket. She settled in to wait, wishing she had her phone to call Combs. It had been a mistake to shut him out. "Hindsight sucks," she said. "Think with your head next time, not your heart."

But there wouldn't be a next time. Not if she could help it. She was done with drama. Tired of hurting the people who cared about her. Like Teddy. A fresh rush of guilt spilled over her. She'd been incredibly insensitive, and he'd been a good friend to her. Like Combs. It was hard to be her friend, but she'd make it up to him. After this meeting, she'd find Teddy and explain. And apologize. Hope he'd forgive her.

Clack-clack-clack!

She jumped, hit the door lock, and scrambled for the gun in her pocket, heart galloping. Shadow barked and snarled, ears slicked back and spittle flying.

A snaggle-toothed man wearing a blue and red ski mask stood beside the door, tapping her window with the blade of a shovel.

Chapter 33

Teddy wished he'd brought his laptop. The detectives hadn't wanted him to come, but they couldn't legally stop him from following them to the veterinary hospital. He had to park across the street, though.

He'd known as soon as they mentioned the veterinarian that September's cat Macy must be involved, but he couldn't think why. Taking the cat seemed a direct dig at September, a way to keep her attention, or maybe gain leverage over her in some way. Of course the detectives focused on the human victim.

September had been desperate to collect her pet. He could see that now, though she'd tried to hide it from him. He should never have ignored her fear.

Detective Combs said she'd left home so quickly she didn't pack or go back for her phone. To him, that sounded like running away. So who was chasing her? Maybe the same person who took the cat? If he'd stayed and heard her out, he could have persuaded her to go to the police, and maybe none of this would have happened.

Any mention of Molly's illness made him crazy. He lashed out against the helpless feeling, and September had been the handy target. It wasn't her fault Molly's disease couldn't be reversed. He'd gotten riled at the suggestion of finger-pointing blame even though Mr. Fish's notes were anecdotal at best, based on rumor and supposition. Sylvester Sanger's reputation tainted the story with a bad smell. Yet being able to do something in defense of Molly, even as ineffectual as running down a bogus story, gave him purpose. It was good to have a purpose again.

The poor vet tech had been beaten to death, and that trumped anything else. Whatever she'd gotten mixed up in, he knew it wasn't her fault. September had worse luck than Job.

The EMTs had given up trying to resuscitate the technician by the time he'd arrived. Now Teddy sat in the clinic waiting room. A large plate glass window offered a clear view of Detective Gonzales doing whatever detectives do after a murder. Teddy wished they'd cover up the poor boy. Another person arrived, maybe the medical examiner, and conferred with Detective Gonzales before kneeling to examine the body.

Teddy clearly heard Detective Combs interviewing the veterinarian. They hadn't bothered to shut the door to the examining room down a narrow hall where they conferred. Doc Eugene said the staff had departed by the time September arrived to pick up Macy, and only the technician and doctor had stayed to release patients.

"September wanted to get her cat, don't know why the rush. She could have gotten him tomorrow but didn't want to wait." The veterinarian's voice trembled, and then steadied. "We usually close at six p.m. on Thursdays, and office hours are limited over the weekend, but we ran late tonight."

Detective Combs's low voice kept a professional tone. "Did you see the attack?" Pause. "So what did you see?"

Teddy strained to hear.

"Tim offered to take the cat to the car while we finished talking. Timothy—that's my technician. God, he's worked here fifteen years!" The veterinarian needed a moment before he could go on.

"I know this is rough. Take your time." The detective spoke with gentle encouragement, and soon the doctor calmed enough to go on.

"September had Shadow with her," he said. "She'd already paid the bill, but wanted to know about the other cat she brought in. I'd left the chart in the back, and by the time I got it, Shadow started barking. Didn't think much of it at first." He laughed without humor. "This is a vet clinic, after all. But then September yelled, and I could tell the barks were serious."

"Serious? How can you tell?"

"Detective Combs, dogs bark for lots of reasons: boredom, during play, excitement. Shadow's barks meant business, they were alarm barks— something threatened or scared him."

"Okay, so you heard some serious barks. What did you do?"

"Ran back to the front. Both September and the dog were outside, and Timothy was. . . Tim was hurt. On the ground." He paused, and Teddy heard him blow his nose before continuing. "I grabbed some towels, a dog blanket I think, whatever I could find to cover him and keep him warm to counter shock. He tried to talk to September. I made him stop, tried to keep him calm, told him help was on the way. I called 911."

"Did you see anybody else? Any other vehicle?"

"September said somebody in a truck fought Timothy to take Macy. Why would anyone steal a cat?" He blew his nose again. "Tim started to crash, so I gave CPR until the EMTs arrived. That's when I realized September was gone."

Teddy shook his head with dismay. September probably chased whoever took Macy, but leaving the scene made her appear guilty as hell.

Detective Combs said nothing for a moment, and then offered, "I've watched those dog shows on TV. Some dogs—cats too?—must be worth a lot of money."

The veterinarian demurred. "Rare breeds go for a pretty penny, yes, but Maine Coon cats are pretty popular. Macy's gorgeous, very nice example of the breed, but I don't think he's ever been shown."

"Why does that matter? My mom had a cat. The vet told her Simba could produce a hellacious number of kittens if she wasn't fixed. That's a lot of potential cash." Combs floated another speculation when the vet didn't act convinced. "Locals know September won the lottery. Maybe somebody's holding the cat for ransom."

Teddy had thought of that. September would pay anything to keep Macy or Shadow safe.

The doctor agreed. "That makes more sense. Champions can produce some high-dollar litters, but that's the exception with cats, not the norm. Macy's neutered. He shouldn't be bred anyway, not with his HCM—that's a potentially heritable heart ailment."

"Heart problems? Is that why September brought him in?"

"Yes. That, and the other cat. Belonged to…Wait a minute, I left the file out front."

Teddy pretended to read the Humphrey Fish pages when the veterinarian walked behind the front counter. Detective Combs hurried after, saw Teddy in the waiting room, and scowled. "Go home. This is a matter for the police." He paused. "That's my file."

Teddy stood, and pushed his glasses up his nose. "I know, Detective, figured you'd need it. But September's like a daughter to me. I want to help."

"Help by going home. Leave the file with me." He turned to the veterinarian as the doctor riffled through a stack of color-coded paper files.

"Here it is. Sylvester Sanger's cat."

"What?" Teddy hurried to the counter, and set Fish's file on the ledge.

"Damn, she mentioned Sly's cat this morning, I totally forgot." Detective Combs's words ran over Teddy's.

Teddy leaned against the tall counter. His mouth had gone dry and he licked his lips before he could manage to speak. Blood from the dead technician stained Doc Eugene's white coat. "What's wrong with it? The cat, that is, why's it sick?" He imagined the file's information scorched his hands, and dropped it on the counter.

The veterinarian frowned. He saw Teddy stare at the red stains, and shrugged out of the white coat and stuffed it into a garbage can. "You a friend of September, huh? That's good. I think she needs friends, but be careful. Her friends have a way of getting hurt."

Detective Combs flinched, and Teddy wondered how close a friend the detective had become. He knew the veterinarian's murdered wife had been September's friend, too.

"This could be related, Detective." Teddy angrily slapped the folder against the counter. He waited for the doctor to open the file, but Doc Eugene eyeballed the file like it was a snake.

Detective Combs shoved the file closer. "He's right. Sylvester Sanger disappeared this morning. He left his cat with September, said he'd been researching some weird new animal disease. We never found Sly's notes. This supposedly is a recap."

"New critter disease? Don't know if it's new. I've got my own ideas about that." The veterinarian opened the file and began to read. "Uh huh, uh huh. Yep. That's what I've seen, too. But mostly in dogs." He pushed it aside and opened up the clinic's file on Sylvester's pet cat. "This is the first cat case I've seen. It's more obvious with dogs. Cats hide, or they wander off and disappear. People notice when dogs forget house training or tricks they've always known." He rubbed his face. "I understand from a few clients they've seen similar behaviors in wildlife, but that's purely anecdotal. I couldn't confirm or deny that."

Teddy pressed for more details. "September told me cats and dogs can get Alzheimer's, like people. They forget things, get senile."

The veterinarian shook his head. "Not exactly. Yes, they can develop brain changes as they age, and some of the amyloid brain deposits are similar to the human Alzheimer's disease. This is different, though." He sounded puzzled. "Cognitive disorder in pets happens with the really old ones. That would be dogs aged nine or more, and cats older than fourteen or so." He tapped the cat's file. "This new syndrome affects old pets, too, but not exclusively. Mr. Sanger's cat Pinkerton is three or four—now, I wouldn't know for sure if it's the same thing without an examination of the brain changes. But I had a dog come in recently, and the owner authorized the necropsy after euthanasia. I'm still teasing out information on that, sent some slides to pathology, but it has me concerned."

"Is it contagious?" Teddy held his breath.

"Contagious?" The veterinarian looked up sharply. "You mean from pets to people? No."

The front door of the clinic squealed open and Detective Gonzales entered. "You want to see him before they take him away?"

"Be right there." Detective Combs turned back to Teddy. "Like I said, you should let the police handle this. Or turn it over to Parks and Wildlife."

The veterinarian shook his head. "Actually, the county health department should be told. If the pathology comes back as I suspect, the CDC will take over the whole thing."

Detective Gonzales perked up. "Health department?"

"CDC? I thought you said it's not contagious?" Combs shrugged. "It's Sly's pet theories about the sick critters, maybe connected with this mess. Could tie in with the perp taking September's cat."

Sighing, the doctor rubbed at a stain that had bled through to his shirt. "Don't want to speculate too much, or cause a panic. But it's likely some sort of environmental contamination. Probably food. Pet food contamination can affect pet owners, too."

Gonzales nodded. "There was a big scare a few years back with pet food being recalled. Like that?" He paused, opened the door and called, "Hold up, we'll be there in a minute." He shut the door and told Combs, "They want to roll. Why don't you take a gander, and I'll finish up in here."

Combs headed out the door. Teddy saw him hurry to the body.

Gonzales crossed to the counter and leaned on it, standing beside Teddy. The small detective made Teddy feel tall, even with his old man stoop. "So it's not contagious to people, but could cause problems if they're also exposed by handling contaminated food. Like salmonella or E coli. Damn, need to call Mercedes—my wife—and tell her to watch the kids around the dog food."

Teddy wished they'd be quiet. He remembered something, a connection with food and memory, but couldn't quite recall. Wait, had his memory jumped the tracks, too? Would he join Molly in madness?

And there it was. His heart pounded and he put a hand to his chest. He whispered the words. "Mad cow disease?"

Chapter 34

The masked man's happy grin faded when he saw September's gun. He stumbled backwards away from the car, holding his hands and the shovel aloft. "Don't mean no harm. Thought you was here to help." He head-jerked toward the ratty truck parked on the other side of the park.

September steadied the gun, aiming at the man's belly. Chris's lessons came back to her: *Don't point unless you mean to shoot, and always go for the biggest target.* She hoped it wouldn't be necessary, but she was ready. "Drop the shovel. Back away. Farther." She yelled the words to be sure he heard through the closed window. When he'd retreated a safe distance she opened the car door and stepped out. "Take off the mask. Where's my cat?"

"Mask?" He ducked his head, hands still in the air. "Oh." He tugged the ski mask over his head. "I ain't hiding nothing. It's colder than a witch's tits." He frowned. "You lost a cat? I love cats, got me a sweet litter over at the barn." He smiled again, showing teeth in dire need of dental care. "Got me some great hunting dogs, too. Nice one you got there." He didn't sound particularly concerned about her pulling a gun on him. "He won't bite me if you let him out. Dogs know good'uns from bad'uns. They always like me."

Her hand wavered, and slowly she lowered the gun, only then realizing she'd not released the safety. She dared a glance over her shoulder, and saw Shadow with his nose poked as far as possible through the opening in the window, wagging tail underscoring the stranger's words. This man wasn't a threat. And he hadn't taken Macy. She remembered the toothpaste-bright shine of the attacker's grin, nothing like this man's broken fencepost smile.

"Sorry, mister. Where'd you get the ski mask?" The attacker had worn an identical one.

"Okay for me to pet him?" She nodded but kept distance between them when he approached Shadow. "He wants out. Okay?" The man asked permission—she liked that—and when she agreed, he opened Shadow's door for the dog to hop out.

"Who are you?" She relaxed when Shadow raced to her side, nudging one hand to get a pet. She watched Shadow's reaction closely, hand still tight on the gun hanging at her side, and stepped on the dog's trailing leash to keep him close. The stranger seemed harmless, if a bit odd.

"Call me 'Felch,' everybody does. They gave all of us official gear with the TV colors." He indicated the ski mask, which now bulged from one tattered pocket. "Not supposed to wear 'em out and about till the launch party tomorrow night, but I didn't have nothing else. Mr. Dietz don't want nothing to get in the way of our big-whammy party, so I try to do what's right but on the hush-hush." He held a finger to his lips. "My own fault I got sick. But nobody else ought to pay for my mistake. Couldn't live with myself knowing what I know and not making the effort." He squatted to meet Shadow on his own level, turning his face away when the pup aimed a slurp at his eyes. "Can't sleep no more. My body clock's all bass-ackwards. So got to hurry while I can still think straight. It comes and goes." He stood again, ambled over to the shovel and stopped. "I know what I need to do. But sometimes the why of it gets all foggy." He walked back toward his truck, his figure flickering from into the lamplight to shadow and back again like a stop-action film.

September's eyes took time to adjust when she slowly followed the man. Stepping from bright into dark shuttered her vision as effectively as blinders. "Somebody took my cat. He stole Macy from the vet clinic." Her voice caught. She squinted from the dazzle upon reentering the next spotlight.

Felch hunched his shoulders, but kept walking. "Your cat's sick, too? Sorry. Hurts to lose 'em, and I've lost several. See, it gets the critters sick lots faster than us people. It can take a critter down in a couple months. With people it's maybe a year." He sounded sad. "I got a few more months, I figure. Had other plans, but now they don't matter none. Got to work fast."

"Wait. Mr. Felch, wait. You're saying there's a contagious animal disease making people—making you—sick?" She hurried to keep up with his long stride. "Infected pets make people sick?"

"Naw, the same thing makes people sick gets the critters, too. All get exposed to it, one way or the other, but the animals die quicker. I think that's because they age so much faster, and kitten brains still developing. And the wild ones, they eat direct from the source."

"Eating? Dying?" She stopped at the thought. This was confirmation of Sly and Fish's wild story. September again hurried to catch up. "It's local, though, right?" Please let it be local, and not the beginning of another debacle like the horrific pet food recall of 2007, when nearly 200 brands from a dozen manufactures were intentionally contaminated. This would be worse if it also affected the pet owners.

He hefted the shovel. "The more they eat, the quicker they get sick. I can't clean up that biggest mess by myself. Can't put 'em all out of their misery. But I can collect the bits that I shared, get 'em back, and get rid of 'em. I been working through my list."

They reached his vehicle and he tossed the shovel in the truck bed. His ski mask fell from his pocket and got kicked underneath when he climbed in after the shovel. Felch stood to tug and aimlessly rearrange the contents.

She stood next to the old truck. "If you didn't take my cat, who did? The man wore the same kind of ski mask as you."

He shrugged. "I warned the reporter when he asked, but Mr. Dietz didn't like that, said it could cause a panic. I can't warn 'em all. Mr. Dietz says the show reaches more folks at once, that he'll make it right, lots faster than me with my lonely old shovel. He promised." He motioned to the dusty pile of dirt in the truck bed, sifting over top of bags of fertilizer and stacks of unidentified boxes, some with garden supplies spilling out. There was barely room for him to stand.

"What does any of this have to do with me?" Shadow pressed against her legs, and she followed his gaze. His attention was focused on something in the blackness beyond the pool of light, and she felt more than heard him begin to growl.

Without hesitation or thought, September ran. In the same motion she lifted the gun. But before she'd taken two steps someone grabbed her gun hand and wrenched her arm behind her back.

September screamed, dropped the gun, and was yanked against a muscular form. She twisted to see, but he wore the familiar ski mask. He forced her to bend with him when he scooped up her gun.

"Hey, what y'all doing? Don't hurt her." Felch stepped forward to tower over them from his perch in the truck bed.

Shadow danced around September and her captor, barks mixed with frightened yelps. He feinted bites at the man's legs.

The man took careful aim at the pup, and September screamed again. She couldn't move, kicking accomplished nothing. She turned her head and bit him hard on the jaw through the mask and tasted blood.

He yelled. The shot went awry. His grip never faltered, and instead of releasing her, he head-butted her temple.

The world spun. She would have fallen if not for his support.

Felch whined, confused. "You promised to help."

September screamed at Felch. "Help me! Make him stop!" Her head whipped from side to side, dark hair flagging an SOS as she searched vainly for help. The nearby schoolyard remained deserted. She, Felch and her attacker were alone.

She watched with incredulity when Felch sank to his knees, head cradled in his hands. "I can't remember what I gotta do. You promised!" He reached a hand toward them, and acted surprised at the gunshot. Red blossomed at his neck. He remained motionless an endless moment before he dropped. A cloud of white dust billowed and quickly settled.

September froze for a heartbeat and then redoubled her efforts. Get away, fight, flee. He'd kill her, kill Shadow, she had to get away, stop him, save herself. She kicked, but her rubber soled boots made no dent against his heavy work boots. "Let me go, you son-of-a-bitch, get off, get off!"

Shadow's hysterical barks grew more frantic. His tail flagged in high jerky movements, and snarls shouted fear and indecision. He grabbed and bit the man's pant leg and tugged, nearly pulling him to the ground. September cheered silently, but saved her breath to fight.

He aimed the gun again. More carefully. At Shadow.

"No!" She knocked his arm, and the shot went wild.

"I'll kill your dog. Like before."

His voice. The old familiar terror iced her veins. Victor, his voice, she'd never forget it. The gun followed the dog's movements. "Don't hurt him!"

"Beg." He shook her a little, couldn't do more with only one arm snugged her vise-tight, but it was enough. "Just like old times. Let me hear you beg."

"Please don't hurt my dog." She couldn't stop the sobs that choked her and could barely speak past the grief. "Whatever you want, but don't hurt him."

"You're so predictable." He laughed, delighted. "Call him off or I'll shoot him."

She swallowed hard. "Wait. Shadow, it's okay. Settle, baby-dog. Wait." Her voice cracked, but turned to steel to issue the commands to save her boy's life. He had to obey. Had to, or he'd die.

"Put this on. Backwards." Victor grabbed her by the hair, and she bit her lip not to scream. He held the gun trained on her, and turned loose her hair long enough to pull another ski mask from his pocket and toss it to her. "Do it." He aimed the gun again at Shadow.

She could run, and he'd kill Shadow and still come after her. "Shadow, hush. Sit. Wait, good-dog." Her voice trembled when he planted his tail. He yawned and whined his distress, licked his lips to signal "no threat" in the hope the scary situation would go away. When it didn't, he watched her with a furrowed brow, clearly conflicted whether to obey or not. "Please be a good-dog, wait. That's it. Wait."

Victor turned the gun toward her face. September took a breath and pulled on the ski mask, eyehole and mouth openings turned to the back. She could see the floodlights filter through, but no details. "Wait, Shadow, good-dog!" She kept calling, the command more a plea and a prayer as she let herself be dragged to the truck. Victor shoved her into the cab and started to climb in after.

With a furious roar, Shadow broke the stay. She heard him thunder close, could imagine him savaging Victor's legs.

God, no! He only wanted to help but he'd be killed. She saw Victor's silhouette, arm raised, pointing. She didn't hesitate.

"Shadow, *show-me* GUN!"

Victor cursed. The gun popped. Shadow screamed.

Chapter 35

Combs watched the EMTs load the vet tech's body into the ambulance, and slowly roll out of the parking lot. No lights. No hurry. He cracked his knuckles and flexed his neck, releasing tension that had settled into place like a vagrant no matter how often he tried to evict the unwelcome intruder.

He turned to the ME who waited nearby, leaning against his car, foot bouncing with impatience. "Sorry for the wait. COD pretty obvious? Blunt force trauma?"

The doctor agreed. "One massive tear caused all the bleeding. Something like a hatchet, some weight behind it but the blade was rather dull. Not so much a stab or cut as a tear. Caught him on the side of his neck and laterally down his chest. Another blow took out one knee and took him down. His right ulna, bone in the forearm, is fractured. Maybe more, but that much I could tell from this prelim."

"Defensive wounds." Combs demonstrated, holding up his right arm in a protective gesture. "The object came down and his arms came up, protecting his head."

"Probably." The ME nodded shortly. "Don't know the order yet, but at least one blow got through his defenses and cracked him a good one beneath the hairline. Likely a concussion, subdural hematoma—a brain bleed—could be what killed him. I'll know more when I get him on the table." He sighed. "There goes my nice, quiet holiday plans. Tell me this won't be a repeat of last Thanksgiving."

"Sure hope not." Back at the brightly lit clinic Combs could see Doc Eugene, Teddy and Gonzales still chewing the fat. Must be the veterinarian's worst nightmare to have this happen. Not only bad for business, but a horrible reminder of his wife's tragic end.

Once again, September was at the center of it all.

His phone rang. He frowned when he recognized the caller. "Hey Melinda. Daddy's working, can I call you back?" She knew better than to call during his shift. Well, to be fair, his regular shift should be over by now. Overtime would be the name of the game for the foreseeable future.

"You gotta come home. I mean, come over to our house. It's important. I'm scared."

He'd been ready to brush her off until the last two words. Combs straightened. "What is it, baby? Scared of what?"

"Somebody stole Mom's garden stuff. We had it stacked up in the garage, and came home and somebody broke in and—"

Combs ran a gloved hand over his head, tipped his face to the sky and mouthed, "Why me?" But he counted to five before answering. "You had a break in. Did you leave the garage door open again?"

"Maybe. I don't know."

"Anything else taken? Or only the fertilizer?"

"Daa-aaad. I don't know! But Mom's gonna freak. You know how she is about her roses. This is supposed to be some fancy exclusive stuff makes them grow like crazy, and you can't get it any more 'cuz the guy who makes it won't share the recipe, and Mom's already pissed I took off with my friends instead of going Christmas shopping with her and—"

"That's between you and your mother, Lindy."

Dead silence. "You don't know, Daddy. It's hard. Mom's acting weird lately. She can't remember anything, and blames me and William. Even Uncle Rick notices. And…and I miss you." Her voice cracked on the last.

Combs's hand tightened on the phone. 'Uncle Rick,' Cassie's new husband. At least Lindy didn't call the man "dad." That would kill him. After the tiff they'd had, he wanted nothing more than to leave Gonzales to the investigation, race to his kids and hug them close. "I know it's hard, baby. Hard for me, too. Hard for your Mom. And you gotta admit, that's not the first time Mom acted weird."

She laughed. As he'd hoped.

"I got to go. But I'll check in later, promise."

"What about the watch party? Mom said I could invite anybody I wanted. There'll be celebrities and swag giveaways, free food." Her voice got small. "Could you come?"

He arched his neck, and blew out his breath. He wanted to say yes. But didn't want to let her down. That happened too often. Better to say no than to disappoint. "Text me the details. I got a new case, but you know I'll be there if I can."

"New case?" Her voice was resigned. She'd grown up with him being a cop. The job trumping family stuff was nothing new. "You'll be careful, right?" She waited for the expected response.

"Careful as a three-legged dog with a fire hydrant. Bye, Lindy." He hung up the phone as Gonzales came out of the clinic. They walked together to the car.

"Everything okay?" Gonzales pulled out the car keys.

"Yeah, fine. Kids stuff. Ex-wife stuff. The usual." Combs pulled open the passenger door and climbed in. "Anything new from the vet? Teddy still playing detective?"

"Yep." Gonzales started the car. He adjusted the blower to keep windows clear. "He's convinced the pet angle is connected. I'm not so sure. Probably wishful thinking because of his wife. Wants something to blame." He changed gear and the subject. "Whatdya know about the stalker situation? You know September better than anyone. Why else would someone swipe her cat?"

Combs agreed. "I'm thinking it's personal. The cat's leverage over September. For ransom? Or something else." He pulled her cell phone out of his pocket. "Maybe we'll get lucky and the call to ransom her cat will come through September's phone."

She'd only told him bits and pieces about her stalker, but more than what Mark seemed to know. Her brother's assessment didn't jive with September's PTSD. "I think the stalker's here. Or someone pretending to be him scared her off. I got a name. And a picture. Victor Grant. Her brother said he was a family friend supposed to watch out for her, but I think instead he took advantage. For my money, Victor Grant is her stalker."

"Makes as much sense as anything. She built that fortress for a reason." The car increased speed. They were headed back to headquarters to write up the report, and later would swing over to the ME's office for further details once the vet tech's body had been processed. "Hard for September to stay under the radar after everything blew up last month."

"True that." Combs stared out the window.

"At least she has the dog with her."

Combs shook his head. "Shadow's a service dog; she never trained him for protection. He scopes out the house and warns of intruders, but I think he's more for emotional support than anything else."

"Whatever. I still wouldn't want to go up against his teeth."

"For the stalker to know about her cat, he must have been around for a while. This wasn't spontaneous, it was planned." He wished September would let them help. There was no way to reach her. Knowing September, she'd gone after the guy to get Macy back. "We need to find Victor Grant. If he's in the clear, then it's something other than the stalker."

Gonzales gnawed his mustache. "We don't know for sure this Grant is her stalker, if she never named him. But whoever it is, probably somebody new to town at least since Thanksgiving. Look at hotels for long-term stays, and apartments for recent rentals. Damn, that's a lot of people. Man, it is the holidays."

"September claimed the stalker killed her husband, but the local PD didn't buy it. I'm betting they at least took a look, even if they didn't clue her in." He paused. "Call Chicago PD, too. Uncle Stan knows people there, and her husband worked SVU there before they got married." Uncle Stan, retired after forty years on the force, still had plenty of connections.

Combs didn't need September to quote chapter and verse. It didn't take an Einstein to scope out what happened. Her sister April had never given birth, which begged the question about Steven's birth parents. Put it all together and it wasn't a huge leap what had happened.

September's stalker found out he had a kid, got pissed, and came after her.

Gonzales's phone rang, and he plucked it from a front pocket and thumbed it on. "Yeah, Gonzales." He listened, and his posture subtly straightened. "Yes, sir. Right away, sir, we're on our way."

Combs braced against the door when Gonzales slowed at the next intersection and pulled a fast U-turn. "What?"

"The Captain." He pushed the gas, hard. "Pecan gleaners in the south of the county, over the other side of Cottontail Mountain, found a pile of bones. A big pile. Deer mostly, probably a hunters' dump."

"Yeah, it's still deer season."

"There's not much left besides bones. Coyotes and other critters picked them clean. Hell of a place to harvest nuts." He pressed the accelerator hard.

"Pickings kind of slim by this time of year." Wild pecans commanded a decent price by the pound, and for some had become supplemental income. Commercial growers used motorized engines to shake down the nuts, but the gleaners banged branches with long poles and scrounged the ground to gather the pecans before squirrels beat them to the punch. Hard work, back breaking to gather up the bounty for not much reward, but that'd put the gleaners nose-to-nose with God-knew-what might be found in the scrub country. "Captain wants a pecan pie?"

Gonzales snorted.

"So what'd they find? Or should I say, glean?"

"A body. Face gone, so are the hands, probably cut off and tossed somewhere else to stymie ID. Wallet gone, too. But Captain says the fellow has a press badge the killer didn't find. Sylvester Sanger."

"Son-of-a-bitch. September was right. Somebody nailed that sorry bastard, and then moved the body."

Gonzales smoothed his mustache. "Somebody tried to kill Sly's investigation when they disappeared him. Another few days among the critters, and there would've been nothing left."

Chapter 36

Shadow banged his nose into the side of the truck when the stranger slammed the door. He jumped high against the side of the truck, barking-barking-barking as loud as he could. He clawed the metal as the truck started to move.

He heard September inside, crying. Shadow tried even harder to reach her.

A good-dog protected his person. She was his family. He'd tried even though the bad man pointed the gun at him. Shadow knew guns could reach out and bite, his ear stung with the memory. He didn't want September to get bit, either. So when she shouted *'show-me'* he nose-punched so hard the gun flew from the man's hand.

But September didn't climb out after the gun fell in the dusty road. Why didn't she come back to him?

Instead, she stayed with the bad man in the truck. It moved faster and faster, down the road and past September's parked car. Shadow barked for the truck to stop, and when it didn't, he chased after, trying to grab the tires with his teeth. He had to stop it from taking his person away.

But once it spun out of the lighted park onto the dark, hard car path, it raced faster and faster, so fast he couldn't keep up. Shadow ran after the truck anyway, chasing the truck into the night and crying for September to stop, to wait for him. But she'd left him behind.

Panting became more important than barking. He needed every breath to chase after them. No matter how hard he ran, the truck sped faster and soon its eye lights faded into the distance. He was left alone in the dark.

Shadow settled into a distance-eating rhythm, head held high to taste the air for the signature odor of the truck that had stolen his person. He loped along, focused only on the thread of scent, one paw padding after another, panting breath and pounding feet a hypnotic rhythm syncopated with his heart. On and on he ran; the odor fresh and blood hot in his nostrils. He didn't need light to see, his ears and his paws kept the path true, straight down the middle of the deserted car path. Without need to think, the scent told him where to turn, and although it grew fainter with time, it pointed the way as bright and sure as sunlight on a good-dog's back.

Trucks and cars followed car paths. Their four wheels spun faster than four dog-paws could gallop, but they always stopped. He'd catch up to the truck and his person as long as he didn't stop. One paw after another. No matter how long it takes. Follow the scent. Turn at the corner, run up the hill. Keep running. On and on. Don't stop. A good-dog finds his person.

Light haloed him from behind and made a dog-shadow leap out before him, but he ignored the shine. When the TOOOOT! sounded, he jumped, but quickly turned back and kept running. The scent pointed. He followed.

TOOOOT! The horn sounded again, and Shadow moved to the side of the road so the car with its shining eye lights could pass by.

"Hey boy. Hey dog?" The car pulled alongside and slowed to keep pace while the stranger talked to him out the window.

But Shadow kept running. Panting harder now. Running slower. But still moving. He couldn't stop. September was waiting for him. When the truck stopped and he caught up they'd be together again. They were family, and family belonged together.

"Dog with a mission, right? C'mon, boy, you're gonna collapse. Why doncha take a break."

Shadow's ears flicked. He didn't need to pee and poop. He didn't know why the stranger suggested take-a-break. He ignored the man's words. Only the scent mattered. The scent ruled. There. On ahead.

He stumbled. Caught himself, and pushed ahead. What was that whistle? His breath. It made whispery whistle sounds. Shadow came to another crossroads, ignoring the car that followed beside him, and paused. He knew which way to go, but paused. Another step. His head hung to the ground and he whined. Step. Pause. Step, step. Breathe.

The stranger's car stopped beside him. "Man, you're gonna kill yourself, dog. Doncha want a car ride?"

His ears flicked again, but he didn't raise his head. For a moment, catch his breath. There, over there, the scent-path continued. He took another step, licked his lips and whined. Panted. Jagged breaths pumping in and out.

"That's it, that's enough." The man got out of the car and walked slowly toward him, and Shadow watched warily. "Car ride?"

He raised his head, and barked at the man. His voice sounded funny. He barked again. *Car ride.* It wasn't September's car. But cars traveled fast, faster than dog paws, maybe faster than strange trucks that stole away a dog's special person.

"You want a car ride, dog? Sounds like a deal." The man opened the passenger door, and stood back.

Shadow whined, looked from the road's scent path to the open door. Finally, he limped to the car and climbed in. It took two tries to jump into the seat, and he leaked a bit of urine on the way in.

"Good-dog, that's a boy." The man carefully closed the car door, trotted around to the driver's side, and climbed in. He and Shadow stared at each other, until Shadow whined and reached out to gently sniff the man's offered hand. "Good boy, you're a beauty, aren't you?" He scratched Shadow's neck, and played with the jingle-sounding dog music on his collar. "So your name's Shadow?"

He cocked his head and barked once, but softly. It didn't occur to Shadow to wonder how the stranger knew his name. People knew things that dogs didn't. That's the way things were. Shadow watched out the window, sniffed the closed glass, and woofed again. He wanted the car to go. To go THAT way, where September had gone.

"Okay, Shadow, chill and rest. And we'll get you back where you belong."

The car started, and Shadow wagged with excitement. His tail thumped. But then he yelped, and pawed at the glass when the car turned around.

They were going the wrong way! He barked and pawed the glass again.

But the strange man only made soothing sounds. And drove Shadow away from any chance of finding September.

Chapter 37

Teddy took off his glasses, plucked a tissue from the box on the front counter and polished them, more a habit than anything. They weren't dirty. But it gave him time to think. He wished the whole situation would go away, but he owed it to September—and maybe Molly—to dig deeper into the story. He hoped it truly was only a "Fish" story.

"It's been a long, hellacious day. I want to lock up and go home." Doc Eugene rubbed his own eyes. "The patients have already been walked and fed, Timothy took care of that before he…" He turned away, busied himself gathering and stacking file folders.

"I'm sorry for your loss." Teddy carefully placed his glasses back on.

"Tim's family needs to be notified. Do I do that? Or the police?" The veterinarian slumped into a chair. "When my wife died, I got a call from the cops. I was out of town at a conference in Houston. It was our thirtieth wedding anniversary, did you know that?"

Teddy didn't know what to say.

"The blizzard grounded planes, and I couldn't get home for three days." The hurt remained raw, his words bitter. "She'd be alive today if it wasn't for September."

"September thinks so, too. And you're both wrong." Teddy held up a hand to stop angry words. "A lot of people were hurt. I lost a dear friend, and I'm terribly sorry for your loss. September will punish herself forever. Yet the only thing she's guilty of was trying to save the lives of her sister and nephew. And your wife helped her do that."

Doc Eugene started to say something, and then shrugged. "Pam never needed to be asked twice, that's true, she loved SAR work, hands on with the dogs to save people's lives." He smiled. "Seeing Shadow today was a treat. He's from one of the last litters Pam bred. I've placed his littermates with people who will help the pups reach their full potential. I don't have time to run a practice and train the dogs, too. And frankly, the dogs that are left—Heike, Uschi and Bruno—just remind me of my loss." He picked up a picture from the desk, of Pam surrounded by her dogs. "Bruno didn't eat for a week, thought I'd lose him, too. God, they were a sight together, especially on the trail. Don't know who enjoyed it more, Pam or the dogs." He turned the picture around for Teddy to admire.

"Good times, too. Right?" Teddy reached out a hand and squeezed his shoulder. "My wife Molly looks the same. But she's only really present now and then." When the veterinarian tipped his head, questioning, he said, "Alzheimer's."

"Aha. Sorry." Doc Eugene stood again and shuffled through the files he'd stacked, pulling one free and opening it. "That's why you're so interested in this."

"Mad cow disease. Here in Heartland." Teddy shivered.

"I didn't say it was spongiform encephalopathy. Far as I'm aware, prion disease has never been reported to affect dogs, but there is a feline spongiform encephalopathy thought to relate to the bovine form. Then there's scrapie, which affects goats and sheep. I don't know what this is, but the signs are similar." The veterinarian met his eyes. "There are other prion diseases that affect wildlife, rarely. Mink get it, and chronic wasting disease affects deer and elk. Again, that shouldn't impact the pet population, or humans. If it did, the CDC would already be here with sirens wailing."

Teddy shook his head. "There was a scare some years ago about infected cows and contamination of the food supply. I thought they cleared all that up."

"Right. There was a major outbreak in the UK back in the 80s and 90s. They test for it now so it can't get into the food supply." The veterinarian shrugged. "Mutations in a gene can cause spontaneous prion disease, no contamination necessary. But in people it's damn rare, maybe one in a million every year, with an incubation of months to decades, so nearly impossible to track even if it gets diagnosed. Creutzfeldt-Jakob disease is the human form, and it's thought the variant of that arose from the bovine disease. The only way to diagnose is to examine brain tissue. Tiny pinprick holes develop in the cortex and turn the brain into a sponge." He tapped the stack of folders. "That's why I sent off samples of that dog's brain, it appeared suspicious. I don't know what this is, maybe something entirely innocuous. Coincidence does happen, you know. Like September associated with another murder." Despite the wry tone, the joke fell flat. "Sorry, I know she's a friend."

Teddy didn't acknowledge the comment. He shared the man's bitterness over life's random attrition. He couldn't shake the notion—hope was too strong a word—that something other than Alzheimer's might be the cause of Molly's illness. Maybe something treatable, if it could only be identified.

Teddy didn't know what mad cow looked like, only that it affected the brain. "They banned beef imports for a while, right? From Canada and the UK. I forget all the details. Me and Molly still had our dogs then, and I remember she wouldn't buy beef for us and switched to a lamb and rice food for the pets." He smiled sadly. "At the time, all the experts said it wouldn't affect cats and dogs, but that didn't matter to Molly. Price of beef plummeted, but nobody bought it for a while. Not if a rare steak could drive you mad."

The doctor shook his head. "A cooked steak is as infectious. Cooking doesn't kill prions."

Teddy leaned on the counter. "If it's mad cow disease making the pets sick, it could affect people, too." He paused, and then asked the money question. "Can it be treated?"

Doc Eugene pushed the file to one side. "I know what you're asking. Alzheimer's disease is heartbreaking, but there are medications that help slow the progression. There's nothing for prion disease."

"Something's making people sick. Not only folks Molly's age, but youngsters, too. I know of at least two people in their thirties recently diagnosed with what the doctors *say* is Alzheimer's disease." He emphasized the word to show his doubt. He poked a finger at the file belonging to the infected dog. "Of course, they'd have to eat the same infected food as the animals, I suppose. How many people feed their cats and dogs steak? How often does wildlife get to chow down on prime rib?"

The veterinarian shrugged. "Coyotes and raccoons eat anything. They're scavengers, raid garbage cans like it's a smorgasbord, so theoretically the same food source could be accessed." He opened the file in front of him. "Then there's the raw feeders and home cookers. Mr. Benson's been feeding his dogs a raw ration for years."

"Raw?" Teddy made a face. "I like my rare beef as much as the next Texan, but that sounds like it's asking for trouble.

Doc Eugene laughed. "The veterinary community's shared your concern for years. Nevertheless, lots of my clients' pets get fed raw or homemade diets. That massive food recall that poisoned so many pets also created a whole new cottage industry. People lost faith in commercial foods and started mixing up their own recipes." He shrugged. "It can be done. Takes more time and there are some downsides. You gotta do it right. Sometimes I recommend home prepared foods, but consider them more of a therapeutic option for special cases. Some of my alternative medicine colleagues beg to differ." He laughed. "There's a reason they call it the *practice* of medicine. Often it's more art than science."

"But you say this Mr. Benson's dog got sick and he feeds raw food? Any of his other dogs sick? Do the other sick pets also eat raw food?"

"He's a hunter. You probably know him from that new reality show."

Teddy made another face. "Not a fan of reality programming."

"Well, it's pretty popular. Mr. Benson's become a local celebrity. He only brought in the one animal, but I'm sure he feeds all his hunting dogs the same. The other animals, don't know if it's the same illness or similar signs. Good idea to research common food sources. I investigated at Mr. Benson's behest. But it could affect commercial pet rations as easily. I think Mr. Benson uses a commercial supplement."

"What's that? The supplement?"

"Usually a vitamin and mineral pre-mix that makes sure the homemade recipe is balanced. Lots of them out there, the internet lists millions of self-proclaimed expert recommendations." He flipped through pages in the file. "It's documented here somewhere. I don't carry such things anymore, not worth the trouble when so much is available cheaper. The internet again." He closed the file. "It'll be a couple of days at least before the pathology on the brain tissue comes back. Until then, we're guessing."

"None of this helps us find September, either." Or helps Molly, he thought. If she'd caught this "new" disease, it'd be trading one horror for another. "If September had her phone, I could've used GPS to find her." At Doc Eugene's surprised expression, Teddy offered a sheepish expression. "You could say I have certain skills that allow me to bypass official channels. Only for good."

"Right. The geriatric Lone Ranger."

Teddy barked a laugh. "I like that."

Doc Eugene suddenly straightened and drew in a deep breath. "I wonder . . ." He held up one hand, and flipped once again through the stack of file folders. "GPS. We've got a new product we're trying out. Tracking device for pets, mostly used to keep hunting dogs from wandering too far. Timothy thinks it'd be—I mean, he *thought* the product would make a great holiday promotion." Awkwardly, the veterinarian corrected his tense. Teddy knew it would take a while before the young man's death felt real.

The doctor pulled out Macy's file, flipped it open, read, and paused. "Well how about that?" He turned the chart around so Teddy could see. "September bought a collar tracking system for her cat. If Timothy's killer still has Macy, we can find him with the cat's GPS."

Teddy's pulse quickened. He pulled the file closer, but frowned. "Wouldn't the unit have to be charged?" The veterinarian handed him a duplicate of the product and he quickly scanned the information, and pointed. "See here? It runs on a rechargeable battery."

"Timothy made a note. He charged the unit and put it on Macy's collar before the cat was released." Doc Eugene smiled again, and reached for the phone. He had one of the detective's cards in his hand.

"Wait." Teddy stopped him. "The unit has to be configured. September didn't have time to do that. Or would she give Timothy access to her phone or computer codes?" The veterinarian shook his head, disappointed. "You define acceptable territory, and then tell the GPS feed to send alerts to a designated account." He paused, thinking.

The veterinarian's face fell. "Oh. Right. Guess that's no help."

"Not necessarily." He polished his glasses. "Did I mention I have skills?"

Chapter 38

September slowly regained consciousness when the ancient truck's jounced movement stopped. Her head throbbed. The driver's side door squealed open, and the shot springs jiggled when someone climbed out. He left the door open—she assumed it was Victor—and icy air laced with a hot, gag-making smell poured in.

She couldn't see. Panic. Had the head blow left her blind? The knit mask itched her face, and memory assuaged the panic but only a little. The blindfold snugged tighter over her eyes and around her head than before so no light leaked through. Her temple throbbed. How long had she been out?

Shadow! He'd shot her dog! Then she remembered hearing muffled barking before she passed out, and could breathe again. Knowing he was still alive, that one small victory made the pain worthwhile.

Careful to remain still, September blinked, testing the limits of her vision. Eyelashes scrubbed against the fuzzy knit mask. She heard steps shuffle outside the truck. Victor probably could see her through the windows. Best to play possum as long as possible. Maybe she could learn something useful, leave a message for would-be rescuers, or even figure out how to escape. She'd escaped before.

After a smitten fan sent her flowers—Forget-Me-Not blossoms—Victor became enraged and threatened to smash Melody, her only connection to normalcy, to life before, to the real September. Once he destroyed the music, she'd be next. September knew her daydream of escape must become a reality.

The chance came three months later, December eighteenth, after Victor escorted her onstage. She seated herself, situated Melody between her knees and took the bow. She didn't look at Victor when he brushed a kiss on her forehead, fearing he'd read her intent. He hesitated, and September forced a smile, prayed he couldn't hear her thrumming heart.

Vic exited stage right and stared as she prepared to play.

September nodded at the conductor, the orchestra played, she placed her bow and fingered the strings, took a deep breath—and stood. She ran into the wings, cradling her cello like a beloved child. Gathering her long skirt in her bow-hand, September raced down the stage stairs into the audience, thundered up the aisle and out through the rear double doors. Audience members began to murmur and rustle but she didn't hesitate, and dashed down the first set of red-carpeted stairs, turned the corner, and continued to the ground level.

She terrified the coat-check girl when she suffered her first panic attack, certain Victor would convince everyone her "mental breakdown" required his personal intervention. But the girl let her in and September burrowed between hanging coats to hide, holding Melody like a shield, like the life preserver she truly was.

A half hour later, Detective Christopher Day and the police team appeared. Victor Grant disappeared.

And now he was back.

The truck jostled with accompanying thumps and grunts of effort. He must be in the truck's bed, moving Felch's body. Felch must have helped steal Macy, even if he hadn't understood the implications.

And what *was* that smell? September breathed through her mouth, but the odor coated her nostrils and clawed at the back of her throat. She could almost taste the acrid, cloying smell. They must be at the county dump. She turned to the window and leaned her shrouded brow against the glass, welcoming the cold but afraid she'd vomit into the knit cover and choke to death. That'd serve Victor right. But she wouldn't get much satisfaction, either.

September heard him drag a large object from the back of the truck. Gravel or sand beneath the weight screed against the metal bed. Her seat jounced again when Victor jumped off the back of the pickup, grunted a few times to drag the object off, and a sodden thump hit what sounded like wet leaves. Sound faded as he dragged the object some distance away from the truck.

Before he could return, September quickly explored her face with her hands. Her wrists were bound by tape. More tape wound around her head and across her eyes over top of the knit covering. That explained her loss of sight.

His face and voice haunted her nightmares. She didn't need to see Victor to know it was him, but the blindfold kept her helpless, and literally in the dark about where they were going. Or what he was doing here at the dump.

There must be something, some way to leave a message. The police would talk to Doc Eugene, and he'd tell them she'd been there. Victor could have taken her at the house, but he didn't. Instead, he left the flowers so she'd run. He wanted her to run, and when she didn't, he took her.

Combs might think otherwise. She'd discouraged his attentions for so long, he might decide he'd had enough. How long could you push someone away before they gave up trying? A brief, clutching grief nearly crippled her before she pushed it away as well.

Her car. They'd find it eventually. She'd left the keys behind. Surely they'd know that wasn't right. Maybe Victor had finally screwed up. She had to do something, leave a signal. She had to trust they would look.

September patted her coat pockets. The noxious rotting odor faded into the background as she struggled to wriggle one hand inside the zippered front. A hard object, long and pointed. And a round cylinder, a pill bottle, no help at all. A pencil might work to scribble a note, or if sharp enough, pierce the tape on her wrists, or stab as a weapon.

She traced the outline and recognized the blunt-nosed Sharpie Marker with disappointment. There was no way she could get it out of her pocket, un-cap and write a message before Victor returned to the car.

This had to be more than payback from the mercenary son-of-a-bitch. It had something to do with Sly; the terrible day had started with him. Then there was Felch's confusion, clumsy gait and insistence on "fixing" some wrong. He said the ski mask was some official merchandise. A TV show, that's it. If she could figure out where Victor fit in, she might still get out of this alive.

She heard Victor returning to the truck. *No time, no time, leave something behind in the truck, something that could come only from her.* He'd notice if she kicked off a boot. She'd cut her nails short to practice cello, and they couldn't leave noticeable marks. No buttons to tear, and the ski mask had contained her tears or blood, if any. She wore no jewelry, so had no watch to drop onto the floorboards, nothing that identified her.

The pill bottle. Macy's prescription. She hiccupped, and grappled to pull it out, and the cap pulled off. Normally the child-proof bottles were a bitch to open. Never mind, it wasn't the pills—it was the label on the bottle that mattered.

She managed to milk the bottle up out of her pocket until it dropped. Most of the small, white tablets scattered down her front. September kicked the bottle out of sight beneath the seat and shifted, brushing off pills caught in the fabric folds of her coat.

Knowing Victor, he'd probably dumped Macy somewhere. Her eyes filled. One more innocent victim because of her. If she didn't survive, Macy's pill bottle found under the seat would convict Victor. That was a damn fine legacy for her beloved cat.

The truck bounced as he climbed back into the cab and slammed shut the door. "So my sleeping beauty awakes."

She refused to answer. But in the back of the truck, another voice replied. "Meowring?"

Macy was alive.

Chapter 39

Combs put a hand up to his mouth, trying to stifle the smell. "That's disgusting." One of the uniforms looked green. "You gonna toss your cookies, do it over by the road. I don't want you contaminating the crime scene."

It had taken more than half an hour to find the place. After traveling down main highways and turning onto twisty farm-to-market roads, they'd come to a graveled path that took them deeper into the scrub. Gnarly bois d'arc trees and a few honey locusts fought for supremacy among the native cedar elm, mountain ash and burr oak. He hadn't a clue how the gleaners found the cluster of pecan trees. Maybe they passed the information down the family line the way granny's pecan pie recipe became an heirloom.

As if reading his mind, Gonzales said, "Won't be thinking about pecan pie the same way ever again." He spoke through a paisley bandanna.

"Love the new style. Like you're ready to bushwhack a stagecoach." Combs coughed, his eyes watered. "Yee-haw. Don't suppose you've got an extra?"

Gonzales shook his head, and the bandanna covering his mouth and nose rippled when he spoke. "But I got some Vicks."

"Gimme." Combs accepted the small bottle and liberally smeared his upper lip. It didn't help. "Don't know how the ME handles it." He acknowledged the little man crouched over the remains.

"Nose transplant. You think?" Gonzales led the way over to the small group of onlookers, the pecan-gathering group who stumbled across the body. Literally. "Which one of you called?"

The older woman raised her hand. "I did." She had a young girl of perhaps twelve clutched tight under one arm, and a lanky pimple-faced teenage boy stood nearby trying to pretend he was bored and failing. All three shared the same dark uni-eyebrows, upturned freckled noses and tiny gray eyes. "Daddy found it." She pointed at an even older man standing with his back braced against the tree. "I got the only phone, for emergencies. This qualified."

"I'll say." The teenage boy wiped his runny nose on his coat sleeve.

Combs noticed none of the family acted bothered by the smell. Maybe long-term exposure deadened smell sense the way overuse of perfume made some women overdo the cologne.

"What's your name?" Gonzales took the lead. The wind had picked up, which made audio recording iffy, so he took notes on the small pad.

"Feeny. Glory Feeny. This here's Gina. That's George Junior, and over there's Daddy. My dad, that is, George Feeny, Senior." The little girl shivered, and Glory gave her shoulders a squeeze.

"You called right away?" Gonzales scribbled the names.

"Yep. Soon as Daddy uncovered the boot. First off, thought some hunter done tossed out an old pair, and Daddy needs new ones so he tried the size. 'Cepting the feller was still wearing them."

"Touch anything else?" Combs took in the family's worn clothes, and the loose fabric bags at their feet. Or maybe other pickings. "Mind if I take a peek?"

"Help yourself." She nudged one of the bags with her foot. Dirty, worn tennis shoes peeked from the cuffs of baggy sweatpants. "All you'll find is nuts." She didn't sound angry, only resigned.

"The pigs got him."

Combs glanced up. The old man stood with eyes closed, loose lips mumbling maybe in prayer. "What'd you say?"

He opened his eyes and repeated. "Just what I told Glory. Them feral pigs got him." The old man's words gave Combs the creeps. "Then when they was finished, the coyotes took a turn. Maybe some coons got in on it. And finally the black birds flocked over top, they're gleaners like us, take the leavings. This here's like a trough for the critters, they kin all belly up to the bar."

"Daddy, that's enough." Glory gave him a look. Combs wasn't sure what it meant.

"You've known about this place for a while?" Gonzales asked the question before he could. "Other people come out here on a regular basis, do they? I'll need the names."

Glory shrugged, but stared daggers again at her father. "Hunters know the spot. Don't know no names. They keep to themselves, and we do likewise." She nodded at the trees. "Don't need no competition for the pecans, and sure don't have no interest fighting the pigs for that garbage. We's poor, maybe, but I feed my kids healthy." Her chin jutted out.

"No disrespect, Ms. Feeny. Just trying to figure out who might have dumped this man out here." Gonzales pulled down the bandanna so she could see him smile. "We appreciate you being good citizens and calling us. You didn't recognize him?"

She shook her head. "Like Daddy said, the pigs got him. Nothing to recognize." She took a breath. "Can I go? Want to get my kids and Daddy back home. We been out here for too long."

"Just a couple more questions, ma'am." Combs thought Gonzales was a better man than him, going without the bandanna filter. He licked his teeth, to be sure the smell hadn't made them melt. "You got out here what time?"

"Don't have no watch. Early afternoon, though. We ate lunch before we came."

"And when was the last time you came here for the pecans? I mean, before this."

"Last week." Glory turned to her son, and he shrugged. "First day out of school for the kids, so we come up here and scouted around. Not too many pecans that day."

"Did you pick around this same area? So the body wasn't here last week. What day was that?" He stared back at the three pairs of tiny gray eyes. The old man wouldn't meet his eyes. Huh. Something there.

"Monday last. Nobody here that day but us." She crossed her arms. "Can we go?"

"Thanks for your time. Yes, you can go. We may have more questions later, so don't leave town." Gonzales paused. "I need your address."

"Where would we go?" She huffed, but readily gave Gonzales the address of the low rent apartment complex where they lived. "Just so ya know, the phone's disposable and almost done. We ain't got a line at the house so you'll have to catch us when you can." She stooped and scooped up the pecan bag, and the teenager grabbed the other two before they all made their way to a distant rust-bucket sedan.

Gonzales tugged the bandanna back into place. "Doesn't help a damn. But I look so cool." He cocked his head at Combs. "You look like a snot-nosed kid."

"It's a choice. Not a good one, but what can you do." Combs breathed through his mouth for a minute, and the wind in his face also helped. "What do you think?"

"The old guy knew more. Glory knows Daddy could get in trouble and wants him to shut his pie-hole." Gonzales closed his eyes. "Damn, and I used to love pecan pie."

Combs shrugged. "So we'll follow up with Daddy when Glory isn't around." They waited for the ME to approach. "Sly disappeared from September's place on Thursday morning and hasn't been seen since, after she claimed to see his dead body. So somebody flew in and scooped him up after she saw him—"

"—or he walked out under his own power and got transported later." Gonzales shuddered. "Hope to God the man was dead before they dumped him. Feral pigs, nasty beasts. Sure do fast work."

The ME ambled up to the detectives, wheezing from the climb out of the trough. "Sometimes I hate my job."

"Only sometimes?" Combs sounded like he had a cold, and tried again. "What's the word?"

"Dead before he got here."

Gonzales let out his breath. "Sly was a low-brow gossip monger, but even he didn't deserve this."

The ME went on. "Several blows to the torso, and the COD appears to be a baseball bat to the head. A Louisville Slugger, to be exact."

"Got your crystal ball mojo going, do you?" Combs forgot and breathed through his nose, and nearly gagged.

"Nope, nothing so woo-woo. Found the baseball bat. Under the body." He motioned over his shoulder to where the CSIs continued to process the scene. "It's pretty distinctive, has the words *King Thwacker* wood-burned into it. Yep, it's an old fashioned wood bat, not a new-fangled modern aluminum or whatever the hell the Rangers use these days. A lot of good that does 'em," he said.

Combs didn't let his surprise show. He grunted. "September's bat. Must have come from her place. She said they had words."

Gonzales picked up the thread. "More than words. Somebody heard or saw the argument, and took the next step. Doesn't look good for her." He held up a palm to stop Combs's reply. "Just saying. Whoever whaled on Sly meant it to incriminate her." His phone rang, and he frowned as he listened.

The ME continued. "We'll have to confirm ID once we get him back to the morgue."

"I thought the responding officer found his wallet?" Combs raised his eyebrows. "No?"

"Wallet's gone, whoever killed him probably disposed of that. Even cut off his hands and bashed in his teeth, obviously trying to hide who he was. And the critters took care of the rest." The ME shrugged. "They missed his press badge, on a lanyard under his shirt. Sometimes we get lucky, when others get stupid."

Gonzales hung up the phone and crossed back to them. "Found September's car."

"Where? She okay?" Combs breathed through his nose again, but this time he was prepared. Damn, he must be getting used it. He wondered if his sense of smell would be permanently damaged.

"At a park next to Heartland Middle School. She's not there. But get this: they found her gun, and it had been discharged."

"Shit." Combs started running toward their car. "Anything else, tell me while I drive."

Gonzales jogged after him, and swung into the car in the same synchronized motion as Combs. "They found a stocking cap on the ground, weird colors. Somebody recognized it. The characters from that reality hog hunting show wear them."

"Hog hunting?" Combs jammed the keys into the ignition and shoved the car into gear. He didn't watch reality TV and had enough of guns during his day-job. "Hogs, like feral pigs?" The car bucked over the uneven gravel road, but began to make better progress once back on the paved FM highway. "There's a whole film crew in town, I think the actors are local but betcha there's some out-of-towners. Wonder if any of them joined the party since Thanksgiving?"

"Haven't had time to canvass motels. But I got a list of possibles, right age bracket and name match to Victor Grant or close derivatives." Gonzales swerved around a squirrel and nearly went off the road. "Damn tree rats," he muttered, and then louder. "Any word from the Chicago PD or from South Bend?"

Combs shook his head. "Not yet. Like you said, it's the holiday. Case moving too fast." His phone rang and he grabbed it and tried to answer, but nobody was there. It tweedled again, and his eyes widened. It wasn't his phone. "That's September's phone." He dug it out of his pocket, and handed the phone to Gonzales to answer. "Put it on speaker."

"It's an unknown local number." Gonzales punched it on. "Hello? Who's this?"

A man's baritone spoke, cheerful and excited, while in the background a dog barked and yelped. "Hey man, I got great news for you. I found your dog Shadow."

Chapter 40

She stumbled, and Victor's bruising grip kept her from falling. September bit her lip to keep from crying out, wouldn't give him the satisfaction. She knew from experience any complaint fueled an increase in the abuse.

They'd driven for quite a spell away from the dump. The smell faded quickly, and she silently thanked the winter wind, but worried about Macy left in the back of the truck. At least Macy was alive. Thank goodness for Maine Coon fur.

She'd managed to surreptitiously collect half a dozen of the Atenolol tablets. Maybe Victor hadn't noticed, but she couldn't be sure. He might simply wait until later to surprise her with his retaliation. Or he might believe himself so in control of the situation, nothing she could do mattered.

September tried to keep track of turns, even counting the number of seconds between them. That always worked in the movies. But she suspected Victor purposely drove in aimless circles for a time to thwart that possibility. Even if her guesses proved accurate, she had no way to know.

Once they slowed and parked, Macy meowed when Victor collected the cat's carrier and helped September out of the truck. The uneven ground sported large tufts of vegetation, maybe grass or winter rye. Icy wind made her hands stiffen and prickle, the Reynaud's syndrome making an expected appearance.

She listened. It sounded like the middle of nowhere. No traffic or train sounds, no street light buzz or any of the subliminal ambiance that saturated every urban setting. Only the crunching of their feet on frozen ground broke the silence. Her fingertips stung, and she could imagine the nails turning blue in response to the drop in temperature. September curled her bound hands protectively into her chest. She'd need as much function as possible if she were to do anything in her defense.

A soft thump prompted another meowed protest. He'd banged the cat's soft sided carrier against something solid. Still blindfolded, she remained helpless to do anything to protect herself or her cat.

They'd entered some sort of a shelter. She could tell by the change in air pressure and smooth feel of hard-packed dirt beneath her boots. September heard the thump of the duffel drop to the ground, and Macy's guttural reply.

"This is temporary." They stopped. He released her arm. She didn't try to run—run where, blindfolded and bound? Instead she shivered elaborately and whimpered for Victor's benefit. Let him think she was totally cowed. He did have control, but overconfidence might create mistakes. Right now, that was her only hope.

Metal on metal rasped followed by the scream of rusty hinges. "Go on, inside, step up." He pushed her, and she reached out with both clenched hands, found the wooden doorframe and felt with a foot for the step before she cautiously climbed inside.

A room. Small, confined. Smelled dusty and musty, like old lawn clippings. Hay?

"Here's your cat."

He shoved Macy's carrier against her shin, and she crouched to touch the webbing, smiling with relief when the cat's cold, wet nose pushed against her hand through the mesh.

"There's a bucket straight ahead of you on the far wall for the obvious bodily functions. A sleeping bag beside it, in case you get chilly or want to sleep. Not much left of the night anyway, it's nearly dawn." He moved around, and she could hear his boots clop on the wood floor. "Got Felch to clean out all the bones. Didn't seem to bother him, but he was an animal himself. Hell, his own shack up the hill isn't much better. And there's a table to your right with a thermos. Coffee, for the caffeine addict." He laughed. "See, I remember, something we have in common. Neither of us could ever get enough coffee." He paused, and she heard him move around the room again. "Collected all your favorite things here. Just for you." He turned serious, and it was all she could do to stand her ground when she heard him draw near. "It's not how I planned. But you'll never leave me again. You need me, September." His arms came around her. Hot breath burned her neck, and she stiffened.

A phone burbled. Victor's arms tightened for a moment before he stepped away. "Rain check."

She said nothing. Didn't move, although her instinct screamed to put as much distance between them as possible. September reminded herself he'd graduated to murder, and he had her gun. He could aim the gun and shoot her and she'd have no warning.

He answered the phone. "Yes, what?" He listened. Aggravation colored his reply. "I've got everything covered, except I need a ride. Felch's truck slid into the dry gulch at the dump site, can't get it out. Yeah, that's why I'm not back yet." He listened. "I took care of Felch. Hey, we agreed, it had to be done. They shoot horses, don't they?" He laughed. "Great movie. Besides, he couldn't be trusted after what he did to that reporter, and too much of a loose cannon. Hell, he'd show up for the party and start wagging his jaw, and we'd be done." Another pause. "Nobody will tie anything to us, after a couple of days there won't be anything to find. You plan what you'll say when he's a no-show at the party tonight. I still need a ride. No, not one of the new guys, they'd have too many questions. Send BeeBo, he can give me a lift to my car. There's still a few loose ends to tie up before the party tonight." Another pause. "Yeah, grabbing the cat smoked her out but there was a minor complication. Felch will take the heat on that, too. I know what I'm doing. Don't worry," he finished, "I can guarantee she won't be a problem."

September sucked in a silent breath. This *was* bigger than Victor's personal obsession with her. If Felch had something to do with Sly's disappearance, then her kidnapping involved Sly's investigation, and his partnership with Fish.

"You'll manage. You don't need me there. Sunny and the other stars will make the appearance; nobody will notice one less goober. Local yokels will believe anything you tell them," he said drily. He lowered his voice, but she could still hear. "No, I need to move tonight, before then. It's personal." He made a frustrated sound. "Oh, all right. But if you want me there, I want my bonus as soon as we wrap. I'll send wire instructions for the rest, but I need traveling money tonight." He listened. "You don't want to test me. I know where all the bodies are buried. Literally." He hung up. Footsteps thumped the floor. The squeal of the door announced his departure.

"Stop! Please, Victor!" She couldn't help the pleading tone in her voice. That wasn't faked.

The footsteps paused, but he remained silent, waiting for what she'd say.

"How long will you be? Can you at least take off the blindfold? I already know your face, and haven't a clue where we are. Besides, there's nobody to tell." She motioned with her taped hands. "I can't do anything taped up and blind."

Nobody knew she was here. What if something happened to him? She could be stuck here for days before someone found her, if they ever did.

"Plans changed." He wasn't happy. "I'll be back tonight, and we can finish our reunion. That sleeping bag isn't the Ritz but it'll do in a pinch. Soon, very soon, I'll be my own man answerable only to myself, but tonight I've got a command performance I can't escape." He paused. "There's no way out. No windows, no lights, new padlock on the door, and nobody to hear you scream, but go ahead and knock yourself out."

His hand touched her face, spider-light against the ski mask, and she jerked away. "Just remember there are consequences to everything you do. That cat you love so much? Treat me nice or I'll wring its neck." The hinges squealed and door slammed.

September gathered Macy's carrier close, shaking as a padlock snicked closed. Soft footsteps faded, and she craned to hear, remaining motionless until the distant truck's engine roared to life. Once it drove away, she wasted no time.

"Macy, I'm gonna get us out of here. I won't let him hurt you. Or me." The cat mewed back and head-butted the mesh. "I know, I know you want out. Me too." First, though, she needed to see. She'd have to risk Victor's consequences. The alternative didn't bear consideration.

She still grasped half a dozen of Macy's pills in one hand, and awkwardly dropped them into one of her pockets so she could use both hands to work off the mask. Depending on how long they were stuck here, she might need to medicate Macy. Or maybe poison Victor? She wondered what effect Atenolol might have on a person.

She wasn't a scared, gullible teenager any longer. Nothing he could threaten would keep her from fighting him. The chameleon lied as a matter of course. For all she knew, this place was a luxury get-away and the bucket a sick joke designed to torment her.

September quickly rolled the breath-wet soggy knit cap upward, uncovering her lips and nostrils. Cold, fresh air invigorated her efforts.

It took longer to work the taped portion off, the pressure against her closed eyelids creating dark sparkles that slowly faded when she tossed the ski mask free. For a long moment she was afraid to open her eyes, afraid it wouldn't make a difference and that Victor's assertion of no windows would continue to block further effort to see.

Macy yowled, and September blinked. Opening her eyes wider, she turned her head. He hadn't lied for once. No windows. But chinks in old planks allowed dim light to filter through. September levered herself upright, and walked carefully across the floor to the wall, placing her eye to a knothole. Moon glow bathed a rough field with light. The horizon had begun to brighten.

Still dark, but near dawn on this icy December morning, so it must be Friday about 7:30 a.m. Victor's meeting was tonight, what time he hadn't said. But she couldn't count on him keeping to a schedule. She needed to make plans quickly and set them immediately in motion.

Her eyes grew accustomed to the dim light, and before anything else, she tried the door. She grasped and shook the handle to no avail.

The hinges were attached on the other side, so even if she'd had the tools, there was no way to access them. Anyway, she'd need her hands free to do anything.

September bit at the tape, and tried to get a purchase on the material. Gaffer's tape, but she couldn't get the right angle to tear it, and Victor had used nearly a whole roll. The multiple layers made it impossible to remove without a cutting edge.

The bucket squatted against the wall, sure enough, with a roll of toilet paper. The small table held a thermos as well as the missing rose lamp stolen from her office. Was it plugged in?

She hurried to the table, and when the sound of her shoes across the plank floor changed, she realized Victor had placed a carpet over the floor. It was hard to tell in the near darkness, but she suspected it had also been taken from her house. He'd chosen things she would have never left behind when running away. These were items meant to furnish a future life together. She shuddered. "Over my dead body." It might come to that.

She found the cord to the lamp, coiled and neatly tied, and dropped to her knees to search for outlets. No outlets, but Melody was there.

She pulled out the cello, and saw the strings were gone. Crap. The A-string might have cut the tape on her wrists. Any of the strings could have worked as a garrote or trip-wire to surprise Victor upon his return. Hmm. Maybe the cord from the lamp could work to trip him?

Because she would NOT go quietly.

Within minutes she'd explored the tiny confines of the room. Old wooden planks made up the floor, four walls, and low ceiling. Multiple empty nail and screw holes peppered the walls where hooks, shelves or other accessories no longer rested. Nothing remained, no sharps able to injure or threaten a captor, and nothing useful to signal a rescue. Originally used as a tack room or for tool storage, someone had transformed it into a bare box, a prison to keep September contained until Victor could spirit them both away.

Macy yowled, the sound a bit desperate. "Okay, I know I promised. We'll figure something out, right?" She hurried to the cat carrier, sat on the floor and zippered open the top.

He eeled out of the container, stretching first one fore paw followed by the diagonal rear leg and then stroked his full length against September's thigh. Macy climbed into her lap, pushing his cheeks in turn hard against her face. "I know, it's been forever, I missed you, too." His purr vibrated beneath her stroking hands. Somehow that made everything better. Fear and panic slowly began to subside, replaced by angry resolve.

The sticky tape between her wrists caught the cat's fur and he flinched and pulled away. Macy sniffed the tape, and tasted it, and then stretched out on his tummy against the familiar carpet and honed his claws.

"Not even your claws will do the trick on this tape," she said. Macy circled the small room, sniffing the floor for whatever animal scents remained and stopped to cheek-rub the few items: the bucket, the table leg, nose-touched the rubber tip of Melody's endpin.

The endpin! September stumbled in her hurry to reach the cello, and released the holding screw to pull out the long metal rod. Light-weight titanium and about two feet long, the rubber stop fit over a sharp point. With effort, she got the rubber end off, braced the rod between her knees and used the dagger point to sever the tape binding her wrists.

"Yes!" She pulled off the rest of the tape and grasped the endpin, swinging it through the air as though testing a bat or fencing an invisible adversary. Though sharp, the light-weight rod designed to enhance tone of the instrument had never been meant as a weapon. "Use what you got, September."

She returned to the cat carrier. After taking Fish's notes to the vet clinic, she'd had no time to discuss them with Doc Eugene or Timothy, after the vet tech was attacked. At least she'd stuffed them inside the carrier. She set the file aside and searched another pocket, pulling out a small spray vial of synthetic cat pheromone used to reduce feline stress. She put it in her pocket, and added the small penlight used for Macy's chase-the-light game.

Feeling the half dozen loose pills in her pocket, she debated giving the cat a pill. Doc Eugene had explained about titrating the dose—starting small and slowly increasing as needed—and had given Macy his first dose before she'd picked him up. She couldn't risk giving him too much and overdosing him.

That made her wonder again what an overdose might do to a person. Atenolol was a beta-blocker. She glanced at the coffee thermos, and for the first time began to feel hope.

Macy pawed one edge of the carpet in a corner of the small room. He sniffed, and then sneezed.

"What'd you find?" He meowed back at her, and she joined him. "Going to help me get the bad guy? Like you nailed them the last time?" She didn't know how soon Victor would be back and there wasn't time to train new behaviors. "Use what you have," she whispered again, her new mantra.

Claws caught on the edge of the carpet, and Macy lifted the covering enough for her to see in the dim light: a cat-size black hole in the floor on the inner wall.

Chapter 41

Teddy had fooled with Macy's GPS setup for nearly an hour. His eyes itched and didn't want to focus. Cleaning his glasses didn't help. Besides, Doc Eugene's tiny office, outdated desktop and slow internet connection made him want to bite nails and throw the computer against the wall.

"Had to create an account. Email is required to send alerts via email or text, so I plugged in my own info. But that's as far as I got." Teddy's frustration made him even more tired. "I don't have a clue what to set the local portal parameters to, without a general idea of Macy's location."

Doc Eugene rubbed his own eyes. "Usually the local boundary is the pet's home. I've got September's address, if that'll help." He yawned. "Sorry, so tired. I've not slept well lately anyway."

Teddy yawned, too. "Doubt either of us will sleep much tonight, either. I mean today. It's nearly dawn." Teddy refolded the brochure with the setup information. "Nifty device, works something like the Amber Alert tracking options for kids, but without all the bells and whistles. The kid version has multiple zones you can define, and as long as the child wears the device, you can get updates every minute or so and track movements 24/7. You can even set it up for when you go on vacation or for the Little League practice park. And it all tracks on your computer or smart phone."

"Nice. Didn't know they had that for kids." Doc Eugene half smiled. "Bet that would drive teenagers nuts, though."

Teddy agreed. "But for the little ones, and the wanderers—like autistic children—it could be a lifesaver. They use a combo of GPS and cell phone towers to track." He tapped the pet tracking brochure. "This system, though, tracks pets with a separate handheld device. You set up the boundaries on your computer, but the handheld detects signals only within about a two-mile range. It alerts when the pet crosses the designated boundary." He made a face. "That's actually to our benefit, most of these pet trackers only work up to about six hundred feet or so. I still need to set up the boundary, make a best guess to get the location within that two-mile limit. We need straight line-of-sight for best case results. And then pray the batteries on the cat's collar last long enough for us to zero in on Macy. Even the kid version of this technology says batteries need a re-charge every forty-eight hours."

"That's a lot of ifs." Doc Eugene picked up the brochure, flipped it over, and read for a moment. "Wait, here it says they have a GPS option."

Teddy nodded. "Yes, but we're dealing with the basic package. The bonus options would get us eyeballs on the cat from a computer map using satellite technology, but there's an extra fee and a forty-eight-hour set up delay." He paused.

"I could pay the fee, that's not a problem." Doc Eugene leaned forward. "I know September didn't intend for Pam to die, or for Timothy to get hurt. Macy is my patient, and he got taken from my clinic, so there's that. I want him found. Besides," he tipped his head, "I hear you've got skills. Maybe the ability to speed up that forty-eight-hour lag time?" He smiled. "I've got my laptop in the car. It's old, but you're welcome to use it if that'll help."

Teddy smiled back. "Funny you should mention that." He flexed his shoulders and rolled the chair away from the desk. "Does your laptop have a mobile Wi-Fi, you know, one of those plug-and-play hotspots?" The veterinarian shook his head. "Then I'll have to run home and get mine." He stood, collected the materials he'd need, and headed to the front waiting area. "Thanks for letting me stay."

Doc Eugene followed with the keys to the front door, but stopped when the clinic phone rang. He sighed. "What the hell, I'm still here. And I need to record a message we'll be closed today, and cancel the appointments. After Timothy's death, I won't ask the staff to come in, not until Monday." He unlocked the door for Teddy, and then trotted back to the counter and leaned over to reach the phone. "All Creatures Veterinary Hospital."

Teddy lifted a hand to wave, and started out the door. It'd be a twenty-minute drive to retrieve his laptop. Figuring out how to track Macy was busywork, though, and there were no guarantees the thief still had the cat or that September was anywhere nearby. But he owed it to September to try. That was all they had.

"Wait! Hey, Teddy, hold up."

He turned, caught the door before it closed and re-entered the waiting area when Doc Eugene yelled. The veterinarian held the phone receiver in one hand. "It's one of the detectives from before. Somebody found Shadow, they want to drop him off here."

"What?" Teddy hurried back into the clinic, and held out his hand for the receiver. "This is Theodore Williams, what's this about the dog? Was September with him?"

"Teddy, it's Combs." He sounded as exhausted as Teddy felt. "Some guy called. He picked up Shadow way the hell out on FM 1417, said he was a dog with a purpose and running down the road at a pretty good clip."

"What was he doing out there? Where's September?"

A pause. "We haven't found her, but her car was identified over at The Gazebo. That's a park next to the middle school. We think someone took her, maybe the same one took the cat. Could a dog follow the truck, maybe track where it went?"

Teddy relayed Comb's question to the veterinarian. "Maybe." Doc Eugene sounded excited. "Shadow sure has the bloodlines for it."

Teddy spoke into the receiver. "If the dog's pickup was, say, within two miles of the cat's current location, and September's with the cat, I can find them. Macy has a GPS on his collar. Tell me the location."

He hung up the phone, eyes shining. "Combs will meet us out on FM 1417 with Shadow. I need to get my laptop along the way. You drive. I don't do night driving. And pray there's enough time for me to finagle the GPS."

Chapter 42

The hole in the floor measured eighteen inches by five inches where one old plank had split and fallen through. Animal fur fuzzed the splintered edges of the opening, clearly used as a critter path into the barn's tack room.

September guessed this was a barn, probably abandoned since wildlife claimed the building. More likely feral cats set up housekeeping, if her nose wasn't mistaken. Cat urine had its own special ambiance. Macy certainly thought the place an aromatic delight.

She crouched to shine the penlight into the hole. "No, stay back." September gently restrained Macy. "We'll play later."

But they wouldn't play, maybe never again. She pushed aside the crippling thought, and stopped him again when he would have followed the light into the hole, the chase-the-light game so ingrained he had only to see the shine to follow its path. He loved cubbyholes, and probably could squeeze his twenty-three-pound body through. But what then? How would she ever get him back?

Or should she try?

September remembered the step up to get into the place. There must be a crawl space under the floor, and the fur snagged on the hole pointed to another exit into the interior of the barn. Maybe an escape not only for Macy, but also for her. No way could she squeeze through. Not yet, anyway.

But if she could pry up another board or two, she could wiggle through. If the crawl space was deep enough. And if it led anywhere besides dead space under the floor. And if Victor was gone long enough. What time was his meeting tonight? Tonight—that meant after dark. So at least several hours, anyway.

Too many ifs. But no other options presented themselves.

Dropping her hand through the hole, September shined the penlight around inside, illuminating the dirt-floored crawl space. A well-worn path led toward the hidden stair step, back into the barn's interior. That must be the way out.

She stretched out on the floor and pushed her arm as far inside the hole as she could reach to determine the depth of the crawl space. Cold ground stopped her hand about two feet down, and she flexed her icy fingers to keep circulation going. Two feet would be a tight squeeze.

She'd make it work. No other choice. She grappled left and then right, blindly, with one bare hand. Fluffy, soft material crinkled with something that sounded like paper and sticky cobwebs. Probably fur, desiccated vegetation, dust bunnies. Nesting material. At least it was too cold for spiders. She hoped nothing inside the burrow would mistake her fingers for hors d'oeuvres.

Reaching far forward, she brushed more wood, possibly the continuation of the wall, and followed its surface until she found another narrow opening. Her arm wasn't long enough, nor could she see around the corner. But if the cats used it to gain access to the crawl space, it must be at least as large as the one into this room. Macy could get out.

"He could die." She said the words aloud, and then wished she could take them back. Sending Macy into the crawl space put him at risk from coyotes, or the sick wildlife. He was a house pet, and had never had to hunt for a living beyond "killing" his toys.

His heart could give out.

As much as she yearned to hold him safe in her arms, she couldn't protect Macy once Victor returned. Staying with her, Macy would die. Sending him away gave him a chance.

She couldn't explain to the cat. If she showed him the hole, would he run, or instead try to come back to her? Would she have to scare him to make him leave? If she survived this—no, WHEN she survived this, would he hate her? Would he forgive her? How would she find him again?

Eight years ago after she'd escaped, she'd put the cello away because Victor might track her through the music. Turning her back on Melody nearly killed her, and she adopted Macy to ease the empty ache in her arms. Macy taught her to laugh again. Pets were safer than people; they didn't pretend or wear a mask.

Shadow could track Macy. He'd survived the gunshot. She'd heard him follow the truck at least for a while. Would he follow this far, track her to the barn? He'd never been taught to track people, and wouldn't know what to do on his own.

September wiped away tears, and with them the fantasy of a Lassieinspired rescue. Once on the scent trail, Shadow ignored everything. On the road and oblivious to danger, he could be hit by a car. Or he could be bleeding from Victor's gunshot. Shadow might be lost, alone and dying. That was the reality. "Baby-dog, please forgive me."

And Macy was damned if he stayed and damned if he ran. He had a chance to survive only if he ran.

She knew what she'd tell clients. Some lost cats traveled miraculous distances to find their way home. The reality was grimmer.

God, she didn't want to make this choice! This was Macy: the furry wonder who had healed her heart with his silly antics, his demands for attention and affection, his never-give-up pestering attitude and brilliant understanding of her moods. Macy gave her the courage to love again, to say yes to Chris and find some peace. For a while.

The big cat burbled and trilled, climbed into her lap and turned three times before settling into the makeshift nest of her crossed legs. He turned upside down, presenting his white chin and chest for scratches, half closing his eyes and increasing the volume on his Mac-truck purr.

He had something on his collar. She frowned, turning Macy around to better examine the object. "Hold still, buddy." She shined the penlight. "Oh wow, I forgot about the GPS!"

A small plastic object had been attached to his collar. Timothy promised to charge the device, so all she'd have to do was finish the setup at home. That is, if she ever got home.

She would! By damn, she would get home again.

"Thank you, Timothy." She stroked Macy, and his purr rumbled the small room. "Once I get out of here, that GPS will bring you home to me. Keep yourself safe until then, buddy, until I can set up the tracking. I promise."

That eased her heart a little. It was still iffy, but she had to take the risk and turn the cat loose. Victor could return anytime now. "Maybe somebody will find you. Wish you could talk. You'd tell them how to find me, wouldn't you?" The cat cheek-rubbed September's face, smearing the tears she couldn't control.

Pull yourself together. What do I do when a lost pet shows up? Even before finding someone to scan for a microchip, what do I do? "Check for a tag."

September quickly rummaged in her pocket and retrieved the Sharpie marker she'd found earlier. "Hold still, Macy." His rabies tag had her name and contact information, just as Shadow's did. But that wouldn't help anyone find *her.*

She turned the cat around, and wrote on the GPS tag. And then for good measure, she wrote in block letters on Macy's white fur apron.

That finished, she reached for Fish's file. Victor's mention of the reporter indicated a connection that might be the key to getting out of this mess.

The thick file contained pages of scribbled notes nearly impossible to read in the dim glare of the penlight. It also included several internet printouts, some dated from several years earlier.

Scrapie. Wasting disease. Prions.

"It's a brain disease." That's what made the animals sick? "Okay, Sly, tell me how they get it. And are people at risk?" That was the issue.

The government cracked down on foreign imports and tightened processing requirements. Today, even pet food manufacturers had layers of inspection to avoid a repeat of the crippling recall. But Felch said the pets and people got sick from the same cause. She skimmed the documents, and found the answer stapled to the back of the file. A slick flier, folded in three, included a red font that shouted the headline.

HOG HEAVEN HOSTS Hog Hell

Hog Hell. Pig hunts. She knew feral pigs made wallows out of plowed fields, uprooted crops, got into garbage and frequented dumps. They'd made a mess of her garden, too, and aggravated the crap out of Aaron.

She wrinkled her forehead, putting it together. Chronic wasting disease affected deer, but hunters harvested deer and took only the prime venison cuts, leaving behind the spine, legs, and head if it wasn't trophy-worthy. People wouldn't eat the deer parts that could infect them—the brain, especially.

But pigs would.

Feral hogs left nothing; they were nature's garbage disposals. They ate acorns, dug up pastures and trashed seeded fields. They'd eat scraps hunters left behind. Like infectious deer parts? And if hogs ate something contaminated by sick deer, and people harvested the hogs…

"Oh, my God. It's the hogs!"

Macy meowed at the exclamation and leaped off September's lap.

That had to be it. Felch and BeeBo starred in the *Hog Hell* show. BeeBo's dog was sick. Felch claimed to be sick, and had a run-in with the reporter, maybe to quash the story's connection to the TV show. Lots of money was involved in making a show a success, not to mention rich endorsement deals for the stars. They had lots of incentive to make the story go away. She read the flier again, and realized what it meant. "Oh dear God, they're feeding everyone at the party!"

Barbecued feral hog would be served at the Hog Heaven restaurant. Tonight. That must be the important meeting Victor must attend. And Piggy Panache gift boxes of what they called "piggy treats" distributed for the holiday gift giving season.

Horrified, she read that the TV show would offer ordering information to viewers. No wonder they wanted to keep any rumors quiet, at least until after the premier. If the meals and the samples were contaminated, a widespread infection could affect thousands or even millions of innocent victims. How long would it take for the disease to cripple the fans?

It sounded bizarre, like one of Sly's wild, made up stories. But a farfetched rumor would kill the show as effectively as the real thing. They must be desperate to keep things quiet.

She didn't know how Victor became involved. Was he one of the actors, too? She'd never seen the show, but that would explain his willingness to protect his job.

Victor knew Sly had talked to her, so he had even more reason to keep her under wraps, and then whisk her out of town. He would have killed her already, if he didn't have other plans for her.

It wasn't about outwitting a stalker anymore. September had to get out before Victor came back. She had to stop the poison from being served.

She nuzzled the cat. "You're not going alone, Macy. Time to get that hole bigger." September retrieved the cello endpin and set to work.

Chapter 43

Dietz took in the packed restaurant with satisfaction. The kitchen behind him bustled, metal clatter of utensils a percussionist's dream. Roast pork, barbecue sauce, grilled corn and coleslaw teased the air in a medley of complementary aromas that ebbed and flowed like a musical cannon.

Picnic tables boasted *Hog Hell* red and blue checkerboard oilcloth. Tall plastic glasses of sweet tea (unsweetened for the unenlightened) sat at each place setting. But most guests of legal age were enjoying the complimentary beer.

Posters plastered rough barn-door walls and featured BeeBo, Felch, Sunny (in suitably revealing attire) and several of their dogs. He'd wanted a couple of the hounds present—some fans acted more passionate about the dogs than the people—but the health department killed that idea.

At the moment, Sunny "The Babe" Babcock flirted outrageously with Humphrey Fish. He'd arranged to have Fish sit at the head table with the cast, ostensibly for interview ease, but actually to keep an eye on the fellow. Sunny had very specific instructions, and so far, she'd followed the script to the letter and stroked Fish's ego while deflecting any mention box problems. Sunny knew who wrote the checks.

Butterflies, not hunger, quivered his insides. He didn't trust Grady. But he had no choice. At least Grady had the balls to get rid of the reporter's body, and stop Felch from doing any more damage. "God bless the hungry little piggies," he muttered, and then smiled and raised his hand when BeeBo entered the restaurant to loud cheers from the patrons.

Fish hopped from his chair and pumped BeeBo's hand when he joined the head table. Dietz raised his eyebrows at Sunny, and she gave him a thumbs-up from across the room. She'd keep BeeBo from spouting off on the forbidden tangents.

They'd been lucky Grady saw the behaviorist talking with the reporter. Containing fallout from that bigmouth's rumor had become a nightmare. His stomach rolled, and Dietz popped three antacid tablets. He didn't want to know how Grady planned to keep the woman out of sight. They were in too deep now to be squeamish, and soon they'd be over the hump, as long as Grady showed up to finish the job.

Dietz had his own plans for some down time with the tasty babe-o-licious Sunny. Tonight set in motion all his future success. Dietz glanced at his watch. Another fifteen minutes until show time. Two big screen TVs gave everyone in the place a great view.

Dietz always was surprised at the cross-section of fans. Hunters should be the go-to demographic, but teenage boys—and even a few girls in the audience reflected the most recent polls. Here and there, well-dressed couples sipped their beverages of choice—mostly Lone Star—with a few overdressed people thinking "premier = evening attire" appearing mildly uncomfortable and out of place.

For the locals, this was the event of the season, though, and anyone able to snag a ticket to the limited seating made sure to attend. Dietz smiled. At least some plans worked.

By the time Felch went south, it was too late to cancel the watch party, even if he'd wanted. Besides, if the worst happened, Dietz had deniability. *He* hadn't killed anyone, or stashed any bodies. *He* didn't know any details. *He* was a producer/director/host of a reality show. The missing Felch was the bad guy here, and with any luck, he'd never be found. And if he were found, Dietz'd be properly shocked and appalled, and lay blame squarely where it belonged: on Grady's shoulders.

Dietz had been a damn fine actor, after all. But so had Grady, and that made him wonder how much of the man's story was true. He popped another antacid.

Grady entered the restaurant, and relief washed over Dietz as he waved him over. "You clean up good." He wore the official show ski mask rolled up to perch atop his head. Grady wore the show uniform of camouflage hunter's garb, with the blood-red hog silhouette outlined in DayGlow on the back of his jacket. Grady saw one sleeve of the new coat was torn and roughly stitched up. "Wait, is that makeup?" He peered closer at the man's face. "What happened? Wait, I don't want to know."

Grady fingered the spot. "Best I could do on short notice. Got bit, but nothing serious."

"She bit you? What the hell? You said everything's under control! Did she see your face?" That was key. He didn't want any more blood on his hands, but if September could identify Grady—and hence, the connection to him—all bets were off.

"Wore the mask like you said. Relax, nobody's the wiser."

"Counting on that." He breathed in, out, in, out, waiting for his heartbeat to calm. "Okay, I'll introduce you. Be the character. Remember, you love hunting and your hunting dogs are your life. The regular spiel. We good?"

Grady nodded, and a goober-grin lit up his face. "Juss fine and dandy." He wiped his nose with the back of his hand, and Dietz grimaced.

"Drawl is fine, but lose the drool. You're not one of BeeBo's hounds." Dietz jerked his head toward the front of the screen. "Let's get the others."

Dietz made his way to where BeeBo held forth at the head table, entertaining the rest of the crew. He tapped the big man on his massive bare shoulder. BeeBo wore his signature camouflage pants and matching vest with a torn, stained—but clean—tee shirt, and he'd knocked the dirt clods off his boots. He also wore the official show hat, as did most of the crew members at the table. Sunny hadn't put hers on yet, probably didn't want to muss her hair. She'd cut the fingertips out of the blue gloves to show off her new manicure. Whatever.

"Hats on, everybody." Dietz pulled one out of his pocket and pulled it onto his head. "We got two hundred of them, one for everybody in the restaurant." The buzzing crowd started to quiet, sensing the evening entertainment was ready to begin. "Hope we have enough. Pass them out, BeeBo. You too, Sunny and Grady. And I'll get this road on the show." He embraced the rush that came with the virtual curtain rising, grabbed the mic at the front of the room and switched it on.

"Everyone having a great time?" The tentative response prompted a repeat of the question. "I said, having a GREAT TIME?" He flashed his practiced host smile when the room yelled back affirmative, and laughed out loud when a table of youngsters made pig-snorting sounds. Soon the whole room took up the noise. He held up a hand to quiet them. "Sounds like *Hog Hell*—music to my ears." Cheers erupted and again he waited for the noise to fade. "I'm delighted you joined us tonight for a special evening, a watch party celebrating the renewal of Heartland's very own reality show, *Hog Hell*. And your stars are here. BeeBo Benson." He pointed, and the room cheered, while the big man's moonlike face beamed with an 'aw-shucks' expression, clutching the trademark unlit cigar between his lips. "Sunny Babcock." More cheers, mixed with wolf whistles as she struck a pose. "And a new cast member you'll see more of soon, Vince Grady." Grady doffed his cap and bowed, to polite applause. "Unfortunately, Randy Felch couldn't be with us tonight." Disappointed sounds and a few boos came from the youngsters' table, and one of the adults shushed them with a stern expression. "Sorry. I'm disappointed, too. Called out of town indefinitely. You ask me," he dropped his voice and stage whispered into the mic, "he got a call to

Hollywood for his own show. But don't tell, it's a secret." The room laughed, and Dietz knew he had them. Nothing better than when the crowd bit on every nugget, it fed their energy back to the performer. Magic.

"I hope you enjoy your own official *Hog Hell* gear. The cap and ski mask combo'll keep your head warm and face toasty on those bitter cold days during a hunt. I can't guarantee they'll protect you from the flu, but it can't hurt. Oh, and it'll advertise the show, too." He leaned forward. "I'm all about keeping locals working. Well, and me paid, too." He laughed again at the happy response.

Most of the kids in the crowd immediately donned the ski masks, and a few of the adult men did as well. The ladies set the caps aside, but that was okay. He wanted as many men as possible out and about wearing the gear in the weeks ahead, to deflect any potential connection to the show if by chance Grady or Felch had been seen during their clean-up efforts.

"The fine people here at Hog Heaven have cooked up a great meal. Hmm, some lip-smacking food'll be served any minute now. And I wanted everyone to know about our new project, a cooking show featuring more ways to roast up those tasty hogs, while getting rid of a problem that damages local economy. That's right, *High On The Hog* cooking show airs right after the New Year, and our first featured restaurant is none other than your local homegrown talent here at Hog Heaven! C'mon out here, Louisa and Jim Sams, take a bow. The owners of Hog Heaven and hosts for tonight's watch party!"

The middle-aged couple hurried out of the kitchen, smiling with embarrassed excitement at the applause and attention. Jim carried a cardboard carton, and Louisa held aloft a holiday themed cellophane-wrapped box like a candy sampler.

Dietz wished he'd thought to have them wear the official cooking show gear, instead of the stained bib-style aprons. The barbecue sauce dripped like blood. But there was nothing to do about it now.

"To help promote *High On the Hog*, we're giving you a sneak preview taste of holiday gift sets we call Piggy Panache, gourmet samplers available for order right now—but you heard it first. It'll be announced on the show tonight." Jim began moving down the aisles, holding the carton for Louisa to distribute the meat samplers, one to each family. "Could I have a volunteer to help? The show's about to start and I know our hosts want to get back into the kitchen to monitor the meal."

A couple of the teenagers from the rowdy table jumped up to take the carton from Jim. "Thanks, fellows." Dietz watched the distribution with interest.

As they received the Piggy Panache treat samplers, men in the crowd immediately tore open their packages to taste the various bacon, jerky, and sausage offerings. The ladies for the most part set aside the samplers with the hat. Dietz guessed many of the gift boxes would end up getting mailed to hard-to-shop-for relatives. "Before you leave tonight, be sure to have Mr. Grady get your name on the mailing list for future special deals. We want to give our Heartland family the first chance at trying out all the great new features."

Dietz hoped they appreciated the samples. The website ordering information listed each package at $29.95 plus shipping and handling, a tidy profit for product that cost him less than $4, and that mostly for the processing and packaging.

He'd keep harping on the "homegrown" angle as long as it paid, but wanted to cash out sooner rather than later. Two potential buyers had already expressed interest, but would probably move the filming to Louisiana where there were better financial incentives for the industry. They had the funds to take *Hog Hell* to the next level, and he'd still get the income from the new cooking show, a helluva safer way to do TV. No more wading through pig shit, or waiting for someone to discover Grady's clean-up attempts.

He switched on the big screen TVs. "And now, without further ado, enjoy the premier episode of this year's *Hog Hell!*" Dietz cranked up the volume, set down the microphone, and took his place at the head table as Grady and BeeBo joined him. He patted Sunny's luscious backside, and felt better than he had in a week.

The waiters moved between the tables with teaming plates of pork, sides of thick onion slices, potato salad, coleslaw, and grilled corn on the cob. Dietz held up his glass of beer in a silent toast to the TV screen as the opening credits rolled, and the rest of the table followed suit. His stomach rumbled, and he laughed. Butterflies gone, it was time to eat.

Dietz had the first fork of tender barbecue pork halfway to his mouth when the police burst through the door.

Chapter 44

"No, go on, get out of my way." Combs pushed the big pup. Shadow again tried to climb into his lap, making it impossible to drive. "Back! Shadow, get in the back."

The dog wouldn't stop crying. "I thought shepherds were supposed to be fierce, buddy. Can you give me a break?"

Combs opened one of the back windows partway. He remembered September always did that. Finally, Shadow pretzeled himself in the front passenger seat enough to turn around and squeeze through the narrow opening between the front seats into the back. He stuck half his head out the opening. And whined some more.

The dog shivered and panted, his sides a bellows until Combs feared he would pass out. The cold temperature made Shadow's breath fog the glass, which then froze in fairy patterns, and Combs couldn't tell if the pup was exhausted or excited. "Maybe both. Huh, boy?"

He didn't know much about dogs. How September communicated with the pup was magical to him, and he hoped that would translate into the dog pointing to where she'd disappeared.

He'd planned to leave Shadow with the vet. But Doc Eugene had given Teddy a ride in his Jeep, so the dog had to stay with Combs. Finding the cat with GPS seemed a long shot at best, but he didn't want to discourage Teddy. The old man had good intentions, and at this point Combs wouldn't turn down any help.

Shadow's tracking ability was their best shot. Amazing that the dog traveled so far from September's abandoned car at the school, more than twelve miles before the Good Samaritan picked him up. Combs figured they'd start at the pickup point, turn the dog loose, and follow Shadow to wherever September was being held.

Combs's phone rang, and the dog woofed. "Hold your horses, I'll get it. Do you answer September's phone for her, too?" Shadow barked again, and stuck his head back out the window. His tail waved. That meant he was happy, right?

He answered briskly. "Combs."

"It's me." Gonzales spoke over crowd noises. "It's a zoo here. More than two hundred people at the restaurant, it'll take the rest of the night to process them. And you're not going to believe this. Everybody here has one of those hats."

Combs groaned. "What about the production personnel? Anyone missing?"

"We got the whole crew in custody. They made it easy, everyone sitting at the head table. Actually, three head tables but one with the stars and host—and Humphrey Fish. He's eating this up, got his audio recorder going, and keeps lamenting the radio station didn't set up a live feed." He made a disgusted sound. "I had no idea it took so many people to point a camera. Some are missing, were outside smoking or whatever, and ducked out the back when we came in. Don't know how many but we'll get names and track them down. A guy named Felch, one of the stars, was a no show. The head honcho says he got an offer and took off for Hollywood."

"You buying that?"

"Shit, no. Dietz—that's the host producer guy—he's squirmy as a cornered rat."

"Nobody named Victor Grant in the group?" Of the dozen or so possibles Gonzales had found, only a few had previous run-ins with the law, and none were recent. "Got that picture of him with September?"

"Yeah, that and a bunch of other possibles." The crowd noise waxed and waned. "Haven't had a chance to show any pictures. If Grant's our guy he probably changed his name. And maybe his face. Don't actors do that a lot? You know, facelift and Botox and stuff."

"What about Felch? He's missing; September's missing. Felch could be our guy. Might not be her stalker, could be somebody wanted to keep a lid on the contaminated pigs rumor. TV folks have the most to lose when word gets out about that." He hesitated. "Listen, people hadn't started eating that mess, had they?"

Gonzales sighed. "Some had, but got it shut down quick. Oh, and I sent your wife and kids on home, figured we could talk to them later."

"My wife?" His foot jerked in reaction, and the car surged. Shadow barked and nose-poked him as if to chide his carelessness. "Cassie? She was there, with the kids?"

"Sorry, I mean *ex*-wife. Yeah, she was here with your two and a table full of teenage yahoos. Good kids I think, but causing a ruckus."

Combs white-knuckled the steering wheel. Melinda had mentioned plans to attend the premier, even invited him. Why hadn't he picked up on that? "They didn't eat any of the, uh, the food, did they?" He licked his lips and cleared his throat.

Gonzales paused, and answered carefully. "Don't know. Hey, they'll be fine. Like I said, we got here as they started serving. I gotta go, but will keep you posted. You do the same."

The phone went dead, but almost immediately rang again. Maybe it was Cassie? Or one of the kids? "This is Combs."

"Detective, it's me, Teddy. Where are you?"

Sighing, Combs relaxed his grip on the phone. "I'm on my way. *We're* on our way, I mean. I got September's dog." At the last word, Shadow nose-poked him again as if to hurry them along. "ETA ten minutes."

"Good. We're at the intersection. And I got good news. The GPS works."

Chapter 45

Nikki crossed her arms and pouted. It wasn't fair. She wanted to stay and see what other exciting stuff might happen next. But Mrs. Harrison, Willie and Melinda's mom, made them all leave the restaurant. Now she sat squeezed in the back seat, in the middle as always, with Hank on one side and Willie on the other.

"Why couldn't we talk to the cops? Everybody else got to stay." Hank leaned forward to speak to Mrs. Harrison. "I could've got a ride back with Dustin and Zeke."

"I'm not responsible for Dustin and Zeke. But I am responsible for you. Your mother trusts me to take care of you. She can decide if you need to talk to the police."

The restaurant was fun, especially when the boys made funny pig noises and got everyone snorting. Nikki giggled at the thought. She loved the Hog Hell cap, and cradled her gift box of treats. Hank already ate his, but she saved hers for Hope-Kitty. "Why'd the police stop the show, anyway?" She stared out the window. The TV people said Mr. Felch wasn't on the show anymore and went to Hollywood. Had he taken Hope with him?

"I don't know." Mrs. Harrison didn't elaborate. She hunched in the driver's seat, neck stuck forward to peer out the windshield, and slowed at nearly every intersection to read the street signs.

"Will Daddy come talk to us?" Willie kicked his foot against the back of the passenger seat until Melinda turned around and glared.

"Your father will talk to you, if that's necessary. But I think the police have more than enough people to talk to at the restaurant." The car nearly stopped, and then sped up again.

Nikki braced herself against the front seat and her seatbelt cramped across her lap. Willie didn't notice, but Hank put his finger to his lips and shook his head when Nikki would have complained about the jerky driving.

She knew Melinda and Willie's dad was a cop. He didn't live with them anymore because they all got divorced. It was sort of like her and Hank not having Daddy home, even though he and Mom were still married. It sure would be nice when Daddy finally came back from the war.

Mrs. Harrison rubbed her eyes like they hurt, and the car sped up. "What a fiasco."

"What's a fiasco? Is that like a Spanish party?" Willie poked Nikki. "Fiasco, fiesta, get it?"

Melinda groaned, but Nikki giggled despite herself, and poked him back. "Good one." Daddy liked puns, too.

"Mom, you missed the turn." Melinda spoke softly.

Mrs. Harrison bit her lip. "My eyes won't focus. We'll go around the block." She peered at Hank in the mirror. "Your mom told me she wouldn't be home for another hour. I left her a voicemail you'd both be with me. She can pick you up from our house." She paused, and then muttered, "If I can find the damn turn. There it is!" She put on the signal, and the car banked sharply.

Hank shook his head. "That's okay, Mrs. Harrison. You can drop us at home. Right, Nikki?" He elbowed her.

"That's right." She took the prompt. "Mom has Hank watch me every day after school. Even though I'm not a baby." She smiled when Melinda met her eyes. "Girl power, right?"

"Totes." Melinda again turned to her mom. "The road is back there. Mo-om!"

"Let me drive! I know the way home, for heaven's sake."

But Nikki thought she acted confused, maybe even a little scared?

She continued to complain. "What an embarrassment. An embarrassment to the city, to the Chamber, and to me personally. And where's the effin' house?"

"Mom." Melinda turned in her seat. "Are you okay?"

"Just dandy." Mrs. Harrison patted her hair. "Need to get a cut, maybe time for a new style. What do you think, Lindy?" The car stopped at the corner with a jerk, and she cupped her face in both hands.

"Um, Mrs. Harrison? Please, you can drop us at home, that'd be fine. It's two blocks over that way." Hank leaned forward and started to pat the woman on her shoulder, and then thought better of it. "Just turn right. And then at the next block turn left."

Mrs. Harrison straightened up. "That whole restaurant situation blows my mind, you know? Got me totally rattled. A fiasco." She cranked the wheel and gunned the engine, and the car slid around the corner. "Hang tight." She laughed, and then stopped at the next corner. "Which way? You, boy, what's-yer-name, you have to tell me how to get there. I've never been to your house."

"She picked us up two hours ago," Nikki whispered to Hank. "What's wrong with her?"

"Turn left here." Hank's hand squeezed Nikki's knee, and she made a silent "ouch" shape with her lips but took the hint and shut up.

The car made the turn and zoomed four blocks before the driver slowed to a stop, well past their house. Melinda mouthed, "Sorry," as Nikki and Hank climbed out of the car. Willie acted ready to cry.

"Thanks for the ride, Mrs. Harrison." Hank opened the car door, and held it until Nikki slid out. "Lindy, maybe you should call your dad?"

Melinda nodded. Mrs. Harrison barely waited for the car door to slam before zooming away.

"Wow, that was epic." Nikki hugged herself.

"Yeah, an epic fail." Hank shrugged, and grabbed her sleeve. "I didn't see Mrs. Harrison drink anything but sweet tea. Weird." He pulled the *Hog Hell* cap down over his face and stared out of the ski mask holes. "It's cold. Let's go home."

She hesitated, and then cocked her head and smiled. "Race you! On your mark, get set, GO!"

She watched him pelt down the sidewalk, ducking through a neighbor's yard and vaulting a low fence. He never looked back.

Nikki turned around, and jogged in the other direction. With a bit of luck, she'd be home before she was missed. If he told Mom about the barn, tonight might be her last chance to see Hope.

Chapter 46

She'd worked for hours, and the hole still wasn't large enough to squeeze through. Although exhausted, September couldn't let herself rest. The sleeping bag shrugged around her shoulders fended off the worst of the cold, and sunlight filtering through chinks in the boards offered work light for a while.

But now the sun had set, and she feverishly worked by feel, trying to conserve the batteries in the penlight. She feared Victor had drugged the thermos, but thirst and a threatening migraine forced her to risk one cup of strong coffee. It tasted fine, and the caffeine held her headache at bay. Not knowing how long she'd be trapped, though, she saved the rest for later. That also reduced the need for bucket use, a vulnerable experience she didn't want to repeat.

Victor had said he'd be back tonight. She had no time to waste.

September leaned on the endpin, and the third board gave way with a satisfying crack. She moved it aside and shooed Macy out of the way. He wanted to push his face into the hole.

"Yes, I know, smells lovely." She wrinkled her nose at the pungent aroma, but Macy purred with delight. "Big enough for you to get through, anyway. Gotta hope the exit out the other end will let your fluffiness out, too."

She couldn't stop revisiting the what-ifs that brought her to this place. If she hadn't insisted on leaving home at sixteen. If she'd blown the whistle on Victor right away. If Chris hadn't thought he could save her. And if she hadn't bought the stupid lottery ticket.

To Chris, the windfall meant they could start a family, no more excuses. The thought of a baby terrified her, and nearly prompted a panic attack. After a horrible fight, Chris stormed out with Dakota while she wept into Macy's fur. An hour passed. Then another hour. She called his cell and the police answered. And she knew, even before they told her about the blue flowers scattered over Chris and Dakota's bodies. No chance to apologize. No way to explain. She never got to say goodbye.

She dropped the cello endpin to fist the tears from her eyes. Wishing the past away wouldn't change the present. But by damn, she'd decide her own future.

September pushed one arm and shoulder through the opening, gingerly followed by her head. While by no means overweight, the opening barely accommodated her shoulders. It'd take at least one more board width to allow her hips to pass. She shined the penlight and the beam lasered the crawl space, stopped by wooden planks on all sides.

"Oh, no. There must be a way out." What she'd thought to be the exit instead was the hollow of a stair step.

Macy head-butted her thigh, and September raked the light one more time around the perimeter of the enclosure, this time at the juncture of dirt floor and planking.

"There! Thank God." A small cone of excavated dirt marked entry to a tunnel originating beneath the stair. The wood was solid but the nails rusty and loose, and the critters had burrowed underneath. Macy would easily fit through. And if she could get one more board pried loose and squirm the rest of the way into the crawl space, September could kick out the rickety step and also escape.

She heard somebody.

"Kitty, here kitty kitty kitty." The nest under the floor muffled the high-pitched voice.

September froze, and then scrambled to pull herself out of the hole. Sounded like a kid. But what was a child doing here?

"Hope, I got treats for you. Are you here?"

What to do? Could the child get her out?

Macy chirruped and then gave a long, drawn out meeerow in response to the "treat" word. Crap!

"Hope!" Footsteps pattered closer.

Decision made for her, September stood, flipping the carpet back over the hole to keep Macy from diving through too soon. "Hello! I'm in here." She crossed the door and pulled, rattled and then banged on it. "I'm trapped, can you let me out?" Macy yowled again, and the footsteps paused.

"What are you doing in there?" The child came to the other side of the door. "There's a lock. It's a new one, wasn't here before. Sort of like the ones on my school locker, but without the combo dial."

"A padlock." Damn, no way to get past that without bolt cutters. "Before? You come here a lot? Do your parents know?" September's heart raced. "Here's what I need you to do. What's your name?"

"Nikki." The little girl hesitated. "I come to feed the cats. Is Hope-Kitty with you? The TV guy said Mr. Felch went away, so there'd be nobody to take care of her. She's a big cat, and I think some of her kittens are still here, too."

"My name is September."

Nikki laughed. "Like the month?"

"Yes, exactly like the month. Listen to me carefully, Nikki. I need you to find an adult and tell them about me."

There was a long silence. "I'm not supposed to be here. I sneaked off from my brother, and Mom'll get mad if she finds out. I'll get in trouble." She sounded miserable. "Mom's allergic to cats."

"Please! You have to get help before . . ." She hesitated. Telling the girl about Victor might scare her so much she wouldn't tell anyone. Macy cried again. "That's Macy. He's sick. I know you love cats, so you'd be helping him, too."

"How'd you get stuck in there, anyway?" It sounded like Nikki pulled on the padlock.

"Never mind, that's not important. Isn't there anyone you could tell? Maybe your brother?"

Nikki didn't say anything, and Macy meowed again and pawed the door. "I'm sorry your kitty is sick," she said, her voice small. "I guess I could tell Hank. He's my brother."

September switched off the penlight to conserve the batteries. The room plunged back into darkness. "Nikki? Do you have a light out there? How'd you see the padlock?"

"My cell phone." Nikki held it up to a crack in the door. "But it goes out and I gotta keep pushing the refresh."

"Nikki! Call 911, call the police. You know how to do that? Tell them September is locked in the barn. You don't even have to give your name, so you won't get in trouble or anything. Call them—"

"Hey, somebody's coming. A car pulled up." Nikki stepped away from the door, and the light from her phone shut off. "It's a man." She sounded relieved. "Betcha he can get that lock off."

"Nikki, no! Run, please run!"

Oh, God. Why hadn't she sent the girl away immediately? That had to be Victor.

Nikki screamed.

Chapter 47

"Let go of me! Let go! I'll tell." Nikki struggled and kicked, but the man was too big and she couldn't get away.

He didn't say anything, and that was scarier even than his ski mask. It matched the *Hog Hell* souvenir cap she wore. "You were at the restaurant, too."

He gripped her arm tighter, right on top of the scratches Hope had left. He marched her back into the barn. Was he mad about Hope? Her lip began to tremble. "Are you Mr. Felch?"

The man paused, and stared at her a long moment, considering. Then he nodded.

"Why'd you lock that lady up?" She wouldn't cry. Her brother Hank wouldn't cry if he'd gotten caught, and neither would Melinda, so she wouldn't either. Despite the silent assertion, a tear dripped off her cheek. "What're you gonna do? Please, Mr. Felch, let me go. I won't tell. Cross my heart."

It was wrong to lie. Mom said so all the time. But Nikki didn't care, she'd tell the biggest lie she could if he'd let her go. And then tell on him anyway! She was pretty sure it was against the law to scare kids. And for sure, it wasn't legal to lock up ladies in barns.

He held a big heavy flashlight like a club and she shivered. She could see lots better than from the light her phone made, before he stomped it and broke it to pieces. Another fat tear slid down her nose. Daddy gave her that phone. Now she couldn't text him or anything.

They reached the padlocked door, he found a key, and unlocked it. Her teeth chattered. He'd lock her inside, too. She remembered the school lesson on stranger danger, and what to do. Run. But she couldn't run. Scream. That she could do.

The door swung open, and Mr. Felch pointed his flashlight into the woman's terrified face. September yelled, "Macy, *KILL IT!*"

Nikki saw a pinprick of light focused on the man's ski mask. Nikki screamed.

Mr. Felch yelled, too, when a furry projectile hit him claws first in the ski mask.

Chapter 48

September dropped the penlight, ferocious in her joy that Macy had escaped. Now it was her turn. She'd dodge past Victor, and run like hell.

She held one of the broken boards like a batter warming up on the mound. September cocked her arm, but before she could swing, Victor thrust Nikki forward into her arms and the weapon fell with a clatter.

He stepped into the room, booted the improvised bat across the room, and slammed the door. Macy had ripped the ski mask from his face, loosened the moorings of a hairpiece, and left his clawed cheeks slimed with bloody war paint.

Not Victor at all. He was a stranger.

Nikki shuddered in September's arms. "You're not Mr. Felch. You're Grady." She turned, and buried her face in September's chest. "I want my mommy!"

Grady? Not Victor. "Sorry, so sorry. I thought you were someone else. We need to get out of here before he comes back." September's arms hugged the weeping child.

"Should have killed that cat when I had the chance."

She gasped. The voice was Victor's even if the face wasn't. She could see a swelling bruise, hidden by smeared makeup, on one side of his jaw where she'd bitten him through the ski mask. Her skin crawled.

He breathed heavily. "Took years to save up for my new face. Just for you. To please you, September." He aimed the flashlight at his face like a spotlight and his smile gleamed toothpaste bright in the glow. He preened in a model's pose. "That damn cat better not have ruined my face. Lost a hundred pounds, too. All for you."

Victor. The shape of his face, the droopy ears, his piggy eyes, his height, but most of all the voice—and those hands, oh God, his hands!—conjured memories. She moved Nikki behind her to shield the child. "It was never about your looks, Victor."

"Then why did you leave me?" He roared, and September scrambled backwards, pushing Nikki with her. Her instinct was to cower; the old buried impulses reborn in an instant.

The nightmare man. The demon haunting her nights and stalking her days. Thief of her childhood. She'd blanked out the worst, but the body's sense memory couldn't forget.

Every touch. Every cut. Every burn, every beating. Every caress. She gagged, and thought she might throw up. She'd survived only because she learned to freeze, become invisible, go to another place in her mind and convince herself the pain and terror were happening to someone else. A different September.

Terrified animals react in one of three hardwired behaviors: freeze, flight or fight. She was an animal. Freeze, so the predator won't see you. Flight, to outrun the hunter, find a bolt hole to hide. . .

"Took a while to find you, and then you were all over the news. The perfect job opened up right in your back yard. Everything came together, the timing was perfect. We're meant to be together, and this time, you'll never leave me." Boasting. Proud of himself. Wanting her admiration.

Freezing made her a target. Running triggered the predator's chase. She took in Nikki, another innocent victim. Only one option left. It was time to fight.

"Let Nikki go. It's me you want. I'll go with you, do whatever you say, only let her go." She hugged the child as a cover to whisper to her. "Hole in floor under the rug. Go!" She pushed the girl behind her. Nikki was the right size; she'd be safe in the crawlspace. Keep him distracted and focused on her until the child was safe.

He waved his hand dismissively, and the flashlight stayed on his figure like a theater follow spot he clearly relished. "You nailed the lid on the kid's coffin when your cat unveiled me." He tsk-tsked. "What a shame. She saw my face."

September's mouth turned to dust. He was right. If only she'd stayed quiet and not asked Nikki for help. If she'd sent the girl away immediately to call the police. If she'd delayed Macy's command. Any of these choices would have kept Nikki safe. If Nikki were hurt, it'd be her fault. So many wrong choices, all wrong. How could she trust herself to get them out?

She had no choice. Survival was up to her.

He waxed poetic, a thespian writing his own script for a captive audience.

"I say *jump*, and Dietz asks *how high*." His shoulders shook as he chuckled. "Had Dietz so worried about that reporter's fairy tale he nearly wet himself with relief when I cleaned up the mess. Even got a bonus lined up. A bonus for us, for our life together, a gift that keeps on giving."

She couldn't stop her lip curl reaction. Victor still didn't get it.

He pointed at her and she flinched. "I remade myself, for you, for us! And you spit on me—again—like you're so much better than me." He took another step toward her, anticipating her scared rabbit response of the past.

No more running. Her heart quickened. Nowhere to hide, even if she'd wanted to. Time to end this, once and for all. Her shoulders straightened, she breathed in-out-in and a weight melted from her heart with the exhalations. She'd been lost for a lot of years, but tonight she'd found herself. September was reborn.

Out of the corner of her eye, she saw Nikki kneel on the floor and finger the carpet. September nodded encouragement but kept her focus on Victor. She'd goad him, distract him until Nikki wiggled through the hole. She'd lure him further into the room, get him tripped up on the sleeping bag, make a dash for the door, and lock him inside. She took a breath, planted her feet, and smiled. "Fixing your outside doesn't change who you are. A bully and a sadist."

He lunged at her, and she dodged but miscalculated. God, he was quick! His fist caught her jaw, and she went down, hard, landing on top of the pet carrier. If Macy had been inside, the cat would have been crushed. *Please God let Macy avoid coyotes—and don't let his heart give out.*

Victor came after September, and she crabbed backwards, feeling the carpet give way to rough wood. "Nikki, hurry! Go, go, go!" Something jangled, and her hand closed around cool metal, recognized it, and raised the cello endpin like a sword above her. It gleamed in the limited light.

Nikki squealed as Victor remained focused on September, following her and standing over her. "A bully? A sadist?" He panted. "You ungrateful bitch. I loved you!" He kicked her, and September cried out. "I took care of you." He kicked again, and she scrambled sideways.

Nikki sat wide-eyed but frozen against the wall, the uncovered hole forgotten before her.

"Go! Nikki, get out, now! Run!"

She jumped, a terrified bunny-scamper aimed not into the crawl space as directed, but toward the closed door from which Victor had stepped away.

Victor easily countered, caught the little girl's arm and shook her. He crashed Nikki into the closed door. She crumbled, fell to the floor.

"No!" September scrambled to her feet.

"That was your fault." Victor snarled. He transformed into a deranged clown figure, the skewed wig flapped and bloody cheeks distorted his features. Grabbing Nikki's coat collar, he dragged her away from the door and dumped her at the center of the room. "I gave up my own career, my own art to make you a star!"

She whipped the endpin through the air like a fencer's foil and the silver gleamed in an arc that kept him at bay. "You never loved me. You wanted to own me, that's all."

He feinted, dancing in and away. His new athletic physique gave him an advantage, and she hoped her tingling cold fingers could keep fast their grip. She caught him on the wrist and the metal rod made a satisfying meaty sound.

He hissed and retreated, flexing that hand—oh God his hands! Fingers that pinched, fists that punched—her nostrils flared with satisfaction.

"You ungrateful bitch, flaunting yourself, making men want you. I did what any man would do to protect what's his, and teach you right from wrong."

She padded in a semi-circle to get closer to Nikki. The little girl curled into a protective ball, knees hugged to her chest and eyes squeezed closed, frozen in fear.

"Bastard! Picking on little girls make you feel like a big man?" She softened her voice. "Nikki, honey, I know it's scary. I'm getting you out of here. Nod if you understand." The child nodded and her eyes squeezed even tighter shut. "I want you to go under that table over there, okay?" Nikki squinted, located the spot, and scrambled beneath the table and hid behind the cello.

September didn't take her eyes off of Victor. She positioned herself between him and the girl's minimal shelter.

He stood between them and freedom, blocking the door as he mocked her. "You've changed. Sound like a mother." He stepped back closer to the opening to guard the door. But she had no intention of escaping. She'd finish this tonight, once and for all. "How are you going to save her? You couldn't even save yourself. Don't make promises you can't keep."

"Hypocrite!" Like a lanced abscess, the vitriol poured forth, using the words to enrage him and lure him in. "Love doesn't lock you away. Love doesn't teach lessons with whips. Love doesn't punish with lit cigarettes on your neck." Her long hair covered the scars, but the emotional hurt might never heal. Fighting back salved the wounds better than any miracle cure. *Closer, just a little more.* She hefted the endpin, balanced her feet well apart, and readied herself for the swing to take him out.

He took another step closer but then backed away, shaking with anger. "You ruined my life, made me a laughingstock. I couldn't show my face, nobody believed I could deliver, not in the concert hall and never again on stage. I had to reinvent myself."

"Good! You deserve every bad thing that happened." She shook with anger, and it felt good, God it felt so much better than fear. "A normal person doesn't rape someone and call it love. A normal person doesn't murder someone's husband. You killed my dog!" Her voice broke.

Be strong. Do this is for Chris. Do it for Dakota. And for Timothy, for the lost Macy and Shadow-pup. And do this for Nikki, who should never have been here in the first place. "I'm not the same scared kid you tortured into believing she had no value without you. I know what you are. No amount of surgery changes that. You're a freak."

He roared, and came at her at last, the flashlight an improvised sledge.

She dodged to the side, stepped in, and with all her strength whipped the endpin. Its shimmer whickered through the air.

He whirled, countered. Banged into the table.

Nikki screamed. Scrambled. The cello fell over.

September reset, followed him, swung again.

He backed away. Face surprised. Then concerned. Finally angry, he retaliated with the flashlight blinding her eyes.

She ducked. Blocked his blow with the endpin. Metal hit metal so hard her finger and arms stung, but she hung on to her weapon.

He pressed the advantage, scooped up the cello—*no, not Melody!*—and swung the instrument toward her.

Shoulder hunched, she spun away to absorb the blow, and fell to one knee with the impact. He held the cello like an ax, and chopped her exposed knee. She saw Melody fall in slow motion, heard a distinct POP before the pain flooded her knee.

September shrieked, fell to the ground, and rolled. The joint screamed, it was never meant to turn that way. Victor tossed Melody aside and swung the massive flashlight toward her face.

She held the endpin overhead between both hands to block the blow. The pin flew out of her hands, and clanged against the wooden wall, rolled and disappeared down the hole into the crawlspace.

Victor leaned down, loose wig flopping, and took his time as he cocked his arm for the killing blow.

Nikki smashed the used metal bucket over Victor's head, and immediately scurried away, gasping with fear.

Her knee. Unbearable pain. *You've felt worse.* September dug in her pocket. She couldn't move, couldn't get away. Could only wait. Her fingers found what they sought.

Victor wrenched off the bucket, face and hairpiece wet from its contents, and flung it across the room at Nikki in disgust. The girl squealed at the impact, and dodged away.

He turned back to September, ripped the bedraggled wig off, mopped the blood from his cheeks, and threw it into her face.

She brought up the bottle of synthetic cat pheromone, and sprayed directly into his eyes.

He screamed, anguished, the alcohol in the suspension burning his ravaged skin and eyes. Victor knuckled his eyelids, dropping the flashlight as he backed away and reached blindly for the door. "I'll kill you for this! You'll die, do you hear me?"

Nikki raced to September's side.

"Now, get out, now's your chance Nikki, go go go!" September waved toward the door Victor had managed to open and stagger out.

Before the little girl could reach the handle, the door slammed shut. The padlock snicked, locking them both inside.

Chapter 49

"You got the GPS working?" Combs couldn't help grinning. What do you know, the old man came through. Maybe something finally would go right. "Man, you're a freakin' wizard."

"Not so much." Teddy's frustration made his voice crack. "Thing is, the cat's moving, and going fast. Gonna to be out of range soon, if I sit here and wait for you."

"What? Why?" He pressed harder on the accelerator. "The cat's moving? There's a range?"

"I'll explain later. Had to jerry-rig the system, and it's like hitting the lottery to even get a reading. Macy goes into a tunnel or behind a hill, and we're screwed. What you want me to do? Wait for you or go after the cat?"

Combs considered the options. "Go after the cat. Odds are Macy's with September. They're making a run for it. Try to get eyes on the vehicle." Whoever the guy was, he hadn't wasted any time racing from the restaurant to collect his victim.

"Won't work, Detective. The GPS isn't following the road, not the way a car or a person would travel. The signal's heading cross-country. I think Macy got away or was dumped. Something must have scared him to death, he's really moving." He sounded anguished. "Have to track him on foot. Don't know if I can catch him. My joints don't listen to me these days."

He didn't have to think. "Do it. Whatever it takes. Get that cat. Maybe

September got a message on him." That'd be like her. And if the cat started running, that meant September might be close by and running, too.

Behind him, Shadow pawed his arm and yawned. "We can find the initial location of the signal, and from there do a ground to ground search. I'll call it in. The guy must have some out of the way place to hold September."

"That could take hours! I don't think we have much time. And besides," Teddy added, "There's no way to know if the first GPS location came from where she's being held. Macy could have been on the run for a while. That's the first spot we registered once I got it going."

"Go after the cat, Teddy. You handle that, and when I get there with the dog we'll see if he can't point us in the right direction."

Shadow woofed, as if he understood every word. Combs hoped he did.

Chapter 50

Shadow stood in the back seat of the car, and stuck his head through the window. He liked the man driving the car because September liked him. His name was Combs, and he acted like an awkward pup around September, but that was okay. If she didn't mind, neither did Shadow.

He'd enjoyed the car ride with Combs, too, because he got to stick his whole face into the wind. Usually the window only opened a crack for the tip of his nose. He leaned further out, most of his neck also feeling the cold wind, and tasted the scents riding the night sky.

He wasn't sure where they drove. But the man mentioned September several times, so Shadow hoped that meant they'd go find her. He wondered why she'd left him behind. It was a good-dog's job to stay with his person, and it puzzled him why she didn't understand. His paws hurt from running after the truck she'd been in. He hadn't caught the truck, but he'd finally caught his breath.

The car slowed, and Shadow nervously licked his lips. Now what? It was dark, but another car's eye lights stabbed the night.

"Stay in the car, Shadow." Combs got out. "Be right back." He closed the car door, and walked over to talk to a smaller stooped man who got out.

Shadow wagged harder when he recognized Teddy. The old man fed him bacon and scratched Shadow's ears.

"My old legs couldn't manage off road. So Doc Eugene's tracking Macy."

Macy? The familiar name made Shadow come to attention, and he pointed his ears forward. Why did Teddy talk about Shadow's cat? He tipped his head and searched the dark roadside with nose, ears and eyes. Macy only went outside at September's house when he wore a harness and leash—a flimsy thing dogs could chew off, not like Shadow's proper *hide-and-seek* harness. When Macy wore that, September followed behind gripping the line.

His heart quickened at the thought, and he arched his neck. Was September out in the dark, walking Macy? Why else would Shadow's cat be here? That must be why Combs and Teddy brought him here, so they could be together. Did they want him to *seek* Macy, like before?

He felt funny when they weren't together. He took care of September, and she took care of him, and they both took care of Macy. That's what family did for each other.

He liked Macy all right, even if he smelled funny, not like a dog at all. But Shadow only felt like himself when he was with September. Sometimes it was hard to breathe when she touched his neck, stroked his ears, and called him "good-dog." A spot inside his chest grew warm and swelled so big he thought he'd burst with the happy feeling.

Right now, icy dread filled his body, different than the cold air, but he didn't know why. September would know what to do to make him feel better. His brow furrowed and he whined, and then lifted his nose into the breeze. Was she here? With his cat? He sifted scents, seeking…seeking…

The two men stood close together talking, and Shadow listened while he continued to test the air. His ears twitched when he heard his name. He woofed, a polite understated sound the way a good-dog should.

Combs turned to him. Shadow wanted out. How to tell the man to open the car door? He needed a closer sniff, to press his nose into the ground where scent clung to grass and pooled in the lees of ditches. Shadow barked louder. Why wouldn't Combs listen?

Then the breeze shifted, and he froze—Macy scent!—and he couldn't stop barking, pawing the door, lunging to get out the half opened window.

Combs raced back to the car. "Hey boy, settle down. Stop, you'll hurt yourself." His voice barked back with disapproval.

Couldn't he understand? Combs acted like he couldn't smell Macy, and Shadow's frustration grew when people ignored important scents. That's why they should listen to good-dogs. The wind shifted again, and Macy scent disappeared.

Shadow howled! He pushed his head and chest through the window opening, and got one foreleg out, too. Out, he needed out. Follow the cat smell, find September.

Teddy hurried to join Combs. "Let the dog out, for God's sake. He knows something. I watched how he tracked Molly." He reached out with an upturned palm. "Want to play *hide-and-seek*?"

Yes! Shadow yelped, and licked Teddy's hand. Teddy understood. He knew the right words. He let the old man's gentle touch push his paw and head back into the car, and waited impatiently for the door to open.

"He's got a long lead still attached to his harness." Teddy put his hand on the outside of the car. "Don't know if he'll pay attention to me, he's pretty riled up. So get ready to grab that line when I open the door." He spoke directly to Shadow. "Wait. You know what that means, right? Shadow, *wait.*"

Teddy made strong eye contact. Shadow yawned, and turned his head aside in polite deference to the older man. He whined, panting with excitement, and backed away from the door. It opened, and he trembled, barely able to contain the urge to leap out.

"Okay." Teddy gave the release word, and Shadow hopped out and immediately dropped his nose to the pavement. "Shadow, *seek.*"

Someone grabbed the leash, he could tell by the tension that tugged his back, but Shadow remained focused on smells. Shadow tracked left, breathing in with quick snuffles and out with short huffs, clearing his nostrils every so often to better read the scents.

Pulling hard, he swerved off the car path, burying his face for a moment in the dry crinkled vegetation mounding the roadside. Mice. Coyote. Bird poop. Old glove. No Macy.

"Don't we have to give him something to smell?" Combs let himself be tugged after the dog.

"I suppose so. But we don't have anything." Teddy spoke softly but with authority. "Shadow, where's September? Find September, big guy. *Seek.*"

Shadow paused, and stared at Teddy, puzzled. He'd never tracked a person. In the *hide-and-seek* game it was a good-dog's job to find other dogs and cats. And September always gave him a sniff-sample to tell him what to *seek.*

Was this a new game? With new rules? He wished September was here. But he didn't hear or smell her at all. That fleeting Macy-scent teased the sensitive smell place deep in his muzzle almost to his eyes. Finding Macy was the next best thing.

Never mind what Teddy said. Dogs knew better sometimes. Smells and sounds never spoke to people like they did to good-dogs.

Shadow put down his head and tracked to the right this time, still searching for any hint of Macy. He snuffled past the mid-line point of the highway, stopped and came back.

There! That smell: that was Shadow pee-smell, there in the road. He'd been here before.

The wind ruffled his fur, and Shadow lifted his face to the stream, tasting and drinking deep of the myriad smells. There. Macy smell.

He leaped ahead, crossed the car path and dove down the embankment into a stubbled field. And hit the end of the line. Shadow tugged and pulled, yelped with frustrated effort, but Combs planted his heels and tugged back.

"What's he doing? Teddy, he's not following the road. I think he found a squirrel or something."

"Listen to the dog. Follow Shadow." Teddy limped after them in a hopscotch gait, and slowed to stumble down the incline off the road.

Shadow whined, lowered his head to the ground and snorted. He paced back and forth in a half circle, the long line taut where it unraveled from Combs's grip. Too slow! He pulled, threw his weight against the harness, and the tension disappeared like fog battered by sun. There, again the Macy smell beckoned, and Shadow leaped ahead, ignoring Comb's exclamation of pain.

Free of the man's grip, Shadow coursed first one way and then the other in a steady, space-eating jog through the field. His nose barely skimmed the grass. The teasing breeze with its intermittent scent shouted louder than any people words and beckoned his paws to hurry, faster, and faster still. To the left. Now to the right. Ahead for a spell and back left again. And—

There! He stopped. Nosed the spot, inhaling deeply, tail wagging with growing excitement. He told himself *good-dog*, but it wasn't the same. He'd found Macy smell at last. Fresh. His cat had rested here a moment.

Fear stink from the cat's paws made Shadow's hackles bristle. He sniffed again, tracked right and then left and centered on the paw pad trail. Macy's path wound through tufts of grass taller than Shadow, and his signature odor marked the frozen ground and everything his fur brushed.

Shadow increased his pace. The cat spore grew ever more fresh. Maybe September would be with his cat, and they could all be together. His leash-line dragged behind, snaking after him through the rubble. It hung on something, and impatiently Shadow jerked it free, and continued to run forward. Up a small incline. Down the other side. There, beneath that tree. The smell so fresh it glowed clear as star-fire in the night sky.

A hiss. Eerie eye glow, a blink and another hiss. Macy, but terrified, not recognizing Shadow. And September nowhere around.

Shadow stopped. His tail drooped with disappointment, and he whined. Macy spit, and Shadow dropped to the ground. That was how he told September he'd found the lost when they played *hide-and-seek*. It also told other scared dogs and cats not to worry, that he was no threat.

He looked away from the cat's eye-shine and yawned to show he meant no harm. And he woofed, but very softly. He didn't want to scare his cat any further.

Macy growled, but then he mewed—a cautious cat question that sounded puzzled. Shadow didn't dare move or stare directly at the cat. In a moment, Macy delicately sniffed the air, stood, and paced carefully toward him.

Shadow couldn't contain himself any longer and stood, tail flagged high and nose-touched his cat. He sniffed Macy from head to toe as the cat rubbed his length against Shadow's front legs.

The cat stopped and lay down, panting. Macy must be tired from running.

September smell covered the cat. Fresh scent, too. Shadow knew she couldn't be far away. But there was no trail on the ground to find her.

"Here kitty kitty kitty. Macy, I know you're there."

Both Shadow and his cat froze, both furry faces swung toward the familiar voice. Macy tensed, ready to spring away until Shadow nose-touched his cheek again and wagged. Footsteps crunched over frozen grass. Macy pressed against Shadow's side.

"There you are!" A light spilled onto the ground from the man's outstretched hand, and he crouched without moving forward any further. "Well, well, and Shadow, too. How'd you get here? Good-dog, you found Macy."

Shadow plastered his ears and wagged harder, but stayed in place when Macy meowed and trotted over to Doc Eugene.

"How about that, the GPS worked." Doc Eugene gathered Macy into his arms, and grunted as he stood. "Shadow, let's go." He patted his leg. "Come, boy. Back to the car."

He barked, and backed away. It wasn't time for a car ride. Dogs got locked inside cars. September wasn't here, but she wasn't in the car, either. Shadow barked again.

"You know better than that. Hell, you knew how to sit and down and come before you left our house as a pup. Pam teaches all her pups before they're re-homed. So COME!" He took a step toward Shadow, impatience in his voice. He juggled Macy, and the cat settled into Doc Eugene's arms, mouth open and still panting.

September wasn't here. But he could smell her touch on Macy's fur even from where his cat now rested. Macy had been with September so recently, her scent spilled off the cat's body in waves. Macy's fur-contact painted Shadow's leg with the faint aroma of her signature odor. Everything the cat had touched, each tree trunk and grass hummock, carried that telltale clue.

He could find September by playing the game backwards. *Seek* in reverse. Shadow would track not where Macy was, but where the cat had been. *Good-dog!*

Shadow whirled, ignoring Doc Eugene's concerned voice, and found the trail. The man's voice faded in the distance as Shadow ran, his nose barely skimming the trail, picking up the bread crumb smell clues along the way.

By the time he'd passed through the wooded area and padded up the hill, he panted heavily and his paws hurt again. The scent was less strong—older—but still distinct when he burst into a clearing and saw the old building. It smelled of dusty wood and sick animals. Raccoons? Stale cat pee from several other cats.

Macy's trail, tainted with fear-scent that burned his nostrils, led inside.

Shadow didn't slow his pace when a car sitting in front of the old building roared to life. The vehicle's eye-lights speared him in the hard-pack soil of the car-path, its tires spun clots of dirt. The car ran at him.

He gathered tired muscles to dodge away. But then Shadow froze in shock when September yelled.

Chapter 51

"Tell me you got something, Gonzales. I got nothing here, and worse." Combs blew on his rope-burned palm, and shook it, wishing he'd worn gloves.

"What happened?" Background noise from before had disappeared. Gonzales must have left the restaurant.

"Met up with Teddy. He rigged a way to track September's missing cat. Seems to've found the signal and that's still in play, but no results yet." He stood outside the car, leaning against the door while Doc Eugene tramped somewhere out in the darkness supposedly hot on the trail—or tail, of the missing cat.

"Don't you have the dog with you? Get it to track."

"Gee, why didn't I think of that?" The heavy sarcasm targeted his own inept handling of the situation. "The dog must have Greyhound in him, he took off so fast. Couldn't keep up or see him in the dark. How do those SAR teams do it?" He'd never had a dog, other than a tiny mop of a pooch belonging to Cassie when they were first married. Muffy could have doubled for house slippers.

"So we got both September's cat and dog in the wind, and they were our best chance to find her." Gonzales sounded disgusted, but then brightened. "Leaned on Dietz and he's in denial about any contaminated meat, says it's a smear campaign born of jealousy." He laughed. "I kid you not, that's a direct quote—born of jealousy. He's one of those woo-woo artsy types, a smug bastard acts like his shit don't stink."

"Any leads? No-shows at the restaurant?" It still made Combs's skin crawl to think Cassie had taken the kids to the event. What was she thinking? Couldn't have predicted a bust, granted, but it didn't sound like his social-climbing former wife.

"Couple names, yeah. The AD—that's the assistant to the director—says one of the cast, a goofy-ass character, goes by Felch, can't be found. They announced at the dinner he's been replaced. Everyone we interviewed so far confirmed that." He blew out a breath, obviously as tired as Combs. They'd both been running nonstop for nearly twenty-four hours. "Still going through the witnesses and taking statements, only about half done. I had to take a break."

"Felch likely?"

"Involved for sure. Got pictures galore, he's on all the posters and other promo material. Felch is a local, but kind of a recluse, one of those back-to-the-land self-sufficient guys. Lives out in the area you're searching, actually, so might want to run by his place if you got nothing else encouraging."

Combs scribbled down the address. Better than doing nothing while waiting on cat schematics. "Good. Who's the other? You said a couple possibles."

"Guy named Vincent Grady, new to the team. AD says they brought him on less than six weeks ago as the set PA, in charge of wrangling the talent and other chores. Best I can tell, a glorified gopher. He's also replacing Felch in the cast lineup."

Combs cracked his knuckles. "Six weeks. Timing's right. About the time the Blizzard Murders hit national wires."

Gonzales agreed. "Grady got a raise and new title. Pissed off the AD something fierce."

"You can stop with the alphabet soup, Gonzales. I left my scrabble board at home."

"Can you spell AWOL?" He paused. "Grady attended the launch party but disappeared in the roundup. Nobody's seen him since."

"You need to lean on this Dietz character. He's the head honcho—director or producer or something, whatever initials they call them. He's got to know something. Tell him he's responsible. Hell, he probably is."

"Great minds." Now Gonzales sounded sarcastic, and Combs cracked his knuckles. "Rattled him like a box of Good 'N Plenties. Told him we found Sly, and I thought he'd shit a brick. You ask me, Dietz already knew about Sly. Got his composure back pretty quick, like those actor guys do, but I could tell he was surprised we found the body. Took Dietz all of ten seconds to point fingers at both Felch and Grady."

"How convenient they're both missing." Combs saw Teddy motioning to him, and pushed off from the car. "I got something. Maybe. Hold on." He crossed over to the old man, and saw Teddy staring off the road, into the dark.

"Something moving over there." Teddy pointed. "I think it's Doc Eugene."

A flashlight wavered, and then steadied as it floated disembodied over the ground. The figure drew closer until they could make out the veterinarian.

Doc Eugene cradled Macy in his arms. "He was running loose. Shadow found him, too, but I couldn't catch the dog." The vet carefully climbed the embankment, struggling with the added weight. "Cat's stressed, too. Got to get him calmed down." He crossed to his vehicle, opened the back and climbed in with the cat. Teddy followed, shoulders stooped, defeated. He started to climb in the passenger side.

"God dammit to hell, can't catch a break!" Combs put the phone back to his ear. "Just found the cat. It was loose." What a waste of time. "I'll go visit this Felch character's place since we got nothing here." He disconnected.

Before Combs reached his own car, Teddy yelled. "Detective, you must see this, we've got something." He adjusted his glasses as Combs jogged over to the car.

"What?" He peered into the car's interior.

"Couldn't see it out in the dark," said the veterinarian. "But Macy brought us a message. Mean anything?" He'd removed the GPS tag, and handed it to Combs.

Someone had written on the tag with black marker. "V. Gra." He met the men's expectant expressions. "We think that's the name of September's stalker. Victor Grant." He shook his head, frustrated. *Or it could be Vincent Grady. Hmm.* "Doesn't help find him. Or September."

"Victor Grant. September mentioned him. She said he had something to do with Sly's disappearance when she gave me Fish's file." Teddy grimaced, apologetic. "I should have mentioned that sooner."

Combs grunted. "That's confirmation, anyway, but it doesn't help find him, either."

"Maybe this will help." The veterinarian held Macy up, smoothing the cat's fur.

Purrs rumbled as the man stroked Macy's white throat and chest, what September referred to as his bib. She'd used the marker to write on his fur. "Do that one more time, smooth a little to the side. Yes, right there." When the fur laid the right way, it was easy to read. "*Barn.* She tried to write his name on the tag, and the location on the fur." Combs pulled out his phone and hit speed dial to reach Gonzales.

Teddy already had his laptop out, balanced on the hood of the car, the mobile hot-spot providing internet access. The screen filled with an overhead view of the area. His fingers flew, and the image grew brighter, and larger.

Gonzales answered. "What you got?"

"Barn. Give me a list, any structure that could be described as a barn in," he looked around, "maybe a three mile radius of this location."

"On it."

Teddy's fingers clacked on the keyboard, and he gasped. "Oh, no." He glanced up at Combs. "I think I found it."

Gonzales came back on the line. "Hey, man, go figure, Felch's address I already gave you has a barn. I'm on my way."

"Meet you there." He turned to Teddy. The man should be happy or relieved, not stricken. "What?"

Teddy's eyes didn't move from the computer, and pointed to a bright spot on the screen. "I hope that's not the right barn. It's on fire."

Chapter 52

Hot pain radiated from her knee outward, encompassed her thigh and throbbed in rhythm with September's pulse. She reached for the flashlight Victor had left behind, and yelled with frustration and agony when her fingers fell short. Any movement made invisible knives stab deeper into the wound, and left her panting.

"He locked the door. Why'd he do that? Why'd he hurt us?" Nikki's eyes reflected twin pools of shock, and a purpling goose-egg marred her forehead. She hugged herself.

September gritted her teeth. Forced herself to slow her breathing. Deep breath in, blow the pain out, breathe in, blow out. *Focus, focus.* "Nikki, can you see anything? There's a crack in the door." *The reason didn't matter. How could she explain Victor, when she didn't understand him herself? Only getting help mattered.*

The little girl peered through the chink. "It's too dark. Wait." She turned her head for a better angle. "I see something. A light. It's a match, I think." She fell silent, and then backed away from the door, stuttering with fear. "Fire, it's a fire. He set a fire!" She pounded on the door. "Let us out! Let us out!" When it wouldn't give, Nikki turned her tear-streaked face. "He's going to burn us." Her voice was anguished.

"No, he's not. Nikki, listen. Look at me. Nikki!" She put command and conviction into her voice, the same tone she'd learned to use with Dakota. And with Shadow. *Would she ever see the pup again? Or Macy? Not if she didn't get them out of here.* "You won't burn. I'll get you out. I promise. Do you believe me?"

Nikki sniffled, but kept tossing worried glances at the door. "Smoke. Do you smell it?"

The acrid aroma tickled her nose, but soon would choke out the limited air in the tiny space. "We have to work fast. I can't move very well, so you'll have to do what I tell you. Trust me, okay?"

"Okay." She sniffled again.

"Bring me the flashlight." September stretched her hand to take it, wincing at even that minimal movement. She covered the expression with a laugh, to reduce Nikki's fear. The girl's deer-in-the-headlights emotions wouldn't take much more.

Using the light as she had with Macy, September pointed the light at specific objects as she talked. "There on the table, see the thermos? Bring that. And over there, the ski mask. Take off your hat, too."

Nikki brought everything to September, kneeling beside her. "Sorry about your leg."

"Me too. You're pretty handy with the bucket."

She wrinkled her nose. "It smelled bad. He's a stupid-head and deserved it."

Laughing, September agreed. "You saved my life, you know. That was brave. Can you be brave a little while longer?"

"I guess so." She looked at the door and pointed. "Smoke. It's getting worse."

The chinks in the old boards leaked foggy tendrils that floated upward to hang in the upper third of the small room. Tinder-dry wood and animal bedding would burn quickly. There wasn't much time.

September opened the canister of coffee, thankful she'd left most of it in the thermos, and poured brown liquid over the two ski masks. "You're too young to drink coffee, Nikki, so I don't want you trying to get a caffeine fix." She winked at the girl to show it was a joke, and got a tentative smile back for her efforts. "It'll feel nasty but you need to wear the mask with the wet parts against your nose and mouth. Breathing through the wet helps filter out the smoke. And see how the smoke stays up high?" Nikki looked up. "That's why we need to stay down low, the lower the better. Okay?"

"But there's no way out. And there's not enough coffee to put out the fire."

Shining the light again, September pointed it to the far corner where the carpet rucked over the hole she'd enlarged. "That's the way out."

Nikki slowly shook her head. "I don't like little places like that." Her lower lip trembled. "Hard to breathe in little places. And besides, it smells."

The girl was claustrophobic? That sucked. "Yep, it smells bad. I think some cats hang out there."

"Hope-Kitty?" Her pitch turned up a notch. "She could burn up, too!" Nikki crawled over to the opening and pulled back the rug, and stared down into the black hole, doubt and fear chasing one another across her face.

"I can't get through that little opening. But you can. Nikki, I need you to go get help." She thought Nikki would refuse, and couldn't quell her own rising panic. At the least, Nikki had to get out and save herself. A crackle and whoosh beyond the locked door created another puff of heavier smoke. "There's not much time, Nikki. You already saved my life once. You're the only one who can do this. I'm counting on you."

Her narrow shoulders hunched forward. "Okay," she whispered.

"Quickly then." September dumped more coffee on one of the ski masks, and held it out to the girl. "Put it on." She watched as Nikki pulled the soggy mess over her head and covered her face, and then donned the second soaked mask herself, and poured the rest of the lukewarm liquid over the carpet. If she couldn't get into the crawl space, her only chance was to roll up in the wet carpet and pray Nikki got help here in time.

First, get the girl safe. "I'll hold the light for you." September took a breath, braced for the pain, and then rolled onto the side with her good leg, and pulled herself closer to the hole, dragging the wet carpet up over her exposed legs. "Hurry, Nikki. The fire's spreading." The flashlight speared through the hole. A pair of eyes reflected the light back before the animal scampered away.

"It's Hope! Hope is really here!" It gave her the needed incentive, and Nikki sat on the edge of the hole, feet dangling through, and butt-scooted forward. She closed her eyes, took a breath and held it, and dropped into the crawl space as though jumping into a swimming pool.

"Never mind the cat for now. Nikki, find the hole, over there." September pointed with her light as the crackling fire sound grew louder. "Hope will come with you. I promise!" The girl had to go now, before the barn collapsed on top of them.

September dropped her head and shoulders through the narrow opening, ignoring the pain in her knee that had swollen to twice its normal size. She pointed with the light. "Go, Nikki, go!"

The girl quickly crawled to the narrow opening, but stopped to check back over her shoulder. The ski mask turned her into a freakish figure. "What about you?"

"I'll be fine." September smiled, but it was hidden by her own wet mask. She steadied her voice to make the lie more believable. "I'm coming right after you, okay? Don't want to slow you down with my bum knee, so you run and get help. Just go, go now!"

Nikki turned to the small opening excavated by animals, perhaps by her beloved Hope-kitty, and dove through. She wiggled until only the bottom of her shoes could be seen. And then they too were gone.

September wanted to cry with relief. Nikki would tell the authorities about Victor, so he'd be punished. She'd won. After eight years of terror, it was over. For a moment she relaxed and closed her eyes. She'd done all that she could.

Heat blasted her legs. She jerked, and her knee punished her for the reflex.

The wet carpet offered little protection. Her butt and legs splayed out on the floor above might as well be bare. Her upper body dangled from the waist through the hole, so she'd survive longer even while her lower extremities trapped above cooked like a roasted pig.

She dropped the flashlight into the crawl space. Her arms reached for the underside of the floor, seeking purchase. She needed leverage.

September strained, and managed to pull more of her body into the hole. Her hips became a cork that plugged the opening. She screamed, and screamed again. Twisted. Squirmed. Clothing tore. Skin ripped.

Her body dropped, knocking her breathless and pressing her coffee-wet mask into clotted fur and dusty spider webs. Craning her neck, she saw her injured leg still caught in the hole above, and September reached up and managed to tug it down. The thumped landing prompted another scream, but why be brave? Nobody would hear her die. Through the hole, light and shadow danced as flames gnawed the old wood above and around her.

September reached for the flashlight, and it clinked against metal. The cello endpin—all that was left of Melody—gave her an adrenalin boost of hope. Her injured leg made the wood-kicking plan impossible, even if she could have turned her body around. But the metal could help her dig her way out.

She squirmed toward the dugout next to the wooden steps. The agony in her leg belonged to someone else. She *willed it so.* Just as she'd gone to that other place during the Victor years, where the torment visited on that *other* September couldn't touch her, she divorced herself from the pain.

The endpin gouged the frozen earth as she sought to enlarge the frozen dirt tunnel. But within two or three strikes, September realized the barn sat on a cement pad with decades of hard-packed dirt over top. The tunnel couldn't go deeper, she couldn't breach the concrete, and the eight-inch height of the opening didn't come close to allowing her through.

Coughing turned to sobs, and she let her face fall into her arms. At least the smoke would kill her before the flames. She imagined she heard barking, and her tears intensified. *Hope somebody finds you, baby-dog. You deserve a good home. Someone to love you.*

"September? Are you there?"

She roused. "Nikki, what are you doing?" She saw the girl's masked face peering through the tunnel. "Get out, get out!"

Shadow barked.

"Shadow? Oh my God, is that my Shadow?" September coughed again. Smoke had begun to seep into the crawl space.

The dog cried and pushed Nikki aside, scrambling to get his head into the hole. "No, get back, Shadow, it's too small." His powerful shoulders made the old two by six boards flex.

"The bad man was in his car waiting. I couldn't leave." Nikki chattered like the youngster she was, no longer cowed but excited by the adventure.

"He almost hit the dog when he drove away. Shadow—is that his name?—heard you scream. We couldn't leave you here."

Her mind raced. "Nikki, I appreciate that, I truly do. You can do one thing for me, but then you have to run. Not walk, you *run* out of here for help." The drill sergeant demand brooked no argument, and she didn't wait for the girl to respond. "Does Shadow still have his leash?"

At the sound of his name, the dog yelped. "Hold still, dog. Um…yeah, it's a long line." Nikki paused. "What should I do?"

All she needed was one board-width. "Hand me the end of the line." She gathered it up through the hole when Nikki poked it through. "Now get the hell out of here, Nikki! Run, run!"

The girl scrambled to her feet, footsteps pounding. A pause. And then a scream of pure delight. "Daddy! Daddy, you're here!"

September couldn't wonder about who might be outside. She couldn't wait for a rescue. Rescue was here. Rescue was a midnight-black baby-dog.

"Good-dog, Shadow, you're such a good boy. You found me, didn't you?" She had to work fast, or she'd kill them both.

Shadow barked. Joy colored his voice, and not a little fear and worry.

September pulled a third of the length of Shadow's tracking line through the excavated hole, pulled it up and over to poke the end out a chink in the first board until it dropped to the ground. She clawed up that end again, and tied it off, leaving plenty of play in the leash for the dog to maneuver. "We're gonna play tug. Want to play, Shadow? Good-dog, this is a new game and I know you can do it." *Please God let him do it!*

He barked again, ready for anything, and backed away from the tethered board.

September found the cello rod again, and attacked the exposed end of the board. Yes! The sharp end of rusty nails still poked through toward her. She pried at the board, loosening them a bit, and then traded the endpin for the metal flashlight. Using it like a hammer, she pounded them to back the nails out of the wood. Some proved so old, they simply broke off, and she quit when the flashlight bent others and made the situation worse.

It was up to Shadow. If he failed, he'd be burned alive with her, unable to break the tether to escape the barn. And if he died by her hand, she wouldn't want to live anyway.

"Shadow, let's play tug." She coughed, cleared her throat, and put a teasing lilt in the game-words. "I've got it, it's mine and you can't have it. Ready, set, TUG!"

He barked, and grabbed the end of the leash in his jaws and pulled. It slid through his teeth. He couldn't get purchase, but the board shifted.

"Again, baby-dog. Ready, set, TUG!"

She timed it, and shoved from her side when he pulled. Once more, the board shifted. But not enough.

It wouldn't work. Not in time to save them, anyway. Think, think! He wasn't trained the way sledding dogs or weight-pull dogs competed. Shadow was trained NOT to pull when on leash.

Except when tracking.

"Shadow! Good-dog, what a good boy! Wait, it's okay, chill." He panted, and then coughed, and pawed the opening in the dirt. "Shadow, let's play *hide-and-seek*. Where's Macy?"

He cocked his head. The fire lit the area enough that she could see the movement through the narrow opening in the board.

She knew Macy was long gone, perhaps never to be found again. She couldn't think about that painful reality now. The cat could save them, though, even if he lived only in memory. Shadow knew the cat's scent, had been drilled to find Macy, and the trail was fresh from this doorway out of the barn. She needed him to run out of the barn, and pull the damn board off the wall, tug it to hell and gone out of the barn. If she couldn't get out in time, at least he might survive.

"Shadow, where's Macy? *SEEK!*"

He didn't pause. He didn't test for scent. Shadow whirled, put his head down, and bulldozed away. He was caught short by the end of the tether, but the board creaked and moved.

"Good-dog, God, you're such a good boy!" She couldn't see through the smoke and tears. "*SEEK, Shadow, SEEK!*"

He did. The board squealed. And it flew free.

Hope raced past September out the opening and streaked from the barn to rejoin Nikki. September followed more slowly, gasping as she found her way by feel. She crawled on hands and one knee, dragging her injured leg, amazed that safety beckoned less than six feet away. It might be too far.

Her eyes wouldn't focus. Were those cars out there? They circled the burning barn, and as she watched a fire truck with flashing lights pulled up.

Shadow barked and howled, and struggled to get back to her. Thank God, somebody held him back. It looked like Teddy, what was Teddy doing here?

She dragged herself another two feet, and paused to strip the wet mask from her face. Better to see than to breathe, she'd hold her breath the last short distance.

September saw Nikki huddled against a man—her father?—wearing military attire. When a puff of wind momentarily cleared smoke he saw September's struggles, and pushed Nikki gently aside to take three hurried long steps toward her.

But another figure outran him, dodging flames to reach her. He startled a massive flock of tree-roosting birds, flushing them into a feathery explosion that blackened the fire-lit sky before the cloud spun, turned in concert, and finally evaporated into the night.

Combs scooped September into his arms, and carried her the last several feet into the fresh air. For the first time in eight years, September felt safe.

Chapter 53

September hobbled into the kitchen, Shadow never far from her side, and smiled at the array of food still to be eaten. Anita bustled from the refrigerator to the stained glass table, replacing spent dishes with refills.

Shadow licked his lips and stared hopefully at his empty dish. Anita took the cue, grabbed a square of cheese and lobbed it expertly toward the bowl. He leaped forward and snapped it out of the air before it landed.

"He'll get fat." But September didn't mind, not tonight. He deserved as many treats as he wanted. Tonight they celebrated the cusp of a new year, and for her, a new life. Shadow made that possible. So had Macy.

"Get out of here. Go entertain your guests." Anita made shooing motions with her green and red lacquered nails, and flipped dark hair over her shoulder that tonight boasted a matching green streak.

"Got to give Macy his pill." The cat lounged atop the refrigerator, supervising the activity. September stroked Macy's white throat, and rumbled purrs spilled forth. Dark stains from the Sharpie-drawn message had yet to fade, but she considered it a badge of honor. She wouldn't inflict the indignity of a bath on the feline hero.

"Pill time, Macy." She shook out one of his prescriptions. He stood and stretched, and then sat and waited for the medicine. "Open." As soon as his mouth stretched wide, she made a tongue-click noise to signal he'd chosen the right behavior, and quickly popped in the pill immediately followed by a sliver of cheese. "Good boy, Macy!" The cat chewed, swallowed, and pawed her hand. She obliged with another treat and followed up with a cheek scratch.

"Will that cure him? Never knew a cat to open wide like that for a pill." Anita smiled with admiration. "Mine'll take my head off if I think about pills."

September laughed. "Most cats hate pills, true. Macy isn't a fan, but the treat trumps the pill. He knows he only gets treats afterwards. I like to think he knows they make him feel better, too." She shrugged. "There's no cure for cardiomyopathy. Doc Eugene says Macy's is the milder form, and the medicine helps." Thank goodness Doc Eugene was a board certified veterinary internist with a specialty in cardiology. Macy would get an annual echocardiogram from now on, to monitor any heart changes.

Macy's DNA test showed he carried only one copy of the gene so he had a more encouraging prognosis. Maine Coon cats with two copies of the A31 mutation were eighteen times more likely to develop problems and often died by age four.

Anita joined September at the refrigerator to scratch Macy's other cheek, and the cat closed his eyes with pleasure. "At least my mutt cats are immune." At September's frown, she stopped scratching, and Macy head-butted her hand until she continued. "No?"

"All cats can get it. Experts suspect the disease happens as the result of a heritable heart gene mutation—that's been proven in a couple of cat breeds, but not all—so responsible breeders screen for HCM to avoid spreading the problem. Persians have an incidence of up to forty percent, Maine Coons like Macy, Ragdolls, American Shorthair, Sphynx—several breeds are known to be affected. But it's in other breeds, and even mix breed cats and ferals aren't immune. They may get sick and die without being diagnosed, so I suppose we can't know the true incidence in pet cats." She stroked Macy's thick fur. "God bless Winn Feline Foundation. They're funding research to find ways to identify and eliminate the disease from breeding programs, and that can help the general cat population—including your kitties."

The phone rang and Anita started across the room to get it. "Who'd call this late on New Year's Eve?"

"That's the business line. Let the machine get it." Tonight she didn't want anything to put a damper on the festivities.

"Forgot to tell you." Anita bit her lip and plucked a Post-It from the wall phone and handed it to September. "Message from some O'Dell woman, there's the number. She sounded pretty upset you'd not returned her calls." She made a face. "About that time the cookies started to burn, and I got so busy with the food, it totally slipped my mind. Sorry."

"That's okay. With pet lovers, everything needs immediate attention even if the problem's gone on for months. I'll call her later." September stuck the Post-It on the face of the refrigerator, and dropped Macy's pills back into a drawer. She leaned against the granite counter top. "Thanks for all this. I couldn't do it without your help. Still have quite a hitch in my git-along."

"Love doing it." Anita wore a silver sequin-encrusted cocktail dress with matching spike heels and glittered like a tarnished tree ornament. "My postage stamp apartment won't fit more'n four people, and I love parties. Only chance I get to wear my sparkles." She eyed September critically. "At least your crutches got retired. Hard to host a party when you walk like Lurch from *The Addams Family.*"

Stifling a giggle, September poured wine into a glass, and sipped. "I don't do sparkles." Hell, she rarely did skirts, either, and preferred sweats or jeans. She'd surprised Combs by wearing a calf-length emerald velvet gown, the long sleeves, high neck and long skirt not only festive but practical. The dress hid both past and recent scars, including the knee brace stabilizing the ACL tear. Doctors predicted a full recovery with strict adherence to rehab.

"Go on. Get back to your party. I've got this covered." Anita sipped her cocktail. "I'll join you in a minute. It's a half hour to the new year, so go stop Fish from being a conversation hog." She made a face. "Maybe not a good choice of words."

September shuddered. It would be a long time before she'd risk eating pork again. Fish, though, had somehow managed to turn the *Hog Hell* debacle into an opportunity. Rather than shutting down the TV show, controversy vaulted it to even greater ratings, and he'd been tapped to replace Tommy Dietz as the host.

Anita was over the moon when Fish brought her on board as his assistant. Tonight was the closest Anita and Fish had come to having a real date. September hid a smile. Fish didn't stand a chance of squirming out of Anita's shiny net.

When she limped from the kitchen into the dining area, September saw several groups scattered throughout the room. As Anita predicted, Fish held forth in one corner, entertaining Detective Gonzales and his wife Mercedes along with Doc Eugene.

She'd hesitated to invite the veterinarian, knowing how he felt about her, but breathed easier when he'd accepted. He raised his glass when she entered, and September smiled back, grateful they'd been able begin the process of reconciliation. She'd promised to spend time with the dogs Pam had loved so much, and perhaps get them back into tracking form. Shadow would enjoy the canine company.

Shadow stayed glued to her side. He'd not left her sight since the fire, not even when she'd gone to the hospital for evaluation. Combs insisted she and her service dog couldn't be separated, and the medics took one look at his badge and her face, and didn't argue.

Combs smiled from across the room and left Teddy to meet her. "You're gorgeous."

Heat warmed her cheeks.

"So are you, Shadow. Handsome, I mean." Combs held out his hand for the dog to sniff, and the pup politely nose-touched. He pressed closer to

September, and stayed between her and the man.

Combs leaned in to whisper to September. "I think he's jealous. And we still haven't had our first date."

She bit her lip, flustered. "Don't be ridiculous." Her hand fell to Shadow's ruff, and the butterflies settled.

Teddy joined them. "What a lovely couple."

What was this, a conspiracy? September sipped her wine and kept her eyes lowered.

Teddy added, "And you're pretty dapper tonight yourself, Detective Combs."

September sputtered. "Good one."

He scratched Shadow's chin. The pup wagged happily. Teddy turned somber when he turned to September. "How's Aaron?"

She took another sip of the wine, and leaned against a chair, more to give herself time than for any need of support. They'd found Aaron wandering, alive but suffering from frostbite, blood loss and hypothermia. And what they all suspected to be a new prion disease, courtesy of *Hog Hell*.

"Not good. They saved his arm." He'd hurt himself, bled all over the garden, and got turned around when he tried to go for help. Aaron exited out the back of the fence and walked more than a mile before he sat down on the shoulder of a road and was found by a passing driver. "He's lucky he didn't die of shock, lucky the weather wasn't worse. They're still running tests." She raised her eyebrows at Combs, asking permission, and at his slight nod, she continued. "Cassie Harrison has it, too."

Teddy was surprised. "That's your ex-wife, right?" Combs nodded. "I understand how Mr. Felch got sick, and the dogs from the show. But Aaron and your ex-wife, what's their connection? The restaurant says they never served harvested feral pig before the launch party."

When Shadow whined and nudged her, September smoothed his brow. He read her emotions as easily as she read music. "Aaron's a vegetarian. He'd never eat barbecue."

Teddy sounded properly shocked. "Hey, Mr. Fish? Can you explain something for us?" From across the room Fish jutted his chin whiskers in acknowledgment and strutted over, the others in his group following. Teddy continued. "You're on the inside track now. So how'd the barbecue get contaminated?"

Fish hemmed and hawed, and September enjoyed watching the little man squirm. "See, I had to sign a nondisclosure agreement. That's part of my new contract." He preened. "Going to bring some Fish style to the show. I'm the new host, you know. Moving the show to Louisiana, though."

Anita guffawed from the kitchen doorway before joining the party. "Everyone knows you ditched radio and got kicked upstairs. Couldn't sign that contract fast enough." She carried a fresh bottle in one hand, and her own cocktail glass in the other. "Anyone? Refills? More cold beer in the fridge. September, say the word when you want the champagne opened. It's twenty minutes till midnight."

September answered when Fish wouldn't. "The CDC has to sort it all out. Felch is dead, and he was already so sick he probably couldn't tell us anything anyway." She sipped her wine. "BeeBo's got to explain what he knows. I don't think any nondisclosure will protect him. Besides, he'll do it for his dogs. The man's a true dog lover. I don't think he had any idea or intention to cause problems. Dietz is the criminal." Dietz and Victor used each other, and in her mind, were equally to blame.

"Dietz claims he knows nothing." Gonzales waggled his empty beer bottle, and smoothed his mustache. "Time for a refill." He hurried to the kitchen.

Combs set his beer on the table and cracked his knuckles. "I don't buy Dietz's denial." He leaned closer to September, and her first instinct was to back away, but she took a breath and tried to relax. "Your theory works for me," he said. "Tell them."

All eyes focused on her, and she licked her lips. The unfamiliar taste of lipstick jarred her for a moment. Shadow pushed against her knee, the good one, and she steadied at his touch.

"I've done some research, and Doc Eugene put me in touch with some experts." She smiled thanks at the veterinarian. "White tail deer can develop spontaneous prion disease. It's called chronic wasting disease." She took a breath. "When hunters take a deer, they don't harvest the whole thing and the waste gets dumped. That's typically the feet, the offal, and if it's not trophy-worthy, the head. Sometimes they take the haunches, and dump the rest of the carcass."

Doc Eugene rattled the ice in his glass, needing a refill but reluctant to leave the conversation. "They're supposed to dispose of the waste properly. Not dump it in a ravine."

"A ravine where other animals scavenge. Enter the feral hogs." September drained her wine glass. "Pigs eat anything. The most common way to become infected with a prion disease is to eat contaminated tissue, most typically the brain or spine."

Teddy sat on the arm of the chair. "Sorry, my arthritis leaves me achy." He cleared his throat. "If I understand so far, infected deer get eaten by pigs, and people eat contaminated pigs. But that still doesn't explain Aaron, if he doesn't eat meat. Or Cassie Henderson, unless that single launch party meal exposure was enough to make her sick."

"I don't think any of them got sick from eating the pigs. Well, maybe the hunter's dogs, and Felch's barn cats." September ran her thumb over the rim of the wine glass so it sang. "Nikki said several of the kittens became sick and died."

Doc Eugene straightened and smiled broadly. "Did I tell you Nikki's parents gave her permission to keep the mother cat?"

"She got to keep Hope? That's fantastic." September would never have forgiven herself if Nikki had been hurt. After the child's terrifying experience, she deserved some happy news. "Between getting a cat for Christmas and having her dad come home, she must be walking on air. From what I understand, Nikki and her brother attended the TV launch while their mother picked up the dad at the airport, for a surprise." She smiled at Doc Eugene. "So did you put in a word to her mom about dealing with cat allergies?"

"You bet I did. Nikki's a sweet kid, totally cat crazy. She's going to help Saturday mornings cleaning kennels and whatnot, in exchange for some basic cat care. I'm a bit short staffed at the moment with Timothy gone." Doc Eugene's voice turned gruff for a moment and then steadied. "I gave my test results to the CDC officials. BeeBo's dog and Mr. Sanger's cat Pinkerton were both positive for prion disease. Maybe a new variant."

Gonzales returned to the group with fresh beer, and handed a bottle to Combs. Mercedes linked an arm through her husband's and sipped her own wine.

Teddy took off his glasses and pointed them at September. "You say only the pets got it from eating the tainted meat?"

"Raw fed." Doc Eugene shrugged. "Probably contaminated with neuro matter."

"But not the people." She sighed, twirled the wine glass again, and then carefully set it down before she accidentally broke it. "It's complicated, but follow me here. Nikki said when the kids visited Felch's barn earlier, they found a pile of bones."

"Bones?" Mercedes hugged her husband's arm and shivered. "He collected bones?"

September cocked her head. "Collected from the hunters' ravine drop, yes. Felch processed them, and sold the result." It explained everything, how the prions were distributed and people were exposed with no contact with the meat. "Felch boiled and charred them and then crushed up the bones into a fine powder, and sold it in bags to gardeners as bone meal fertilizer."

Teddy's stricken expression spoke volumes. "Molly bought a dozen bags of fertilizer a couple years ago from a local man. Bet it was Mr. Felch. I shared them with the local Master Gardener club when she had no more use for it, and even took a couple bags over to Sunnydale Nursing Home." He rubbed his eyes, and put glasses back on with trembling hands. "That day you brought Shadow, we found Molly out in the garden area with one of the bags. Maybe she knew what had made her sick. She tried to tell me."

September hugged him. "It's not your fault. It's not anyone's fault. Felch tried to make a buck recycling natural materials. Lots of people do that, and never have a problem. Besides, this is only a theory. But it would explain why Aaron and Cassie contracted the illness, too, if that's what they've got." The fault lay in Dietz trying to cover it up.

Doc Eugene drained the watery dregs of his drink. "There have been documented cases of prion disease contracted by inhaling contaminated material, like bone dust."

"We've rounded up all the bags we can find." Gonzales smiled at his wife. "Felch tried to be a good guy. He was on a mission to retrieve all the bags. That's what he meant by damage control."

Combs agreed. "Dietz wants us to believe that Felch killed Sly, but there's no evidence of that." He took a long pull on the beer. "I think Grady killed him to shut him up and didn't expect September to find the body, or call the police. Then he told Dietz he'd clean up the mess in exchange for a cut of the show proceeds. We found a newly signed agreement in Dietz's office." He bent toward September. "He left Felch's truck at one of the dump sites, with Macy's prescription pill bottle under the seat, like you said, so that ties his vehicle to your kidnapping. No prints from Grady, though, so it's circumstantial, not a slam-dunk."

September resisted the urge to ask about leads on Victor, aka Grady. He'd disappeared, left Dietz holding the bag, and she feared the chameleon had again escaped justice.

At her urging, the CSIs collected claw trimmings from Macy, so they had Victor/Grady DNA. He wasn't in any criminal database, though. To prove him guilty they had to catch him first.

It'd been two weeks. He'd disappeared before for years. The thought of him at large, at any moment able to again victimize her or someone else, made her want to scream. She shook herself and forced a smile. She wouldn't let anything spoil this night.

"This is a party. Enough of the gloom and doom, let's concentrate on the positives." September picked up her empty wine glass. "Anita, time to break out something stronger."

"After the champagne, sure." Anita took her glass. "But we've got some toasts first, and only bubbly will do the trick."

Her brow furrowed, but September waited as Anita and Fish bustled to the kitchen and returned with champagne for everyone.

Fish took the floor. "I've got the first toast. To a new career." He winked. "Sometimes you can turn a sow's ear into a silk purse."

Everyone laughed, toasted, and sipped.

"Me next." Gonzales held up his cell phone and winked at his wife. "Not even Combs knows this. Got the word a few minutes ago when getting my beer. The Captain has impeccable timing." Combs groaned. More laughs. "Victor, aka Grady, is in custody"

Mercedes and Anita gasped and then gently clinked glasses.

The room rocked. September grabbed for anything to stay upright. "They caught him? Really?" Combs's arm tightened around her shoulders. "They caught him."

He beamed. "Best news I've heard all day. Here, here!"

She couldn't stop smiling as she lifted her glass, and nearly choked when she tried to swallow the beverage. "He'll try to wiggle out of it."

"That cat's DNA evidence combined with eye witness accounts—yours and Nikki's—nail his balls to the wall." Gonzales flinched when Mercedes punched him for the language, but everyone laughed. A giddy atmosphere overtook the room.

"Me next. First, sit down here." Teddy pulled forward one of the dining room chairs for September and hurried to the office/music room next door.

Puzzled, but too happy and excited to object, September seated herself in the chosen chair. She smoothed the soft fabric of her dress, and leaned forward to rub Shadow's ears when he settled beside her. The rest of the guests watched her face with smiles of anticipation.

"Close your eyes." Combs touched her shoulder.

"What's happening? Not sure I like where this is going." But she did as he asked. "Everyone's in on this, I suppose?"

Teddy's limping footsteps approached, muffled on the deep carpet. "Hold out your hands."

She did. And encountered a cool hard surface, silk smooth, familiar. Her eyes flew open.

"A cello?" She saw each excited face, all claiming the group gift, and her heart expanded, too full to contain all her emotion. "You got me a cello." She took the bow Teddy presented with a flourish.

"That pole thing that sticks in the end? It's there." Combs pointed at the metal endpin that had helped her escape, and she bent down to release it, biting her lip to stop the trembling. "We recovered that from the barn. Part of your first cello, right?" Combs's hand on her shoulder squeezed, and she put hers atop it and squeezed back. September didn't bother wiping her eyes.

"I don't know what to say. Except thank you." She sniffled, and held up her glass. "To my friends."

"To friends," they echoed.

The clock began to strike midnight as Macy strolled into the room and curled up beside Shadow on the floor next to her. September stroked a hand from the cat's domed head to the dog's arched neck. "And to chosen family."

Shadow barked at her words, licked her hand and banged his tail. September had no doubt they thought with the same mind, and loved with the same heart.

Everyone echoed the toast. "To chosen family."

"And to new beginnings." Combs stared into her eyes, and this time she met them without flinching away.

"Yes, to new beginnings." She smiled.

He touched the gorgeous scroll of the instrument. "Play something?"

September quickly tested the strings, adjusted the tuning, and settled the cello between her knees. Where Melody had been as dark as her own sable hair, the face of this instrument shone as bright as the unfamiliar but welcome hope now filling her heart. She set her bow on the strings. "I'll call you

Harmony," she whispered, and began to play a new joyous song.

The room fell still, listening, as the clock chimed midnight, announcing the beginning of the New Year.

Macy's "ack-ack-ack-ack" lion cough answered the cello's sweet voice, and Shadow tipped up his head and added his howl, a raucous trio the most beautiful sound of all.

"Everyone's a critic." September laughed, but didn't stop. She'd never stop playing again.

EPILOGUE

Claire O'Dell clutched the phone, willing it to ring. She'd lost count of the times she'd called since last November, begging for help. But never a reply. How unfair, how wicked to help one child, but sentence hundreds of others to this purgatory of uncertainty.

She and Mike gambled on a miracle for Tracy, and got it. For a while, they basked in the glow of their little girl's transformation, and marveled at the six-year-old's unlocked abilities. But as Tracy's medicine cost drained savings, tempers flared. Worry filled every waking moment as the remaining doses in Tracy's bottle shrank.

No parent should suffer such anguish. The joyous dream became a nightmare. What had they done? Tracy would suffer horrendous side effects caused by a sudden withdrawal. They tried to hide their worry from Tracy. But somehow, she knew.

This morning, Claire's worry transformed to horror. Last night sometime, while Mike worked double-shifts, Tracy vanished along with her last bottle of precious pills. Before Claire could unfreeze her brain to react, to call Mike, to do anything, her best friend called, equally terrified for her autistic son. Lenny had also disappeared, taking Tracy with him.

With the clock ticking, Claire made frantic plans. She'd call Mike from the road, so he couldn't stop her. She knew where they'd gone: Heartland, Texas, where their miracle derailed. All because of that meddling woman.

She'd make September Day fix this, somehow, some way. Tracy's life depended on it.

FACT, FICTION & ACKNOWLEDGEMENTS

Publishing a debut novel is nearly impossible. That's a fact. A second novel is even more difficult to accomplish. That's also a fact. For me it's taken more than twenty years for fiction to become a reality. In dog years I should be dead.

I come from the nonfiction world and love intertwining fiction story elements with fact. But what's real, and what's fantasy? My publisher Bob Mayer writes "factual fiction" so I'm borrowing from him to offer nuggets related to this story. As September might say, here's the Cliff's Notes version with some additional resources for those curious for "just the facts" in HIDE AND SEEK.

As with LOST AND FOUND that launched this dog viewpoint series, much of this book is based on science, especially dog and cat behavior and learning theory, and the benefits of service dogs. A vast number of veterinarians, behaviorists, consultants, trainers and pet-centric writers and rescue organizations offer their incredible resources and support to help make the pet-centric storyline as accurate as possible. Find further information at IAABC.org, APDT.com, DWAA.org and CatWriters.com.

FACT: The *show-me* game is real, created by trainer Kayce Cover as a vocabulary game used with a variety of animals, which my own dog loves to play. See http://synalia.com/

FACT: The German Shepherd Dog on the cover is a real nine-month-old titled tracking dog that achieved her TD at age six months. Yes, that's a girl on the cover! (Don't tell Shadow…) Gillian Salling, a tracking dog expert and owner of Fernheim German Shepherds, graciously allowed her gorgeous and talented Uschi Von Fernheim, TD to serve as Shadow's cover dog model.

FICTION: Shadow's viewpoint chapters are pure speculation, although I'd love to be able to read doggy minds. However, every attempt has been made to base both Macy and Shadow's motivations and actions on what is known about canine and feline body language, scent discrimination and the science behind the human-animal bond.

FACT: Some of the pet characters in HIDE AND SEEK are based on real-life pets. Fifty terrific names were suggested with over 4100 votes during the "Name That Dog" and "Name That Cat" contest. Marci DeLisle suggested **Pinkerton** in honor of a favorite longhaired feral tabby cat with a bright pink nose surrounded by white fur. Pinkerton considered himself the resident security guard for the feral cat colony. Patricia suggested **Hope,** which seemed incredibly appropriate and actually helped focus the theme of the book. Patricia is a double winner, also suggesting the dog name **Rocky** for Teddy and Molly's much beloved heart-dog of the past. I made Rocky a twin to the current therapy dog at the nursing home, named Trixie. **Trixie** received an astounding 805 votes and was suggested by Kristi Brashier who lives with the real-life Trixie described as a very dark red Golden Retriever diva dog, whose goal in life is to have everyone pet her and tell her she's pretty. Trixie is also known as the neighborhood thief because she retrieves things from the neighbors. The winners received advance copies of the book, their pets' namesakes serving heroic roles in the book, and my eternal gratitude. Watch for future "Name That Dog/Cat" contests for future stories.

FACT: Therapy dogs can work wonders when partnered with Alzheimer's patients. Emotional support dogs also partner with a variety of people, from children to adults, including those suffering from post-traumatic stress disorder (PTSD). Not only dogs, but cats, parrots and other critters may be suited to become one of these incredible helpers. Learn more about pet-people partnerships at http://petpartners.org (formerly Delta Society).

FACT: All cats are at risk for hypertrophic cardiomyopathy (HCM), even that random-bred rescue beauty sleeping on your lap. Gene tests for the disease are available for a few select cat breeds including Maine Coon cats. Research funds are needed to make tests more widely available and ferret out the cause(s) of HCM and other cat-specific illnesses that take our cat friends from us far too early. As an added bonus, research into pet diseases often has applications and benefits to human health. The Winn Feline Foundation http://www.winnfelinehealth.org) is worthy of your support in this endeavor. Give generously—it could save your cat's life.

FACT: Canine cognitive disorder has been widely recognized in dogs. The brain changes appear to resemble some aspects of human Alzheimer's disease and drugs beneficial for humans appear to help dogs. The illness is found less commonly in cats. Studies indicate a combination of drug intervention, special antioxidant diets and behavior modification and training games (use it or lose it, to prevent "brain rust") can actually reverse some of these old-pet behaviors. The AKC Canine Health Foundation http://www.akcchf.org/ and Morris Animal Health Foundation http://morrisanimalfoundation.com/ fund research into these and other vital animal health challenges.

FACT: Feral pigs are such a huge environmental problem in Texas that experts agree there's no way to hunt, trap or barbecue our way out of the mess. You can learn more about feral hogs here: http://www.invasivespeciesinfo.gov/animals/wildboar.shtml

FACT: Prion diseases can arise spontaneously in nature and affects a small percentage of people each year. And yes, during the 'mad cow' scare, a few documented cases of cat infections were reported. A good place to start research is http://www.cdc.gov/ncidod/dvrd/prions/

FACT: Human cases of prion disease have been associated with inhalation of infective bone dust. Hey, some things you just can't make up!

FICTION: There is no evidence to support the notion that feral pigs contract prion disease by eating infective deer remains, or that barbecued feral hog poses risk to humans. The shivery notion arose from my decidedly twisted imagination.

FACT: This book would not have happened without my PAW-some tribe of friends, family and accomplished colleagues. Cool Gus Publishing, Bob Mayer and Jennifer Talty created an author-friendly professional venue for "outliers" with unique vision to succeed and support each other's success. My Cuchara gang continues to inspire and support my crazy notions and helped birth this book and many others during our times on the Mountain. Special thanks to my first readers Kristi Brashier, Dr. Lorie Huston and Frank Steele for your eagle eyes, spot-on comments and unflagging encouragement and support.

I am incredibly indebted to International Thriller Writers and the Debut Authors Program. The people who make up this organization are some of the most generous and supportive folks I have ever met, and my fictioning journey would never have become a reality or continued without this organization. Steve Berry's inspiring address to the 2013 Debut Class was the kick in the furry britches this writer needed to git-er-done and write the next book. And the next. And the next after that. I'm wearing my bunny slippers with teeth and loving it!

Finally, I'm grateful to all the cats and dogs I've met over the years who have shared my heart and sometimes my pillow. These days, Magical-Dawg and Seren-Kitty are my furry inspiration for all-things-pets. And of course, deepest thanks to my husband Mahmoud, who continues to support my writing passion even when he doesn't completely understand it.

I love hearing from you. Please drop me a line at my Bling, Bitches & Blood blog at AmyShojai.com or find more pet-centric books at https://www.shojai.com where you can watch for the latest dog-viewpoint THRILLERS WITH BITE!

<u>**SEPTEMBER'S STORY CONTINUES in SHOW AND TELL…**</u>

An animal behaviorist and her service dog race a deadly storm to expose a treacherous secret others will kill to protect.

A BLACKMAILER returns to sell a deadly cure.
A MOTHER'S DENIAL dooms millions of children.
AND A DOG shows true loyalty…when he runs away.

*"**SHOW AND TELL** is one of those rare thrillers that hits you in the heart as well as the head. Amy Shojai hits the ground running and never slows down. Damaged souls of the two and four-legged variety join forces to rescue others along with themselves. Riveting, wholly satisfying …makes us care."* --**Jon Land, *USA Today* bestselling author**

KEEP READING for a sample of **SHOW AND TELL!**

A September Day and Shadow Thriller

SHOW AND TELL

Book Three

AMY SHOJAI

Copyright

Second Print Edition, February 2017
Furry Muse Publishing
Print ISBN 978-1-944423-21-6
eBook ISBN 978-1-944423-22-3

First Published by Cool Gus Publishing
First Printing, December 2015
COPYRIGHT © Amy Shojai, 2015

FURRY MUSE
PUBLISHING
P.O. Box 1904
Sherman TX 75091
(903)814-4319
amy@shojai.com

Chapter 1

Eighty pounds of German Shepherd vaulted onto her bed and startled September from a sound sleep. She froze, mouse-quiet in the dark. Her heart trip-hammered in concert with the dog's low, bubbled growl that shook the bed, the vibration more felt than heard.

The downstairs clock struck five times. Clouds moved aside for moonlight to spill through the wooden blinds, painting the room silver with black shadows. The dog leaned closer. White-bright fangs glistened from his sooty muzzle, and September didn't need to see Shadow's expression to understand the dog's warning.

Shadow had good reasons for everything he did. He'd saved her life more than once.

The big black dog licked her face, and she pushed against his muscled chest, urging him off the bed so she could rise. His hackles continued to bristle despite her soothing touch, a warning she couldn't ignore. He was concerned, but not in full protection mode. Probably a furry trespasser. Better to see what had him on alert. She hadn't said a word, and didn't need to. The two partners were so in sync with each other, they might as well have read each other's mind. Shadow's tail flagged with excitement, anticipating her command to *check-it-out,* his signal to investigate and ensure no danger loomed.

Before she could move, a coffee-dark streak of fur leaped into her arms. The cat's bottlebrush tail echoed Shadow's concern, and September's mouth turned dry with fear. She briefly hugged Macy and brushed aside her long disheveled locks that matched the Maine Coon's fur. Even the stark lock of white hair at September's temple matched Macy's snowy bib. The cat's tilted green eyes, twin to September's, glowed a stoplight warning. Macy shivered. Even the cat reacted to Shadow's concern.

The dog's concern heightened the foreboding that had lived inside September as long as she could remember, despite knowing the ghosts from the past couldn't hurt her. It had taken a year since moving home to Texas for her to begin to heal. Shadow's solid presence and the purring warmth of Macy anchored September in the here-and-now. *They* were real. *They* were chosen family. The crawly sensation on the back of her neck mocked her newfound confidence.

September jumped out of bed, berating herself and silencing the what-ifs. Shadow's alert had been silent, not the full-on bark-warning given for a household intruder. Besides, the house alarms hadn't triggered. She took a calming breath with that realization. Clear the house, and then check the grounds outside.

With a plan in place, September hugged Macy again, and plopped the cat back onto the bed. Best to lock the cat in her bedroom and keep him out of harm's way. Macy didn't need more stress on his heart.

She showed the cat her closed fist. He obediently sat and began self-grooming, a way to calm himself down. September wished she had the ability to self-medicate with purrs.

September cautiously opened the bedroom door, stepped outside with the dog, then closed and latched the door. Shadow pressed against her, and she knelt and gave him a quick hug before signaling with the silent hand-wave command to *check-it-out*.

He bounded ahead, a silent black wraith invisible in the dark. She could track his progress from his thumping paw-jumps down the stairs, claw scrabbling on the wooden entry, and huffing breath as he tasted the air from room to room.

Finally, after clearing the house, Shadow raced back up the stairs, sat before her, and barked once. Her shoulders relaxed, and her grin nearly split her face.

"Baby-dog, what a good dog!" Not such a baby-dog anymore, with his first birthday nearly here, just a week after Valentine's Day. Her first shepherd Dakota taught her to love again, but Shadow became her heart.

She followed him down the stairs, encouraged when her knee gave barely a twinge. After surgery repaired the injury, physical therapy— what she called specialized torture—had her nearly back to normal even though she hated water therapy. After weeks of therapy, she could tread water for twenty minutes without breaking a sweat.

September paused in the office/music room. Playing her cello honored the memory of her old instrument. The gift from Combs and her new circle of friends meant perhaps a new life was possible, too.

September debated calling Combs to come check out the house. But no, she had to take charge of her life. Calling for help meant her stalker still controlled her from his jail cell. Courage meant moving forward despite the fear, and she wanted to be independent.

She still couldn't believe someone like Detective Jeff Combs— handsome, smart, accomplished—wanted to be with her. He'd promised no pressure, yet he wouldn't take no for an answer. So after several "not-a-date" casual lunches or dinners with friends, a couple of coffee meetings, and countless phone calls and texts, September surprised herself by saying yes to a for-real formal date.

Butterflies threw a party in her midsection. It felt good.

The kitchen's stained glass windows usually splashed the slate floor with peacock colors but sunrise wouldn't arrive for another two hours. Several phone messages beckoned on the landline reserved for her pet tracking and behavior consulting business, and September resisted the urge to review them. They could wait.

Shadow insisted something outside needed attention. It was his job to *check-it-out* whenever they returned home, or visited somewhere new. Anything different—a sound, a smell—could set off his alert, and she'd rather Shadow err on the side of caution. Even if they found nothing she didn't want to discourage the dog by ignoring his concern. Training never stopped, after all. She'd learned the hard way to trust her gut, and her dog. Shadow yawned and stretched, but his tail continued to signal his agitation.

Six months ago, she'd have locked the bedroom door and called the police. No more, not after what she'd survived in the last few weeks. She'd take her dog for a walk, and check out the property, like any other normal person. *Let it be a squirrel or raccoon.*

Shadow spun and twirled, nearly running into the wall in his excitement when she slipped on her coat, and stuffed bare feet into mud-caked garden shoes. She grabbed his leash on the way to the door.

"*Sit. Wait.*" She bent to hook the leash to Shadow's collar, and unlocked the kitchen door to the back patio, keyed in the security, and switched on the outside lights. If someone intended harm, the lights would either flush them out or send them scurrying on their way. With luck, any interlopers would be kids taking a dare to trespass on the notorious property. Nobody had any legitimate business being out here so early at five-frickin' o'clock. She slammed the door shut. It had a nasty habit of unlatching and swinging open in the wind.

No stars broke through the overcast sky, and the setting moon's glow tarnished heavy clouds. She should have pulled on a pair of sweats. The down-filled coat, a remnant from her years in Chicago, made her look like the Michelin Man, but covered only her upper thighs. Despite the muggy atmosphere, her bare legs chilled in the sixty-degree temperature.

She couldn't walk too fast in the sloppy garden shoes, and the dog adjusted his gait but remained insistent. Every time he paused to sniff, she found herself dodging one of the dozens of wind chimes she'd hung from every available spot. They served as a low-tech security system. The tinkle of bells, clatter of shells, and rattle of pottery shards played a counterpoint to the clop-shuffle-clop of her awkward shoes on the brick pathway.

She stepped off bricks and into grass when they rounded the house, and the soil squished. The rain finally stopped last night, at least for a while, but the countywide flash flood warnings continued. February more often unleashed ice storms that coated trees, broke branches and downed phone and power lines, so nobody complained about the extra rain. Except maybe her garden, if the plants hadn't drowned. Maybe they'd all die, and she'd have a good excuse to get rid of the roses that had become thorny memories of past pain.

Shadow led her to the wooden ladder next to the carriage house/garage. She'd created the set up as part of his training. You never knew what a search might require of a tracking dog, even climbing a ladder. She'd never met a dog so hungry to learn new things. He sniffed the area thoroughly before moving on.

September scanned the end of the driveway. A pair of carriage lamps on each side spilled light through the bars of the closed green gate, throwing jailhouse shadows in her path. No traffic lit the county road. She started to relax. Maybe the intruder had left. Shadow hadn't alerted to anything yet. *Trust the dog.*

He slowly made his way down the drive, and stuck his nose through the gate, tasting the air. He huffed, and pulled harder, and she noticed an old car parked some distance away, half hidden beneath a live oak. Her throat tightened as Shadow delicately sniffed one side of the gate. His nose hit the ground.

Okay then. She squared her shoulders. "*Seek,* Shadow. *Seek!*"

He towed her quickly up the other half-circle of the drive. September could barely keep up and cursed her decision to wear the sloppy shoes. Shadow dragged her up the front steps, exploring the front door's brick landing. Her heart thumped faster.

The dog continued to track his prey. He pulled September off the side of the front steps, across the lawn and padded quickly around to the other side of the house. They'd made a full circle. The dog moved faster and faster, signaling the target was near. His head came up.

Shadow's tension traveled up the leash and she trembled in response. His bristled fur made him look half again as large when he stalked stiff legged toward the kitchen door that now stood ajar. No wind had tugged it open; she'd latched the door securely.

His deep-throated roar shattered the quiet. September grabbed the leash with both hands to contain Shadow's sudden lunge. He wasn't a Schutzhund-trained protection dog, but after what they'd gone through together, Shadow had every right to be defensive when a stranger invaded their home.

September put a hand on his ruff, and he quieted into a down position, but continued to shake and huff with tension. She had to steady her own voice, outrage as much as fear fueling her emotions.

"Who's there? I'll send in the dog." At her words Shadow lept to his feet. This time, September didn't correct him, but watched when Shadow whined and cocked his head, listening. She wished she'd collected her gun from the SUV's glove box while they'd been near the garage, or brought along her cell phone to call Combs for backup. Screw being self-sufficient, she'd welcome some help. But they were on their own. She'd have to trust Shadow to do his job.

September leaned down, stroked both sides of Shadow's face, and he wagged at her touch. She unhooked the leash but held his collar a moment longer, and whispered. "Good-dog, Shadow. You know what to do." She spoke the command full-voice. "*Check-it-out,*" and released his collar.

Shadow sprang forward, claws scrabbling on the slate floor of the kitchen. He paused, then dropped his nose and traced the scent of the stranger's tread. September edged inside, and stood in the doorway to watch him work. His tail wagged with excitement. Shadow loved hide and seek games.

He tested the edge of the table where someone must have touched before he raced from the kitchen to the adjoining dining/living room. September hurried to keep up, but he easily outran her.

She didn't bother to switch on lights. Scent lit up rooms for a dog brighter than any lamp. Shadow raced into the dark living room, sniffed past the big table and across the carpet until his claws tap-danced on the wooden entry, with September in his wake.

September nearly ran into Shadow when he stopped to nose the handle on the front door. The deadbolt and other locks remained engaged, though. His head whipped around, attention drawn to the music/office room. A split second later, September heard the soft sobbing breath, too, and tore after the sound.

Shadow blocked the doorway, lay down, and barked once, his signal of a successful find.

The soft snuffling came from the kneehole of the desk. Someone as small as a kid. They'd have to be small to have wiggled through the bars on the green gate.

"Come out. I know you're in there." September took a cautious step into the room, and finally turned on the stained glass lamp. "Good-dog, Shadow. *Wait.*"

A girl called back. A tremor in her voice. "I only want to talk. Please don't send the dog after me."

Shadow wagged and stuck his head forward, but didn't break the *wait* command. He'd gotten better about that. His attitude, more excitement than defense, bolstered September's confidence. If the dog showed no fear, she'd trust his judgment.

"Come out from under there. Shadow won't hurt you. Unless you do something stupid." She stood with elbows wide, chest out, and tried to quiet her noisy breathing. Nobody showed up at five in the morning and walked into a stranger's house.

Shadow tipped his head, looking quizzical as the stranger finally pushed the chair away from the desk, and cautiously crawled out of the hiding spot.

"Where'd you come from? Who are you?" She softened her words for Shadow's sake when his ears went down and he yawned and turned away. Despite his scary size, shepherds were sensitive and he didn't like loud voices.

"Came from Chicago. Claire O'Dell." She answered quickly, but moved with slow caution to put the chair between herself and Shadow. "I parked outside your gate, I rang the bell, and when nobody came, I walked around the house. I've called you before, but you never answered, never returned my calls." Her tone became strident. "So I had to come. Beg you to help."

Not a girl, but a petite woman stood trembling, gaze locked on Shadow. Claire's head barely came level with September's shoulders. The whites of her eyes shined in the dim light, and she held up her hands in surrender. "Is he going to bite me?" Her voice traveled up an octave.

"No, he won't bite. Sit down already." September's exasperation made Shadow slick back his ears. "But stop staring at him, no dog likes that." She waited until Claire perched on the edge of the desk chair. "I'm calling the police."

"Oh no, you can't." She wrung her hands. "If you call the police, my little girl will die." Claire sobbed.

Shadow broke his *wait* command. With an apologetic glance at September for disobeying, he trotted over to the stranger, and licked clean her tears.

Chapter 2

Kelvin Quincy's dreams had come true. He'd waited ages for this and couldn't wait to rub everyone's face in his success. Not that he would. He'd act modest and classy, like the stuck up District Attorney, but he'd gloat on the inside.

Kelvin nursed two decades of professional hurt. He'd been passed over for promotions, denied raises he deserved, and relegated to the background time after time. His credentials should have put him over the top when he ran for DA, but instead, the public bought into the pretty skirt, prettier face, and Lollipop TV sound bites.

He couldn't do sweetness and light if you dunked him in syrup, even though he'd never lost his west Texas drawl. On a woman, it sounded sexy but it turned Kelvin into a backwoods hick. His acne-scarred face, balding head and geeky-good grades didn't help so he'd compensated with bodybuilding and tattoos in college and gone overboard. Now Kelvin tried to cultivate a classier appearance. Most of his extra income went toward three-piece suits (not those cheapo off the rack kind, either), silk bow ties, designer suspenders, and tailored shirts with French cuffs and signature cuff links.

Kelvin got into the law to see justice served. He'd been a team player. But he gave and gave and gave, provided the brains and behind-the-scenes support, and stayed invisible with nothing to show for his good works. Although surrounded by less qualified and talented individuals, Kelvin ran a hamster-wheel life while others received acclaim and praise. *If you ain't—aren't—the first horse over the finish line, you get real damn tired of the view.*

No more. This time, *Kelvin* would get the credit. *Kelvin* would be a hero. Sure, he'd have to bend the rules a bit, but the world celebrated shades of gray. It'd be worth stepping up to help kids, put away a bad guy, and line his pocket at the same time. This time *Kelvin* would get everything he deserved and more. Win-win, all the way around. Well, except for the nasty-ass guest he expected anytime.

The intercom buzzed. Kelvin had a tiny office space in the first floor of a converted warehouse. They hadn't yet turned on the AC, so he ran the overhead fan on high. It squealed and wobbled and he prayed it wouldn't unscrew itself from the ceiling. Part of the rent included a receptionist to serve the entire building, but she apparently had stepped away. Kelvin pressed the button to answer.

"It's me, Sunny. Open up."

He smiled, and pushed the release. "Come on in. He's not here yet."

Sunny Babcock sashayed into the tiny office, her neon orange hair in a ponytail, and pulled up one of the rolling chairs. She folded her lithe figure into it. "Tell me again why you don't have the cops staking out this place? They've searched for this guy for six months."

"Don't ask questions. That's the deal." He came around the desk and balanced his narrow butt on the edge. "I'm paying you good money to do as you're told, Sunny. Already gave you the background on this and paid up front. And there'll be a whole lot more, a huge bonus, when we pull this off. So don't second guess."

He'd been Sunny's defense attorney on some minor brush-ups with the law over the years. They'd gone to high school together, and later both got into tattoos and hunting at the same time. He'd lost his taste for hunting, but not tattoos, or Sunny. They had a history, and Kelvin had intimate knowledge of one of Sunny's illegal passions. That's why he needed her in on this. It also gave him more leverage to keep her leashed.

"Fine. You pay, I'll play." She narrowed her sky blue eyes. "I'm already on the inside, but you have to promise I walk away clean. These folks don't take kindly to informants. I need enough to disappear after."

"Sure, Sunny. I need your eyes and ears letting me know the exact time and place for the meet. We need to catch them in the act, not too early or too late. Can't be like last time, where all the witnesses protected each other. And if you hear even a hint that something could derail this, squash it flat." She'd helped him out as a freelance investigator in the past, but he'd never before had so much riding on a case. "You vouch for me, and get me on the inside." For once, his biker tats and low profile would work to his advantage. "Once the event's a go, there's no turning back. I'll call it in, give you the high sign. Get the hell out of Dodge before the cavalry arrives."

"You sure you got the stones for it? Takes more than my say, Kelvin. If you want to be more than a *spectator*, it'll take more than money. Give them something that's, shall we say, indicative of your intentions."

"Like what?"

"I'll set up intros, and as good faith, you deliver some bait." Her brows knit at his expression. "Don't ask. You know exactly what I mean. You won't keep your hands clean on this one. To catch a fish and especially monster whales, you need bait." She nodded. "That's how you play your part to prove you're serious. Sooner rather than later, too."

Damn. He smoothed his shaved head, stood and walked back around the desk so she wouldn't see his expression. Nothing for it, though. If it would put a stop to everything, then a bit of sacrifice would be necessary. The buzzer sounded again.

This time the receptionist announced the visitor. "Doctor Gerald Baumgarten to see you."

Sunny stood, and Kelvin straightened and buttoned his coat. "Yes, send him in." Kelvin walked to the door, opened it and kept his face carefully neutral.

The Doctor stood so tall he had to duck to miss the ceiling fan. He wore a floor length bat-black cowboy duster that turned his pale face and silver hair ghostly. His expression didn't change as flat gray eyes scanned the cramped space, flicking over and dismissing Sunny until finally lighting on Kelvin.

A chill raised gooseflesh, but Kelvin didn't react. He closed the door and motioned to an empty chair. "I'm Kelvin Quincy. This is Sunny Babcock, my associate. An honor to meet you, sir. We've heard a lot about you." He stuck out his hand.

The doctor stared at the hand, and took a seat without shaking. "What?"

Kelvin glanced at Sunny. "Excuse me?" Kelvin hurried to the chair behind the desk and urged Sunny to sit. She shook her head, and instead leaned against the wall, pursing her lips and watching.

"What have you heard about me, Kelvin Quincy? You said a lot."

Sunny started to say something but the Doctor cut her off.

"I know you. From TV. Hog Heaven, episode 21 and 27, Sunny "The Babe" Babcock and her handsome hounds." He cocked his head. "Where are your handsome hounds?" He swiveled his chair to include Kelvin. "Do you have handsome hounds, too?"

His monotone voice and metallic eyes gave Kelvin the creeps. "Uhm, well I have one dog. A big guy, but he wouldn't hurt a flea."

"Dogs don't hurt fleas, fleas hurt dogs. They bite dogs, the flea saliva makes allergic dogs itch and they carry tapeworms, *ehrlichiosis*, *babesiosis*, Lyme disease, Rocky Mountain spotted fever, and plague." He paused. "Dogs hurt dogs, too. In fights. You know about dogfights? I need a dogfight, people who fight dogs. Bad people, but useful. You will connect me with these bad people. That's the deal we make today."

Kelvin opened his mouth, closed it, and indicated Sunny should take the lead. She stepped forward. "Gerald, I can—"

"Doctor. I am *Doctor* Baumgarten. You will show me respect, Sunny "The Babe" Babcock." His voice didn't change, but his weird silver eyes made her flinch.

It took a lot to make Sunny flinch. For the first time, Kelvin noticed the gun peeking out from beneath the Doctor's coat, and understood why he wore the duster in this decidedly off-season warm weather.

"Sure, sorry about that, Doctor." Sunny smiled.

She managed to sound pleasant, but that didn't fool Kelvin. He knew her background, knew she hid her feelings instinctively—hard lessons learned as a teen from her bastard of a father—but Kelvin knew her tells. She flexed her fingers, full lips flattened, and the muscle in her jaw twitched. She'd better keep that temper of hers in check.

"I know dogfights, Doctor," she said. "There's a convention, a really big one, in a few days."

"A few? Definition: several or many or three. A couple means two or several. You said, *a few days*. How many days, exactly?"

Before she could respond and possibly blow the deal, Kelvin interjected. "Six days. This weekend. If this damn weather holds."

"Bad words. Lazy language." The Doctor stood up, his coat flapping, and reached for the gun.

"Oh shit...I mean, shoot. Sorry, that slipped out. Please. I'm sorry." Kelvin held out his palms in a conciliatory gesture. "You're right, no cursing, that's not polite. Doctor, please sit down. My apologies."

Kelvin pulled out a handkerchief, monogrammed to match his French cuffs, and mopped his brow. This loose cannon needed to be taken off the streets, for sure. He debated abandoning the plan and calling the cops for half a second, but couldn't let go of the glory he'd gain for bringing down everything this "doctor" stood for.

"Six days." The Doctor left the gun holstered but didn't sit. "Plans made cannot be un-made. I pay you to give me the time and place. Nothing must stop this event. My associates will attend this event to prepare delivering miracle medicine for many children." He paced. "I promised Mother to continue our important work. A promise made cannot be un-made." He stopped pacing. "Promise: a declaration or assurance that one will do a particular thing or that a particular thing will happen."

Kelvin knew that the freak blizzard last November hadn't stopped the Doctor's Rebirth Gathering, either. They'd caught his mother, the brains behind the outfit, he'd always believed, but the Doctor got away. Kelvin could call the cops now but they'd take the credit. No, better to be patient and spring the trap later so they'd catch both the Doctor and his entire drug crew. That would make anyone's career, and show the bozos in Heartland they'd snubbed him for the last time. Now Kelvin had baited the trap, and he needed to lure the Doctor the rest of the way in before slamming the door.

"I'll find out the time and the place." Sunny licked her teeth. "How much?"

Damn it, why can't she keep her mouth shut? "I'll take care of you, Sunny. This deal is between me and the Doctor."

The tall ghost-man stuck his hands in the pockets of the long coat, and pulled out a banded stack of bills from each. "First payment." He tossed a bundle first to Kelvin and then Sunny. "Another when you give me time and place. And final payment when our work is successful and I'm far far far away."

"Holy Jes—" Sunny clamped her mouth shut before finishing the oath.

Kelvin experienced the same surprised delight. A hundred-dollar bill on each side sandwiched the inch-thick bundle. He'd finally get out of this shit-hole of an office. But he didn't dare say that aloud. "It's a deal." He stuck out his hand again.

The Doctor stared. "Germs on hands make people sick. Do you want to make me sick?"

"No, of course not." Kelvin dropped his hand.

"That's good. You now will make me a promise. That's a written or oral declaration given in exchange for something of value that binds the maker to do, or forbear from, a certain specific act and gives to the person to whom the declaration is made the right to expect and enforce performance or forbearance." The Doctor paused. "Repeat after me: *I promise, Doctor.*"

Kelvin shrugged. "Okay, I promise." Kelvin held one hand behind his back, crossing his fingers like a scared kid. He smiled, faking confidence but sweat trickled down his neck.

"That's good." The Doctor turned to Sunny. "Now you say it, Sunny "The Babe" Babcock. Say, *I promise, Doctor.*"

She didn't hesitate. "Yeah, whatever. I promise Doctor." But she didn't look up. She instead busily counted her stack.

"Promise made cannot be un-made. Make it happen." For a moment, the Doctor's face creased into a forced but practiced smile, one he clearly intended to put people at ease.

Instead, it gave Kelvin more chills than the gun's presence.

Chapter 3

September carried the pot of coffee to the stained glass table, topped off her own "son-of-a-peach" mug, and poured Claire another cup.

The woman offered a tremulous smile, pushed black curly hair out of her blue eyes, and took a sip. Shadow nudged her with his nose, and Claire tentatively patted his head. "You'd think he's mean with that scary ragged ear, but he's actually nice." She sounded surprised.

"Shadow and I consider that a badge of honor." The gunshot that took Shadow's ear tip could have killed her instead. Shadow had every reason to be suspicious of strangers, yet he still met the world with wide-eyed puppy optimism. She shouldn't be surprised he'd responded to Claire's tears the same way he did hers. Dogs read and reacted to emotions much more strongly than people imagined. Shadow had a gift for knowing when and how to soothe distress.

"Thanks for not calling the police." Claire stopped petting Shadow, and he whined and nosed her hand.

"It's only a reprieve, until you tell me what this is all about." September took another swallow. Something told her she needed to get fully caffeinated to meet this day.

"I drove straight through the night, thank God the roads were good this time. So tired, I'm not thinking straight, or I never would've come into your home. I've never done anything like that before." Claire's swollen eyes must have cried miles of tears. She suffered from terminal bed head, endearing on a youngster but tragic on an adult. The constellation of freckles dusting her nose and cheeks stood out in stark contrast to a ghost-pale complexion born of weeks of worry. "There's a lot of things I've never done before. Things change when you have kids." The words were bittersweet.

"You got that right." September rose and crossed to Shadow's food bowl. So many things these days reminded her of Steven, her sister's autistic son. She'd first trained Shadow to be Steven's service dog. Legally, she had no kids, other than the four-legged wonders she lived with. And she liked it that way.

Shadow rose, shook himself, and eagerly headed to the filled dish September set on the floor. "Must be pretty important to drive from Chicago to break into my house. What's the deal?" She opened a drawer, took out a bottle of pills and rattled it, and Macy appeared in the stairway. "Don't mind me, I need to feed and medicate the troops."

Claire stared as the shaggy twenty-pound feline gave her a cursory once over, pointedly ignored her further, and leaped from a standing start to the top of the refrigerator. "Like I said, I tried to call you. Left a bunch of messages since last November, and never got an answer."

September froze. So, that's what this was about. "Macy, pill time. Open." The cat obligingly opened his mouth to accept the tiny pill. September made a "click" sound with her tongue, and Macy trilled with eagerness for the treat reward.

"Did that cat just. . .? Never mind." Claire turned away, swallowed a slug of coffee, and then studied the empty cup as though it held answers to the universe. "My daughter Tracy just turned six. She's autistic."

Like Steven. "I can't help you." She'd put that horror behind her, and wanted no reminders. Besides, it was a police matter now. September filled Macy's bowl with food, and set it on top of the refrigerator out of dog nose-sniffing range.

"My husband and I, we prayed for a miracle. And we got it."

"Claire, I can't help you." She stared into the sink, refused to turn around. Her sister April prayed for that same miracle for Steven, and it nearly got them both killed.

"They took all our savings; we'll lose our house. Maybe our marriage." She knuckled her eyes, and her voice turned fierce. "But it's all worth it because we got our Tracy. Our little girl."

September finally faced Claire. "But that has nothing to do with me. Don't you understand? I'm sorry, but there's nothing I can do, even if I wanted to." September resented Claire's stinging litany. "My sister pulled me into that mess. Steven got out of the hospital, the psych ward, last month, and April's still recovering from being shot." September crossed to the smaller woman, and spoke with gentle firmness. "People died, Claire. I'm sorry about your daughter, but Tracy isn't the only one hurt, and I can't go back in time and make it go away. Believe me, I wish I could. At least the people responsible are in jail." She took a breath, knowing what Claire wanted. "There's no more medicine."

"You're wrong." Claire straightened in her chair, and pushed the cup aside. "Not everyone is in jail. That's why I'm here. Those of us at the last Rebirth Gathering got a supply of the medicine, and a promise we'd get refills as needed. We get the medicine every six weeks by mail as long as we pay." She sounded bitter.

The news hit September like a gut punch. "The Ghost? Gerald Baumgarten? He's still selling that poison?"

"DOCTOR Baumgarten." Claire corrected her, still defending the lunatic. "It's not poison. He saved my daughter, and hundreds like her, from being locked inside themselves. I'll be forever grateful for that. He says the cost went up because he had to go underground." Her chin jutted out with accusation.

Shadow leaned against September's thigh, and she absently stroked the dog's neck. He could tell when her stress levels skyrocketed, and right now, Mt. Vesuvius was a sparkler in comparison.

Claire's voice shook. "Three nights ago, Tracy disappeared, and it's your fault."

September's legs turned to Jell-O. Another child lost, needing to be found? She couldn't play that emotional hide and seek game, not again.

"I can't call the police. They'd take Tracy away. They only care about catching the Doctor. They'd be like you. Prejudiced because of what happened, never mind our children's needs. I can't let that happen, not to Tracy, not to any of the kids." Claire clenched her fists, clearly struggling for control.

Shadow whined and pushed against September. "I'm sorry, I truly am. But you're wasting time. How could a six-year-old get all the way here from Chicago?" She'd escaped that city nearly a decade ago, and would never willingly return. Bad enough she visited the place in her nightmares. She'd never move forward as long as the past kept dragging her back. Her mouth turned sour, signaling an imminent flashback, and September sank to the floor and opened her arms to Shadow's insistent nudging. She grabbed him like a furry life preserver.

"Tracy came here. Where it all began." Claire sank to the floor next to September, and spoke with a mother's passion, begging for her child's life. "Soon as we discovered her gone, I called my friend Elaine. Her son Lenny also got the treatment last November, and he disappeared the same time. We think they're together."

It made no sense. "Kids on the Spectrum often wander. You can't know they're here." That's why she'd originally trained Shadow, to keep Steven safe. Shadow only became her service dog when Steven spent months in the hospital after the drug fiasco. "Just call the police. You wouldn't need to say anything about their meds."

"Lenny took Elaine's van. We know they're on the road, and we know they planned to come here." She pulled a folded piece of paper from her pocket, smoothed it, and handed it to September. "I don't know why they're here, but Lenny left this note."

September reluctantly took the page, torn none too neatly from a spiral bound notepad, and smoothed it against the slate floor. It featured a beautifully rendered drawing with a few block letters. She saw a van traveling on a road, complete with patched tires and rust spots. A boy with short brown hair sat in the driver's seat, while a pretty girl with freckles and black pigtails peered out the passenger window, holding a green dinosaur in one hand and pill bottle filled with blue and white capsules in the other. The detail amazed her.

"It says, 'No worry Tracy and me fix.' Nothing about coming here." September tried to give back the page.

Claire tapped one corner of the page at the end of the highway. "There, see that? They're both on the highway, Lenny driving and Tracy with her medication and Grooby, the dinosaur. And there at the end of the road, the destination."

September stood up. "It's a city, with the red sunset reflecting in the windows. Lenny's a talented boy, but it could be any city."

"Look closer. Lenny's art communicates both literally and symbolically. Sometimes it's hard to understand but Elaine's gotten very good at reading his messages." Claire stabbed the paper again. "There are exactly twelve pills left in Tracy's bottle, and they left three days ago so she has only two or three days left before they're gone.

You know what happens when they stop taking the meds. I know you do. It happened to Steven, I read about it in all the news reports. "

September flinched. Other children, including Steven, suffered psychosis when the medicine stopped. Her nephew stole his father's antique gun, wounded the Doctor's mother, and a near miss blasted Shadow's ear. Only intensive therapy over the past several months allowed Steven to leave the Dallas hospital but he'd never be a normal child.

"Please, September. Look again. And then if you don't see what Elaine and I saw, I'll ... I'll go away and leave you alone." Her voice broke.

Reluctantly, September examined the paper. A frantic parent saw special meaning in everything, and she had no wish to deny that hope, and hurt Claire any further.

Damn Gerald Baumgarten to hell. His accomplices including his recovered mother awaited trial, but he'd escaped, disappeared despite the manhunt. She wondered if the authorities knew the lunatic's vision survived, and that he continued to devastate families with his quack drug, while sucking them dry of hope and funds. No parent deserved such anguish. Now Claire wanted to drag September back into the nightmare.

"Right there, at the city destination. In the windows. I saw it driving in over the hill into town as the sun came up over the buildings. What do you see?" Claire prompted, eyes impossibly bright.

Squinting, September held the page closer and then sucked in a breath. Rendered in intricate detail, Lenny had drawn signature buildings of Heartland, Texas in stylized but recognizable detail. To make the point irrefutable, what she'd thought to be sunlight reflection instead named the place. In the window of each building shined a tiny red heart.

Claire smiled with triumph. "You see it, don't you? You do."

September looked from the page to the woman, and Claire's expression acknowledged her triumph; gaining a reluctant ally. Even if she'd wanted to, September couldn't deny that Claire had won this round.

Hands on hips and voice fierce, Claire stood as tall as her petite frame allowed. "You're going to find my daughter."

Chapter 4

Detective Jeff Combs took the rinsed plates from his daughter Melinda, and added them to the dishwasher. He kept an eye on her younger brother, Willie, as his son dumped clean laundry on the couch. The boy soon had sorted a small pile of his own socks and underwear. Melinda rattled silverware under the faucet, and dropped them into the dish rack.

Combs treasured these times spent with his kids, even on mundane chores. He didn't get much time with his kids since the divorce. It had been a rough few years for their family, especially Melinda, his little drama-queen.

"Hey Melinda." Willie snagged a pair of his sister's hot pink undies, wrinkled his nose, and twirled it in the air around his finger, making sure she could see. "These'd make a great sling-shot." He launched them toward her.

Her face flushed red. She'd turned thirteen, and no teenage girl wanted her brother—or her dad—to notice, let alone handle, her undies.

Combs hid a smile.

She tried to snatch them, missed, and the dog grabbed them and ran, a white streak of fluffy fur. "Dad. Make him quit." Melinda chased down Kinsler and had to play tug with the terrier mix to retrieve her underwear. The dog shook his head and sneezed, the tan saddle spot and contrasting ears striking against his snowy coat. Combs could swear the dog smiled, dark eyes twinkling through the curtain of disheveled fur.

"Quit bothering your sister. Finish folding your own laundry." He tried not to laugh. He'd been a pest to his sister at that age, too.

Willie launched another bit of lace toward the dog. "Kinsler likes them. Hey boy, go guard second base."

He'd named the dog after Ian Kinsler when he still played for the Texas Rangers. Willie wanted to change Kinsler's name when Ian deserted The Rangers to go play ball for the Detroit Tigers, but Combs convinced him that would confuse the dog.

"William Stanley Combs, stop bothering your sister and put away your laundry. I promised Rick you'd get chores done before he brings your mom home from the hospital. You may have the day off but I have to work. Detective Gonzales picks me up in fifteen minutes."

He'd never imagined such an arrangement when Cassie left him for Rick-the-Prick. Normally Combs wouldn't lift a finger to help his ex-wife and her new husband. She'd been a bitch during the divorce, and made him fight to get joint custody. Now with her inability to care for their kids, and her CPA husband's fourteen-hour tax season rush, he could sue for sole custody, but couldn't afford the court costs. Besides, he didn't want to put his kids through that tug-of-war, and his job schedule with the Heartland Police Department made time a challenge.

So, he made a deal with the devil. It gave him a guilty sense of satisfaction to know Cassie would hate being beholden to him, even if these days, Cassie wasn't aware of much.

Melinda caught the dog and retrieved her underwear. She stuck her tongue out at Willie when she thought Combs couldn't see, a gesture far younger than her teenager status. "Stupid dog. Now they need washing again, yuck." She disappeared into the laundry room.

"You need to cut your sister some slack, champ." Combs finished rinsing and loading the breakfast dishes, and closed the dishwasher.

Willie slowly folded his clothes. "Uncle Rick says you're only helping because Mom's sick and won't get better."

"That's a lie." Melinda flounced back into the room. "Tell him, Dad." She punched Willie on the arm. "Don't say things like that, it's bad luck. Besides, they can cure all kinds of things, even cancer these days. Right Dad?"

Combs pretended to wash his hands, to give himself time to form an answer. "I'm not a doctor, Melinda. I don't know if it's like treating cancer. Rick hasn't shared any details." Before her scowl melted into tears, he hurried to add, "But you're right. Lots of new medicines and treatments happen all the time."

She punched Willie again. "See, brat? And you're folding wrong."

He clutched his arm. "Bossy-pants."

"Stupid face." She squealed when the dog leaped onto the pile of laundry, splitting the pair, barking and dancing, scattering the clothes onto the floor. "Daddy. Make them stop."

"Both of you, that's enough. Melinda, pick up the clothes."

"But Dad, Willie's the one—"

"Don't want to hear it." He turned to Willie. "Take your dog outside. Keep him on the leash, or he'll try to catch every squirrel on the planet. And stay out of the mud, or I'll hose you both off. With ice-cold water. Got it?" He rubbed his eyes. Probably not a good incentive. Both Willie and the dog would relish a game of hose tag.

Willie ducked his head, and whistled for the dog. Kinsler barked—he had an extraordinarily loud bark—and the pair clambered noisily out the door into the fenced back yard. Before Willie could attach the leash, the dog dodged away. Combs sighed.

Melinda glowered. "Not fair. He's such a brat lately. Why does he always get off the hook?" She picked up the spilled laundry, and threw each piece one by one back into the basket. "Now he and Kinsler'll track all over and I'm the one who has to clean up the mess. Uncle Rick's barely here anymore." She sulked.

"Nobody said life's fair. He's your little brother, and now you're a teenager, I expect more from you. This isn't easy for any of us. I need you to take more responsibility." He crossed and pulled her into his arms. God, she was so much like Cassie, a redheaded firecracker ready to explode. She stiffened, and pulled away from his hug. That hurt but didn't surprise him.

"He won't listen to me." She turned her back, concentrating on the clothes. "How can I be responsible if Willie won't listen?"

Combs ran a hand through his hair, and then searched his pocket when his cell phone buzzed. "I'll talk to him, okay? Dump Willie's on his bed. He can fold his own stuff later. Wouldn't want you to touch boy undies."

"Oh, Dad." Melinda scooped the remaining laundry back in the basket, and carried it down the hall.

The phone call brightened his mood. Talking to September always made him smile, especially since she'd finally relaxed enough to go out with him. He couldn't wait to surprise her with his belated Valentine's Day plans. She refused to go out that day, saying it made things too serious, but that didn't mean he couldn't turn a later date into a romantic evening. She needed someone to spoil her for a change.

Melinda called from her brother's room. "Dad, it stinks in here."

"Then hold your breath." He answered the phone, still smiling. "What can I do for my favorite lady?"

"Hi Jeff, sorry to bother you at work."

He didn't correct her, and checked the clock. Gonzales should be here any minute. "No problem, the day's still young. What's up?"

"Can you recommend a private investigator?" Her voice sounded hushed, as if she didn't want someone to hear.

Combs crossed to the front door to watch for his ride. "Why? What's wrong?"

"Don't worry. It's not for me. A friend asked."

Melinda came back into the room, and checked the oven. "Your breakfast burrito is ready."

Combs mouthed 'thanks' as Melinda poured coffee into a mug and secured the lid before he answered September. "Sure I can't help?"

"For now, she wants to keep it private. I found out this morning when she dropped by the house a couple hours ago."

He checked the clock and frowned. Awfully early for someone to stop by. She sounded nervous, too, and he wondered who among their friends needed a P.I. He knew all of September's local friends. She'd not been back home in Heartland long enough to make many new connections.

"There's a guy I considered working with last year." He'd nearly left the police force when summarily demoted over a scandal. It ultimately blew over but had been the straw that broke his marriage's back. "If he's available, I'll ask him to reach out to you directly." He cleared his throat. "On another note, I want to pick your brain about an animal issue."

She laughed. "Kinsler acting up again? Or your sister's cat, Simba?"

"Kinsler's a mess. Acts demented around squirrels and keeps digging out from under the fence. But your cat tips did the trick." Simba had been Mom's cat and probably still missed her, hence the litter box indiscretions.

Melinda leaned across the counter. "Is that September? See if she'll take the mutt off our hands." She batted her eyelashes, clearly not meaning it.

Combs shook his finger at her. He knew she loved the dog as much as Willie did, if not more. "September, we're working on something up your alley and the Captain authorized you to consult on the case. We got a lead on a dogfight ring."

Her voice turned cold with outrage. "Here in Heartland? That's disgusting. What is wrong with people?" She took a beat, and he could imagine her finger combing her hair, a nervous but endearing habit. "Does this have something to do with the dogfight bust two weeks ago in Oklahoma? You know, the ASPCA has a whole division devoted to shutting down dogfights. They even have a veterinary forensics team. That's how they nailed Michael Vick."

Combs turned around when a car honked outside, and nodded at Melinda when she held out the hot burrito in a bag, with the coffee ready. "Listen September, Gonzales just got here. We can meet later, and I'll share what I can and pick your brain."

"Sure. I'm in and out today, too. Got a consult about a stray cat that ought to be a hoot. I keep waiting for the number of AWOL pets to diminish, now that the wildlife die-off has abated. And then thanks to you, I'm playing cello over at the theater." He could hear the smile in her voice, and was delighted she enjoyed the gift so much.

She'd created a unique business tracking lost pets with Shadow. Combs admired her ability to celebrate happy reunions as well as accept sad outcomes. The latter seemed to outnumber the live finds. He knew from his own experience with missing persons that finding the body, while tragic, also offered closure to loved ones. Maybe it was the same for pet owners.

"Have a good show at the theater. Do I say break a leg? Or a string?" Combs grinned when she laughed. After he disconnected the call, he quickly texted a brief note to the P.I. for September. He set his phone down beside the coffee. "Where's my coat, honey?"

Melinda retrieved it from the back of one of the kitchen chairs. "You promised to talk to Willie."

"Right, right." He hurried to the back door, cracked it open and shouted into the back yard without stepping outside. "Willie, listen to your sister. When I'm not here, she is the boss of you." He winked at Melinda, and she smiled back as he shut the door. "Melinda, you watch your brother. It's a boy rule to be obnoxious to older sisters, so you'll have to put up with it. Okay? I'm counting on you."

The horn honked again. Melinda offered the bag in one hand and coffee in the other, and once his hands were full, she held the door for him. When she got back inside, she didn't notice he'd left behind his phone.

Chapter 5

September hated withholding details about Claire's missing daughter from Combs. She sympathized with the woman, but she couldn't help directly. Hooking her up with the private investigator salved her guilt.

Claire reentered the study that doubled as September's music room, dabbing her face with a clean hand towel. "Thanks for letting me freshen up, and for helping me find Tracy. And Lenny, too. I promised to keep Elaine updated." Her smile hinted at the attractive young woman beneath the frazzled worry.

Bracing herself for an argument, September tried to let Claire down gently. "I want to help you, I really do."

"I read all the newspaper stories about how you found Steven after he got lost in that blizzard. And how that dog saved your life." Claire watched Shadow and took a seat on the nearby piano bench. "Tracy doesn't have much time." She leaned forward, elbows on her thighs. "You know this town, know the people, and have resources that I don't have."

September had only a handful of connections and Claire's refusal to inform the police cut out Combs. It still amazed her that Combs not only forgave her involvement in his mother's death last November, but also had become one of her dearest friends. Maybe even more than that.

September took a breath, cutting off that thought. "I still think you should call the police." She raised a hand to stop Claire's protest. "Just tell them Lenny's a runaway, or it's a joyride gone on too long, or something. The police can put out a bulletin with the license plate. You have the number?"

"Sure. But I can't risk it." Claire balled her fists. "Believe me, I've thought everything through. If the police find Tracy before we do, they'll call CPS and they'll take my daughter away. You said you'd help."

"I've contacted a private investigator to help."

"Oh." Claire bit her lip. "I thought you'd do this by yourself." Her voice rose, worry the constant undertone. "I can't afford some fancy investigator."

It wasn't her problem. If she had any hope for a normal life, a future without the threat of flashbacks and panic attacks, she couldn't subject herself to constant reminders of the past.

"Claire, I appreciate your confidence in me, but I train dogs and cats, help solve behavior problems, and sometimes Shadow helps me find lost pets." September shook her head. "I don't find missing kids, that's not what I do. You need a professional for that."

"But you found Steven."

"He's my nephew. My sister begged me to help, I couldn't say no. And I got incredibly lucky." She leaned forward in the chair, elbows on her knees. "A private investigator—"

"I drove straight through the night to get here and you blow me off, won't even try?" Claire rose, a thunderous expression making her ugly. "You're a selfish, despicable person, September Day. You got called a hero, but what about Tracy and the other kids? You made the cost go up. If it wasn't for you, Tracy could still get her medicine. She'd be home safe." She breathed heavily, and impatiently swiped tears away.

September bowed her head. Claire and the other parents believed their own version of the truth. The fees would have gone up regardless, but Tracy and Lenny going missing added to the tragedy. "I'll pay for the P.I., but that's all I can do."

"That's right. You can afford to throw money at your problems. I read about your lottery winnings. Must be nice."

September hunched her shoulders. She couldn't save the world, and had enough trouble taking care of herself, despite what the public might think. The winnings had been enough to move home to Heartland, buy this house and renovate it, but medical costs—she owed it to Steven and her sister April—had depleted the balance substantially. That didn't matter, as long as she had a chance for a life now, one without drama.

She cleared her throat, fidgeting. "Do you have a place to stay?"

Claire sank back onto the piano bench, and dropped her face into her hands. "What am I going to do?"

September felt even more like a heel. "You're going to rest. Stay here. I can do that much, there's two extra bedrooms. You can't do anything until I hear from the P.I."

Claire, ready to collapse from nerves, exhaustion, and worry, could have been a lost child herself. "Thank you. I don't mean to be such a bitch; I know I'm asking a lot."

"You're a mom. I get it. And in my world, being a bitch isn't such a bad thing." September's phone ping reminded her the day's busy schedule meant leaving Claire, a virtual stranger, alone in her house, and was surprised it didn't bother her. Well, not much. In the past, the thought might have triggered a panic attack. She *was* better. Besides, with a little luck—and Claire deserved good karma—the promised help from Combs should quickly take Claire off her hands.

Claire yawned. "I am exhausted. But wired, too, you know? There must be something I can do."

"Keeping busy helps. Shadow and I have to go to a behavior consult." Before Claire got upset again, she explained. "We won't be gone long. What's your cell?" They traded phone numbers.

"Tracy took her iPad, and Lenny has a cell phone." Claire yawned again. "The voicemail is full from me and Elaine calling. I don't think it's on. Elaine said Lenny didn't take his charger so the phone may be dead. Both of them do better communicating digitally than verbally."

That sounded familiar. Steven used his iPad or computer almost constantly, a major complaint from Mom, who did the lion's share of caring for the boy these days. She wondered if that would work in Claire's favor. Maybe the P.I. could get the signal traced. She kept the thought to herself, not wanting to add false hope to Claire's already stretched nerves. She also needed to let Combs know about the pill distribution scheme without betraying Claire's confidence.

"While I grab a shower, why don't you put together information for the investigator?" September moved to her small desk and brought up the computer's word processor. "Make a list. What they're wearing, any unique habits, likes and dislikes or behaviors, the car license plate, email and phone number, online sites they frequent, anything and everything. I haven't a clue what could help, so don't leave anything out."

She left Claire busily typing away on the keyboard. Shadow followed her up the stairs and stood guard as September quickly showered and dressed. Macy made a point to apply full body rubs against her legs. "I know, you hate me washing off all your good cat smell, don't you, buddy?" He trilled, and led the way from the bathroom, pausing to nose-touch Shadow before galloping down the stairs.

The doorbell rang. Shadow raced to the front door and waited impatiently for September to join him. On the way, she peered into the nearby office to check on Claire. She had dozed off, head on the desk, and September put a finger to her lips, signaling Shadow to keep silent. That might be the only rest Claire got until they found Tracy.

A tall, lithe figure moved in front of the stained glass sidelights, but sparked no recognition. Shadow snuffled loudly at the bottom of the door, his tail an agitated metronome. His hackles rose and a low growl bubbled deep in his throat.

The bell rang again, followed by knuckles rapping on the door. "Hello?" An impatient voice called out. "Detective Combs sent me, said you need a P.I."

September's shoulders unclenched. "Hold on, let me get the locks. Shadow, *sit. Wait.*" He yawned loudly as she unlocked the several deadbolts. The door swung open, and September stared. The woman was drop-dead gorgeous, with doll-bright orange hair and a china complexion despite swollen blue eyes and runny nose.

"You must be September Day. You're surprised, I get that a lot." The woman dabbed her nose with a tissue. "My business associate got the request and passed it on to me. I'm Sunny Babcock." She noticed Shadow, and her smile widened. "Oh, what a handsome fellow. I adore dogs, have a couple of my own." She held out her gloved fist for a sniff. "What's your name, puppy?"

Shadow slicked back his ears, bared his teeth, and snarled.

Chapter 6

Combs cracked his knuckles as he sat in the passenger seat of the unmarked car. His partner flinched. "What? This?" He cracked them again.

Detective Winston Gonzales pulled the car into the lot outside the police station. "You'll be sorry. It'll turn your knuckles huge and grotesque."

"Says who?" Combs reached for his thermos of coffee, black-no-sugar, after taking a bite from the triple-decker cheese, bacon and sausage breakfast burrito Melinda had made. He had to make up for Gonzales's health kick.

"My granny says so. Grannies always know. They'll tell you so." The smaller man took another bite of his veggie wrap, then carefully wiped his black mustache with a paper napkin as he chewed and swallowed. "September won't like you with grotesque knuckles. Besides, your knuckle cracking makes my teeth hurt as bad as scratching a blackboard."

Combs winced. "You had to say that? And never mind about September." But he smiled.

Gonzales eyed Combs's food choice. "Better than cookies and caffeine, I suppose. Eat up, we've got a meeting in ten minutes." He took another bite, sipped his drink, and balanced the O.J. on the dashboard.

Even seated, Gonzales exuded the confidence of a bantam rooster, and never hesitated to face down men twice his size. Combs could have been partnered with anyone once reinstated as a detective, and counted himself lucky this time around. They'd both been previously partnered with the same career-climbing piece of work, and ironically ended up together.

Others on the force cracked wise about the Mutt and Jeff size difference, but they'd stopped laughing when Combs and Gonzales cleared cases in record time. Because of that success, they'd been tapped to lead the local investigation of a wide-reaching drug ring, operating in a loosely connected group of small cells scattered throughout the Midwest and southern states.

"Talked to September this morning." Combs sipped his coffee.

"Late night into early morning, eh?" Gonzales lifted one eyebrow.

"Wiseass." *He wished.* "She called while I was with the kids. Wanted a favor, so I asked one of my own."

"She going to consult? Yes!" Gonzales pumped his fist, and nearly knocked over his drink.

After the recent Oklahoma bust, one of the perps angled for a reduced sentence with insider info, and connected dots between the drug ring and its distribution system. When Combs cross-matched drug busts with dogfight complaints, the pattern became clear. Now they had departments in five states involved. All they lacked was a dog expert.

It'd been Gonzales's idea to pick September's brain. Combs resisted. He wanted to protect her, and was reluctant to involve her.

"Let's keep it to consulting offsite, Gonzales. Answering questions, suggesting leads, that's enough. She's been to hell and gone." He'd let work take precedence over family in the past. He wouldn't repeat that mistake with September.

"She's stronger than you think." Gonzales held up his hands, palms out. "It's the Captain's idea, his call. And you said she said yes."

"Fine." He wadded the paper bag. Combs could run interference with the home team. Hell, they might not even need September's help, once the Chicago team weighed in.

"Sure, Combs. Whatever you say." Gonzales dabbed his mouth. "Just don't tell September you're keeping her in bubble wrap. She'll go off on your ass."

Combs grinned. True enough. She'd always had a prickly self-preservation designed to keep people at arm's length. That defensive attitude had mellowed now that she finally felt safe. She acted more confident, more relaxed, but took offense at the slightest inclination she received special treatment. Combs tried to respect that and balance it with his desire to shield her from any further hurt.

Combs gulped the rest of his coffee as Gonzales crumpled the wrapping on his own breakfast. They headed inside, Combs adjusting his tie and brushing imaginary crumbs off his coat. Gonzales's perennial spit polished appearance had no need of spiffing up.

Captain Felix Gregory stuck his head out the door of his office as soon as they entered the bullpen, and signaled them to hurry. Through the frosted glass door, Combs could see a tall silhouette.

Gonzales spoke before Combs had a chance. "Sir, we've got our dog expert on board. September Day agreed to consult."

Combs stifled a curse, and covered it with a cough. Sure, the Captain needed to know. He'd have preferred to share that info himself later, if and when they needed her expertise. "She may not be much help. But she'll refer us to resources and answer questions." He glared at Gonzales.

Before they went inside, the Captain stopped them, his voice hushed. "You will extend every courtesy and treat our guest with respect throughout this investigation. Work as a team, no grandstanding, and no keeping secrets to one-up each other. Do I make myself clear?"

Gonzales had to crane his neck upward to meet the Captain's gray eyes. "Of course." He pointedly didn't look at Combs.

Combs wondered at the caution. Neither he nor Gonzales had ever cared about the glory, only wanted justice done. Like all the other cops and detectives on the force, they worked each case with that in mind.

The Captain spoke as he led the way across the room. "We've come full circle." He opened the door, took his place behind the desk, and offered a tight nod to the visiting detective who waited. "Y'all already know each other, so skip the happy reunions for now. Detective Doty, bring us up to speed from the Chicago end."

"Yes sir." Detective Kimberlane Doty towered over Gonzales and stood eye to eye with Combs. She didn't offer to shake hands, unconcerned by the men's reaction.

Combs[s stomach tightened, and a sudden sour taste paralleled his opinion of the woman. He did his best to maintain a stoic expression.

She hadn't changed. Doty still sported the white-blond flattop haircut, tailored pants and jacket, and Amazon warrior stance. Always a competent if not flashy investigator, she'd relied on subterfuge and manipulation of informants to get the inside track. It had gotten a young girl killed on Combs's watch, but Doty managed to wiggle away and leave her then-partner Combs holding the bag. The firestorm nearly destroyed his career, and Combs doubted he'd have returned to the force if Doty hadn't transferred to Chicago.

In Combs's experience, horses don't change their spots. He leaned against the wall, watchful, waiting to hear what she pitched.

Doty pulled out a stick of clove-flavored nicotine gum, noisily unwrapped it, and stuck it in her mouth. "Like the Captain said, we've got a déjà vu situation, gentlemen. That Oklahoma bust two weeks ago produced more than rumors. These drug runners are a cut above the usual scum. Or a cut below, depending on how you view the situation." She popped her gum.

"Distributing through dogfight rings, that's a new twist." Gonzales pulled out his note pad. "Drugs always have a presence, but not in such an organized way."

"True, Gonzales. But we got a sample of what they're running." Doty grinned, making them wait. "Damenia. Sound familiar?"

Combs stood away from the wall. "You're shitting me!" That's why Doty came back to Heartland.

Gonzales licked his pencil and jotted a note before looking up. "Damenia's not a recreational drug the usual suspects get a jones for. Whoever's selling has a very specialized market." He glanced at Combs.

Combs leaned forward. "Doty, that's got to be random. Damenia doesn't produce a high. Nobody's going to get rich off that."

"Give me a little credit. And somebody got rich off it." Doty crossed her arms.

"Sure, I get that." Combs looked at the Captain, and got an encouraging smile from Gonzales. "Why're we going down this old rabbit hole? It's been what, four months, for God's sake. This is the first time it's resurfaced, and the entire country from the FDA and every initial agency out there's been on high alert watching for the stuff." He cracked his knuckles. "With respect, our guest from Chicago jumped the shark on this one."

Doty opened her mouth, but Gonzales cut her off. "Even if there was a black market for Damenia, what parents attend dogfights to pick up a prescription for their autistic kid?" He seemed to enjoy the exchange, too.

Doty's lips pooched out as though she tasted a lemon, clearly unsettled by the challenge to her assumptions. Combs knew that must be a rare experience for her.

Combs kept his voice neutral. "Everybody knows drugs and dog fighting go together. But tying a few pills back to the Blizzard Murders takes us in the wrong direction. We all want to nail the one that got away, but not by ignoring the whale in the bucket. Let's concentrate on the dogfights and drugs angle, shall we?"

"Does seem you're trying to wrangle zebras, Detective Doty, when cows'll do." The Captain leaned back in his chair until it touched the wall. "I'll buy the connection with North Texas. But why now?" His chair creaked. "We've got a dogfight expert on retainer, so let's get her in here." He swiveled to face Combs. "Get the Day woman on the phone and find a time the three of you can confab."

"September Day?" Doty's lip twitched, not quite a sneer but close enough. "Talk about a reunion."

Just like that, the blonde drew blood. Combs's jaw ached with the effort to stay cool. "No need to involve her, not at this point anyway. I'm still waiting for Doty to convince us Damenia isn't her personal McGuffin."

The Captain rocked forward on his chair. "Ms. Day's expertise will be needed regardless." He motioned Doty to continue.

"Thank you, Captain." She unwrapped and stuffed another stick of gum into her mouth. "Timing is suspicious. Remember, we questioned all the families, and they clammed up about any and all details."

Gonzales still wasn't buying it. "So? We figured they got a supply that'd keep them stupid and happy for weeks, maybe even months."

Combs grudgingly put it together. "And it's been months. What would happen if all those kids ran out of Damenia at once?"

"Exactly. Crazy-time. It started about two weeks ago in Chicago. Runaway kids, lots and lots of them." Doty's cud pooched out her cheek until she could've been a cowboy dipping an entire can of Skoal at once. "When I got the tip about Damenia showing up at the dogfight bust, I started looking for more runaways."

"How many kids this time? How many dead?" Gonzales turned green, probably thinking of his own kids.

"Five kids in three different states so far. No deaths yet, but a dozen or more injuries." Doty popped her gum. "They're not attacking anyone this time. Instead, they steal cars, hitchhike, and borrow bikes, all running away from home. Most injuries result from vehicular collisions." She popped another stick of gum in her mouth. "Some are so young they can't see over the dashboard. We talked to the parents and got nowhere. Sound familiar? Five for five of the kids were in that roundup last Thanksgiving." She smiled with satisfaction. "My partner's heading up a team to debrief all the parents, and hope at least one will spill. But they're scattered across several states, so it's a jurisdictional issue. It'll take time."

Combs rubbed the back of his neck and wished for another cup of coffee. Doty assumed a lot.

Gonzales didn't buy it, either. "Pretty thin, Doty. I'll concede the timing could work for withdrawal symptoms in the kids. But why not psychosis like last time?" He chewed his mustache. "And all the kids running south at the same time? That's not coincidence. Kids that age don't plan." He tapped the pencil against his teeth. "Three states? Dios."

"Doty, do you really believe those kids are being influenced by—"

"Don't know what's going on with the kids." Doty glared. "But they're a piece of the puzzle. Think of them as one symptom of the bigger disease." She held up her hand, counting on each finger. "Drug ring connects to dogfights. The dogfight connects to Damenia. Damenia connects to these specific kids. And the kids connect to Gerald Baumgartner."

The Captain squeaked his chair, put the flat of his palms on the desk and stood. "Detective Doty, great speech. Still damn thin. What else you got?"

Gonzales snapped his notepad closed. "Dazzle us, Doty. I would love for you to dazzle us."

Doty popped her gum again, looking like the cat that ate the canary, and Combs wanted to shove the cud down her throat. She'd been playing them.

Combs leaned forward. "What haven't you told us?"

"I got someone on the inside." Doty reached out and patted Combs on the shoulder. "For over a week now, I've had an informant infiltrating the local dogfight scene. Something's going down, and soon."

"Is that so?" The Captain didn't sound any happier than Combs. "Detective, I've already made clear to Gonzales and Combs that this team shares information and holds nothing back. I expect no less from you."

"Of course, Captain, my apologies." She didn't sound sorry. "Guess we all got caught up in brainstorming, but at least now we're all on the same page. Last message from my guy said he'd get us the fight location."

"Great. That's news worth waiting for." Gonzales flipped open his notepad again.

"Who do you have on the inside?" Combs looked at Gonzales and shrugged. He had to hand it to her. Doty never stuck in a toe when she could jump in with both boots. "I still think your kid connection won't float. Someday we'll nail the Doctor, but I'm happy to slam the door on the drug distribution."

The Captain nodded. "Get us the day and time, and we can put eyeballs on the site, catch the whole slew of 'em with their britches down. When's your guy's next check-in?"

For the first time Doty looked uncertain. "Benson is supposed to check in every 48 and it's been three days now." She shrugged. "Can't count on civilians."

"Benson? Not BeeBo Benson?" Combs throat grew tight.

"Yeah, you know him? The guy from that hog hunting show. He knows the area, knows the players, and knows Pit Bulls. He said, and I quote, 'A feller who'd abuse a critter was lower than pond scum.'"

"Sonofabitch! Doty, did you ever meet the man?" Combs shook off Gonzales's hand when he tried to hold him back.

"Detective Combs. Stand down!" The Captain's command stopped Combs in his tracks, but his fingers still itched to wrap around Doty's scrawny neck.

"Never had the pleasure. We talked on the phone." Doty's face turned as expressionless as granite. "He's pure West Texas good 'ol boy." Her voice grated with temper. "He said an older cousin introduced him to dogfights when he was a kid, and he hated it so much, he decked them. At first he wanted nothing to do with the idea, so I appealed to his civic duty." She jutted her chin. "He acted particularly incensed that kids might be involved. Said it ruined his cousin for life."

Gonzales looked ready to tackle her himself. "BeeBo is a child in a man's body. And you sent him undercover? He couldn't lie to save his life."

She didn't back down. "He seemed fine to me. Insisted he wanted to help, after I explained the situation." Doty licked her lips, and reached for the pack of cigarettes she no longer carried, and then dropped her hand. "If he's slow, even better. Nobody'll consider him a threat, or believe he'd be working with the police."

"We got to check on him." Combs whirled and strode across the room.

"Combs, leave it. Benson is Detective Doty's informant." The Captain paused. "Doty, you started this operation, so finish it. I want this drug ring shut down. And for damn sure, I don't want any civilian casualty."

"Yes sir. It's under control." Doty glared at Combs.

A uniform officer knocked on the door and without waiting, stuck his head inside. "Captain, we just got a call on a missing kid—"

The Captain held up a hand to stop him, and aimed steely attention at Combs and Gonzales. "You two, take that call. See if it ties in with the other AWOL kiddoes. After that, liaise with September Day and get as much information as you can about dogfights, the people involved, and what to expect. I want a full report by shift's end. Got it?" He took a seat behind the big desk, and waited a beat, looking at all three of them. "What the hell you waiting for? Get out of here."

Chapter 7

Kelvin shed his clothes, trading French cuffs and tailored suit for soiled and patched jeans, a Texas First tee shirt with ripped off sleeves, and scuffed steel-toed boots. He tugged a black knit cap over his bald head, hoping it wouldn't itch and drive him nuts, and pulled on a sleeveless denim vest with an assortment of badges. The patches were legit, from his crazy motorcycle club days, even though the club had long since disbanded. He hoped they'd add to his cred.

Hercules sprawled on the bed, soaking the cover with dog drool and thumping his tail each time Kelvin turned his way.

"What do you think?" He posed, flexing his biceps so the tats of snakes undulated along his arms.

The dog wagged, stood up and shook his 240-pound tan torso, black muzzle spraying drool across the room. His collar tags jangled, bed springs squealed and the headboard thumped the wall like a seedy hotel room's amorous neighbor. Kelvin smiled wistfully at the thought, knowing he'd had his last taste of Sunny. If not for her pillow talk last week, he wouldn't have connected the dots that brought the Doctor within reach.

"Only good times ahead. New apartment and better class of neighbors and clients, just you wait, Hercules. Maybe even a doggy girlfriend for you." He'd counted the wad of cash three times, and had the $10,000 stashed in a yellow sock and locked in the top desk drawer at his office. You couldn't deposit that much cash without pointed questions being asked and paperwork required. Time enough later to figure out how to manage the windfall.

To reap the full rewards, though, he had to pay in blood—not his own, but innocent blood. He walked to the bed and opened his arms to Hercules, welcoming the heavy heat against his chest when the Mastiff leaned into his embrace. They'd been together six years. He'd want to kill anyone who offered to hurt Hercules. So would anyone with half a heart. Something must be broken inside of Sunny. Now, he'd have to play a gruesome price to buy the trust needed to gain insider access to the dogfight ring.

"Not you, boy. Never you." Kelvin thumped his palms on the dog, and Hercules panted happily.

It'd only take a couple to satisfy them. Surely, he could wrangle up a couple of strays. Besides, people who let pets wander didn't deserve to have them. He told himself it'd be only a day or so before he called in the authorities, not enough time for anything bad to happen to them. Kelvin didn't know if he could live with himself otherwise.

But he had no choice.

His phone beeped, signaling an incoming call. Kelvin hurried to the adjoining bathroom vanity where it charged next to the sink, and recognized the sender.

"Got the location and the time." Sunny quickly rattled off directions, and he scribbled them down. "Here's the deal. You deliver three animals to the location today. Better hurry, before the storm hits. There's dumpsters on the property. Put 'em inside one of those."

"Dumpsters? I thought they were supposed to be alive?" His stomach tightened. "That doesn't give me much time." He unplugged the phone and carried it back into the bedroom, and sat beside his dog.

"Yes, alive. Open the lid and drop them in. You can toss some hot dogs if you want. With all this rain, there should be plenty of water to drink. It's not like they'll be in there for long."

He closed his eyes. If Sunny had been in the same room with him, he would have smacked her, never mind he'd never struck a woman in his life. He'd make an exception in her case.

She must have read his mind. "Hey, this isn't some sweet-and-fluffy Disney adventure, Kelvin. I'm the messenger. If you don't have the stones for it, my guys won't let you inside."

"Right, I know." He stroked Hercules, imagining reproach in the dog's eyes.

"This is a test. You won't see them, but they'll be watching your every move. I want the rest of my money, what's coming to me." Her voice turned fierce. "So don't mess up. That would reflect poorly on me, too."

"Yeah, whatever." This was his party, and he had the most to lose. He knew what the dog men did to fighters that disappointed, and could guess his fate, should he fail in any of myriad ways. "Maybe there's another way."

She blew out breath with exasperation, and he imagined Sunny tossing her neon locks. "Figured you'd try to weenie out on me. I need the money, Kelvin. I've got plans, gotta get the hell out of this stinking place and start over. You can't trust anyone here. It's all empty promises, lies and disappointment."

God, she'd played the victim card again. In her world, everyone was out to get her. "Sunny, hear me out. That referral I pitched your way, over to that old renovated Victorian, 205 Rabbit Run Road? I'll double your fee."

Combs's text had been insulting. *Detective* Combs now. He hadn't been so high and mighty last year after his demotion. Combs came to Kelvin begging for a job. Kelvin strung the cop along for a while, figuring Combs would still have inside connections even as a tainted ex-cop that could prove helpful with Kelvin's clientele. But once reinstated, Combs no longer had the time of day for Kelvin Quincy. Until now.

Sunny laughed. "Figured it wasn't worth much or you'd do it yourself."

He grit his teeth. He couldn't let anything distract him from nailing the Doctor's drug ring, but couldn't tell Sunny that. At the same time, Combs knew Kelvin never turned down a job. Doing so could make the detective suspicious, when Kelvin couldn't afford cop noses in his beeswax, so he'd referred the job to Sunny. "You already agreed to take the job, Sunny, I'm just sweetening the deal."

She waited a beat. "I'm playing with you. Already on the job. I never turn down a bonus."

The P.I. job would keep Sunny out of his hair until he could figure a better way to manage this whole thing. Maybe he'd send the Doctor to the designated spot, and let Combs know. The detective would owe him. He'd heard Combs was a stand-up guy willing to share credit. Kelvin wouldn't have to mention the $10K socked away, literally.

"As for this deal, Kelvin, I won't let you back out."

He laughed so hard, he shook the bed. Hercules sneezed, joining in with a doggy laugh, and his collar tags jingled again. Kelvin was many things, but he was not a dog killer. *Drop in a dumpster? Sheesh.* "Sunny, what kind of leverage could you possibly have?"

"I took care of BeeBo, like you said. Squashed him flat. So to speak."

His shoulders tightened and he stopped laughing. "What do you mean?"

She drawled, voice dripping with treacle and seeming to enjoy every word. "Got word about BeeBo asking questions, sniffing around. I did my own sniffing, and sure enough, it smelled to high heaven like bacon." The honey turned to brimstone. "BeeBo's cousin turned me on to his little game. We go way back." She giggled. "Then when BeeBo called me to help out with his undercover sting, I couldn't resist fixing our problem. The poor simple soul had a little accident with his gun."

He leaned forward, and shouted into the phone. "You *shot* him? Are you crazy?" His voice raised an octave and he leaped to his feet. "You crazy bitch. If he's undercover, a suspicious death won't help our cause." Murder had never been part of the plan. He was supposed to be one of the good guys.

"Don't take that tone with me. I'm not stupid, I quizzed him first. He hadn't reported to his handler, not yet, but was going to. I couldn't wait. He'd already been out to the site. Had a kitten he must've pulled out of there. I hate cats." She sniffed. "I'm still so stuffed up with allergies I can't breathe. If I hadn't taken care of business, you and me and the Doctor wouldn't *have* any business."

Kelvin pulled off the black stocking cap and threw it across the room. "That's dandy. That's it, Sunny. I'm out. Bad enough this deal involves murdering dogs. But you killed a *man.* They'll never buy that a gun guy like BeeBo got careless. You're on your own." He'd call Combs, come clean and the devil takes Sunny and the Doctor and the whole shitty mess.

"Before you click off, hon, you should know about my insurance."

He hesitated. She sounded positively gleeful, and he couldn't bring himself to disconnect. Not until he knew what the witch planned. "What? What insurance?"

"The police investigation will turn up a rabies tag that doesn't belong to one of BeeBo's *dawgs.*" She drawled the last word, the way BeeBo would have said it. "Now, you give that big old Hercules-boy a pat for me, y'hear? Always loved the way he jingles his collar."

Chapter 8

His feet squished with each cautious backward step, and Larry froze and prayed the slight noise wouldn't raise an alarm. There were dogs out there, a lot of them. Pit Bulls.

Every horror story he'd ever read about the murderous beasts flashed through his mind. A single bark would alert whoever had staked them out here in the middle of nowhere. If they were guard dogs, he didn't want to find out what they protected.

A half mile back, his car hydroplaned off the pavement when he stupidly crossed a low spot covered by running water. Now that his MiniCoop sat up to its headlights in black mud, and the weather knocked out cell phone service, he'd never make track practice in time. Coach would have a cow, not to mention his dad once he found out about the new car.

Larry lifted one foot and winced at the slushy sound it made coming free of the ooze. The sticky muck turned his feet into black snowshoes that nearly tugged off his sneaks. Larry carefully scraped them against a nearby tree and lamented his Christmas track shoes, barely worn, were ruined. His eyes pricked and he silently berated himself to suck it up. After all, he'd turn seventeen next week. Maybe Mom would replace the shoes for his birthday.

Not likely. They'd been too expensive the first time and the gift was supposed to count for both Christmas and birthday combined. Ditching the car made the shoe issue pale in comparison.

Wind panted hot breath against his face. This had been a year for weird weather, and the February temperatures mimicked May, excessively warm even for Texas. The breeze swirled his curly hair into his eyes. His girlfriend was right, he needed a haircut. If he'd listened to Melinda, he'd be getting shampooed and trimmed in downtown Heartland, instead of hiding from a pack of devil dogs. Larry hoped they couldn't smell his fear. Fear smell made them crazy, or so he'd read. Even he could smell his rank sweat, like he'd already run a marathon.

He sheltered behind a stand of burl oak, but the naked limbs did little to screen his presence. The wind rattled dry-bone branches, and he shuddered, remembering the recent news accounts of bone yard dumps. Maybe the dogs belonged to hog hunters like from that reality show? At least they'd rounded up and arrested all the bad guys. Larry relaxed a bit with that thought, until lightening strobed a dark cloud, and a simultaneous BOOM! made him wince.

The dogs didn't like the thunder, either. A couple of young ones yelped. Some had empty metal barrels laid sideways on the ground, but the makeshift shelters squatted in the same muddy swill that hobbled Larry's feet. He heard the rattle of the enormous chains that tethered each dog, even the pups, collar-to-stake-in-the-ground in a scatter-shot pattern around the remote clearing. Poor dogs, they couldn't help their nature. Was it necessary to chain them up like that? Must be to keep the dogs from killing each other. Everyone knew Pit Bulls were bloodthirsty beasts eager to attack innocent bystanders. They must be something powerful if they needed huge chains to restrain even the babies.

He hoped they'd focus on each other long enough for him to get away. Hell, he'd run farther distances before, and in the rain, too. This would be a great story to tell Melinda and their friends at school. At that thought, his chest puffed out. She'd be impressed.

Larry had only plodded down this chewed up drive to find a house, homeowner and phone connection, or maybe a truck that could pull him out. When he'd seen the dogs staked in front of the cement block barn, he'd stumbled off the gravel drive to hide behind scrubby trees. He debated whether to beat a more hasty retreat, or slog through muck to take advantage of the half-assed shelter of the trees.

An engine revved behind him. Larry crouched, heart thumping, and started to flag down the driver for help. Whoever owned those dogs, though, might not take kindly to him trespassing. Before he could make a decision, the mud-spattered truck pulled up next to him, rolled down the window and stared, pockmarked face grim. The driver's bare arm boasted snake tattoos writhing from wrist to shoulder.

A massive canine with close-cropped ears, nearly as broad as it was tall, rode in the truck bed with front paws balanced on the roof of the cab. A short chain kept the beast anchored to the truck. It stared at Larry but remained silent.

"That your yellow car back there, swamped beside the road?" In answer, the Pit Bulls leaped up and stood at the ends of their chains barking, most with lowered heads and wildly wagging tails. Both the man and his gigantic dog ignored them. "I said, is that your yellow car?" The driver raised his voice over the barking.

Larry swallowed hard, and nodded.

"Figured somebody needed help when I saw that. Glad my Hercules didn't have to get out in the mud to find you." At the name, the dog in the back wagged his tail. "Don't stand there in the rain. Hop in, I'll give you a ride. Got a rig in the back ought to yank your car back onto the road."

Larry straightened. He swallowed, but saliva had turned to dust. The big canine—Hercules?—perched in the back of the truck stared at Larry while the Pit Bulls barked.

Shifting sideways half a step, Larry scanned the area, curly hair whipping in the stiffening wind. Dogs at the barn, scary stranger beside him, the monster dog in the truck, and nowhere to hide.

"What're you waiting for? Get in the truck. Bet your folks won't be happy you got your car stuck." He smiled with sympathy when Larry flinched. "Get in the truck, kid." He put a hand out the window, and the huge dog leaned forward to sniff and lick the snake tat on his arm.

"Does he bite?" Larry wanted to kick himself for asking. What did it matter? He had to run and take the chance. He'd had a few close calls during runs, and even one butt-nip from a Toy Poodle, so embarrassing he'd told no one, not even Melinda. He imagined the bright-hot pain of Hercules's giant teeth grappling his legs.

"All dogs bite in the right circumstances."

Larry stumbled a half step backwards.

"Hell, kid, take a breath already. I'm trying to save your ass." The big man wiped his acne-scarred face with a paisley kerchief. "Hercules puts the fear of God into some of my clients. I'd never tell them this, but he wouldn't hurt a fly. He's more a wrestler. He don't—I mean, he doesn't bite. Mastiffs pin you to the ground but never leave a mark." He paused, and added impatiently, "I got things to do. And I'm trying to do you a favor. I just want to get you out of here safe and sound, and get that toy car of yours back on the road. Do we have a deal?" It wasn't really a question. "Get in the truck."

Larry gulped. "Absolutely, sir, whatever you say." He took a couple of steps toward the truck, stalling and doing his best to clean the rest of the muck off his running shoes. He'd sooner face the chained Pit Bulls than climb into this guy's truck.

The gravel drive sat above the mucky field on one side while more scrub trees blocked the other. He could be halfway back to the main road before the driver could turn around and give chase, or release good old Hercules from his tether in the truck bed. Larry consciously steadied his breathing, psyching himself the way he did at the start of any track meet.

The man leaned over and swung open the passenger door to the truck. "Don't worry about the other dogs, either. Even if unchained, they might lick you to death. Pit Bulls love people. They only hate each other, same as lots of terrier breeds that are dog-aggressive." He chuckled. "All that hoopla about being mean does give folks pause, though, so they keep their distance. But a well-bred Pittie would sooner kill itself than harm a human." He craned his neck to follow Larry's progress around the back of his truck.

The gravel drive, littered here and there with a muddy puddle, beckoned with open invitation once Larry cleared the tailgate, and he didn't hesitate. With the truck between him and the stranger, he put his head down and sprinted.

The truck's engine snarled. Shit. The guy hadn't taken the time to turn around. He'd shoved it into reverse to come after him.

The Pit Bulls had gone nuts, too, barking and snarling. Larry imagined them lunging, breaking each massive chain one after another. He tucked his chin and increased his speed.

Overhead, thunder crackled. Dark shadows dance across the road. The truck's tailgate loomed. Hercules rode the bed like a surfer, silent and watchful, and strained against his tether.

Before the tailgate smacked him, Larry vaulted off the embankment. Within two steps, mud mired his feet. Damn. He tripped and fell forward. His braced hands sank wrist deep into black soil.

The truck revved. The dog man shouted. "Kid, what the hell you doing?"

Sobbing, Larry clawed to push himself upright. His thighs and calf muscles screamed against the weight of the clay. When his feet and hands sank deeper still, the mire anchored him in place. He crouched with eyes wet and chest heaving.

The weight of Hercules hit the end of the tether at the right angle, and snapped. The dog tumbled from the tailgate, landing on the incline at the side of the gravel drive. The trucker opened his door and clambered out.

"Hercules, STAY. Come, boy. Come." The man scrambled to retrieve the tether, and hissed when it screamed through his bare hands when the beast couldn't stop his forward motion.

Hercules hit Larry high in the shoulder. Larry opened his mouth to scream, anticipating the crush of jaws, but instead the dog yelped and floundered in the sticky muck as hobbled as Larry.

"Hercules, oh God no! Kid, hang on, hang on."

The dog flailed for solid footing, and then lunged, forelegs grasping Larry's waist. Larry caught a glimpse of the man's terrified expression before Hercules pushed his face deep into the cold muck.

The Mastiff rode his shoulders, claws scrabbling for paw hold.

Larry struggled to lift himself upright. Mud filled his ears and muffled the stranger's frantic shouts and the dogs' barks. Larry flailed, kicking legs churned, and he craned his neck side to side. His mouth filled with black dirt.

For one last sane moment, Larry calmed himself enough to reach down, down, impossibly far, seeking rock, tree limb, anything solid for leverage to push up out of the soup. But his hands met no resistance.

Lungs burned. Eyes snapped open into the grit that tears couldn't wash away. Screams bubbled tar pit slow from his mouth, and he inhaled, choked on black cold death.

Larry convulsed. Sludge cooled super-heated nerves, almost a balm, until all went black.

Chapter 9

Shadow braced himself in the back seat. The big car jolted down and up again when it lurched off the regular car-path. He stuck his nose in the window crack, making wet streaks on the glass with his nose. A low tree branch switched against the car, and he flinched back.

"Sorry, baby-dog." September reached through the metal bars that separated him from the front seat. He slurped her fingers. "Just chill. When we get there, we'll play Frisbee."

He thumped his tail to show he understood. Shadow loved fetch-games, but the happy words couldn't change his disquiet.

He'd growled at the scary woman. Oily acrid scent rolled off her gloves in waves, covering up the clean dog smell underneath. He wondered why she needed guns when she had dogs to keep her safe?

Gun stink made his lip curl. Guns made ear-hurting noises, and could reach out and bite dogs and their people from far away. He didn't like or understand guns. Teeth were better, even for show. Good-dogs don't bite, not ever, even when scary strangers deserve biting. But instead of listening to a good-dog's warning, September shushed him. She knew best, but he remained alert until the stranger drove away with the crying lady.

Despite her rude intrusion into his house, the weeping woman hadn't worried him. When he smelled the salty wet on her face, he knew she posed no threat.

September couldn't enjoy the scent-colors that filled the world. He did his best to show her these hidden treasures, wanted to share his joy. Usually she listened to him, reading the lift of his ear or shift in his posture, but sometimes Shadow didn't know how to explain. If dogs detected smells and sounds hidden from people, then humans must know things dogs couldn't understand.

People knew names for so many things, and he loved learning new names in the *show-me* game. People made cars run faster than any dog, and he relished wind-taste that blew through car windows. Shadow half closed his eyes, licked his nose, and stuck it further out the window to catch the scent-stream. Bliss.

The car slowed, and tires crunched when they made a turn. He stared ahead, tipping his head to one side for a better view. The path unraveled in front like the paper roll Macy-cat liked to steal.

Shadow saw a small wooden-sided house, its yard messy with tall uncut brown grass all around. He stood on the seat, wagging as the car came to a stop. To one side, a chain-link fence with a cement floor enclosed half the yard, empty now, but he smelled two dogs. He wagged harder, his tail raised with excitement. He couldn't stop the small whines of anticipation when September released her car-harness to get out.

"Sorry, Shadow. *Wait.*"

He yelped in protest. He knew what *wait* meant, his least favorite word. He needed to do his job, lead the way, *check-it-out* for danger the way he always cleared their house when they returned home.

"Everything's fine. Scariest thing here is the stray kitten BeeBo rescued, and a frightened kitty won't appreciate you nosing around." September took in the empty dog yard and frowned at the mud-crusted truck parked under a nearby carport.

Shadow wagged again, and whined hopefully. He loved September talking to him, even if he didn't understand all the words. He understood the emotions and intent, so the words didn't matter.

"His truck's here. Maybe BeeBo's out with Dot and Teddy. Can't have them come back and discover you baptizing their personal space, so you have to wait. I won't be long, I promise." He panted and pawed the window. "Give me a break, you're not hot. Okay, I'll leave the blower on. How's that?" She restarted the car and flipped a switch so that wind from the front of the car ruffled his fur. September slammed the car door, and stuck one hand to the barely opened window for him to nose-touch. That made him feel better. A little.

Shadow sighed, and watched her walk up the path to the front door, climb the stairs, and knock on the door. And wait.

She knocked again and called out. "Hey BeeBo, you home?"

An eerie keening howl rose from behind the door. Shadow came to full attention with the *DANGER!* cry from the strange dog. His fur bristled when September's back stiffened. She glanced at him, and he woofed and stood up, willing her to return, let him out to protect her from *DANGER!* the dog's howling fearful threat *DANGER!* inside the house.

"BeeBo? Everything okay?" September's voice shook.

A second dog joined the first's lament. Hysterical woofs mixed with frantic yelps and mournful howls. September reached for the door handle, but before touching it, pulled her hand away as though from a flame.

Shadow added his bark to the chorus, wanting, needing to reach September. He barked louder, but she ignored him, stepped off the porch, and disappeared around the side of the house.

He whined, frustrated. She'd left him behind. He paw-slapped the window, clawed the door, frantic. Dot and Teddy's horrific howls of loss infected him with worry.

September screamed.

Shadow howled. He braced one paw on the door-ledge and wedged his nose further out the window. The glass abruptly scrolled down, and he didn't hesitate. A good-dog protected his person. Shadow vaulted from the car window, and dashed to join September.

***

She bit her fist to stop another scream. The dirty window offered only a cloudy view, but enough for September to recognize the giant shape mounded in the middle of the floor. A long gun of some kind balanced against his torso. She couldn't see his face, but a dark stain pooled beneath his bulk, and smeared paw prints surrounded him. Did his chest rise and fall? Could he be alive, with so much blood everywhere?

His dogs were inside. The white dog, Dot, peered back at her with what BeeBo called her "stare of death." She'd never seen the red dog so still, and only the duet of howls told her Teddy was alive.

Before she could unfreeze her legs, Shadow sprinted around the corner, kicking up mud when he skidded to a stop at her side. "How did you? . . . Crap, forgot the child locks again." He poised to leap up against her, and she crossed her arms and leaned into his space to back him off. "Good-boy. Sit."

She'd love to bury her face in his ruff. But BeeBo needed help. "Stay close." She welcomed his warmth pressing against her thigh as she hurried back to the front porch, pulled out her phone and dialed 911.

September shared her name, BeeBo's address, and as much information as she knew to the dispatcher. "I can see through the window, he's on the floor. There's a gun nearby, and lot of blood."

"Is he alive?"

"I don't know. Going to try the door now." She paused. "Send animal control, too. His two dogs are with him." Shadow pushed in front of her to block the door, fur bristling. "I've got my dog here, too." She had to secure Shadow. Dot and Teddy had every right to protect BeeBo from a strange human and dog entering their house.

"Shadow, car ride. Now." Her voice turned drill sergeant sharp. He hesitated, but when she moved, Shadow whirled and beat her back to the SUV. He leaped into the rear seat through the open window. "*Wait.*" September opened the driver's side, scrolled up the rear windows, punched the child-lock mechanism, and shut the door. She ignored Shadow's wail of protest and returned to the porch.

September called to the two dogs through the door, making her voice calm but cheerful. "Dottie, here pup. Teddy, good boy. Who's a good dog? I'm coming in, you remember me." Teddy had always been extra protective. She grasped the knob, cracked upon the door, and the smell hit her. Dog poop and pee. And underneath, the coppery stench of old blood that made her stomach crawl up to her throat.

The smaller white dog, Dot, crowded close to September, trying to climb up her leg as she stepped inside. Teddy, the red nose Pit Bull, crouched beside BeeBo and continued to cry. "Good dogs, that's the way. Let me see." You could never predict how a dog might react in such situations. Even though they knew September, she trod carefully. She couldn't help BeeBo if the dogs wouldn't let her.

"BeeBo, do you hear me?" She stepped around the blood as best she could. Much of it had dried in a sticky dark stain near the big man's head. September knelt beside him, and checked his neck for a pulse, but his cold flesh didn't lie.

The red dog growled. "Teddy, good boy, you're okay." She slowly withdrew, and spoke into the phone. "He's not breathing. I think he's been gone a while. The gun . . ." Her eyes filled with tears.

"Wait for the authorities. The ambulance is on the way, and the police will dispatch someone shortly. Don't touch the gun. Was he suicidal?"

September frowned. "I don't think so, but I haven't known him long. He knows...I mean, he knew a lot about guns. I can't imagine he'd be careless with one." She wondered why the dogs were inside, when BeeBo's phone message made such a point about keeping them away from the rescued kitten. So far, she'd seen no sign of the cat.

"Don't touch anything. Leave the house, and wait outside, can you do that for me?"

"Sure." It broke her heart to see the dogs' grief. They knew. Dot huddled and shivered against the door, while Teddy interspersed whimpers with low growls, still intent on protecting his master. September clicked off the phone, stuck it in her pocket. The dispatcher couldn't mean for her to leave the dogs in here. It would take time for animal control to arrive, and she didn't want the police delayed by upset dogs.

Especially with anything that looked like a Pit Bull. Like most APBTs, Dot and Teddy fell all over themselves to please people, but still suffered the bad reputation media often fostered. September couldn't do anything now for BeeBo, except protect his dogs. She'd get both dogs to their kennel, and settle them safely away from the police circus that would only stress them further.

"Dottie, c'mon good girl, let's get you out of here." Teddy might calm a bit once Dot left the building. The girl dog dropped to the ground and dramatically rolled over. The right side of her face was brown, with a black dot giving her a jaunty make-believe black eye, and the rest of her face white like her body. BeeBo always pointed out Dot's eye shadow smudge over her left eye, and lipstick dark lips, saying they made her a glamour dog. September blinked hard, and wondered what would happen to the pair with him gone.

She had extra leashes in the back of the SUV and various other dog and cat consulting paraphernalia. BeeBo trained his dogs to respond to voice and hand signals unique as himself. She'd only seen him work his dogs once, and hoped she'd remember and they'd respond.

September fumbled with the drawstring on her sweatpants, and pulled it free. She half crouched, turned sideways toward Dot, and called. "Yoo-hoo, comy-yup-pup." She patted her leg at the same time, and Dot put her head down and wiggled toward her, flailing her tail as she bared teeth in a classic submissive grin. "Comy-yup-pup, good girl, Dot." Quickly, she threaded the drawstring cord beneath Dot's collar, stood up, and moved toward the door. "Who's a good girl? Dottie's a good girl." The dog pressed hard against September's leg, waited patiently until the door opened and followed with unmistakable relief to the kennel gate. "Kennel-up, good girl, Dot."

September latched the gate behind Dot, and trotted to her SUV to get a sturdier leash. Teddy was bigger, stronger, and probably less willing. She also grabbed a couple of bandannas, and liberally sprayed them with a commercial analogue of a dog pheromone. She stuffed one in her waistband and carried the other with the leash back to the house. At least Shadow remained quiet. Having him near kept her calm, able to focus on getting the dogs out. She'd need a Shadow-fix after this, once the authorities came.

Before opening the door, she called again to Teddy to warn him. Nothing worse than a startled, hyper-vigilant dog. "It's me again, Teddy. Want to see the handsome fellow." She moved inside and latched the door, avoiding direct eye contact with the stressed dog. "Comy-yup-pup, Teddy." She stood sideways, a few feet away from the entry, crouched down and patted her leg again. "Comy-yup-pup." September wadded up the treated bandanna, and tossed it halfway to the dog.

The dog whined and stretched his neck toward the cloth, sniffing. Mother dogs produced the pheromone while nursing puppies, and it soothed fear even in adult dogs. September hoped the chemical signal would take the edge off Teddy's fear-aggression. Luring Teddy away from BeeBo also reduced the chance the dog would want to guard. "Comy-up-pup, let's go see Dot."

Teddy sniffed BeeBo's face, nose nudged him, and when he gave no response, the dog stood and shook himself. That released the invisible cord tying Teddy to his body, and he rushed to meet September. The big red dog nearly bowled her over trying to get into her lap.

"Good-boy, such a good doggy, sweet baby, I'm so sorry, honey." September babbled, but the words meant less than the emotion. Teddy wriggled as the leash clipped to his collar. September pulled the bandanna from her waistband and knotted it through the collar like a bow tie. The other one she'd attach to Dot's collar.

She kicked the wadded bandanna on her way to the door. Before she could retrieve it, a streak of fur sprinted from beneath a nearby chair, grappled the cloth with tiny claws, and skidded into September's ankle.

Teddy immediately stuck his nose into the kitten's face and got a snout full of claws for his trouble. It must be Fuzzit, the rescue cat that BeeBo mentioned. Before September could scoop him up, the tiny kitten shimmied up her pant leg and chest to reach her chin. She tucked the trembling baby under her shirt to contain it on the trip outside, tugged Teddy's leash, and led the dog to join Dot in the fenced yard.

Shadow woofed from the car, and she hurried to meet him. "I promised you fetch-time, didn't I?" She'd never felt less like playing a game, but it would be therapeutic, reduce her stress, ward off the panic attack clawing the back of her mind. She couldn't leave until the police arrived and took her statement. But first, she needed to situate the kitten.

September popped the SUV's rear hatch, and snagged the small fabric duffel-shaped cat carrier in the rear of the compartment. After she zippered the tiny kitten inside, she collected the stack of dog toys, stowed the carrier on the front seat, and opened Shadow's door.

As soon as his paws hit the dirt, Shadow nosed the scent path to the front porch, hackles raised. "Shadow, no. Wanna play fetch?" She sing-songed the magic words, knowing that the happy association could change a dog's attitude.

Shadow's head whipped around at her words. When she waved one of the disks in the air and then wrist-flicked it away from the house into the next field, he flew after the sailing toy. September's shoulders relaxed as he snatched one after another from the air, and raced back to drop them at her feet. He paw-danced with impatience, urging her to toss the next.

Cars appeared at the end of the narrow lane, quickly closing the distance. A black and white led the way, followed by an unmarked vehicle September recognized. Her shoulders tightened. Not Combs, anyone but Combs. There must be other detectives in Heartland.

"Shadow, that's enough. Bring." She watched as he gathered up the Frisbees, neatly stacked them, and returned to her carrying all six of the toys. September deposited them in the SUV and got Shadow into the back seat, rolled the window partway down, and waited.

Officers from the black and white disembarked, but she only had eyes for the tall lean detective climbing out of the unmarked car. Her studied composure began to crumble. She wanted to run to him, hide her face against his broad chest, and feel the warmth of his arms.

Before she could say a word, Combs stomped across the gravel drive to join her. White tension marked the corners of his mouth, deepening the cleft in his chin, and she flinched in surprise at the fury in his tone.

"What the hell are you doing, playing games in the middle of my crime scene?"

Chapter 10

Combs turned away from September, fuming. He motioned to the uniform officers. "Secure the scene. Let me know when the coroner arrives." He glared at September, and then turned from her hurt expression. He'd been on the way to interview the missing boy's parents when they got the call about BeeBo. So much for Doty handling things.

He couldn't believe September had discovered the body. Again. Media would gnaw that bone like a starving dog.

Gonzales offered quietly, "You want me to talk to her?"

He grunted, not trusting himself to speak but shook his head and waved Gonzales toward the house. When the smaller man took the hint and walked away, Combs strode so quickly toward September, she shrank against the car and Shadow offered a warning bark. That took him aback. Combs tried to soften his tone but the words still sounded accusing. "You found the body?"

September's catlike green eyes narrowed, and she crossed her arms, her tone equally defensive. "BeeBo called for a consult." She gestured toward the dogs in the pen beside the house. "They were inside with him, already contaminated the scene. Didn't want emergency folks to be delayed waiting for animal control." She spoke so fast the words barely made sense. "Took me a while to get them out. The animals, I mean."

"You know better than to disturb a crime scene." She'd let her concern for the animals rule her actions but Combs acknowledged she had a point. They couldn't process until someone removed the dogs.

"I couldn't leave them in there. It was heartbreaking." Her voice caught, then steadied and she pushed mahogany hair out of her eyes. "They tracked blood everywhere, and Teddy—he's the red one— wouldn't let me close enough to see if BeeBo was alive. I had to try."

Combs rubbed his eyes. "Okay, yeah, I get that." He offered a conciliatory smile. "Seeing you here surprised me, that's all. Dispatch didn't say who found the body. Can't quite wrap my head around you being here. "

"Neither can I." She hugged herself again.

He noticed the dogs had retreated to an igloo-style house and huddled so tightly together they could have been a two-headed dog. "They're calm enough." He strained to see. "Is that blood? Were the dogs injured?" Something dark stained the white one's lower flank. "BeeBo was a dog guy. What he didn't know about his dogs you could fit in a thimble. Never figured he'd need your advice."

Her arms tightened across her chest.

"That didn't come out right." Combs mentally kicked himself. September didn't know Doty recruited BeeBo to infiltrate the dogfight ring, but that wasn't his info to share. Combs wanted September as far away from this case as possible. "Okay, tell me top to bottom what happened, what did you see, you know the drill."

"Don't you want to read me my rights? Or record my statement? So you can check later to see if I change my story?" The sarcasm didn't suit her but he probably had it coming.

He put out a hand, wanting to pull her into his arms, and knew he couldn't. Not here. He'd make it up to her later. Right now, they both had to keep a professional distance. "Let's start over, okay? Finding a dead body doesn't do great things for my personality."

She finally offered a tentative smile. "Me either. The sooner we get this over, the quicker I can get out of your hair."

He leaned against the car door, and absently scratched Shadow when he stuck his big head out the window. "Gonzales has the recorder, and sure, you'll have to tell it three ways to Sunday. I need a general time line for now." She played with the zipper on her coat, avoiding his eyes. "I'm not mad at you." He wanted to throttle Doty,

though. "I'm angry you had to discover another victim. Now tell me—
"

"Victim?" Shocked, September stuck her hands in her pockets and shivered. "You haven't even been inside. BeeBo was shot, yes, with that fancy gun he inherited. I figured he wasn't used to it and it went off or something."

Combs caught her arm. "Walk with me." She started to follow him away from the car, and Shadow yelped. When September raised her eyebrows, Combs sighed. The pair was a team virtually joined at the hip. "Sure, bring the mutt, he's already trampled all over the field." Shadow hopped out, leaned briefly against September's leg to get his head stroked, and then raced ahead at her signal. "Now, tell me what happened."

She spoke in a rush, walking so quickly he barely kept up with her long legs. "BeeBo called about Fuzzit, the stray kitten he found." She told him the rest. "The kitten is in a carrier in my car."

That made more sense. Dogfights used all sorts of "bait" to train the bloody sport, and if BeeBo got close enough to rescue the kitten, he also could have learned about Damenia. The Doctor had killed before to protect his mission. "Animal control will take it."

She made a face. "But the kitten is so young. The city shelter will expose it to all kinds of things. Let me handle it?" She put a hand on his arm. "What difference can it make?"

He hesitated. They'd need to have someone examine the dogs and the kitten for evidence. He couldn't forget that September's cat Macy provided evidence last Christmas. Blood from beneath Macy's claws matched her stalker. Juries loved that kind of evidence. "Okay, no shelter for the cat. But you can't take it home either." Cats weren't his thing, and he'd been grateful his sister agreed to take Mom's old cat Simba.

"I'll give Doc Eugene a call, he's got a quarantine room."

"Perfect. I'll sign off on any fees incurred. Tell him we'll try to get the cat seen in the next 48, sooner if possible. I don't know how long evidence can be preserved on a cat. They're self-cleaning, right?"

She rolled her eyes. "Right. Like an oven. Now it's your turn. Why do you say murder?"

"I didn't say murder, I said victim."

"Don't play that game with me, Combs. You said I disturbed a crime scene." The contrasting white strand of hair nested among sable tresses blew across September's lips, and she impatiently smoothed it behind her ear. "You've got uniforms out here, so why do you need two of Heartland's detectives? You suspect it's more than an accident." Shadow raced back to her, carrying a stick he'd found and pressed it into her hand to throw. She tossed it and they watched him bound away. "BeeBo grew up with guns, and I don't buy him being careless." She wiped her eyes. "His dogs were the world to him. But it did seem weird Dot and Teddy were inside."

"Weird? I figured BeeBo slept with them." The joke fell flat. He knew September slept with Shadow, but that was different. He couldn't help a bit of jealousy, of a dog, no less. "No offense." Hell, he kept eating his foot today.

"Lots of owners share their pillow with their pets, not only us PTSD folks." She answered softly, but her fists clenched.

"Truce, okay? We're both on edge." Hair blew across her face again. Combs reached to push it aside, and she jerked away, and then relented. He cupped her face, started to say something else, and then pulled back when the coroner arrived.

Combs, September and Shadow walked back to her car. He caught her arm. "What was weird about the dogs being in the house?"

"BeeBo didn't trust them with the kitten. He'd kept Dot and Teddy in the kennel, so it strikes a sour note they were all in the house."

Combs pointed the coroner to the house as Gonzales came out the door, snapping off disposable gloves. The small man ducked his head in greeting to September, and she offered a tight smile in return.

"It's a mess in there." Gonzales's mustache twitched. "Dogs tracked blood everywhere, but the prints are dry and the blood pool under the body congealed. The coroner will give us a timeframe." He pulled out his digital recorder. "I know you already told Combs, but give me the Cliff's Notes version and we'll get you out of here." He winked at Combs. "He knows where to find you for details."

She quickly recapped what Combs already knew.

"Wish you hadn't moved the dogs." Gonzales clicked off the recorder. "We've got shoe prints, one set is probably BeeBo but the other's too small. To cross all the t's we need to eliminate you from the trace."

She shifted her weight as if her feet had betrayed her. "I have a change of clothes in the back of my SUV." She stroked Shadow's face. "Do you need Shadow's paw prints, too?"

"And the cat," said Combs drily. "Dealing with a Noah's Ark."

Gonzales didn't hide his disgust. "Not the way the Captain wanted us to liaise with you. We can do the consult here, or head downtown."

Combs made a "zip it" gesture with his fingers.

September frowned. "Consult? In this investigation?" She turned to Combs with surprise. "What does all this," she waved a hand toward BeeBo's house, "have to do with dogfights?"

Gonzales kept the recorder going.

"Tell me." Her jaw tightened.

Combs cracked his knuckles and stretched his neck, but the tension wouldn't leave. "Several departments, including Heartland, are on alert." He hesitated.

Gonzales picked up the narrative. "The fights move around. Every time the investigation gets close enough to shut it down, it disappears. Oklahoma, Louisiana, even Kansas. Now we got word they're here. Somewhere in North Texas."

Her mouth gaped. "You think BeeBo was involved in dogfights?" She laughed, and then choked off the garbled sound.

"I didn't say that." Combs glared at Gonzales, and the smaller man took the hint. The less anyone, including September, knew about the operation, the better. She was an outside consultant, period. Although after this, she might refuse to help at all.

September connected the dots anyway. "BeeBo couldn't hurt a fly. I watched him melt into a blubbery mess when one of his dogs got sick. He'd have nothing to do with that abomination." Her brow smoothed and she took a staggered step backwards, and caught herself against the car. "Did you get him to snoop for you?" She breathed heavily, outraged.

Combs reached out for her, but September danced out of his way.

"That's perfect, just perfect. Just because BeeBo has Pit Bulls." She fought tears. "I can imagine all the arguments." She knuckled her eyes. "You encouraged that gentle soul to cozy up to dog abusers, put himself at risk." Her eyes widened. "They did this! How could you?"

Combs flinched. She'd pretty much nailed Doty's argument, and his suspicions. To his mind, Doty might as well have pulled the trigger. He pinched his lips white with the effort to stay silent. Right now, the best he could do for September and the case was to shut his mouth and let her rage.

"I'm not a simpleton. I know dogfights attract gambling, illegal guns, drugs and who knows what else." September whirled, her lightening-streaked dark hair a storm cloud spilling over her shoulders.

"BeeBo never would have agreed, unless you told him it would save dogs."

Gonzales interrupted her tirade. "You're making assumptions not in evidence." He gestured with the recorder. "We don't know that BeeBo's death had anything to do with the dogfight ring. You'd agreed to consult on the case."

She leaned against her SUV as though fearful she'd fall to the ground. September ignored Gonzales, refusing to break eye contact with Combs. "Tell me you didn't ask BeeBo to sniff around the dogfight ring."

"I didn't." He kept his eyes steady. "Neither did Gonzales."

She didn't back down. "Someone did."

He hesitated, but couldn't lie to her. "You know we can't share everything about investigations, and sometimes we don't agree with every decision . . ."

"Oh God." Her voice broke. Color drained from her face until her complexion matched the moon mark streak in her hair. She pushed past Combs and yanked open her car door, and searched for her keys. It took three tries to find the ignition. Shadow whined from his perch in the back seat and yawned.

Gonzales held up a hand. "Hey, you can't leave yet—"

September ignored Gonzales but stared up at Combs with brimming eyes. She slipped off her shoes, thrust them at him without a word, slammed the car door, and drove away.

Chapter 11

September knuckled her eyes with one hand, driving as fast as she dared with the other. Hard-to-miss potholes turned the car into a bronco ride. Shadow bounced once too often and yelped when his nose banged the bars separating him from the front seats.

"Sorry. I'll slow down." She stuck her hand between the seats, and he nosed and licked her palm. The contact helped, as always.

The lump in her throat wouldn't go away, though, and she hiccupped a muted sob. Poor BeeBo. She didn't know which hurt worse: his senseless death, or Combs's investigation putting BeeBo in harm's way. She blinked hard when Shadow again licked her hand.

She'd planned to thank him for sending the private investigator, and let him know about Damenia's reappearance without betraying her promise to Claire. But BeeBo's murder left her reeling.

September knew cops made tough choices. That didn't make it any easier to accept. During her short marriage to Detective Chris Day, she'd seen him agonize over cases. He'd always protected her and refused to discuss details. Chris rescued her, kept her safe, and introduced her to the joy of tracking dogs. After Chris's murder, she'd run home to barricaded herself behind dozens of deadbolts, and kept everyone at a distance, even her family. Shadow broke through, insisted they belonged together and convinced her that chosen family was every bit as important as birthright. September dared to hope she'd have a future, maybe even with Combs.

"Stupid, stupid, stupid." She pounded the steering wheel in rhythm with her words. She hadn't considered if she could live with the tough, unsavory choices of a detective. What did it say about him? She'd never thought much about it with Chris, but at that point, in her life, she'd been in hibernation mode.

She wanted the dogfight ring shut down, too. Combs wouldn't confirm it, but he didn't deny BeeBo's involvement, either. There had to be a better way, without risking innocent lives.

Maybe Mom was right after all. She kept trying to set September up with men that were more "appropriate." Wouldn't that be a laugh? She pressed hard on the muddy gas pedal, icy sock feet as bruised as her heart.

"Who needs him, right Shadow? You're my best boy anyway." She checked the mirror, and smiled when the black dog laid his ears back. She could hear his tail thwacking against the seat cushion. "Want to go see Doc Eugene?" He barked, and wagged faster, and that tickled her.

Doc Eugene had treated Shadow for several injuries, yet instead of associating the clinic with scary pain, Shadow adored the veterinarian and his staff. Most of them, anyway.

Pulling into the parking lot, September noticed the new office manager's car parked in the only handicapped spot right next to the front door. Typical. Robin Gillette probably didn't want to get her hair wet in this rainy weather. While efficient and thorough, something bothered Shadow about the woman and as a result, September treated Robin with respectful caution.

"You didn't like Sunny Babcock, either." Shepherds typically acted reticent around strangers, and September worked hard to counter Shadow's natural suspicion. As a service dog, he needed to be calm and nonthreatening in public, as much to counter her own PTSD as to be welcome wherever she might go. He acted more comfortable around kids, probably because of his training with Steven.

Dog savvy folks like Doc Eugene usually turned Shadow into a fuzzy puddle of wags, so September wondered why he'd taken such an instant dislike to Babcock. The woman had worked on the same reality TV show with BeeBo, and had her own brace of hog hunting dogs. But people sometimes took an instant hate-at-first-sight dislike toward each other. So could dogs.

She plugged her cell phone in the charger and left it in the car. Shadow jigged and whined in the back seat when September grabbed the cat carrier and juggled it out of the car before releasing him. He immediately scoped out the best places to baptize with a blissful expression as he sniffed up all the juicy Pee-mail messages left by clinic visitors.

Her sock feet squished despite avoiding puddles. September scrubbed her face with the cuff of both sleeves. She'd only recently begun wearing a bit of makeup again. What a waste. Now, tears had turned her into a clown. She could blame it on the pouring rain. She stopped for the moment to stare at the glowering sky. Grabbing the armful of dry clothes and boots from the back of the SUV, she balanced them atop the carrier and slammed the hatchback shut.

"Shadow, let's go. Take your leash." He bounded to her, took the leash in his mouth, and she followed him to the clinic doorway. After elbowing open the lever handle she pushed the door closed, and left a dirty sock print on the kick plate. September made a mental note to clean it off before Robin noticed and complained.

Shadow paw danced around the empty waiting room, claws ticking like tap shoes on the tile. He ran to the front counter, jumped up to peer over the edge, ears forward and tail waving. His ears fell and he hopped down and dropped his leash when Robin stood up and glowered.

"I told you before, he should be on a leash. Carrying it doesn't count." Her disapproval extended to the muddy footprints, both dog and human.

September didn't bother to acknowledge the old argument. "Is Doc Eugene around? Need to talk with him about this kitten." She set the carrier on the counter and the baby stuck a paw through the grill. "And I need to change clothes."

"Another charity case, I bet." Robin said something under her breath and started to take the carrier. "All these freebies cost the clinic money. The Good Samaritan Fund is nearly depleted."

"It's a rescue, yes, but a special case." September shifted the carrier out of reach. She gave in to temptation. "Please tell your *boss* I'm here. I'll wait."

Robin stepped away, her back stiff. "I just mopped the floor, you know, and appointments could come in at any time. Why don't you wait in the dog room—number three—and stop dripping all over."

She flipped her hair as she whirled, and this time September caught the muttered, "Cheapskate."

Shadow leaned against September's thigh and whined, so she stroked his ears. "Don't let her get to you. She wants to be in charge, and gets pissed when reminded she's not." Robin knew about her lottery winnings and thought, like much of Heartland, that September had money to burn. She didn't know and probably wouldn't care that most of the money was gone. Robin would be equally surprised to learn September funded the Good Sam program that paid fifty percent of care costs for un-owned critters, if the rescuer agreed to pay the other half.

September heard arguing voices. Crap. Robin probably redirected her aggravation toward someone else. People did that with spouses and kids after a bad day at work where they couldn't talk back to the boss. Even pets did it, lashing out against other pets or owners when they couldn't reach the preferred target.

Reading her disquiet, Shadow nudged her and picked up his leash. He tried to push it into her hands, implication clear.

She laughed. "We'll go soon." She gathered the carrier and clothes, and led the way down the narrow hallway to the examining room Robin indicated. If the woman hadn't acted like a jerk, she'd have mopped up the mess herself.

The kitten stuck paws out of the carrier front once more. "Poor baby, this has been quite an ordeal for you." She crooned and touched the little paw, encouraged when it didn't withdraw. The kitten flinched and yowled when she touched the other bloody paw. "What a brave little cat." It clearly had suckered BeeBo, a confirmed dog guy, into championing its cause. She wondered where he'd found the tiny thing.

A soft knock on the connecting door made Shadow alert. He cocked his head as the door opened and a young girl peeked around. "September? Hi Shadow." Nikki fell to her knees and opened her arms, and Shadow turned into a blithering idiot dog. He fell on his back, legs splayed and tail waving, making blissful noises in his throat as Nikki rubbed his chest. "Robin said to tell you Doc Eugene's busy, and that I should help. And she said to blame you that I get to mop again." Nikki smoothed her white-blond hair behind each ear, and giggled. "I'd rather mop than muck out the kennels any old day."

September grinned. "When you work with animals, crappiocca happens." She motioned to her clothes. "I'd give you a hug, but you'd get soaked, too. Can you babysit Shadow and the kitten for me while I get changed?"

Nikki nodded, and at mention of the cat, left Shadow waving his paws in the air to peer in the carrier. "Aw, what a cutie."

"That's Fuzzit. Don't let him out, and don't touch him, not until I talk to Doc Eugene, okay? It's sort of a quarantine situation."

"It's sick?" Nikki peered closer. "He's got a torn claw. Poor baby."

September gathered up the clothes. "Shadow, *wait*. Be right back, I'll bring some treats." He stood and shook himself, and whined a soft protest, but didn't argue.

She rushed to the small bathroom in the rear of the clinic, in a hurry to get inside before Robin interrupted again. Quickly she shucked out of her outerwear, and peeled off wet socks. The dry jeans and old but clean sweatshirt warmed her chilled skin, and a paper towel dried her feet. The work boots would fit loose and probably rub on bare feet but she didn't have a dry pair of socks. She wouldn't have to wear them for long, though, and could change once she got home. September checked the mirror. That explained Robin's expression when she'd showed up. She washed away streaked makeup. She couldn't do much with her rat's nest hair, though.

She bundled the wet clothes and carried them back to the exam room, surprised to see Nikki playing the *show-me* game with Shadow.

Nikki held a cat magazine in one hand and the leash in the other. "This is *magazine*." She held it out. "This is *leash*." Shadow cocked his head, and panted happily as she held each an equal distance from her body. "Shadow, *show-me* LEASH."

He leaped forward, and nose-poked the leash.

"Good-boy." Nikki preened. "He did it for me, too."

"Yes, he's a good boy. By the way, he knows the word *book* for magazines, books, anything like that, so it's less confusing. Short names work best." She stroked his head. "He's smart, but we have to give him a little help."

"Can we teach him new words?" Nikki searched the exam room for something else to name.

"His head will explode soon, he knows so much." The game taught Shadow names of objects. September used *show-me* more as a way to practice their communication and keep his attention sharp. But people delighted in seeing the trick demonstrated. In practical terms, a service dog learned the names of many objects in order to partner with the human. Although she'd never planned it, more than once the lessons learned in the *show-me* game had saved her life.

"I tried to play with my cat Hope, but she won't pay attention long enough. Unless there's food involved."

September dumped the clothes on a nearby wooden chair. "I've not taught the game to Macy. Cats have shorter attention spans than dogs, and different motivations. And not every dog has the focus or interest, either. All pets are individuals, Nikki."

"That's for sure." Nikki crossed to the cabinet and pulled open drawers for a likely pair of objects. "Maybe he already knows everything."

"He likes to play the game anyway. We can use things he already knows." September rummaged in her damp clothes and found the car keys, and drew the dog's attention to her. "Shadow, this is *light*." She thumbed on the laser light that Macy adored chasing. "And this is *sock*." She dangled one of the wet socks she'd shed. "*Show-me* SOCK."

Shadow pounced forward, and grabbed the soaked material, and then shook it and tossed it in the air. It landed with a soft "splat" on the tile, and Nikki giggled again.

"Wait, I know." Nikki pulled out a small tablet. "How about this?"

September took the device, frowning, and tried to think how it appeared to Shadow, and what other objects he already knew might correspond. "Hand me that, too." She pointed, and Nikki passed her the coffee mug from the sink with lettering that spelled, "Real Doctor." She'd bet it had been a joke-gift from the veterinarian's late wife.

Shadow watched with interest. He already knew that she called all drink containers "cup" so that made it simple. "Shadow, this is *cup*." She held out the mug and he sniffed it. "This is...*tablet*." September held the objects, one in each hand, out to her sides. "*Show-me* CUP." He nose poked the mug, and she didn't move either object. "Good boy. Now, *show-me* TABLET." He happily touched the tablet, and tried to take it from her.

"Ew, dog drool." Nikki, delighted, took back her tablet and wiped the surface with her sleeve. She scrounged for something else, opened another drawer, and pulled out a pair of shiny bandage scissors and held them up with a question in her eyes.

September pointed to a jar of treats on the counter. After all, she'd promised him treats. This would be a real test for him, something new compared to something he wanted. Shadow licked his lips when the treat jar lid clinked, but sat patiently.

"Shadow. This is *treat*." September held one in the palm of her right hand. She took the scissors from Nikki in her other hand, and held it carefully, pointed away from the dog. She hesitated, and decided on a name. "This is *knife*." He glanced quickly at it, and then back to the treat hand. "Shadow, *show-me* KNIFE."

He bounced forward, and nose-bumped the scissors and then scooped the treat out of her other hand. Nikki gasped as the scissors took flight and rebounded against the opening door.

Doc Eugene entered. "Sounds like a party in here." He bent and picked up the scissors.

"*Show-me* game." September shrugged an apology.

"You mean, the show-off game, right, big fellow?" Shadow slicked his ears down and rubbed against the big man, happy with the attention. "Nikki, could you put these away, please? Oh, and these, too." He handed her the bandage scissors along with a pair of bolt cutters. "Thanks, dear. I'll call you if I need you." He watched as the girl scurried out the room. "I should have so much energy."

"You use bolt cutters in a cardiac practice?" Doc Eugene served as both a general practitioner for dogs and cats, and a veterinary heart specialist. He'd diagnosed Macy's hypertrophic cardiomyopathy.

"Yep. And sadly, not the first time I've needed to use them." He rubbed the back of his neck. "Newly adopted dog came in, only been with the owners a week or so, and he suddenly turned vicious. Snapped at their kids. They were heartbroken, but wanted him euthanized, said they couldn't risk giving him to somebody else."

September's heart constricted. "Extra furry, right?"

Voice grim, he added, "We sedated him, and shaved his neck. Found exactly what you'd expect. A puppy size chain collar digging into his skin. Somebody put it on him months ago and didn't bother to remove it when he got big. Had to use bolt cutters to get it off. We cleaned him up, and physically he'll recover. He even wagged his tail, licked my hand after it came off." He pulled off his glasses, polished them. "Amazing the resiliency of pets."

"So the owners? . . ."

"They're willing to try. My bet is on the dog. Sweet little guy." He cleared his throat, and adjusted his glasses. "Now, Robin said you have another charity case." His smiled at her expression. "Don't let her get to you. She's trying to show me how to turn more of a profit. Is this the kitty? What's the problem?"

Quickly she told him, and watched his expression darken. "BeeBo was a good man. Who has his dogs?"

"Animal Control was on the way. I left before they arrived."

"So the police need a safe place for this kitten until they can collect any evidence?" He frowned. "The isolation room is empty; we can quarantine there."

"I was told it wouldn't be more than a day, two at the most. Tell Robin the city will pay. And if it's longer, I'll take care of it." September knew BeeBo would have done the same for her.

"Never mind about the payment." Doc Eugene's expression changed. "Are you all right?"

At the kind words, her eyes filled with no warning. "No. I am not all right." She grabbed a tissue from the nearby dispenser, and blew her nose. "I found a man dead."

He patted her shoulder. "Of course you're upset. Don't worry about the kitten. You take Shadow home and play some Frisbee, why don't you?"

At the F-word, Shadow tipped his head, and woofed as if in agreement.

September collected her clothing, Shadow's leash and the car keys, and returned to her car. Her feet slid up and down in the boots. But before she could start the car, her phone rang.

She saw two missed calls and a text, all from Mom. None were from Combs, and she choked back disappointment. She told herself she didn't want to talk to him anyway. Besides, he had his hands full with the dogfight ring.

"Yes Mom, sorry I missed your calls."

"Where are you? The curtain goes up in twenty minutes. I told the director how professional you are, and now you've embarrassed me, and—"

"Wait? There's a performance today? You said rehearsal."

"They changed it from a brush up to a performance after the run sold out. The entire cast, orchestra, and crew, not to mention the theater board of directors, are all here. You know how important this is for Steven, too, and for me. I'm the hostess for the after party." Her voice went up a notch. "If I tell them, they can hold curtain for maybe ten minutes. Are you coming or not?"

Crap. She'd let her family down too many times already. Besides, she didn't have anything better to do. Not like she had a date or anything. "I'll be there."

Chapter 12

Nikki crooned to the cat and put her hand against the front of the stainless steel cage. The kitty cheek rubbed and clutched her hand through the bars. "Let's get you a clean spot, okay?" She'd already spread fresh newspaper in the adjacent cage, and quickly opened the door to move the patient away from its soiled temporary home. "Don't be embarrassed, kitty. It's the anesthesia makes you wet the bed, it's not your fault. And your mommy will come pick you up soon, so you can go home."

She briefly cuddled the cat, but carefully avoided the spay stitches on the sore tummy. Nikki loved volunteering at the clinic on weekends, and had learned bunches from Doc Eugene. Mostly she kept the kennels and cages clean, walked the dogs and played with the cats.

Ever since Daddy came home from deployment right on time for Christmas, Mommy smiled more and Nikki and her older brother Hank got to do more stuff on their own. Hank wasn't so bossy anymore, either. After all, she'd finally turned ten years old, a very responsible age. Daddy said so.

For Christmas, she got to keep her rescued kitty, Hope, even though Mommy got sneeze-attacks around cats. And for her birthday a week later, Doc Eugene invited her to come learn how to take care of Hope and other animals on weekends. Today school closed for teacher business or something, so she got the day off and extra time at the clinic. For the first time ever, she got to watch a surgery.

Mommy thought it'd be gross and didn't want to let her. But Daddy called her his "littlest hero" because of how brave she'd been during the fire. He told Mommy that if she wanted to be an animal doctor, they had better find out now.

Turned out, it wasn't near as ooky as she expected. Blue paper covered up the prepped pets, with a little open spot for the surgical site. The opening centered on the tummy for the girls, or what Doc Eugene called "nether regions" for the boys. She loved seeing their upside-down kitty faces, so cute under the paper. Doc Eugene showed how to put ointment in the eyes, to help protect them.

Nikki gathered up urine-soaked paper, wrinkling her nose as she dumped it into the trash. Then she sprayed the cage with a cleaner, wiped it out good, and added more clean newspaper to the bottom.

"All set in here?" Doc Eugene stuck his head in the door. "Any problems? Everybody waking up okay?"

"Just finished. Tuxie sure is a stinker, though."

He walked down the bank of cages, checking each of the five recovering felines. "Remember what I told you about boy cat urine?"

"Yep. The girl cats think it's kitty cologne." She walked to the sink and used a bunch of liquid soap to get rid of the smell. "But when they get neutered, the smell goes away."

"Well, it's not as pungent anyway. Cat pee still smells like cat pee." The black and white Tuxie reached out and hooked Doc Eugene's sleeve with his claws, until he stopped and gave the cat some attention. "What did you think of the surgery?"

"Kind of neat. Hank said I'd pass out from all the blood. But there wasn't hardly any." She'd had worse nosebleeds.

"I sure didn't want you to pass out."

"It's way more complicated than I thought." Nikki smoothed her special veterinary assistant smock, powder blue with cartoon cats, dogs and bunnies on it. "You got to weigh them, figure out how much sedation to put in the shot, then get them ready."

"What else?"

"Put on a heart monitor and...put that tube thingy down their neck."

"Intubate, right. And?"

"Hook up the gas anesthesia. Put them on a heating pad. Then you got to scrub in." She ticked each item off on her fingers. "Can I do that sometime? Wash really good and put on gloves and gown and mask and all?"

"You think you'd like that? Help with surgeries someday?"

"Not only help. I want to DO the surgeries and be a vet."

Doc Eugene walked to the door. "You keep that focus, Nikki, and it'll happen."

She fairly glowed. Nikki pulled her tablet out and activated her favorite app, and quickly posted an update to the private Show And Tell group of a bunch of kids from all over. Somehow, it was easier showing and telling stuff to strangers than people you saw every day. Nikki shared everything with the group, especially happy stuff. Almost immediately she got several "likes" and started to post a picture of Tuxie when Robin stuck her head in the door.

"Nikki, stop messing around and go walk the dogs." Robin spoke with a broad West Texas drawl that got on Nikki's nerves.

"I just got finished." Nikki hunched her shoulders and stuck the device back in her backpack. She liked the dogs well enough, but Robin always made sure Nikki got the truly nasty kennels to clean. As much as she admired Doc Eugene, she disliked the new office manager he'd hired. She was all cotton candy sweet in front of the veterinarian, batting her heavily made up eyes and swinging her hips, but morphed into a tyrant dishing out scut jobs as soon as he turned his back. Nikki ducked past the big woman who nearly blocked the doorway, and turned toward the dog kennels on the other side of the building.

Nikki nearly reached the far door before Robin stopped her again. "Have you soaked the instruments? I showed you how to get them ready for the autoclave. If I have to tell you every single thing, I might as well do it myself."

Then why don't you? But Nikki didn't dare voice the words. She suspected Robin tried to get Nikki fired. She didn't know why Robin hated her. "Do you want me to walk dogs, clean kennels, or do instruments?" She tried to make her voice soothing the way she talked to her skittish cat Hope.

"Don't take that tone with me, young lady." Robin's eyebrow piercing bobbed up and down. "You smart mouth me, and I don't care how much Eugene likes you, your narrow little butt is gone, charity case and all."

"What do you mean? I'm a volunteer. I just want to learn stuff."

"I just want to learn stuff." Robin mimicked her with baby talk. "Give me a break. I work my butt off, and take any overtime I can get to cover rent and make car payments, buy groceries, pay off loans. You waltz in here, spend a couple hours a week petting puppies and kitties—"

"Well duh. I'm a kid. My parents don't make me pay for food, except special snacks I get from my allowance." Nikki covered her mouth, tickled at the thought. "And I can't drive, so why would I want a car?" She couldn't help rolling her eyes.

"I wanted tickets to that sold out musical, but you whined and cajoled and Eugene gave his tickets to you. It's your day to volunteer, but I have to work." She stomped down the hallway toward her, and it was all Nikki could do to hold her ground. Robin stuck her face close, and her fierce whispers smelled of beef jerky and Dr. Pepper. "When you work for free he doesn't have to pay me overtime. And on top of that, he gives you all your cat food and meds and even the spay surgery for free. *For free.*"

Nikki started to deny it. She'd seen Daddy give Doc Eugene money for Hope's care. But she also remembered her parents argued over the cost. Was it true? Had she embarrassed Daddy? But that meant she needed to work even harder to pay and make it up to Doc Eugene, never mind what Robin-the-Rat said. She drew up her chest and stood tall and proud, the way Daddy said soldiers stood, and never took any guff. "We're not a charity case either."

"Just go clean up the dog poop. That's all you're good for." Robin stalked away, opened the door to the front reception area, and closed the door.

Blinking furiously, Nikki whirled and banged through the door to the dog room. A Chihuahua yelped in surprise, and a big black mutt recovering from anesthesia lifted his head, tried to stagger to his feet, and instead banged his tail against the floor.

Nikki retrieved her tablet and let the hurt flow in an impetuous burst of misspelled words to the Show And Tell group. Nobody knew who Nikki-Kitty was anyway, so what could it hurt?

Before she could stow it away and begin to muck out the poopy kennels, the "bing" announced a message reply. Her eyes widened. She got more than a simple "like" this time. It came from Kid Kewl himself, the owner of the whole super-secret group.

"Hush little Nikki, don't be mad.
I'm gonna fix, turn your sad to glad."

Chapter 13

Singers on the stage moved with practiced ease as they awaited their musical cues. Seated above the actors toward the rear of the orchestra loft, September counted the measures silently, attention divided between the conductor at the front of the orchestra and soloist poised on the balcony across the way. The baton raised, cue given, and September's extended right arm danced her bow across the strings in a syncopated drumbeat of sound while her left hand fingered the strings. The eerie driving rhythm, echoed in the rest of the string section, built the desired tension and had the attentive matinee audience on the edge of their seats until all fell silent save for the celesta's single delicate music box chord.

"How...could I ever know," sang Lily-the-Ghost.

With a smile, September leaned forward, long hair spilling over her shoulders only a few shades darker than her cello. She embraced the cello she'd named Harmony like a mother comforting her child. Musical tension released along with her shoulders with the audience's collective sigh. Harmony's tenor strains blended molasses-rich to complement the actor's mint-fresh soprano soon joined by the tragic hero's tenor.

The lyrics cut too close to home. Guilt, shameful secrets, lives destroyed, all remained too fresh and September funneled the pain into each bow-stroke until music washed clean and transformed emotion into pure bliss. Music saved her sanity once before, and she'd only recently dared to play again after a year's long hiatus. She had no reason to hide anymore. Music wouldn't betray her and might even complete the healing.

Playing might give Mom reason to be proud of her, for a change. Her parents, Rose and Lysle January, sat in the front row in the audience to cheer their grandson in the children's chorus. This was eight-year-old Steven's theatrical debut.

Steven still didn't talk, but when Grandma Rose discovered he communicated most easily with rhymes and singing, she arm-twisted the theater director to include him in the children's chorus. September doubted how much Steven enjoyed being around so many people, but one didn't question Rose January. Especially about her grandbabies. She was always right. She'd tell you so, herself.

Thunder shook the theater, real thunder, not the electronic sound effects already used several times during the show. The actor playing Lily hit a high note, the shimmery tone pure, true and clear. Archibald strained to hit his high tenor part of the duet. His voice cracked into an unfortunate squeak, but quickly recovered. Shadow, positioned next to September, added a soft baritone moan of complaint, turning the duet into a trio.

September gave the "shush" signal, but Shadow continued to moan-sing along with the actors. When the tenor's voice again failed to reach the appropriate note, Shadow's arrroooo climbed the scale in a two-octave arpeggio that rivaled the singers' ranges.

Her face warmed at the orchestra director's dirty look, but she kept playing. How could she stop? September could imagine Mom's reaction and risked a quick peek over the railing to the audience below. Dad hid a smile with his program, but Mom sat stiff and unyielding, ignoring the doggy trumpet-blat.

At least the rest of the audience didn't realize it was a dog. The first act had struggled with feedback from the mics, after all. The actor playing Archibald turned red-faced but sang with renewed vigor, determined to out-sing Shadow's enthusiastic counterpoint.

A rest came in the music, and September again signaled Shadow to shush, but he thought it was a game. Other musicians giggled, some outright laughing with delight. September mouthed a silent "sorry" to the director but his expression forgave nothing. His nostrils flared while the baton beat the air.

The duet came to a close and Shadow's commentary quieted. She whispered to him, still aware the director watched. "Good-dog, Shadow, good shush." Praise the good, ignore the bad while gritting your teeth. That took practice, but the effort worked much better than the alternatives. "Here, take care of Bear. Bear is lonely." She nudged the dog's stuffed toy with one foot, giving him something legal to do with his mouth other than howl. He grabbed it, propped one paw over it, and began to nurse on its misshapen head.

She readied herself for the finale, grateful for the end of the performance but dreading the after-party. Mom planned the shindig for the entire cast and crew, more to showcase herself as a donor and her grandson Steven. After Shadow's impromptu solo, September knew she'd be the target of hurt and angry glares from actors, the directors and most especially, Mom-the-perfectionist.

The rest of the performance finished note-perfect both onstage and off. The applause faded, and September cleaned her bow, wiped rosin from the strings and closed the cello score. The rest of the players put away their instruments, most smiling at her on their way downstairs. A few spoke to Shadow, but none offered to pet him. They were locals. They knew her history, and respected his working dog status despite his lapse in etiquette.

Dr. Parker Belk, the orchestra director, weaved through the chair obstacle course until he loomed above her, and September flushed again. They'd only met briefly two hours ago, when he'd introduced her as the substitute cellist.

She forced herself to meet his storm-cloud-gray eyes. "I'm so sorry." She put one hand on Shadow's head, and the dog wagged but didn't release his toy. "It's my fault, I need time to prep him to the singers." Shadow had never been around singers. He'd probably considered singing to be a human howl.

"Your mother told me you were a professional, and I appreciate you sitting in at the last minute. Sight-reading the score, that's impressive. But Rose said nothing about your pet wolf attending the performance." Parker straightened his red bow tie, and smoothed the black tuxedo jacket, making September feel even frumpier in the old jeans and tracking boots she'd not had time to change.

"He's a service dog." She turned off the stand light and rose to face him. He stood a head taller than her five-feet six inches, but not as tall as Combs.

"A service dog should have better manners. Don't you have to take a test to get a license or something? Why doesn't he wear a vest?"

"You're right, he shouldn't have howled. Beyond that, you're misinformed." There was no test, license or identification required of service dogs. In fact, under ADA guidelines, even business owners were only allowed to ask if a dog provided a service, and what the dog was trained to do.

September accepted the cello case he handed to her. She expected him to march off in a huff.

He was right. But he didn't have to be a jerk. "I said I'm sorry, Professor Belk." She kept her voice low, but Shadow immediately dropped his Bear-toy with a whine.

"Call me Parker." He smiled, the first time she remembered seeing anything but a scowl, and it transformed his stormy expression and took years off his age. "I hate this monkey suit but can't change until after the meet-and-greet with donors. You're coming, too." He gestured at Shadow. "Bring the wolf, so they know it wasn't me this time criticizing the performance."

The turn-about caught her by surprise. The vertical scowl lines framing his wide mouth smoothed, replaced by a dimple at one corner of his crooked smile. She smiled back, but she couldn't quell disquiet. "Okay, sure. There's a week until the next performance, plenty of time to work with Shadow before then. He won't howl again."

"Oh, that's right. Rose said you trained him yourself. Everyone's doing that now." He rubbed his chin. "My sister-in-law got one of those Internet certifications so she could take her little poufy dog on planes for free."

She stiffened. "Excuse me?" She hated fake services gaming the system. It just made it harder for those with legitimate animal partnerships. September put a hand on Shadow's brow, and steadied her breathing.

Parker didn't seem to notice he'd offended her. "Thanks for filling in on such short notice. You saved my bacon."

At the *bacon* word, Shadow cocked his head and licked his lips. September made eye contact with the dog and shook her head and his ears drooped with disappointment. She sheathed her bow into the front-case slot, and noticed the other musicians had already left.

When her phone pinged, she checked the display and noted three missed calls, all from Combs. She quickly pocketed the phone, and her music-induced high drained away quicker than a toilet's flush.

"You have to come to the party." Parker's request held a note of pleading. "I hate these things, but it's expected. Everybody knows everyone, but I'm a newbie to the theater like you. Besides," he leaned forward and whispered, "Rose made me promise to get you there."

That explained a lot. Rose never did anything without a reason. She wondered if Parker was Mom's latest matchmaking target. September took a moment, appraising him. Heck, why not? They at least had music in common. That was a hell of a lot less stressful than dead bodies.

Shadow pressed against her. "I'm okay, baby-dog." She touched his ruff and her breathing steadied. Mom would have a cow if September had a panic attack here, in front of the folks Rose wanted to impress.

Her phone buzzed in her pocket. September pulled it back out to check. Combs again. She declined the call, and pocketed the phone.

"Let me carry your ax?" Parker didn't wait for her answer. He grabbed the cello's backpack straps, slung Harmony onto his shoulders, and headed for the stairs. "You coming?"

What choice did she have? "Shadow, let's go. Bring Bear."

Shadow thundered down the cement stairs and waited for her impatiently at the bottom. September kept one hand on the railing, habit after her knee repair surgery. This could be good, reconnecting with fellow musicians, people she understood and with whom she shared common interests. She'd make a ten-minute appearance at the party and be polite to Parker. At least she had a good excuse to dodge Mom.

Thunder boomed again, and the lights flickered off and back on. "What fun, it's a thunder party, right Shadow?" She joined the dog at the foot of the stairs, jollying him with her happy voice as she reattached his leash.

He offered a muffled woof, the Bear-toy still clenched tight in his jaws, and shook the stuffed toy hard while his tail flagged high. The sight of his bullet notched ear was a stark reminder of past danger they had faced. Better to focus on music. Anyone with half a brain would choose rim shots over gunshots.

Parker stopped, eyebrows raised. "Thunder party?"

"Some dogs fear loud noises, especially thunder. So ever since Shadow was a baby, we've had thunder parties with fun games and treats when it got noisy." That probably had helped Shadow get through his close calls, although she hadn't planned it that way.

She followed Parker from the backstage to the floor of the stage. Actors mingled with fans, mostly family, and accepted bouquets, hugs, posed for pictures and signed programs. Most of the musicians stood in an awkward group to one side. September moved to join them, until she saw Parker dodging between bodies to cross the stage. He still carried Harmony over his shoulder.

"Parker, wait." He made a beeline to her parents. Crap. Into the lion's den. Now she had to explain Shadow's disruption with the whole world listening.

The play director stood chatting with Mom and Dad, and Rose gave Parker a brief hug and then searched the room for September. Parker bent to greet Steven, and the child turned away, his green eyes stabbing September from across the room.

She hadn't seen Steven since that horrible day last November. He'd grown since then. And he acted so formal, not like a child at all, despite his frail frame. Steven stood military straight, but when Mom reached to stroke his white-blond hair, he shifted away like a skittish cat. Mom urgently beckoned September to join them.

Shadow whined, leaning back against her legs. September smoothed the dog's black brow, unconsciously mirroring Mom's comforting gesture. Far from dodging away like Steven, though, Shadow leaned into her palm wanting more. He dropped Bear-toy and shivered a bit, and then pulled back on the leash not wanting to move. "What's wrong, baby-dog? You've never been scared of thunder before."

***

Shadow stared at all the strangers milling about and talking with loud voices. He only recognized a few. Nikki saw him and smiled, and he wondered if Doc Eugene might be there, too. Shadow's tail stirred until she turned away to talk to Steven. His tail fell.

Steven had grown taller, thinner, and somehow *sharper* than before. Shadow shivered when Steven stared into his eyes. His-boy had never done that before, and Shadow slid his eyes aside, the way a polite dog should.

All around him, strangers laughed and talked so loudly it hurt a good-dog's ears. He felt unsettled by Steven's odd behavior. He trusted September, but she acted distressed, too. That made Shadow worry. Her smell always changed before she had a scary-gone time, when her heart hammered and she panted like something chased her, and she fell into a deaf-blind-screaming fit. In those times, she couldn't hear him, or see him. Shadow warned her before a scary-gone time happened, and sometimes September kept it at bay. When she couldn't, Shadow protected September until she knew him again.

Her smell hadn't changed. But it might. September tried to be brave, but he could always tell when she struggled. So, Shadow pressed close to her side to keep her safe. Nobody told him he should. Shadow figured that out all by himself. He was smart that way.

In the before, a lifetime ago when Steven had been his-boy, Shadow kept Steven safe. September showed him how. He stayed close beside Steven so his-boy didn't wander away, and barked loud to warn adult humans when Steven needed help. Shadow learned how to understand what September wanted him to do when she told him to *sit* and *down* and *wait*. He learned not to pull too hard or lag behind on the leash, especially when Steven grabbed hold of the leash, and that he should always stay with his-boy.

September played games that made him think hard and wag harder when he finally figured out what she wanted. September made a "click" noise with her mouth and gave him a treat when he guessed right, until he didn't have to guess anymore. He knew many words, like "phone" and "cello" and "Macy-cat." He'd learned some things all by himself, too, including "car ride" and "Frisbee" and "bacon." He really liked bacon.

Steven never talked but sometimes he screamed. Shadow wondered why. He yawned, and peeked quickly at Steven again, relieved that his-boy no longer stared. Staring made his skin prickle.

Long ago, Shadow decided he should teach Steven the joys of playing tug and fetch, tummy rubs and running fast-fast-fast. Instead, Steven stacked rocks, or made things spin, boring games for Shadow. Before, his-boy never looked at him, not directly. And Steven never ever petted him, even though Shadow ached to be petted. Maybe if he knew how to make the click-mouth-sound, Steven would understand.

Shadow nudged September with his nose, and her hand dropped to smooth his brow. That made him feel better. She'd been a constant in his life even in the before-time when Shadow lived at Steven's house. She understood Shadow even when he couldn't make click-noises to explain. She petted him—BLISS—and scratched his hard-to-reach spots. September never yelled if he made mistakes. When he did something right, she called him "good-dog" until he thought he'd melt with delight. He liked pleasing September and being called "good-dog" even more than getting a treat. Unless it was bacon.

He didn't *try* to love September. It simply happened. And now they belonged to each other.

Seeing Steven made his heart jump with concern. Fur stood off his shoulders at the memory of Steven pointing the gun, the scary-pop sound and acrid smell when it bit his ear. Ever since that day, he'd lived with September and been a good-dog for her, keeping her safe from bad dreams and bad men. He didn't want to get close to Steven ever again.

Shadow whined, and nudged September's thigh again with his nose. He wanted to go home, take a car ride back to their house. Macy waited for him there. His Frisbees were in their car. His life belonged with September.

"What's wrong, baby-dog?" He could tell she didn't want to talk to Steven or the people around him. But her voice made everything better, and he licked her hand to tell her so. He jumped up, surprising her. He wasn't supposed to, but needed her arms around him. She scolded him with a laugh that said she didn't mean it.

Shadow didn't object when she scooped up Bear-toy where he'd dropped it, and tucked it under her arm. When she tugged his leash, Shadow reluctantly followed, but he kept his eyes down, away from Steven. His tail tucked.

She wouldn't, would she? Hand his leash to Steven? His tail tucked tighter at the thought and he whimpered. Humans did things that made no dog-sense sometimes. Shadow wanted to please September, but not if it meant going away from her. He'd do anything to stay with her. She belonged to him, they belonged together.

Why had Steven come back, unless he meant to take Shadow away? That would hurt worse than the gun-bite.

His whimper became a steady whine. He debated digging his feet into the rough floor. Shadow had chosen to disobey September before, when he knew—knew for certain—that she was wrong. This time he wasn't sure, and the confusion and worry made his head hurt and heart ache. Before he could decide, September's phone made a funny sound and she stopped to talk.

Her scent changed and then her voice. Alarm fluttered his stomach when she asked, "Who is this? Why do you have Detective Combs's phone?"

Shadow didn't recognize the young voice on the other end of the device. Only that the girl sounded terrified.

"Melinda?" September stiffened when she said the word, and Shadow nose poked her thigh, but she ignored him. "Willie's gone? Oh my God."

Cocking his head, Shadow studied her face. The whites of her eyes and wrinkled brow matched her words, and her scent became brittle with the rush of energy. September waved at the adults across the room, and pointed to her phone. He couldn't help his paw-dance of relief when she did an about face.

"Let's go, Shadow."

They hurried back through the crowds to the rear door of the building. Together. A team. Away from Steven.

Chapter 14

September ran from the crowded stage. A lost child trumped anything Mom had planned. No time to discuss or explain, especially with Steven within earshot. She couldn't guess how much her nephew remembered about his ordeal. No need to remind him.

"Let's go, Shadow, time for car ride." He woofed and pranced and she let him off the leash. Thunder rattled the building again, but this time he didn't react. His earlier fearful behavior she ascribed to the strange place and crowd. September regretted leaving Harmony behind, but trusted Parker would lock the cello in the box office until she could collect her.

As they left the building, the sky dumped buckets of rain. Heavy winds pushed water into waves skittering across the pavement and sheets lashed her tangled hair. Crap. It had been cloudy and warm when she arrived, so she'd left her coat in the car. With no other choice, the pair ducked and ran to September's SUV parked half a block away. She thumbed the key-lock, waited for Shadow to leap into the back seat, slammed his door and then dove into the front.

Wicked gusts caught the driver's door and it took two tries to slam it shut. Cold water poured down September's neck, and she swiped her face with a drenched sleeve. In the back seat, Shadow shook, splattering the inside of the car.

"Gee thanks, baby-dog." In response, he wagged, slicked back his ears and poked his nose through the metal grill that kept him from claiming the driver's seat. September reached back, and smoothed his soaked face. Her sweatshirt stuck to her skin. She gathered her soaked hair to one side to wring it out on the passenger side floor. *At least it's not a blizzard.*

The slate-color clouds churned, black edges tattered flags streaming with the wind. Occasional lightening strobed the area into an eerie stop-action movie.

After she started the car, September crept from the parking lot, leaning forward to peer through windshield wipers that snick-snacked but still couldn't clear her view. The deluge cut visibility to nil, but they couldn't wait. Shadow could track Willie's dog, and with luck, they'd be together. Any hope for a successful search ticked away with every minute delayed, and rain diluted scent while wind chased it away and made it harder for Shadow to track. But they had to try.

Before she'd gone half a block, a dashboard light alerted her to an unlatched door. She must have keyed open the rear hatch of the SUV. She pulled to the side of the road, and Shadow watched with interest when September caped her down-filled coat above her head to run and slam shut the rear door. The piles of blankets and tracking equipment stored in the back would need drying out later.

Although she knew the address, September had no reason or desire to visit the Harrison residence before today. Combs's kids lived with his ex-wife Cassie and her new husband Rick Harrison in a two-and-a-half story brick monstrosity designed to shout their elevated social status to the world.

After fifteen minutes, the overhead faucet shut off. Gutters on each side of the street overflowed, creating whitewater the overtaxed drain system couldn't handle and leaving only the crown of the street free of runoff. September un-crunched her shoulders and sat back in the seat, steering toward the middle of the road to stay clear of the flood swell. After so much recent precipitation, North Texas had been under flash flood warnings all week. Weird weather for February. September worried the temperature would drop and create a statewide skating rink.

Ten minutes later, with no traffic to speak of, September pulled into the Harrison's drive. Shadow stood and made concentric nose prints on the window. His tail thwapped against the back seat.

"Shadow, *wait.*"

He yawned, and muttered his opinion, then turned away and pawed at the back seat. He woofed, and pricked his ears. Maybe he wanted his tracking gear she'd stowed in the back of the SUV. Shadow sometimes read her mind, and September liked to think she also tuned in to his thoughts.

She preferred Shadow with her, but better to question Melinda first. She left the keys in the car, hit the window child locks, and switched on the radio to her favorite classical station.

Cold gusts turned September's wet hair to a chilly mop that trailed over her shoulders nearly to her butt. Quickly she snugged tight the zipper on her oversize coat, the poufy padding more suited to snowstorms than rain. Even the damp cover helped cut the wind.

Before she could ring the bell, Melinda swung open the massive double doors. Red wavy hair framed her heart-shaped face. "You came." She peered past September toward the car. "You brought him? The tracking dog?" She swiped her palm against one eye.

September pushed into the foyer, and wrinkled her nose when her sodden clothes dripped on the spotless white marble. Who in their right mind designed an entry with white marble? "Where's your stepdad? Did you call him?"

Melinda and hugged herself. "He's with Mom. Getting more tests." She pushed the door closed, and crossed her arms. "He couldn't do anything anyway. It's all about Mom. They don't have time for us." Her bitter tone spoke volumes.

Cassie suffered from a rare brain disorder that mimicked Alzheimer's, one of half a dozen or so in the region affected. September personally knew of two others.

"I'm sure that's not true." She had to say that, although Melinda probably was right. Rick naturally focused on his wife over his stepchildren. September understood the girl's resentment being saddled with Willie, and unable to hang out with friends. "Don't you have the number for Detective Gonzales? He's with your dad."

"I didn't want to get Dad in trouble leaving his phone and all." She looked away.

"Uh huh. Yes, I'm sure that wouldn't go over well." September couldn't resist the dry jab. Far more likely, Melinda lost track of time and knew she'd be in trouble when found out she'd let Willie out of her sight.

"Dad's busy. He's told me before I shouldn't call him during shift." Her voice rose. "You're supposed to be some dog tracking expert or something, so I called you." She jutted her jaw.

"Show me where your brother left the house. And could you loan me a towel?"

September gingerly tiptoed across light tan carpet to avoid leaving footprints. Once she reached the ceramic tile of the kitchen, she gratefully wiped her face with the hand towel Melinda offered.

The girl gestured to the hallway, voice defensive. "I was on the computer in my room. Doing homework. I heard Willie yell something about the dog. He's always trying to get me to take Kinsler out, especially when I'm in the middle of something. It was his turn, and besides, I didn't want to get my new leggings all muddy."

"That's the least of your worries." September walked to the kitchen door to check out the window. The back of the house boasted a good half acre of lush grass contained by a privacy fence painted to match the shutter's white trim. Standing water pooled in two corners of the yard, slowly draining beneath the wooden barrier. "He went out here, and through the gate? It's still ajar." She could see a narrow alley that divided this property from the neighboring house.

"Why anyone would want that dog is beyond me. He poops in the house, chewed up my fav boots. But Willie loves him." She wiped her eyes on the hem of her shirt. "Willie plays make believe with bad guys and stuff, pretending to be a super-cop and Kinsler's his partner."

Pretending to be his father.

"I heard the door open and Willie yelling and screaming. By the time I got in here, the back yard was empty."

"Why didn't you go after him?"

"I did. I'm not totally horrible, he *is* my brother." Melinda indicated her splattered leggings. "Ruined them chasing after Willie. He knows I'll get in trouble if he gets hurt." At the last word, she deflated. "I got to the gate in time to see this ginormous baby-poop-brown truck zoom away. And Willie wasn't there."

"You checked with the neighbors?"

"Yes. Yes, I checked. I'm not an idiot." She tossed her hair. "Sorry. But we're wasting time. For a while, I thought Willie hid to get back at me? But when it started storming, I knew he wasn't fooling." She grabbed a lock of wavy red hair and twisted it, a nervous habit that had left one side shorter than the other. "I tried to call Dad first. That's how I knew he left his phone when it went to voice mail and I heard it beeping on the table. Yours was the first name listed, and the first time I dialed sort of by accident. And then I thought, why not?" She took a breath. "So what about tracking Willie? We have to find him. Dad will kill me." Her chin trembled. "Willie thinks he's so grown up but he's only ten. Only a little boy."

September awkwardly embraced the girl. "It'll be okay." She'd bet anything Willie took shelter with a neighbor, and, like many little brothers, relished getting payback for being dismissed. Melinda hadn't mentioned the truck before, though, and that worried her. "I'll take a quick look, okay? But you have to call your dad. No arguments. Give me his phone."

Reluctantly, Melinda handed it over and September quickly scrolled through the contacts to find Winston Gonzales. "You know his partner, Detective Gonzales, right? Call him, explain who it is and ask to talk to your father. And you tell him what's going on."

Melinda's shoulders tightened but she nodded. "Don't you need your dog?"

"Shadow's trained to track other pets. So unless Kinsler is with your brother, Shadow probably wouldn't be much help." Besides, she still expected to see Willie trudge sheepishly out of the shrubbery once an adult ordered him inside. "Make that call. Now." She turned to the door.

Her wet tracking boots squeaked on the tile, and bare feet chaffed inside without socks. September dreaded going back out into the wind, and took a moment to pull up the hood on her coat. At least her feet wouldn't freeze. She hurried out the kitchen door, and trotted across the yard.

Sod squelched beneath her feet, and the atmosphere smelled of ozone. Her skin prickled with goose bumps that had nothing to do with the sudden temperature drop. September almost turned back to get Shadow.

She reached the wooden gate, and paused once she stepped through. The alley, more of a sandy pathway, served as shortcut through a field that separated two halves of the subdivision. The Harrison's home perched on a slight incline with the back yard leading downward to a natural runoff, dry most of the year, but now a raging torrent. Willie would have had to cross the water, and she prayed he'd not taken the chance. Too easy for a small child to be swept away. Heck, she wouldn't attempt crossing, either.

Heavy rain hadn't erased deep tire ruts that supported Melinda's account of a big truck. It had spun out to escape the mire. The drive foundation might be solid, but anything off the road hadn't a chance. She saw nothing as fine as a child's footprint, or dog's pad mark.

Lots of scrubby burl oak, cedar elm and mountain ash lined both sides of the drive, all barren of leaves, and offering no shelter to hide a small child. "Willie? William Combs, if you hear my voice, come home right now." She yelled as loud as she could, and paused to listen for a reply.

Nothing.

"Will-eeeeeeeeeeeeeeee!"

Something fluttered in a nearby tree. September cautiously stepped off the roadway, slaloming down the muddy incline, and grabbed a branch to steady herself. She plucked the blue and white scarf from the limb, each end festooned with the Dallas Cowboys star, something a little boy would love.

Lightening crackled and September jumped when a fingernail of light scratched the blackboard clouds. Rain pattered around her, the storm ready to reprise its assault.

She wheeled, and ran back the way she'd come, slipping and sliding in the muck as she cornered through the gate. September clutched the scarf close, as if shielding the fabric would extend protection to the child. She burst through the kitchen door, and nearly ran headlong into a wild-eyed woman.

"Who the hell are you?" A whip-thin lady with sharp features and flyaway red hair stalked her, brandishing a butcher knife. "And what are you doing with Willie's scarf?"

Chapter 15

The truck lurched, and the dog in the back of the truck yelped again. Kelvin forced himself to ignore the cries of the "bait." Their sacrifice would put an end to a much larger horror, but that didn't assuage his guilt. At least the cats had stopped yowling. He needed all his attention for the uneven road.

He'd snagged the cats from the "free to good home" parking lot give-away next to the Wal-Mart. The woman's worry changed to grateful relief when he agreed to adopt them all. That moment would haunt him, and he damned Sunny for forcing his hand.

Sunny mocked his "humanization" of his dog Hercules. She treated her own dogs well, in the same way she cared for her guns and truck, but considered them replaceable tools. She treated people the same way, as either assets or expendable. Loyalty had a price, and emotion had no part in Sunny's life. The fires of childhood abuse forged her, so Kelvin didn't blame her brokenness, any more than he blamed a copperhead for its nature.

She demanded he get his hands dirty, too, as insurance he wouldn't hang her out to dry. Kelvin needed Sunny's unsavory contacts to spring the trap and be a hero. That would absolve him. Hell, if he hadn't taken the kittens, they'd be dumped somewhere else, and die anyway. This way, their sacrifice made a difference.

But compared to the high school kid, stealing a few animals barely rated. In this part of the country, anyone with half a brain knew what chained Pit Bulls meant, so it didn't surprise him when the kid ran. Hercules hadn't meant to kill the kid. Hell, the dog had been hysterical when Kelvin finally got him back to the truck. Nobody could know, not even Sunny. That'd give her insurance he'd never be able to pay off.

Kelvin couldn't have the cops bust the fight ring and disrupt the Doctor's plans before Kelvin could spring the trap.

If he hadn't got so rattled, Kelvin would've jacked the kid's car out of the muck and dumped it somewhere before running Hercules home. On his way back to address that little detail, the muddy stray dashed in front of his truck like a belated Christmas present. Kelvin slid to a stop, it waited for him, wriggling and wagging, and even slurped him across the face when he scooped it up. He slammed the kennel grate in the dog's face and tried to ignore the betrayal he imagined in its eyes.

The rain came down in sheets and he needed all his attention to keep the truck on the narrow lane, grateful when he could increase the turtle pace on the narrow drive. Kelvin slowed to a near stop, turned, and punched the gas and the truck jackrabbited onto the road. But he couldn't outrun the pungent wet-dog odor of the stolen dog that clung to his clothes.

He squinted at the dark clouds that turned day to twilight. The wipers flailed in an effort to keep the windshield clear, and the inside of the glass fogged despite the dashboard blower. Kelvin cracked opened his window to help clear the steamed glass. A prickly sensation tickled and raised hairs on the back of his neck and the rain abruptly stopped. The hum of tires on wet pavement changed when the truck slowed for the final turn.

He pulled onto the narrow pathway and rolled the window the rest of the way down. The ditch now rushed with water, and the kid's tinker-toy yellow car was gone.

Kelvin continued slowly down the drive, puzzling what that meant. Good that the car no longer flagged this turnoff like a hazard warning. If the flood took the Mini Cooper away, he must be living right.

But Sunny's friends had eyeballs on the area. If one of her cohorts saw what happened to the kid, and moved the car for the leverage, Kelvin figured he'd just bit into a shit sandwich. He needed to pick Sunny's brain without giving her more ammo to screw him.

He pulled out his phone, and tried to get a dial tone. The weather played havoc with reception out here. Kelvin climbed out of the truck, and walked toward the rear of the vehicle before a couple of bars appeared on the phone promising better connection. Sunny answered on the first ring.

"Sunny, I picked up some bait like you said. Something happened, though, got to change plans."

Her voice crackled through static on the line. "I get paid anyway, whatever happens. That's the deal." The wind picked up so much Kelvin had trouble hearing Sunny's response.

He covered one ear and ducked his head, leaning against the truck bed to use as a windbreak. "A car got stuck in the mud, right off the road." He felt more than heard the hiccup in his voice and hoped Sunny didn't recognize the emotion.

"Did you go all Good Samaritan and help 'em out?" Sunny dropped the mocking inflection. "Keep him away from the barn, that's the main thing."

"I never found the driver." The lie came easily on the heels of relief. "I hope he caught a ride. If your friends caught him snooping, he wouldn't live to tell about it."

"True enough. Only reason they let you get close was my recommendation. It's a payday for them, too, if we don't screw it up."

"Right, that's what I figured. Anyway, now the car disappeared, and I didn't touch it." He kept his tone neutral. "Your friends again?"

Sunny paused. "Not that I heard. Whoever gave him a ride must've collected the car, too."

Kelvin half smiled. She didn't know. That didn't mean her friends didn't have him on video, though. "Maybe flood waters moved it. But you said they monitored the area. Is it cameras or what?" Lightening cracked and Kelvin jumped when a chorus of yowls erupted from the twin kennels in the truck's bed. "Could your, uhm, associates have moved it?"

Her answer again mixed with static proved too garbled to understand except for the last word: payday. Leave it to Sunny to have her priorities straight.

"I got to go, Sunny, it's fixing to storm something fierce. Don't worry, you'll get your money."

Her final jab came crystal clear. "Deliver your end of the bargain, Kelvin, and get those animals over to the barn or you'll have more than hail to worry about."

Kelvin disconnected without answering. Lightening crackled again, and rain rejoined its dance with the wind. Time had run out for the cats and stray dog in the back. He'd thought the price steep enough in terms of innocent lives, until BeeBo and the unnamed kid tipped the balance further into the red zone. He'd make sure their lives counted for something.

The truck lurched as Kelvin climbed back inside. In another day or two, it wouldn't matter if Sunny's associates knew anything or not. Once rounded up along with the Doctor, the cops would dismiss any fantastic claims they spouted as desperate fabrications.

He shoved the truck into gear, and drove slowly toward the hidden barn, already planning how to get the animals from the truck into the dumpsters. It'd take three or maybe four trips. He didn't have a carrier, so he'd have to tote one by one while dodging a path through the chained Pit Bulls. They wouldn't bother him, but probably considered smaller pets as prey. The truck hit a pothole, and the bucking movement jarred something loose in the truck's bed.

One of the kennel doors sprang open. It slapped to and fro in the growing wind. Kelvin took his foot off the gas when the three cats spilled out. The littlest one, the color of dark honey and probably just as sweet, climbed up something dark that moved. Kelvin twisted in his seat to stare, as the truck continued to coast.

The dark shape became a youngster. The boy tucked the small orange cat inside his coat and scooted on his butt to the passenger side of the truck bed. Kelvin cursed when the muddy white stray dog followed him. The boy boosted the pooch up and over the side of the truck. It yelped when it landed.

Kelvin watched with disbelief as the stolen "bait" escaped. The boy turned back, maybe to gather up the last two cats, saw him, and yelled. Kelvin slammed on the brakes.

"Run! Kinsler, run run run!" The boy vaulted over the side of the truck to follow the dog.

Kelvin leaped from the truck, cursing, but didn't attempt to stop the boy. He stood and watched him pelt down the muddy trail, never once looking back. He waited until the boy disappeared from sight and then Kelvin collected the remaining cats, and delivered them to their destiny. They'd have to be enough.

Chapter 16

The fire in his lungs finally made Willie stop, but he still couldn't catch his breath. He stumbled off the side of the road to hunch beneath sheltering limbs of a live oak, leaves sparse but still green despite the weather they'd had. He propped himself against the tree before his noodle-weak knees gave out. The little cat inside his jacket shivered and mewed, and its tail slipped out. He tucked it back inside, thinking the waffle-colored tabby had the longest tail he'd ever seen.

Willie peered around the tree, and breathed easier at the empty road. He'd lucked out. Either the nefarious bad guy couldn't turn his truck around quick enough to chase, or he had more important stuff to do. Like maybe steal more kids' dogs and cats.

"Kinsler? Where are you?" Willie thought the dog was right behind him. "Kin....sler. Come here, boy, come on, let's go home."

Waffles shivered and yowled in answer. "Hey, it's okay, little guy. Kinsler probably caught a whiff of squirrel and took off again. Dang dog lets his nose talk him into trouble. That's what Melinda says."

Melinda would know what to do. For a girl, she was pretty smart. At least Kinsler got away from the dog thief. Maybe he'd sniff his way home.

Willie's teeth chattered. It'd be cool if he had a fur coat and could sniff his way home like Kinsler, but he couldn't see three feet before him through the curtain of rain. He winced when something stung his cheek. He looked at the sky. Pea-size beads of ice peppered the ground and shredded leaves for thirty seconds, and then stopped. His soaked jeans stuck to his legs, and when lightening crackled, he scrambled from beneath the tree. Trees attract lightening. He learned that at the school safety assembly about tornadoes.

Tornadoes were awesome. Not when they hurt people. But the combo of wind and hail and lightening played out like video games where superheroes fought above the clouds, and thundering artillery drove evil doers away. He bet the dark fluff in the south-west sky was a wall cloud. Willie always thought it'd be cool to be a storm chaser.

But storm chasers only talked about the excitement. Nothing, not even hugging the cat in his arms, relieved the feeling of *aloneness*. He looked up, as if from the bottom of a dark, enormous pit with no way out. Clouds pushed down, down, down until he couldn't breathe, and his stomach clenched the same way a roller coaster flip-flopped your insides. Daddy would know what to do. Melinda would get mad. But Mom wouldn't even know he was lost, or care if he never got home. That sucked the worst of all.

"Don't be a stupid-head." He said it out loud, to buck up his courage, and the cat purred. "Wasn't talking to you, Waffles. But guess we're in this together."

Willie's wet clothes chaffed and itched his legs when he cautiously climbed back onto the road's crest. His shoes slipped every third step but he took care to dodge channels cut in the bank as water sluiced down. Hair dripped into his eyes, making it hard to see. The ditch on both sides of the road collected brown water that churned and nibbled and swallowed whole chocolate-color chunks from the bank. As he watched, the water level rose so fast it lapped nearly to the spot he'd previously stood.

Lightening zippered across the sky, and Willie picked up his pace down the middle of the road heading toward town. Rain took a breather and the wind didn't push quite so hard, but the spider web itch on the back of his neck never let up. Creepy.

Distant headlights drove Willie to the brushy growth off the road. Only the truck guy and his creepy minions dared to be out…and stupid-head kids. He figured these minions wouldn't be cute cartoons, neither.

One step off the solid pavement sent him sliding toward stinky ditch water. Willie wrapped his arms tighter around the purring

Waffles, squared his shoulders, and slowed to a determined walk in the opposite lane. Dad said attitude got you through tough situations, so he'd be tough.

The van—it was a van, not the brown truck, he saw with relief— slowed to a crawl. "Drive on, drive on, drive on," he whispered to himself, and kept his eyes averted, sure if he made eye contact, his head would explode.

But the van pulled alongside him, stopped, and the driver cranked down the window. A kid maybe his sister's age stuck his head out the window. A girl younger than Willie with black braids rode in the passenger seat clutching a stuffed purple dinosaur.

"Storm coming, bad storm. Get in, get safe. Bad storm, high winds predicted. Based on Fujita-Pearson Scale, storm will cause considerable to severe damage. Very dangerous situation. Golf ball size hail which is ice falling from sky, and F2 or F3 tornadoes. Fascinating tornadoes but deadly, too. Why outside? Get in." The boy cocked his head when Willie's rescued cat meowed. "Storm bad for cat, too."

Willie grinned. "Tornadoes are cool. I'm sort of a storm chaser. Want to be one, anyway." Rain began to spit again so he hurried to the rear door, levered it open and climbed inside. "I'm Willie. Sure glad you showed up, it's a long walk back to town." He opened his jacket and the orange cat spilled out, took a couple of unsteady steps, and then shook wet from its fur.

The little girl squealed and clutched her toy. "Grooby hates wet." She turned around in her seat, as much as the belt would allow. "Sixty-seven percent chance tornadoes hit Heartland."

The driver nodded. "Tracy knows numbers. Lenny knows tornadoes. And maps. I'm Lenny. She's Tracy." His gaze slid away.

Kinsler did that with his eyes, too. Willie hoped Kinsler found a safe spot out of the storm, or sniffed his way home. Dogs were supposed to have some sort of homing instinct. He read about that in The Incredible Journey book.

The boy behind the wheel shoved the stick shift and gears grated before the van shook and began to move.

Willie studied the two kids. They talked weird, but he didn't doubt they were smart about numbers and storms. "We're not going back to town? We could go to my house." He wanted to go home, but at least he was out of the rain. Mom always said beggars can't be choosers, so he couldn't complain.

"Basement?" Lenny kept both hands on the wheel, his knuckles white when sudden wind shook the van. When Willie shook his head, Lenny sped up the van.

What if a tornado hit his house? Melinda was there by herself. "One time we all huddled up in the bathroom. Hail took out the front window but everything else was okay." Ground shifted too much in North Texas to have a basement. He didn't know anyone who had a storm shelter, either. Most times, bad storms magically moved around or turned away from Heartland, and only hit the outskirts.

Tracy fiddled with a tablet, then held it up. Willie could see a multicolored schematic of weather radar moving in real time across a digital map.

Lenny tapped the screen. "Safe spot, there." He slowed the van, peered through the windshield past the flack-flack-flack of wipers, and turned off onto a hidden gravel pathway.

Crowding tree limbs scraped and pushed against the van like witch fingers guarding secrets. Willie yelped when a particularly large limb thumped the windshield. A star-shaped crack appeared. He remembered the drainage ditch on both sides of the road, and hoped the narrow road wouldn't wash out before they got to Lenny's safe spot. And that it truly was safe.

Dad would call the road a pig path. Willie wondered where feral hogs hid when tornadoes threatened.

The three remained silent, bracing themselves as the van struggled up a slight incline to higher ground. Lenny slowed the van, and pointed. "Down there is safe. Tornado jumps over low land."

Willie checked out windows on both sides of the van. The road straddled a man-made dam. A livestock tank on the right gave way to a steep dirt slope on the other, where a cement barn squatted halfway down screened by an army of massive bois d'arc trees. The building seemed solid, all right.

The overgrown drive veered to the left and downward, and Lenny drove slowly, babying the van. But almost immediately, the tires lost traction in the saturated ground. The van skied sideways, crabbing downward until earth completely gave way.

Tracy shrieked, Willie yelled. The van slammed the rear wall of the barn. Waffle's percussive spit-hiss morphed into banshee yowls after Lenny's head made a melon-like "thonk" on the windshield. Silence.

Then a pack of dogs howled.

Chapter 17

Shadow wondered why September ignored the stowaways in the back of the SUV. When they jumped in the car at the theater, he'd noticed right away. Maybe it was a game, hiding under blankets. Shadow liked games. The kids only came out after September left the car to go into the house without him.

"Good-boy, Shadow." Nikki reached to scratch him. "Thanks for not giving us away." She turned to speak to Steven. "Now what? September left the keys, but I don't know how to drive. Do you?" The hitch in her voice, and rising inflection, partnered with her wrinkled brow, spoke of worry and concern.

Shadow still fretted what Steven wanted. But he liked Nikki. She gave him treats, played the *show-me* game, and scratched his chin the way he liked it. And she smelled like cats. Shadow liked cat smell.

The squeal of wet tires stopped right behind their car and made the two kids squeak and dive back under the blankets. Shadow arched his neck and pricked ears at the strange man who got out, followed by an odd lady moving with strange twitches. She had flyaway fluffy hair even longer than September's. He poked his nose out the window crack, tasting the air when they walked by.

The lady's smell mixed sweat and perfume, medicine and fever. It reminded him of the vet clinic, only without the companionable animal smells. The man's breathing hurried fast as his feet, while his shoulders hunched against the rain. Wind tossed the lady's mane over her face, and then away, and when Shadow glimpsed her wild eyes, his ears went flat. He muttered a growled caution to himself.

What to do? September was inside. Strangers near his person, without Shadow to protect, made his heart race faster than Macy chasing a toy.

His suspicion and frustration grew when the pair reached the door. The man fiddled with the handle to make it open, jingling keys— Shadow knew that word from the *show-me* game—while the woman made high pitched whines that hurt a good-dog's ears.

Shadow furrowed his brow and ran to the other side of the car to see better as the man opened the door. The sick-smelling lady scuttled inside. He whined and pawed the window. He should be with his person, to protect September and warn about sick-smelling people and strange men opening doors.

Sometimes when he pawed car doors, the window scrolled down. Shadow didn't know why this didn't happen every time. The fact it happened at all offered enough incentive for him to try every time, especially when a good-dog needed to be with his person.

People knew many things that dogs didn't. September told him to *wait* and good-dogs did what they were told. But dogs knew many things, too, sometimes more than people did.

He pawed the door, scratching the window and the side of the panel, while anxious whines spilled from his throat. Maybe Nikki would open the car door for him? Shadow checked, but the two kids still huddled under a pile of blankets, not even a twitch to betray their presence. They smelled scared, the acrid scent laser bright. He heard muted sounds that must be the whiny lady's voice even through the closed door of the house.

"Willieeeeee!"

Shadow ran to the other side of the car when he heard September's worried cry. From somewhere behind the house. He relaxed a bit. The strangers inside weren't near her after all.

He didn't know what the "willieeee" word meant, but it had the same tone as when she called Shadow to come. Was September calling another dog? He only liked to come when treats or toys were involved. But he came anyway, because he wanted to be a good-dog for September.

Would she give that willieeee-dog a treat? He listened hard, past the sizzling-bacon-sound of rain on the roof, and paw-swiped the door again.

This time, the window opened. Delighted, Shadow hopped out and stood on the pavement for a moment, sniffing the foot treads of the strangers while rain pelted his black fur.

The door to the house opened again, and Shadow's head came up. The strange man left the door ajar, and called over his shoulder. "Watch your mother, my phone's in my car."

Shadow dashed away when the man jogged toward him, and redoubled his pace at the man's startled cry. He bounded to the rear of the house, nose up to seek September and the willieee-dog she'd called. Running feet slapped a sodden drumbeat, and Shadow recognized September's quiet gasps for breath. No longer worried, now she sounded scared.

He barked as he ran so she'd hear him and know not to be afraid. He'd protect her, just as she protected him. That's what family did for each other.

Shadow found the fence, and followed it around the backyard border, barking again and again until he reached the open gate. He quickly scanned the large yard, and found September in the open doorway of the house. Her tight posture, both palms up in a warding off gesture, screamed danger.

Each splashing leap brought him closer. At first, he ignored September's voice, intent on reaching her as quickly as possible.

"Shadow, *wait*." She didn't turn, just held her palm toward him, to reinforce the command.

He skidded to a stop shy of the cement paving stones. Shadow whined, and took two slow steps closer to within nose-touch reach.

"Good-dog, Shadow. *Wait*." September backed up a step, too

Peering around her leg, Shadow saw the wild-eyed woman in the middle of the room, waving her hands around. Something silver-bright glinted in one of her fists. A young girl stood at one side, mouth a silent "o."

"Where's my son? Where's Willie, what have you done with Willie, he's not here, where's Willie?"

Shadow recognized the "where" word. September often prefaced a *seek* command with this word. He looked around, wondering what she'd lost, waiting to be told what to find.

September offered the woman a length of fabric, the sort of thing people wore around their neck because they didn't have enough fur to stay warm. September spoke with calm, but Shadow read the underlying emotion. He tensed, prepared to throw himself at the threat.

"Mom?" The young girl found her voice. "Put down the knife. Please?"

Knife? Shadow knew that word, too. He watched the lady's hand. There were no treats in her other fist.

"Who are you? Where is my son?" The words came fast and loud, jumbled together so Shadow couldn't pick them apart. The sick-smelling lady moved erratically, her head whipping back and forth so her mane-like hair covered her face. She stalked toward the young girl, jabbing the knife in the air. Shadow took a stiff-legged paw step closer, putting himself between September and the knife.

"Melinda, go!" September jerked her head and the girl sidled sideways and then turned and ran. Her footsteps thumped away to the front door, and Shadow heard it swing open. His ears rang when she screamed for help.

Shadow sidled closer. He leaned hard against September's knees, using his weight to push her back. He snarled silently when the strange man rushed into the room. Shadow showed his teeth, not wanting to bite, merely to warn away the danger.

September put a hand on Shadow's head. At the unspoken request, he lowered his lips but divided his attention between the man and the distraught woman.

"Go 'way go 'way go 'way." She jabbed the knife at the man, too, and he backed up without saying anything. "Where's Willie? My husband is a cop, go 'way go 'way go 'way."

Shadow knew the words meant bad things because September flinched like she'd been hit. Shadow nose-poked her thigh, and she finally made eye contact. Her posture changed. His tail lifted with anticipation, knowing she'd made a decision. Her hand on his head stroked with purpose, and she whispered for him only. "Good-dog, Shadow, wanna play *show-me*?"

He wagged, but remained silent. Shadow watched her face, confident now she'd taken charge and could tell him what to do. How to fix this. Together they could do anything.

"Back, back." Shadow took a step backwards, and cocked his head when both the man and girl retreated, too. The wild stabbing motions subsided. September kept her voice conversational, but the command in the tone made people as well as good-dogs pay attention and obey.

The lady started to cry, an ugly sound that made Shadow's ears fall flat. Her hands dropped to her sides like fluttery birds falling from the sky.

"*Show-me* KNIFE." September's voice cracked.

Shadow rocketed forward, and nose-punched the back of the lady's hand. She screamed. But the knife spun away, shiny and bright. It clattered against the floor.

"Shadow, BRING KNIFE."

Without hesitation, he dove for the object, and gingerly grasped the widest part. He ignored the man who had rushed to embrace the sobbing lady. Shadow triumphantly carried the prize to September.

"Good-dog, what a brave boy." With relief in her voice, September pocketed the knife and welcomed Shadow into her arms. "I must have unlocked instead of locked the windows, thank goodness."

Across the room, the young girl's angry voice made Shadow's ears hurt. "Nice trick. But can he find my brother?"

Chapter 18

Kelvin opened his office door and waited, shifting his weight from boot to boot. He'd not had time to change, and the black clay that stained his dingy clothes chilled him to the bone. The Doctor strode toward him, open coat flapping so much Kelvin expected him to shed feathers and caw.

Water stained the calf-length duster from the shoulders halfway down the man's back. He carried no umbrella, and wore no hat. Rain tarnished his long silver hair, making the stalk of his neck appear too thin to support his head. His hair dripped, running down both cheeks, mimicking tears Kelvin doubted the man had ever shed.

"You have the place. The time." The Doctor didn't bother to wipe his face, only stood in the doorway and dripped.

"Come in, we need to talk. Yes, I've got the location and time." Kelvin crossed to his desk and pulled out a map. Sunny had refused to give him anything in writing, and it took him forever to find the site based on her directions. He had too much riding on this to risk the Doctor claiming the directions weren't clear.

He used a red Sharpie marker, wrote a #1 on their location, a #2 at the barn, and drew a line along appropriate roadways to connect the two. "Paved road most of the way. This last bit here," he poked the map with the marker, "dirt drive that follows along a levy. Narrow, my truck barely cleared the trees. Probably better for you to send in a few small vehicles than a double-wide that'd get stuck." He offered the map. "There's dogs staked out front, but they won't bother you. Just stick to the path leading into the barn. You'll want to store your—uhm, product—on the second floor, in the loft. Fights are in the pit down below, so you can do your business privately. It's not fancy, but you get what you asked for."

The Doctor tipped his head, peered at the map, but didn't take it. "What time tomorrow?"

"About that." Kelvin dropped the map on the desk and moved to put distance and solid oak furniture between them. "Sunny said her guys won't pit the dogs in bad weather."

The Doctor straightened. "Dogs don't fight in rain?"

"That's not it." Kelvin figured the dogs fought anytime, anywhere, as commanded and offered welcome respite from boredom. He figured the times between fights, chained up alone and without hope, must hurt like hell on earth.

"Rain makes dogs sick?" The Doctor stared. "Mother's Pomeranian hated rain. Made him sick. Neptune died." The man's silver eyes nearly disappeared with saucer-size pupils.

He's on the same shit he pedals to the kids. No wonder he's antsy. "No, rain doesn't make them sick. But it keeps customers away."

"Doesn't keep my team away. We mail medicine. Neither rain nor snow nor—"

"Not talking about your customers, Doctor. These dogfight guys, they've got their own clientele, some of them moneyed thrill seekers who bet huge numbers. They don't want to get their cufflinks wet."

"Wet cufflinks? Why—"

"Never mind the jewelry, it's a figure of speech. They don't want to get out in bad weather, okay? So it doesn't make financial sense for the fight to happen if nobody comes out to play."

"Current weather report posted a flash flood watch for this county. Possible destructive winds." He sounded like a computerized weather announcement.

"Right. That's right, Doctor. And they're talking possible tornado watch that's likely to last through the weekend." He didn't mask his frustration. Bad enough he had to deal with these scumbags and dirty his hands. If it weren't for Sunny's threats, he'd call the whole thing off and make tracks out of town. "Doctor, these fellows like to watch other creatures get bloody, but don't want to risk the wind mussing their hair."

"You made a promise."

"Yes, I made a p-promise." Kelvin took a breath. Hell, he hadn't stuttered since high school. "Sunny says they already canceled tomorrow's show."

"She promised, too." The Doctor put both hands to his face, wiping the wet upwards from cheeks to forehead, and smoothing hair from his brow. He left his big hands on his head, manicured nails grasped fists full of hair, tugging, tugging. "Promise is a contract." Tug. "Promises to Mother can't be un-done." Tug-tug. "You," tug-yank, "promised." Yank!

A tendril of wet hair fell to the floor. It made a red stain.

"Hey, stop. What're you doing?" Kelvin winced, reached out and immediately pulled back. If the guy wanted to snatch himself bald, so be it. "They canceled tomorrow, and moved up the time. Same place, but happens tonight, to beat the weather."

"Tonight?" The Doctor dropped his hands, one still clutching a hank of hair. "You promised. Sunny promised." The hand, hair still clinging, reached for his gun. "Broken promises reap punishment. You will keep your promise."

"You bet, Sunny and I have every intention to keep our promise." Kelvin rubbed his own bald head. "Those guys that set up the dogfights, though. They didn't promise. It's on them, not on me or Sunny, don't you see?" The Doctor blinked slowly, and Kelvin halfway expected those lizard eyes to shutter above a flicked forked tongue tasting the air.

When his hand moved away from the gun to a phone, Kelvin breathed again. The Doctor punched in a single number, listened, and spoke quickly with what must be latitude and longitude designations. "You have current batches addressed, ready to mail. Move them to the event site now. Yes, immediately. Call me to confirm delivery. We distribute tonight." He disconnected, dropped the phone in his pocket, and smoothed his mussed hair with the other.

"There, see? All fixed." Kelvin smiled, silently congratulating himself the meeting hadn't gone completely south. "Just means we finish our business that much faster." *And stop your money-grubbing kid-destroying plot.* He had the cops on speed-dial, once Sunny left town with her crazy-ass threat.

The Doctor pulled a stack of bound bills from his pocket and tossed it on the desk. "I keep my promise. Last payment tonight, after distribution." Another creepy slow blink. "When you keep your promise." He whirled, coat furling like a comic strip bad guy as he started for the door.

"Wait. Are you forgetting?" Sunny would throw a fit. Hell, she'd play her "insurance" card if she didn't get her share. "What about Sunny? I'm supposed to collect for her."

The Doctor whirled, and the coat flared outward again. "Already paid Sunny "The Babe" Babcock when she shared vital news that you killed BeeBo."

Kelvin sat down so hard, his teeth jarred.

"Sunny cried and cried and cried. She liked BeeBo. I liked BeeBo, too. But I understand you tried to help me, tried to keep your promise." The Doctor donned one of his fake smiles. "I never cry. Mother says real men don't cry, so I never cry." He took three long strides toward Kelvin, and stood above him, a lean black wraith. A thin trickle of crimson ran from his torn scalp down his forehead to the corner of his eye, a ruby tear that grew and grew. "Do you keep your promises?"

"Promises are sacred. You bet." Kelvin stared, waiting for that red drop to fall.

"That's good." He strode to the door, but instead of leaving, the Doctor shut and locked it, and pulled out a chair and sat down. "I'm good at keeping promises. And secrets. I'll help you keep yours as long as you keep mine." The red droplet trickled into the man's pale eye, creating bloody tears that spilled from his slow lizard blink.

Chapter 19

Combs flinched when the hail, now marble size, continued to hammer his car, sounding like a B-movie gunfight. Gonzales tipped his head toward the house. Combs hunched his shoulders and swung open the passenger door at the same time as his partner. "We'd better make a run for it before it gets worse."

The two men sprinted to the front porch, Combs with a forearm sheltering his face. The hail shredded the umbrella Gonzales wielded, and he dropped it with a disgusted sound. "Dammit. My kids got that for me for Christmas."

"All umbrellas are alike. Get another one." Gonzales had twin four-year-old daughters, and his son had just turned nine.

Gonzales shook his head. "I tried swapping something once when Finnegan B. Goldfish went belly up, and the kids caught me. Mercedes said they would. Moms always know. Nope, I'll have to 'fess up and tell the truth." He smoothed his mustache. "The umbrella saved my life in a battle with the Ice King."

Combs laughed. The front door swung open, so he turned it into a cough instead.

A balding thin man with a portly woman stood in the entry. She twisted a sodden tissue, dabbed her eyes, and spoke in a choked voice. "Come on in out of the mess. You the police, right? Here about Larry?"

"Mr. and Mrs. Samson? I'm Detective Combs, and this is Detective Gonzales. You've still not heard from your son?" Combs followed the woman into the house, Gonzales following closely behind. They took seats around a plain kitchen table.

"He's a typical teenager, sometimes forgetful, but a good boy. He's seventeen, almost. His birthday is next week." Mrs. Samson rubbed swollen eyes, and sniffled. "Larry never came home last night. And he didn't call."

Gonzales set a digital recorder on the table and thumbed it on, but also scribbled on a tiny notepad. "Forgive me for asking, but is your son autistic?"

"Autistic?" Mr. Samson rocked backwards. "No." He shared a confused glance with his wife.

Combs gave a slight shrug when Gonzales looked at him. Doty's missing kids were much younger, but they had to ask.

"Has he ever stayed out all night before? Without telling you?" Gonzales continued the rhythm of the questions.

"Never." Mr. Samson took off thick glasses and cleaned them on his shirttail. He cleared his throat. "He had track practice yesterday after school, but never showed up." He turned to his wife. "You have his latest school picture?"

She produced a large color image of a clean cut beanpole thin young man. His smile shone bright with braces. A few bright pimples blushed his cheeks.

"Friends?" Combs leaned forward on the table to accept the picture. Mrs. Samson gestured at the coffeepot, and he shook his head with a tight smile.

"His girlfriend called here last night." Mr. Sampson took his wife's hand. "Otherwise, we wouldn't have known he missed practice. They were supposed to meet after, and she said he was a no show, and not answering his texts."

"She's too young for him. I worry about that." Mrs. Samson crossed her arms. "She's only fifteen, way too young. Larry should date girls his own age."

"She's a good kid, she can't help if she looks older. I was older than you, and we turned out okay."

"That's different." She sniffed.

Combs figured the sore subject could have something to do with Larry's disappearance. Once Melinda turned sixteen, the age they'd agreed she could formally date, he'd be a wreck. She already pestered relentlessly to drive. He'd given in since the skill could help her disabled mother in case of an emergency. "My daughter is a newly minted teenager, and I love her to death. But Melinda wants to grow up too fast, and keeps secrets. Kids that age do. Are you sure the girlfriend isn't protecting your son? Is he in trouble?"

"Melinda? Your daughter is Melinda Combs?" She turned to her husband. "See? He says she's *thirteen*, I told you she's too young."

That knocked the wind out of him.

Mrs. Samson grabbed another tissue and blew her nose. "Larry would never worry us like this. You should have let me talk to Melinda when she called."

"Are you saying Larry's girlfriend is my daughter? Dating a seventeen-year-old?" Secrets, indeed.

Gonzales rapped on the table to get everyone's attention. "Focus. We'll worry about Melinda later. When did you last see or hear from your son?"

The couple spoke at the same time, words overlapping. "Yesterday morning..." and "Breakfast." Mr. Sampson grabbed his wife's hand again. "Go ahead, honey."

She gathered her thoughts, and repeated. "Breakfast yesterday morning." Her words spilled faster. "We make a point to have family time every day. Larry's school and extracurricular stuff make it hard to have dinner together, except Sundays after church. So, breakfast is family time, every day, without fail. Yesterday we had oatmeal and OJ but Larry was in a rush, because he convinced his dad," her eyes raked him with disapproval, "to borrow the new car. He wanted to show his friends and take them to Sonic after track practice. Except it turns out, he meant to meet up with that—I mean, your daughter." She spat the last words at Combs.

Mr. Samson took up the story. "Apparently, Melinda headed over to track after school and he wasn't there. Coach was pissed he was a no show, but his buddies swore he'd been in school."

Combs cracked his knuckles, regretting he only saw Melinda on weekends. She hadn't said a word to him this morning about the boy. "Buddies? We'll need names." Combs clearly read the terror in the couple's faces. He struggled to keep his face neutral, be the detective and not the dad. Nothing could be worse than a missing child.

Thunder cracked, and Gonzales jumped and swore, then smoothed his tie as if that would also calm his nerves. Hail turned windows into snare drums. "Maybe he got caught in the storm. It rained heavily last night. What kind of car does he drive?"

"Mini Cooper, black over yellow. Larry picked the color to match the school mascot, The Hornets." Mr. Samson rubbed his face. "He's a good driver, extremely responsible like we said. I'll get you the license number, but I shouldn't think there are too many that color."

Someone's cell phone pinged, and reflexively, Combs reached for his and only then realized that pocket was empty. How'd that happen? He never went anywhere without it.

Mrs. Samson's sour voice interjected. "He used to hang out with Zeke somebody, and a Henry or Hank, I think. But ever since he started dating Melinda, I don't know how much time they've spent together."

Mr. Sampson cleared his throat, struggling to keep it together. "I spoke to Melinda last night about 7:30 or so, and then tried to reach Larry. His phone kept going to voice mail. I even tried texting. He told me once that phone calls are *so yesterday*." He tried to smile, but his lips trembled and the expression wouldn't stay in place.

Mrs. Sampson tore tiny pieces from the tissue and rolled each into tiny balls as she spoke. "I called Zeke, and he hemmed and hawed and finally said Larry mentioned staying with Hank for the night. So I tried to reach Hank but got no answer there so I left messages. Wanted to drive over to check on him, but he wouldn't let me."

Her husband looked stricken. "Boys that age, they don't want their mom checking up on them in front of their friends. Larry has never given us reason not to trust him. I wanted to give him a pass this once, you know, and then kick his butt later if he screwed up. You have to let kids learn from mistakes." He wouldn't meet his wife's glare. "I was wrong."

Combs seethed, understanding Larry probably spent the night with Melinda. Before he could respond, Gonzales gripped his shoulder and shook his head.

"He didn't stay with Hank?" Gonzales's phone pinged again. He scribbled on his pad with one hand, and pulled out his phone with the other.

The woman shook her head. "Like you said, kids cover for each other. I spoke to Hank's mother an hour ago. She put him on the phone and made him explain, and then we called you." Her voice trembled. "Last night after I talked to Zeke, he texted Hank not to answer his phone. They thought Larry and Melinda had a whatdyacallit, 'hook up' and didn't want to get them in trouble. The two of them had it all figured out, except Larry didn't show up, and Melinda got worried and called us." Grudgingly, she added, "At least she did call."

Combs took a breath, wondering how often the pair had "hook ups?" He'd talk to Melinda later, and do more than talk to Rick-the-Prick. Cassie wasn't responsible.

Right now, the missing boy had to be his focus. "Larry left class at what time? About 3:30 or so?" He checked his watch. "So he's been missing about 18 hours."

Gonzales stared from his phone to Combs, and nudged him. "Says the call is from you. Somebody have your phone?" He answered, listened, and mouthed, "It's Melinda," and held it out to Combs.

Puzzled, Combs took the phone from his partner. "Must have left my phone this morning." He walked into another room, out of sight of the concerned parents, before he spoke. "We'll talk later, Melinda. I know about Larry. I'm so disappointed in you." He struggled to keep his cool, more hurt than angry. "I'm with his parents now. I'll call after shift."

"Daddy? I'm sorry. Please don't hang up." The girl's voice quavered, nothing like the usual brash know-it-all. "This isn't about Larry. I mean, I'm worried about him, too, but…"

His smile faded. "Is it your mother again? Sorry, honey, but Rick needs to deal with her." *Rick needs to step it up if he wants to keep custody.*

"Daddy, Willie's gone." She told him the rest. His face drained of color.

He ended the call and he rushed back into the kitchen. Out the windows, a weird twilight gloom painted the afternoon sky a sickly green that mirrored the expression on both parents' faces, and now on his own.

Chapter 20

September stumbled and caught herself on a tree but Shadow bulldozed on, towing her in his wake. Head down and nose tasting the ground, the German Shepherd acted impervious to the brambles that hobbled her own progress. September frowned when she recognized the ring tone—Combs phone. *Melinda again.* She started to thumb it off before answering, then quickly answered without breaking stride.

"Have you found him? Where are you?" Panic in Comb's voice sounded barely under control. "Melinda says you've been gone nearly forty minutes."

She stiffened. He must have rushed home to retrieve his phone. "No sign yet, but Shadow picked up a scent that could be Kinsler."

"Forget the damn dog. Find my son." His cop's cool cracked along with his voice.

She kept her own temper. "Shadow tracks pets, you know that. If they're still together, tracking Kinsler is the best bet." The black dog flicked his ears at the sound of his name, impatient to continue the trail. "Shadow's hot after something, and I don't want to discourage him."

Combs took a steadying breath, but his clipped tone remained frosty. She could hear a weird staccato clattering in the background.

"Weather guys upgraded the tornado watch to a warning. I've got pea-size hail. Where are you?"

She peered at the dark sky. Wind blew a nose-wrinkling smell of ozone, and lightening carved zigzags across the clouds but the rain had taken an intermission. "We're off FM 680 heading northwest. On foot with Shadow about midway across the field. Rain will muddy the trail, literally, but we can't stop until we find Willie or the trail goes stale."

The hail sound grew louder over the phone. "You're in the path. It's traveling about 30 miles per hour so it'll hit you in less than twenty minutes, maybe sooner. I'm on my way." His voice cracked again, clearly struggling with mixed emotions. "You need to find Willie quick, and take cover. I don't want to think about him out in this weather." He paused. "Or you."

The afterthought hurt, and shame followed. Willie was his son. She was merely some woman he'd known for a few months. "I know about tornadoes, remember, I grew up here. Even Chicago and South Bend had their share of bad weather." She brushed hair out of her eyes, and wished she had tied it back. "We've got no hail, not even rain at the moment but the window's fast closing. Got to run."

"You are the most stubborn, infuriating woman."

She said nothing. This wasn't the time or place. With tornadoes added to the mix, a little boy's life was at stake.

His tone softened. "Don't want to be scraping you off the pavement, either." The noise increased. "Dammit, the hail is getting bigger. I'll be there soon as I can. September, I don't want to lose either of you."

He disconnected before she could say anything, thank goodness. She wiped her wet face. Rain, only rain, she told herself, but her throat ached. Better to make a clean break now than hang on and hope the situation would change. People couldn't hide their true selves forever. They could lie to others, or even themselves . . . She needed to decide who she was, and what she wanted. "Dogs never lie, right Shadow?"

He cocked his head, questioning.

"Never mind. We've more important stuff, right?" She squared her shoulders. "*Seek,* Shadow, *seek.*"

He wagged again, and yelped before turning to sniff at the beckoning trail. Shadow knew what to do. This time, it wasn't about a wildlife die-off spilling into the pet population.

Melinda said her brother saw someone snatch Kinsler. Why steal a dog, when the city shelter offered near give-away adoptable animals?

Kinsler was priceless to Willie, but the dognapping made no sense. Unless it had been about luring the boy away, and hurting Combs. As a detective, he certainly had enemies.

For now, the reason didn't matter, only finding the boy. September pushed with renewed determination through brambles that clawed her passing. Gloves offered protection more from the stickers and branches than the cold. Shadow ducked beneath branches and weaved through clotted overgrowth. She clutched the tracking line in one fist, keeping it taut without dragging too much on Shadow's harness, and used the other to push aside errant branches that threatened to whip back and slash her face.

The sun played hide and seek with billowing clouds, snarling September's coffee-colored mane until it appeared spun from the storm. It had already rained more—snowed more, too—this past winter than she could remember. The area's flash flood warning worried her more than the threat of distant hail or potential tornado. Thankfully, the scent trail followed higher ground. So far, anyway.

September studied the clouds with worry. If the sky broke with another downpour, rain would dilute or erase the trail. Shadow was good, but he wasn't a Bloodhound.

Shadow increased his speed, tail waving with excitement and breath huffing as the scent became fresher, drawing him ever faster along the invisible path only a tracking dog could detect. His eagerness made her hopes soar. He rarely got this excited anymore. Finding remains (or nothing at all) depressed Shadow as much as her.

Dogs needed success and hope, and finding the living rewarded Shadow as much as the relieved pet owner. They'd followed the highway in the direction of the brown truck, and then Shadow veered from the road. She didn't want to give Combs false hope, but if Willie remained with his dog, the fresh trail increased the chance of a happy reunion.

Her jeans caught and hung on a fallen branch and she had to stop to untangle the fabric. Shadow pulled and hesitated when she didn't immediately follow. He huffed impatiently.

"Give me a minute. Close, are you?" He woofed as she straightened. "Okay, baby-dog, I'm ready." He still hesitated, so she repeated the command. "Shadow, *seek.*"

He whirled, and eagerly ran into the thickest overgrowth. That would be the trail a squirrel would take, and tease Kinsler to follow. She shielded her face, turned sideways and scrambled through the stand of scrubby saplings. Some of them had already begun to bud in response to the unseasonal warming trend. Ducking under a massive branch, she stepped onto pavement, one of the many farm-to-market roads that crisscrossed the rural regions of North Texas. September sighed, her shoulders sagging. She expected Shadow to cast back and forth and lose the trail, as he had so many times in the recent past. She guessed the missing dog got loaded into a vehicle and whisked away.

But Shadow kept tugging. If anything, his urgency increased until she had to trot to keep up with him. They ran, following the highway. Maybe the dog gave up on the critter chase and headed back toward home. Wouldn't that be wonderful, to find Kinsler and Willie hiking back to Heartland?

Veering across the pavement to the other side of the road, Shadow dove off the embankment, dashing her hopes. *Please, don't let him be hit by a car—either one of them.* Shadow slid on his haunches and finally put on the furry brakes at the bottom where more of the scrubby undergrowth sprouted.

"Shadow, *wait.*" She didn't need him yanking her headfirst into a tree. While he impatiently watched, September carefully climbed down, one gloved hand grasping thick hanks of Johnson grass to brace her descent and avoid turning an ankle or worse.

When she joined Shadow, September smoothed his brow while she took in the plowed, open field. Black waves of sludge resembled cold grease on a griddle, left behind after flood waters receded. It smelled spoiled, like rotting road kill, and made her wonder what sort of wildlife drowned in the deluge.

Water carved a trench down the middle of the field where a narrow bright ribbon of water still ran. Sooty banks of mud flanked each side, the smooth surface marred here and there by detritus washed up and left stranded. The glassy flats invited the unwary to tread the surface, but she knew better.

Shadow learned the hard way. He sprinted toward a dark object situated perhaps ten feet off the road. Almost immediately, he recoiled and tried to backpedal but his front legs sank into black muck nearly to his shoulders.

He yelped and strained backwards, churning the mud. September made an effort to speak with calm authority. "Steady, baby-dog. *Wait. Wait,* good-dog." He settled, but she could see his chest heave and the whites of his eyes roll. "I'll get you out, you're fine." The black mud was more annoying than dangerous, but Shadow didn't know that. He could hurt himself trying to clamber out.

September grasped the tracking line with both gloved hands, and pulled with steady pressure against the harness. "Okay, Shadow, let's go. C'mon, baby-dog. Back, back." He strained his haunches again, and with a sucking sound, the mud let go. Shadow scrambled backwards, lifting each paw in turn with a nearly comical expression of distaste. The black clay-filled soil coated each foreleg, and she knew the clammy sensation wouldn't be pleasant. "You need a bath." He found a somewhat level spot on the embankment and shook himself, hard, and September laughed when mud spattered her face. "Yeah, guess I deserved that."

He sniffed one paw and then lifted his head, tasting the wind. Shadow's tail stirred the air and he woofed low in his throat and then barked again, louder. He took a step toward the dark figure, but immediately retreated when one paw again encountered the mud. Shadow made eye contact with September, barked and deliberately lay down.

September peered toward the object. At first glance, it appeared to be nothing more than a pile of debris, coughed up by the recent rains sluicing down the side of the road embankment. Shadow barked again and a dark figure stirred, and lifted its furry head.

"Good-dog, Shadow. Good find." He'd located the missing Kinsler. Maybe Willie was with him, she had to check. Shadow beat his tail against the ground.

"Willie? Willie Combs, are you there?" No answer, but the boy could be unconscious.

Lightening flashed, and the wind sprayed rain against September's cheeks. The terrier mix barked and began to yodel. He stood, perched precariously on the mounded island he'd found, tail flagged high with excitement but not daring to leave the secure footing. Mud stained his white fur gray, clear up to his neck. A good head shorter than Shadow, Kinsler was lucky he'd found a perch before the mud dried like cement and encased him in a permanent trap.

She searched for something to reach the small dog. A tree branch tossed atop the mud might offer him enough incentive to scramble within reach.

Any loose limbs, though, had already washed along the small tributary in the wrong direction to offer any help. She needed a few two-by-fours or plywood flats that, once tossed across the mud, would support her weight. She had some at home in the garage. That would mean leaving Kinsler, trudging back through the thickets, driving home and coming back, with fingers crossed the dog would wait. Not likely, especially when the storm broke. And she couldn't risk the wait if Willie was there.

As if to confirm her fears, the little dog leaped from his perch and promptly shrieked and floundered. Within seconds, he'd managed to mire himself up to his chin in the mess. Shadow jumped up and added his own barks to the chorus. "Shadow, *wait*. Settle, good-dog." She squinted against the rain, and sighed. Wishes got nothing done. She had no choice. Time to get dirty.

September searched one of her coat's enormous pockets to find Shadow's short six-foot leash and tethered him to a burl oak. "You *wait*, baby-dog. *Wait*." The leash served more as a reminder than anything, and she didn't want to worry about him trying to come to her rescue.

She unhooked Shadow's tracking line and looped one end around the base of the same tree. Next, she stripped off her boots, rolled up her jeans, and shucked out of the jacket as well. Good thing she hadn't replaced her socks, they'd simply weigh her down. She'd count on luck that her bare feet would only get dirty, not cut.

Stepping forward, September winced at the icy mud. She'd better do this quickly, or her feet would go numb. Keeping one hand wrapped around the tracking tether, she slowly and methodically worked her way toward Kinsler.

"You're okay, boy, I'm coming." She crooned a singsong chant to the small dog, as much to keep Shadow calm as to halt Kinsler's struggles. She had to drag each foot high and step forward before repeating with the other foot. Taking too wide a step threatened to make her slip or trip (or both) and topple her into the mess. She moved the wrong way, and her recovering knee protested with a sharp burst of pain.

The closer she came to the dog, the deeper grew the mud until it reached above her knees. The dog had to be perched on something, or would have sunk to his neck or deeper. He wriggled and barked repeatedly at her, his tail stirring the mud, but he'd learned his lesson and refused to move. Cautiously she drew abreast Kinsler, and saw nothing resembling the boy. Crap. She moved slowly, not wanting to bruise her feet on whatever stump or felled tree supported him.

"Good-dog, you're a good boy, here we go now." September dropped the tracking line onto the surface of the mud. She'd use it to pull them back to the road, once she had the dog in her arms.

September grasped Kinsler by his collar and shoved her other arm into the mud beneath his belly, ready to flex her legs to pull against the grip of the sludge. "Poor puppy, I've got you now, going to get you home." Lightning and thunder made her jump. The clouds stopped teasing and rain poured in earnest.

The mud held on for an endless moment, pulling off one of September's gloves before it let go with a weird lip-smacking sound. The dog squirmed happily in September's arms, reaching up to slurp her face. Her sweatshirt as well as her jeans turned stiff with plastered muck. She stripped off the other ruined glove and dropped it, tucking the dog under one arm and caught up the tracking line with her other hand. She half turned, wrenching free of a tree branch that had temporarily hitched a ride on the dog up out of the muck.

It let go and fell back with a splat, most still sunk beneath the muck but the near end resting on the muddy surface. As September watched, the rain washed it clean revealing not a tree branch after all, but a clenched human hand.

Chapter 21

Beneath the blanket in the back of September's car, the air became stale but neither of them made a move. Nikki jumped when September's car door opened again. She turned her head to meet Steven's eyes, but his expression didn't change. It never did.

Someone hopped in the driver's seat, and turned the key to start the car. Had September come back? What about Shadow? She'd seen the dog jump out the window—how smart, she'd never known a dog could open windows like that—but he'd been gone when she peeked out. Soon after that, another car zoomed up and Nikki hid again, but not before she recognized Detective Combs.

He was Willie and Melinda's dad. Nikki and Willie went to the same school, but Melinda was popular, older and very glamorous with a track star boyfriend in high school. Nikki wished she could be more like Melinda, with long cheerleader legs, copper hair and a cute figure that looked so grownup. Not like Nikki's mousy straight hair, stick figure and dowdy Goodwill clothes.

But Kid Kewl's plan would change all that. Otherwise, Nikki never would have risked hiding in September's car, or convincing Steven to come, too. Steven was weird, but okay for a little kid. She worried what she'd got them into, and for the first time doubted Kid Kewl's plan.

Nikki thought for sure Detective Combs would discover them in September's car. She'd practiced what to say, but wasn't a good liar. For sure, she'd keep the Show And Tell site secret or she'd never be part of the cool kids. Besides, the awesome plan would help her family. And a bunch of other kids, too.

Thank goodness, she didn't have to make up a story. Detective Combs went inside and out again, quick as you please.

The SUV jerked into gear, and peeled out of the driveway. Nikki heard soft sobbing. She pulled aside the blanket, and sneaked a peek over the back seat.

The driver tossed red hair over her shoulder, and pounded the steering wheel, talking to herself. "I'm sorry, so sorry, Daddy, I'll find him. I'll make it up to you, promise I will."

Nikki popped all the way up. "Hey Melinda? You okay?"

The girl shrieked, eyes wide in the mirror, and nearly drove off the road.

Hanging on to the back of the seat, Nikki braced herself and pulled the blanket off Steven. "Sorry, didn't mean to scare you."

The car stopped. Today, Melinda wasn't glamorous at all, not with black smears under her eyes from runny mascara. "What the hell are you doing back there?" She rubbed her nose on one sleeve. Gross.

Steven sang an answer in the same tune from the Secret Garden part he'd performed:

Mister Scary, quite contrary,
Now it's your turn to know
Shivery yells, and shotgun shells,
For pretty pills all in a row.

Melinda's eyes grew large. "What does that mean?"

Nikki flexed her shoulders and her backpack shifted. "He's weird. Steven won't talk, he sings. No offense," she turned to Steven. "You got a nice voice and all."

"I don't have time for baby riddles. I've got to find my brother." Melinda turned around in the seat, hands shaking on the steering wheel. "I let my brother get lost, my boyfriend stood me up, and now my dad thinks I'm a slut." Her chin trembled.

She didn't sound like the cocky, popular Melinda Combs anymore. Nikki squirmed up and over the rear barrier into the back seat, talking as she came. "That's not true. Your dad is a hero, and heroes don't think stuff like that. Not about their kids. You aren't, are you? A slut, I mean?" Nikki stared at the older girl. Her clothes weren't slutty at all.

"It's not being a slut when you're in love." Melinda spoke with conviction, and then in a smaller voice. "Besides, we never did anything. Larry got scared and didn't meet me. Maybe he doesn't really love me." Her eyes welled. "And now Willie chased off after his stupid dog, so I had to call Dad's girlfriend to find them, and—"

Steven tap-tap-tapped on the hatchback window, and hummed the music over and over.

Melinda said nothing, but reached down and released the lock. The two girls waited as Steven carefully hopped out of the back, folded up the blankets, smoothed them back into the stack, shut the hatch and walked to the front passenger door. He slipped inside, fastened his seatbelt and shut the door, and silently held out his hand to Nikki. She sloughed off her backpack to dig out his tablet. The backpack held supplies Kid Kewl said they might need for their adventure.

"September Day is your dad's girlfriend?" Nikki leaned forward, the dog bars a barrier between the two front seats. "She's nice. Knows all about animals."

"Well, she can have that dumb old dog of ours; he's liable to get Willie hurt or even killed. And then Dad will never forgive me."

Dogs are scary, not ordinary,
When forced to fight, you know.
To be the cure, save a wag or purr—
When you tell and show.

Melinda stared at Steven, but he focused on his tablet as he finished singing. "What is he talking about?"

Nikki grimaced. "There's a very bad man, he's hurt a lot of kids. He hurt Steven, and hurt Steven's mom, and who knows how many other kids. Steven is autistic. That means—"

The boy ducked his head, but kept on working on his tablet.

"I know what autistic means." Melinda huffed. "Wait. Isn't he September's nephew? The kid she had to find last Thanksgiving during that blizzard?"

Nikki nodded. "The bad man who got away? He's back. Now he's hurting pets, too. Stealing pets."

"Stealing pets? Did he take our dog?" Melinda scowled. "You can't possibly know that."

Nikki turned to Steven, but he was no help. Kid Kewl's online forum was secret, so she couldn't explain. And as a cop's kid, Melinda might let something slip and get the forum shut down, what Kid Kewl called *the hive brain* where everyone pooled his or her special talents for important projects. She wasn't sure why they invited her into the group, when all the other kids knew about complicated things like math and computers and weather.

Melinda was closer to a grownup than to the kids in the forum and grownups were funny and always suspicious. "Never mind how we know. There's a bunch of us working together to catch this bad man, get the medicine all the kids need and take back the money he stole from their parents."

Melinda flipped her hair. "What, you're going to catch that Doctor guy when even my dad can't find him?" She sniffed. "My dad caught his mother."

Mister Gerry, no more scary,
Now it's your turn to go—"

"Shut up, already." Melinda cut him off. "That's creeping me out." She turned to Nikki. "I've got to find my brother. You two can come or get out, but I'm not in the mood to play babysitter."

Nikki smiled. "But you're part of the plan. That's why Kid Ke...I mean, that's why we decided to hide in September's car."

"You two are seriously creepers. I can't go home, my Uncle Rick will have fits because I took off in September's car. Hell, she may be back already with Willie." She hesitated, clearly debating what to do.

...time to tell and show.

Nikki explained. "When we left the theater, we sneaked into September's car because we knew she'd go to your house, to search for your brother. We know why Kinsler got stole. Why all the pets got took."

"How do you know my dog's name? I never said." Melinda sneaked a peek at Steven's tablet, and he covered it with a hand. "What's going on? How do you know stuff?"

"The dog thief works for the Doctor. We know where he took Kinsler." Nikki leaned forward, needing to convince the older girl to stay with them, to be the driver. That was key to Kid Kewl's plan. "You want to make it up to your dad? Drive us to the dog place. That's where you'll find Willie, too."

Chapter 22

Dime-size hail grew to nickel and then quarter size and dimpled the mud flat all around September, increasing in velocity as she stared at the hand for an endless moment. Kinsler yelped when ice pinged off his head. Startled, September ducked her head and slogged back toward solid ground. Combs's storm arrived right on schedule.

A body. Or at least and arm and hand. Adult size. So, it's not Willie.

"Thank you, God." She breathed out in a rush, the relief palpable, but then guilt furrowed her brow. What kind of awful person gave thanks for a stranger's death? Somebody missed him, or maybe her. She couldn't tell the gender. She wouldn't dare try to move the body. The poor soul got caught in a flash flood. She had to call Combs.

Shadow woofed when September clambered up the embankment and set the smaller dog on the ground. The two dogs circled and jockeyed for position, each trying to sniff without being sniffed. September managed to attach each dog's collar to either end of the doubled up tracking line. That left one hand free while keeping the pair under control, or so she hoped.

"Ouch!" Hail pummeled her back, and September searched for any sort of shelter while fumbling in her pocket for the phone. A dark wall cloud threatened, classic preamble to funnel cloud activity, so she prepared herself for ditch-diving if something swooped out of the sky.

To the left, the dirt road led back to the highway, with no shelter in sight. September swung right. She scraped off as much muck as she could and put on her coat and boots, hating the clammy gritty sensation but needing the protection. "This way. Come on, let's go." She jollied the dogs into a trot, grateful when the size of the hail decreased but worried the lull in wind signaled worse to come. At least the drive canted downward. A low position in relation to the elevated highway should prove protective. They ran, and she fumbled for her phone to call Combs. He picked up on the first ring.

"You find Willie? Is he all right?"

She could hear the thunk and ping of hail from his end of the phone connection, but it had abated around her. "No. I found his dog, but not Willie. But there's a body."

He said something, but the words garbled. "...breaking up. Say again. What about Willie?" He barked the last words.

"Combs, I can't understand you. Have to take cover, it's bad here. Found a body but it's NOT your son."

She disconnected and pocketed the phone. Ahead, the narrow road dipped down toward a cement barn that clung to the side of a steep embankment. Three large green dumpsters butted against the near wall, while a cleared dirt space in front of the storage building held a dozen or more rusty metal barrels turned on their side as shelters, with a dog chained next to each.

September stopped short, recognizing the Pit Bulls and what that meant. She took half a step backwards when a couple of dogs noticed her and roused from their enforced boredom. Shadow barked, tail flagging, and pulled against the tether, eager to meet-and-greet all the potential canine friends.

"Shadow, no. *Wait*." Her voice whip-cracked the command. The Pit Bulls, none in good health, leaped or in some cases staggered to their feet. She noticed young ones also dragged logging chains they could barely lift.

She'd wager the rest of her lottery winnings they figured in the dogfight ring. Kinsler tugged at the leash, and another puzzle piece clicked into place, betting BeeBo's rescued kitten came from here. Dog men used small pets to teach gladiator dogs to fight and kill. Or be killed.

Bile burned her throat. Her knees gave way, and she sat down, hard, in the middle of the road, rain no longer an issue. Shadow pushed himself into her arms, licking her face, and she buried her face in his black ruff.

September tried to call Combs again but couldn't get a signal. Sadly, animal abuse often wasn't enough to involve the police, but the attendant guns and gambling made dogfights worth their attention. Shutting down dogfights cast a wide net.

And drugs. She reeled with sudden insight. What a brilliant, twisted notion, to distribute the Doctor's poisonous autism "cure" under the protection from a dogfight ring.

She pocketed the useless phone, and scrambled to her feet. Wind had died, hail had stopped, and a yellow-green sky colored the chained dogs in a hellish glow. Static crackled her hair into a Medusa's crown, and all the dogs howled in sudden concert as if cued by a conductor's baton.

She couldn't see it, but the freight train sound signified a funnel cloud. She needed shelter, had to drop below the tree and road level. Inside the cement barn offered the best shelter.

The dogs strained against their chains, staked between her and sanctuary. Shadow and Kinsler couldn't pass without risking a bloody war they couldn't win.

"Good-dog, Shadow, stay with me." They were dead if they stayed on the road, if not from the twister, then from wind-tossed debris bulleted with enough strength to penetrate cement.

The roar increased. No more time. She had to risk threading a path past the Pit Bulls. They'd all die without shelter. September ran in a fast limp, sore knee hobbling her progress. She scooped Kinsler into her arms and shortened Shadow's leash to keep him close to her side.

A horn honked behind September. Startled, she whirled. Her own SUV hurtled down the dirt path straight toward her.

Chapter 23

He stared at his phone. Combs forced himself to relax before he crushed it—he wanted to throw it—and took a deep breath before hitting re-dial. He pressed the phone hard to his ear, plugging the other ear to mute the thunder and wind that shook his car.

"What'd she say?" Gonzales flinched when simultaneous lightning strobed and thunder boomed. "Dammit, Combs, get us to cover. We're no help to your son or to September if we get blown to Oz."

Combs shook his head. He ground his teeth to keep from cursing. Fury mounted when the connection failed. Failure all around. The connection had been bad, but he'd heard enough. He'd ask if she'd found Willie. Her answer broke his heart.

"*. . . found Willie. . . It's bad...a body...*" And the phone went dead. He closed his eyes, willing her to answer, for the call to go through. Damn the storm, damn the dog, damn September, she promised to find him. Alive. ALIVE, dammit.

Gonzales raised his eyebrows, silently asking again. Combs lowered his phone. He couldn't repeat what September had said. That would make it—*NO! Not his little boy!*—a reality.

Wind pummeled the car. Tornado sirens raged, coyotes answering in an eerie chorus. They'd only traveled a mile or so out of town. Combs knew the general vicinity of September's search but the storm meant no chance in hell of finding them. He slumped against the steering wheel. *Too late anyway, what does it matter. God, make this a bad dream. Let me wake up.*

"Son of a bitch." Gonzales never swore.

Combs recoiled as if splashed with ice water by the vision out Gonzales's passenger window. Snakes of black spun earthward from the distant wall cloud, lightening etched gashes in the dark sky. *Holy shit.*

"It's coming, Combs, it's coming. Get us out of here. How about, uhm, now? Now would be a good time. Vete de aqui, ve rapido, Go-go-go-go!"

A muffled Niagara Falls roar filled his ears. A sudden adrenalin spike transformed Combs from apathy to flight. He shoved the car into gear. Tires squealed, the U-turn barely held the road, and he floored the gas. "Where?"

"Don't care, just go, ve rapido, fast fast fast." Gonzales half turned in his seat. "Man, I need a raise." He turned back around. "First solid building we find, we get inside. Cars are deathtraps in a tornado."

Combs knew that. "If they don't want to let us in?"

"They will. We're the cops. People love us." Gonzales smiled.

He ignored the lame joke. He owed it to his partner to get them to safety. But how could he care about being alive, staying safe, when his son... Willie hadn't had a chance. *Don't think, just go.*

The engine screamed into town, the car rabbiting and swerving as the twister rode their bumper like a hound sniffing blood. He had to drive perpendicular to the storm path. Combs took a hard right, almost nailed a lamppost, and sped halfway up the block before he recognized a familiar business. A brick building. Glass on the front but as he recalled, the place had a storm cellar, rare in this part of the world.

"Hold fast." He fishtailed into the parking lot. Both men vaulted out before the car engine stopped and raced to the door of Doc Eugene's veterinary clinic.

The vacant waiting room, normally bustling this time of day, offered no shelter. Floor to ceiling windows offered a great view of the parking lot and death by glass should the storm punch through.

"This way." Combs loped down the hallway, and dodged through the door to the first examining room, into the treatment area. "Hey Doc? Where are you?" Gonzales reflexively ducked and cursed again when something thumped the roof of the building.

"Who's there?" Doc Eugene's muffled voice came from behind another closed door. Gonzales and Combs hurried to join him.

"Detective Combs? Detective Gonzales, too? What're you doing here? Don't you know there's a tornado?" The small room, not much bigger than a walk-in closet, served as storage for the vet clinic's pharmacy and other supplies. Doc Eugene and a flamboyant heavy younger woman huddled on the floor beneath a shelf, in the far corner. She appeared peeved to see them.

Combs and Gonzales pushed inside and closed the door. The overhead light flickered in concert with thunder. All four gasped when another clatter-thump buffalo stampede crossed the roof.

"You said he had a storm shelter." His quivering mustache belied Gonzales's steady voice. The man might have been asking for a veggie wrap, extra hot sauce.

Doc Eugene snorted, but made room for the two detectives. "A lot of good it does me. Flooded last week, and still a foot of water and God knows what else swimming around in the sludge." He pushed his glasses up his nose. "No way to get the animals in here, but we've only a few including BeeBo's kitten that September dropped off earlier. This is the next best thing to a storm cellar: an interior room with no windows. And plenty of pain meds, pet food and fluids." He laughed, and then nudged the woman beside him. "Robin, these are the detectives I told you about. They're going to find the sick bastard who killed my Pam."

Robin ignored the detectives. She put an arm around Doc Eugene's shoulder as if to comfort him. When he shrugged it off, Robin's nostrils flared and she stared at her hands.

Doc Eugene's wife, Pam, had been Shadow's breeder. She'd died during the Blizzard Murders last November, along with Combs's mother.

Gonzales answered the unspoken question on the veterinarian's face. "We had to outrun the storm. The funnel hadn't touched down yet, but was snapping at our heels." He turned to Combs. "Hope we still have a car when we get out of here." He pulled out his phone. "I've got no bars."

Combs sank to the floor, and slapped Gonzales's leg. "Get down. We'll worry about the car later." He pushed against the wall, knees bent and arms circling them. Now they'd escaped the tornado, he couldn't stop thinking about September's call.

Gonzales checked the shelves filled with various medications, shampoos and other pet products. He picked up one of the pet collar tracking devices. "Sell many of these? Sure saved us a ton of time, when September went missing."

Doc Eugene took off and polished his glasses. "After all the news stories, I can barely keep the collars on the shelves. The company even gave September the technology and all upgrades for life."

The building shook, and Gonzales braced himself. "Damn. Didn't know I'd think back on the drought with nostalgia." The lights went out. The overhead stampede became constant.

Combs closed his eyes, and let tears run unchecked. How had Melinda let this happen? What would he tell Willie's mother? Would Cassie even understand? He was helpless, hopeless and angry, and oh, so much alone.

Chapter 24

Claire gasped and jumped when lightening crackled, and banged her head on the passenger side window of Sunny's big green truck. She prayed Tracy and Lenny were inside somewhere, and not out in Elaine's old rickety van. Weather alerts and warnings continually beeped and buzzed on Sunny's phone.

"Now what? We've been driving in circles for hours." Her initial hope after meeting the striking P.I had faded. Sunny hadn't done anything, except drive around and text.

Sunny didn't answer. Every once in a while, she got a text that made her eyes flash with temper. As if on cue, the "ping" of her phone announced another message. "Hold the wheel." She turned her full attention to the phone.

Claire wrinkled her pug nose, but leaned over to steer the truck while Sunny texted her reply. "What's it say? Is it about Tracy? Have they found the van?" Sunny said she'd sent the van's license to her connections, and promised quick results.

"Not everything is about you."

Sunny's terse reply hit below the belt. Claire's hand on the wheel jerked, and she over-corrected, nearly driving them off the road.

"Son of a bitch. What is wrong with you?" Sunny grabbed the steering wheel, and steadied the truck. "I took on this case as a favor.

Now you want to wreck my truck? That's a custom rig in the back, special made by friends in South Texas." She pulled into a mini-mart gas station, shoved the truck in park, and half turned in her seat. "Did you ever think maybe these kids don't want to be found? I ran away a dozen times, for good reasons."

Claire sniffed. "Don't be ridiculous. What a horrible thing to say. They're children, they're scared. You said you could find them, easy-peasy you said."

"I may have overstated. One of my guys saw a van matching the description in an area—" Her smooth brow furrowed. "No, couldn't be your kids. Never mind."

"Let's go!"

"It's a stretch. Trust me on this. Don't want to waste time."

"And driving around the past several hours has been so productive? Sunny, we have to do something. My little girl is out there." Thunder rattled the windows. Although the rain had abated, the threat remained. "She's out in this storm, scared, alone." Claire leaned toward the taller woman. "Do you have kids?" She had to make Sunny understand the urgency. The woman acted like Tracy and Lenny were a couple of lost pets, or something.

Sunny shuddered. "Nope. No kids for this one."

Probably a good thing. "That old van isn't reliable. They could be stranded somewhere. If you know where they were last seen, we should go check."

When Sunny's phone "pinged" again, and the woman focused on the message, Claire lashed out. "If you can't or won't go after them, tell me where to go and I'll find Tracy myself."

"I've got to make a call. It's private. Sit tight." Sunny exited the car, taking the keys with her as if she feared Claire might take off without her.

Claire flushed. "You're being paid to help. September said she'd pay you. Tracy's only six, Lenny barely sixteen. They're children, for God's sake." She pounded a fist against the window. Sunny waved but headed into the store, phone pressed to her ear.

Now what? Claire threw back her head, and stared at the roof of the truck, then unbuckled her seat belt. She might have taken the car if Sunny had left the keys. She'd already broken into a house. If she didn't know better, she'd think Sunny meant to stall or even prevent Claire from finding the kids. Wind shuddered the car, and splashed a new deluge against the windshield.

What had September told the P.I.? Maybe Sunny was a cop. Her stomach tightened. Claire only knew what she'd seen on television shows, but the woman's actions hit a sour note.

Worry tainted everything with suspicion. Claire sighed, and gave herself a pep talk. "Can't do this alone, you have to trust somebody." She had to give Sunny the benefit of the doubt. She could be frustrated, too, just doing the best she could.

Claire thumped her head against the headrest two or three times, as if the action would reset her brain. Then she sighed, considered the brightly lit store, and opened the door. Might as well make a potty stop while she could.

Claire hurried to the toilet. She heard someone in the wheelchair accessible stall, and when she recognized Sunny's boots under the door, Claire silently entered the next stall and quietly closed the door.

Sunny's hushed, angry voice echoed. "...Because I know you, Kelvin, I knew you'd get cold feet. And I can't let you screw this up for me. Damn straight, I threw you under the bus." She laughed quietly. "Do unto others before they do unto you. I've been a step ahead of you all the way. Yes, twenty thousand is a nice nest egg, but nothing compared to an additional ten thousand coming." Venom filled her voice. "Admit it. You planned to get me out of your nonexistent hair with this missing kid stuff, and it didn't work. Lucky for us both."

Claire clamped a hand over her mouth to stifle her surprised gasp. Claire prayed Sunny hadn't noticed her.

She guessed not, because Sunny kept talking, tone increasingly sarcastic. "I'll tell you exactly what I mean. The kids you sent me to find? They're autistic." She paused. "Yeah, right, one hell of a coincidence. And get this. My guys saw the kiddo's van in the vicinity of tonight's show." She paused. "No, we're fine. The mom's clueless, but the kids know something. It's creepy-strange, as if they're on a mission. They drove themselves all the way from Chicago, for God's sake."

Dropping her face into her hands, Claire breathed slowly through her open mouth while black sparkles danced before her eyes. She carefully sat down on the toilet, being extra careful to make no sound, afraid she'd faint if she didn't. Her pulse drummed so hot and loud in her temple she worried Sunny would hear.

"Kids complicate things, but I got us covered." Sunny's anger had cooled to practicality. "I'll ditch the mom. No, I won't shoot her unless I have to. Miss Clueless can't hurt us."

Claire's teeth began to chatter, and she clamped her jaw tight.

"Why don't you do it?" She paused. "Oh, you're with the Doctor right now? Doesn't want to get his hands dirty, I guess." She snickered. "Sure, I'll drop off the mom, and reconnoiter the barn, secure the product and make sure the kids don't get in the way." Sunny paused. "Hell, they're kids, six and sixteen, and autistic besides. What can they do? You worry too much, Kelvin."

Before she could change her mind, Claire slipped out of the stall and ran. The door banged open and closed, and she nearly knocked down the clerk on her way outside. She couldn't tell the store clerk any more than she could call the police. It hadn't sounded like a joke. Claire couldn't make Sunny suspicious by calling a cab. Besides, Sunny knew where Tracy was.

Claire dashed through the pouring rain and climbed back inside Sunny's truck. She calmed her breathing, and practiced an innocent smile for when Sunny returned.

"Didn't mean to take so long. You need to pee?" Sunny showed her teeth but the expression raised the hairs on the back of Claire's neck. The truck pulled out of the parking spot.

"I'm fine. Too worried about the kids, I guess." Claire cleared her throat when it squeaked. Water dripped from her coat, and she stammered. "I mean, I started to go in but saw you leaving. So I hurried back to the car." She forced a laugh. "Guess I got a little wet."

Sunny stared, her face expressionless. She turned away, pressed the accelerator, and the car skidded as it peeled out of the lot.

Chapter 25

Shadow howled. His ears hurt. He shook his head to relieve the fullness, but stayed pressed next to September. He'd stay near even if she didn't have the leash so short he could barely move.

A sudden burst of wind came from all directions at once. His whiskers tingled, and he flinched at the booming overhead noise. He tucked his tail, shivered, fighting the urge to squat and pee. Shadow shook his head again and his ears popped.

Wind wailed, and tree limbs tore free to skitter across the ground like wingless beetles. He pushed against September, willed her to acknowledge him and maybe stroke his face. She always knew what to do.

But she didn't touch him. Her arms cradled the other dog that smelled of black mud and sour terror.

"Good-dog, Shadow, stay with me." Her voice jittered, squeaky and shrill, and made him shake in sympathy. She pulled him toward the distant stone house, beyond the chained dogs with distant hopeless eyes.

All around, the roar increased while sky flashes made his skin tingle and fur crackle. September ran toward the chained dogs, tripped and caught herself, and galloped on, her hand tight on his leash. Shadow leaped by her side, eager to get inside.

A familiar-sounding car engine roared and Shadow slowed, tugging against the leash. The horn beeped, cutting through the wind's howl, and September stumbled to a stop. They turned. A car headed toward them. September yanked his leash and he darted with her as she dove to the side of the road. September ran up to the car when it skidded to a stop. She had to yell over the roar of the storm. "Melinda, shove over."

The driver's and rear doors swung open at the same time. September dumped the small dirty white dog into the front and took her place behind the wheel. Shadow leaped into his back seat. He wagged and slurped his friend Nikki across the face as the girl removed his leash, but dropped his ears when he noticed Steven. His-boy ignored him, though.

The wind rocked the car, pushing it sideways on the road. September screamed. A gust hit the open door, and it peeled off the car. She screamed again, and then the car raced down the road, fast, and faster still, toward the stone house.

A limb slapped the car, and the small dog yelped. Speeding, bucking, shuddering, the car shook Shadow back and forth like Bear-toy. Nikki and Steven screamed too, and clung to each other.

"Hurry!" Melinda wailed from the front seat, and hugged the little dog so hard he squealed.

Shadow snarled at the nightmare vision out the back window. A dark twisty cloud fell from the sky and snapped at the car.

Rain and ice pounded the roof, sounding like many guns biting all at once. Shadow cringed. He watched wide eyed when September weaved through the doghouse barrels, aiming for the open barn door.

One of the doghouses lifted off the ground and tumbled away, and a second quickly followed as though kicked by a giant invisible foot. Young ones cowered and cried, flinching as hail thumped all around and hit them repeatedly.

Just as the car's nose poked through the barn door, a sonorous racket grew and the car lifted and smashed back down. Shadow wailed. He slammed against the side window, the new floor of the upside-down car. Nikki and Steven piled on top of him.

"Out, everyone out. Away from the door, hurry." September's shaky voice shouted over the wind noise. She opened the passenger door, now above their heads, and help Melinda out first. September passed the little dog to the girl, and then helped Steven through the crushed front seats. September clambered out and levered open the back passenger door.

"The dogs." Nikki's anguished voice rose over the wind.

"No, Nikki. We can't help them. Give me your hand." September reached in and Shadow licked her fingers. Nikki turned away and wiggled into the rear of the car. The crash had unlatched the hatchback. "Nikki wait."

"They'll die." The girl squeezed out of the back of the car, hunkered down, and sprinted toward the chained dogs.

Chapter 26

The wind out-shouted September's screamed warning. She yelled again, but Nikki ducked her head and scurried to the first chained dog. She crouched beside the trembling youngster. The girl ignored the driving rain but flinched when the hail thumped the middle of her backpack. At least she had that minimal protection.

"What's she *doing*?" Melinda hugged Kinsler while Steven simply stared, silent with wide eyes. "The tornado will get her, what's the *matter* with her?"

"Go take cover. Go on." September gestured toward the dirt pit dug several feet deep in the center of the cement building. "Crouch down and cover your heads. Take Steven. I'm counting on you, Melinda. Go."

Melinda grabbed Steven's hand, and still clutching Kinsler, she headed for the pit.

September had to get Nikki to safety, but also protect Melinda and Steven. "Shadow, *go-to* Steven. Keep him safe." She gave him a quick hug, then squirmed into the crushed SUV. The car blocked the barn door completely. The only way out was through the open hatchback.

Her knee whined when it cracked against the car but she didn't listen. September narrowed her eyes against flying debris. She prayed the hail wouldn't knock either of them unconscious, and dashed to the girl. She yanked Nikki's backpack to get her attention. The storm's noise drowned out easy conversation.

Nikki's face reddened with frustrated effort. "I can't get it off." She screamed over the wind noise. "His collar's too stiff." The young tail-wagging Pit Bull pushed into Nikki's lap hampering her efforts.

"You'll get us killed." She tugged Nikki's arm, but the girl wrapped her arms around the pup, refusing to leave. With frantic fingers, September struggled with the pup's collar, too, but it was hopeless. "We'd need to cut it." She dug in her pocket for the knife Shadow had knocked out of Cassie's hand during the *show-me* game. Even with the sharp blade, it would take too long to saw through the stiff leather.

Nikki's smile lit up her face. She reached into her knapsack, and pulled out Doc Eugene's bolt cutters.

"What else you got in there?" September sheathed the knife back into her pocket with such force the blade sliced through fabric and caught in the padded batting lining. She took the bolt cutters from Nikki and cut the chain tethering the pup to the stake. "Now let's go."

Nikki shook her head, and mouthed something September couldn't hear, pointing to the next dog, and the next.

"Dammit! I'll do it. You go!" September waved the girl toward the barn when her screamed words tore away in the wind. She stood and grabbed Nikki by the arm, ready to drag her back, but the girl released her Pit Bull pup, pulled away and ran to the next dog.

Had she been alone, she'd not hesitate to rescue the dogs, so September fought grudging admiration for Nikki. As the adult, she had to put kids first, no matter what.

September sacrificed five seconds to consider options as the sky boiled black, and the swarming cicada-buzz grew deafening. Her ears popped with pressure change, but she couldn't tell the funnel's location. Hell, it could be a mile away or directly overhead, flatten the barn and leave her untouched. No way to predict, no way to get Nikki away from the dogs, and no way she could abandon the foolish child. *All you can do is the best you can do.* A sudden calm filled her with purpose, and she raced with the bolt cutters to the next dog.

Nikki soothed each dog and held collars steady for September's snick through the chain. At their release, the dogs slunk low to the ground, wagging and sticking close to their heels, either unaware of freedom or relishing the attention more.

The last dog, a massive adult male with a scarred head as wide as his chest, leaned into her arms as September cut him free. "Back to the barn." The storm out-shouted her words, but Nikki understood when September waved the bolt cutter.

The hail increased in size and velocity, pounding all around. The adult dogs, although frequently struck, made no sound but stayed close to Nikki and September as they hurried toward the shelter. An army of icy bullets machine-gunned the barn and Nikki squealed and covered her head. Then her arms dropped to her side, and the girl fell face forward onto the ground.

September stumbled and fell, surprised when her knees splashed into soggy ground salted with the chunks of ice. The roar of the storm out-shouted anything she might say. Bright crimson sheeted from the girl's scalp where hail had clubbed her brow.

The open rear hatch of the SUV beckoned. Before September could stagger upright to lift Nikki, Shadow leaped from the car and raced toward her. "No. *Wait.*" Heart in her throat, September also gave Shadow the *wait* hand signal, and breathed again, when he skidded to a stop.

The young Pit Bulls milled around her legs. At least the storm distracted them from aggressing toward each other, or Shadow. September had to get Nikki, herself and Shadow back through the SUV gateway. As she watched, one of the nearby dumpsters tipped over and blew hard against the barn, metal lid flapping like cardboard. The train-like chang-chang-chang-chang noise relentlessly approached. All but the scar-faced dog scattered.

September grunted as she hefted Nikki over one shoulder. Shadow hesitated, and then disobeyed and raced to meet her.

The Pit Bull eyed him, face and forelegs crisscrossed with a jigsaw puzzle of scars. Mangled ears pinned back, he offered a broken-toothed snarl, and stood foursquare braced and ready for a fight. Shadow put on the brakes but didn't take his eyes off the dog.

"No. Shadow, stay with me." She couldn't hear her own voice, and prayed he'd listen. No time left. Must choose. Prevent the fight…protect the girl. . .

The twister tore into view, uprooted trees like weeds and tossed the second dumpster across the yard. "Shadow, COME. Stay with me." Anguished, September left Shadow to race the last few yards to the SUV, pushed Nikki's limp figure inside, and turned back to watch. "Shadow. Shadow, come boy, baby-dog, come on. Pleeeeese . . ." Her throat shredded raw with screams, shielding her eyes from debris, she watched Shadow's standoff from inside the SUV, willing her dog to run, run, return to her.

The Pit Bull would take him down if he turned tail. Shadow knew it, too.

The two dogs circled each other, Shadow backing away and turning his head as the older, more experienced fighter stalked him.

She couldn't abandon him. *Screw the storm.* September grabbed the bolt cutters to race to Shadow's defense. Then Nikki stirred and started to wail, and clutched September's arm.

"Don't leave me. It's coming, it's coming, don't leave me!" Frantic eyes wide, blood streamed from the child's sliced brow.

September dropped the tool, and gathered the girl into her arms. "I'm here, hold on, we're going to be okay, hold on." More debris flew past the SUV's open hatch. Shadow and the Pit Bull continued to circle each other.

Lightening staggered across the sky accompanied by a simultaneous "boom." A tree branch barely missed the open hatch of the SUV. It impaled the cement wall of the barn. Another one might not miss. September strained to see, but the two dogs had disappeared.

Baby-dog, stay safe, God I'm so sorry, please forgive me . . .

September wept as she pulled the hatch closed and thumbed the key-fob lock, praying she'd not cut off Shadow's only chance for survival.

Chapter 27

The white dog scared Shadow more than the weird wind or thumping ice from the sky. The dog's body language threatened, and his tormented eyes and teeth promised pain.

He ached to follow September and Nikki back to the cement building, but couldn't allow this danger-dog to chase them. Shadow weighed less but the shorter dog's muscles, scars and smells told stories of bloody conquests. Shadow didn't dare turn away. He had to be brave and strong and create a furry barrier between the warrior dog and September. Nobody told him to do that. He simply knew.

Wind made it hard for a good-dog to hear. He strained to see September's progress. He wished he could smell or hear her but scent mixed together into swarms quickly scattered by rain. Ice hit him like Steven's fists during a rage, and Shadow winced and yelped with each blow. The white dog remained stoic and focused, though, ignoring cold thumps shooting from the sky, staring, staring hard at Shadow with pale eyes.

Shadow knew this territory belonged to the other dog. Shadow wouldn't want strangers in his place, either. He turned his head, and lowered his tail. He backed away, edging closer to the barn and September. With her out of sight, he didn't feel quite as brave.

The other dog stalked closer, snarling. His short white coat bristled, even the raw swollen wounds with little fur. He had only ragged stumps for ears, making it hard for Shadow to read his mood. The heavy chain swung from the dog's collar, and dragged furrows in the mud. He raised a forepaw, the leg crisscrossed with scars.

Shadow's brow wrinkled, he licked his lips and again turned away, a silent declaration: *no threat.* The white's close cropped ears and frantic tail said one thing while his offered paw contradicted the message. Shadow yawned, and backed away, his placating signals obvious.

The other dog charged, stopped short, and placed the paw heavily across Shadow's shoulders. Close up, the dog's sour stink of infection mixed with bitter rage.

The dog lunged at Shadow's throat.

Shadow ducked and whirled. A shattered tooth creased his skull and carved a ragged line down his cheek. Shadow snarled, his teeth snapped air, a warning despite the near miss.

The sky boomed. Big metal boxes tumbled and lurched toward him. Shadow yelped and danced sideways, but the cacophony elicited not even an eyelash twitched from the white dog. He stalked relentlessly forward, ignoring or unaware of the tower of black smoke twisting at the far end of the road. It chewed up and spit out trees, stones, and dirt as it staggered forward. Shadow's ears felt stuffed, so full they might burst.

Scarface sprang.

Shadow whirled, and left behind a mouthful of thick black fur in the other's jaws. When a branch scuttled across the ground, Shadow spun away from the massive wind-torn limb. It lifted into the air, clubbed the white dog and spun up into the sky.

Scarface screamed a choked eerie sound that rivaled the storm's shriek. He threw himself onto his back in a silent plea, eyes screwed tight. He didn't fight, just accepted the beating sure to come. The sharp aroma of dog pee rode the wind.

Before the white dog's confusion cleared and he scrambled away from the approaching funnel, Shadow fled in the opposite direction, back to the barn, to September. He needed to be with her, and keep September safe if Scarface returned. She'd know what to do about the black wind, and the ice balls that turned the ground white.

Shadow put paws up on the car's back window to peer inside. He barked, calling, pleading, *don't forget the dog.*

But he'd disobeyed. He'd only wanted to keep her safe from the white dog. That was his job. He barked again, but September didn't come. He pawed the glass, then hopped down and frantically searched for a way under or around the car.

The two remaining metal boxes banged against each other, their lids lifting and slamming closed like hungry mouths. Shadow cried out as two ice missiles hit his flank and the car glass simultaneously. September didn't come.

Shadow raced for the meager shelter of the dumpster tipped on its side. He timed his movement until wind lifted the cover a dog's width, and dove inside the metal box. Ice balls pounded and echoed as they tried to batter their way inside. The box stank of fear, feces and misery.

The box lifted slightly, and fell. Again, and then again it tumbled and rolled one way, and back the other direction. Shadow yelped, wailed, and finally fell silent. He crouched against a corner and curled into a tight ball of misery. No light penetrated the metal box, and the icy scabrous floor, filthy with animal stink and blood, made him shiver. Sounds of the outside storm echoed and hurt his ears as the wind raged.

After a long time, longer than a good-dog could say, the wind slowed and finally stopped. The plink-thump-CRACK! of ice missiles disappeared. Shadow stood and shook himself, and flinched and yelped at the bruises and the hot sting from the bite slicing his face. He nosed the heavy lid, but it stuck on something outside the box and wouldn't open. Shadow barked, and pawed the lid with frustration. Trapped.

A growl answered, followed by a whine and a hollow thumping sound. Shadow sniffed. His hackles rose. Another dog shared the big metal box.

Chapter 28

A sudden eerie silence proved more frightening than the storm's violence, but September refused to move. She kept her eyes squeezed shut. She held Melinda circled tight in her arms, and the girl's trembling form in turn crouched protectively over Nikki and Steven. All remained silent, except for Kinsler, who keened and shivered.

September wanted to cry, too, but not in front of the kids. She couldn't think about Shadow, or would dissolve into a useless puddle. She had to be the adult. September cautiously opened her eyes and released her grip on Melinda. "Everyone okay?"

Melinda lifted her head. She turned loose of the kids and hugged herself. "Is it over? Will it come back?"

"Nikki, how's your head? Steven, you all right?" September waited impatiently for a response.

Steven remained silent, but Nikki nodded, then winced, and gingerly touched her blood-soaked hair. September pasted on a cheerful expression to hide her concern. Head wounds bled a lot, even when not serious. She hoped it wasn't serious.

Kinsler squirmed from beneath their feet, shook himself hard, and sniffed the bloodstained ground. The 18-foot square dogfight pit offered an ideal storm shelter. Three-foot-high plywood walls framed the space on two sides, reinforced by stair-step stacks of straw bales piled halfway to the loft.

Ironically, the same space had meant death or worse for the dogs forced to compete within its walls. The Pit Bulls she and Nikki had freed stood a better chance fighting the tornado than surviving this arena. September prayed they'd evaded the storm.

And God, please let Shadow be all right.

Any hope of finding Shadow hinged on escaping the barn. September scrambled to her feet to assess the damage.

Her SUV blocked the main entrance but the wall had collapsed around the vehicle. The car had taken out the loft ladder, too. Overhead, steady rain fell through where the metal roof peeled back like a pop-top lid.

The small loft above and three remaining cement block walls retained most of their integrity. A pushed-in section marred the back wall, where a small door and three shuttered windows suggested another way out.

"Melinda, watch the kids." The older girl had already begun to clean up Nikki's cut brow. Steven's attention remained glued to his tablet, probably playing a video game. Maybe her phone reception had returned. She checked, but had no bars.

September noted the scratch line in a corner of the square pen as she vaulted over the plywood wall. She tripped on a washtub positioned nearby, empty now but used to bathe fighting dogs before they entered the ring to be sure nobody "cheated" by putting poison on the fur. The opposite corner would have the same diagonal scratch mark, she knew, where the so-called "dog men" held their canine contenders at the ready before the "referee" gave the signal to release them and begin the fight. She shuddered.

Once past the divider, she saw more dogfight paraphernalia. A modified spring pole hung from an overhead beam, consisting of a length of rope and rubber tubing dogs were encouraged to grab and hang from to condition neck and jaw muscles. September knew BeeBo also provided a spring pole for his dogs to have fun, but she found nothing innocent about the contraption in this context. Out of place in the rustic surroundings, a modern electric-powered treadmill stood against one wall. The attached logging chain, similar to the ones she'd cut from the dogs' collars, made it clear the treadmill served as one more tool for conditioning the canine athletes for the blood sport.

The machine's presence meant power, if she could find a switch. Daylight faded early in February. With the SUV totaled, and storm still lurking, September had no intention of hiking out with a bunch of kids. Best to hunker down and wait for help. Lights would shine a welcome beacon to speed rescuers to find them, especially once the sun set. Only gray light filtered through the gash in the roof, but even as she watched, it grew dim.

On the wall behind the treadmill, September found a power bar with a bright orange weatherproof cord that trailed up the wall and disappeared through the ceiling into the loft. She toggled the switch, and floodlights blazed from the rafters, spotlighting the dog-fighting pit bright enough for an ESPN special.

Melinda stood up and cheered, and September turned back with a smile and a thumb's up. Nikki wobbled, though she kept a firm grip on Kinsler's collar. If she had a concussion, Nikki needed a doctor sooner rather than later.

"Let me see if I can get the back door open." September hurried to the far end of the barn.

The lights revealed the cat mill and she cringed. Designed like a miniature horse walker, trainers harnessed the dog to the long spoke projecting from a turn-style and lured him to chase the living bait held in a cage beyond his reach. This built up the dog's conditioning as well as increasing prey drive.

September hurried past, averting her eyes from the sad mound of fur trapped inside the cage. She gasped and stopped short when the fur moved. "Hey, there's a cat." And still alive, despite being cramped inside a space too small for it to stand.

"A kitty? Where?" Nikki finally roused, and stood up woozily.

September motioned to Nikki to stay put. "Keep hold of Kinsler or he'll scare it." She didn't want to explain to the kids about the cat, or God help her, the rape-stand over there used to keep breeding pairs of fighting dogs from killing each other.

The cat mewed and cheek-rubbed the side of its cage as she struggled to get the door open. He hadn't been inside long. She saw no waste in the cage or dropped beneath in the dirt of the barn floor. September knew that bait animals, often rabbits or cats, didn't last long, so this cat won the lottery. Otherwise, after the "training" session, the bait became the dog's reward. She'd like to "reward" the sickos with some of their own medicine.

The striking green-eyed cat sported a brown tabby "cap" on his head, tabby coat covering his back and tail, and underneath, snowy legs, chest, muzzle and tummy. His friendly demeanor had enabled the catnapping. The thieves hadn't even bothered removing his collar or nametag that clearly spelled out, "Boris Kitty."

She feared he'd run away—hell, she wouldn't blame him—but September couldn't bear to leave him inside the wire contraption. "Stay close, big guy." She crooned soothingly as she messed with the opening, hoping he wouldn't spook and zoom away. "When we get out of here, I'll do my best to get you back home."

As soon as the confinement opened, the cat leaped out of the wire basket, and scaled September's shoulder to nuzzle her cheek. He draped himself around her neck like a sack of potatoes, and the vibration of his purr made her smile for the first time in hours. "Guess that's as good a place as any. Hang on, Boris Kitty."

September fought the déjà vu sensation. Only eight weeks ago, she'd nearly died while trapped inside another barn when it caught fire. With the wooden loft drowned by the storm, not even a direct lightning strike would ignite this barn. Still, she didn't want to stay inside any longer than necessary. That the storm had abated didn't mean it couldn't return with renewed violence. As if in agreement, thunder boomed.

Keeping one hand on the cat as much to calm herself as to balance the perching animal, September hurried to the far wall. She tried the door, but it jammed from something wedged outside, and wouldn't budge. Long metal bars secured shutters covering each of the windows, effectively keeping any inside light contained. Scheduled fights likely took place at night. Whoever ran the show didn't want light leaking out and giving them away.

After removing the rebar brace, she swung open the first set of shutters. Glass had shattered from the outside in, and fell with a music box crinkling sound. A blue metal surface butted up solid against the opening, with no way through.

September moved to the next window, pulled away the brace, and found a repeat of the broken glass and blue wall. She banged on the metal with frustration, before moving to the third, final window.

Startled, the cat dug nervous claws into her coat collar. "Sorry, Boris Kitty. My bad. You're right, nothing gained by getting angry." She pulled and tugged the final rebar until it released. September lost her balance and fell backward on the ground. She heard an answering thump from the blue metal.

The cat scrambled to keep his perch on her shoulders, and then abandoned her and ran. Wet soaked through her pants, and September put down a hand to brace herself. Where moments before the floor had been dry, now she sat in a wet spot that slowly grew as she watched, pooling from cracks in the cement blocks at the foundation level.

The banging came again, followed by faint shouts. September scrambled to her feet, and wrenched open the final set of shutters. The opening revealed the passenger side glass of a blue van pressed against the barn's shattered window. Willie Combs thumped and yelled from the front passenger seat, a dark haired younger girl peeking from behind him while a teenaged boy slumped behind the steering wheel, motionless.

Chapter 29

Shadow cautiously sniffed the direction of the strange, spotted dog. Elevated levels of testosterone in the youngster's pee labeled him an adolescent. The pup crouched in the farthest corner of the dumpster, banging tail echoing in the metal box. A short length of metal loops hung from the pup's collar, and clanged against the filthy floor when he shifted. Shadow arched his neck and stretched his nose closer, and the pup whined and rolled onto his back, his tail whipping back and forth in an abject show of deference.

Shadow yawned and turned away, giving the youngster a chance to compose himself. When the pup slunk forward, crawling to reach Shadow, whimpering as he came, Shadow stood stiff and slowly waved his own tail. He allowed the youngster to lick his face and eyes. The spotted pup dropped to his back without prompting, and wriggled as he offered Shadow an up-close personal sniff. Recognizing the pup posed no threat, Shadow gave him space to stand. The dog rolled happily to his feet, dripping from the pooled water in the bottom of the metal box, and shook, spraying wet in the close space.

Happy to have a new dog friend, Shadow rested his chin on the smaller dog's shoulders for a moment before turning to the exit. He needed to find September. His paws splashed in the puddles that got deeper inside the box, and Shadow nose-nudged the edge of the plastic door-lid beside him. It should be above him, except that the metal box had tipped on its side. It wouldn't move. Something pressed against the plastic from the other side, so that he couldn't budge the covering. Now water leaked into the bottom of the metal box from the saturated ground outside. As he watched, a steady stream ran inside.

Shadow followed the bottom edge of the door lid, and push-tested every few inches until he reached the far corner where it gave a bit more. He pushed harder and managed to stick his nose through the opening. He pulled back when it tightened on his neck, and tried to jerk free. Shadow pawed the plastic, thumping and clawing to no avail. His feet stung with cold, and he splashed with each step.

The pup shouldered beside him, and pressed a blunt muzzle to the base of the plastic. He dug paws for traction and leaned one shoulder against the plastic surface. When it gave a bit more, Shadow wasted no time, and pushed his nose, then face, and finally shoulders through before it tightened and held him in its jaws.

Whining with sudden concern, Shadow struggled but couldn't move. He backpedaled, but couldn't pull himself free that way, either. A big tree outside held the dumpster lid shut.

He had to get out-out-OUT, and find September. Shadow yelped and struggled, but the plastic held tight.

Behind him inside the metal box where he couldn't see, the younger dog leaned against his flank, and Shadow stiffened with concern. He couldn't defend himself, or get out of the way. Shadow panicked when the pup scramble under him. He pedaled and flailed when the smaller body wiggled beneath his tummy. But the youngster didn't make a sound, only squirmed and clawed in the mud until he'd escaped through the door-space held open by Shadow's body.

Shadow closed his eyes when the pup again licked his face. He pulled and tugged and squirmed, but still couldn't get free.

His jerking efforts to escape startled the pup so much, the youngster dodged away, but stopped short. Shadow stared, and cocked his head. The dangling chain from the collar caught on something, and held the spotted pup in place. Shadow sniffed the metal links, and twisted to see them disappear beside him under the plastic lid cover. The pup yelped, and tugged, and the lid cover jostled.

Struggling but now silent, the young Pit Bull braced his paws, ignoring the water that had risen knee deep. He pulled, pulled, and pulled again. With each tug, the pup's neck and shoulder muscles bunched and relaxed, and Shadow felt the lid shift, slightly releasing pressure that clamped him in place. Shadow dug his own claws for purchase, and when the pup gave one more wrenching yank on his collar chain, Shadow pushed out of the metal box the same moment as the pup's chain popped free.

Shadow shook himself hard, and briefly nose-touched the pup. He saw the metal box still rested against the hard wall of the barn. September's car poked out the doorway. He needed to find her.

As Shadow splashed his way to the car, the spotted puppy whined, and lifted each paw in turn in reaction to the deepening water. The youngster scrambled onto the fallen tree that leaned next to the dumpster they'd escaped, heavy chain still dangling from his collar.

After a quick sniff around September's car, Shadow knew she hadn't come out yet. But he could find no way into the building. The water level flowed around the base of the barn, more from one side than the other, and instinctively Shadow headed toward the higher elevation past the dumpster, uphill to the water source.

He had to duck and weave to find a pathway through scrubby trees that sheltered the side of the stone building. A loud metal noise sounded overhead, and Shadow flinched when the roof waffled in the wind. Would it take flight like a bird and soar away? He'd seen big birds grab little animals. Would the roof-bird chase a good-dog and carry him off, too? Shadow hugged tight to the building, and hurried to reach the back of the barn.

The ground became steeper when he rounded the corner. The barn backed up against a big hill covered with grass and scrubby trees. A dark scar cut down one side of the hill. It looked like a dog had dug for varmints. Now water ran down the trench, overflowed, and bled mud across the grass.

A big boxy car, bigger than September's, sat at the end of the channel and Shadow wondered how it got there without a car path to ride. It leaned against the backside of the barn. Someone moved inside the car. Shadow cocked his head when someone shouted from the barn.

"Get back. Cover your face."

He recognized September's voice when she called from inside the barn. Shadow charged ahead despite the scary thump-thump-crash-crunch sound as he raced toward the big car. He barked, and barked again, frantic for a way to get past the car and into the barn to reach September.

Despite his barks, September never answered. Instead, she waited until the boy inside the van shook off pieces of glass. She helped him climbed out the car window into the barn, and never looked at Shadow at all. That made his tummy hurt with worry.

Maybe September couldn't hear or see him. The water's noise covered up a good-dog's barks, and he knew people couldn't hear as well as dogs. Shadow dodged to one side as the van shifted when a small girl also climbed out. He froze in momentary shock when September crawled out the barn window into the van. Shadow whined and licked his lips, relief mixed with concern for her safety. She'd come for him, after all! He expected her to call to him, make eye contact and tell him what to do. But she only crouched over the motionless driver.

The van shuddered and slid forward, riding a sudden shift in the ground. Shadow's surprised barks mixed with frightened yelps as a rush of deeper cold sluiced over his paws. Above him, the hill moved, turf sliding downward like a green blanket unmaking a bed. Water spilled over the top and sides of the dark flayed wounds. The hill split. One side fell away.

Shadow leaped high, as high as a good-dog could, and landed on the slick front surface of the car. He scrambled to keep his footing as the van surged and bucked in churning water. His throat ached and tummy soured with distress that only contact with September could soothe. He barked, his warnings louder when September still ignored him. She had to hear, it was a good-dog's job to keep his person safe.

She hadn't come before when he called. But he'd disobeyed her *go-to* Steven command. Maybe she didn't want him anymore?

Shadow dug at the splintered windshield and bit at the crystal fragments that glittered and broke away. His bark escalated to a scream that sprayed the glass with bloody saliva as the van shifted and lurched, battered by the rising tide of the flash flood.

Chapter 30

He's okay, thank you God, Shadow's all right. The relief made her want to shout, but September had to trust he'd stay safe until she could get Lenny into the barn. The van shifted again, taking the windows out of plumb. She had to hurry or the passage into the barn would slam shut.

She hunted for and found a pulse. Lenny's blue lips and labored breathing scared her more than his bruised face. He'd not worn a seatbelt, and the old van had no airbags. The impact not only cracked his head on the windshield, the steering wheel probably caused internal damage. Moving could kill him.

The van lurched, and Shadow's barks turned hysterical. "I hear you, baby-dog." God, she had to get the kid out, and help Shadow. "I won't leave you again."

No choice, she had to move Lenny now, or they'd all die. September yanked and tugged to drag him from behind the wheel. She looped his arm over her shoulders and supported Lenny's waist with her other arm.

Water carved twin channels down the sides of the reservoir's breached dirt dam. The gushing stream eroded the van's precarious perch and it lifted with a stomach-dropping action.

Shadow shrieked. His paws clawed for purchase as he surfed the hood of the van. "Hang on, baby-dog." September prayed he'd keep his grip. Once they got inside, the old cement structure should buffer the strong current. She pulled the boy with all her strength and thrust his head and shoulders through the opening.

"Grab his shoulders, pull-pull-pull." September knelt on the seat, and eyed the water spilling into the bottom of the van. She shoved Lenny's legs through the aligned windows as Melinda and Willie pulled the lanky teenager into the barn.

The van bumped with a sudden herky-jerk movement with the loss of Lenny's weight. September grabbed to steady herself, angrier than scared when the barn window slipped out of sight.

Shadow yelped, still clinging to the hood of the van. "Good-dog, what a brave boy." At her voice, he slicked back his ears, and nosed the ragged opening in the windshield. If she could knock out the rest of the glass and climb onto the roof, maybe they could ride out the flood together. Staying inside risked entombment in a watery coffin if the van toppled in the current. Shadow would never survive.

September pushed at the windshield, and immediately realized the futility. Hail or impact with the barn created starburst splinters, but laminate held the safety glass together. It would take time and tools to remove the entire window, which likely would knock Shadow off in the process.

The van jerked again, and September screamed. It caught on something, and slowly spun before slamming back into the wall. Shadow somehow maintained his wobbly balance, and she gasped with relief.

The water kept rising. The next surge would take them.

With the windshield holding her captive and the passenger window flush against the barn's cement wall, the driver's window offered the only escape. Every movement she made risked unsettling the van's temporary anchor and launching Shadow into the flood. September carefully shifted her weight, knelt on the driver's seat and tried to roll down the window. It wouldn't budge.

She'd used the rebar to break the van window, but had dropped it inside the barn. September searched for something else that would work. Other than a few candy wrappers on the wet floor, the van was clean. She popped the glove box, and again came up empty.

The van canted backwards. Water settled in the back half of the vehicle. Shadow barked and pawed the windshield, then climbed halfway up the spidered glass as it shifted to near horizontal. She had to get out. Now.

She hammered the window with the heels of her palms and then fists. Shadow barked with each blow. The window didn't budge. September searched the dashboard for something, anything to use. She pulled out the van's keys from the ignition, and jabbed them at the window, then tried her own SUV keys using the casing from Macy's laser pointer. She felt for the knife in her pocket, but after slicing through the fabric, it nested between inch-thick padding. After failing to extricate the blade, she gripped the knife through the coat fabric and stabbed the glass. The tip of the blade punched through the fabric, but the bare metal tip broke off and barely left a scratch. Nothing worked. She scooped up a handful of change, tried to score the glass with a quarter, and then threw it at the window with a scream of frustration.

The van lurched and settled. Water lapped above the seat. The current increased. September spied something white on the seat between her knees, picked it up and reacted with horror at the bloodstained porcelain tooth torn from Lenny's mouth. With revulsion, she hurled it away. It pinged the glass.

The driver's side window shattered.

Without hesitation, never questioning what had happened, September crawled out of the window. The van began to roll. She scrambled to get free of the vehicle, and used the sill as a step to vault onto the roof of the van.

Shadow already waited for her there, wagging and crying. "Good-dog, what a brave boy." She grasped his collar with one hand and the roof rack with the other to get her bearings. The van roof, only a temporary island of safety, would either sink, flip them off or spin away on the growing rush water.

Beside and above them, the loft offered the only hope. The tornado had sheared away part of the roof and wall. Good luck for them, since it offered access they otherwise wouldn't have. September carefully stood. That put the raw edge of the loft at shoulder height.

"Shadow." She kept her voice upbeat more for herself than for him. He'd easily read her terror, but she had to be resolute so he'd trust to do what she asked. She wouldn't leave him behind again, but there'd only be one chance to save them both.

Once Shadow made eye contact, she patted the high-placed floor of the loft. She prayed she'd keep her balance, her bad knee wouldn't betray her, and that the van's modest anchor held for another thirty seconds. He'd made vaults higher than this. She patted the loft floor again. "Shadow, JUMP."

He didn't hesitate. Shadow vaulted, stretched front paws and clawed for purchase when they caught the loft floor. September boosted his haunches the last little bit.

Relief flooded September, but she couldn't waste time. She heard the remainder of the dam crumble behind her and a wall of water gush forward.

She leaped for her life, and grabbed hold, forearms braced on the loft floor. Below her dangling boots, the van tipped over, and spun away in the deluge. September inched forward, swinging her good leg up and catching her heel on the edge until hot breath and teeth tugged her collar. Shadow's boost provided the extra needed to roll into the loft.

Panting, she lay on her back. Shadow stood over top of her, licking her face and making crying dog sounds.

September sat up and pushed the dog away. The sounds were not Shadow, but from below, inside the barn. Mixed with Kinsler's howls, kids screamed.

Chapter 31

The hail switched off as the heavens called a temporary truce, but Combs didn't move. He hunkered on the floor of Doc Eugene's storage closet, knees drawn up and face pillowed in his arms. The pain and denial grew, not wanting to believe September's message. Willie, his bright, exuberant son, so young, strong, and happy...no. He wouldn't let his imagination go there.

Damn the dog. Damn the storm. And double-damn September for failing Willie.

Lights flickered back to life, but Combs kept his head down. He heard the others labor to their feet, and surreptitiously scrubbed tears from his cheeks before taking three or four gulping breaths and lifting his head.

"Let's see the damage." Doc Eugene opened the door and exited the tiny room, closely followed by Robin. "We're still standing." He disappeared into the front of the vet clinic, his footsteps sneaker soft as he canvased the building. Robin trailed him.

Gonzales held out a hand to help Combs up. "You look like hell. Storm's over. For now, anyway."

Combs jerked away, and stalked out of the room. His throat ached. "Over for us. Willie's still out there." He couldn't tell Gonzales about

September's call. To say it out loud made it real. Magical thinking, sure, but he didn't care.

"What did September say? She didn't find him?" Gonzales took out his phone, checked it and grimaced. "Still no bars."

He turned away, and grudgingly spoke. "The message broke up. Wasn't clear." Combs clung to that thin thread and the hope that September wouldn't relegate such news to a voice mail.

Doc Eugene came back into the room. "Lots of limbs blew down, some power lines, too. Robin's car looks like someone worked it over with a baseball bat. Don't know if yours will start or not. But my SUV has barely a scratch, except a honey locust branch scratched one side." He sniffed. "Bizarre weather keeps getting more and more strange." He saw Combs checking his phone. "The office landline is dead, too."

"I'll check the car." Gonzales turned to Combs. "Better touch base with Doty on the radio, find out the state of the county. I don't care if the car's a lumpy-bumpy mess, if it runs." He squeezed Combs's arm. "I got kids, too. We'll find him." He hurried out the door.

Doc Eugene raised his eyebrows.

Combs answered. "Willie's out in the storm."

"For heaven's sake, why would he do that?" Doc Eugene held out a palm in a placating gesture. "Forget I said that. He's a kid. Doesn't need a reason."

"He went after his dog. September's tracking with Shadow, but I can't reach her." Combs shrugged. "Her last message mentioned Willie, but was garbled."

Gonzales returned. "Car's got two flats. I reached Doty, though. Cell towers are down all over North Texas, and flooding disrupted cable between those still standing." He held up his mobile phone. "Meet my high-dollar paperweight." He pocketed the device. "Told Doty about your boy and she promised to get a team out ASAP. But she said lots of people need help." He cleared his throat. "Headquarters got a tip about the dogfight ring. They're set to go. Tonight, in a couple hours. She tapped us to follow up."

"My son's out there. She expects us to check some half ass tip when Willie's missing?" Combs barked a humorless laugh. "She can go screw herself."

"Is the Internet still up?" Doc Eugene hurried to the reception area and booted the computer. "I shut it down during the storm, it'll be a minute."

"The 'net probably is hit or miss, depending on your provider." Gonzales took a step toward Combs's angry pacing. "About that tip. Doty said every account in the department got an email from some hacker calling himself Kid Kewl that detailed the time and location. Some old barn off of FM 691."

Combs wanted to punch something. Punch someone. Doty's face would do.

Gonzales gnawed his mustache, and hesitated. "Isn't that the area September headed?"

He nodded. "But nothing's happening tonight. No dogfight, no drug deals. Doty's bust won't happen, none of the players will be out in this weather." Combs spoke with forced politeness. "Do what you need to do, Gonzales, but right now I could care less about Doty or my job. I'm going after Willie."

Doc Eugene interrupted. "If the Internet works, you can track Shadow by his GPS collar. I know he wears one. You said September mentioned Willie by name, and Shadow never leaves her side. Find Shadow, you'll find Willie."

Combs remembered the GPS system they'd used before. "She's got her house defined as the home territory. When September's pets wander beyond that designated area, her email gets an alert."

It worked similar to Amber Alert tracking systems used to keep kids safe, something Combs wished he'd got for Willie. Parents could get updates sent to a computer or smart phone about the child's location every minute or so and track movements 24/7, even define new areas for after school events or vacation destinations. For pets, the bare bones design used a combination of cell phone towers and GPS to track movement. It worked with a handheld reader.

Gonzales sounded hopeful. "We can give the barn a once over and work the GPS angle at the same time. Doty won't have to know."

Combs moved closer to the computer. "The hand held device has a two-mile range. A desktop won't cut it. We'd need a laptop or tablet with mobile hot spot. Last time our friend Theodore Williams, the geriatric hacker, set that up but since his wife died, he's not been around much."

The computer started up and Doc Eugene launched the browser. The icon spun forever, but nothing came up. "You're right, that's not going to work." He stuck his hand in his pocket, and plucked out his car keys. "But I remember the way to Teddy's house. Let's go."

Chapter 32

Lightening clawed the sky, but September didn't flinch, numbed by what had come before. She only gritted her teeth and shivered when the clouds once again turned on the spigot. Shadow pressed close beside her.

From her vantage, she saw the tank's partially breached dam continue spewing water. Two-thirds of the dike held the rest of the water at bay, but as she watched, the artificial current down each side chewed at the barrier. She swiveled, gauging the rate of rising water inside the barn, its rush buffered by cement block walls already weakened in the storm. Once the dike surrendered—not *if*, but *when*—anything inside would drown.

The roof and loft already sliced and diced by the tornado exposed the barn interior to punishing rain. The low windows she'd opened to reach the kids now allowed water to sluice inside like a dam's open floodgates. Her elevated view mimicked first balcony seats at a macabre theater production, and she carefully edged forward and craned her neck when the kids screamed again.

Melinda, Willie, and Steven clung together. Lenny sprawled unmoving at their feet. The little group hunkered on the first level of an island of stacked straw bales that abutted one side of an eight-foot-long horse panel, a wire grid barrier defining that side of the dogfight pit. The rising water lifted the bale and the kids rocked a bit before climbing to the next tier to join Boris Kitty. They left Lenny, and September worried the boy might roll off into the water.

Willie wailed again. "He wiggled and slipped out. Get him. Please, get him, Nikki." He jerked his arm but couldn't escape his sister's grip. "I can't swim, please get Kinsler."

September followed Willie's gaze, and her stomach lurched. A bucket floated by, banged against her SUV that still blocked the exit, and performed a drunken pirouette before the current sucked it beneath the car. Nikki slowly plodded through the rising water toward a bobbing white bundle.

Shadow woofed under his breath. He watched with interest, but kept a wary distance from the edge of the drop off.

It only took a few inches of rushing water to knock adults off their feet, and a little girl like Nikki wouldn't have a chance. If the dam broke, the surge of additional water would batter her against, or trap her beneath the car. Once sucked through the narrow breach and tumbled out the other side, not even an Olympic swimmer would survive.

Nikki didn't understand the risks. Her empathy for stray cats nearly got Nikki killed in the burning barn, too. September quelled the urge to shout, "Hurry up," because slow and steady offered better footing. "One step at a time, don't trip, Nikki."

"I'm okay. But his head's under water." Nikki stopped, scooped up the dripping dog and turned back to the bales. Limp and unresponsive, Kinsler flopped in the girl's arms, and September's heart sank.

"Is he okay? Is Kinsler going to be okay?" Willie scrubbed anguished tears from his eyes. He pulled away from his sister's restraint, but fear of the water kept him rooted in place.

September didn't blame the boy. Water made her queasy, too. She couldn't bear to put her face in it. "Everyone, stay right where you are." Her voice whip-cracked with authority. "Nikki, hook your hands in the wire grid on the horse panel. That's right, that's the way." She held her breath until the girl slogged close enough to roll the small dog up onto the level where the kids crouched.

"He's not breathing." Willie stroked long white fur away from Kinsler's face. "He's not breathing." Willie hovered over his dog, and his sister helped Nikki climb out of the chilly water.

The boy's pleading expression unnerved September. In his world, adults had all the answers, and were supposed to make everything better. Poor kid. First the divorce, then his mother's illness, and now he'd watch his dog die. She hated adding another failure onto his young shoulders, but she had no time to waste on a hopeless cause. The kids' safety and getting them into the loft before the dam broke took priority.

"Listen to me. The water's going to get worse really fast. Everyone must get up high, quick as you can." Straw stacks gave them height, but the bales floated, and would become unstable once the dam broke. The loft was the safest location, but her SUV smashed the loft's stairway.

The spring pole's rope moved back and forth in the breeze. Able to sustain the ferocious grip and gyrations of a Pit Bull hanging by his jaws, it certainly could support the weight of each child. But the lowest end hung a good five feet above ground now covered with over a foot of water. Rope-climb drills in Phys. Ed. class when she was a girl spawned universal kid nightmares. September doubted she'd be able to do it, let alone tiny Tracy. They needed something foolproof. Like a ladder.

Even then, the kids couldn't lift Lenny. Shock alone could kill the boy, if his injuries hadn't already. "Melinda, there's a couple of horse blankets on one of those top bales. Yep, where Boris Kitty is resting. We've got to keep Lenny warm."

Willie remained focused on his dog. "Nikki, you work for a vet." His voice trembled, the implications clear. "There's stuff you can do to save him. I saw it on TV about pet CPR."

"I never learned how. September knows." Nikki leaned over Kinsler and felt his chest, then held her palm in front of his nose. "He's not breathing. And I can't feel his heart." She jutted her chin. "September, tell me what to do."

September fumed. They couldn't waste the time. At least Melinda had covered up Lenny as best she could. The orange cat Willie called Waffles decided to snuggle beneath the injured boy's neck. Maybe they could secure the bale in place—

"My dog, what about Kinsler?" Willie yelled, frantic.

Shadow whined. He hated raised voices. More to placate Willie and keep him busy than with any hope for success, September barked out instructions. "Melinda, you're the tallest. Pick up Kinsler by his rear legs. That's right, upside down. Now swing him. Back and forth. With more energy." That often jump-started breathing. Chest compressions required a flat firm surface, not spongy straw bales, and even a veterinarian had trouble performing the ideal 100-120 compressions per minute under the best of conditions.

With Willie's urging, Melinda took the dog by his hocks and swung him back and forth several times. The white dog flopped and dripped water like a sodden stuffed toy.

Nikki interrupted. "It's not working. What about mouth to mouth? Doc Eugene promised to show me but—"

September didn't wait for her to finish. *No time, no time, she had to get the kids to safety.* "Nikki, you still have your bolt cutters? Good. Willie, you work on Kinsler. The rest of you do exactly what I say, no questions and no hesitation. Got it?" She couldn't get down there to do the work, so they'd have to pull together.

They all agreed, eyes wide and frightened.

"Willie, sit down and put your dog in your lap on his back." As he situated himself, September pointed to the metal grid next to the stacked straw bales. "Nikki, those panels come in sections. Cut one loose. It'll be about four bale lengths apart, probably wired together."

"I'm ready, now what?" Willie cradled Kinsler and waited, ignoring Nikki as the girl carefully climbed back into the water and searched for the far edge of the horse panel.

September turned to the two youngest. "Steven and Tracy, you need to help, too. Melinda, work with them. Cut free the baling twine that holds together the bales. Choose the ones that won't matter if they fall apart, we need the twine."

"What do I do about Kinsler?" Willie sounded panicked.

"Willie, do nose-to-mouth rescue breathing. Kinsler's mouth won't seal right so wrap your hands around his muzzle. Yes, that's right. Now open your mouth, and put it over top of his nostrils and mouth." The boy didn't hesitate. "Keep his neck straight so it's a direct shot into his lungs. Gently blow two quick breaths, like you're blowing up a paper bag."

He did it and then pulled away. "His chest moved."

"That's good, Willie. After every two breath-puffs, pull away to let the air come back out. Keep doing that. Don't stop." Sometimes it took quite a while before pets breathed on their own. Sometimes they didn't. But she couldn't tell him that. Better that he remained focused. And calm.

"I got one end cut." Nikki splashed to the other end of the wire grid panel while the first part sagged in deepening current. September wondered why the girl didn't shiver in the cold water. Adrenalin kept them all warm, she guessed.

"Stay close to the bales, and keep a hand on a safe anchor." September told herself that would give Nikki time to escape if the breach came. The truth was, she didn't know. But they didn't have any choice.

Melinda tugged ineffectually at the sisal on one of the bales. She screamed her frustration. "I need a knife!"

The broken knife still poked through one side of September's coat. She grabbed the handle through the fabric and tried to work the blade free. She'd toss it to the kids, and pray her aim wouldn't hit them or fall short and drop it into the water.

Nikki continued to struggle to cut loose with the other end of the panel. Without the horse panel, they wouldn't need the twine, and without the twine, they couldn't use the panel. September checked the state of the dike, and her breath quickened. No wonder the water level increased. The rest of the barrier could go at any moment. And the damn knife wouldn't come free.

Steven brought a two-foot scrap of twine he'd found and pushed it into Melinda's hands. Her brow furrowed. She wouldn't take it at first, until he began to singsong instructions.

"See-saw, Margery-Daw,
Cut the thing with the string.
See it saw, Like a claw,
Make a sling, Cut the string…"

September frowned. Maybe he had learned this trick at the theater. Worth a shot. "Melinda, do what Steven says. Take that bit of twine, slip one end under the bale strap. Now grab both ends of your piece and pull up. That's what he means, *make a sling.* The weight of the bale holds it taut, you see? Now use your short piece and saw back and forth."

Melinda's face lit up when the maneuver cut through the strap like butter, and then she stiffened. Boris Kitty had climbed up her pant leg and draped himself around her neck. She dumped him off.

"Good job, what a team. Melinda, you cut them, and Tracy and Steven collect them." September balled her fists, frustrated she couldn't lend a hand. "Next, tie all the pieces together, end to end, to make two strands long enough to stretch from here," she patted the loft floor, "clear down to the ground. Hurry." Best to have enough and double or even triple that amount of twine to add strength. She'd not yet worked out how to get the twine up to her level.

Boris Kitty once again vaulted high, this time clawing up Melinda's back. With a cry, the girl twisted, stood, and tried to shake him loose but he kept his grip and shimmied to reach her shoulders. She peeled him off and set him none too gently on the bale beside her.

"Done." Nikki stood with one hand still clutching the bolt cutters, and the other entwined in one end of the horse panel to keep it from sinking into the tugging current. "Now what?"

Willie yelled with frustration, his face red from worry and exertion. "It's not working. He's still not breathing." September winced at the accusation in his voice.

She saw a bit of sharp wire sticking out from the panel. Desperate times call for Hail Mary measures . . . "Nikki, cut off that wire, and straighten it out like a needle. You're going to do acupuncture on Kinsler."

Willie's eyes grew large. To Nikki's credit, she acted excited. She followed September's directions explicitly. "Take the sharp end, and jab it to the bone in the midway point of Kinsler's philtrum. That's the slit below the nose and above the lips. Jab it HARD and wiggle back and forth." Needling this alarm point stimulated the release of adrenalin—veterinarians call the drug epinephrine. That might be enough to jump-start the dog's heart. "Don't stop, keep wiggling it and pressing hard."

Ten seconds become a lifetime watching for signs of life in someone you love. When Kinsler gasped, Nikki jumped backwards with a squeal. The dog took another breath, and then yelped. He struggled weakly in Willie's happy embrace.

Melinda shouted, too, and Shadow barked with excitement in what September thought to be celebration. But no. It was Boris Kitty again, this time perched atop Melinda's head, a climbing maniac determined to scale the heights.

September smiled. She knew exactly how to get the twine into the loft.

Chapter 33

The spring pole system, anchored with a triple-wrap of steel cable, sprouted from a crossbeam even with the loft floor. The attached industrial-size spring looked like it came from a garage door. A well-worn rope hooked to the spring, and ended with a frayed, chewed up double knot that swung slowly back and forth.

September checked below. Steven and Tracy sat beside Willie who kept a firm grip on Kinsler's collar. The little dog appeared recovered, and September didn't want to tell the boy Kinsler could still collapse. All near drownings needed follow up medical care, but at this point, that was the least of their worries. She still hadn't a clue how to get Lenny up into the loft. *Concentrate on those you can help.*

The two girls pushed one of the floating bales directly beneath the suspended rope while dragging the metal horse panel grid behind them. September knew the panel only weighed about fifteen pounds, but the eight-foot-by-fifty-inch dimensions made it a pain to manipulate. It'd make a keen ladder, though, something all the kids could climb. They'd hoist it up with twine and secure it to the crossbeam, once they got the twine up to September.

"Nikki, stay low on the bale. Help steady it for Melinda." The older girl wore Boris Kitty like a stole, and his tail thumped with agitation.

September didn't blame the cat. If she had a tail, it'd be bottlebrush with fear.

Melinda carefully stood on the floating bale, directly below the spring pole rope. The kids had already threaded one end of the twine through Boris Kitty's collar. Melinda grabbed the end of the swinging rope, using it to steady her own balance, and then held it next to her neck. Nothing happened.

"What'll I do now? He won't go." Melinda peeled the cat off her shoulders with one hand, and tried to hang him onto the rope. He twisted and clawed at her shirt.

"No, don't try to force him. It has to be the cat's idea." September watched in horror when the girl lost her grip and Boris Kitty fell into the water. The current immediately whisked the feline toward the swirling exit. "The twine, catch the twine." September prayed the collar wouldn't give way. Many cat collars break away, for safety reasons, so a cat wouldn't catch on something and strangle.

Nikki caught up the end of the long spool of twine they'd gathered, and towed the hissing cat back. Before she could collect his furious form, he clawed his own way onto the floating straw bale, shook himself and each foot in turn, and leaped for Melinda's pant leg.

She squealed as he climbed her body, scratch graffiti testament to his displeasure. This time Boris Kitty didn't stop at Melinda's shoulders. He spat in her face, paw-clutched the rope she still held steady in one hand, and scaled it quicker than a furry Tarzan, the lightweight baling twine trailing from his collar.

"It worked. Now what?" Nikki stood in the water beside the bobbing bale, and grabbed the other side of the metal grid.

The soaked cat, met by Shadow's inquisitive nose, smacked the dog soundly and streaked across the loft floor. Shadow started to follow. "No, Shadow. *Wait.*" Cowed, he did as she asked. September wanted to shout with joy, but still needed to retrieve the hissed off cat and collect the twine. He'd vaulted to the top of a stack of wardrobe boxes stored in one corner.

The cat ignored her. Shadow whined with concern as September walked the balance beam to reach the other side of the barn. "Hey there, Boris Kitty. Can I call you BK? What a brave cat, and such an athlete." She crooned to him and avoided eye contact, crossing to him in a curving pattern. One wrong move and the spooked feline might self-launch into the rafters, destroying their plans.

But for once, luck was a lady. BK ignored her to studiously groom away water from his soaked fur. She picked up the trailing end of the twine, and collected it hand-over-hand as she approached the cat until able to untie the string from his collar. He purred his forgiveness. "Aren't you a handsome, brave fellow?" He mewed, head-bumped her hand, and returned to his tongue bath.

Shadow woofed and pranced where he waited on the far side of the loft. September planned to set up the makeshift ladder on the far side, but time had run out. She'd need to tie it off on this side, and quickly.

"Girls, weave twine back and forth through the end of the grid. Do it now." She watched impatiently. "That's right. Now tie it off. A couple of knots are fine, I'll do more once it's up here. Y'all lift and support the bottom, feed it up as I pull from this end."

They lifted and all eight feet of the flexible fence snaked out of the water. September gathered the twine into a pile beside her. "Good, good, now hold it steady while I secure the top."

The makeshift ladder wasn't ideal but the best she could do. September wrapped twine around the crossbeam, through the wire grids and back again, doubling and tripling the strands. The kids watched from below, finally understanding what she had in mind. This side of the barn actually worked better, because a double tier of straw rested directly beneath the panel making the first step up an easier reach.

They heard the roar when the dam broke. The surge of water rocked Nikki and Melinda's bale, and the girls shrieked. They clung together when the straw surfed backwards. It smashed into the other bales where the other children perched.

"Hang on. Everyone, stay together." September watched helplessly as the bales lifted in the sudden swell. Shadow rushed to her side.

The flood uncorked the SUV from the bottleneck at the barn's doorway, bulldozing it away. Lenny's straw bale, closest to the exit, bobbled and twirled. Steven lurched; his tablet flew from his hands and landed between Lenny's legs, startling the small orange cat that still nestled on Lenny's chest.

Steven grabbed for Lenny's sleeve, but missed, slipped, and pitched into the water. Steven never made a sound, but his mouth opened in a shocked "o" of horror. He dog paddled to keep his head above water, but the current battered him like a cat playing with a mouse.

"God, no!"

When September screamed, Shadow pressed hard against her side. She hugged him tight and trembled, but her muscles refused to obey the mental command to go after the boy. Save him, save Steven. It's what any normal mother would do.

Shadow stared into her face, gently licked September's tears, and pulled out of her embrace. He whirled, and without hesitation, Shadow dove off the loft floor into the water below.

September screeched as her dog—her heart—disappeared beneath dirty swirls of water. The water depth had risen past his shoulders, running so swiftly it easily knocked him off his feet. She leaned forward, staring, ivory knuckles clutching the edge of the loft.

She couldn't catch her breath. Her hands, feet, even her legs tingled. September willed Shadow to reach Steven. Her pulse drummed so loudly in her ears, it out-shouted the flood.

He lunged, snapped and snagged Steven's jacket. Shadow's grip swerved the boy's trajectory enough to lob Steven against Lenny's floating bale. Steven managed to claw a grip into Lenny's bale strap with frantic fingers.

The bale bobbed, dipped, and disappeared out the barn door with the two boys, Shadow helplessly swept in its wake. As if to underline the blackness of despair, the overhead floodlights sputtered out.

Chapter 34

Nikki shrugged off Melinda's weeping embrace. She had to shout over the rush of water. "What do we do?" They couldn't go after Lenny and Steven. But they couldn't stay here, either. Their perch on the straw stack bobbled.

The other kids stared anywhere but at Nikki, the way kids avoided eye contact if a teacher asked a difficult question. Willie clutched his dog with one hand and held tight to Melinda with the other. Tracy hugged her dinosaur and rocked. They were no help.

"What do we do? The flood's getting worse." September didn't answer. Nikki craned to see into the loft, but September had moved back from the edge out of sight. Maybe working on some kind of plan? "Hey, September, where are you?" She hoped the woman wouldn't do something stupid, the way grownups sometimes did out of desperation. Nikki wanted to cry.

The bales heaved upward and tipped, and everybody squealed, even Nikki. "September, we got to do something now." The whole stack shifted toward the open doorway, a hayride gone terribly wrong. One more big wave and the water would squirt them out like jelly from a doughnut. They couldn't wait for September. They had to finish her plan themselves.

The crazy ladder beckoned, but the bales had shifted so much, they'd have to wade yards of water to reach it. Nikki caught up the extra baling twine—they'd cut far more than they needed—and patted Melinda's arm.

"What?" The older girl shivered uncontrollably and whimpered. Her tangled hair and runny mascara turned her face into a freaky Halloween mask. The collective bales, now a floating island, bobbed sideways. The whole stack slowly traveled toward the open barn door, and hung because the top tier of the straw wedding cake proved too high to pass through. It might scrape off any minute, though. The mountain of straw ground against the dirt floor. Flood pressure pushed from one side and sucked from the other, creating a temporary dam that slowed the outflow. When the top scraped off, they'd stream away with the rest of the bales.

Nikki thrust the twine at Melinda. "You're biggest, you have to go first. Tie one end to your belt loop. Then you." She poked Willie. "Put Kinsler inside your jacket and zip it. You'll need both hands."

"What are you talking about?" Melinda's attention sharpened. "Go first?" But she threaded the end of the twin through belt loops, without being prompted a second time.

"I'm next to tallest so I go last." Nikki had grown a bunch in the past two months, and stood a head taller than Willie despite being the same age. "Tracy goes ahead of me, because she's littlest."

Nikki's hands shook and her tongue wanted to stick to the roof of her mouth. At least she knew how to swim. Willie said he didn't know how, and there was no way Tracy could cross the water without help. Nikki scanned the loft again. She hoped September would be there when they climbed into the loft.

Now that the bales had moved, the swaying horse panel's eight-foot length still left a four-foot gap to the floor of the barn. Nikki measured the best route with her eyes. A direct path, though shorter, risked the tug and push of the current. Better to sidle off the bales and use them like anchors as they moved to the far wall first. "There." She pointed, and explained as the other kids finished stringing themselves together. "September has the ladder all ready. We just have to reach it without getting drowned."

Willie snorted. "Yeah, getting drowned would suck. Ask Kinsler." The dog's head poked outside his jacket like Wack-A-Mole and Willie pushed Kinsler's head back down. Willie's complexion matched Kinsler's pale fur.

Nikki figured she wasn't at her best, either. Her favorite shoes looked ruined, and her jacket would never recover, but at least she wasn't swept away like Steven and Lenny. And Shadow. Before she could dissolve into a blubbering baby mess, Nikki pinched herself, hard. That hurt. But it worked.

Their bales shifted again. Nikki reached out and grabbed Tracy to keep her steady. The little girl didn't notice, simply clutched her soaked dinosaur and rocked faster and faster. "We've got to go. Now."

Nikki gave Melinda a shove. "Wait, you mean into the water?" Melinda wrinkled her nose.

"It's either that or fly. Go ahead, step off real careful. Willie, give her your hand." Nikki paused, and when Melinda hesitated, her tone sharpened. "You want to die? You want all of us to die?"

"Okay, I'll do it. Willie, don't let go." Melinda sat on the edge of the bale, and let her feet drop into the cold brown water. "Nasty, stinks like a sewer. I'm going, already." She clung to Willie's hand and slid off to stand in the water, adjusting to the tug of the current. If the stack of straw let loose in the doorway, the current would turn into a water shoot and blast them out.

"Steady yourself against the bales." Nikki had already been in the water and knew what to do. Melinda gained confidence after a couple of steps. "Get to the wall, and wait for Willie. Once he's there, follow the wall until you reach the metal wire fence."

Melinda nodded, but said nothing, biting her lip in concentration. She reached the wall, and waited for her brother to draw near.

Willie joined his sister. "Go ahead, Melinda." Nikki talked as loud as she could without screaming, so they could hear her. "Hug the wall, and be real careful you don't slip because there's nothing to catch you. That's the reason for the tether, see? It's our contingency." Dad always said a contingency was the most important part of any plan. Dad was the smartest person she knew. Well, Doc Eugene was super smart, too, being a veterinarian and all.

Melinda moved more quickly. She reached the near edge of the suspended fencing and grasped the wire, but tripped and went chest-deep in the water.

Willie yelled and started toward his sister.

"Stay where you are, Willie. Keep the twine tight so you can reel her in!" Nikki held her breath.

"I'm okay." The older girl dragged herself upright, spitting and making a face after getting a mouthful of the runoff. "Willie, don't go toward the middle. There's a rut or something in the ground." Melinda turned back to Nikki. "What about the little one?"

Nikki had it all figured out. She spoke softly to Tracy, explaining exactly what would happen. She wasn't sure if the girl understood but talking worked with the spooky feral cats at the clinic, and they didn't understand people talk, either. Doc Eugene and September said tone of voice meant more than words, so she spoke with confident encouragement and hoped Tracy understood.

Tracy stopped rocking long enough to let Nikki lift her. With the girl's legs and arms firmly wrapped around her waist and neck, Grooby trailing down her back, Nikki took a first careful step into the water. She moved sideways, clawing deep with both hands into the bales to anchor herself along the way, until she reached Willie.

"Now you. Along the wall, Willie, to Melinda at the grid." He made hurried progress and soon joined his sister. "Melinda, how about you moved to the far edge of the fence to hold it steady, while Willie holds his side. Hang on tight, though." She waited until they sloshed into position. Was it her imagination or had the water got deeper, but the current slowed? Whatever. They couldn't stop now.

"I need some help here. Willie, make sure you have a good grip on the panel. Yeah, that's good, hook an arm through. Now find your end of the twine, and keep it tight as I come to you."

If she slipped while holding Tracy, they'd both head out to sea unless the twine held. September said it would hold. But they only had a single strand, while September used multiple thicknesses to secure the fence-ladder. "We don't weigh much, though, do we Tracy?" The little girl squeezed her neck, and Nikki smiled. "I'll take that as a yes." She took a breath. *Here we go.*

The tether tension Willie provided, along with leaning one shoulder hard against the barn wall, gave Nikki enough extra balance. She only slipped once, and thank goodness, quickly recovered. Finally, they all stood beneath the suspended horse panel. Water now reached Melinda's butt and stood well over Willie's waist.

"Now what?" Melinda waited for direction.

Nikki examined the cross beam above. It wouldn't be easy to climb the metal fence, and tricky to get from the beam to the solid floor of the loft. They'd come this far, though, and she wouldn't give the other kids any reason to doubt their ability. Dad said that, too. You had to believe, before you could do. *I believe, Daddy.*

"Tracy first." Nikki unwrapped the girl's arms from her neck. "You can do this. I'm going to hold you up to grab hold, and Melinda and Willie will hold the bottom steady. Climb, and don't look down. Climb like you do the monkey bars at the playground, okay?"

Nikki worried the girl would freeze, or cling to her and yell or something equally dumb. She was clean out of ideas if that happened. But happily, Tracy gripped Grooby between her teeth, and scrambled quick as a squirrel up the ladder contraption. "Wow, good job. Tracy, you're a champ." She turned to Willie. "You next. Watch out for the dog."

"Got it covered." Willie had tucked his jacket into the waist of his pants to secure Kinsler. "If Tracy can do it, so can I."

Nikki didn't appreciate the girl-slam, but at least it gave Willie incentive. Real heroes got scared, too. They didn't let the brain freeze shut them down. "So make like a monkey already."

He made a face, and hooted his chimp impression, but let Melinda give him a boost up before he quickly climbed the fence.

Nikki's shoulders relaxed. September's idea worked great.

"Now you." Melinda wiped hair out of her eyes. "I'm the tallest, like you said. I can get up that first step on my own, but you'll need me to give the first boost. And I'm the oldest. You've done enough; I got to step up, too." She dropped her voice. "Girl power, right?"

"Girl power." Nikki smiled. "Okay, we got this." She searched with her foot under the water to find Melinda's braced knee, balanced briefly on one foot while grabbing the wire, and pulled herself up.

With only one person steadying the make-do ladder, it wanted to shimmy as Nikki climbed. It took her twice as long to reach the loft as the first two kids, but her arms already ached from holding Tracy. Finally, she grabbed the beam, and crab-walked to the solid loft floor.

Nikki sank to her knees, so relieved she wanted to cry. She looked around, and saw the other kids around September, who sat in one corner of the loft with her knees drawn up, shaking and crying and acting totally weirded out.

She wanted to find out what was wrong, but had to wait for Melinda. Just as the older girl grabbed the wire handholds, the topmost wedding-cake bales broke off. The straw stopper unplugged and the rest of the bales washed out the barn door like bumper cars. The sudden outflow swept Melinda off her feet.

Chapter 35

The water tasted of dirt, animal dung and dead bugs, fermented grass and bitter bark. Shadow sputtered, struggled to keep his head above the tumbling torrent, and lunged once more. He grabbed and latched onto cloth. A familiar scent, one never forgotten, filled him with confusion.

Protectiveness. Affection. Distrust. Fear. Memory of the "otherness" of his-boy pointing the gun that bit a good-dog's ear.

He gulped air in panting breaths. Small scared whimpers escaped but he didn't dare let go his grip on the coat. Nose thrust hard against Steven's back, Shadow's jaws ached with tension and his stomach churned. When his flank smashed into something hidden beneath the rush of dark water, he nearly lost his grip, but didn't yelp. Shadow drew his paws up tight, helpless, riding the whims of the water.

His-boy's odor crinkled Shadow's nose, the bite-sharp terror spilled through Steven's clothing more potent than the cat pee dribbling from the little orange cat. Smells choked his throat. Water filled his ears, muffling the flood's roar and cat's screams. Shadow wanted to shake his head. But he clenched his jaws and hung on.

Bam!

The sodden bale hit, stopped, tipped downward. One of Lenny's arms flopped into the water. Shadow's hold broke loose when the bale reared high, a legless horse vaulting a hidden obstacle.

He flailed; paws churned to find solid purchase, and turned water to filthy froth. The wet, muddy bank beckoned, only a dog-length distant. Current tugged him away.

Steven's arm whipped out. His-boy grabbed Shadow's collar, and kept his other fist latched onto Lenny's bale. Steven had grown in the time away, and his legs were much longer than Shadow's. When he found his feet, Steven stood chest deep and braced himself against the surge.

Shadow reluctantly met Steven's eyes. Neither of them liked eye contact with strangers, and after all the time that had passed, they were strangers. But something had changed. The "other-ness" in Steven's eyes remained but it no longer spoke of danger.

The floating bale bucked again. Shadow's collar tightened. Steven swung him through the water closer to the bank where shallow water pooled.

Shadow didn't think. As his paws touched, he clawed and scrambled out of the water. He shook himself so hard, he nearly fell over. He panted and shivered at the same time, then in one convulsive heave, threw up.

The current continued to push wreckage along the water's surface. An underwater tree had hooked the bottom of the bale. The tree bobbed up and down in the current. When down, the bale tried to squeak over the branch, which then boosted it up again.

Steven waited until the bale dipped low, then grabbed something shiny and flat from between Lenny's legs. With a smooth gesture, he Frisbee'd it toward Shadow.

Shadow lunged and caught it. He recognized it from the earlier *show-me* game. Steven didn't smile, but sensed his-boy's approval. He wagged.

Shadow cocked his head when the orange cat yowled with each bounce of the floating bale. He wondered why the cat didn't jump off and race to higher ground. Macy-cat picked a safe tree to climb and wait for Shadow to *seek* and bring him home. But this cat didn't move, merely kept his claws secured in Lenny's shirt, and burrowed closer to the boy.

Steven clung to the bale, wading with careful small steps to reach the bank. He had to let go of the bale to climb up like Shadow, but kept slipping back into the water. The bank's soggy mud turned loose of trees and grass so there was nothing his-boy could grab. Boys don't have claws like dogs.

Shadow put down the tablet he'd caught, and slowly put one paw and then another on the fallen tree. His weight held it steady. When Steven reached out, Shadow stretched his neck and grabbed the end of Steven's coat sleeve, and tugged.

That gave his-boy enough help to scramble up on the tree limb. With both Steven and Shadow standing on the slender trunk, though, the limb sank further beneath the current, bouncing the straw bale and giving it enough leeway to pass over the temporary snag.

Steven sprang at Shadow, and Shadow nearly dodged away. But something told him to stay still.

"Good-dog."

Shadow pricked his ears with surprise. His-boy had never told him that before.

He held still, marveling at Steven's gentle touch. His-boy quickly pulled off Shadow's collar and tossed it toward Lenny, just as the current again captured the bale and swirled Lenny and the cat out of sight.

Chapter 36

September screwed her eyes tight against the flames. Her flesh blistered, charred and fell away. She struggled to breathe in the super-heated furnace of the burning barn. Her legs, cocooned in an ever-tightening noose, strangled every effort to escape. She clawed, flailed and bucked to get out, crawl away, to survive. A heavy weight crushed the air from her chest and pinned September to the hard pack dirt.

From far away Shadow yelped, followed by an anguished howl. Oh God, don't let him burn, too! Wet flame licked her face, and September screamed, screamed, screamed for a lifetime and only fell silent when her raw throat and heaving lungs failed. The relentless heat bathed her face again and again. Barks and whines cut through the fog of horror, hot air fanned her neck, and she recoiled — then recognized the sensation with a sob of relief. Not a furnace blast, but anxious dog panting. Canine whimpers sounded a counterpoint rhythm to each attention-seeking slurp-kiss aimed at her eyes and mouth. His icy nose shocked her out of the flashback.

Her heart still hammered its marathon sprint, and her entire body shook with chills despite the heat flushing her face. September kept her eyes closed. She told herself to breathe slowly, and managed to curtail gasps and unclench still tingling hands. Thank God, she had Shadow, her sweet baby-dog, to keep her safe, to anchor her in the real world.

"Good-dog, I'm okay." Shadow knew better, but saying the words gave her a goal. She put up a hand to block his enthusiastic face kisses. His wet fur was wrong.

Kinsler, the white terrier mix, got in one more slurp before she pushed him away. Shadow? She sat up with a gasp, disoriented.

Still in the barn. A different barn. Cold and wet, no choking smoke or flame. Tornado. The flood. The kids. Lenny. Steven.

A choked sob caught deep in her lungs. Her fault, her terrible fault. Steven, her dirty reminder, fruit of the trauma she'd never ever escape. But she'd never wished him ill, even put her life on the line to save him.

Then Steven was gone. And she was glad.

She was a monster. Only just for God to punish her, she deserved it, the taint on her soul she'd never scrub clean. But not Shadow, why punish him? His loyalty, his love, his innocence. They shared one heart. She'd bleed to death from his loss. The mind-numbing grief threatened to suck her back into the void.

Kinsler nose-poked her again, and more of her surroundings came into focus. Willie rode her legs like a pony. "Willie, get off."

The little dog scampered around, as the boy dismounted. "You were moaning and flailing around, and I didn't want you to roll off the loft."

Her scowl silenced him. She pushed away the dizzy hopelessness before she fell back down the rabbit hole. September steeled herself. Get over it. Life wasn't fair. She wasn't meant to love, or be loved. *Accept it. Move on.*

"How'd you get up here?" She was afraid to ask about the other kids. She had no more grief to spend.

"It worked. That ladder thing we built, it worked." Willie couldn't stand still, excited and happy, a kid on an adventure. "Nikki made us work together. Tracy's over there," he pointed to a corner of the loft, "and Nikki's helping Melinda climb up. Everyone's okay. Well, except for Lenny and Steven." His smile faded but his words remained hopeful. "Maybe they'll be okay, too."

She didn't answer. Easier to accept their deaths, ignore the hollow emptiness, and work to save the living. There'd be time later for a lifetime of regrets.

She wanted to scream to the heavens the depth of her loss. But she wouldn't dare, not when children's lives were lost. Her silence would be the worst betrayal of Shadow's trust.

The wooden floor and upper walls reverberated as if a semi rammed the structure. Dust and straw sifted from the ridgepole. Water gush increased to a roar.

September scrambled to her feet. "What was that?"

"No no no!" Nikki crouched above the makeshift ladder. She nearly lost her balance when the floor shuddered. "Hang on, Melinda." Her frantic expression implored help.

September rushed to Nikki's side. Below, Melinda had a double-fisted grip on the bottom "rungs" of the horse panel, but her legs trailed in the water that poured out the open barn door so fast, the girl couldn't stand up.

"I'm slipping. I'm going to fall." Melinda's shriek made the rafters ring.

"No. You will *not* fall." September's temple throbbed and fists clenched, damned if she'd lose another kid. "Nikki, move back." September searched the loft for something, anything, to help.

Across the loft, Tracy poked around a stack of dusty wardrobe boxes. "Dammit, what are you doing? Leave that alone, Tracy." For the first time September noticed the baling twine that trailed from Tracy's waist across the floor. She looked sharply at the other kids. "Are y'all tied together?"

Nikki nodded, pointing to twine that dangled from her waist over the edge of the loft. If Melinda lost her grip and water yanked her away, Nikki and the rest of the kids would jerk along like the tail of a kite. It worked both ways, though. They could give Melinda a toehold if they could keep from tumbling off the edge.

In the dark corner above the boxes hung a metal contraption with a large pulley that ran on an overhead track attached to a high beam. September had seen fancy multi-pulley contraptions re-purposed into lamps in antique stores, but this hay trolley worked. Melinda needed the extra boost to get her footing. This would work. Because it had to work.

"Nikki, cut loose that twine, but hang on to the end for all your worth." September rushed to the trolley as she spoke, caught and tugged the end until it followed, jerking along the overhead track. "Now give me your twine."

"I'm slipping. My hands feel numb." Melinda twisted and turned in the current.

"Don't try to stand, not yet. Going to get you some help, sweetie, hang on." Working fast, September threaded Nikki's end of the twine through and over the large metal pulley. "Melinda, when I say NOW, I want you to pull as hard as you can and grab the next rung up. Okay?"

Gathering the slack, September wrapped the twine around both hands, shouted, "NOW!" and pulled down with all her strength. The twine cut both palms, but the reel gathered the twine and levered Melinda upwards. September released one hand to get a grip further up, and sensed Willie take up the excess cord behind her and add his weight. She couldn't see Melinda's progress, but the weight and steady movement told her the girl must be moving. When Melinda's red head poked over the edge, September dropped the twine to grasp the girl's arm and pull her the rest of the way up. Willie grabbed her other arm, and the two fell into each other's arms.

September sat down on the wet floor, hardly noticing the burning cuts. She put her face in her hands, but had no more tears. Numb was good. Numb didn't hurt. If she started feeling again, her heart would shatter.

At least the kids were safe. She had to let Combs know and tell Claire she found Tracy. She wondered if Nikki's folks knew where she was. Happy endings for some, numb for the rest.

Her phone still had no signal. Even if it didn't go through, she sent a text to both Combs and Claire.

One of the wardrobe boxes, nearly as tall as Tracy, toppled as the little girl pulled threadbare clothes off the hanger bar inside. Rattling pill bottles spilled out all over the floor. Tracy crowed and danced around the loft with Grooby. "Told you so, Willie, told you told you. Magic pills."

Chapter 37

Claire sat statue still in the passenger side of Sunny's green truck. The woman hadn't said a word since leaving the convenience store. Finally, Claire could stand the silence no longer. "Where are we going?"

"Shut up. I'm thinking." Sunny stared at the sky, clearly worried. She finally glared at Claire. "I know you heard. You were in the bathroom."

Instead of terror, the weight of uncertainty lifted and a calm clarity descended. She lied, and prayed the near truth would suffice. "I only heard the last part, something about a barn and the kids. And dropping me off somewhere." Claire puffed herself up, knew she had to play this right. "I won't get in the way. I don't care about anything except getting my daughter back."

Sunny's face darkened. Claire wondered how she'd ever thought the woman beautiful. Sunny's high cheekbones could slice skin and her snarl bared feral teeth, but she only pressed harder on the gas.

Claire recognized the sign for Rabbit Run Road. Within minutes, the big truck pulled up behind Claire's ramshackle car parked outside of September's gated drive.

"Get out." Sunny sat stony faced.

"I want to go with you, and find my daughter. And Lenny. They're out of medicine by now. You can't handle both at the same time." She unbuckled her seatbelt, gambling the woman wouldn't hurt her. She had no choice.

"Go. Now. Before I change my mind." A small vein throbbed in Sunny's neck. "That wall cloud's ready to birth serious weather. Take my advice, and get under cover."

Claire spoke earnestly, but her nostrils flared. "If you had kids, you'd understand. A mom does anything for her kids to keep them safe. Anything."

Sunny reacted as if slapped. A flush climbed her throat.

Claire didn't stop. "You wouldn't know about that. TV star and model perfect, probably everything comes easy for you. Okay, fine. I'm going, I'm going." She climbed out, slammed the truck door and ducked her head against the returning rain. After thumbing the key fob, she climbed into her car, and shouted over the rising wind. "You can't stop me from following in my car."

Sunny rolled down her window and pointed a gun with a barrel the size of Texas. "You don't know me, bitch."

Claire wailed. She slammed the door, and covered her head with both hands. *Stupid, stupid.* She fumbled for her phone. Two shots popped, not nearly as loud as she expected. Her car shifted. Sunny had shot the tires.

Another shot and the driver's window shattered, spraying glass over Claire's crouched form. The fourth came with an explosion of white-hot pain that bloomed below her right shoulder and came out her front. Claire screamed, screamed again, and waited for the final shot that would end her life.

"Shit." The truck's engine roared, and it raced away.

She didn't move. It hurt to breathe, so she knew she wasn't dead. Her phone. Call the cops. Stop Sunny, or she'd hurt the kids.

Claire grabbed the steering wheel with her left hand to lever herself upright. Slicing heat traversed her chest. The bullet had entered her back and exited below her right breast. Blood soaked her coat. It smelled raw and rich, a meaty aroma that made her gag. Retching, nothing coming out. Gasped until she caught her breath. Claire wadded and rolled the bottom of her jacket, picked up her right hand and placed it over the wad, commanding herself to hold it tight.

Her phone pinged, blinking on the seat between her knees. She picked it up, read the text message from September, and began to cry. Claire didn't question or care how it happened; only that Tracy was safe.

She coughed, and tasted blood. She might die. She might never see Tracy again. Claire had to speak to her, hear Tracy's voice, one time, that's all she wanted. Carefully, Claire balanced the phone on her knee, scrolled to find September's number and dialed.

September answered at once. "Claire? Claire, thank God the phone's working, don't know for how long. You got my text? Tracy's fine."

"My daughter, want to talk to her." Hard to breathe or to speak. The whole side of her body weighed a million pounds. It didn't hurt so badly now, though.

"I need you to call the police. Ask for Detective Jeff Combs. Tell him—" The connection filled with static before again clearing. "...barn loft. Don't know how long it'll stand, the tornado hit us hard. Hello? Hello, are you there?"

Hail the size of gumdrops pattered the windshield, quickly growing in size and velocity. The sky blackened and temperature dropped twenty degrees in the space of ninety seconds. No wonder Sunny raced away. "Tornado. Coming at me."

"Claire! Where are you? Take cover."

"My car. At your house."

"Get out, get out, cars are deathtraps, go to the house. Damn, you'll never get inside, I made that house a frigging fortress."

The shattered window glass fell from her lap in a glittery heap as Claire stepped from the car. She thumbed the phone onto speaker, and dropped it into her coat's breast pocket. September's frantic voice continued to yell instructions. "The garage, go to the garage. Hurry."

"Need to tell you." Claire held both hands over the bloody hole beneath her breast, amazed she could still move or speak or breathe. "Sunny works for the Doctor. She's coming to the barn to get the pills. Tell Tracy I love her." She reached the side of the house, and leaned there to catch her breath. And couldn't. "Can you hear me?" She staggered against the wind, no longer ducking or even acknowledging the hail. "Sunny shot me." Another push, the garage over there, only a little farther to reach safety.

The tornado hit, taking the entire garage and half of September's house with it. Roses lifted into the air with clods of black, and swirled in a delicate dance. Claire's car sat untouched.

Chapter 38

September redialed when the connection failed, but Claire's number went to voice mail. She prayed the woman reached cover on time. Her garage, actually an old-fashioned carriage house, had withstood nearly a century of weather, after all.

Sunny Babcock's involvement made no sense. September didn't know the woman, had only briefly met her after the debacle involving the hog hunting reality show. Combs met Sunny there, too. And when she reached out to Combs this morning for P.I. help—had it only been this morning?—he sent Sunny.

A horrible idea reared its ugly head. When Combs arrived at BeeBo's, he'd been angrier than she'd ever seen, more than her presence justified. Last year, the Doctor and his mother had an insider on the police force, Combs's own partner. . .

The kids surrounded the stacked boxes of Damenia pills, chattering with excitement, especially Tracy. The bounty would relieve Claire's financial worries, too.

Steven no longer took Damenia. She hadn't wanted to know about his treatment, wanted nothing to do with the child. He reminded her of an ugliness she'd never erase, but it wasn't Steven's fault. Too late to make it up to the boy—or herself.

According to Claire, Sunny could show up at any moment. She'd have no compunction about eliminating witnesses, even kids. September squared her shoulders. Too late for Steven, but saving these kids might save her soul, if God even listened anymore. After losing Shadow, she doubted the Big Guy had any time for her. It was all on her.

For now, they were safe from the flood. But with no way out of the loft, they might as well have taped bullseyes to their backs.

It worked both ways, though. Sunny had no way to get into the loft, and didn't know they were here. They could hide. Claire's call to the police would bring Combs to the rescue.

"Tracy, leave that alone. It's evidence." The little girl stuffed a double handful of pill bottles into her jacket pockets, while Boris Kitty sat inside the open box, batting vials around.

"It's *her* medicine." Nikki sounded defensive. "That's why she and Lenny drove all the way from Chicago. Finders keepers." She put her hands on narrow hips.

Tracy ignored September and stuck several more vials in her pockets. "Eighty-four pills per bottle times 30 bottles, two pills a day, 1260 days 180 weeks 45 months 3.75 years. Not enough." She abruptly sat on the dusty floor of the loft, and pulled out her tablet from an inner pocket. "Internet is up." She fiddled with the screen.

No need to argue. Let her keep the medicine, for now. Hiding the kids took priority. "The man who made the medicine—"

"The Doctor." Nikki had appointed herself spokesperson for the little group. "That's what Tracy said." Her gaze shifted up and to the left, telling September the girl fudged the truth. As if to cover sudden nerves, Nikki fished Boris Kitty from the box and draped him over her shoulders.

September didn't care how or where Nikki got her information. "Tracy's mom called. Someone's coming to collect the pills. We need to hide, or it could get dangerous." She scanned the loft. A pair of ramshackle bookcases, one against a wall and the other shattered across the floor, spilled back issues of Sporting Dog Journal and Certified Contender Report across the loft. Illegal as hell, the publications recorded which dogs won and tracked winning bloodlines. A few cardboard cartons filled with who knows what sat nearby. None were large enough to hide one kid, let alone the whole group.

"The storm blew everything to smithereens." Nikki scratched under the cat's chin. "Only place to hide is behind the stack of boxes. Or inside them." She rolled her eyes.

Smiling, September hugged Nikki. "You're brilliant."

"Careful of the cat." Nikki turned away, incredulous. "You don't mean actually get *inside* the boxes. We won't fit, they're full of stinky old clothes and Tracy's medicine. We can't throw it out, or she'd see." She pet the cat, defiant.

"She? You know who's coming?" September grabbed Nikki's arm when she tried to walk away.

"Uh, no. How could I know that?" Nikki looked away again. "She, he, whoever. There's nowhere to dump the clothes so *the person* wouldn't see and suspect something."

"Sunny "The Babe" Babcock. It's a she. Will be here in six-and-a-half minutes. That's 390 seconds." Tracy kept fiddling with her tablet.

September stared, then grabbed the tablet from Tracy, expecting a CSI-like satellite view of a car speeding toward them. Instead, she saw a rudimentary BBS where posters could message each other. It reminded her of early days on the Internet.

Nikki snatched it back before she could read anything. "That's private." She returned it to Tracy. "It's a kid thing, our secret club. We're not allowed to go on Facebook. We're not hurting anything." She spoke too fast, and blushed.

She dismissed the childhood angst. She had no clue how Tracy knew about Sunny, but the fact she did lent credence to the predicted arrival. September stared toward the road. It sat thirty feet away, and nearly level with the loft elevation. Six more minutes and Sunny would be here.

"Everyone, quickly dump clothes from the boxes out the back of the loft into the water. Hide the pills in these magazine cartons. That'll make room for you to get inside." The Doctor transported the medication in mislabeled wardrobe boxes so nobody would search past the musty clothes.

"There are five boxes but six of us if you count Kinsler." Willie stuck out his jaw and she could see his dad in his belligerent pose. He clutched the dog and looked ready to argue his cause if anyone suggested leaving Kinsler behind.

"Kinsler goes with you. I'm too big for the box. It's getting dark, she won't see me. I've got a plan." She didn't like it, but had no choice.

September upended the two shabby cartons. Medical supplies spilled from one, including syringes, hemostats and suture material probably used to patch up dogs. The other carton contained a dozen or more plastic dagger-like objects, some with bite marks and blood on them. Break sticks, inserted behind the gripping dog's premolars to persuade him to release, usually were made from wood. September dumped them onto the floor with distaste.

The pill bottles overflowed the empty cartons, testament to the many customers the Doctor still controlled. September set the cartons atop the toppled bookcase, scooped the remainder into the prone shelves, and scattered armfuls of the fight publications to cover them up.

"Quickly now. Inside, everyone inside." September lifted Tracy into of the first box. "Turn off your tablet. If it makes noise and Sunny hears, we're sunk." She shut the lid, and reused the old tape to secure it closed.

"You next, Willie. I'll hand Kinsler to you once you're inside. Promise to keep him quiet." Willie folded himself into a Buddha pose and she handed the subdued dog to him.

Nikki and Melinda hopped into their respective boxes after September cupped hands for a boost up. "You sure this will work?" Nikki stared up at her from the bottom of the box, thin arms hugging her knees. "Where will you hide?" Worry etched her brow.

"I'll hang out. Literally. I want to try out that homemade ladder. Y'all got to climb it, and now it's my turn." September tried to smile, but quickly gave up. "I don't know what sort of equipment Sunny has. I'm banking on her taking the boxes one by one."

Clouds finally had started to break apart. The nearly full moon offered the only illumination, streaking the loft with sinister gloom. Good.

"Sit real quiet, like mice. Cover up your mouths if you need to when she moves your box." September shivered. "Melinda, she'll probably leave keys in her truck. Once everyone's out and Sunny comes back for the last box, y'all take off."

Nikki shook her head, and started to pop back out of her box. "Leave you? That's not happening." Her lip trembled.

"That is SO happening, Nikki. Go to the police, drive like your lives depend on it." September shut their boxes and loosely taped them shut like the others, so they could easily get out.

From inside the closed wardrobe, Nikki yelled. "What about the cat?" Boris Kitty meowed, and hopped onto the top of the highest box.

Headlights pierced the gloom. "Too late, she's here." September stage whispered, not sure how far her voice would carry, now the storm had passed. A green truck with a high rack-hunting rig tooled down the road, and jerked to a stop.

Chapter 39

When the big truck rumbled down the road toward the barn, Shadow followed Steven and hid with his-boy behind a stand of scrubby trees until it passed. He poked his long, black nose out to scent-test the wind. The engine sounded familiar and made Shadow's hackles rise, but he didn't know why.

Shadow wanted to race back to the barn. September waited for him there. She'd be worried, and he grew more anxious the longer they stayed apart.

The water had carried them a long way. They'd only walked back a short distance because Steven couldn't run as fast as dogs. Boys don't have as many paws. But September wouldn't want him to leave Steven, and above all, Shadow wanted to please her.

Steven found a big rock and sat on it, shivering in his wet clothes while he stared and poked at the shiny Frisbee-tablet. Shadow whined, wanting to follow the truck. Maybe the driver would find September and the other kids. That would be a good thing. Still, the wet fur on the back of his neck itched and quivered, increasing his unease.

He put a paw on Steven's knee, but the boy nudged it aside. Shadow whined again, and then woofed sharply.

"Shhh." Steven made the hush-sound again.

Yawning with nervous frustration, Shadow peered from Steven to the distant barn. September waited for them. Why was his-boy sitting there, shivering? Going back to the barn meant finding September. She always knew what to do. His tummy grew warm when he thought of her, even though his wet fur chilled him in the wind. With exasperation, Shadow nose-poked Steven, using his muzzle to lever his-boy's hands away from the device. September always laughed when he did that. It was his job to tell her when she needed a break.

"No-no-no! Like I say, go away." Steven clutched the tablet before it fell. "Ready to yell for show and tell. Go away, right now, today." He slapped Shadow's nose.

Shadow squeezed shut his eyes. The slap didn't hurt. But it reminded him of Steven in the long ago time, when his-boy got so angry Shadow had to lie down and hold him and never flinch away from his fists. September taught him what to do. Now when September cried out and flailed at invisible threats, Shadow did the same to keep her safe.

He debated what to do. His-boy was safe, out of the water. And Steven said go away. It was a good-dog's job to do what people said. He still didn't feel right about leaving.

In the distance, the truck door slammed and a woman cursed. That decided Shadow, and raced to reach the big truck.

It sat at the edge of the broken car path, a short distance from where water cut the road in half. The driver stood in the brightness of the truck's eyelights, talking into her phone. Her voice sounded familiar, but only when the wind shifted and he caught her scent did Shadow recognize the woman. She'd visited that morning, smelling of gunpowder and death.

Chapter 40

Kelvin recognized the caller and answered immediately. He quelled his first impulse to rip her a new one. Sunny should have checked in long ago. The plan had been flawless, until she screwed it up. He'd grown more and more flustered the longer he sat with the Doctor virtually breathing down his neck. The crazy-eyed bastard had begun polishing his gun twenty minutes ago.

"Who calls?" The Doctor moved from his post in front of the closed office door, to hover like a vulture spying a meal. He leaned on the desk, the gun dangling from the other fist.

"Sunny." Kelvin struggled not to shrink away.

The Doctor held out an imperative hand, but Kelvin shook his head and turned away to talk. He could still salvage the situation. Maybe she had good news. He forced himself to speak calmly. "I want you to—"

"Kelvin, I don't care what you want." Wind buffeted Sunny's phone. "Is the Doctor there? Tell him there's no way to retrieve the product."

Done, screwed, over and out. Kelvin shouted into the phone. "Tell him yourself." He switched the phone to speaker, clunked it down on the desk and backed away, distancing himself from Sunny's failure.

She spit the words, a cornered cat with claws extended. "I'm at the barn. Correction, I'm parked on the last bit of road, at least 20 feet away. The road washed out, it's all under water. No way to get to the barn." She laughed bitterly. "There'll be no big show tonight, sweetheart, not with all the dogs drowned. Everything's under water. Hell, half the loft is gone. Tornado probably took the drugs, too."

The Doctor's free hand rose to his scalp, grasped a lock of silver hair, and twisted. "Promises made," he whispered.

Kelvin parried with persuasion and sympathy. "Sorry about the dogs, Sunny. But we made a deal. You don't have a choice."

"Forget the dogs." She snorted. "Hell, most were has-beens, only a few good prospects. Kelvin, there's always more dogs. And the Doctor can make more pills."

"Find. A. Way." Had they been fists, Kelvin's words would have bloodied her face. "If it's there, get it out. That's why you're being paid." She had no idea what tightrope they walked. The venal bitch cared most about money, so he'd use the only leverage he had.

"I already got paid. Most of it, anyway." She paused, amusement in her voice. "The Doctor's making you all flustered. Take a chill pill, Kelvin. Maybe he'll loan you some meds."

"Sunny "The Babe" Babcock, you have been paid for services not yet rendered." The Doctor yanked a twist of hair from his head, and idly painted the gun with the hank.

"Yeah, well, the tornado had other plans." Her sarcastic retort made Kelvin's stomach drop. She thought distance kept her safe. He took another step backwards.

Twist, yank. Another silver lock fell. "You will arrange for another event to fulfill our agreement. And you will secure the product for this future event, at your own time and expense."

"Why should I?" She taunted the man, clearly enjoying herself. "It's your party, Doc. Give me one reason I shouldn't pack up and leave you to clean up your own mess."

Kelvin took another step backwards. If he could reach the door . . . He stopped when the Doctor raised his gun.

"I'll give you two reasons, Sunny Babcock. Reason number one. Do this and I will pay you Kelvin's share as well."

Licking his lips, Kelvin slowly shook his head as the Doctor pointed his gun. No chance to change his mind. He could see the Doctor's decision in his pale eyes.

For the first time, Sunny sounded cautious. "Kelvin might object. What's the second reason?"

In concert with the gun's "pop-pop-pop" Kelvin's knees unhinged. The triple-punch blazed fire into his middle. He pressed both hands to his gut, wobbled, and then keeled over. His face smooshed against the floor. The carpet smelled of mouse turds.

"Reason number two. The police will discover you killed Kelvin for his share, unless you finish the assigned task."

Another "pop-pop" sounded, followed by the opening squeak and rattle of the top desk drawer dumped to the floor. Kelvin's money-stuffed yellow sock rolled under the desk. From his vantage, he watched the Doctor scoop up the blood money he'd never get to spend. The money never mattered, not really.

The Doctor picked up the phone, talking as he walked, until his fancy snakeskin boots stood inches from Kelvin's face. He closed his eyes and held still when the man's toe nudged his neck. Possum time.

"Since I no longer have confidence in your trustworthiness, Sunny Babcock, I will meet you at the event destination. You will transfer the rescued product into my safekeeping. Don't disappoint me." The Doctor's pointed boots moved away, then the office door opened. "Broken promises reap punishment." He tossed the phone at the desk, and slammed the office door.

Kelvin's eyes flew open. His phone. He'd be dead soon. But there was still time. To do what mattered most. To be a hero.

***

Shadow watched the woman's back stiffen. Her fist clenched and she shoved the phone back into her pocket. Then her shoulders slumped, and she paced back and forth in the eyelight beams, looking first at the barn and then at her big truck.

Shadow watched curiously when she backed the truck dangerously close to the road's chewed up edge. She got out and climbed into the back of the truck bed, and began adjusting things. Metal pings and thunks made loud clattering and he slicked down his ears. She squatted and with a grunt, lifted a metal rack contraption upward until a clacking sound locked it in place.

Shadow cocked his head and he huffed beneath his breath when she climbed the platform sprouting from the truck's bed. A long metal ladder was heaved upward, too. Shadow knew about ladders.

But she didn't prop the ladder against anything. Instead, she balanced the ladder on the top platform and then tugged and pulled a rope contraption until the ladder grew. Shadow nearly barked with surprise when it kept expanding, sticking out like a tree limb. It clanked down with a muted thud on the top of the open dumpster, but kept growing longer and longer.

Shadow had never seen a ladder move sideways through the air instead of up against a wall. It stopped growing when the end touched the cement wall just below the open side of the loft.

The woman at the truck took a careful step onto the ladder, balanced herself, and then hurried along the metal pathway she'd created, graceful as a cat on a fence. She reached the end of the ladder, grabbed the edge of the loft, and hiked herself inside.

Chapter 41

Combs sat in the passenger side of Doc Eugene's SUV, bracing himself as Gonzales pushed the car's limits. The veterinarian sat in the back, probably wishing he hadn't insisted on coming.

The GPS idea to find Shadow should have worked. *Should* being the operative word. They'd arrived at Teddy William's house in good time only to discover several days' worth of newspapers stuffed in the front door. Combs had his cell number, but with the towers down, no way to reach him. Without someone like Teddy massaging the technical side, they'd wasted their time.

Gonzales slammed the brakes, and both Combs and Doc Eugene stifled curses. Half a bois d'arc tree blocked the road. He shoved the SUV into a lower gear, cranked the steering wheel, and plowed off the road around the barrier, scraping up the car's side on his way around.

"Sorry, Doc. Now you've got matching scratches." Gonzales took off again.

"Insurance covers storm damage." Doc hung onto the back of Combs's seat. "Lucky we didn't slide into the water, though."

The county road barely cleared runoff that surged alongside the drainage ditches on either side, spilling over the road in each low spot.

Combs stiffened every time they slowed to clamber through one of these runoffs. It didn't take much to hydroplane off the highway.

Somebody's phone buzzed. "Hey, that's my phone." Doc Eugene answered, and quickly shut it off with a grimace. "Robin checking in. She's heading out to check on a friend."

Combs dug out his phone to call September. He looked at messages first. One from Kelvin, the P.I. he'd referred to September, but nothing from her. He scrolled through text messages next.

Gonzales's phone beeped. "Yeah this is Gonzales." He pulled the phone away, and whispered, "It's Doty."

"Tell her to—" Combs cut off the rude comment when he saw September's text. He read it again, and then a third time, suddenly realizing he'd stopped breathing. Without a word, he reached out a hand to grip Gonzales's shoulder. His face split with the biggest, sappiest grin of his entire life.

Gonzales mouthed, *what?* "Uh, hold a minute." He held his phone against his thigh. "Willie?" He took his foot off the gas, letting the car coast.

At first, Combs couldn't speak. "Text from September. Don't know when it came in, but she says Melinda and Willie are with her. They're fine. The dog, too." Combs thought he might cry, and didn't care. "What is Melinda doing with her?" He didn't care about that, either. His kids were okay. Safe. And so was September. That mattered, too. A lot.

Doc Eugene leaned forward to pat Combs on the arm. "Where are they?"

"Didn't say. Her house, I guess." Combs leaned back, and felt his tightly wound spine crack and relax for the first time in hours.

The car drifted to a stop, and Gonzales shoved it into park in the middle of the county road. No danger with the highway deserted. Residents knew to stay inside during tornadoes, and the clouds hinted the weather might return.

"Let me get back to Doty before she chews me a new one." Gonzales slapped the steering wheel. "Now we won't have to kill ourselves to find this barn. Hell, we're already in the neighborhood." He picked up the phone.

While Gonzales dealt with Doty, Combs tried to call September but only got voice mail. He left a brief message. Later, he'd show her the extent of his gratitude. Curious, he thumbed the voice message left by Kelvin, and frowned when he only heard a long silence followed by heavy breathing. "That's weird. I got a heavy breather call from Kelvin." Gonzales's pissed expression stopped the banter before it began. "What?"

"Doty was at Kelvin's office. He's dead. Shot."

"What the hell?" The euphoria over his kids' safety evaporated.

Doc Eugene leaned forward again. "Do I know this Kelvin fellow?"

Gonzales ignored the veterinarian. "Kelvin always aspired to get ahead. This time, he must have sucked up to the wrong players." He put the car back into gear. "Doty said they found a dog tag in BeeBo's hand. Belonged to Kelvin's mutt." He smoothed his mustache. "He was up to his BVDs in this dogfight stuff. Kelvin had a wadded up map in his fist, with directions to that same barn our tipster shared."

Combs grunted. Didn't sound like the dog-loving Kelvin he knew. "Money makes people do crazy-ass evil. Let's drop Doc Eugene somewhere." Now his kids were safe, he could focus on the job.

"No, I'm fine. I'll ride along. Won't get in your way. Robin locked up the clinic, but nobody's coming by with this storm." The veterinarian leaned back and crossed his arms. "Besides, it's my car."

Much as Combs liked Doc Eugene and appreciated his help, they couldn't worry about a civilian and work, too. "We'll leave you with September and I can check my kids. It's on the way."

Gonzales chewed his lip. "Where'd you say she they holed up? Hope it wasn't her house. That whole area got hit by the storm."

Combs's gut clenched.

Gonzales wouldn't meet Combs's eyes. "We'll swing by. Like you said, it's on the way."

Chapter 42

September watched Sunny through a crack in the loft wall. The streaming headlights sparkled the water, and revealed an insurmountable path from the barn to the truck. She'd nearly decided to let the kids out of the boxes—no way Sunny could collect them without a fire truck—when the hunting rig rose and a hunter's spotlight turned twilight to day.

The ingenious jerry-rigged affair looked precarious. Sunny somehow had secured the foot-end of the extension ladder to the top of the hunting rig. From there, it stretched horizontally toward the loft, supported at the midway point by the dumpster's rim. The ladder extended further from there to reach the barn wall, ending about three feet lower than the loft opening.

That meant the boxes containing the kids must drop off the loft floor, land on the horizontal ladder, and be scooted the entire length back to the truck. Missed aim at any point would send the boxed kid into the floodwaters, below.

What a stupid idea, to hide the kids in the boxes! Even if Sunny had a gun, it would have been better to surprise ambush her.

Sunny's balance beam performance rated a perfect ten as she danced along the ladder toward the loft.

Crap. Too late to change plans even if she wanted to.

Just before Sunny reached the barn, September climbed down the makeshift wire ladder. As long as Sunny focused on the boxes, she'd be safe.

But almost immediately, footsteps approached September's hidden roost. She clambered around to the other side of the grillwork, putting the floor between her and a clear sight line. Her arms trembled, making the grate shimmy back and forth.

Sunny focused overhead, though, and grabbed twine that still hung from the hay trolley. She rolled it along the overhead tracks probably back to its original position over the wooden pallet of stacked boxes.

The woman muttered and cursed. Moving straps creaked and the metal rollers squealed. "I ought to shove the whole mess into the water. That'd show him. Blackmail me, will you?"

Alarmed, September climbed higher and cautiously peeked over the edge. Sunny shed her jacket, flung it angrily across the floor, and her truck keys spilled out and scattered the collection of break sticks.

So much for Melinda driving the truck to safety.

Boris Kitty lounged on the highest box, a feline king surveying his domain. "Shoo, cat. Get the hell away." Sunny poked at the cat until he hissed and jumped off. "Hate cats. Even BeeBo had a stinking cat."

Sunny's back strained with each tug on the rope she'd strung from the leather harness cradling the pallet. As she pulled, the pallet shifted, tipped, but finally rose enough to clear the wooden floor. Sunny booted the pallet to swing it over and out of the loft.

It took four tries before the pendulum swung far enough, and Sunny let the rope drop. The pallet thudded against the outside of the cement wall on the backward swing. September heard a muffled yelp. She winced, prayed Sunny hadn't heard, and that Willie could keep his dog quiet a bit longer.

Sunny kept working. Her bare arms flexed as she slowly lowered the pallet onto the ladder. Once in place, she released the rope, and bent, hands on her knees to catch her breath. September saw three parallel red stripes on her neck. Cat scratches.

The truck keys glinted. Teased. She had to get them to the kids.

Sunny gingerly stepped off onto the ladder. September heard her grunt again, and the soft scree of the wood pallet shoved across metal.

"Screw this. One by one, then."

September peeked out, and started when Boris Kitty stared at her, front paws tucked under and sitting only a few feet away. She continued to sneak peeks as Sunny nudged the first box off the pallet, and shoved it steadily on metal ladder "tracks" to reach her truck's platform. September pulled herself up onto the loft floor to be out of sight when Sunny returned, and worried there wouldn't be room for all of the boxes on the high rack platform. Sunny confirmed her worst fears when she bent her knees, lifted and then dropped the box into the truck bed several feet below.

One gasp or scream from inside the box, and Sunny would know. September held her breath, but whichever kid hid inside the first Trojan box must have stayed silent.

Sunny hurried back up the ladder to retrieve the next box, and September timed her descent to stay out of sight. Back and forth the woman toiled, tugging and pushing boxes and dumping them into the bed of her truck. The cat crept closer to the opening in the loft floor until he peered down at September, tail flicking. She hoped Sunny's obvious dislike of cats would keep her from investigating Boris Kitty's interest.

September's up-and-down exertion made her biceps throb and hands sting from clutching the thin wire. The truck keys rested well out of reach. Maybe she could climb up and grab them the next time Sunny went to the truck. But if caught, she couldn't match the athletic woman, and the gun would come out. No, better to wait until the final kid-in-the-box reached the truck. She couldn't fail these kids, the way she'd failed Lenny and Steven. And Shadow.

Boris Kitty stared at her. His tail thumped, jostling one of the break sticks so it rolled a few inches along the floor. Maybe the cat could help.

September grappled in her pocket for her SUV keys. She switched on the laser light Macy loved. Aiming the red dot at the floor right in front of the cat, she held her breath and then smiled when Boris Kitty followed the lure, pouncing and chasing it across the dusty floor. Once he reached the far side of Sunny's keys, September jiggled the laser on them. He obliged by pouncing and swatting the rattling bundle across the loft closer to her. Another paw-swipe like that, and she'd be able to snag them.

Not winded in the least, Sunny ran lightly up the ladder toward the final box. Instead of the repeat of past efforts, she vaulted back into the loft and crossed to collect her jacket. And keys. Sunny saw the cat, and aimed a foot to boot Boris Kitty off the loft into the floodwaters below.

The cat spit and dodged, the kick missed. The laser light fell into the water. September lunged and grabbed Sunny's ankle, toppling her to the floor.

Sunny shrieked, caught herself on her palms, and immediately rolled onto her shoulder and back to her feet.

September grabbed for the truck keys.

Sunny kicked them. They slid and jangled across the loft, and stopped near the final wardrobe box. The cat chased them down, and crouched over the keys, growling. Sunny straightened, ignored the cat, and drew a knife from her boot.

September scrambled to stand. Her hand closed on one of the breaking sticks, and she crouched low, jabbing it toward the other woman.

Sunny laughed. "When I bite, I don't let go." She feinted with the knife, smiling when September twisted and fell as her knee failed. Sunny moved in quickly, grabbed a handful of September's hair, and shook her like a dog worrying prey.

September screamed. Her scalp caught fire, and blinding tears filled her eyes.

"Let her go!"

Oh God, Melinda had climbed out of the box. "Get out of here. Call your dad."

"What the hell?" Sunny pivoted, yanking September's hair while keeping the knife at her throat.

"I did, I already called Daddy. Let her go, the police are on the way." Melinda's gaze slid up and to the left. A lie. Maybe Sunny didn't see.

The keys. The keys, there on the floor, right next to Melinda, guarded by the cat.

"One word, one move, I slit her throat." Sunny growled the words.

Melinda's eyes grew big.

The cold blade pressed harder, hot pain laced September's skin.

"Jeff Combs's kid." It wasn't a question.

The knife cut deeper. Scalding warmth trickled from her neck. September struggled to stay still.

"Damn Doty. If that bitch detective hadn't sicced BeeBo on us, we'd be free and clear."

Detective Kimberlane Doty had sent BeeBo undercover, not Combs after all. September stifled a sob. He'd been killed by Sunny, someone he considered a friend.

September widened her eyes, and purposefully stared from Melinda to the cat on the floor, and back again. Boris Kitty fell on his side to bunny-kick the jingling set of keys. Back and forth, she stared, girl to cat, until Melinda followed her gaze. The girl tightened her lips and nodded understanding.

"Now!" September yelled.

Melinda dove for the keys, snagging them away from the cat. Reflexively, Boris Kitty grabbed Melinda's collar, and hugged the girl's neck as she awkwardly clambered back out of the loft onto the ladder.

In the same instant, September used both hands to drive the point of the break stick backwards, deep into Sunny's thigh.

Sunny shrieked. Her knife plunged into the churning water. The woman tumbled backwards, following her knife. One hand entwined in September's dark mane jerked September to the floor.

She acted like a human anchor, holding Sunny aloft as she dangled by September's hair. Scalp screeching, September's fingernails tore against chinks in the wooden floor. She slid ever closer to the edge.

Something hard pressed through September's coat.

"You're coming with me, bitch." Sunny's face twisted with determination and hate.

September punched the knife's broken blade through the coat's hem, and slashed as she pitched over the side.

Chapter 43

Shadow watched and worried as the woman brought boxes from the barn. Each time, the truck lurched when she dropped them into the back. He waited, though, hoping to see September emerge from the loft.

When the shrieks came, Shadow exploded from his hiding spot beneath the truck. He raced to the edge of the road. How to reach September? Water surrounded the barn, making it an island impossible to reach. The ladder offered a path, but hung far over his head. Not even Shadow could leap that high into the stranger's truck.

Shadow's heart banged hard in his chest. He danced forward, close as he could get to the edge of the water. He didn't like the cold wet. But he had to reach September.

A disturbance made him look up. Kids appeared in the back of the truck, silent as they watched Melinda scurry along the ladder. She moved with jerks, fits and starts, not like the smooth dance of the strange woman. And she wore a fur collar around her neck. It moved and smelled like cat.

Melinda jumped down from the high platform into the back of the truck to join the other kids. They yelled and cried out so loud it hurt a good-dog's ears and made it hard to understand.

Melinda yelled louder than all the others. "We're going."

Willie wailed. "You don't know how to drive."

"I'll learn." She ran to the truck cab, and the other kids noisily followed.

Shadow swiveled his attention between the loud kids and the quiet loft.

The truck growled to life, made a grinding sound, and jerked into motion. Its tires spit mud and sticks at Shadow when it sped away. One end of the ladder fell out the back and thud-splattered in the mud. The truck disappeared down the road, taking the light with it.

Another scream pealed from the barn. Shadow barked, and barked again, crying out to September. A woman dangled over the water, holding fast with both hands to something overhead.

September? He couldn't tell. Shadow ran to the fallen ladder, now within reach, and sniffed the metal. Different than the wooden one in his garden. But he had to try.

Something shiny-bright flashed above the dangling woman's hands. Her yell choked off when she plunged into the water. Another woman, this one with short hair, spilled after her through the loft hole, but caught on the metal grid. Clouds blew apart and moon glow shined down.

"Shadow? Baby-dog, is that you?" September's raw voice overflowed with disbelief, hope, and then elation. "Thank you God, you're alive."

He howled again. His forepaws tested the ladder. She was there, so close. He *needed* to be with her.

"*Wait*, Shadow. Good-dog, *wait* for me."

He hated that word. But he trusted September. She knew things dogs didn't know. He could relax now she took charge. The relief in her voice made his heart sing, and he sat down to wait for her. He panted anxiously, yearning for her touch, wanted to taste her face. He wanted a nap. And maybe some bacon. Shadow licked his lips, and yawned.

Mud splattered his fur at the same instant he heard the POP!

Shadow jerked away. He'd focused so hard on September that the rumble of a car running without lights snuck up on him. The gun reached out again to bite him, and he dove into the brush on the other side of the road.

He snarled as the boy-thief climbed out of the car, the gun gripped in one hand and Steven in the other.

Chapter 44

Her head throbbed and September fought dizziness from the near scalping. Her jagged knife-cut hair fell in her eyes, blinding her as she clung to the horse panel. She'd lost her knife, but survived. Sunny had disappeared, swept away by the waters.

Seeing Shadow made her want to laugh and cry at the same time. Weak with relief and arms trembling, September dragged herself up the horse panel back into the loft. She had to reach Shadow, hold his solid warmth in her arms, and never ever let him go. September carefully stepped from the loft onto the ladder, just in time to see Shadow dart out of sight.

A heartbeat later, the strange car pulled up and disgorged her worst nightmare. The Doctor who haunted her nightmares yanked Steven from the car. September choked back a cry. Steven lived! She sank to her knees with relief. Maybe she wasn't such a monster after all.

The real monster stood below. The Doctor raised the gun, and as he fired, Steven squirmed enough to skew his aim. A bullet splintered the cement block beside her.

She reflexively covered her head. He shot again, this time on her other side. Playing with her. September forced herself to stand. The moonlight shined the metal ladder, and water reflected its glow, illuminating her as clearly as a spotlight. If she tried to duck back into the loft, he'd kill her before she reached safety. She wouldn't give him the satisfaction of cowering.

He aimed again, and then cocked his head and lowered the gun. "I'm going to kill you, September Day. No more interfering. Medicine must be delivered to save the children." He ignored Steven's struggles, the tiny boy less than a gnat of annoyance. He raised the gun again.

"I'll dump this ladder. Then try to get your precious poison." She could do it. September shifted her weight, and the ladder shuddered and clanged. The once horizontal ladder now canted at about a thirty-degree angle, barely clinging to the corner of the open dumpster at its midway point. Knocking it off meant there'd be no way to get to the loft until water receded.

"Sunny Babcock retrieved the product at my behest. She likes money. People do anything for money."

"Sunny failed, you miserable mental defective. I've got your product right here." Nothing to lose. "And you'll lose, too." If she could prod him enough, maybe he'd come after her and let Steven go.

"So the product remains in storage." It was a statement, not a question. September imagined his brain clicking away, mental gears calculating what that meant.

She shifted backwards a bit, so when she kicked away the ladder, she'd have a chance to pull herself inside. "Let Steven go, right now, or I'll take down your only chance to recover your *product*." She sneered the final word.

His bloodless smile chilled her. "I can make more. Delay means more children suffer. More blood on your interfering hands." He flexed the gun back and forth, back and forth. Stimming. The self-comforting repetitive behavior increased with stress. Maybe the Doctor needed another dose of his miracle drug.

She taunted. "It's not about the kids, it's never been about the kids. Or the money. It's playing god, turning people into puppets to make you important." *C'mon, get mad.* "You give nice, decent autistic people a bad name." He might be brilliant, but his stunted emotions offered a weakness she'd used before. Get him riled enough, and like dogs and cats, analytical thought couldn't function alongside fear or fury.

She rocked the ladder, and it shifted closer to the edge of the dumpster. The green box rocked as water continued to surge around it. "You scared, Gerald-baby? Should be. I beat you before, put your sicko bag of scabs Mommy away. You're only brave shooting unarmed women. And abusing dogs. How's it feel, knowing you'll never see your Mommy again?"

The stimming grew worse. Steven squealed, his arm in a vise.

This time, she wouldn't let him get away, even if she had to use herself as bait. He vanished too easily, and had resources nobody could match. And by God, she owed it to all the lives he'd ruined, to Lenny and to Claire. To her sister, and Steven and Tracy, and so many more.

If she could get him into the loft, she could dump the ladder and trap him until the police arrived. When Combs arrived. She'd been wrong about him, wrong about so many things.

"What you going to do, you sick bastard? Son of a bitch, go on, make your move."

"Bad language, lazy language. Shut up shut up shut up!" He shook Steven into submission, steadied his hand and aimed the gun.

Chapter 45

The boy-thief's posture changed. Before, he'd been relaxed and unhurried. Now his shoulders hunched, breath panted and his scent screamed DANGER! and made Shadow bristle and bare his teeth.

September stood over there, up high on the ladder against the loft. But Shadow knew guns could reach out and bite from far away. His notched ear twitched at the thought, and his tummy tightened when the pale man steadied his wobbly hand, and pointed the gun.

At September.

He didn't wait for direction, his heart told him what to do. He sprang, paws digging deep in the muddy soil, and leaped high to muzzle-punch the gun away.

At the last second, the man spun, flinging Steven to the ground. He adjusted his stance, ignoring September to aim at Shadow.

Shadow grabbed for the gun. So did Steven. The gun spat.

Steven squealed, swinging from the boy-thief's arm. He'd jogged the gun enough for aim to go wide.

"Steven, run!" September screamed and rushed down the clanging ladder, but Shadow didn't move his eyes from the pale man. "Shadow, good-dog, *go-to* Steven."

His ears rang from the shot, making September sound far away. He snarled at the gun's acrid oily stink.

"Demon dog bit me." The tall man's voice shook. "Sick of dogs. Sick of ungrateful kids." He brushed off Steven, set his legs apart, and aimed with both hands. The empty eye of the gun stared back and followed when Shadow danced forward and back.

September cried out with desperation. "Run, Steven, get away. Please Shadow, please go."

But Shadow didn't budge. Sometimes dogs knew better than people. Even smart people like September. As long as the gun sniffed after him, it couldn't bite September or his-boy Steven.

The man reeked, the whites of his eyes shined bright as the moon. Shadow heard the man's heart thud so hard and loud it might come out of his chest and his pungent breath wheezed like Bear-toy's broken squeak.

Steven ducked around the man's spider legs, and dashed for September on the metal ladder.

"No, no, no, run away." September's anguished voice shook, her hands waved Steven away.

The boy-thief tracked Steven's scrambling escape and Shadow's challenge at the same time, head moving side to side.

Shadow's lips curled when the man's concentration wavered. He adjusted his posture so his head, neck and back flowed in one smooth line. His tail, only the tip, jerked as he watched the pale man's eyes return to him. Once the bad man's attention moved from Shadow's family, calm descended, surrounding him like September's embrace.

Good-dogs don't bite. But Shadow wanted to be a bad-dog if it meant protecting September and Steven. This man needed biting. He remembered the dry taste of fabric, the flex and give of muscle, the salt-bright blood smell. He wanted that taste on his tongue again, to rend this man's flesh. To punish. To protect his family.

Shadow dodged left, ducked right, and charged. The gun popped, and white-hot pain creased his neck. But his teeth crunched, bones broke, and he tasted blood. Shadow shook the hand and pulled hard, snarling without releasing his grip, relishing grim satisfaction at the man's ratcheting screams. The gun fell in the dirt.

"Shadow, good-dog. Hold him." September moved to meet Steven at the halfway point on the ladder.

He put down his ears and wagged at her happy encouragement. And hung on. September would make everything right.

The boy-thief kicked Shadow hard in the stomach. With a gasp, he let go, and struggled to catch his breath. His stomach cramped.

"I'll kill you dead dead dead!" He shrieked so loud, Shadow winced. When he scrabbled with his good hand for the gun, Shadow snapped the air in warning. He didn't want to bite again. The man tasted bad.

The pale man's expression changed. The pain in Shadow's gut and neck slowed his reaction. He couldn't stop the man's spider climb up the ladder toward Steven and September.

Chapter 46

Almost before the SUV stopped, Combs bounded from the car to climb over, around and under trees tumbled across the front of September's property. The gate hung by one hinge, and a battered old car he didn't recognize sat nearby.

The tornado's pick-up-sticks game left the proud brick fortress in rubble. Barely half the house stood, the rest blown away to God knows where. The old carriage house on one side had vanished.

A rescue worker tried to stop him, until he flashed his badge. "Who's in charge?" The man pointed, and Combs raced to a cluster of firefighters and two police officers, their expressions grim. "Anyone? Did you find any survivors?" Combs stuffed his hands in his pockets to keep them from shaking. September said his kids were fine. Now this?

"No sir, Detective Combs." The firefighter scanned the area. "Found one body. Female, dark hair, early to mid-thirties."

Combs slumped against the wall as Gonzales caught up to him. "They found September." He croaked the words, tongue thick. "No sign of the kids." Doc Eugene trotted up, too, but Combs didn't care enough to make him leave.

"Uh, Detective? Sorry, I understand you knew her. We're waiting on the team to process the crime scene. We've not moved the body."

His eyebrows rose. "Show me." Combs followed the man, Gonzales in his wake. Doc Eugene trailed them until Combs glared and the veterinarian stepped back.

The body—*too small for September*—sprawled face down. Sudden relief switched to worry, wondering where she'd gone. This woman had been shot, the bloody wound clearly visible. The tornado probably finished the job. "Who is she?"

"Claire O'Dell. That's the I.D. in the car by the gate, anyway, but she doesn't resemble her license anymore. There's blood in the car, too. The wound is through and through, so the bullet could still be in the car."

"O'Dell. Where do I know that name?" Gonzales scribbled notes in his ever-present pad.

One of the firefighters yelled, bent over, and picked up something dark that struggled and then settled in his arms. "Found a cat."

Combs motioned Doc Eugene forward. "Must be Macy. That cat has nine lives." September would be relieved, once he found her. And his kids. "Take care of Macy for us, Doc?"

The veterinarian cradled the big Maine Coon in his arms. "We'll wait for you in the car. Lucky I came along after all, eh?"

Gonzales stayed to talk with the first responders, while Combs followed the veterinarian to the road to examine O'Dell's car. It wasn't locked. He opened the passenger door, pulling on gloves first. Keys remained in the ignition. Despite the bunged up appearance from the hail, the inside of the car was tidy, except for broken window glass and the dark stain against the driver's seat back. He poked the hole in the upholstery, noting it went clear through. Perhaps they'd find the bullet in the back.

Combs opened the glove box, and leafed through the papers. He found registration and insurance naming Mike and Claire O'Dell. A purse on the floor produced a wallet with a few crumpled bills, and the driver's license of a pretty snub-nosed woman. He also found an intricate picture, probably drawn by one of the woman's kids. He frowned, reading the inscription.

No worry Tracy and me fix.

Two kids in a van. One with a pill bottle. He squinted, and held the page under the overhead light. Everything clicked when he focused on one tiny detail. The pill bottle label named the patient, Tracy O'Dell, and the medication. Damenia.

"Gonzales," Combs yelled, "We gotta go." He slammed the car door, taking the colored picture with him. When he hit redial again, the number still went to September's voice mail.

The smaller man ran from the destroyed house and they met at the SUV. Combs thrust the drawing at Gonzales. "You can't see it without a light, but trust me. The pill bottle with that little kid says Damenia."

"No shit." Gonzales handed back the picture. "Her kids?"

"I think so, yes." He slapped his forehead. "That's why O'Dell sounded familiar. Claire O'Dell was one of the parents we questioned at the Rebirth Gathering last November."

"Right. There were nearly 200 kids, all with at least one parent, and not one said a word. And that was a single Gathering, we don't know how many others came before." Gonzales opened the car door and climbed behind the wheel.

About one out of every 88 children fell into the Spectrum, a 78 percent increase in the last ten years. Parents of these kids were ripe for the Doctor's pitch. "Her kids must have run away, like Doty said. O'Dell figured out they headed here, and contacted September to help. That's why she wanted the P.I." He paused, and snapped his fingers.

"Kelvin." They said the name at the same time.

"Kelvin already had a shady deal going with the Doctor. Bet you my pension the Doctor killed Kelvin." Combs's phone rang. Maybe it was September. He answered without looking. "Combs here."

"My guy says you're at your girlfriend's house searching for AWOL kids." Doty, in a perpetual state of pissed, sounded ready to explode. "A whole shit-load of delinquents just got pulled over driving some god-awful pick-'em-up truck without a license." She breathed heavily. "Now you're all caught up on your freaking family ties, are you ready to do your job, Detective?"

"Wait. What?" Combs ran a hand through his hair. "You found my kids?"

"Found your son, your daughter, couple of pets and their joy-riding friends." She laughed without humor. "Patrol saw them weaving all over the road, with some sort of high metal rig hanging off the back. Redheaded girl behind the wheel said she belonged to you." She grudgingly added, "They appeared to be fine, but I instructed Patrol to transport to the hospital and check everyone out."

Combs closed his eyes, and breathed with relief.

"They tell a wild story we gotta sort out, and mentioned Pit Bulls. And September." She continued, acerbic as ever. "Why is she always involved when something goes sideways? Don't know what you see in her, Combs. But according to your kids, they weathered the storm with September in a barn. So you and Gonzales get out there, now."

The news made his heart sing despite Doty's prickly tone. He didn't know how or why she'd ended up there, but he had no doubt they'd find September at the barn. Combs quickly brought Doty up to speed on the O'Dell woman's identity, and what it meant, and disconnected. Doty promised to send backup.

Doc Eugene leaned forward. "Did I hear right? The kids are fine?"

Combs nodded. "Let's go get us a bad guy."

Gonzales started the car. "Hang on tight, Doc. What do you know about dogfights?"

Chapter 47

September crouched to keep her balance on the ladder but finally fell to her knees as the crab-climbing Doctor wobbled it side to side. It clinked and clanged a broken bell chorus, and barely clung to the corner of the dumpster.

Steven scurried higher, with the Doctor in plodding pursuit. If she could get the boy into the loft, she'd dump the ladder, sending the Doctor to join Sunny in the hellish flood.

"Take my hand." September reached for Steven, careful not to move too far and tip them all off. Better to let Steven come to her.

Shadow ran back and forth at the far end of the ladder. He'd been silent before. Now his barks became yodels of frustration. Her joy at his survival turned to fear he'd be killed, and then fierce pride how the uncertain puppy had become a confident protector. She hadn't taught him that, but he'd improvised when needed. God, how she loved him.

September had to trust Shadow to protect himself while she focused on Steven's safety. The kids must have called Combs by now. She could hang on until the cavalry arrived. Didn't have a choice.

The Doctor couldn't grip with his savaged right hand. He still made creepy progress bracing his elbow and gripping with the good hand. He stopped, grabbed one edge of the ladder, and shook it until Steven's small hands lost their grip, and slid backwards within the Doctor's reach. Steven yelled and kicked at the pale man's face.

"Hang on, Steven. I'm coming." September scooted on her butt in an urgent race to reach Steven before he fell. The Doctor showed his teeth in what passed for a smile, grabbed Steven's ankle and yanked.

The ladder rocked, still barely gripping the dumpster's edge. The metal box bobbled and dipped, halfway floating in the tide. Only their weight held the ladder in place.

September caught a cloying stench of animal feces, infection and wet dog. Something white moved inside the dumpster, but she couldn't take the time to look.

She grabbed one of Steven's hands. "Let go of him, you bastard." Her hands ached but she couldn't let go.

Steven became a tug-toy between her and the killer. The child's soprano screams sang discordant counterpoint to Shadow's baritone yodels.

Then the dog fell silent. The ladder shook. Behind the Doctor's oblivious form, Shadow crawled up the ladder one careful paw-tread at a time. A raw scrape bisected his head; a bloody crease carved an opening in the side of his neck, and his face dripped blood into the water below.

September screamed again, this time to keep the Doctor's attention. One unknowing kick would knock Shadow into the water.

Shadow had returned to her twice. He couldn't survive another immersion, not with such severe injuries.

Steven kicked the Doctor in the teeth, knocking the Reaper's grin off his face and September wanted to cheer. He recoiled backwards, and Shadow's jaws snapped closed on his ankle. The man gasped and released Steven. The Doctor tried to regain his balance, but fell sideways from the ladder, dragging Shadow with him.

The Doctor belly flopped, folded across the edge of the foul dumpster, head inside and legs dangling outside. Shadow still clung to the shrieking man's ankle, rear paws trailing in the floodwaters. Suddenly the man's screams cut off. He shuddered, and fell limp.

September poised to dive after Shadow. It was her turn to save him. But when the dumpster began to move, she reflexively grabbed Steven. The ladder tipped sideways, and they hung for an endless moment before splashing into the icy flood. To save Shadow, she'd have to let go of Steven.

The dumpster drifted with the water. Shadow's jaws remained clamped on the Doctor's leg.

Shadow's big brown eyes met September's with an expression of acceptance that seemed to last forever. She had no words, but he knew. He always knew. His eyes closed, he unclamped his teeth, and sank beneath the water. The metal dumpster floated the Doctor away.

September clung one-handed to the partially submerged ladder. She struggled to keep Steven's head above water. Moon glow cast diamonds over the frigid flood. She'd had no choice, and no more tears to give. Only prayers.

Please God, take care of my dog.

Chapter 48

Combs stood aghast when he saw the barn. Or what was left of it.

The cement frame carried less than half a roof, leaving most of the wooden loft open to the weather. The flood swelled four feet high around the base, turning it into an island that might wash away any minute. The sibilant sound of the water reminded him of snakes. He hated snakes. Floods flushed out all kinds of creepy crawlies. Now that Willie and Melinda were safe, worry for September knotted his gut.

Uprooted trees and other debris created beaver dams that clogged the new waterway, hitching along in fits and starts before pieces broke loose and surfed away. Nobody could survive unless able to anchor to something solid.

Combs, Gonzales and Doc Eugene slowly climbed out of the SUV. The veterinarian collected an odd-looking gun from the back of his car that Combs knew held tranquilizer darts, in case Pit Bulls posed a problem. He and Gonzales both carried flashlights. So far, though, he detected no sign of life.

Gonzales walked closer to the edge of the road, and peered up and down. "If they held dogfights here, the water has done a number on any evidence." He headed to the abandoned sedan, with the driver's door still open, and poked his head inside. "Keys in the ignition. An iPad on the passenger seat. Is this September's car?"

Combs shook his head. And Shadow, he never left September's side. He gazed up at the distant loft. If she was there, they'd need a hook and ladder to get her out. "Hellooooo! September, you there?"

A dog yelped. "Shadow? Hey boy." Combs searched for the author of the sound, his flashlight spearing the gloom. On the far corner of the barn, nearly out of sight, slanted green metal thrust up out of the water, a fallen tree partially obstructing and holding it in place. "There, is that a dumpster?" It had overturned, and a white dog with spots clung to the top.

Doc Eugene adjusted his glasses. "It's a pup. What do you know; we've got a dogfight survivor after all. Somebody cut its chain." Heavy links hooked to the dog's oversize collar clanked and chattered against the metal box. "No way to reach him, though. Smart not to swim. The chain would drag him down."

"Have to wait for the level to drop." Gonzales examined the sky. "The rain stopped for now. If it doesn't start up anytime soon, flood water recedes pretty quickly."

Combs eyeballed the debris field both on the ground and in the water surrounding the barn, searching for any motion. Hope tightened his throat when he saw the bundle of clothes, then recognized hangars stuck in the mass caught on an extension ladder half submerged in the flood. Damn. Just showed how tornadoes created havoc, dumping the contents of someone's closet from miles away.

Gonzales, still at the strange car, examined scuffmarks in the ground, and then reached for his gun. "Combs, I got shell casings. It's a .45, consistent with a semi-automatic, same as at Kelvin's office."

"Doc Eugene, go back to the car." Combs pulled his own gun, and speared his light over the ground. "The Doctor had a Remington Rand." There were lots of those World War Two surplus guns still in circulation. "Here's another shell. And another." He scanned left and right, and then hurried toward the brink of the drop off. "I got the gun." It sat in a puddle next to the road.

Gonzales cocked his head. "Hear that, Combs?" He surveyed the area, brow wrinkled in concentration. "I could swear somebody's singing."

"...down came the rain,
and washed the spider out..."

***

She imagined voices, including the bark of a dog. Not Shadow, she knew his voice.

September stirred, tried to raise her head, and gave up. She'd managed to pull Steven onto her lap, one arm locked around him while she hooked the other through the overhead ladder rungs. She didn't have the strength to pull them both out, and wanted to hang on and catch her breath.

When dumped clothing from the wardrobe boxes swam out of the barn, she'd been grateful it covered them both. She didn't fight the sodden mess. By comparison, the worn material kept cold wind from further chilling their forms.

Steven still shuddered with cold, but September felt warm. She'd stopped shivering. And wanted in the worst way to close her eyes for a nice nap. But not yet. Not until he was safe. "Steven. Steven." She tried to shake him a little, and panicked when she nearly lost her grip on the boy. "You have to climb out. Can you do that? Grip the ladder rungs, and climb out."

She wondered why her words slurred. Steven acted like he didn't hear her or understand. But even a little kid should be able to manage. "Up up up, climb out. Ona ladder, get in the car." He'd be warmer, safer inside the Doctor's car. The Doctor wouldn't need it anymore. That thought made her want to giggle, but it took too much effort.

The police would come soon. Somebody called them. Couldn't remember who. "A little nap..." They'd wake her when they came. Her eyes drifted closed.

Steven started to sing. Little boy soprano, like an angel. Rude audience, shouldn't talk . . .

If the voices would stop, she could sleep. Asleep, she could dream. About Shadow. Her baby-dog. He'd gone away, hadn't he? She'd done something to make him go away, couldn't remember what. The deep ache of loss hurt, hurt, hurt, God please, she wanted to hold him one more time, tell him sorry, so very sorry. She'd laugh and he'd lick her face, and beg to chase Frisbee and shake his Bear-toy and play sniff-the-cat to drive Macy nuts and wag-wag-wag so hard his tail hurt when it hit her legs and she didn't care but God, the love and acceptance in his big brown eyes, no blame, no judgment, only love and more love and silly sweet baby-dog cocking his head and sticking toys in her face to make her laugh.

September held out her arms. She could feel him, his furry black warmth in her arms, and clung tight to him, happy again, never wanted to let him go, but still he slipped away, away, away . . .

***

"She's there. End of the damn ladder. Doc, hold it steady." Combs couldn't believe he'd nearly missed her.

September trailed in the water, barely floating and anchored only by one elbow hooked over a rung. Her waist-length hair had been hacked off, ragged, close to her scalp. The child, could that be Steven? clung to her, repeating the singsong nursery rhyme.

"September, hang on, I'm coming." Her blue lips never moved, and her eyes remained closed.

Doc Eugene and Gonzales held the end of the extension ladder while Combs climbed to reach the pair. He had to pry Steven from September's arm, and then handed him back to Gonzales. Steven continued to sing as Doc Eugene wrapped him in a blanket and carried him to the warm SUV.

Combs slipped into the water to reach September. He gasped at the temperature and his teeth chattered. He could stand in the four-foot flood, but the current greedily sucked and dragged, eager to swallow him up. He hand-walked the overhead rungs, and kept one hand gripped on the ladder, and gently unhooked September's arm. Her icy skin shocked him.

"Doc, call the paramedics." They had to warm her up. "You got anything for hypothermia?"

She stirred in his arms. Her green eyes didn't focus. September began to cry. "He's gone he's gone he's gone, oh God, he's gone, my fault." She looked around wildly. "Steven. Lenny? Did you find Lenny, he's a kid. And Shadow, oh my poor baby-dog." She wept.

"Steven's safe. Put your arms around my neck. Come on, put your arms around me, honey." Combs looped his left arm about her waist, and used his right on the ladder to pull them along.

September tried to hook one arm on his waist, but it kept slipping off. The temperature quickly sapped his strength, and he wondered how long she'd been in the water. Combs reached the bank, and handed her up to Gonzales.

He pulled himself out and as soon as their weight came off, the ladder slid from the dirt bank and sank beneath the filthy water.

"Let me." Combs took the blanket Gonzales offered and cocooned it around September. "Come on, honey, talk to me." He shook her. "Talk to me, September."

September blinked, and recognized him. "Are you real?"

With a cry, he hugged her. "Yes, I'm real. You're safe, the ambulance is on the way. Steven's okay, too. All are okay." He smiled, holding and rocking her. "Now that I found you, September, I won't ever let you go. I love you."

But her eyes overflowed. "I love you too, Jeff. But I've lost Shadow." She turned her face into his chest, sobbing.

Chapter 49

September hugged Macy. He cheek-rubbed her face and nuzzled her short wavy hair as though they'd been apart for years instead of a single day. Six days ago, the hospital insisted she stay, but she'd signed herself out after one night against the doctor's orders. She'd been frantic to reunite with her cat, the only thing left of her family, and had visited Macy every day since.

"He missed you." Doc Eugene smiled.

"Thanks for keeping him." She forced a return smile. "Mom isn't a cat person." *Or a dog person. Not that it mattered any more.*

"No problem. He's welcome to stay as long as you want. Macy has become a favorite around here."

"What's Robin think of that?" September hadn't noticed the sour woman the past few days.

"Had to let her go. She wanted more than I could give."

"A raise?"

He hesitated. "She'd been helping herself to more than the cash drawer. Pills missing, and a whole stack of my prescription pad. The local pharmacists called when my signature looked off. I'd already caught her mishandling a couple of the dogs." He shook his head sadly. "Did you know she was BeeBo's cousin? Makes you wonder what turns some people on the wrong path. Anyway, I turned her in but I don't think they've caught up to her, yet."

"I'm sorry." She knew about misplaced trust and betrayal, had experienced enough to last nine lives. She looked around the clinic, still stroking Macy. "Guess you'll need a new office manager, huh?"

He chuckled. "Nikki's already campaigning for the job. That kid can't get enough of the animals, especially the cats. She loves showing Macy off. Surprises the heck out of clients when he takes his medicine without a fuss." He took off his glasses and polished them on his smock as he spoke, avoiding her eyes. "I'm sorry about Shadow. But he's the reason we found Lenny. Well, with help from Steven's mad computer skills."

She stiffened, and then made herself relax. Doc Eugene meant to make her feel better.

She'd been out of her mind with grief, and insisted they search for Shadow's GPS signal. They'd found the dog's collar looped over Lenny's ankle, when Steven used his iPad to track the signal as neatly as any computer geek quadruple his age.

Lenny had floated over a mile on his straw bale before it hung up on a tree. He suffered internal injuries but would survive, in part due to the protective warmth of the young orange cat that refused to leave him. A miracle. The boy's parents agreed that Lenny could keep the little cat Willie insisted they name Waffles.

Mom wouldn't stop talking about her genius grandson. Despite Steven's irksome rhymes, September made an effort to connect. She needed to, for herself as much as him.

Of course, Mom got on her nerves even more. Nothing new there. It sucked not having a car. Or a house. She hadn't decided whether to repair, rebuild or relocate. A clean break would put distance between her and painful memories. Besides, Heartland wasn't truly home, and hadn't been for years. She couldn't pretend any more. Even her family acted uncomfortable around her, and she couldn't blame them. Coming back to Heartland had been running from the past, and she no longer needed to run. Now she could choose. Live in the present, and plan a future.

But until the insurance claims processed, she'd put up with being an uncomfortable guest in her parent's home. Mom treated her like a fifteen-year-old again, before all the bad stuff happened. But she'd put up with it, for now. Mom couldn't compare to the conflict she'd already survived.

These days, September walked eggshells without Shadow to keep her grounded. Surprisingly, she'd suffered no flashbacks. Stress and memories triggered the attacks, and both were a package deal with her family, another good reason for a fresh start. Even the rescued animals conjured memories. That's why she'd turned down the offer to take BeeBo's dogs.

After the news broke, pet lovers rallied to adopt the furry victims, including Kelvin's sweet dog Hercules. September wanted to scream when they found Sunny two days ago trying to sneak across the Mexican border. It wasn't fair a murderer survived when Shadow had perished saving innocent lives.

Sunny even tried to blame Kelvin for BeeBo's death, and might have gotten away with it, if not for the torn claw festering in her neck. September had no doubt forensics would confirm the claw came from the kitten BeeBo rescued. Fuzzit now lived the life of Riley as Doc Eugene's clinic cat.

Boris Kitty and his person celebrated a joyous reunion filmed by local TV news crews, and started a blog featuring the hero cat. Delays continued over the spotted Pit Bull puppy's adoption, though a waiting list clamored for the honor. The police considered him evidence. Samples of his blood, sent to the Pit Bull DNA database, would trace his bloodlines back to breeders and others for prosecution in the sordid dogfight business. A forensic veterinary team continued to collect evidence at the barn.

Her phone rang, and she checked before answering. Parker Belk again, the orchestra conductor from the theater. She sighed and let it go to voice mail. She'd already told him she wasn't interested. Thankfully, the other cellist recovered enough to play the rest of the Secret Garden run. She'd pick up Harmony later. Macy and her cello were the only two things of value she had from her old life. Time to start a new one. Maybe even tonight.

The front door binged bringing a warm glow of anticipation. She handed Macy to Doc Eugene as Combs appeared.

"Ready?" He crossed to shake the veterinarian's hand before turning back to her. "I like your hair. Different, but I like it."

Mom insisted on a makeover: hair, makeup, the works, even a new outfit with a tailored emerald blouse to match her eyes, and a slinky white skirt. But September drew the line at dying the white streak. It looked even more pronounced with the short hairstyle.

September blushed when Combs put an arm around her waist, and brushed her cheek with a kiss. But she liked it. "Yes, I'm ready." They had a long overdue Valentine's make-up date.

She'd promised herself she'd smile and act happy, despite her aching sorrow. For Combs. He deserved that, and she did care for him. Loved him, in fact. She had a hard time saying so, or showing it. Tonight, though, she'd show him. Or try to. Wasn't sure she knew how. She blushed again.

"I've got news first. Not to spoil the mood or anything." Combs scratched Macy's ears, and the cat purred. "We found Larry Pitts."

"Who?" Doc Eugene leaned forward.

"September found him first, I think." Combs turned to her. "Remember when Shadow tracked Kinsler?"

"Oh my God. The hand." The dog had perched on top of a body. How had she forgotten?

"That was Larry Pitts. Young high school kid, only seventeen. Found his car swamped not too far from his body. He had scratches on his back and neck consistent with dog claws." He rubbed his face. "Haven't told Melinda yet, not sure what to say. It's different, when you have kids."

September touched his arm. "I know. And I'm sorry."

Doc Eugene frowned. "But you don't think Kinsler—"

"No, he's too little. Larry had been missing before Kinsler went AWOL." Combs snorted. "Damn dog still goes nuts for the squirrels, but now we've Kinsler-proofed the fence." He cleared his throat. "We also found the Doctor." He nodded at September. "Just like you said. Dead."

"Good." *Another chapter closed.* "Where?" She wouldn't apologize for being glad.

"About six miles from the barn." Combs kept petting Macy as he spoke. "Inside a floating dumpster, an appropriate coffin for a very bad piece of garbage. He'd been mauled." He avoided meeting September's eyes. "No sign of the dog. Or dogs. Forensics will figure it out."

"Shadow saved me. He died for me. But he didn't kill the Doctor." She stuck out her chin. "I'm glad that evil man got what he deserved. Poetic justice, if one of his canine victims sent him to hell." She sounded like a monster, and for once, she didn't care. "Did you find the drugs?"

He scowled. "Not a trace. Must have all floated away when the loft collapsed. I'm thankful you and the kids were well away by then."

She forced a smile. "I'm ready if you are. Let's go."

September liked the weight of his arm around her shoulders. She leaned against Combs as they walked together to his car. "Where are we going?"

"To a secret garden." He smiled, and took her hand, lacing their fingers together before opening the car door for her. He waited as she pulled her long skirt inside. "I hope you like it, that it's okay." He shut the door, and cracked his knuckles.

He's as nervous as me. Somehow, that made September relax.

They drove in companionable silence until she recognized the route. When he turned on Rabbit Run Road, she finally spoke. "My house? But there's nothing left. You said so."

He shrugged. "There's some of it left. Enough of the important parts, anyway." He cleared his throat. "I know with everything that's happened, you've got no choice except to move forward. To do that, you have to start somewhere. Right? Put the past in perspective so you can build on it and make a new future?" He rubbed his face. "Hell, I don't know what I'm saying. Maybe this was a bad idea."

Although puzzled, she reassured him. "It's fine. I want to go, need to see. Only I wasn't planning on it tonight." She reviewed her outfit, carefully chosen for a romantic evening, and sighed. September steeled herself, but still wasn't ready.

The old Victorian had stood for over a hundred years. Previous owners let it go to seed. It had been the designated witchy house when she was a kid, but had always intrigued her and made her sad, like an old dog once loved and now neglected. So, when September returned to Heartland last year, she'd bought the place, determined to restore it to its former glory.

In the process of creating her own personal safe haven, she'd created a gorgeous, glorious prison. The tornado had torn away the locks, ripped bars off stained glass windows, and destroyed the fancy security system. Only the shell of the haunted house remained. She wondered if ghosts ever stopped haunting the living.

They drove through the broken front gate, pulled into the circle drive and stopped. Combs waited, silent.

She took a big breath, smiled at him and pushed open the car door. "Since we're here, why not look, right?"

He got out, and hurried to meet her. "It's not all wrecked." He took her hand, and tugged her across the brick sidewalk past the missing carriage house to the back of the house. "Wait." He dropped her hand, hurried over to the damaged wall, and flipped a switch. Outside lights lit the back garden.

September's mouth fell open. A gentle breeze moved dozens of wind chimes, creating fairy music. A stained glass table from her kitchen now sat on the grass, and held two place settings. A picnic basket waited for them, and a small stained glass lamp shined a cheery kaleidoscope on the brick walkway. "I can't believe anything survived."

"Like I said, not everything was trashed. Your brother's lamp and the table were untouched. The living room, too. The piano didn't make it, though. Sorry."

"Oh my heavens, the roses. That perfume. I wanted to rip them out. But now, oh my." She walked quickly to a busy plant covered with tiny pink blossoms, and another nearby boasting white starbursts. "The rain, all that cursed rain. It brought the roses back to life."

"Ripped some away, too." Combs pointed out several bare spots sandblasted by the storm. "And there." He pointed up, and she saw a bright rambler transplanted to the eaves, spilling a profusion of butter-colored petals in the wind.

Awed, she sighed. "That's Fortune's Double Yellow. Way too early for it to bloom."

Combs smiled. "Texas roses are tenacious; they bloom and grow wherever they land."

"Guess the bare spots make room for the new. For the future, maybe?"

He smiled, and held out his hand. "There's food. Don't worry, it's catered, I wouldn't dare try to cook. But it smells pretty yummy."

Before she'd taken two steps toward the table, a sound stopped her cold. "Did you hear that?"

"Hear what?" He held the chair for her, but cocked his head. "September?"

It came again, a soughing carried on the wind she felt more than heard. She took another step toward him. "You must hear that. Please, tell me I'm not crazy." Her breath quickened. *Please, not now.* But it didn't feel like any flashback she'd had.

"Are you okay? I'm here." Combs wrapped her in his arms. And then he stiffened when it came again.

"You heard it too. You did." And she tore out of his arms, running, running, stumbling, getting up and racing toward the sound, the whimpering cry, the voice she'd heard every night in her dreams for a week, certain it would never come again. "I'm coming, I'm coming!"

Combs raced with her, matching her step for step, their breath as one. There. Now louder. He stopped when they saw him. Combs let her go on by herself.

Shadow stood on the other side of the garden fence. Covered in caked mud from paw to shoulder, muzzle and neck stained with blood, she could count his ribs. He couldn't get through to reach her, but tried with all his might to force his way in. His voice nearly gone, he still warbled his happiness with garbled, heart-breaking gasps.

September dropped to her knees as close as she could get. "Oh baby-dog, my sweet boy." She pushed her arms through the fence, trying to hold him, to touch him, but the bars kept them apart. Her hand came back red with blood. "He's hurt."

Combs grabbed her waist and lifted her, and she struggled. "No, no, no I can't leave him; we have to get him help." And he set her gently down on the other side of the fence.

Then Shadow was in her arms, burrowing his head into her neck, licking her face, tail bruising her—oh, bliss. And Combs had leaped the fence.

"I'm not leaving either of you." His strong arms encircled them both. "You're my family. This is where we begin."

Chapter 50

Nikki hurried to the mailbox. It would come today, it had to come today. Kid Kewl told her exactly what to do.

Her parents had been scared at first, then madder than she'd ever seen. She couldn't explain why, either, and that made it worse. At least she hadn't been driving when the cops pulled them over. Melinda being a cop's kid meant she embarrassed her dad. That couldn't be good.

At first, Mom said Nikki couldn't volunteer at the vet clinic anymore. She thought she'd die. Nikki called up Doc Eugene to tell him, and instead Robin got on the phone and gave her what for. Doc Eugene must have found out, because then he came over and talked to her folks, said how much he depended on her, especially now that Rotten Robin was gone. Wow. How lucky, to have a friend like him, otherwise, she'd still be grounded until she was old, like thirty or something.

But after today, it'd be worth all the upset. Between the money they'd found in Sunny's truck, and the cash Steven found in the Doctor's car, her parents would be rich.

It made her guilty the others insisted she take it all. Melinda called it blood money, and said she couldn't touch it because it could get her dad in hellacious trouble if somebody found out. Tracy and Lenny only wanted pills. Nikki guessed that's what happened when you got addicted.

She could care less if the money had blood on it, or not. It spent the same. But Nikki knew her parents would question where it came from. Kid Kewl had promised to help. So, she asked him what to do.

"Send a little in a letter,
And that riddle makes it better.
A bit won't alarm or do any harm.
A little at a time will be just fine."

So she decided to mail cash, a few hundred dollars at a time, to her parents. She used Doc Eugene's printer to address a bunch of envelopes. And every couple of weeks, she'd stick one in the mail from the clinic, addressed to her folks.

Kid Kewl said he read the idea in a fiction book. He must be really smart. She saw the mail truck coming down the street. Now, she and her parents wouldn't be a charity case anymore. Heck, they could even *give* to charity if they wanted to.

***

Tracy ran and jumped into Daddy's arms and hugged him tight-tight-tight. Too bad he still acted sad all the time, and she wondered when Mommy would come home.

He hadn't asked how she got so many bottles of magic pills. A bunch spilled out somewhere during the adventure, and the police people tried to take them from her. So, she made lots of noise and screamed and Grooby might even have bit someone. But they let her keep two bottles.

Kid Kewl said it was enough. He said twice-exceptional kids like them made exceptional things happen. She liked being a 2e kid.

Tracy excelled at numbers the same way Lenny aced maps and other kids shined at different stuff like peeping inside long-distance computers, tracking phone calls and postal codes, making art and singing, and bunches of other things Tracy didn't understand. Twice-exceptional, her teacher said. But that was okay. A single kid alone got ignored. But all together they fixed things for their parents and for themselves.

Grownups said she and Lenny and the others were different than everybody else like it was a bad thing, but Tracy knew better. *We're exactly the same, only different.* With their magic pills, they'd still be twice-exceptional kewl-kids, too. Tracy couldn't wait.

Daddy set her down without a word, and walked to the clock on the counter. It had stopped. He wound it up tight, so it made the tick-tick-tick sound she liked. "Time to take your medicine, Tracy."

She smiled, and ran to him and opened her mouth. Instead of one pill every twelve hours, she'd take 1/2 pill every eight hours. She'd number-juggled the days-minutes-seconds for new medicine times. Before long, she'd need less and less. And soon, very soon, no more pills at all. Kid Kewl had everything planned.

She still hadn't told Daddy about the secret. The adventure had barely begun.

EPILOGUE

Shadow whimpered, and leaned hard against September's leg. He liked Doc Eugene, but the hospital smelled of strangers, and resounded with cries of scared cats and dogs. Not even petting and treats made up for all he endured, shivering but stoic while the doctor took care of his many hurts. Now, the thru-thrump of September's heartbeat jittered like a puppy gallop, making Shadow's tummy flutter in sympathy.

"He'll be fine, September. Healing nicely, and lucky he only lost one toe to frostbite. We saved his tail, and the fur should grow back soon. There's just this one stubborn place he won't leave alone. It's got to come off before he does more damage." The man scowled, and Shadow flattened his ears, and thumped his tail.

September stroked Shadow's brow. "Can I be with him?" Her heart still raced. "I mean, just as you put him under for the surgery?"

She held him steady on the cloth-covered table, her scent a balm calming him even before the medicine made him yawn. Shadow leaned against September, safe in her arms, his-person, his everything. Eyes fell closed, muscles relaxed, and the clinic faded away…

Shadow dreamed. Dreamed of another place. Of a different girl. Dreamed of Lia saving a good-dog from the hungry flood. And of the beautiful, sweet-smelling puppy-girl Karma, who warmed his heart.…

FACT, FICTION & ACKNOWLEDGEMENTS

Thank you for reading SHOW AND TELL, and I hope you enjoyed this third book in the September Day series that began with LOST AND FOUND and continued with HIDE AND SEEK. I feel like I've won the lottery, to write about my passion and share these stories with the world. There never would have been a second book, and now a third one, without YOU adopting these books. (Can you see my virtual tail wag?)

My writing pedigree tips heavily toward the nonfiction side of things, so when I began writing novels, the journalist on my shoulder continually whispered in my ear. Fiction by definition is, as September would say, made up crappiocca. But in order for readers to suspend their disbelief, there needs to be a scaffold of truth holding it together. My first fiction publisher Bob Mayer writes "factual fiction" and I love that concept so much, I'm stealing it. Below, you'll find the Cliff's Notes version of what's real and what's fantasy.

As with the other books in the series, much of SHOW AND TELL is based on science, especially dog and cat behavior and learning theory, the benefits of service dogs, and the horror and reality of dogfights. Suspense and thriller novels by definition include mayhem, but as an animal advocate, I make a conscious choice to NOT show a pet's death in my books. All bets are off with the human characters, though.

I rely on a vast number of veterinarians, behaviorists, consultants, trainers, and pet-centric writers and rescue organizations that share their incredible resources and support to make my stories as believable as possible. Find out more information at IAABC.org, APDT.com, DWAA.org and CatWriters.com.

FACT: The *show-me* game is real, created by trainer Kayce Cover as a vocabulary game used with a variety of animals, which my own dog loves to play (http://kaycecover.synalia.com)

FICTION: Shadow's viewpoint chapters are pure speculation, although I would love to able to read doggy minds. However, every attempt has been made to base all animal characters' motivations and actions on what is known about canine and feline body language, scent discrimination, and the science behind the human-animal bond.

FACT: Real-life pets inspire some of the pet characters in SHOW AND TELL. I've held a "Name That Dog/Name That Cat" contest for each of the three novels thus far in the series. This most recent contest resulted in 46 dog and 81 cat name nominations and a total of 16,930 votes.

Patricia H. named **Hercules,** the Mastiff belonging to Kelvin, based on a dog she met during pet sitting. Debbie Glovatsky's yellow tabby boy **Waffles** won the honor of being rescued by Willie and later saving the life of Lenny—Waffles is a blogging star known to have an extra-long tail and an adventurous mancat nature. Another cat blogging star, Kelly Hoffman's feline alter ego **Boris Kitty** (a kitty from da hood) shines in the "Tarzan cat" scenes and, I'm told, is also a climber, leaper, shoulder-percher extraordinaire. Karyl Cunningham suggested the name **Fuzzit** for BeeBo's rescue kitten in honor of her 18-year-old cat Anubis, nicknamed Fuzzit, a real-life friend of **Simba**, also mentioned in the story. For BeeBo's dogs, Lynette George suggested **Teddy**, a beloved protective red Pit Bull from her childhood, and Kristi Brashier nominated **Dot**, a glamour girl rescued Pit Bull who is also a diabetes alert service dog. Finally, Theresa Littlefield's squirrel-fanatic dog **Kinsler** won the honor to be Willie's run away dog. Congratulations and THANK YOU to all the winners. I think they all deserve treats. Maybe even bacon!

FACT: Therapy dogs can work wonders when partnered with autistic individuals. Emotional Support Animals (ESA) also partner with a variety of people, from children to adults, including those suffering from post-traumatic stress disorder (PTSD). Only dogs and guide horses for the blind can be service animals trained to perform a specific function for their human partner, from becoming the ears for the deaf, eyes for the blind, support for other-abled and alert animals for health and physically challenged individuals. Learn about the differences and the benefits of pet-people partnerships at http://petpartners.org. You can also find out about "fake" credentialing services that hurt legitimate partnerships in this blog post: http://amyshojai.com/fake-service-dog-credentials/

FACT: Dogfights are a sad reality in much of the world. All of the paraphernalia described, from break sticks to the cat gin, spring poles to rape stands, are real. It's also true that law enforcement now has veterinary forensic specialists available—think of it as animal CSI—to nail these bad actors. The flood in SHOW AND TELL would be problematic but tests from the living dogs or any remains found could help find out a great deal. Animal fighting is already a federal crime and dog fighting is a felony in all 50 states. That's due in part to the relationship between the fighting events and illegal gambling, guns and drugs. Here in Texas, it's still quite a problem where sometimes whole families attend including little kids. Children brought up in the culture of dogfights consider them normal, and perpetuate the horror. To combat the crime of dogfights, the Missouri Humane Society, the ASPCA, the Louisiana SPCA, and the UC Davis Veterinary Genetics Laboratory collaborated to establish the first ever database. Find out more about Canine CODIS here:

http://www.vgl.ucdavis.edu/forensics/CANINECODIS.php

FACT: Pit Bulls are not inherently "evil" or "aggressive." Because of their heritage, these dogs have an increased propensity for dog-on-dog aggression, as do many other terrier breeds. Pit Bulls do not bite people more readily than other breeds. Sadly, that statistical distinction goes to German Shepherds. (Don't tell Shadow!) All dogs bite, and every breed has challenges, so be educated and prepared for whatever animal friend steals your heart.

FACT: Kinsler's resuscitation accurately depicts nose-to-mouth rescue breathing. The acupuncture "alarm point" does work, and has been known to resuscitate stillborn puppies and kittens up to twenty minutes after pronounced dead.

FACT: The porcelain cap from Lenny's tooth used to break the van window theoretically could work. Windows designed to withstand blunt force, like car windows, can break a household knife. Any sharp sudden strike with the right force and location could cause the glass to shatter. I just liked the idea of using the tooth, after seeing this YouTube video, enjoy! https://www.youtube.com/watch?v=llu-ckEe5cQ

FACT: According to the CDC and others, Autism Spectrum Disorder (ASD) affects about one percent of the world population, and about one in 68 children. The challenges facing these children and their families vary from mild to severe, and can prove devastating to those who love them. Some of these gifted individuals rise far above their challenges (think of Temple Grandin and Albert Einstein for example). These types of characters make great fodder for fiction authors, even if "twice exceptional" or 2e children may not be the average. After putting Steven, Tracy, Lenny and their parents through hell in the first book LOST AND FOUND, it seemed only fair to turn SHOW AND TELL over to them for their heroics to shine through. Refer to these resources for more information on ASD: http://www.cdc.gov/ncbddd/autism/data.html

http://psychcentral.com/lib/autistic-and-gifted-supporting-the-twice-exceptional-child/

FICTION: I created the fictional drug Damenia supposedly borrowed from an Alzheimer's treatment. However, drugs for dementia and psychotropic drugs offer mixed results when treating autism. Off-label drug use in children is controversial but does happen, particularly with informed consent of parents. At times, the benefits are enormous and other times potentially devastating. Some psychotropic drugs cause psychosis, and oftentimes, abrupt withdrawal from a drug protocol causes unexpected consequences. However, there is no evidence to support the notion that withdrawal from an approved ASD treatment would cause any of the outcomes described in my thrillers. I made it all up.

FACT: Court cases have convicted people based on animal evidence, such as Fuzzit's torn claw embedded in Sunny's neck, or cat hair found on the defendant. Actually, I wanted to use cat hair DNA evidence, but after Sunny spent so much time in the water, that idea didn't wash. Literally.

FACT: Both dumpsters and straw bales float. I checked.

FACT: This book would not have happened without an incredible support team of friends, family and accomplished colleagues. Cool Gus Publishing, Jennifer Talty and Bob Mayer made these thrillers with "dog viewpoint" a reality when many in the publishing industry howled at the notion. Special thanks to my first readers Kristi Brashier, Carol Shenold and Frank Steele for your eagle eyes, spot-on comments and unflagging encouragement and support. Wags and purrs to my Triple-A Team (Amy's Audacious Allies) for all your help sharing the word about all my books. Youse guyz rock!

I continued to be indebted to the International Thriller Writers organization, which launched my fiction career by welcoming me into the Debut Authors Program. Wow, just look, now I have three books in a series! The authors, readers and industry mavens who make up this organization are some of the most generous and supportive people I have ever met. Long live the bunny slippers with teeth (and the rhinestone #1-Bitch Pin).

Finally, I am grateful to all the cats and dogs I've met over the years who have shared my heart and oftentimes my pillow. Nine year old Magical-Dawg (the inspiration for Shadow) and nineteen-year-old Seren-Kitty, along with newcomer Karma-Kat inspire me daily.

I never would have been a reader and now a writer if not for my fantastic parents who instilled in me a love of the written word, and never looked askance when my stuffed animals and invisible wolf friend told fantastical stories. And of course, my deepest thanks to my husband Mahmoud, who continues to support my writing passion, even when he doesn't always understand it.

I love hearing from you! Please drop me a line at my blog https://AmyShojai.com or my website https://shojai.com where you can subscribe to my PET PEEVES newsletter (and maybe win some pet books!). Follow me on twitter @amyshojai and like me on Facebook: http://www.facebook.com/amyshojai.cabc

READ FIRST THREE CHAPTERS!

FIGHT OR FLIGHT (Book #4)

A dog trainer with special abilities. A dead body with hidden secrets. Solving the case will take more than animal instincts.

.

PART 1 BORN to LOVE
(*February*)

Chapter 1

The flash flood swirled Shadow down, down, and scraped him head over paws against the muddy bottom before thrusting him up in a stomach-wrenching rush. He gasped, and his yelp became a strangled gargle when water smothered his cry. Deafened by the roar, scent blinded and sight dimmed, Shadow struggled to tell down from up, wind from flood. Forelegs churned the water to dingy froth, and he struggled to keep his black shepherd's muzzle above the surface.

The night's frigid air set fire to his flayed cheek. It would be easy to give up and let the torrent take him and erase his pain. But Shadow had to return to his family. To his boy, Steven. And to September. Especially to September, his person. She needed him. And he needed her.

He gasped and snatched another two breaths while he could, without wasting further air on fruitless wails. Shadow timed gasps to match the roller coaster surge that swept him along before he fetched up hard against a floating tree.

Shadow yelped when the trunk caught his tender middle where the boy-thief had kicked him. He thrashed and managed to scrabble a toehold across one limb. Weakened by his recent battle with the bad-man and now the wicked current, Shadow couldn't pull his 80-plus weight any higher. He clung to the limb while the flood snatched at a good-dog's fur and tried to swallow him whole.

Neither the sting of his scraped cheek, fire on his neck, nor his throbbing gut could compare to the empty ache inside. He'd left his family behind, without a good-dog to protect them. The bad-man could return to hurt them. September couldn't protect Steven or even herself, not without Shadow by her side.

On the bank ahead, Shadow spied a car. He barked for help. Cars meant people, and people helped good-dogs. But the water's roar swept his cry away. He barked with anguished frustration when the women stared back at him, without any offer to help. Shadow caught a whiff of their scent, which shouted names louder than any human scream—Robin Gillette and Sunny Babcock—before the tree floated him out of sight.

The tree he rode caught on something below the water's surface, and spun in slow circles in the current. Shadow managed to lunge enough to pull himself onto the trunk. When the tree's underwater anchor let go, Shadow crouched and braced himself against a thick upright limb. But after only a short distance it thumped into a metal dumpster tumbled about by the twisty black cloud. Shadow stiffened, sniffed cautiously, but detected no sign of the hated boy-thief, just stale garbage and animal stink.

Shadow waited another heartbeat, but his perch didn't move any closer to the bank. So he levered himself upright and took slow, shaky steps. The tree dipped and the overhead limb slammed the metal box with clanging blows, until it broke.

Loss of the limb spun the trunk and spilled Shadow back into the cold water. Energy spent, only the thought of September spurred him to flounder and hook one foreleg across the bobbing tree. His eyes half closed, as he floated helpless in the chill water, and yearned for a home that seemed a world away.

Chapter 2

Lia Corazon squinted at the clouds muddying the North Texas horizon. Wind whipped her goldenrod hair into a tangled froth, pulling it free of the hazel-green kerchief that matched her eyes. Parallel furrows etched her brow, but she couldn't change plans over the weather. It'd be close, but with luck, the storm would hold off long enough to get this meeting behind her.

She stooped to tighten the laces on one shoe, stood, and then trotted in an exaggerated loping gait across the fenced yard. A pack of black puppies galloped after her, their rust colored muzzles yapping with excitement. A couple out-paced her, with the rest satisfied to tag along in her wake.

Her words jollied them along in a high-pitched singsong designed to ramp up excitement. "Puppy-puppy-puppy, that's the way, who's gonna win?"

Once at the far end of the enclosure, Lia leaned against the chain link. The cool metal soothed heated skin through her damp sweatshirt, and she mopped her brow with one pushed up sleeve. February should still be cold, but the weird muggy weather that frizzed Lia's hair also frazzled her nerves. So much depended on today's client. At the thought, her pulse jittered in her throat.

Time to take charge of her own life, though, even if it kept her sideways of the prim-and-proper grandparents who'd raised her. That's why she'd dropped out of college two years ago and "gone to the dogs" (as Grammy called it). Now Lia was smack-dab on the cusp of making her own dream come true. Never mind that Grammy and Grandfather expected her to fail. It all depended on the new client. If all went well, Corazon Boarding Kennels would become a reality.

The glamor of belonging to the Corazon dynasty had worn thin many years ago with the hobbling demands of her grandparents. She'd had her fill of mucking out horse stalls by the time she graduated to training yearlings. Between Grandfather's character-building work demands, Grammy smothered Lia with society commitments. Of the two, she preferred mucking out stalls. The older she got, the better Lia understood why her mother ran away during a family vacation, and eloped.

Nevertheless, she'd stuck to the family's plan until two years ago. Her first mentor, Abe Pesquiera, sold his business to Lia before he died. He'd had faith in her, and Lia's success training Karma honored his memory as much as it validated her dream.

She needed to calm down. She needed a puppy fix.

"Puppy-puppy-puppy! Come-a-pup!"

With ears flopping and stubby tails held high, excited yaps spilled from nine furry throats as the nine-week-old Rottweiler babies raced to meet her. "Puppies, COME." She used the command with intent. She liked to imagine she shared a special level of communication with animals, as had her mother. Once they responded to the chase-and-follow game, she associated the command word with the action.

Lia didn't use the clicker anymore—too easy to lose—and instead preferred a tongue-click to signal THAT (click!) was the desired behavior. She'd already taught the pups a handful of commands in a series of games designed to reward their natural puppy curiosity and urge to play. *It's a tough job, but somebody has to do it.* She grinned.

Thirty-six short furry legs churned, with some of the pups preferring to chase and wrestle each other rather than complete the recall. But over half of the litter, five sleek black and rust beauties, responded to the command and raced to reach Lia.

"Oh you're so smart! What smart brave puppies, good COME."

She clicked her tongue as the biggest girl pup, the one wearing a purple collar, skidded into her ankles. Lia rewarded the puppy-girl with the stinky-yummy liver treat all the pups wanted. She watched the girl-pup chew with relish while the late comers milled and whined about her legs in a furry sea of disappointment. "You snooze, you lose. Life's not fair, puppies. Gotta be quicker next time."

At first, all the pups got the reward, so they knew the stakes. Now at four months of age, the litter had reached the puppy delinquent stage. They already knew a lot—how to sit, down, come and walk nice on leash—but tested boundaries and often ignored lessons they'd nailed last week. Lia called it their "make me do it" phase, so she increased the stakes at each training session.

For the past four days, only the winner of the recall race got the prize. The sharpest pups understood right away, and those that didn't care weren't the best training prospects anyway.

Lia knew from hard experience that life wasn't fair and not everyone got to win the prize. Dog life worked the same way. For the elite in this litter, the race-game prepared the Rottweiler pups for their future role as police dogs. The technique spurred those puppies with the correct temperament to respond to her command without hesitation in order to win a reward. Her mentor, Abe Pesquiera, had taught her that trick, one of the best ways to train a reliable recall no matter the age of the dog. God, she missed Abe.

Not all pups were police dog material—maybe one or two would qualify—but all could still be delightful companions or canine partners in other ways. All dogs benefited from training, and a reliable recall saved dog lives. Lia's job prepared them for life with people, no matter what that role might be. After all, Lia was nobody's pick of the litter, either.

As if that thought summoned the call, Lia retrieved her buzzing phone, not surprised at the caller. She debated whether to answer, but knew Grammy wouldn't give up. Not until she got her way.

"I'm in the middle of training, Grammy." Lia pulled a tattered rope toy out of her other pocket and dragged it across the brown grass for the puppies' pleasure. Two of them went after it. Purple Collar girl won the prize by shouldering her brother aside. The pup grabbed hold and tugged, growling with ferocious ardor and Lia grinned as she held on. "And I've got a client on the way."

"In this weather? You realize the county is still under a tornado warning." The gentile southern drawl masked hidden steel as inflexible as Grammy's helmeted coiffure.

Lia rolled her eyes. "Yes, I know. My phone alarm keeps going off." She eyed the clouds again as she walked back toward the kennel, towing the tugging puppy with her. The rest of the litter followed, all hoping to snatch more of the tasty liver reward.

"I don't know why you're so stubborn. We have a storm shelter here. Let us help out." Grammy pronounced, and you were expected to comply.

William "Dub" Corazon and his wife Cornelia lived on a 4000-acre spread that had been in the family for over one hundred years. Corazon

Stables bred and trained champion cutting horses, born and bred to manage cattle and "cut" the selected animals out of the herd.

"I'll be fine, Grammy. I have responsibilities here."

Grandfather had never had much to do with Lia. She'd catch him watching her from a distance, his spicy aftershave vying with the cigar smoke that wreathed his scowling brow. Grammy tried to tame Lia's wild streak with strict curfews, home schooling and stifling supervision.

Grammy grew insistent. "For heaven's sake, your grandfather and I just want you to be safe."

She bit her lip. Grammy and Grandfather wanted to "help" when it suited them. They'd told Lia no often enough. *Let it go, Lia.* The client would be here any minute, they'd conclude their business, and Lia would never have to beg crumbs from the Corazon table again.

Lia smiled when Miss Purple Collar switched her focus from the tug toy and attacked Lia's moving feet. *Need to capture that behavior, and put it on command.* "Grammy, you've already said I can't bring the dogs."

"Of course not! They're dogs. And they don't even belong to you." Grammy tittered. "We don't bring our *horses* into the storm cellar, nor the prize bull. Just one of them is worth more than—"

"I know, you've said it before. *Worth more than all of Lia's pipe dreams combined.*" Lia mimicked Grammy's condescending tone while she glanced around, taking in the decrepit building and grounds. "The dogs are my responsibility, and so is this property, even if one of your horses costs more."

Thunder grumbled overhead, echoed in the phone Lia held. "Be reasonable, Lia. Storm's coming. Grandfather and I just want what's best. You've received every advantage, the best education, introductions into the proper social circles. Yet you prefer to mix with . . ." She hesitated, and Lia knew it was for effect. Grammy had never been politically correct.

"I'm an adult. I get to make my own decisions." Lia couldn't hide her exasperation.

"You are a *Corazon*, you have a position in this community. Don't waste your talents on losing propositions. Your grandfather would happily support your choice of an *appropriate* career." She spouted the same old argument. "Instead, you take every opportunity to embarrass your family. People laugh at us, they laugh at you. Don't throw it all away—"

"Like my mother?" It always came back to that. The all-powerful, all knowing Corazons chose an *appropriate* career. Never mind what Lia might want.

Grammy remained silent. Lia pictured Cornelia's ice blue stare, flared nostrils and creamy complexion that had no need of Botox. She imagined Grammy smoothing her perfect platinum hair with shaking, bejeweled fingers. Mention of Lia's dead mother was the one weapon guaranteed to crack Cornelia's carefully crafted image.

Lia had never known her mother, described as petite with dark gold hair and fair skin, a firecracker personality and looks true to her northern Spanish heritage. *I wonder if I look more like my father, whoever the hell he might be.*

She took a shaky breath. "I'm not *her*, Grammy. I can't ever be Kaylia, no matter how much you and Grandfather push." *Or how hard I try.*

"That's certainly true."

Lia gasped, and then squared her shoulders. They'd become very good at hurting each other. She fingered the flowers on the old baby bracelet for courage. She never took it off, in part because she couldn't resist poking an ant's nest. Lia had found the baby bracelet and an antique braided leather lariat several years ago, hidden away in a box of Kaylia's things Grandfather hadn't managed to destroy.

Grammy had a conniption and refused to discuss their provenance. Lia asked Grandfather about the lariat, made in West Texas, according to a tooled maker's tag. He turned red, blustered and stammered, and threatened to disown her if she ever asked about that *no-account bastard* again.

She hadn't. But she still wondered, and had promised herself to ferret out the truth, someday. Meanwhile, she honored her mother by wearing the bracelet, and worked Kaylia's lariat until she could out-rope anyone. She kept the lariat handy, hanging on her office wall.

"Why make everything so difficult, Lia? I'm sure the dogs and everything else will be just fine. Everything's insured, after all, and can be replaced. Come home."

Just like her to think living creatures were replaceable. "This is my life and my home now! My future. None of it's replaceable." She'd gone to her grandparents for a loan but her dream wasn't appropriate for a Corazon and they'd refused. She couldn't help thinking they wanted her to fail.

"Oh Lia, don't be so melodramatic." Grammy's drawl turned brittle. "Go on then. I'll tell your grandfather you'd rather huddle up with those worthless dogs that don't even belong to you. Just pray that failing business doesn't collapse into rubble around your ears. Go ahead, since that's more important than your family." Grammy disconnected.

Lia touched the bracelet again. It'd be different if her mother had lived. Why had her mother's mysterious Romeo abandoned them? Abandoned *her*. Lia always imagined Kaylia died of a broken heart when he left, but nobody spoke of the details. Lia had been born. Kaylia died. Her father hadn't wanted them.

Except her name on the baby bracelet—her *real one*, not the short version the Corazon's gave her—told a different story. The bracelet's dainty plumeria flowers framed a name spelled out in tiny individual letters:

Apikalia.

She'd looked it up. The flowers and the name were Hawaiian. It had to mean something.

Angry with herself for rising to the old bait, Lia bent down and scooped up Miss Purple Collar. In order to tell puppies apart and keep track of health and birth order, each wore a color-coded collar. She relished the smell of puppy breath when the baby slurped her face, and Lia kissed the top of her smooth black head. "How about we play a new game? We'll call it, *TRIP*. Sound good, puppy-girl? My little Karma?"

This one attracted all kinds of trouble, but Lia liked her attitude and drive. "You like that name, Karma?" The puppy cocked her head and slurped her face. "Good girl, Karma!"

If Grammy and Grandfather considered her a mutt, a *poi dog* unworthy of the Corazon name, so be it. Dogs loved you no matter what. The Karma-pup didn't care about unknown fathers or dead mothers

Apikalia meant *my father's delight*. Had he chosen her name? Or was it her mother's wishful thinking?

Too many unanswered questions. Lia wanted—no, she *needed* to know where she came from before stepping into her future.

Lia bounced Karma in her arms, and hurried to round up the rest of the litter. Everything depended on what happened today. Failure would mean a continuation of the Corazon's *told-ya-so* hell.

Chapter 3

Karma struggled in Lia's arms. She hated restraint. The girl's hugs didn't hurt but reminded Karma of her mother's discipline. Even though Lia had the right to tell Karma what to do—she was the leader, after all—the unpleasant sensation made Karma squirm.

Her littermates bounced around the girl's feet, and Karma tried to enjoy her elevated view from Lia's arms. The familiar building they approached meant home and safety, but it shut out the best sniffs and sounds. The sniffs and sounds that made life exciting and fun. Karma yearned for adventure, to explore beyond the wire walls of her kennel, and to escape the protective flank of her dam, Dolly. Even at her young age, Karma's confidence outshone that of her mother and siblings combined.

A loud rumbling growl sounded overhead. She strained to look upwards. Did a dog hide above? Dark billowing shapes mounded and surged as far as she could see, perhaps pushed by the same invisible breath that combed the grass of the nearby field.

"Puppy-puppy-puppy, COME!" The girl's sharp command had the litter surging through the open wired door, back into the kennel where Karma's dam waited—shy as always and curled up tight in a corner. A handful of treats tossed onto the pavement prompted a rush of squeals and happy barks. Even Dolly roused enough to claim a few morsels.

Lia's arms tightened when Karma squirmed, she wanted her share of the treats. "Not you, puppy-girl. We've got a new game to play."

Karma barked and grinned. She knew two of those words. Sometimes she learned words all by herself. She was smart that way.

What would happen when both *play* and *game* words came together? Her short black tail stood straight up, and her entire back end wiggled. That happened a lot when she recognized happy words.

The girl unhooked a target stick hanging on the wall before she set Karma back on the grass. The pointer helped Karma know where to look while learning new games.

Cold mud squished under Karma's feet as she bounced across the yard. The wet on her paws reminded her of another urgent need, and Karma trotted off a short distance to squat. She didn't even wait to be told to *take-a-break*. She finished and looked around with a hopeful wag. Sometimes she got paid for peeing. She liked it when that happened.

But not this time. She cocked her head and focused on Lia for some clue about the game. Karma knew many of the mouth-sounds people used, the important ones like *tug* and *play* and *Karma*, and the sniffing game where she got to ferret out treats hidden around the yard. She also knew the less exciting words like *come* and *sit*. Karma loved hearing her new name because it signaled something fun would happen. But she didn't care as much for *sit* or *come*. Beckoning sniffs, sights and sounds distracted and led her astray. But if treats or a game of tug were involved, Karma could be persuaded to do most anything.

She took a moment to sniff the warm wet spot she'd made—self-smell made her feel happy and safe—before racing after Lia's churning feet. The skipping shoes triggered her instinct to chase-chase-chase, to grab and grapple and wrestle.

People covered their feet, muffling the good sniffs that came from between their toes. Karma wondered why Lia avoided the delicious feel of grass and dirt on her foot pads. How did people nibble an itchy paw? Balancing on two instead of four paws must be hard, too. How did people run at all without bare claws to dig into the ground for grip? Maybe that's why people ran so slow and funny.

The girl stopped and lifted one of her shoes and wiggled it just as Karma skidded to a stop within nose-touch range.

Karma tipped her head at the swiveling foot, and looked up at the girl's face, seeking a clue. Karma knew the rules of the game. She had to guess what the girl wanted, and when she got it right, Lia would make a CLICK-sound with her mouth and give her a treat. Even better than the treat, guessing right made the girl smile and laugh. And that made Karma's chest swell with a warm happy feeling. She wasn't sure why, but she liked that. A lot.

The girl extended the tip of the long target stick, and Karma focused on its movement. She'd learned to pay attention because it often gave clues about the game. When the tip came to rest on top of the girl's elevated shoe, Karma stretched her neck forward until she nose-poked the foot. Immediately, she heard the CLICK mouth-noise that said she'd guessed right. Karma couldn't help drooling, and smacked her lips after she gulped the treat without chewing.

She looked from the girl's smile, and back to the target stick, wagging her back end so hard she lost her balance. She liked this game. Touch the foot, get a treat. Easy.

Next, Lia girl put her foot on the ground before tapping the shoe with the stick. Without hesitation, Karma bounced forward and nose-poked the shoe again, and stared up with her mouth ready even before the CLICK sounded. She chomped the treat, head swiveling to follow Lia's next move.

When the girl turned her back and trotted away, Karma gave chase. Her four paws overtook the girl, and this time she didn't wait for the target stick to direct her action. Foot movement through the long grass mimicked prey and she pounced, grappling the girl's ankle and mouthing the strings on the foot covers. The "click" mouth-sound came, just as the girl tumbled forward and rolled onto the ground.

Karma released the girl's foot and danced away. She'd never seen people fall over. How exciting! She bounced forward again, growling and yapping with excitement. When the girl moved the target stick back to the same shoe, Karma nose-poked the foot, but stood puzzled when no CLICK followed. She poked the shoe again. Nothing. One last nose poke, and then with frustration, Karma grabbed the shoestrings and tugged.

CLICK!

With delight, Karma took the treat. She returned to the shoestrings, grabbed, growled and tugged, even shook her head to subdue the shoe.

CLICK! A whole handful of treats fell from the girl's hand.

She didn't know where to sniff and gulp first. Snuffling through the grass to collect the bonus reward, Karma's brain processed the game as the girl regained her feet and trotted to the other side of the yard to repeat the lesson. Karma abandoned the few treats left, because the excitement of the new game offered way more fun. Karma dashed after Lia, eyes focused on the girl's moving feet. This time, she needed no prompting, and tackled the shoe, ferocious play growls and happy yelps filling the air. She wriggled with delight when the girl didn't fall at once, instead tugging back and struggling to step forward. What fun, a tug game with chasing.

"*TRIP!* What a good *TRIP*, good girl, Karma. *TRIP!* That's it, *TRIP!*"

Karma continued to grapple the girl's foot, understanding few of the words but registering the percussive final word and the repetition. She wasn't sure just yet and continued to test and refine what the girl wanted.

She bit harder—it felt good to bite—so she adjusted her grip and tugged, too. When the girl fell forward, rolling onto her side, Karma let go and danced out of the way. But that garnered no CLICK sound. Lia stuck out her foot, shook it and repeated, "*TRIP!*" So Karma launched herself once more at the shoe, biting it, and even clasping and humping against the girl's foot in the ultimate display of dominance.

"Good *TRIP*, what a smart Karma, good-dog. So you like the *TRIP*-game? Good girl, Karma." The girl laughed and pulled out a handful of treats, tossing several for Karma to find in the grass. While Karma collected the yummies, the girl adjusted the padding on her lower legs before standing and starting the game again.

Each time they played, the girl changed something. Not much, just a little bit. Just enough so Karma had to think and figure out what was different. She watched, smelled, and listened to every detail, paying exquisite attention to the girl—what she did, what she said, and especially Lia's facial expression. Every wrinkle of her brow, flare of nostril or quirk of Lia's lips spoke to Karma. The treats didn't matter as much as figuring out what the girl wanted.

More than anything else, Karma wanted to please the girl. So much so, she only struggled a little and didn't growl at all when Lia scooped her up in a hug to end the game.

Get FIGHT OR FLIGHT

at all fine bookstores!

ABOUT THE AUTHOR

Amy Shojai is a certified animal behavior consultant, and the award-winning author of more than 30 bestselling pet books that cover furry babies to old fogies, first aid to natural healing, and behavior/training to Chicken Soupicity. She has been featured as an expert in hundreds of print venues including The Wall Street Journal, New York Times, Reader's Digest, and Family Circle, as well as television networks such as CNN, and Animal Planet's DOGS 101 and CATS 101. Amy brings her unique pet-centric viewpoint to public appearances. She is also a playwright and co-author of STRAYS, THE MUSICAL and the author of the critically acclaimed September Day pet-centric thriller series. Stay up to date with new books and appearances by subscribing to Amy's Pets Peeves newsletter at www.SHOJAI.com.